◄ BOOK ONE ►

THE GIRL & THE GALDURIAN

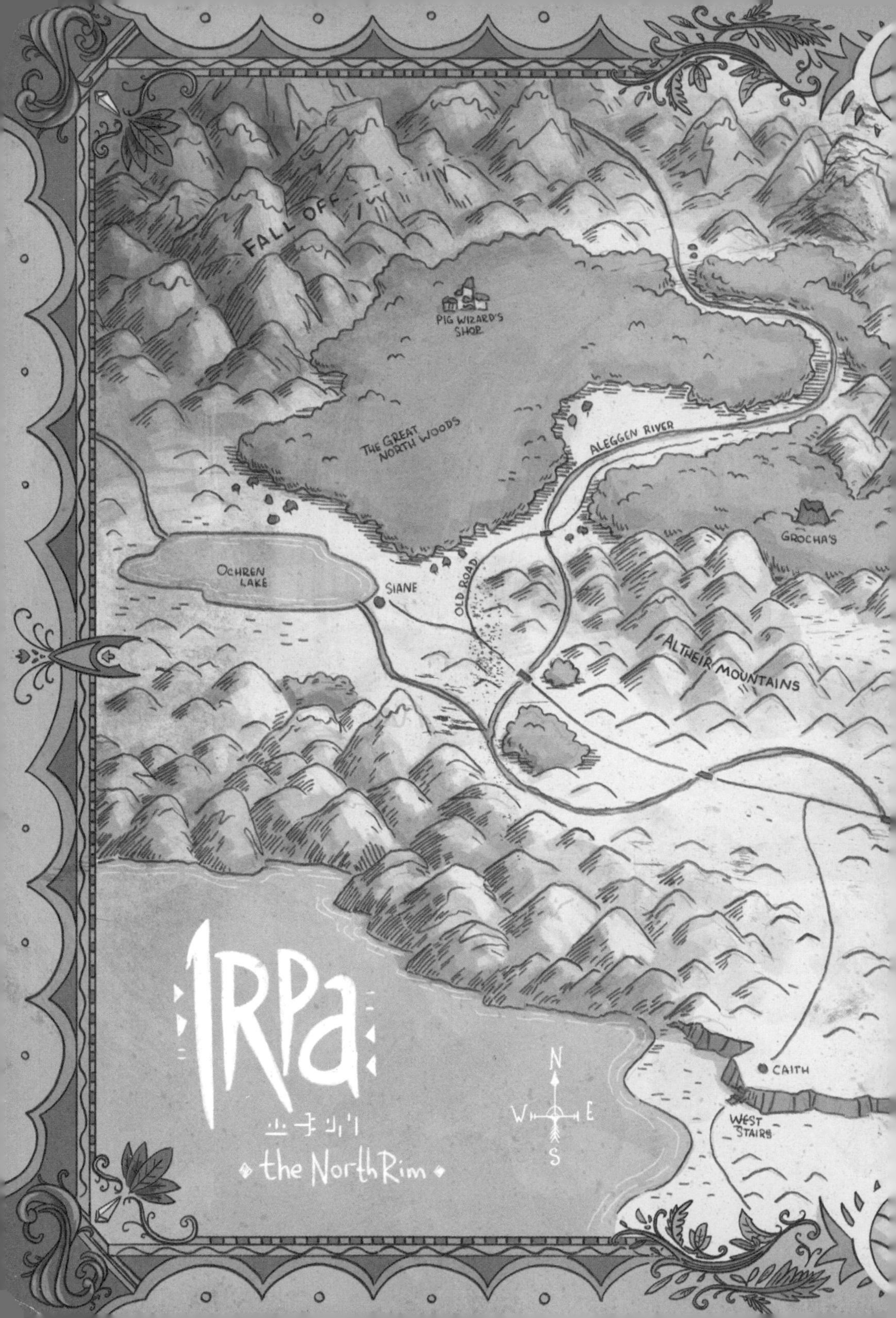
FALL OFF
PIG WIZARD'S SHOP
THE GREAT NORTH WOODS
ALEGGEN RIVER
GROCHA'S
OCHREN LAKE
SIANE
OLD ROAD
ALTHEIR MOUNTAINS
IRPA
the NorthRim
N
W
E
S
CAITH
WEST STAIRS

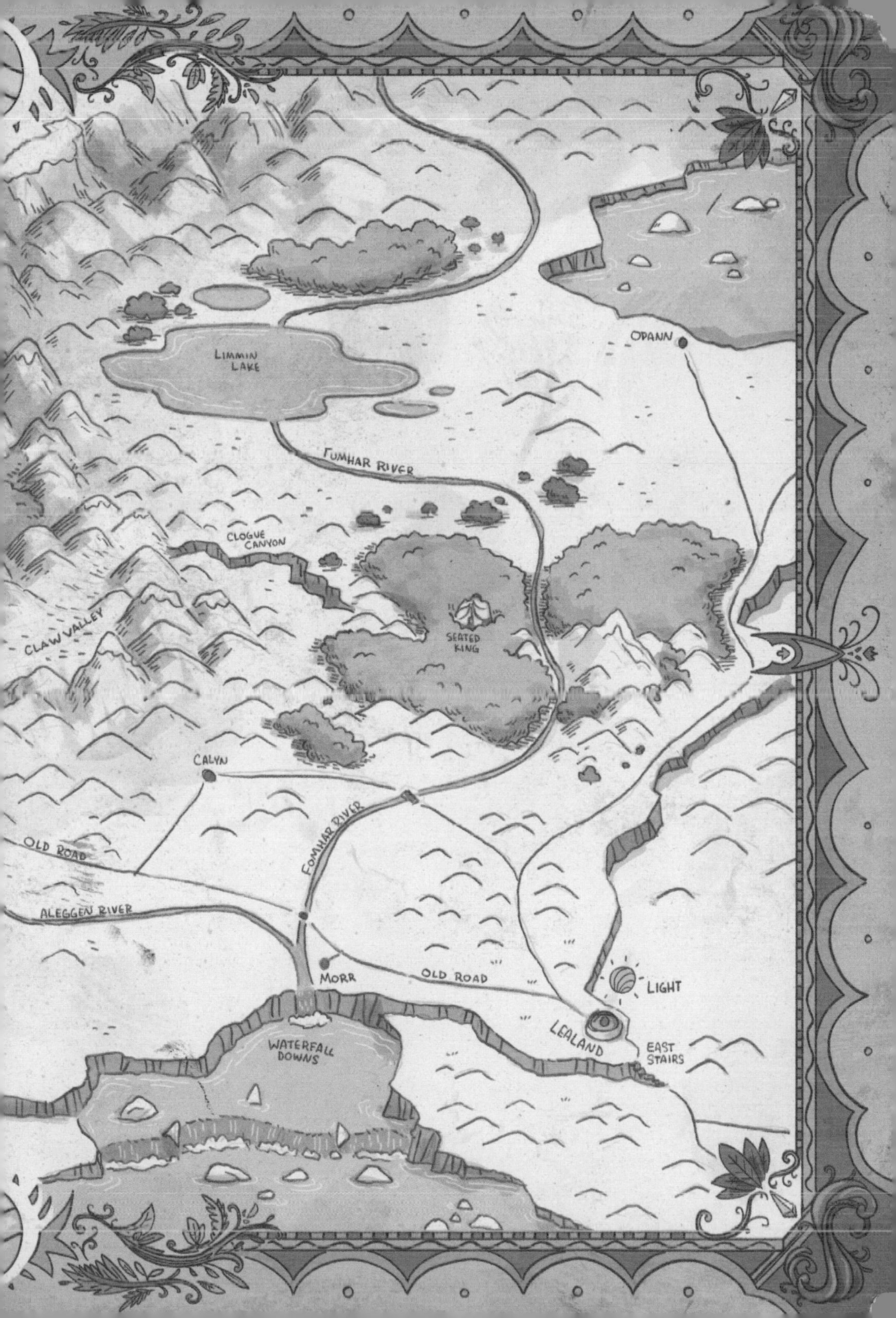

OPANN
LIMMIN LAKE
FUMHAR RIVER
CLOGUE CANYON
SEATED KING
CLAW VALLEY
CALYN
OLD ROAD
FOMHAR RIVER
ALEGGEN RIVER
MORR
OLD ROAD
LIGHT
LEALAND
EAST STAIRS
WATERFALL DOWNS

Walking with a friend in the dark is better
than walking alone in the light.

—Helen Keller

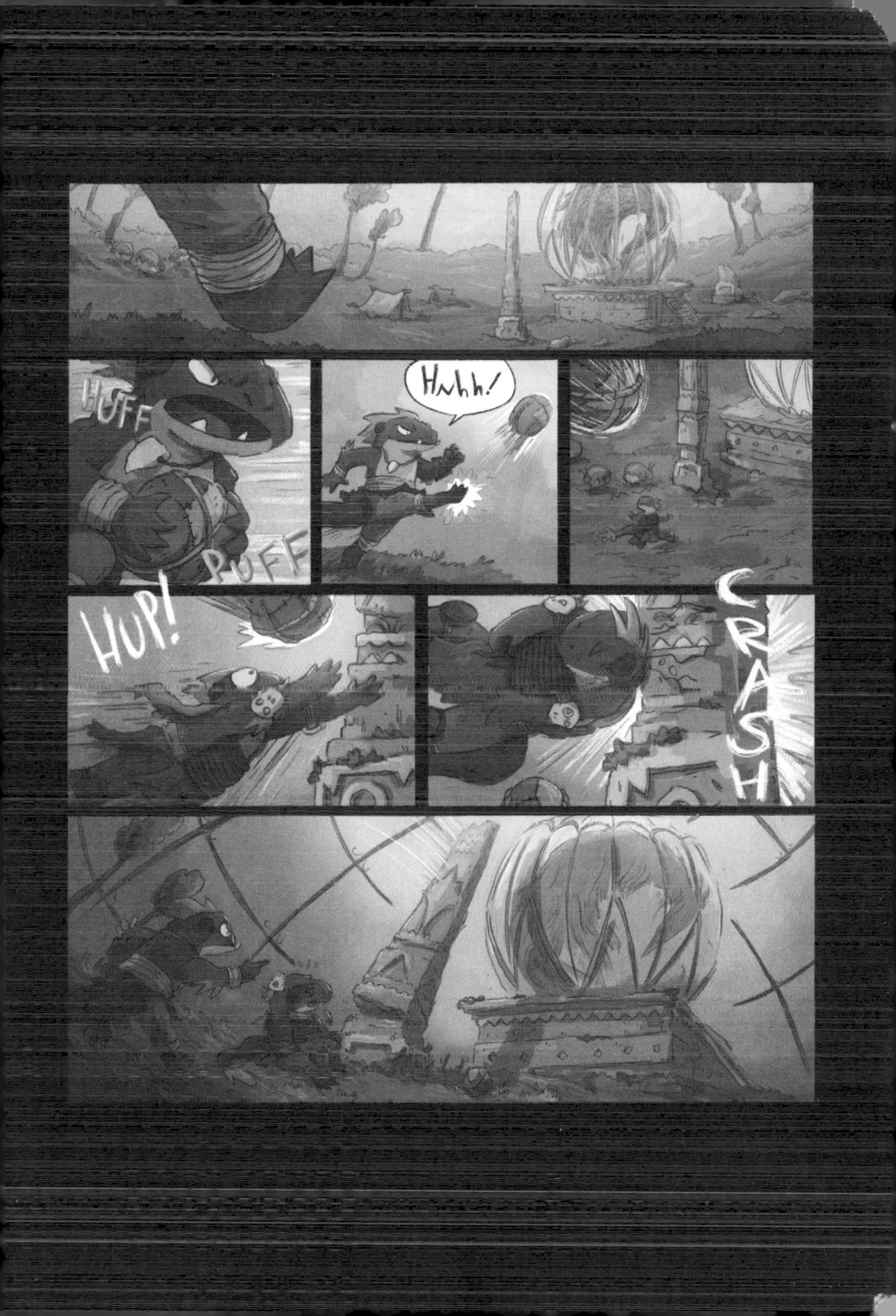
HUFF
PUFF
Hnhh!
HUP!
CRASH

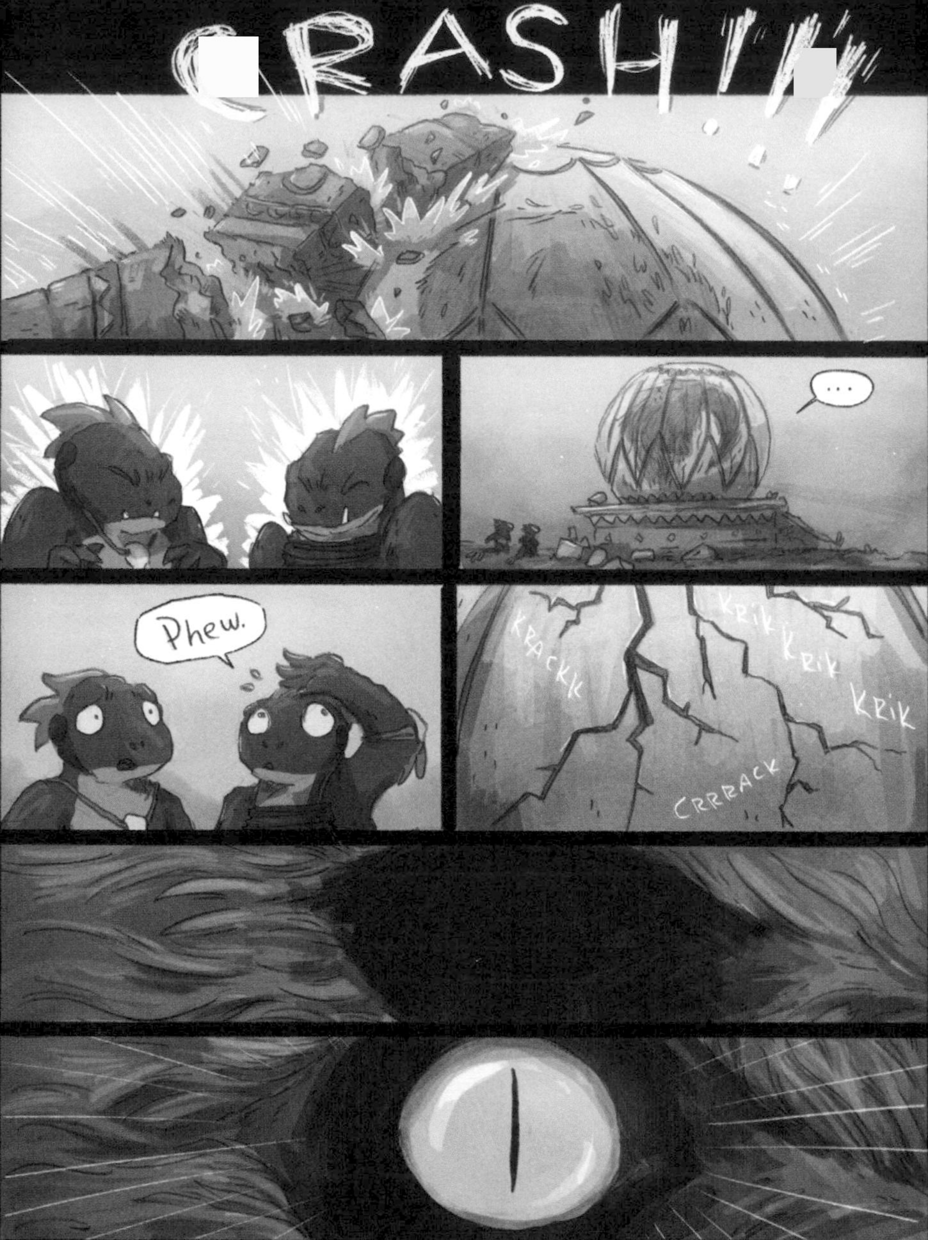
CRASH!!!
...
Phew.
KRACKK
KRIK
KRIK
KRIK
CRRRACK

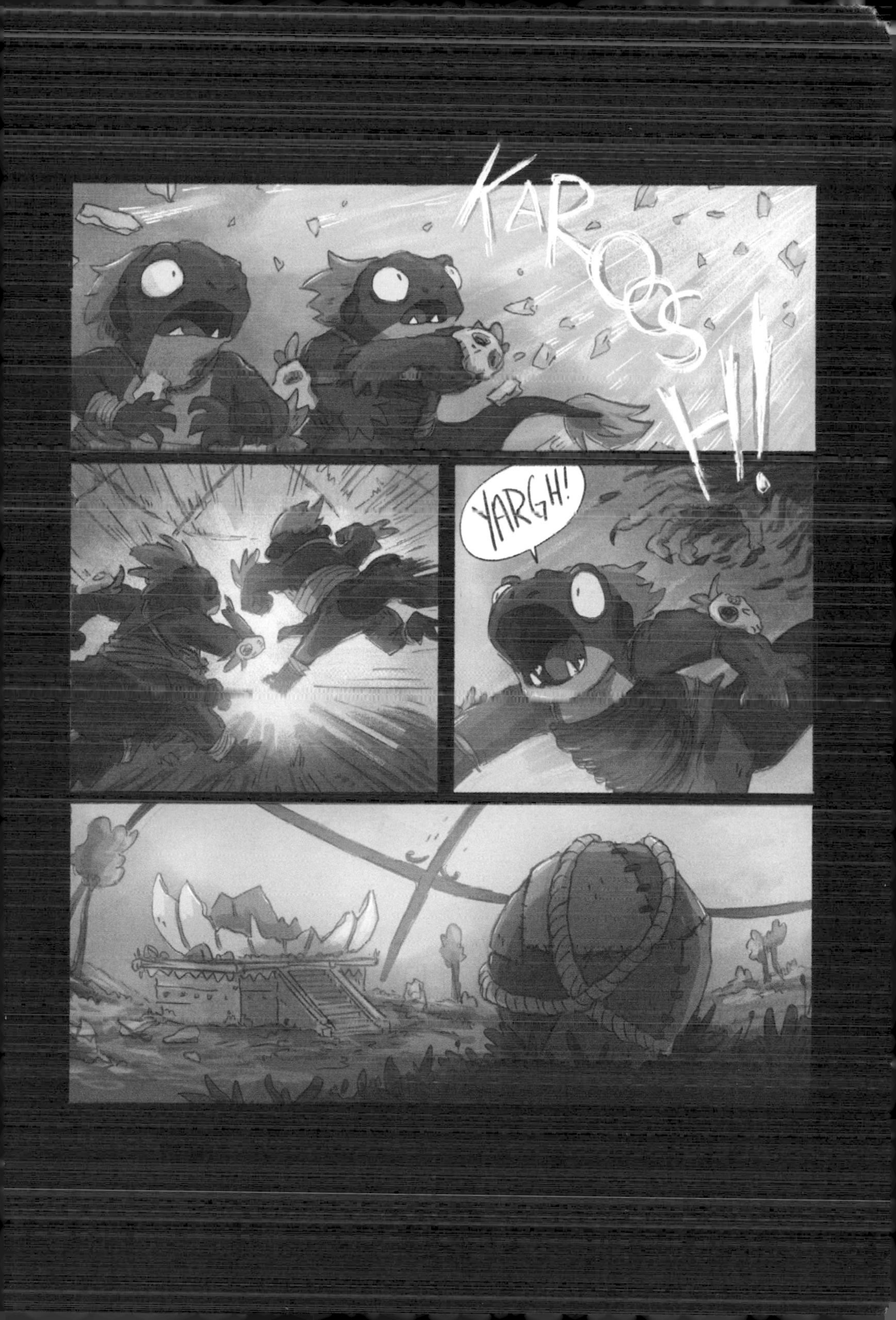
KAROOSH!!
YARGH!

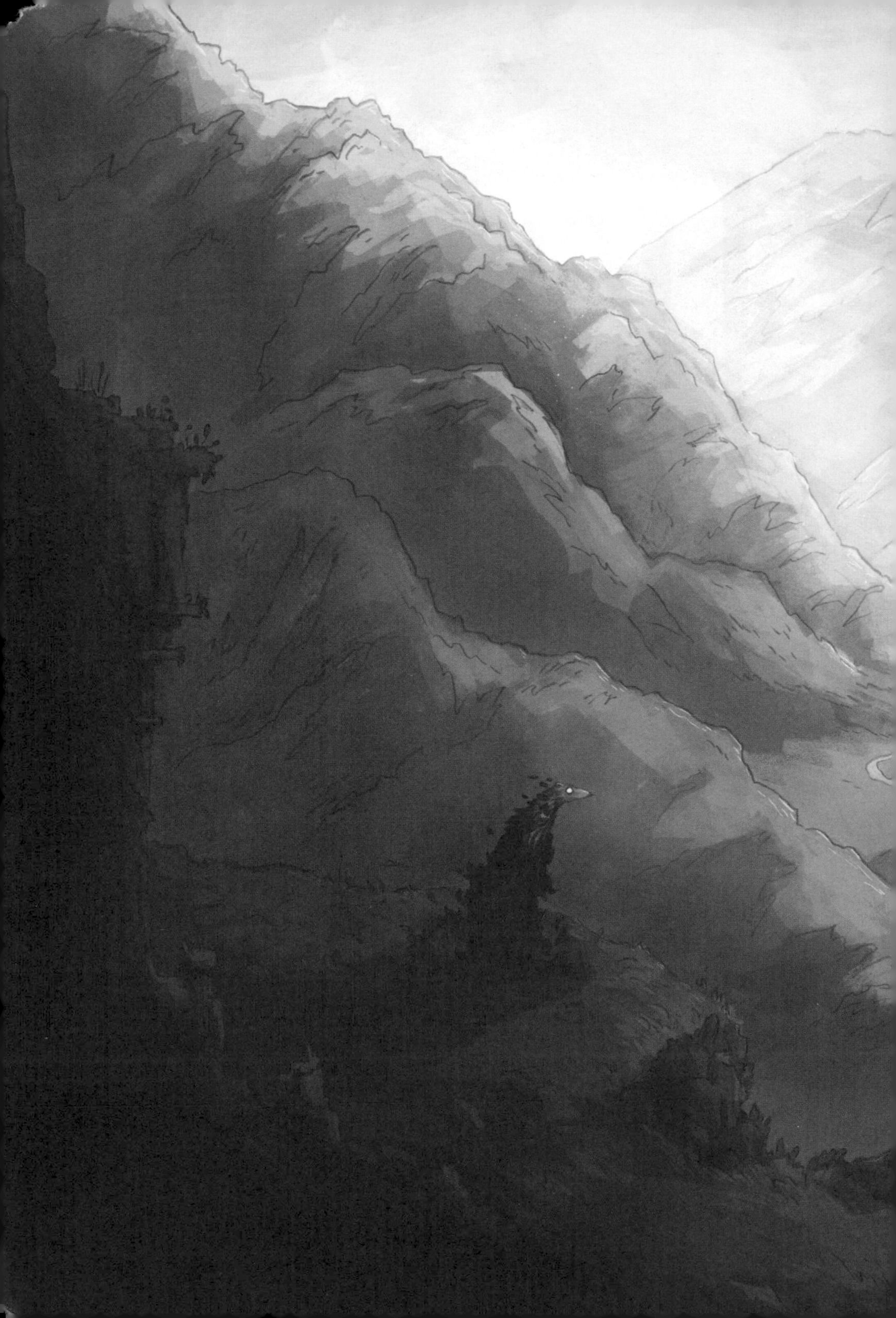

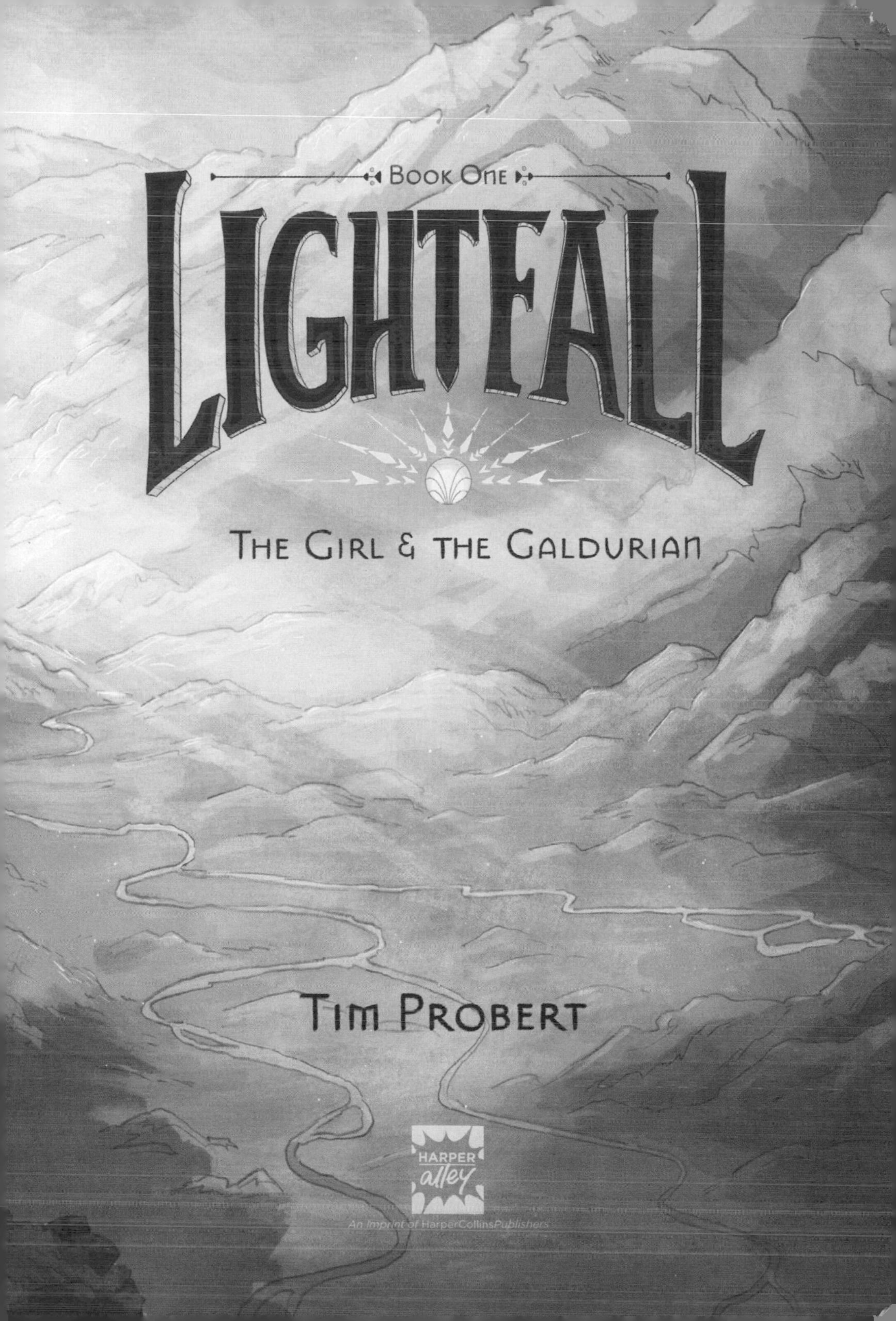

Book One

Lightfall

The Girl & the Galdurian

Tim Probert

Harper Alley
An Imprint of HarperCollinsPublishers

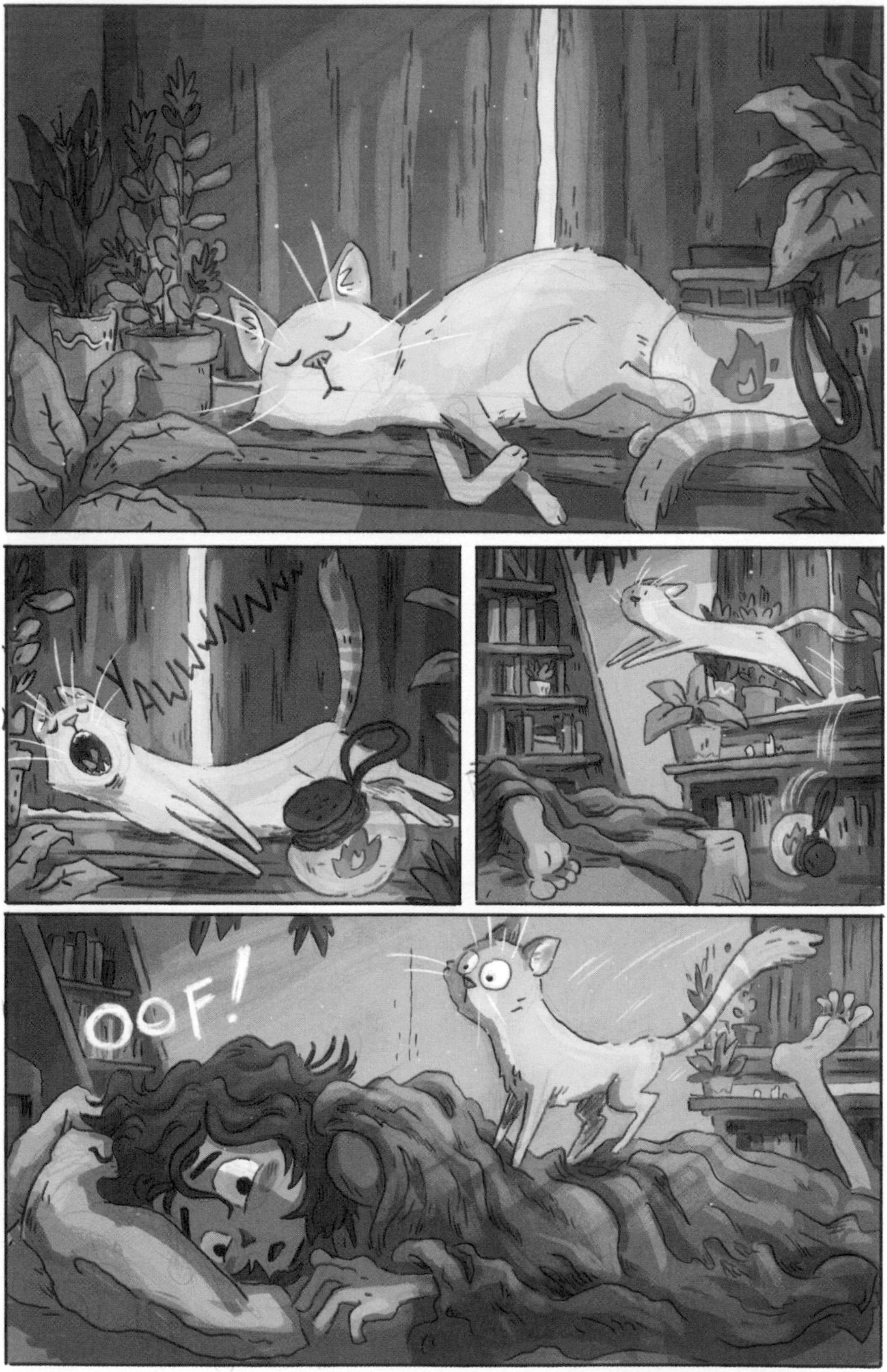
YAWWNNNN
OOF!

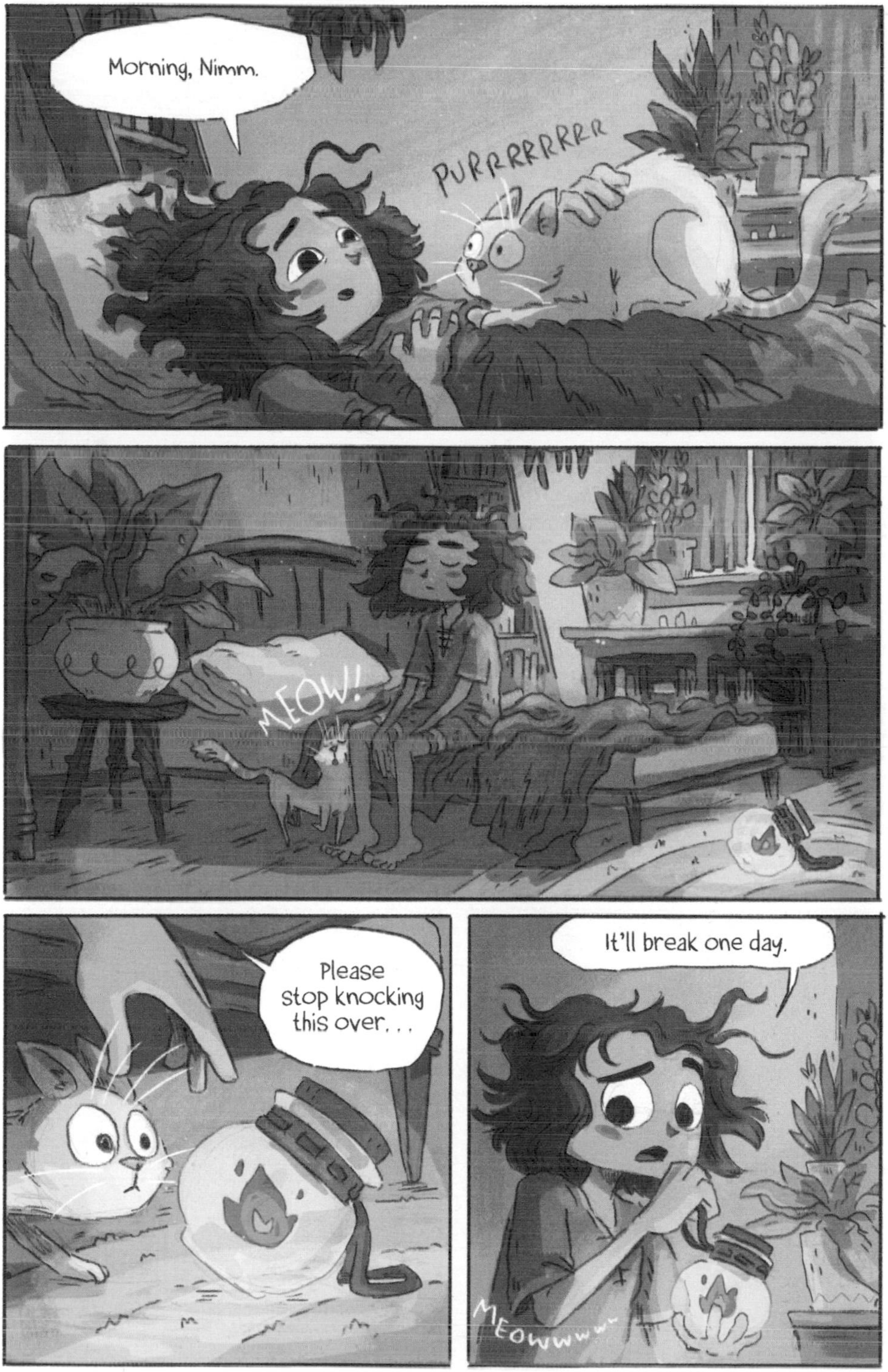
Morning, Nimm.
PURRRRRRRR
MEOW!
Please stop knocking this over. . .
It'll break one day.
MEOWWWW

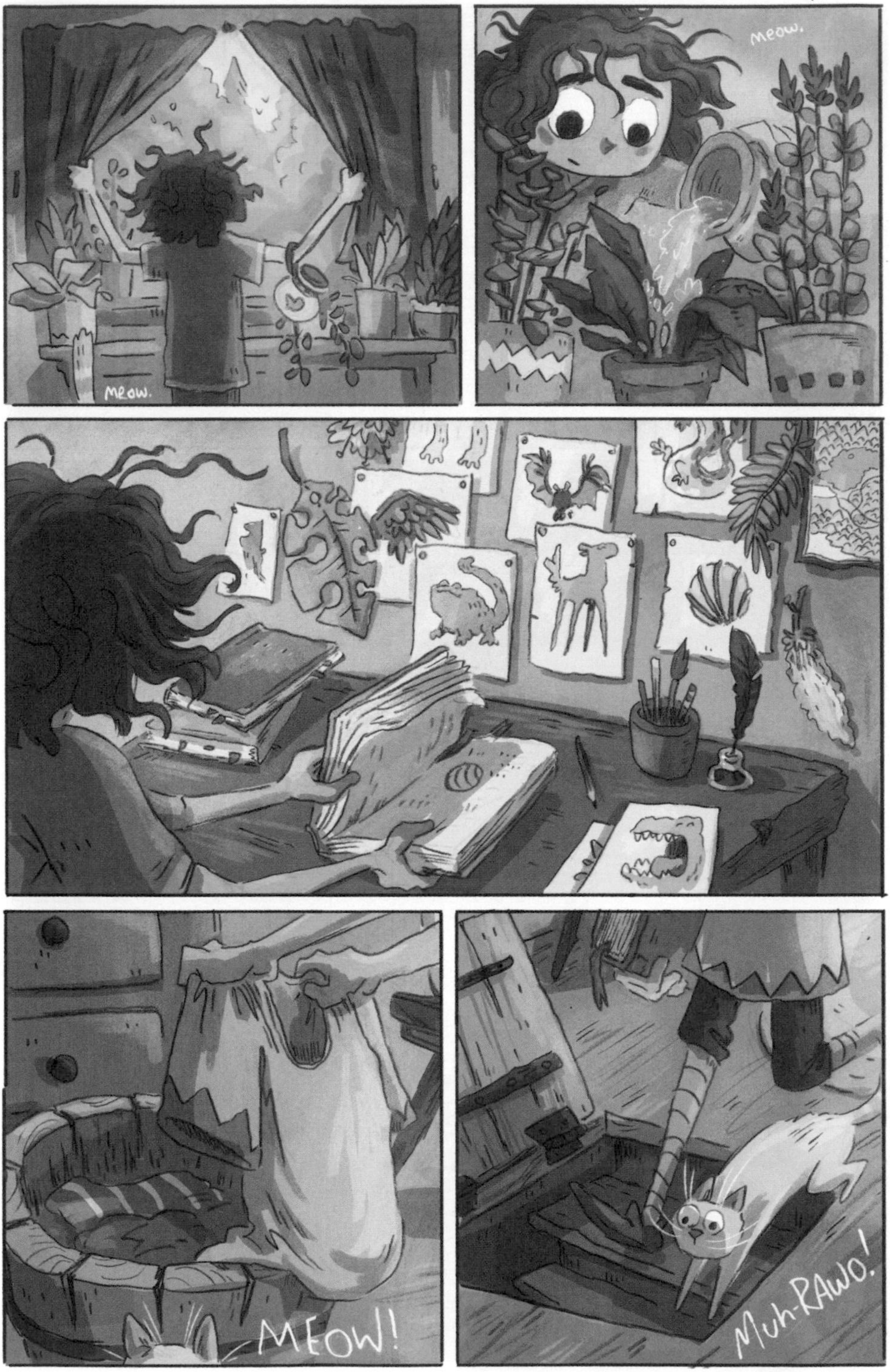
Meow.
Meow.
MEOW!
Muh-RAWO!

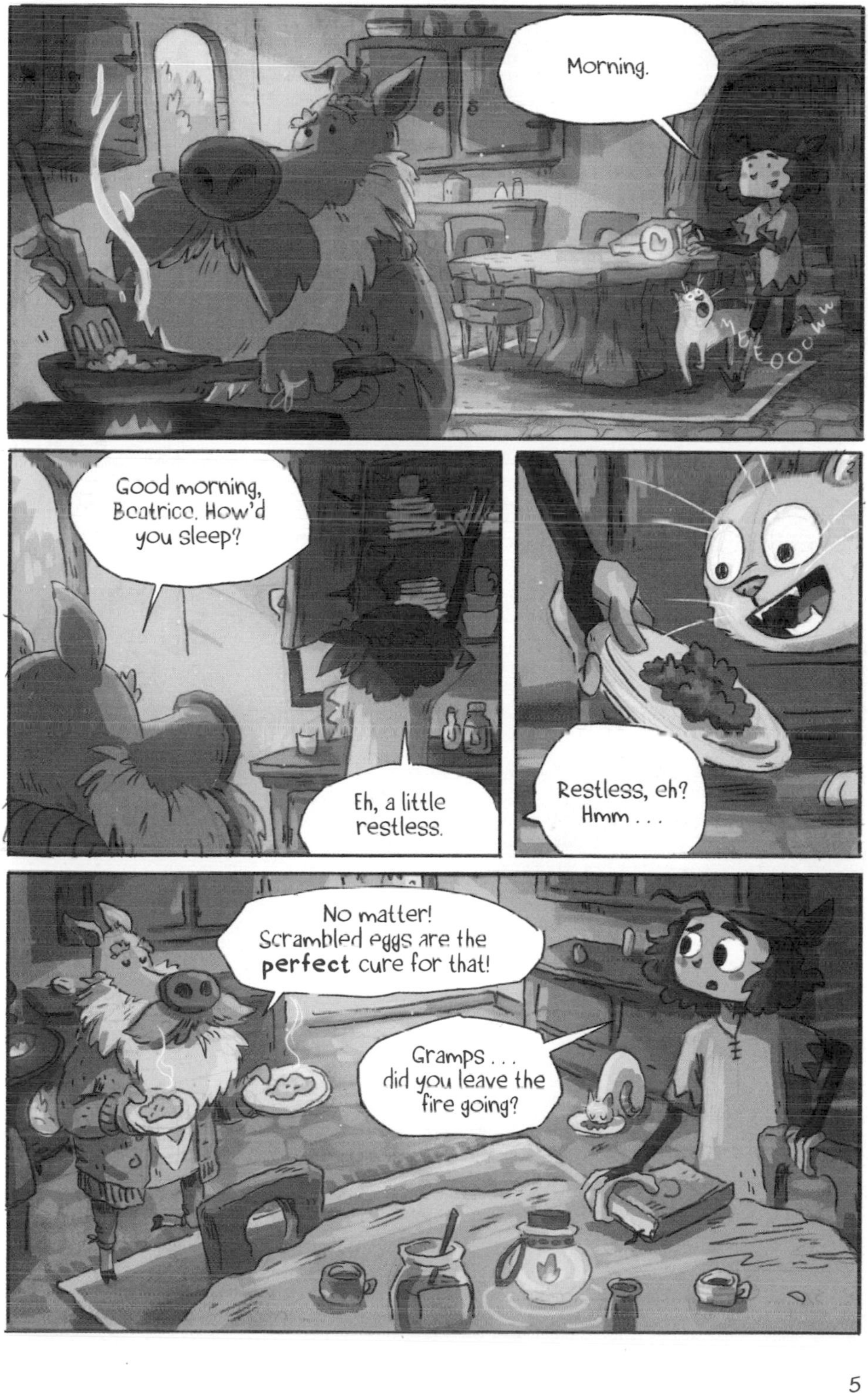
Morning.
MEEOOOOWW
Good morning, Beatrice. How'd you sleep?
Eh, a little restless.
Restless, eh? Hmm . . .
No matter! Scrambled eggs are the **perfect** cure for that!
Gramps . . . did you leave the fire going?

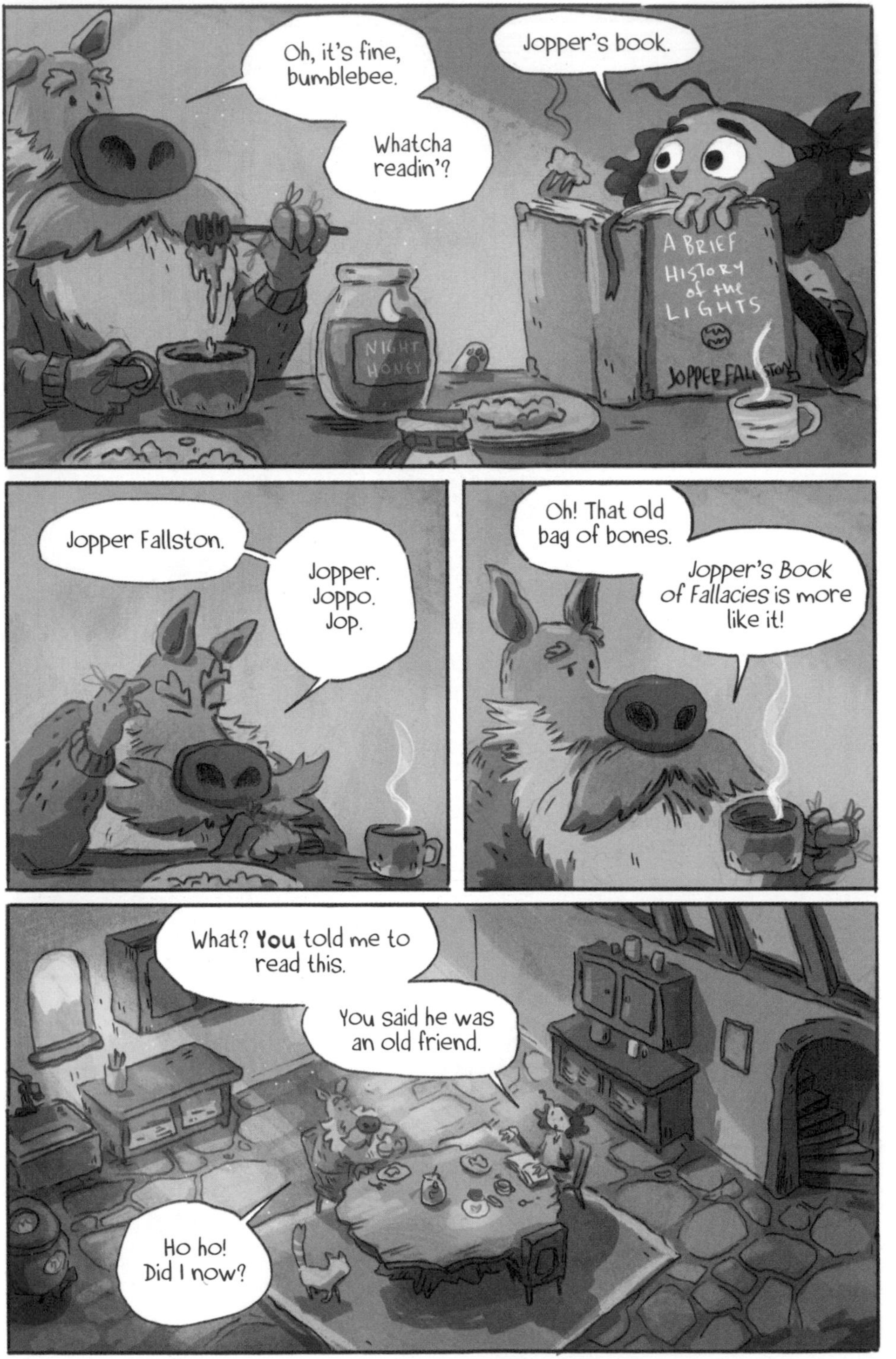
Oh, it's fine, bumblebee.
Whatcha readin'?
Jopper's book.
NIGHT HONEY
A BRIEF HISTORY of the LIGHTS
JOPPER FALLSTON
Jopper Fallston.
Jopper. Joppo. Jop.
Oh! That old bag of bones.
Jopper's Book of Fallacies is more like it!
What? **You** told me to read this.
You said he was an old friend.
Ho ho! Did I now?

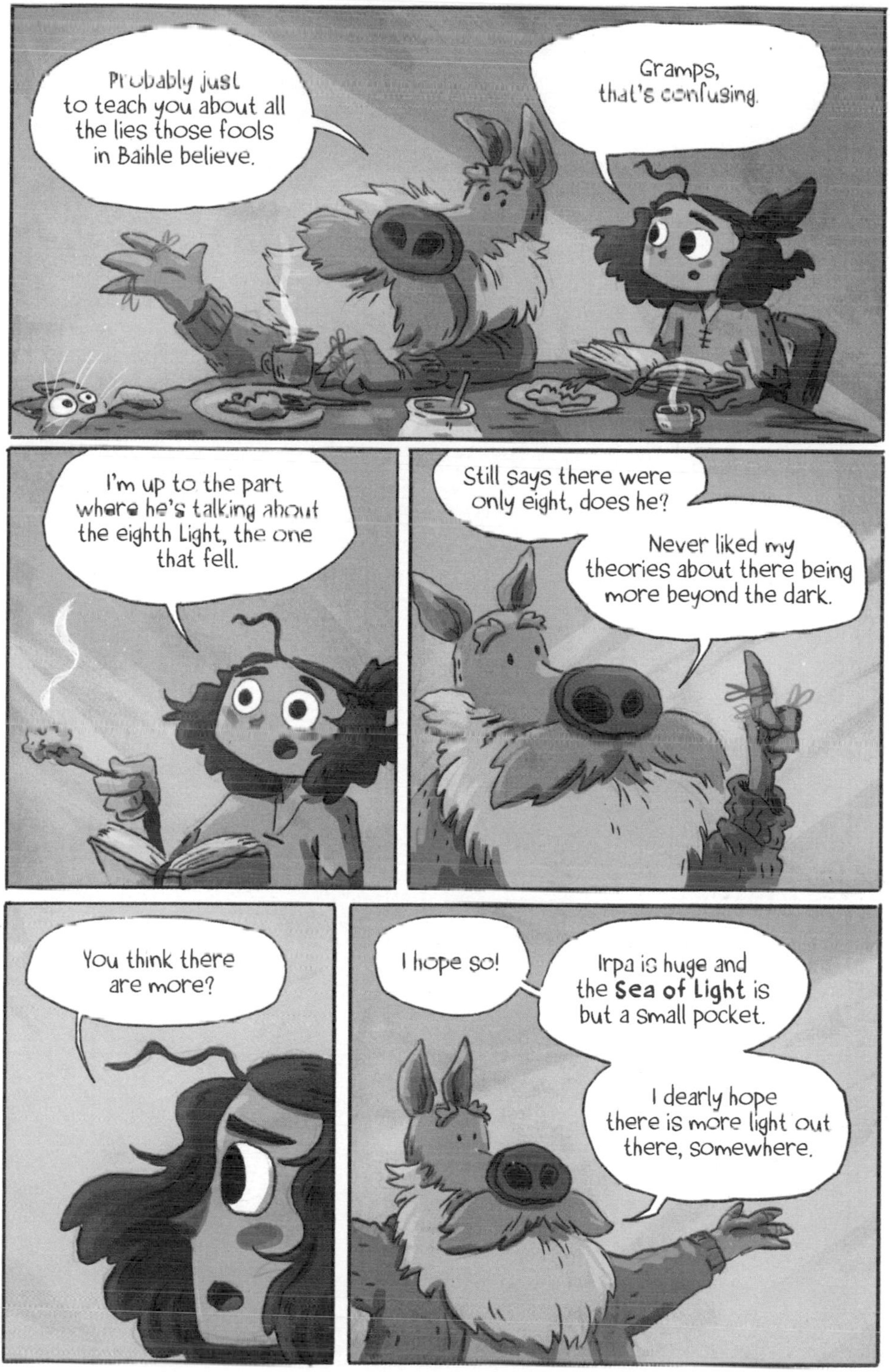

Probably just to teach you about all the lies those fools in Baihle believe.
Gramps, that's confusing.
I'm up to the part where he's talking about the eighth Light, the one that fell.
Still says there were only eight, does he?
Never liked my theories about there being more beyond the dark.
You think there are more?
I hope so!
Irpa is huge and the **Sea of Light** is but a small pocket.
I dearly hope there is more light out there, somewhere.

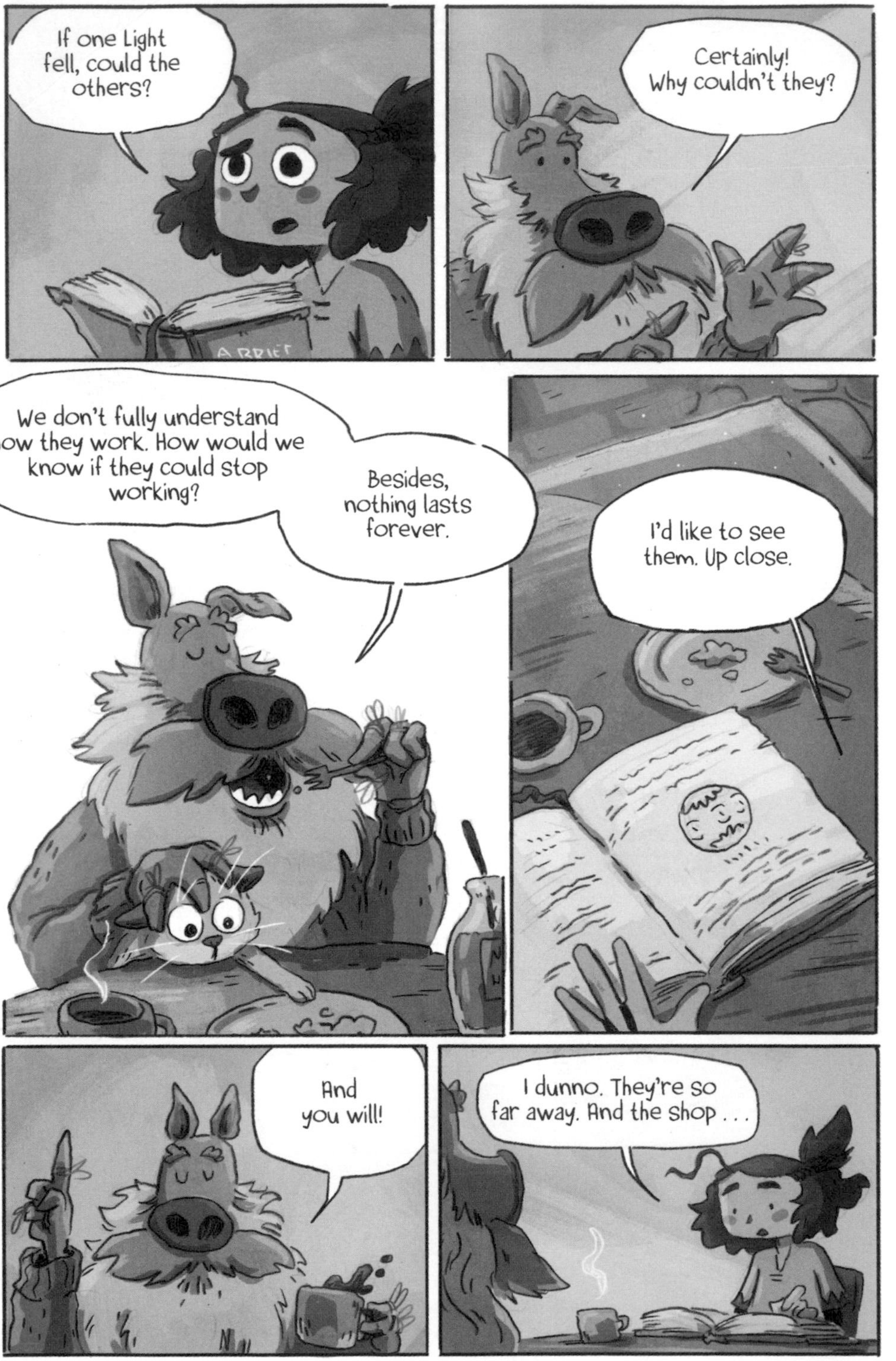
If one Light fell, could the others?
ARBIE
Certainly! Why couldn't they?
We don't fully understand how they work. How would we know if they could stop working?
Besides, nothing lasts forever.
I'd like to see them. Up close.
And you will!
I dunno. They're so far away. And the shop . . .

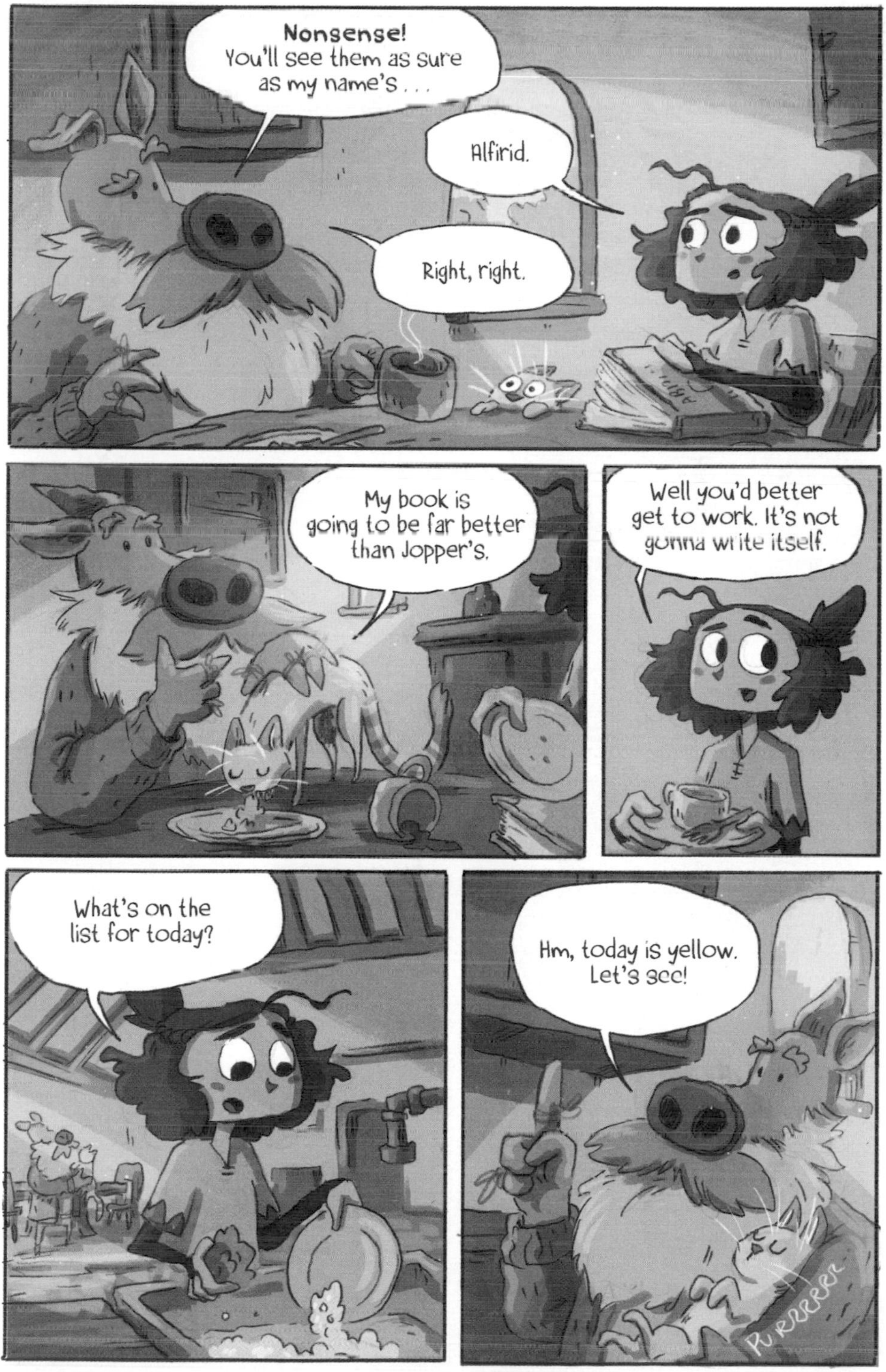
Nonsense! You'll see them as sure as my name's . . .
Alfirid.
Right, right.
My book is going to be far better than Jopper's.
Well you'd better get to work. It's not gonna write itself.
What's on the list for today?
Hm, today is yellow. Let's see!
PURRRRR

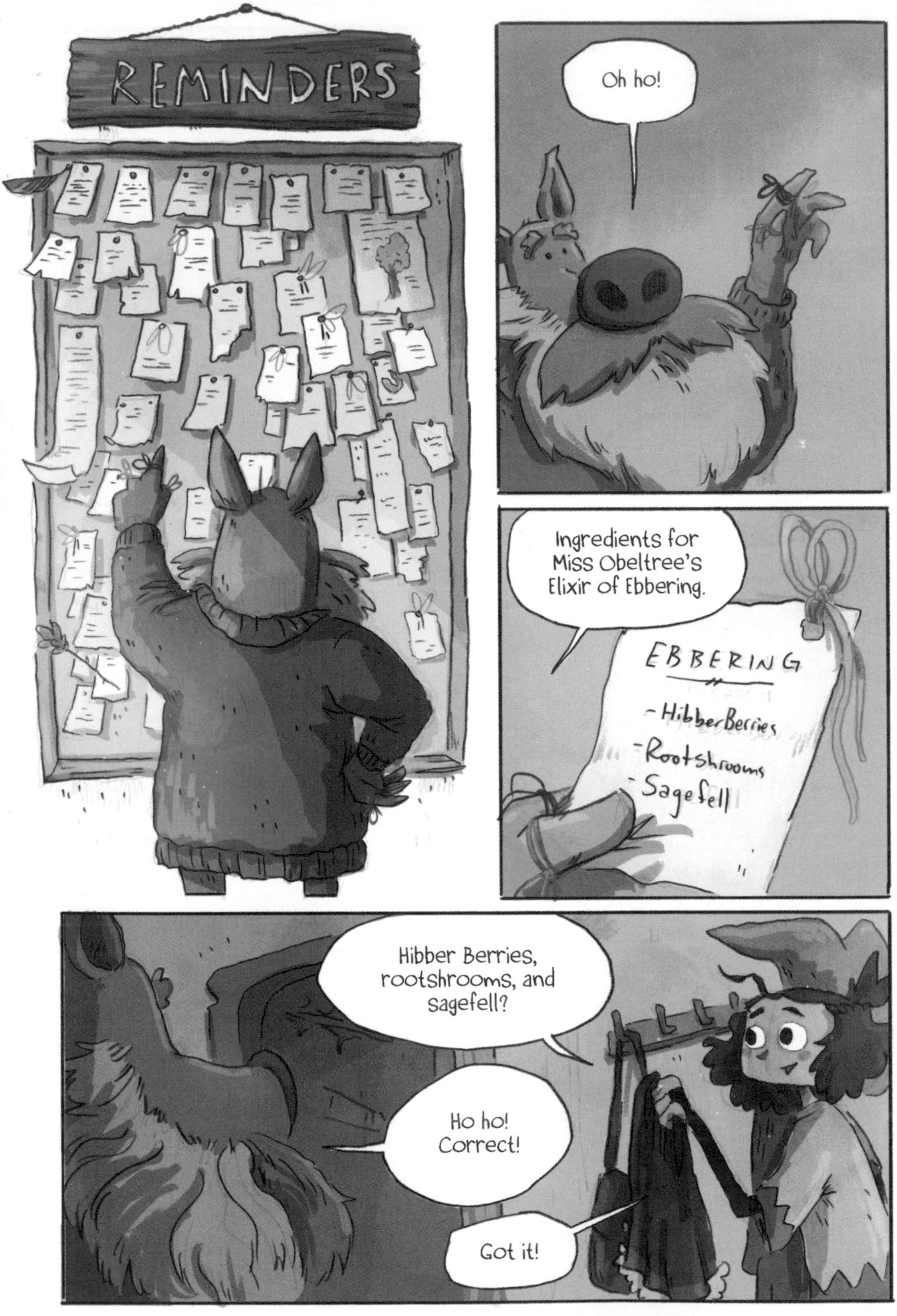
REMINDERS
Oh ho!
Ingredients for Miss Obeltree's Elixir of Ebbering.
EBBERING
-HibberBerries
-Rootshrooms
-Sagefell
Hibber Berries, rootshrooms, and sagefell?
Ho ho! Correct!
Got it!

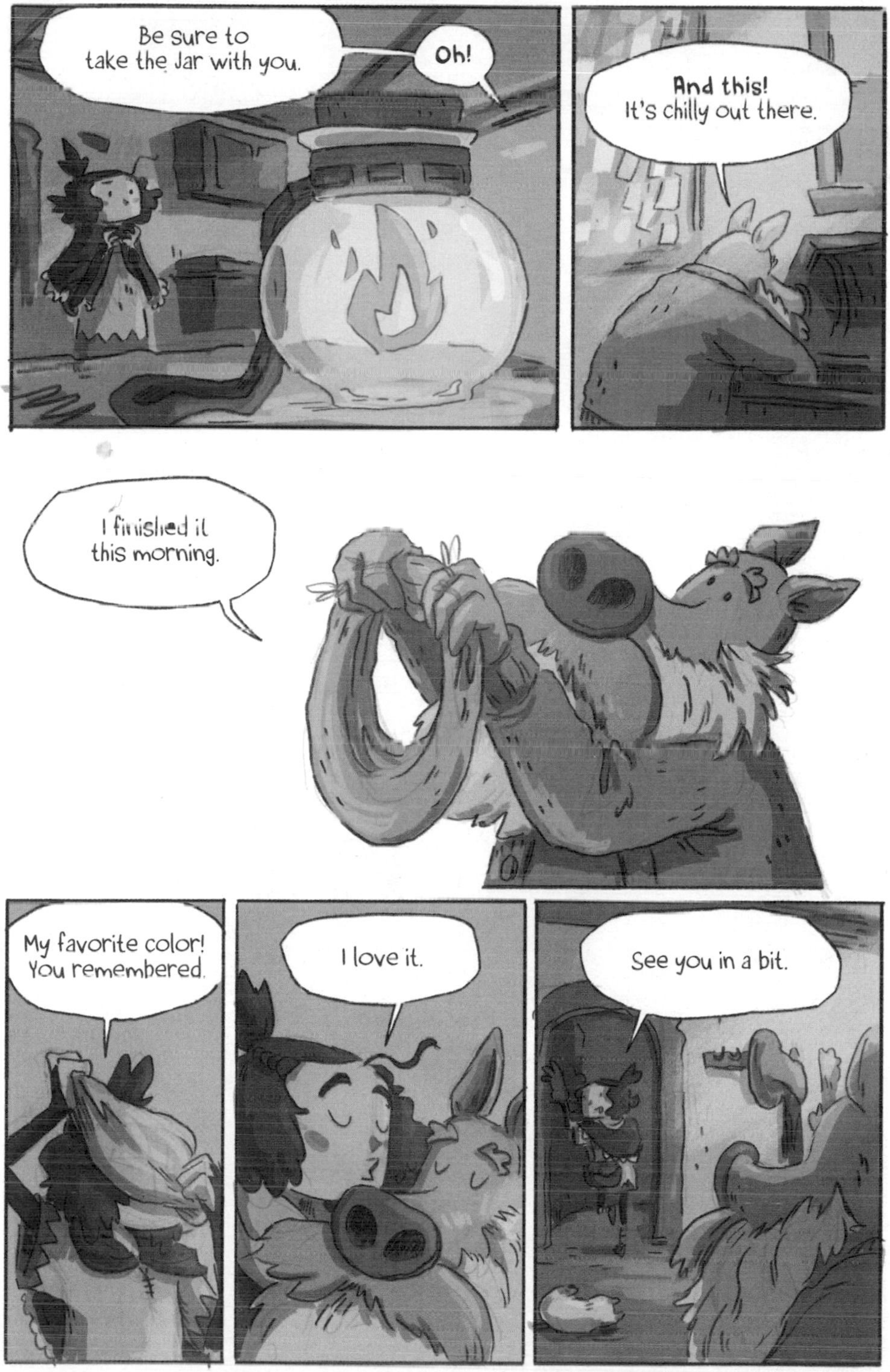
Be sure to take the Jar with you.
Oh!
And this! It's chilly out there.
I finished it this morning.
My favorite color! You remembered.
I love it.
See you in a bit.

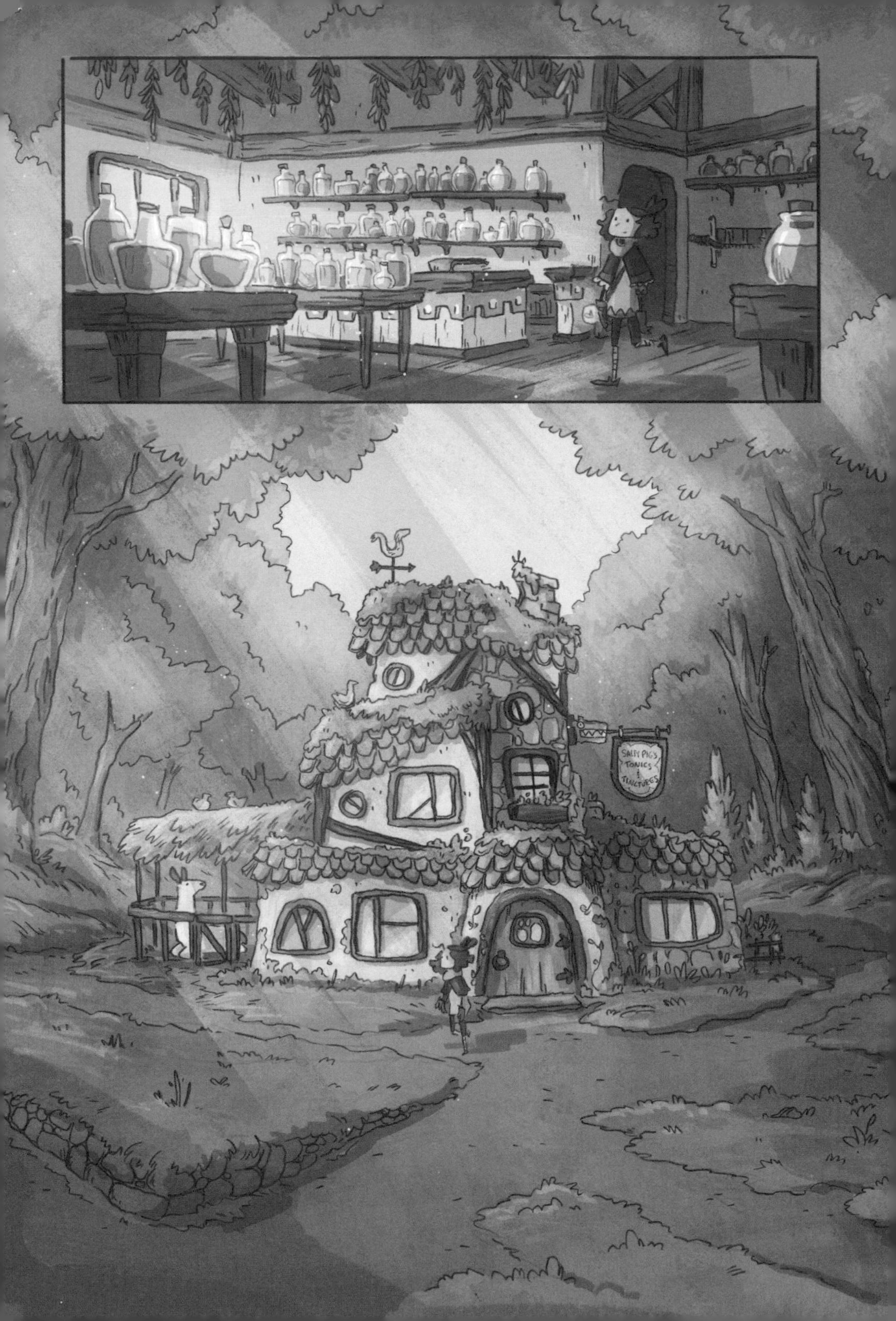
SALTY PIG'S
TONICS
&
TINCTURES

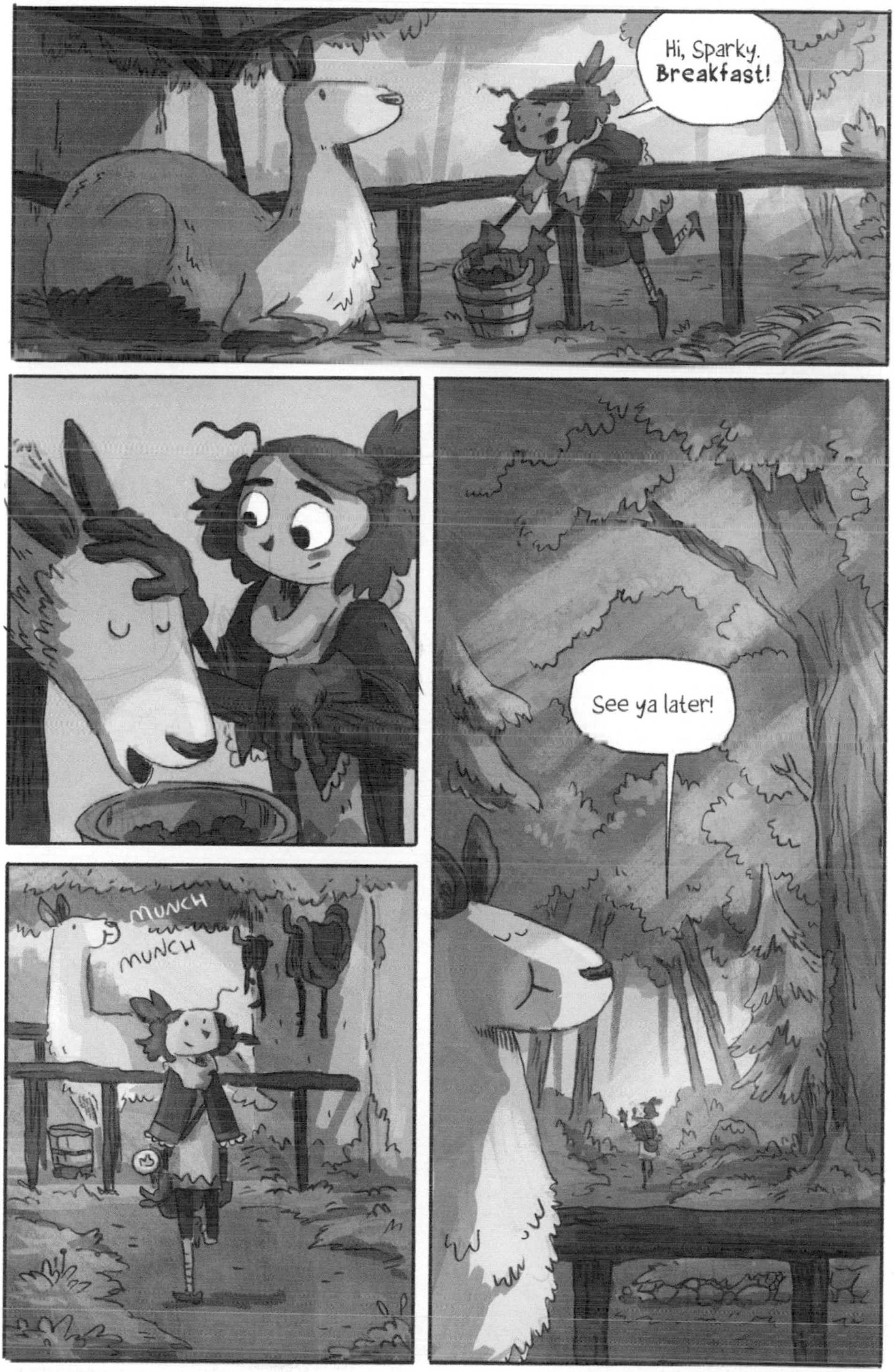
Hi, Sparky. **Breakfast!**
MUNCH
MUNCH
See ya later!

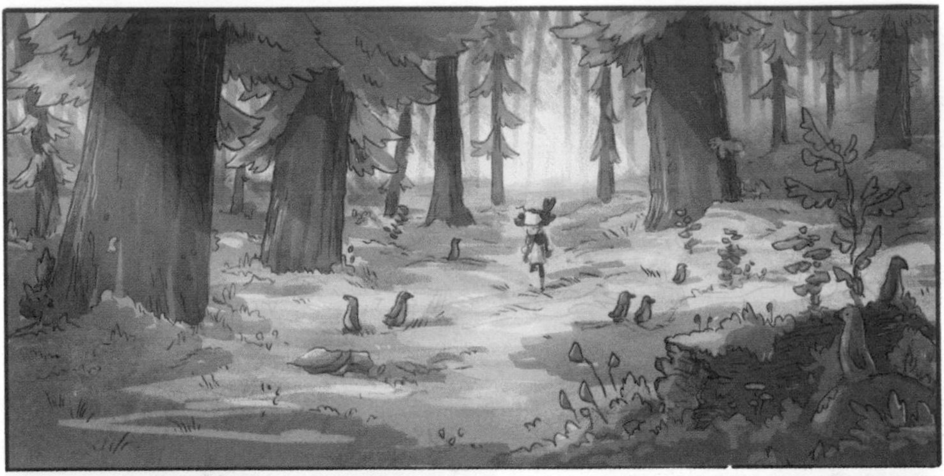

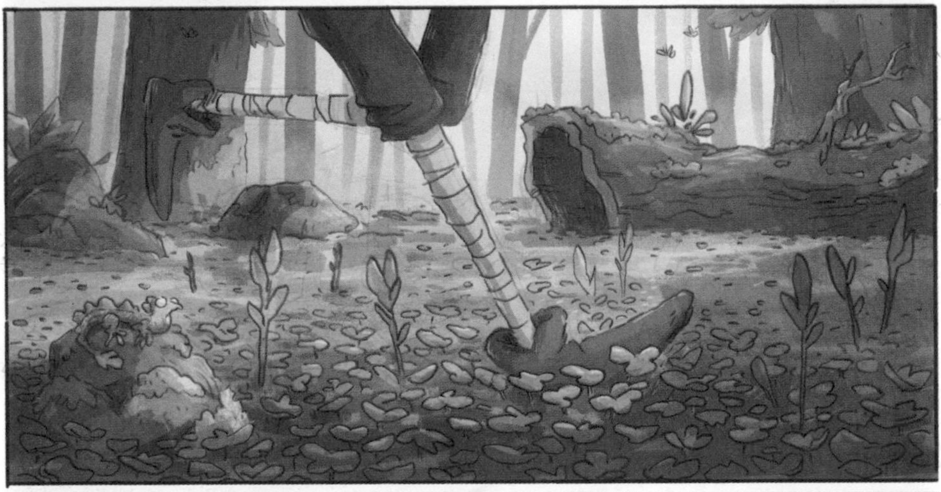

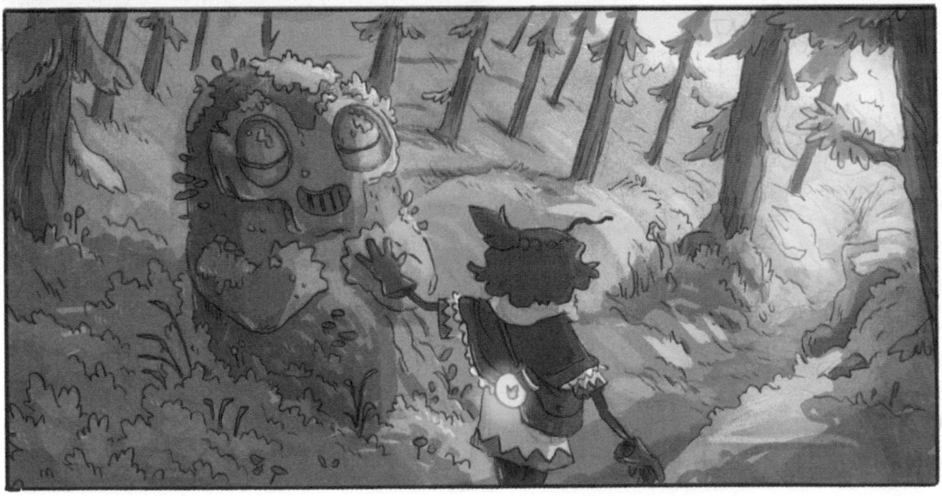

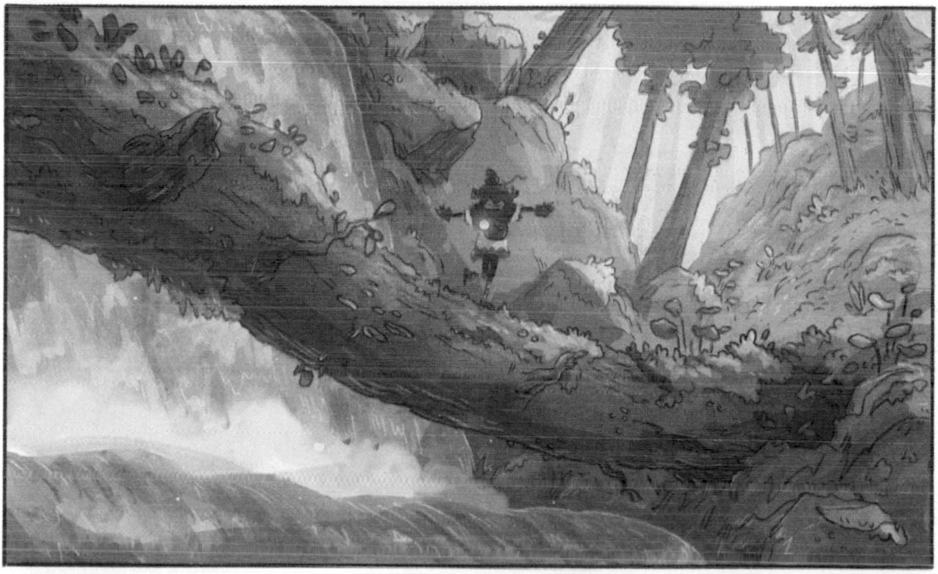

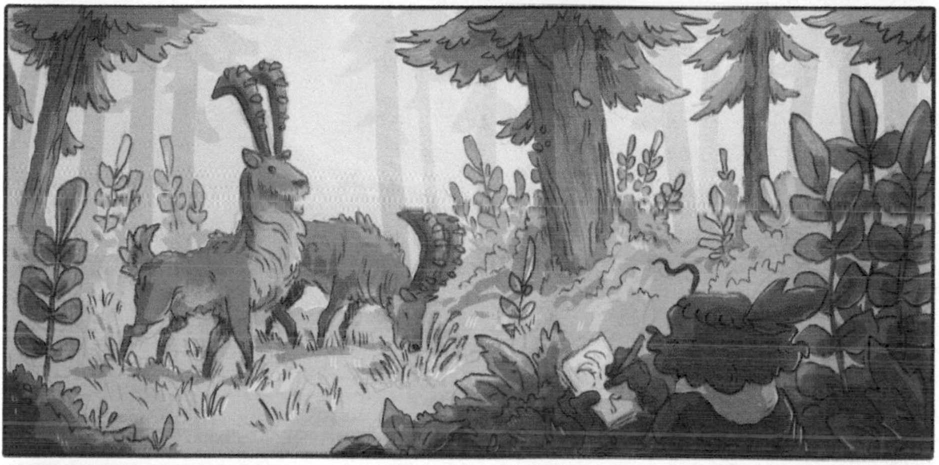

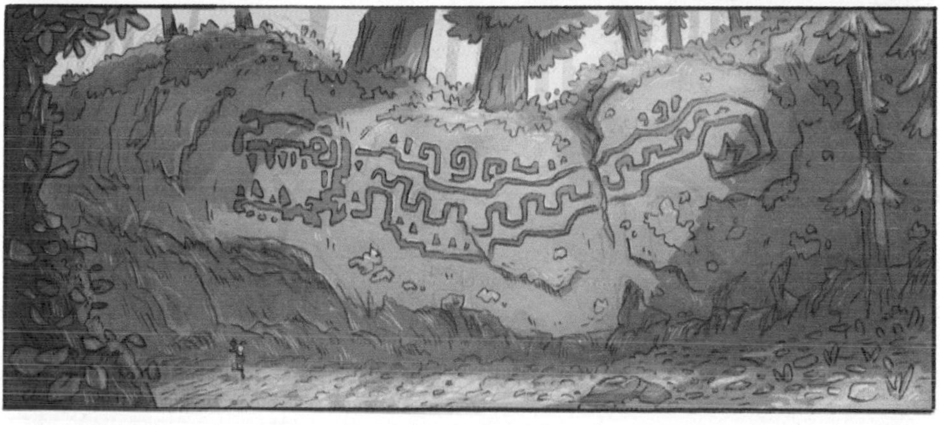

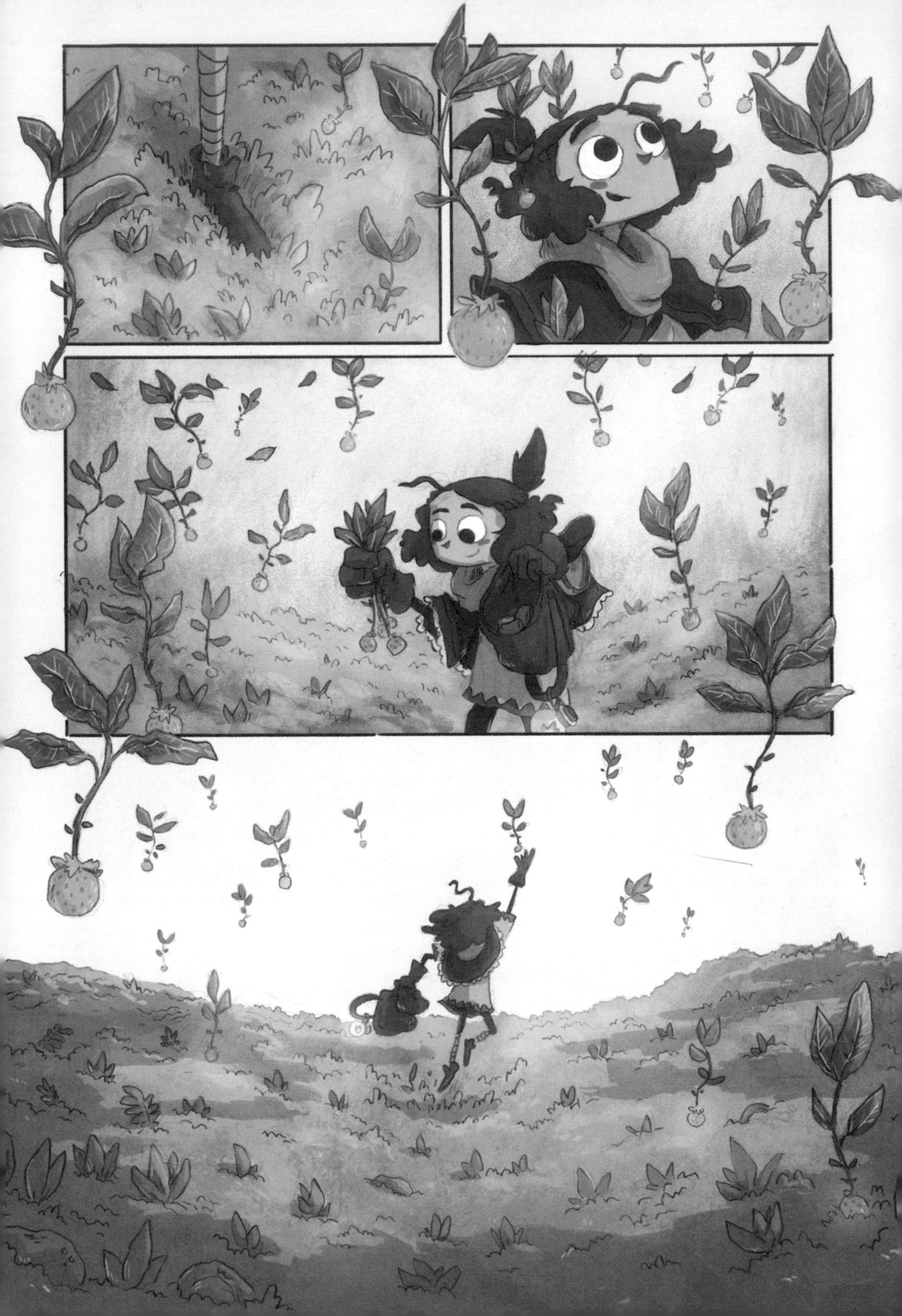

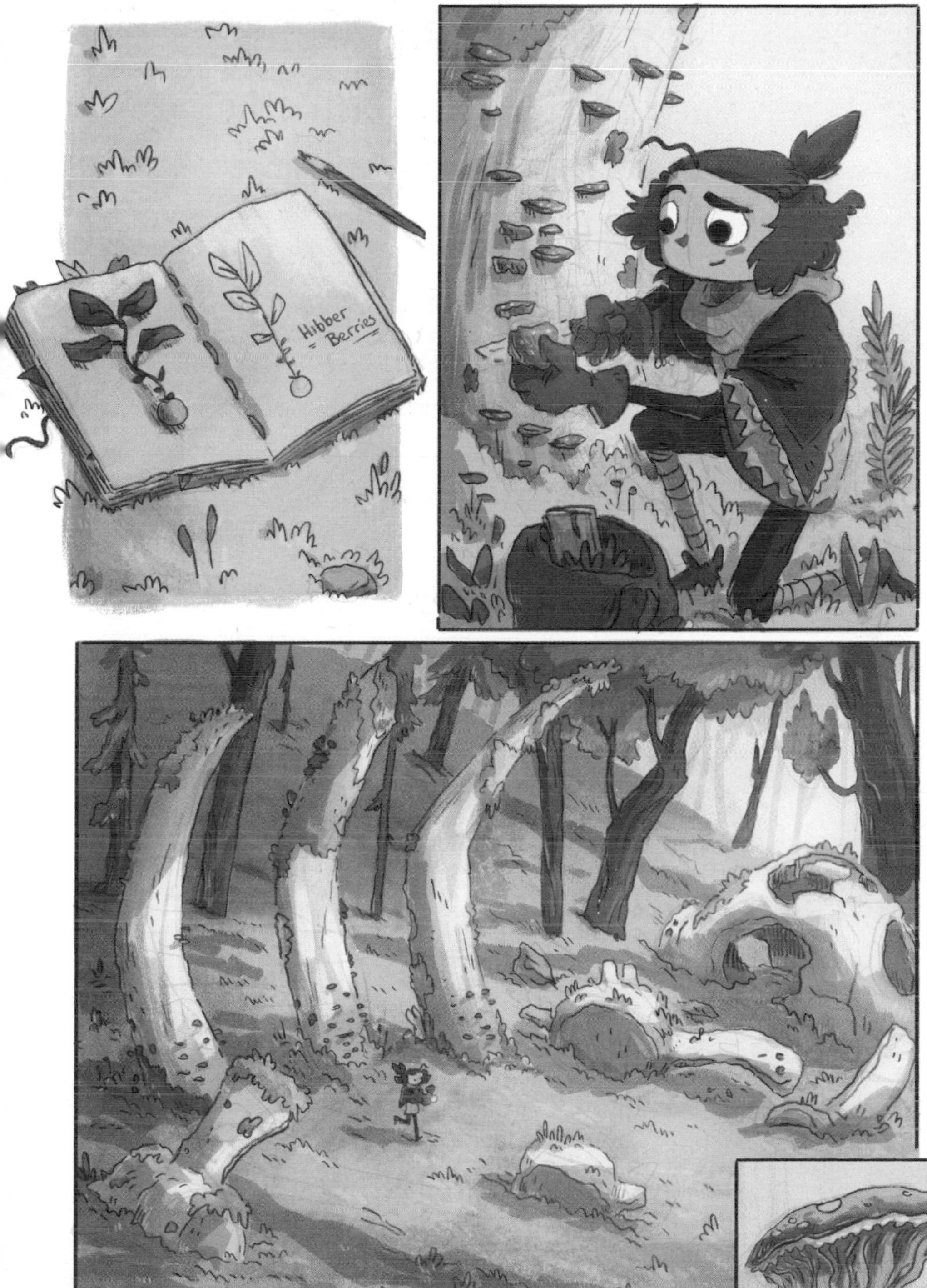
Hibber = Berries
Rootshroom

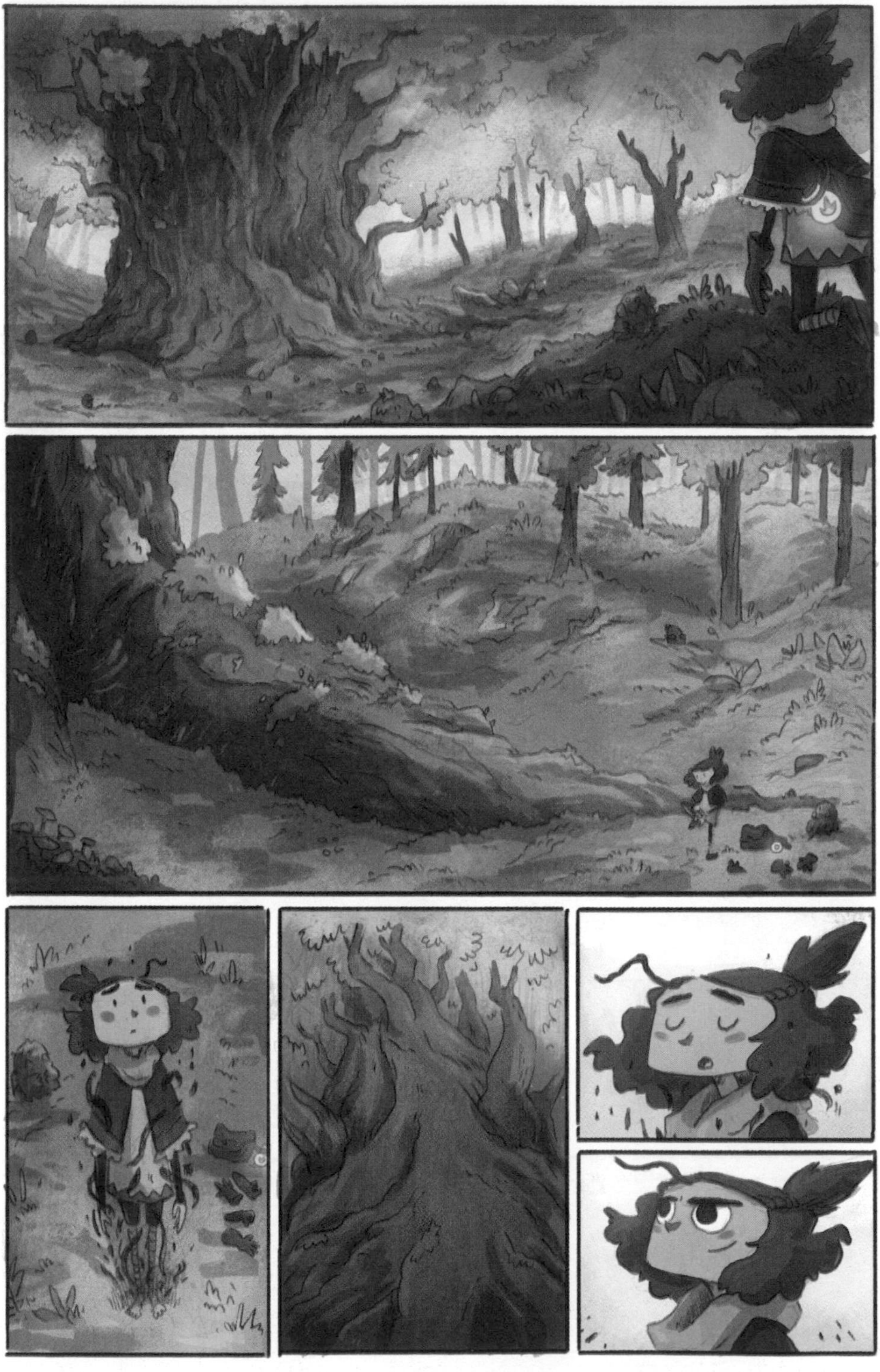

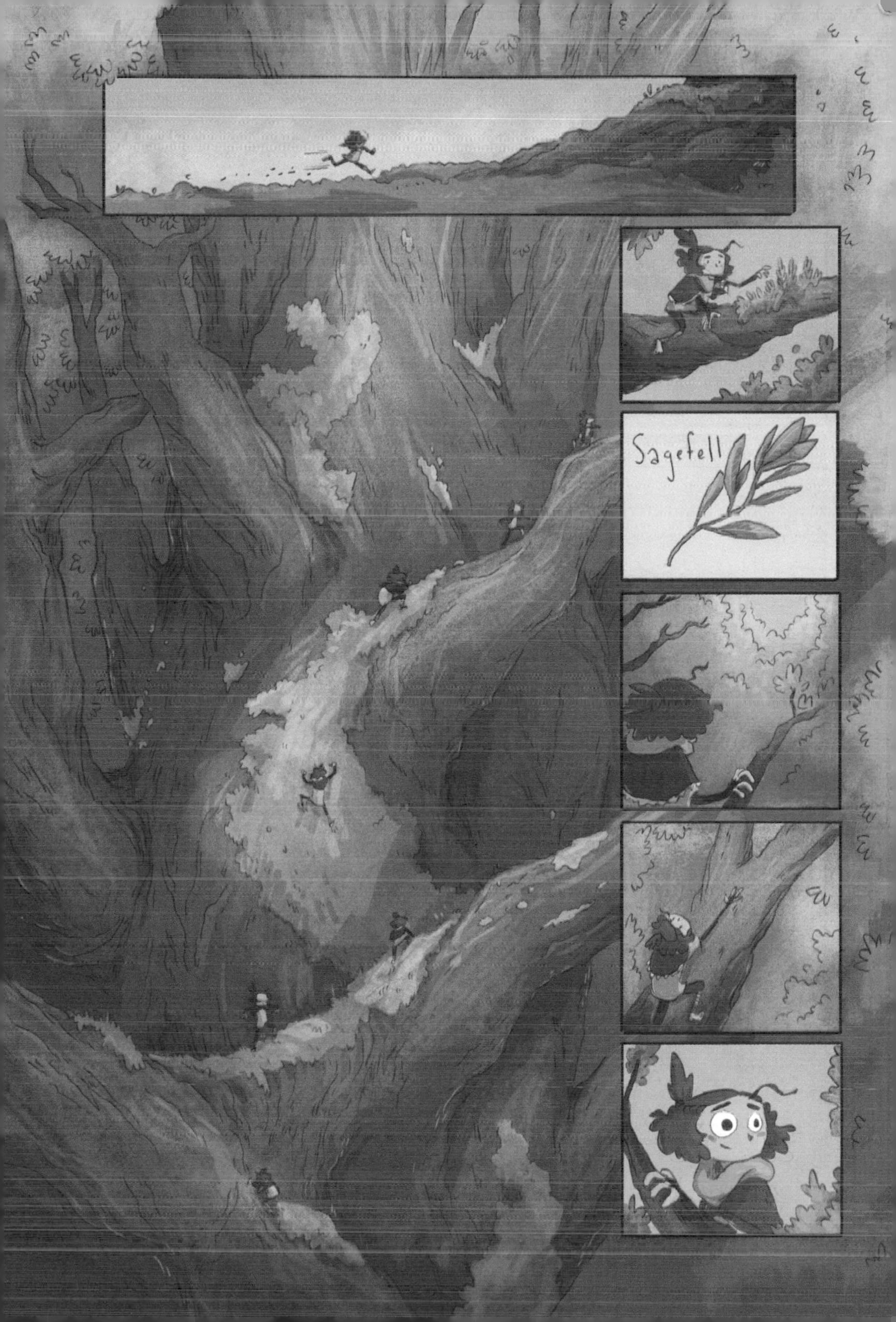
Sagefell

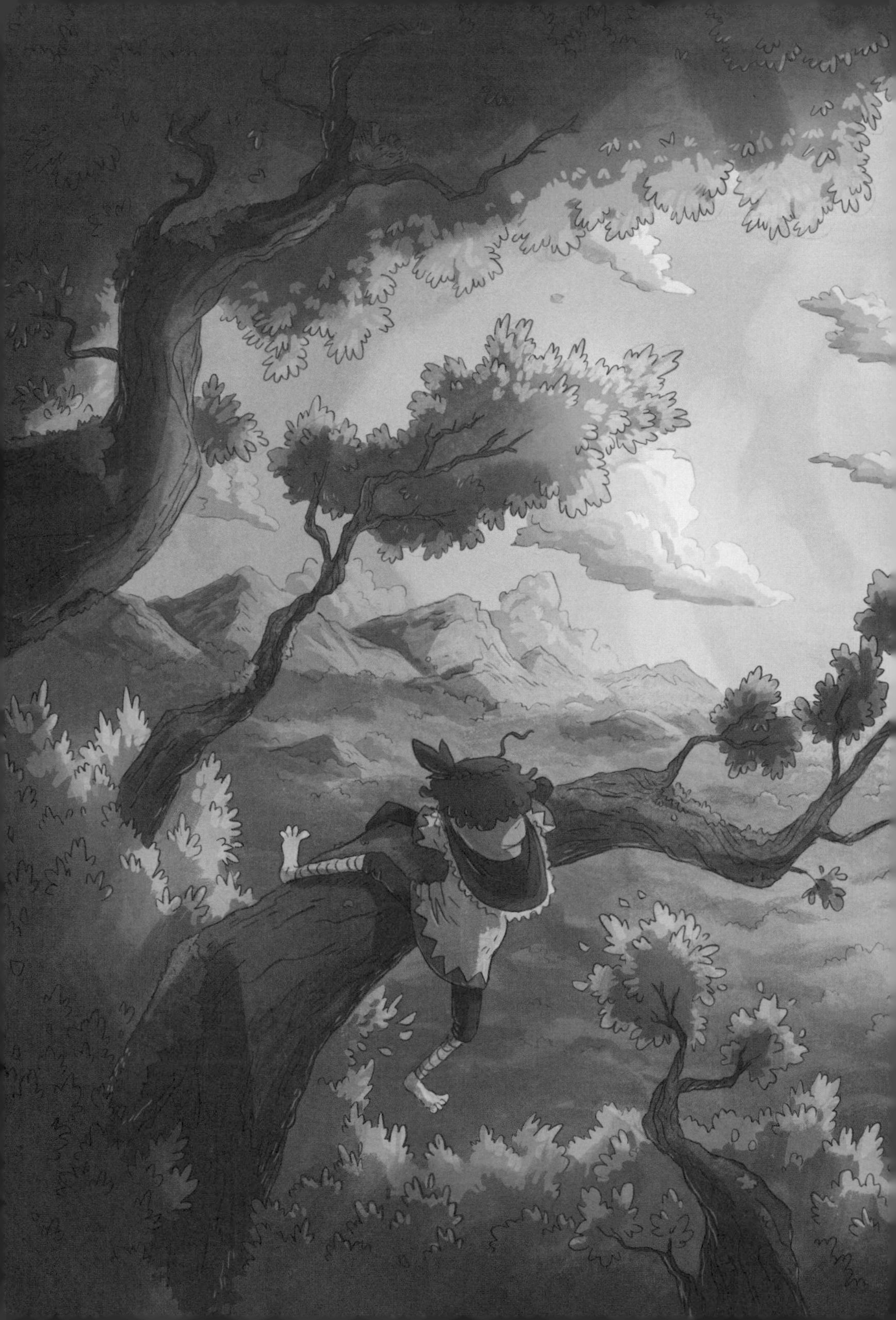

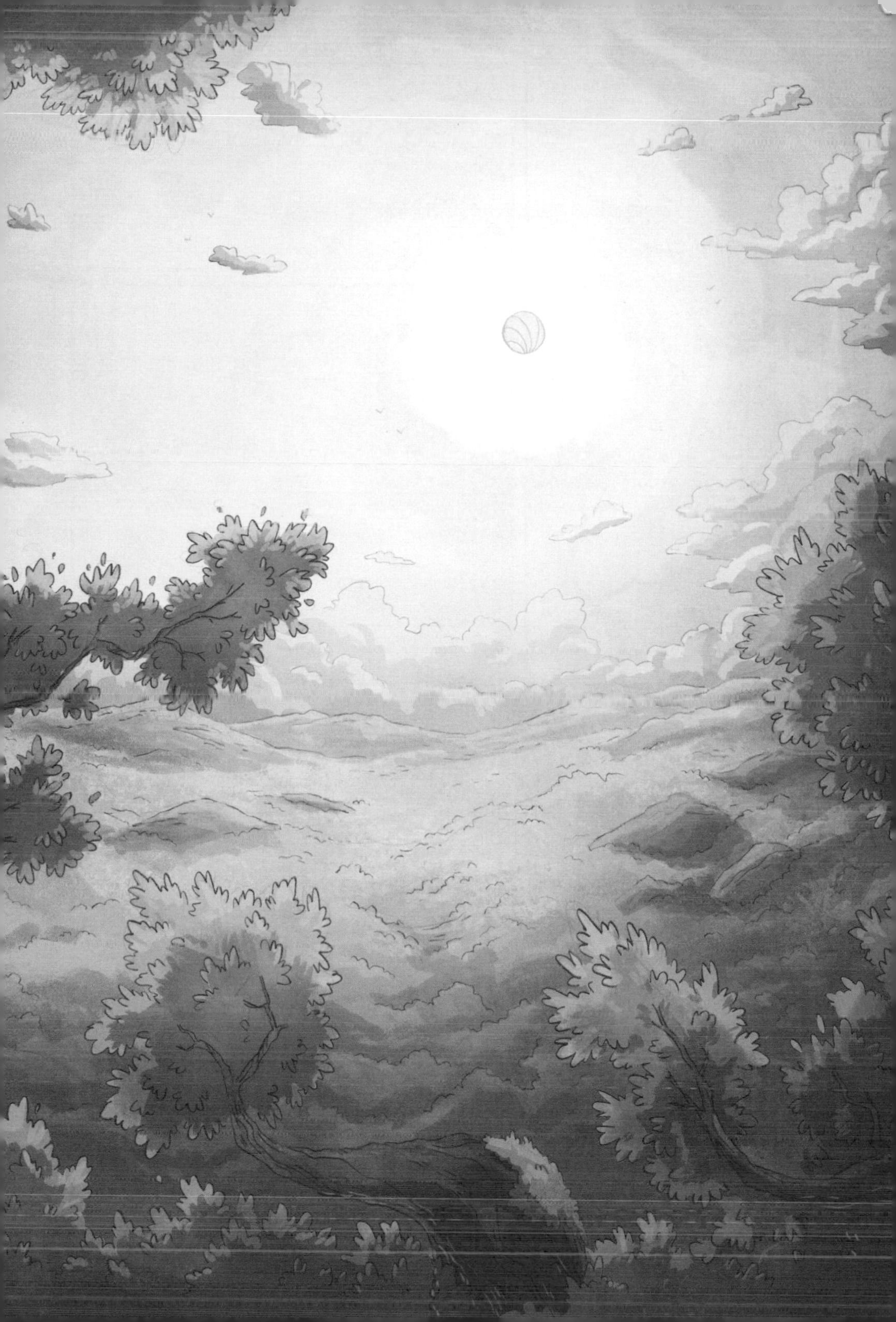

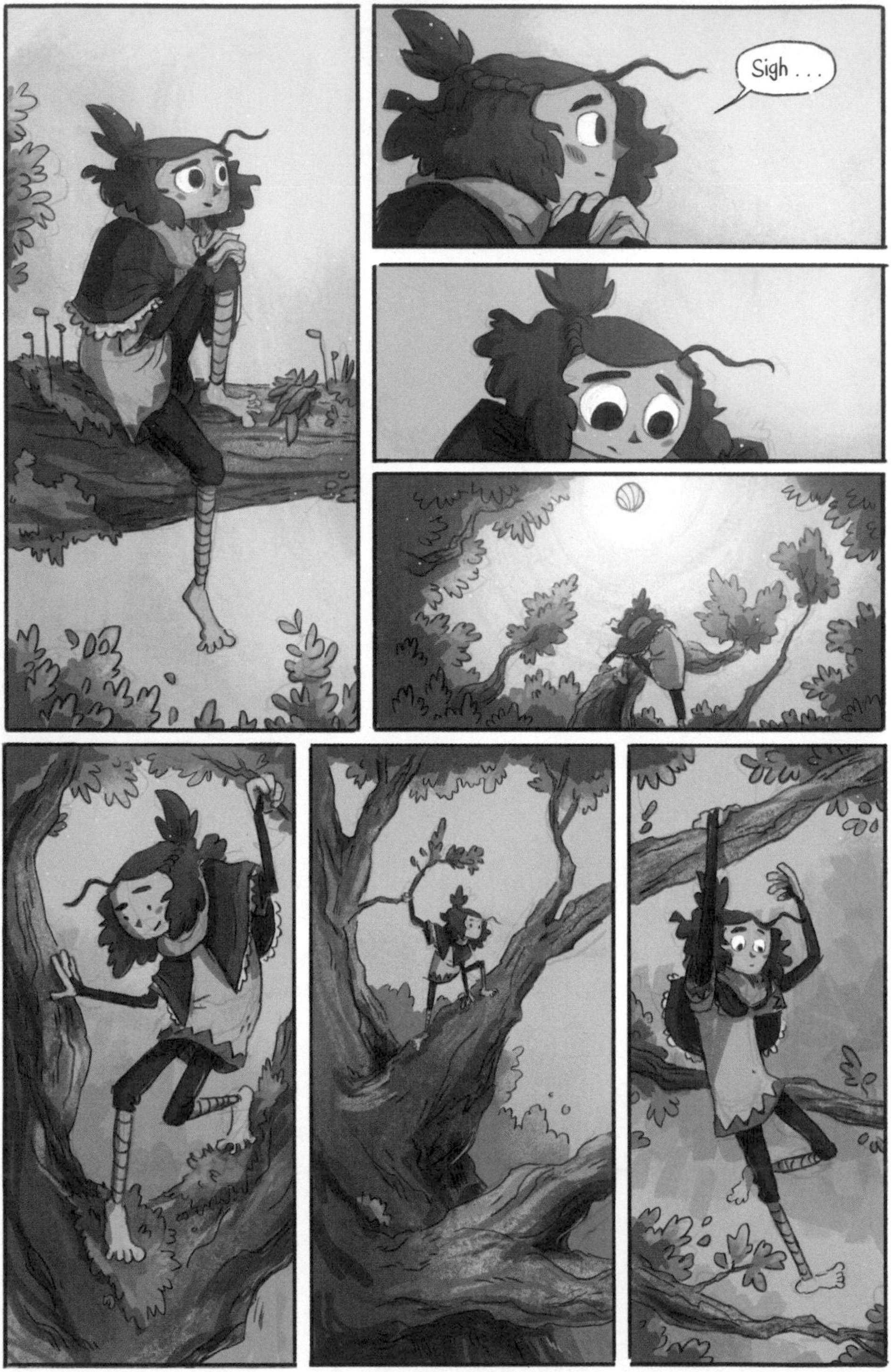
Sigh . . .

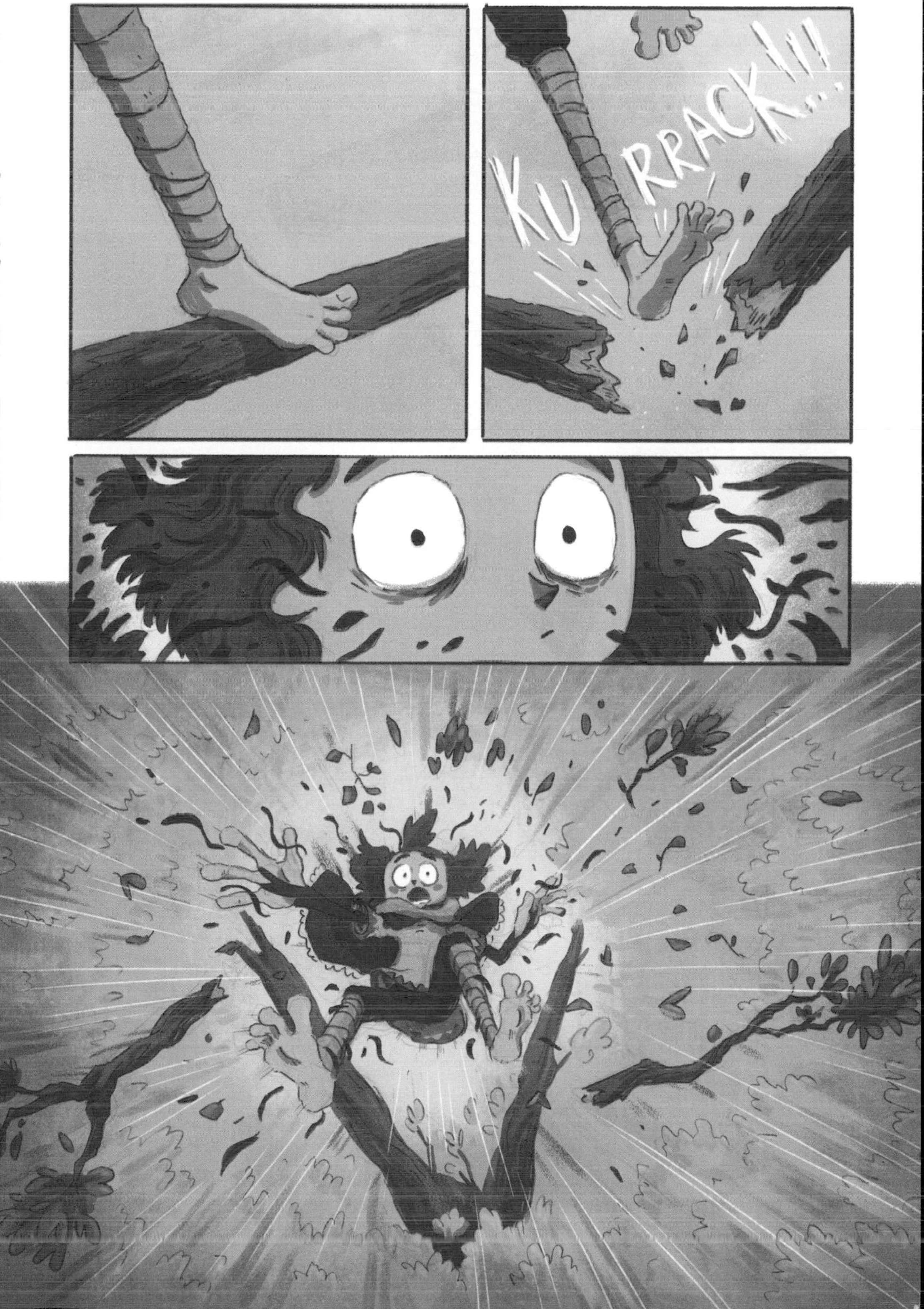
KURRACK!!!

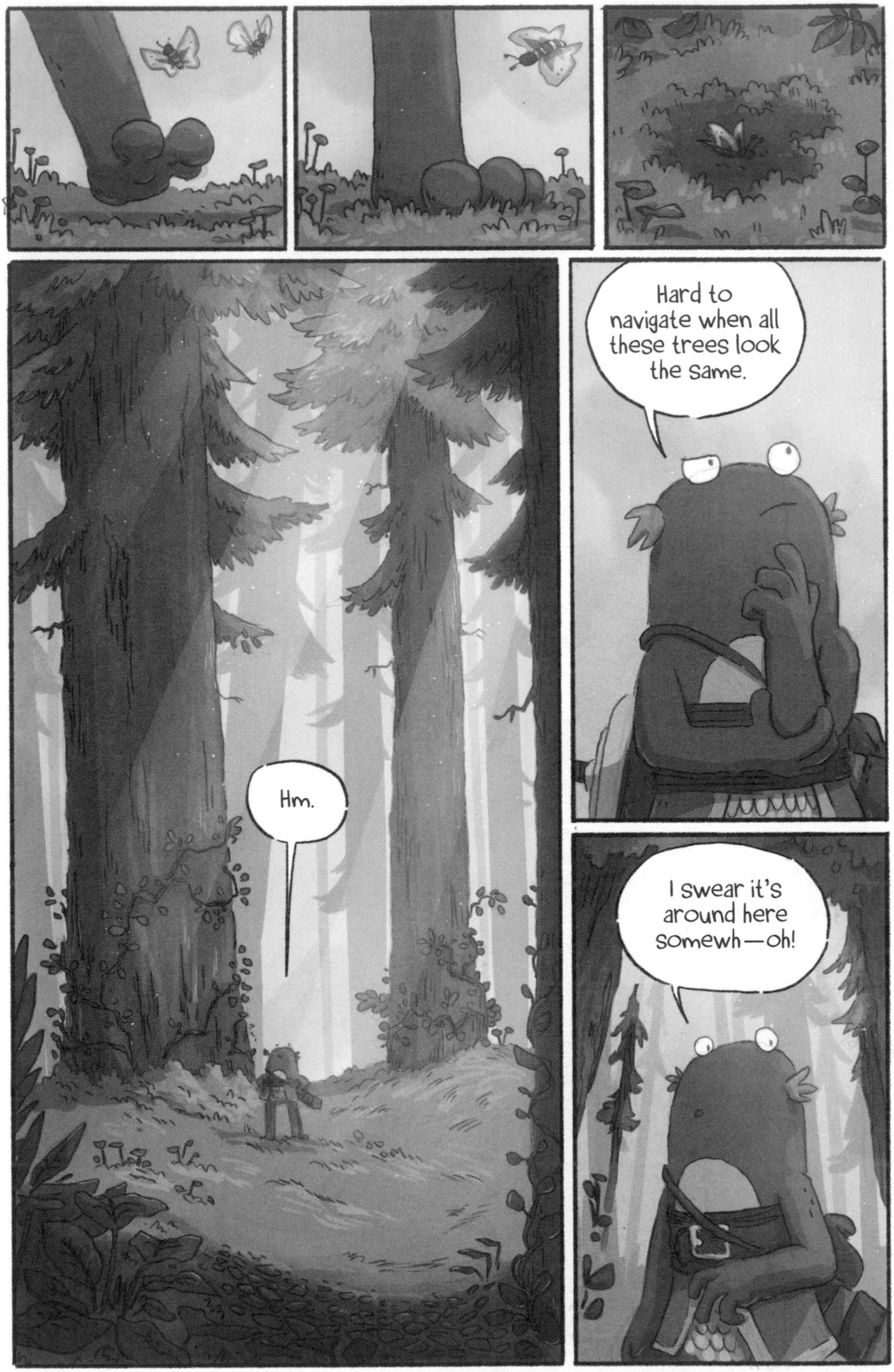
Hm.
Hard to navigate when all these trees look the same.
I swear it's around here somewh—oh!

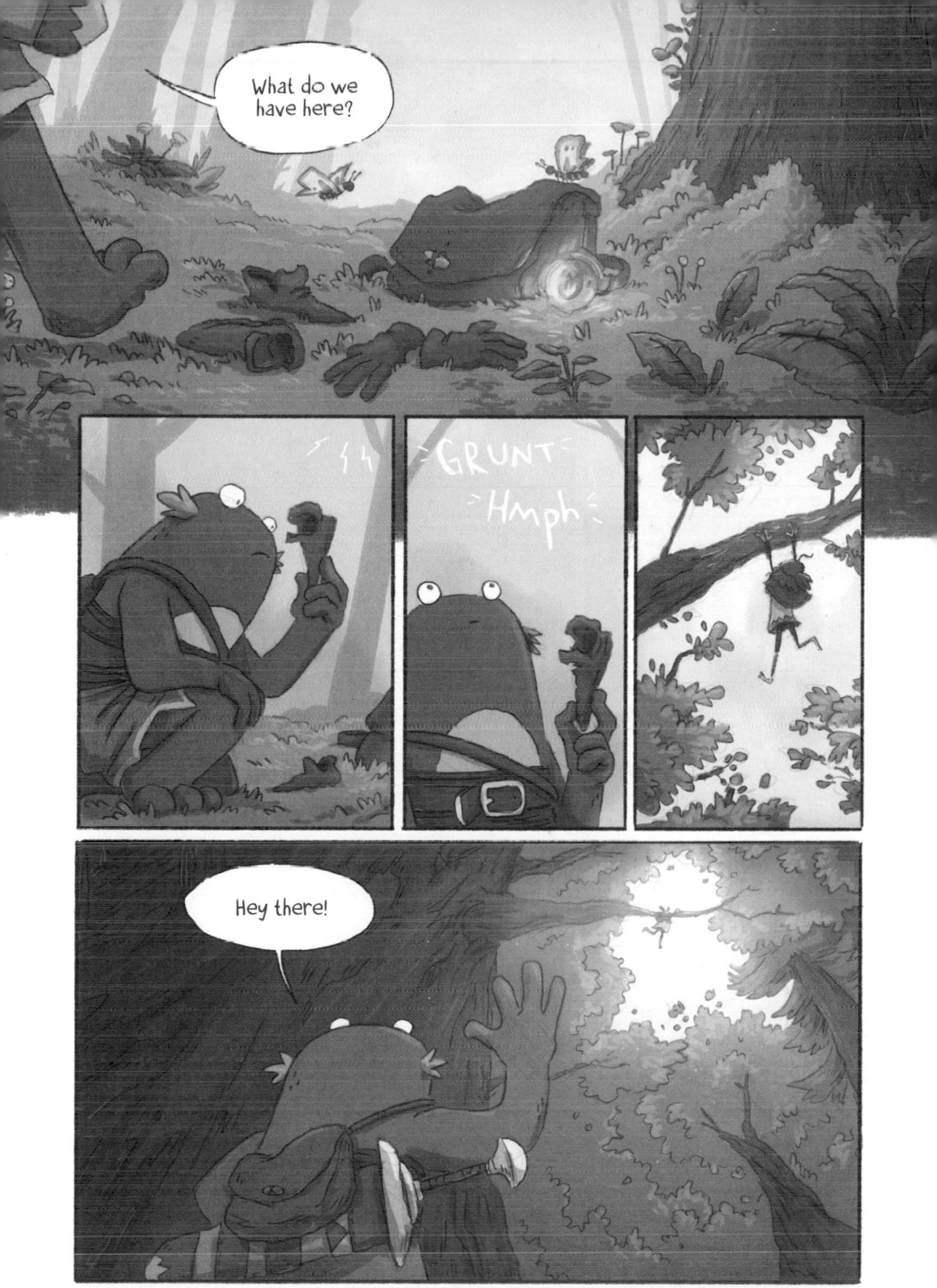
What do we have here?
GRUNT
Hmph
Hey there!

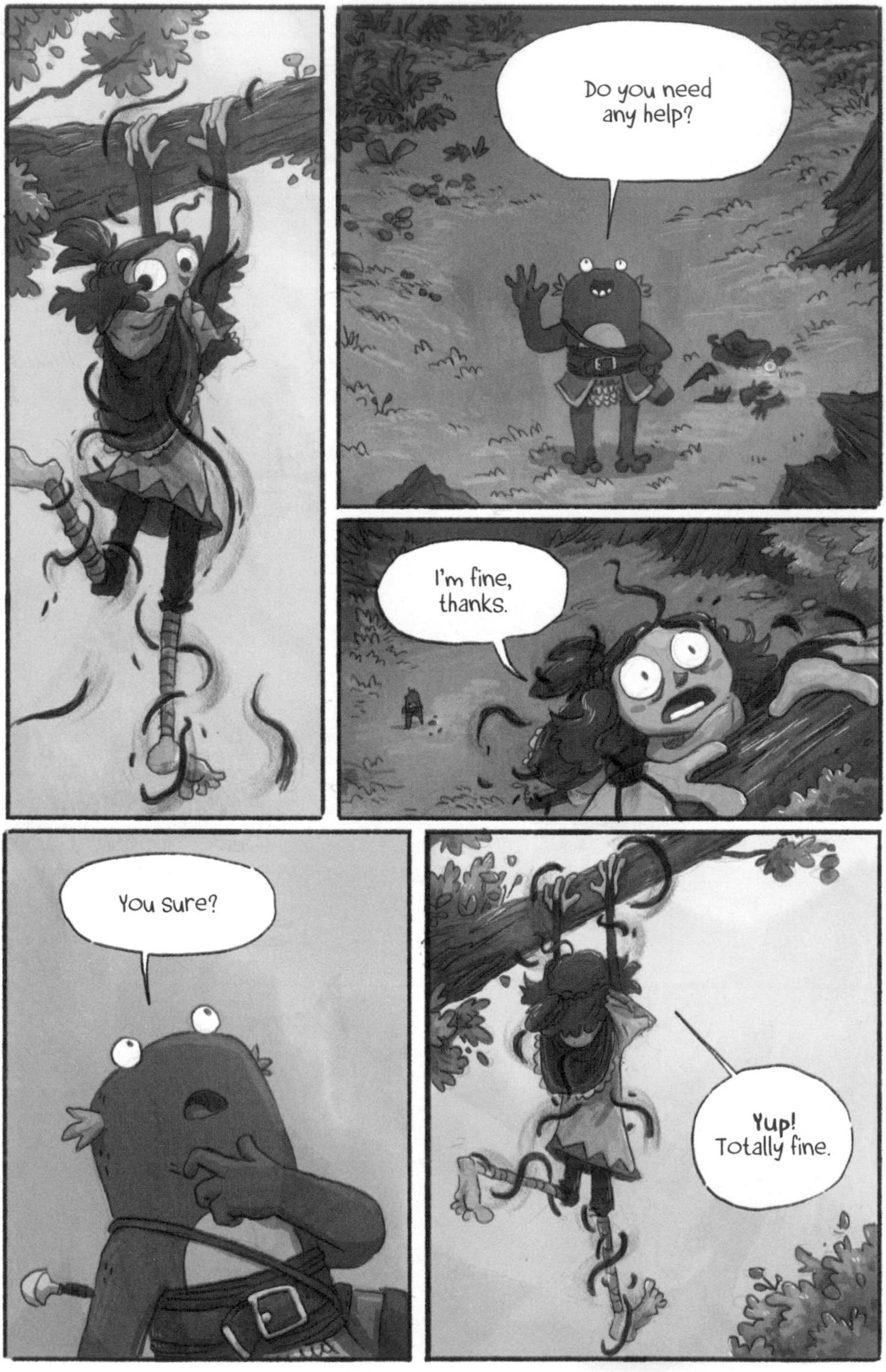
Do you need any help?
I'm fine, thanks.
You sure?
Yup! Totally fine.

Tell ya what—

Just let go and I'll catch you.

Catch me?! You'll **eat** me!

Eat you?! HAHA HA HA!! I'M A Vegetarian! HA HA HA!!

Well, I do eat eggs. And the occasional fish.

But you don't look like an egg. Or a fish, for that matter.

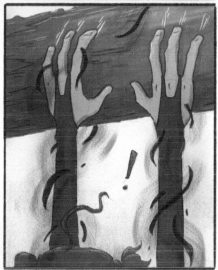

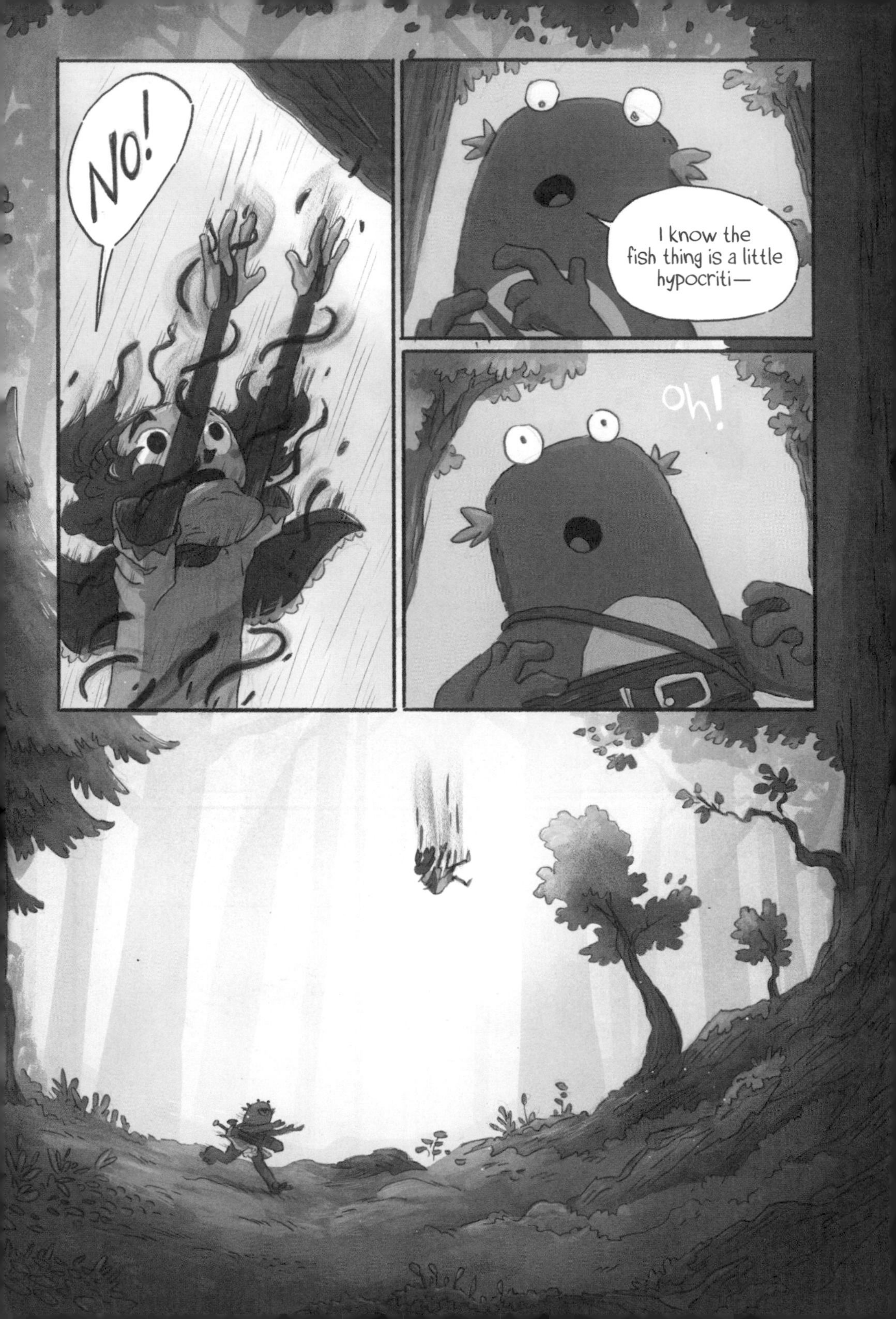
No!
I know the fish thing is a little hypocriti—
Oh!

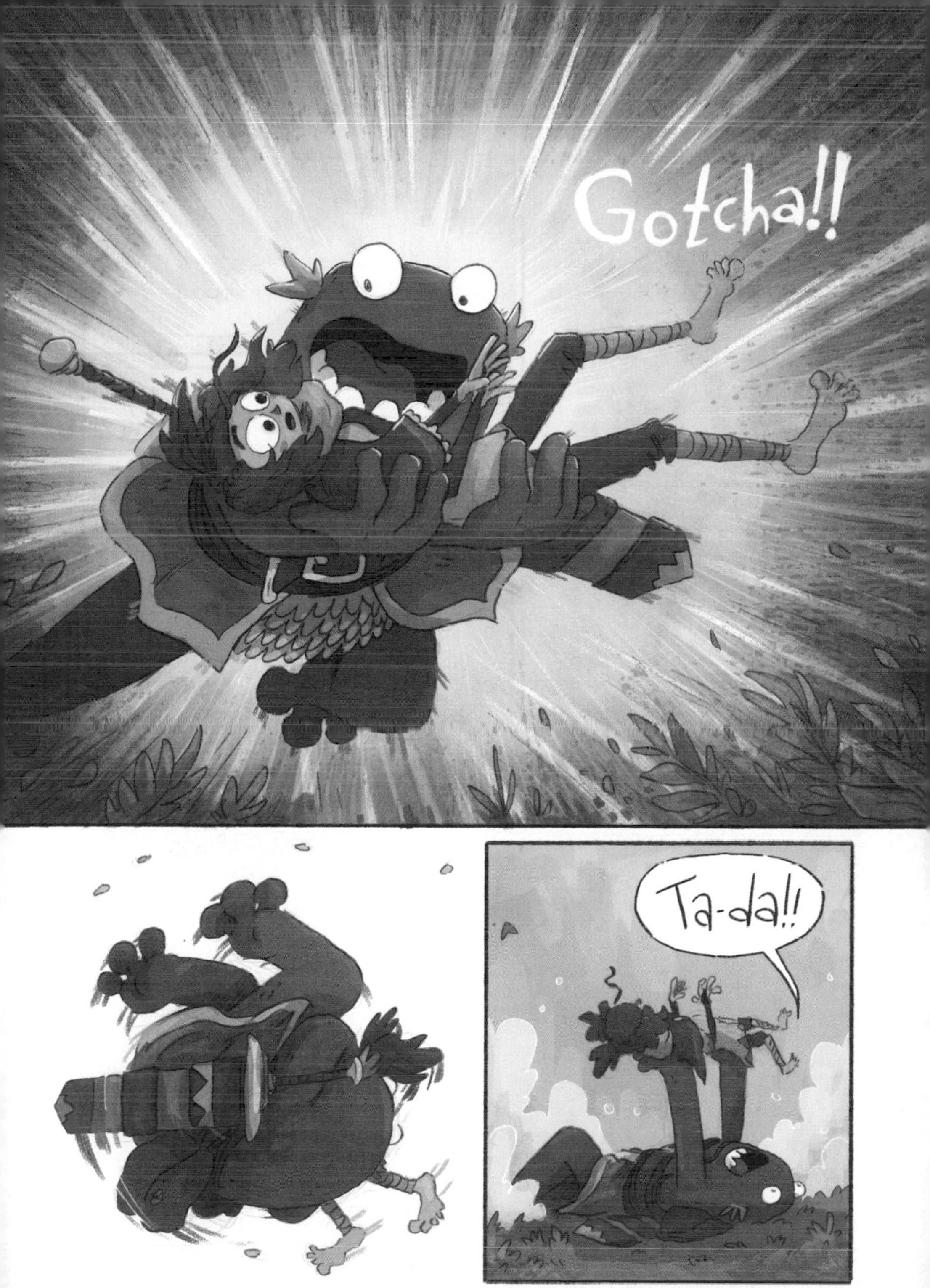
Gotcha!!
Ta-da!!

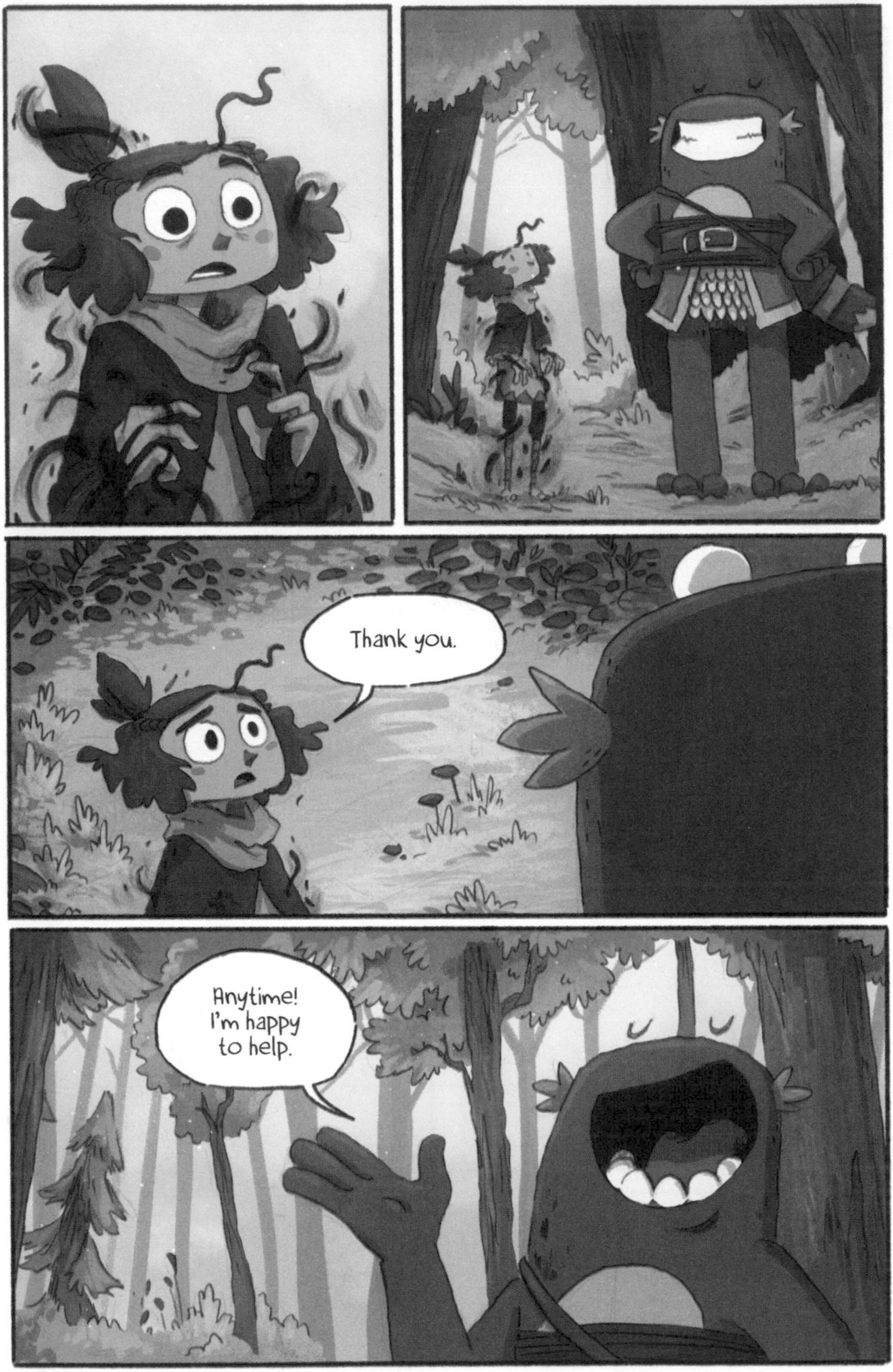
Thank you.
Anytime! I'm happy to help.

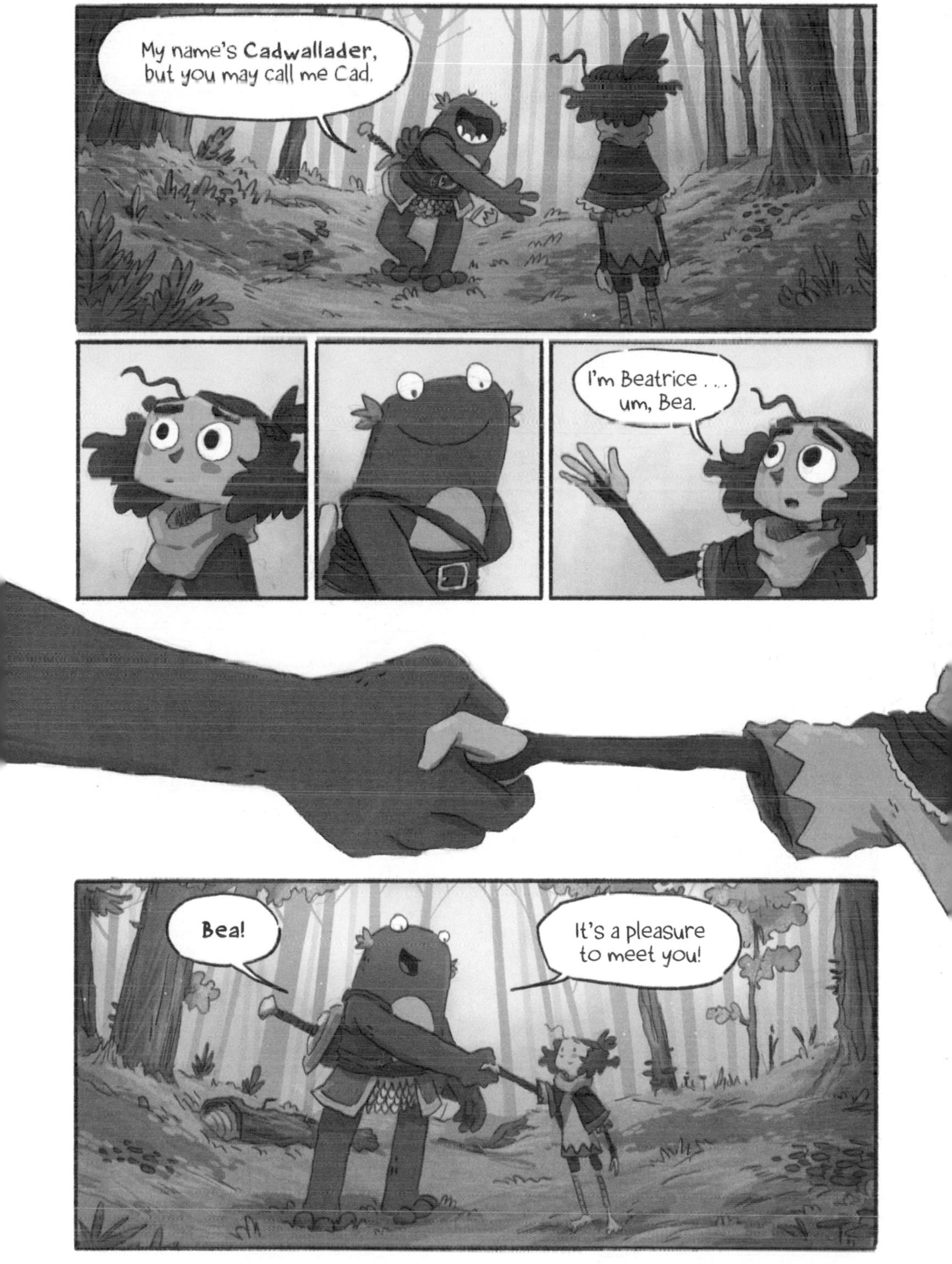

My name's **Cadwallader**, but you may call me Cad.
I'm Beatrice . . . um, Bea.
Bea!
It's a pleasure to meet you!

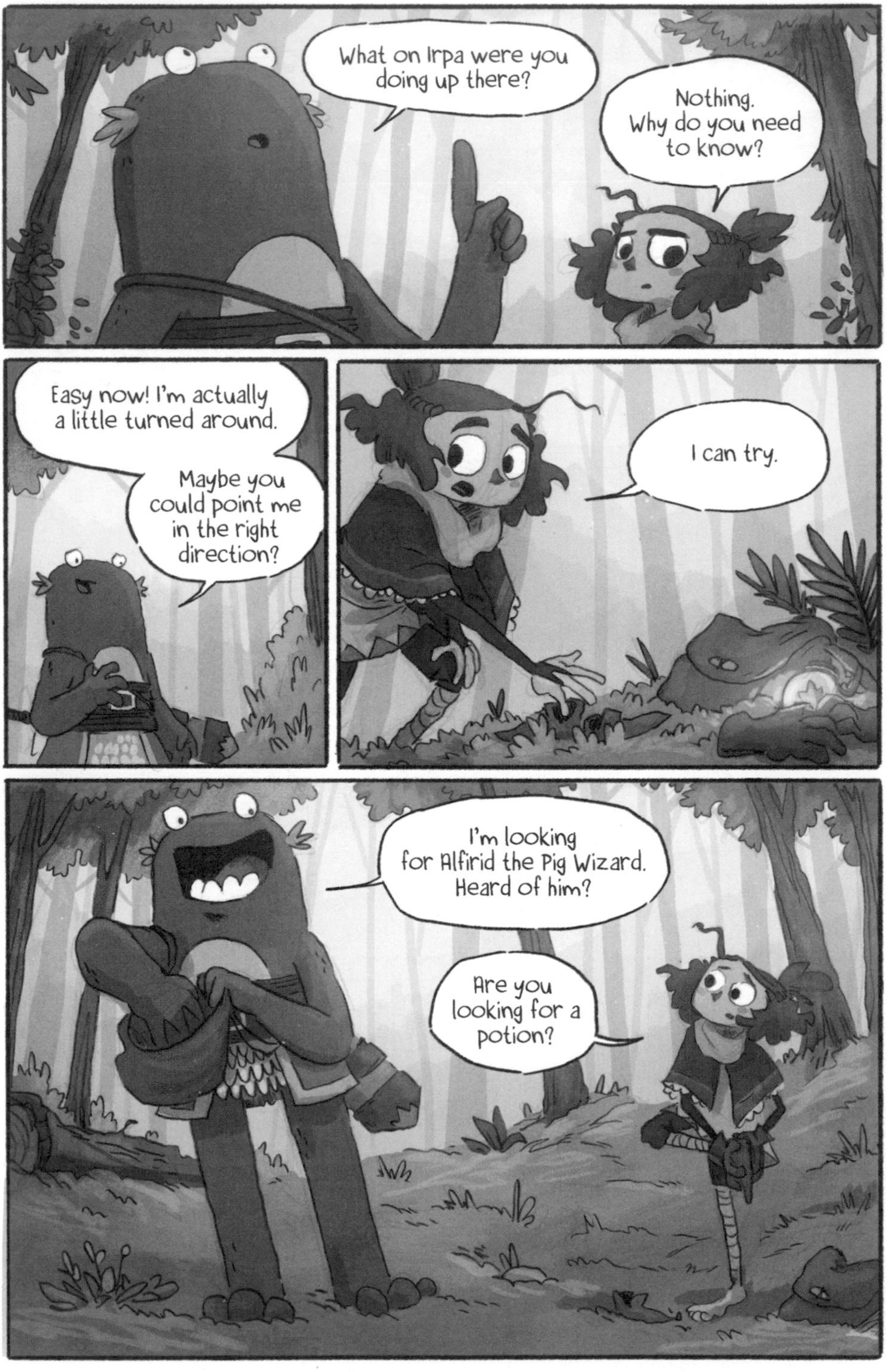

What on Irpa were you doing up there?
Nothing. Why do you need to know?
Easy now! I'm actually a little turned around.
Maybe you could point me in the right direction?
I can try.
I'm looking for Alfirid the Pig Wizard. Heard of him?
Are you looking for a potion?

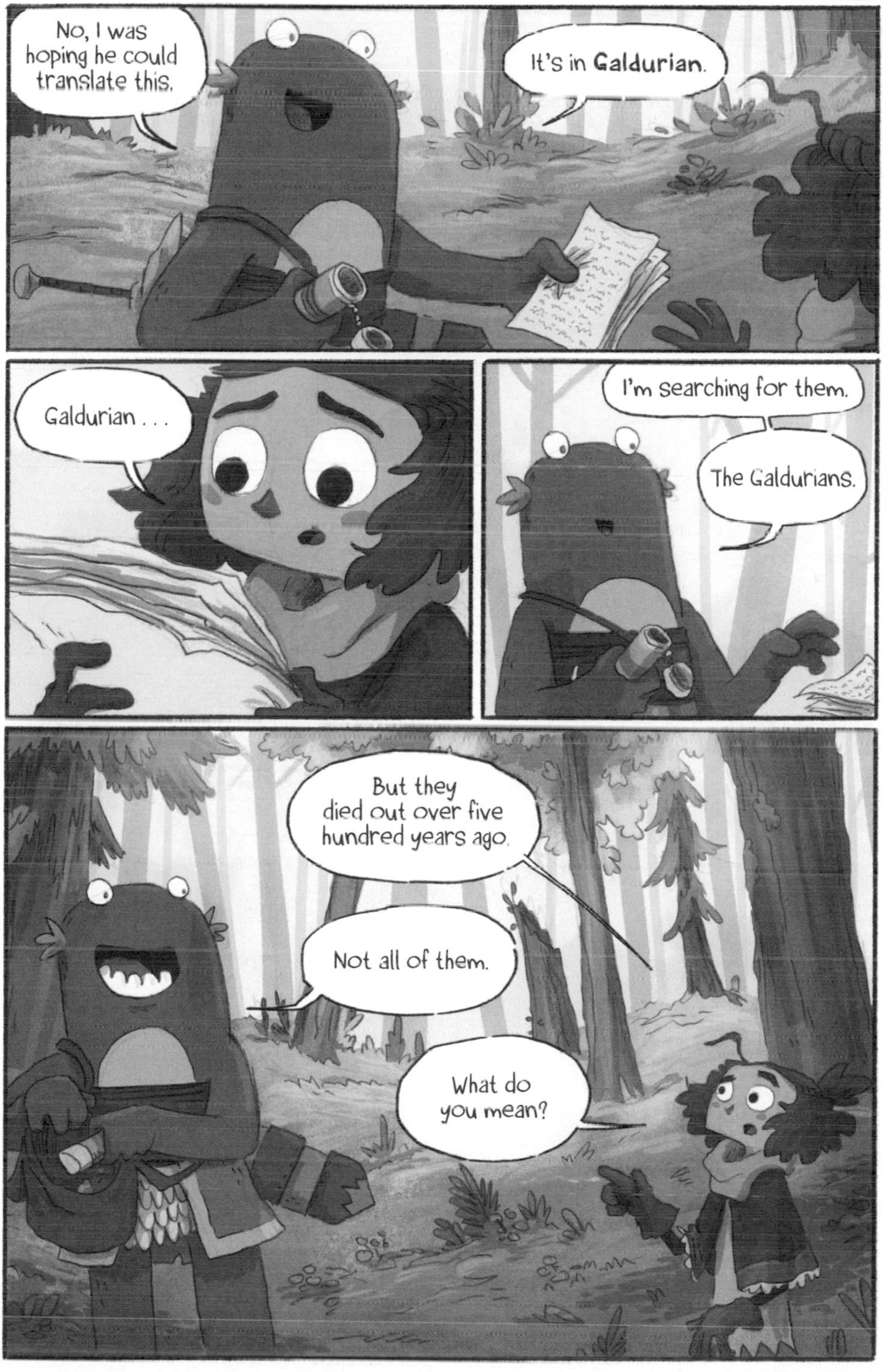
No, I was hoping he could translate this.
It's in **Galdurian**.
Galdurian . . .
I'm searching for them.
The Galdurians.
But they died out over five hundred years ago.
Not all of them.
What do you mean?

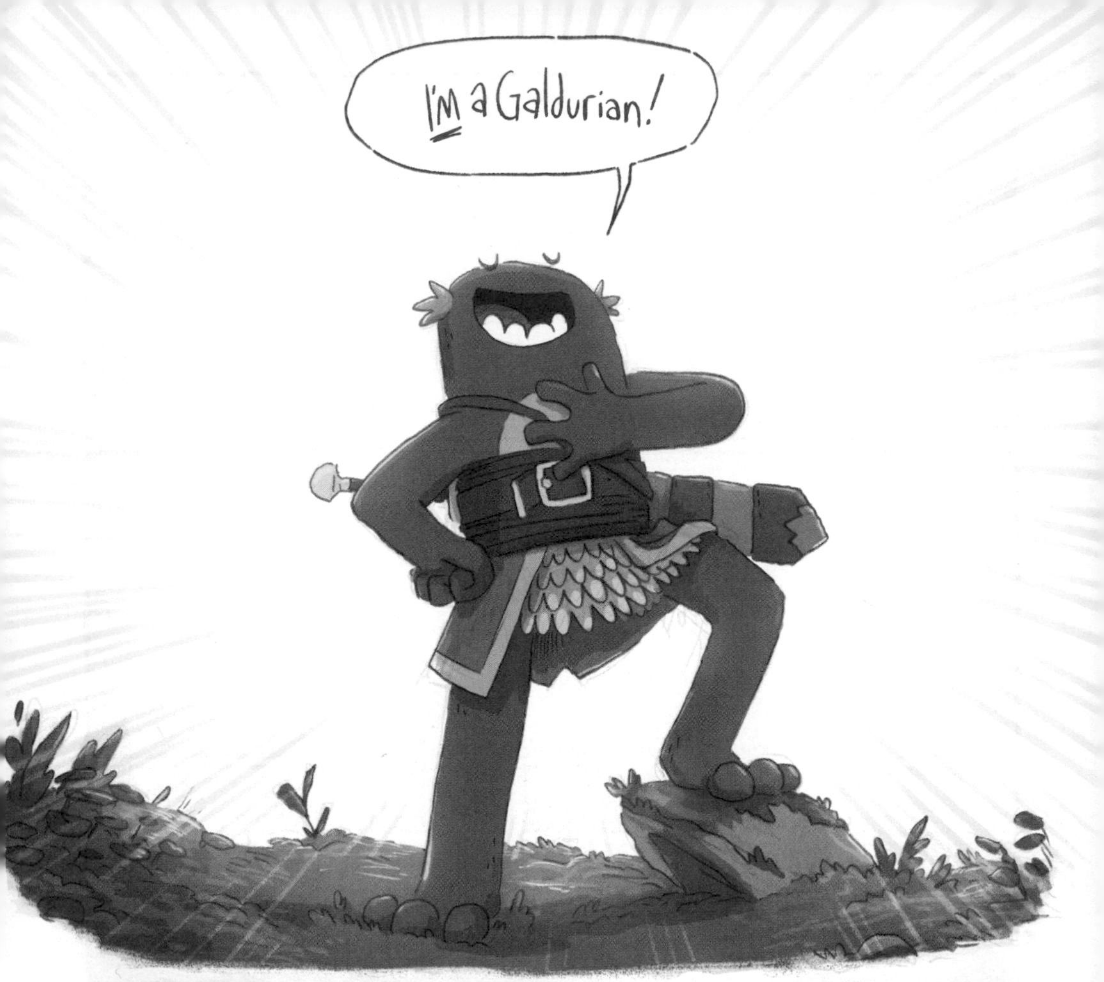
I'M a Galdurian!

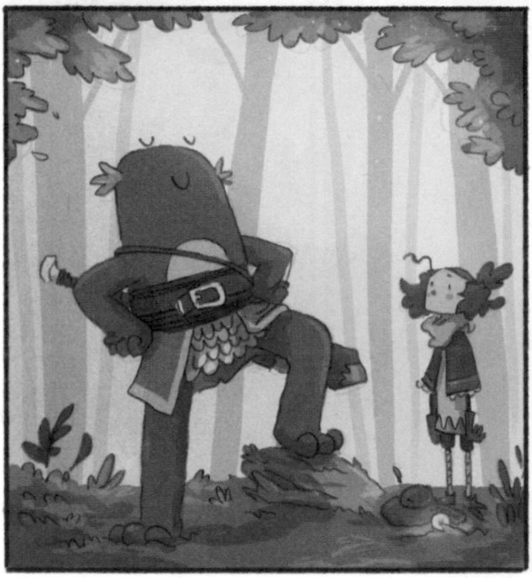

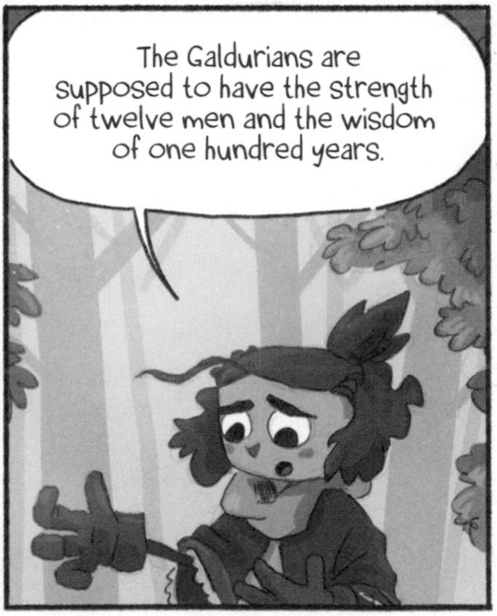
The Galdurians are supposed to have the strength of twelve men and the wisdom of one hundred years.

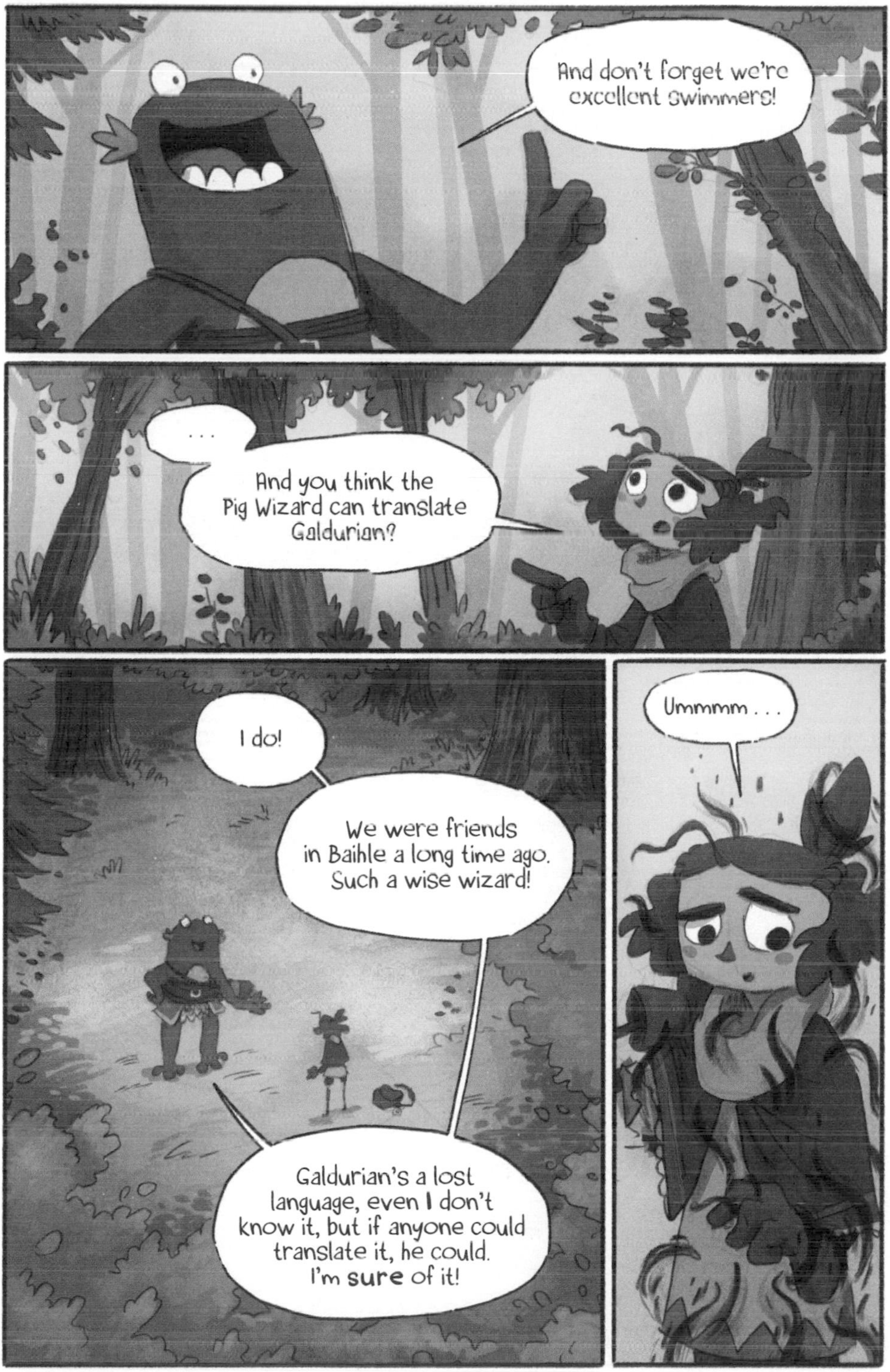
And don't forget we're excellent swimmers!
. . .
And you think the Pig Wizard can translate Galdurian?
I do!
We were friends in Baihle a long time ago. Such a wise wizard!
Galdurian's a lost language, even I don't know it, but if anyone could translate it, he could. I'm **sure** of it!
Ummmm . . .

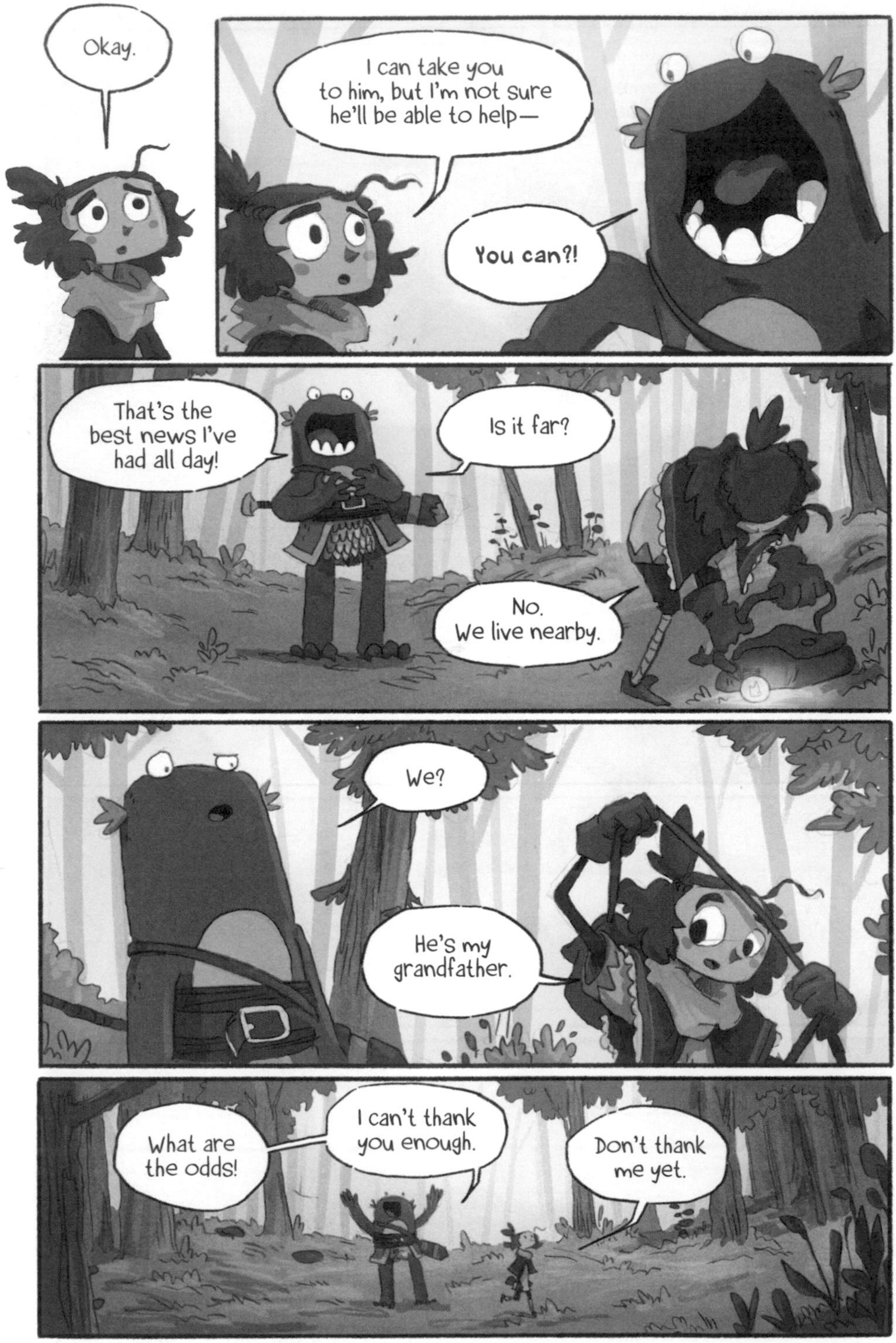
Okay.
I can take you to him, but I'm not sure he'll be able to help—
You can?!
That's the best news I've had all day!
Is it far?
No. We live nearby.
We?
He's my grandfather.
What are the odds!
I can't thank you enough.
Don't thank me yet.

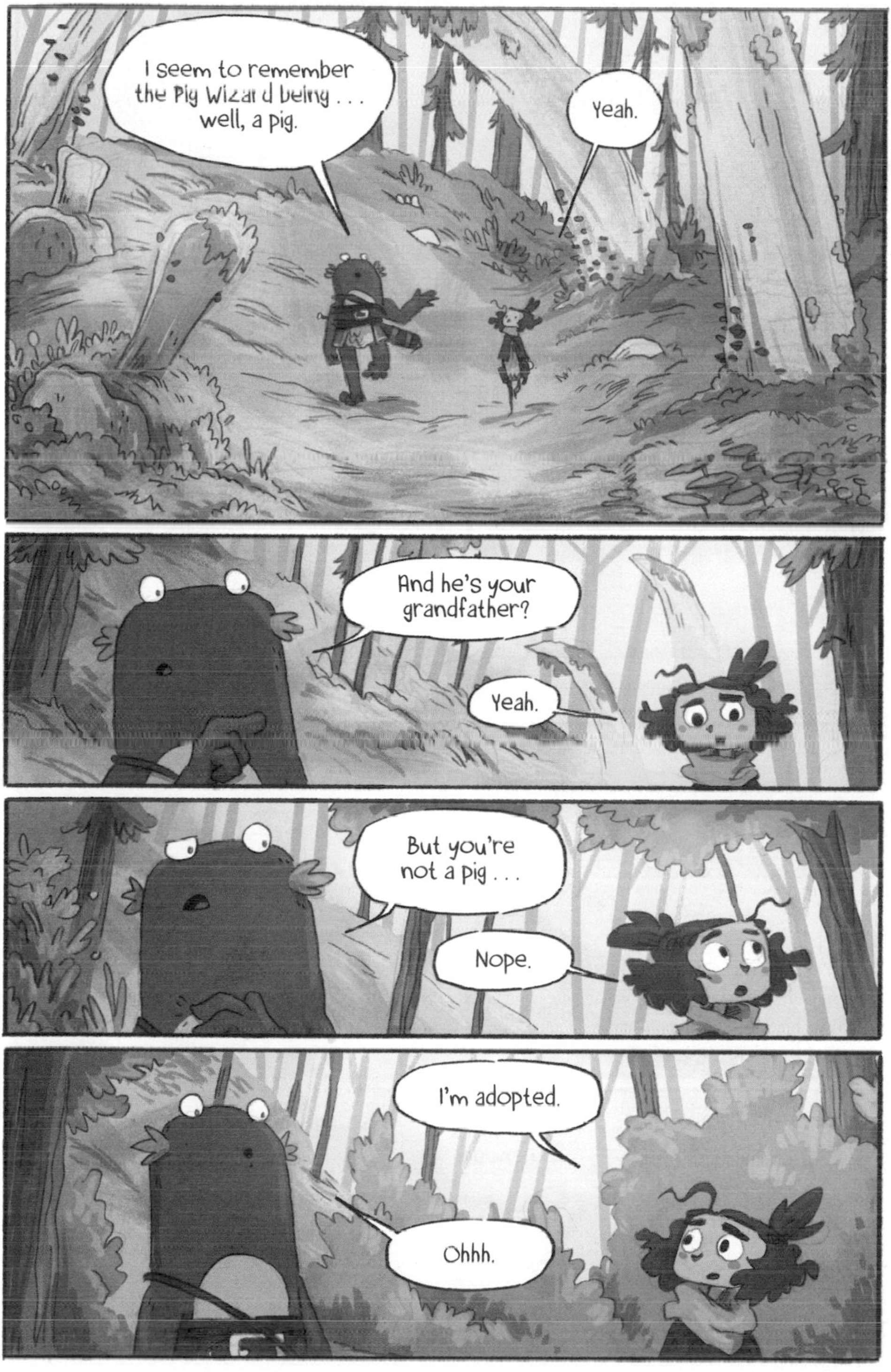
I seem to remember the Pig Wizard being . . . well, a pig.
Yeah.
And he's your grandfather?
Yeah.
But you're not a pig . . .
Nope.
I'm adopted.
Ohhh.

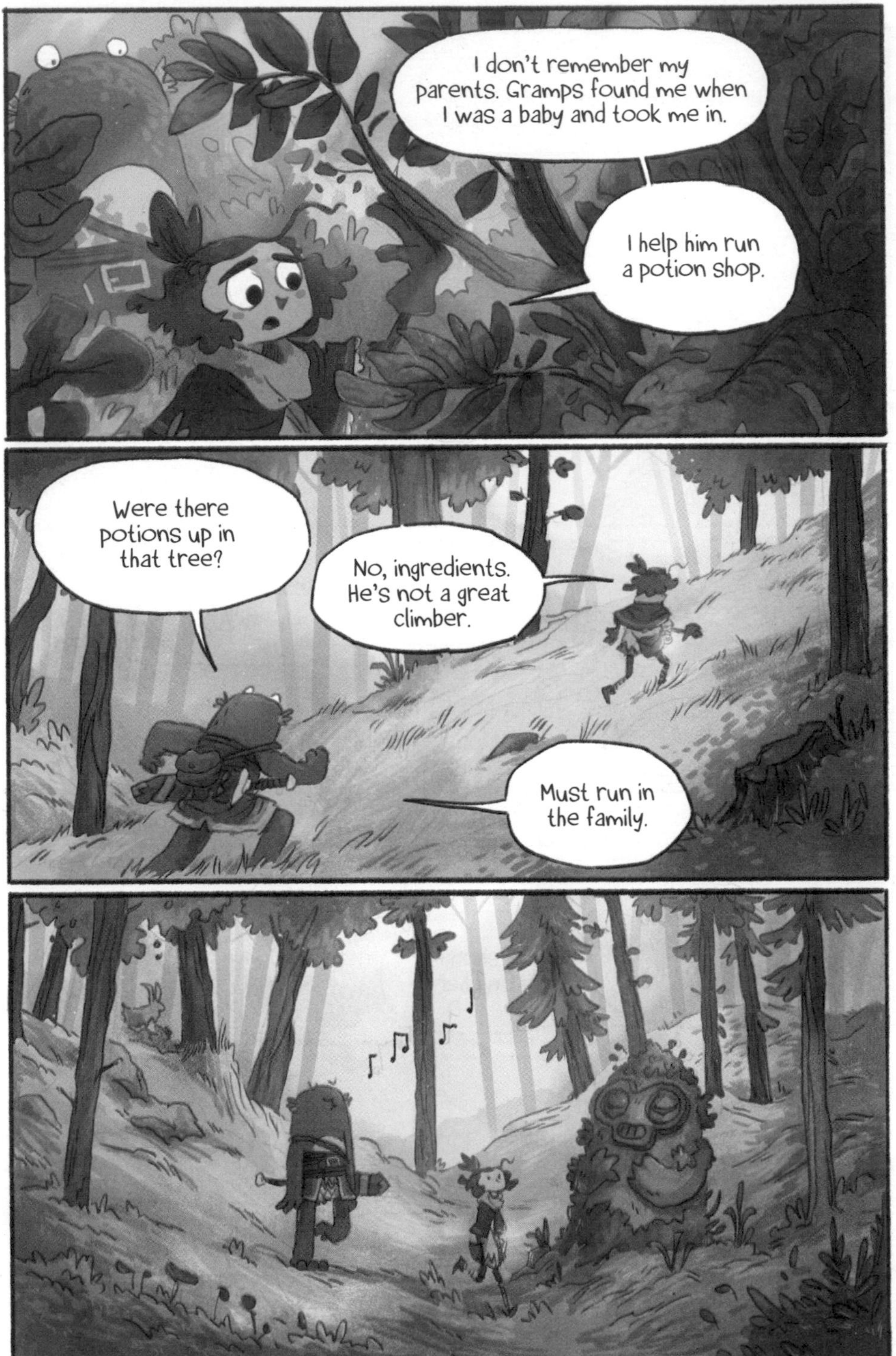
I don't remember my parents. Gramps found me when I was a baby and took me in.
I help him run a potion shop.
Were there potions up in that tree?
No, ingredients. He's not a great climber.
Must run in the family.

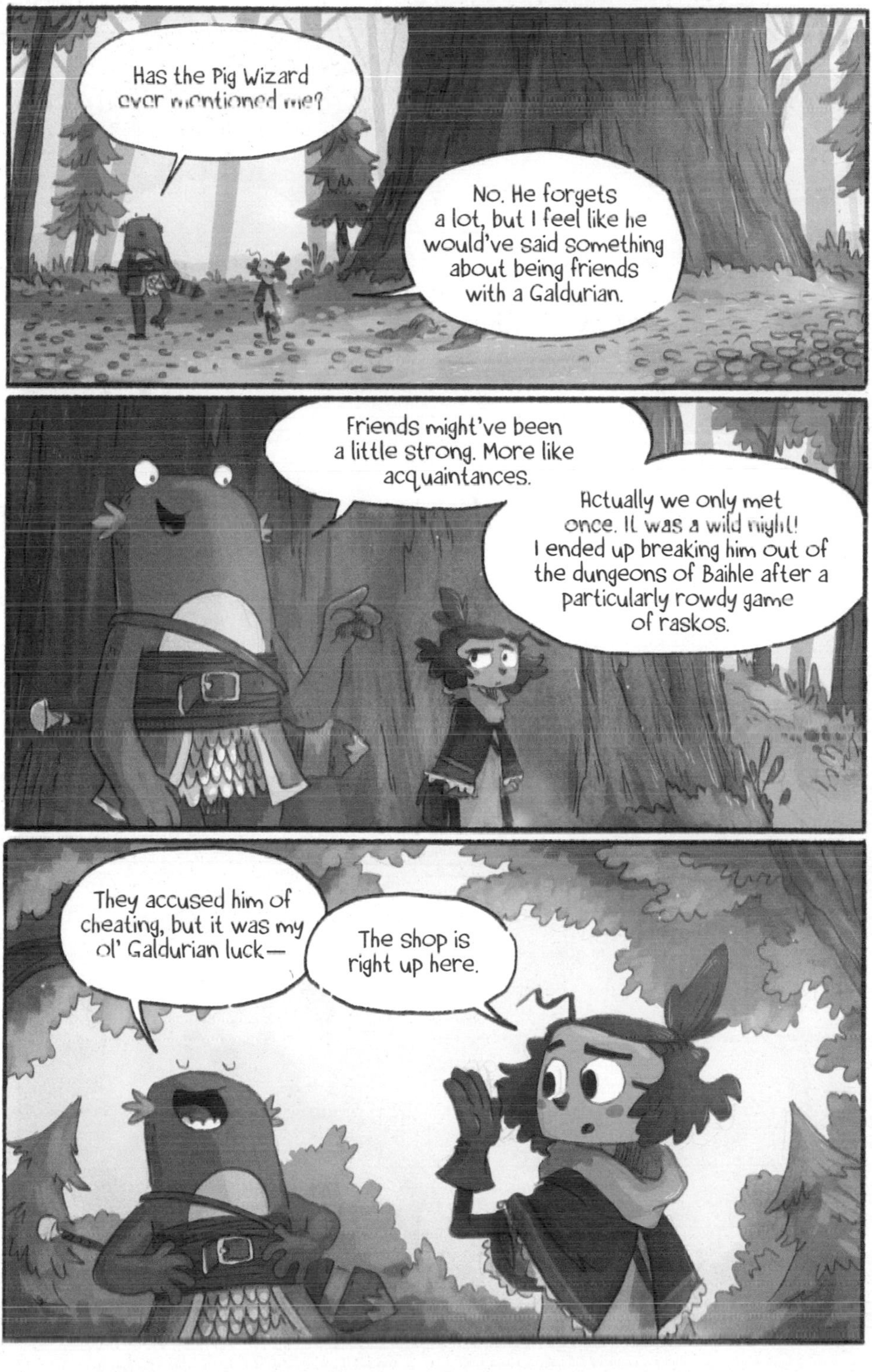

Has the Pig Wizard ever mentioned me?
No. He forgets a lot, but I feel like he would've said something about being friends with a Galdurian.
Friends might've been a little strong. More like acquaintances.
Actually we only met once. It was a wild night! I ended up breaking him out of the dungeons of Baihle after a particularly rowdy game of raskos.
They accused him of cheating, but it was my ol' Galdurian luck—
The shop is right up here.

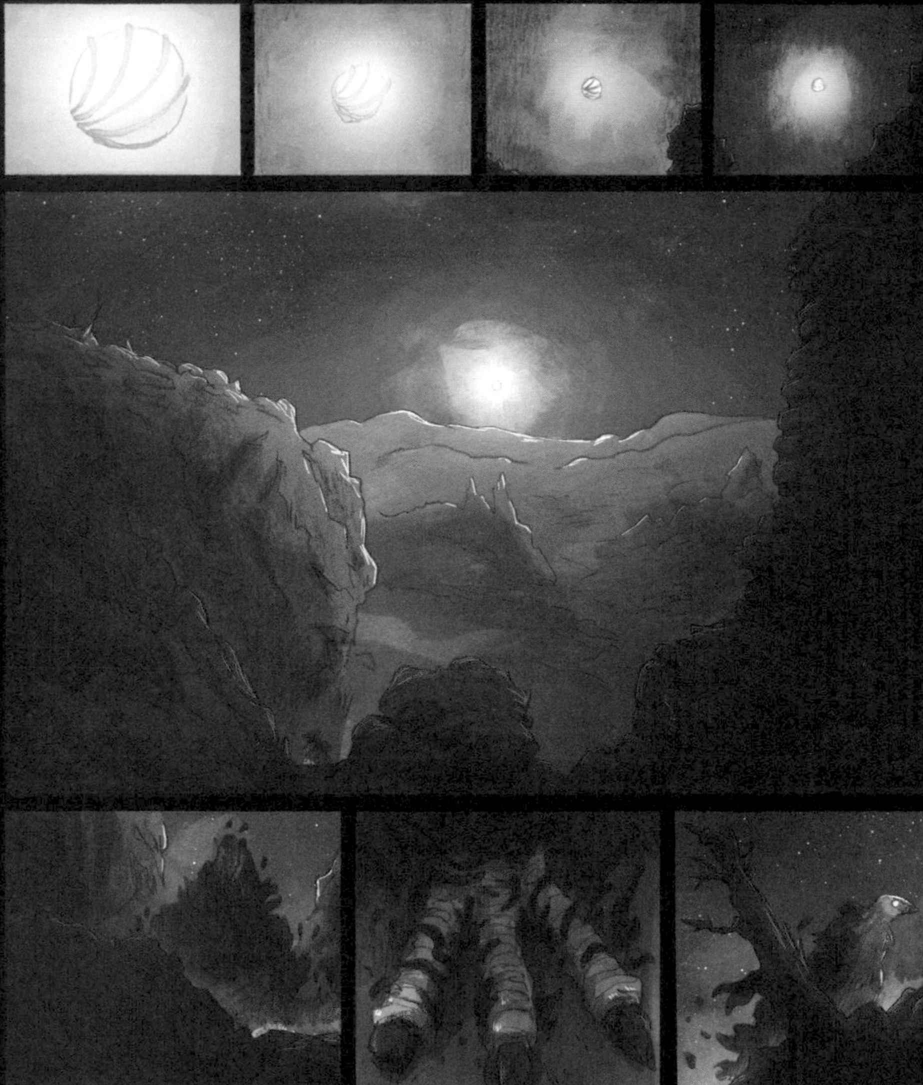

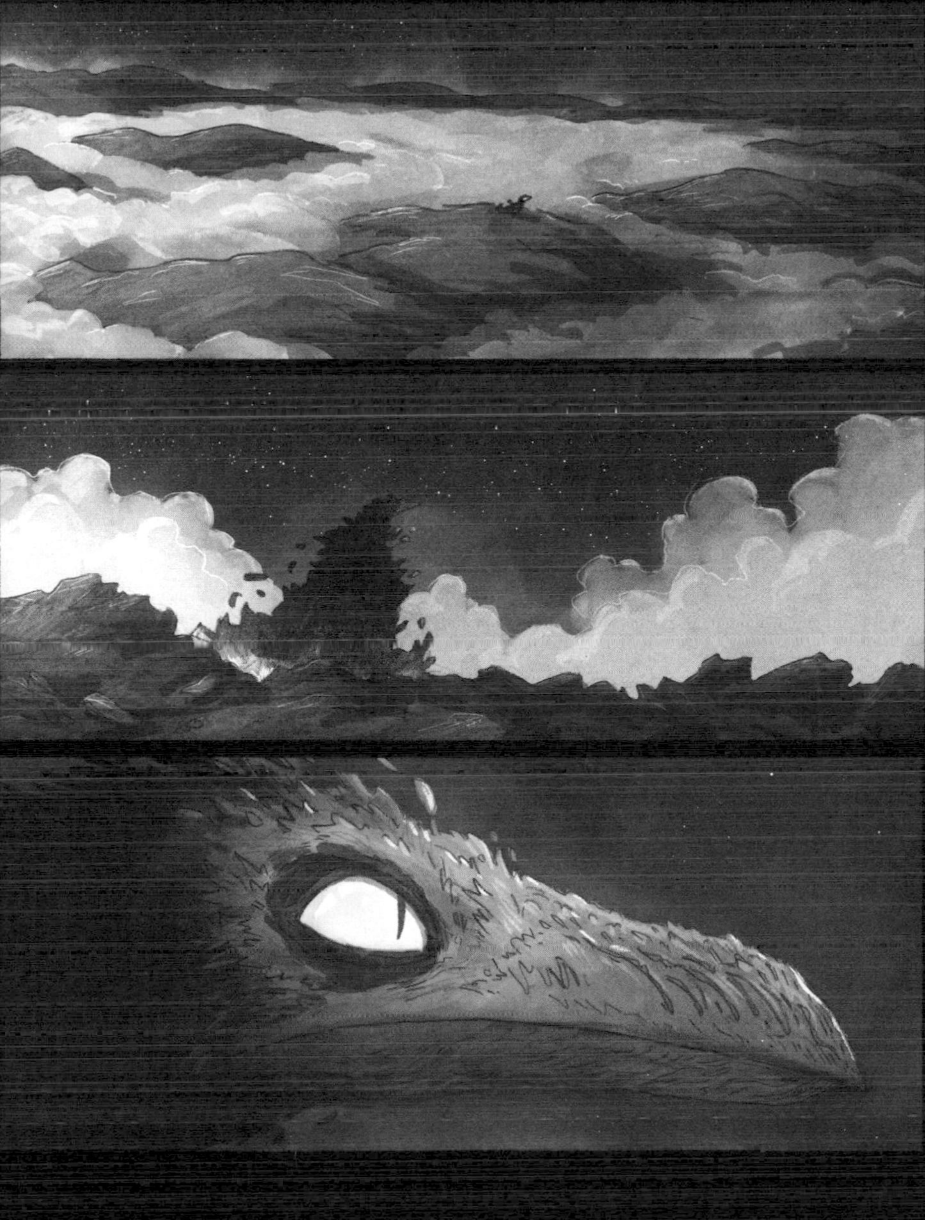

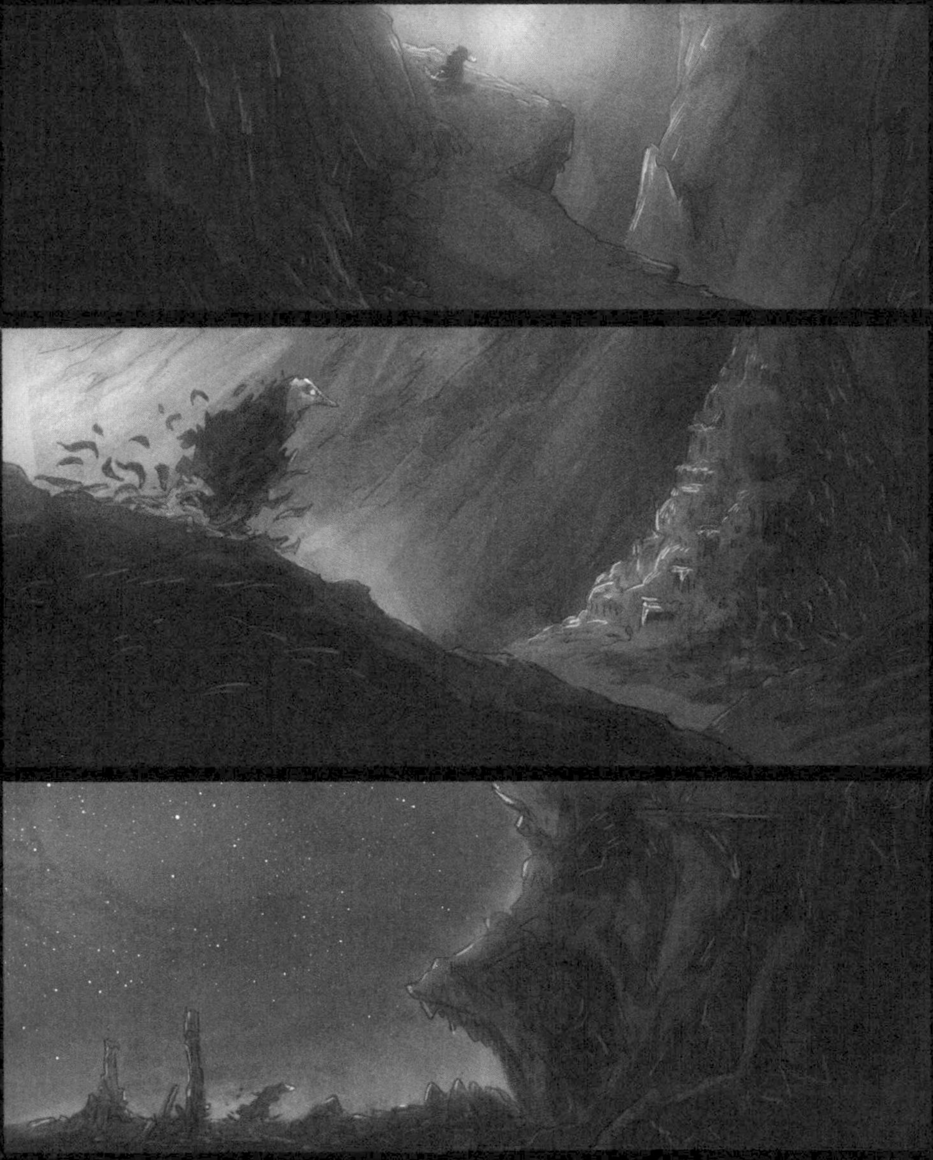

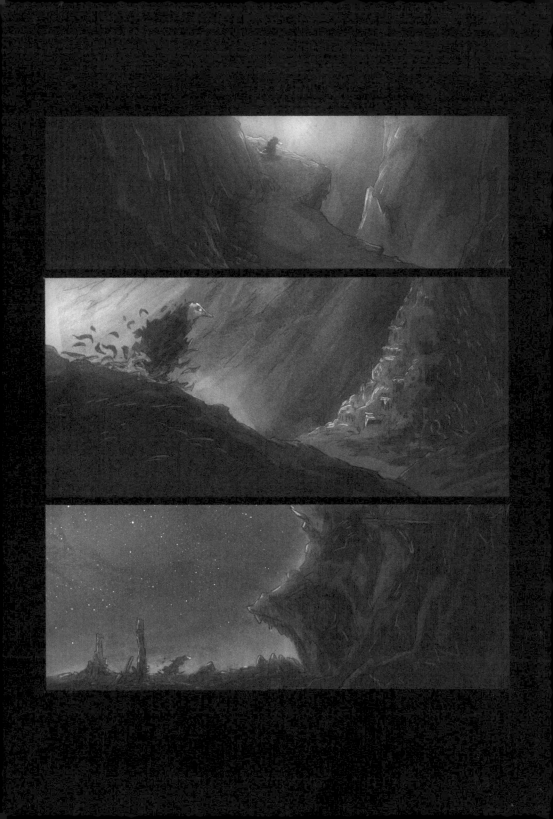

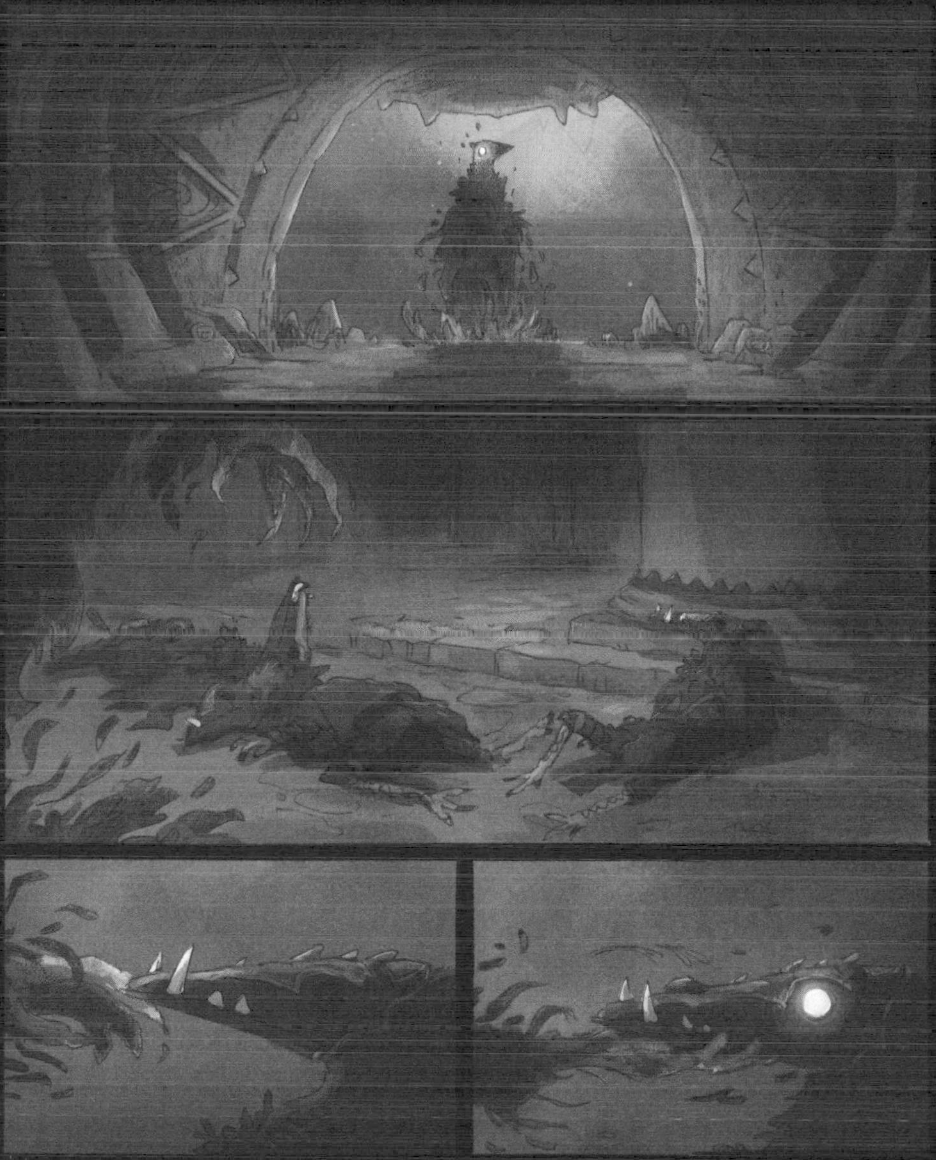

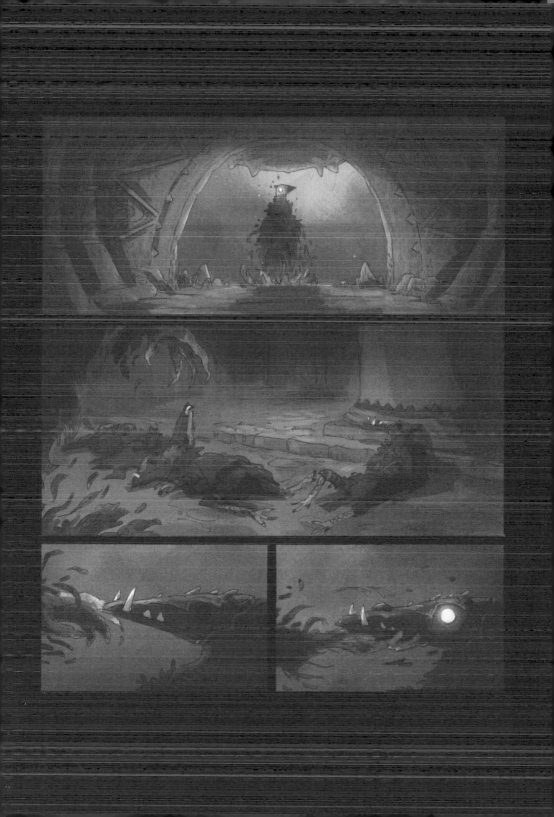

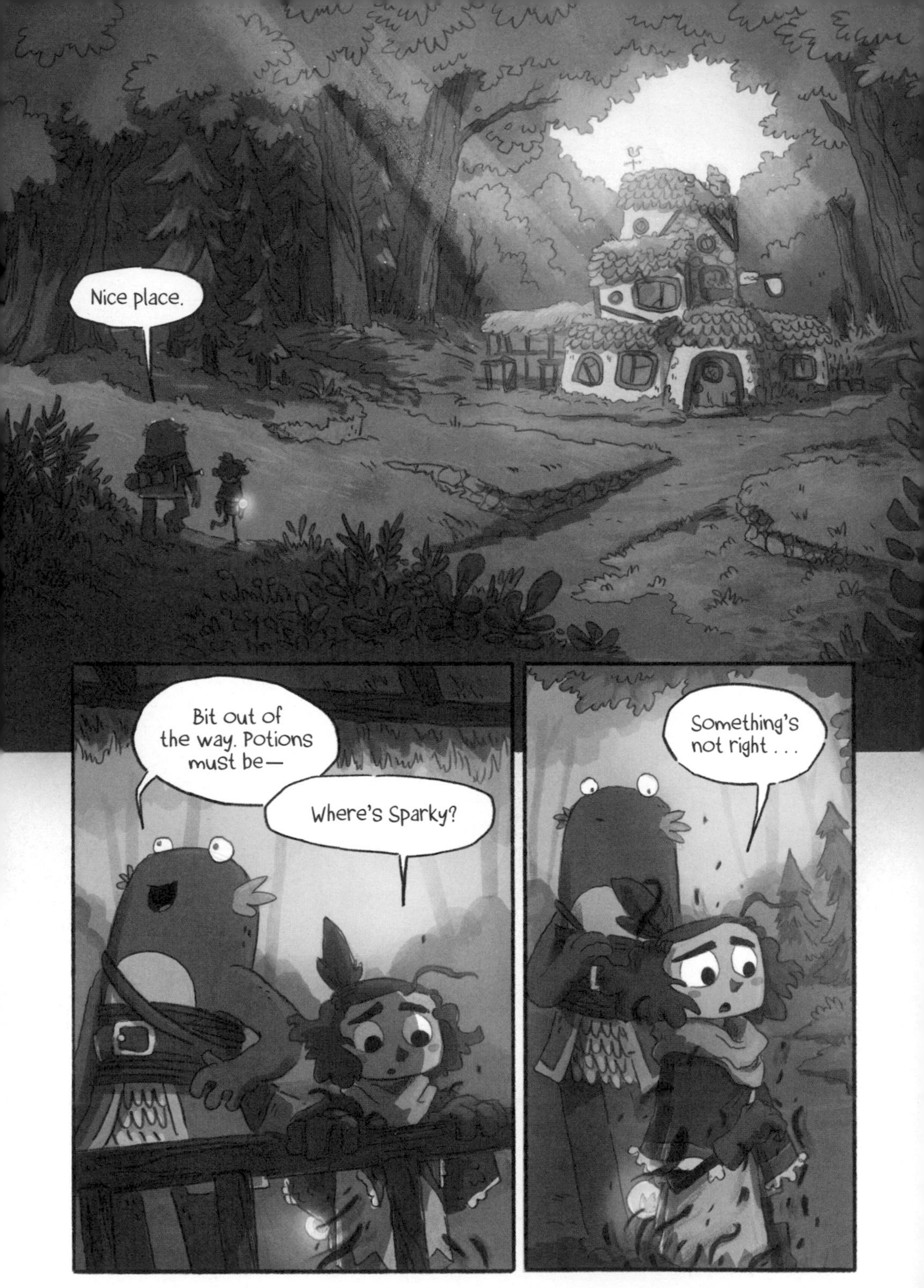
Nice place.
Bit out of the way. Potions must be—
Where's Sparky?
Something's not right . . .

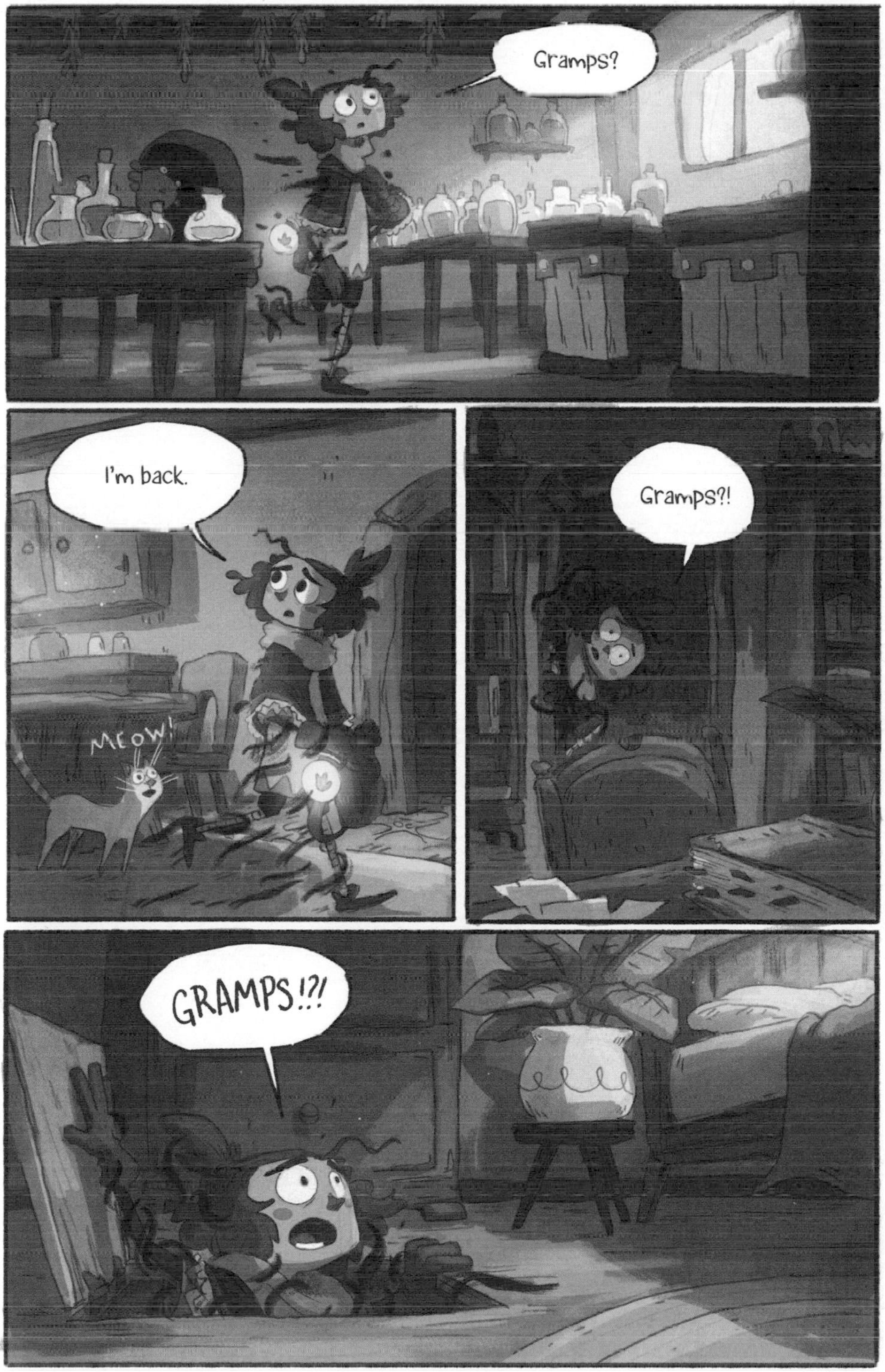
Gramps?
I'm back.
MEOW!
Gramps?!
GRAMPS!?!

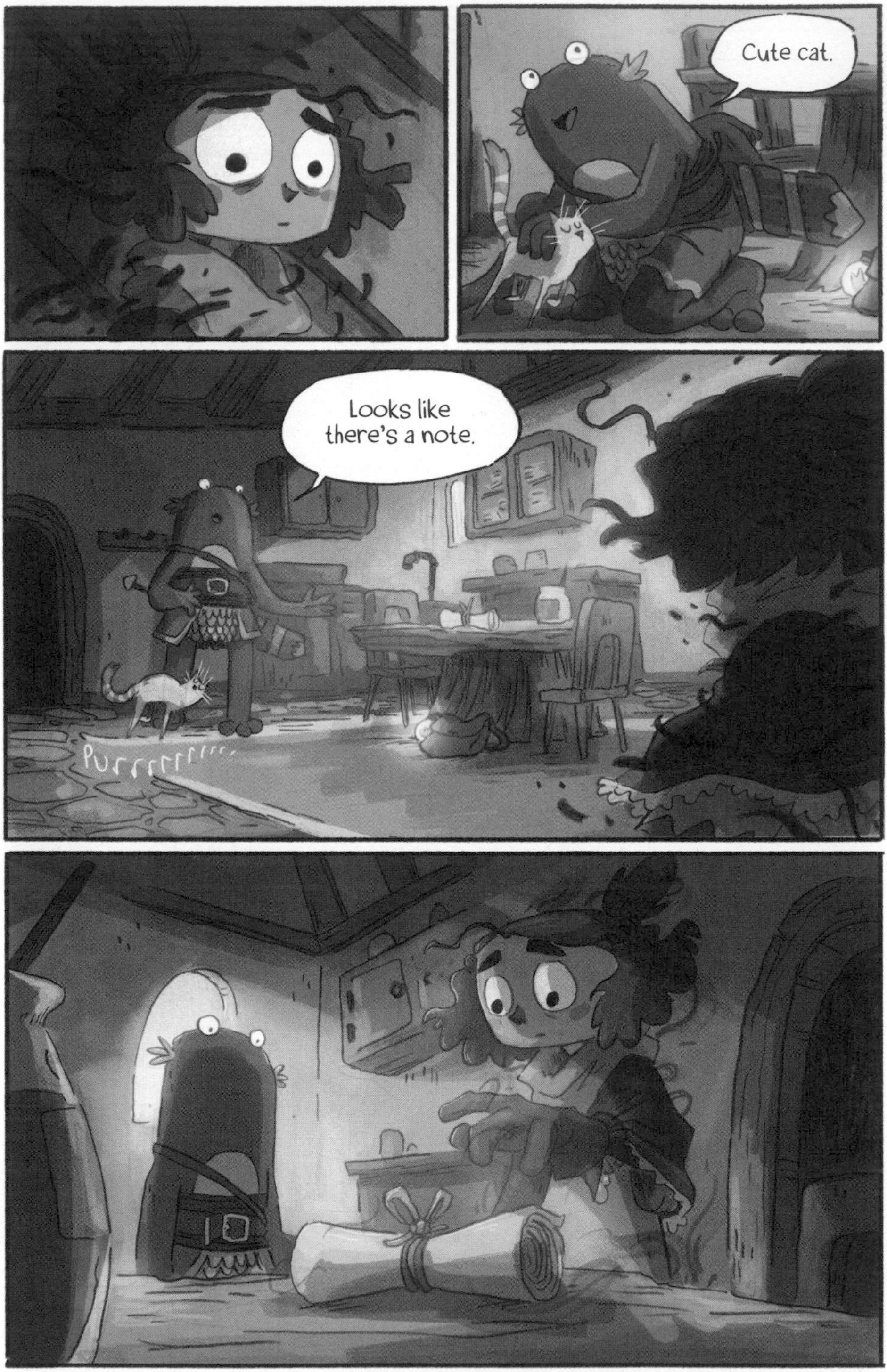
Cute cat.
Looks like there's a note.
Purrrrrrr

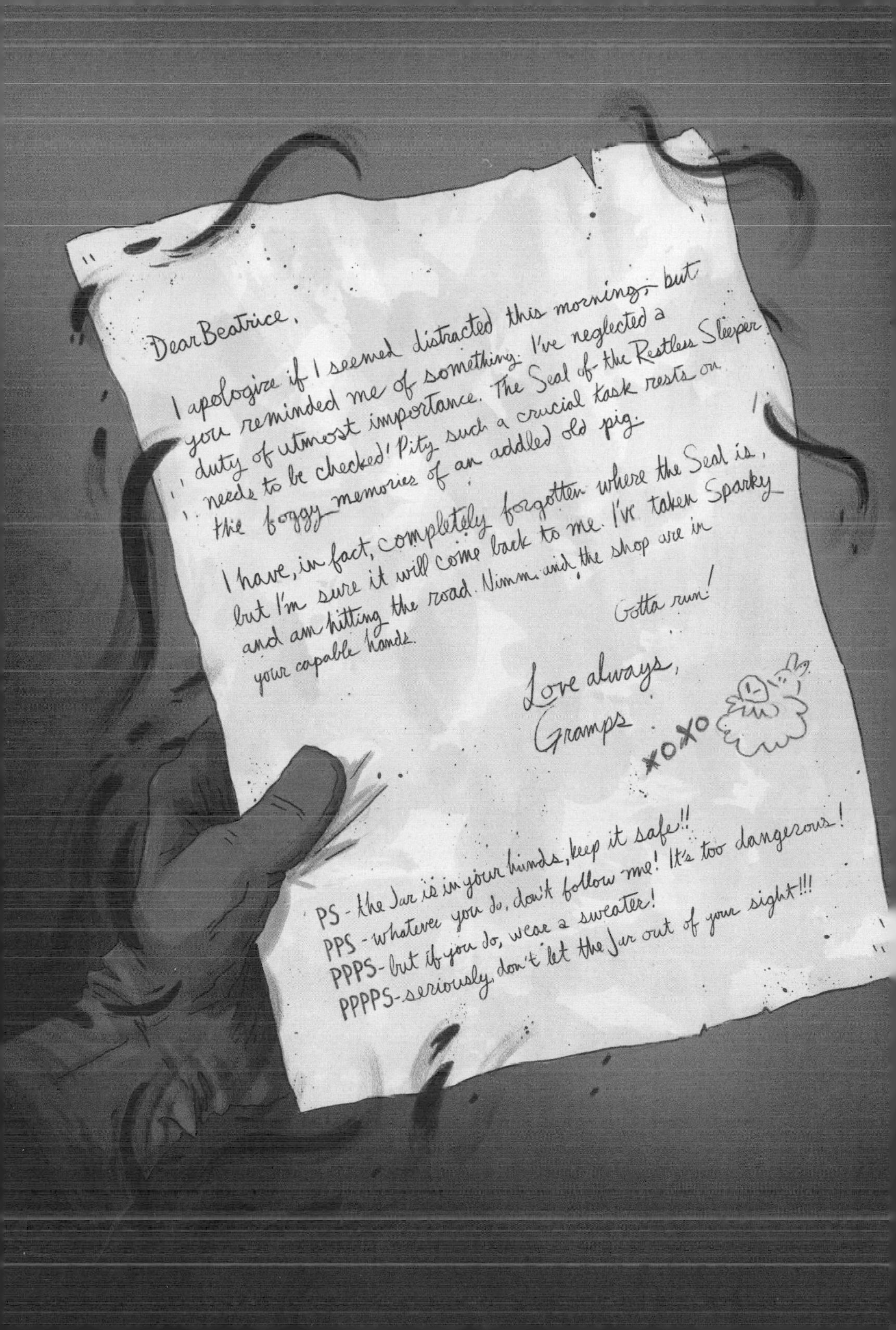
Dear Beatrice,
I apologize if I seemed distracted this morning, but you reminded me of something. I've neglected a duty of utmost importance. The Seal of the Restless Sleeper needs to be checked! Pity such a crucial task rests on the foggy memories of an addled old pig.
I have, in fact, completely forgotten where the Seal is, but I'm sure it will come back to me. I've taken Sparky and am hitting the road. Nimm and the shop are in your capable hands.
Gotta run!
Love always,
Gramps
XOXO
PS - the Jar is in your hands, keep it safe!!
PPS - whatever you do, don't follow me! It's too dangerous!
PPPS - but if you do, wear a sweater!
PPPPS - seriously, don't let the Jar out of your sight!!!

The **Seal** of the **Restless Sleeper** needs to be checked!

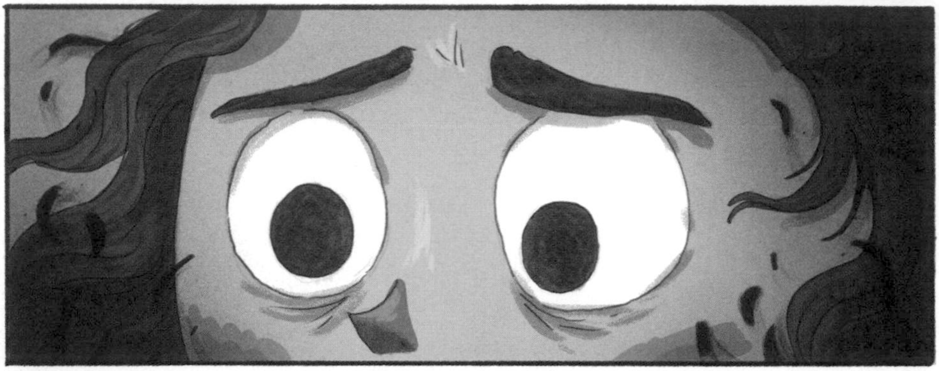

. . . hitting the road . . .

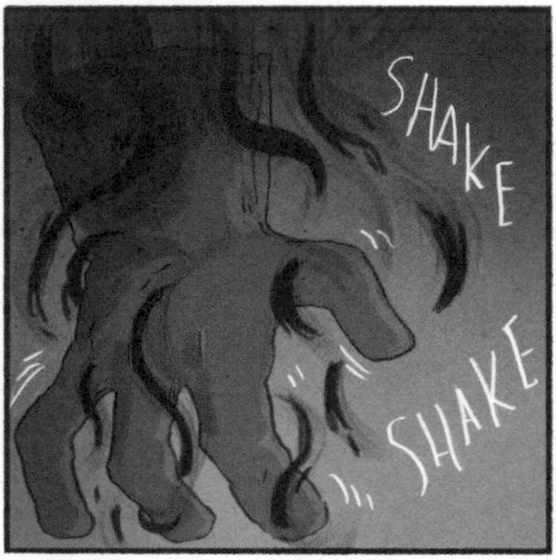
SHAKE
SHAKE

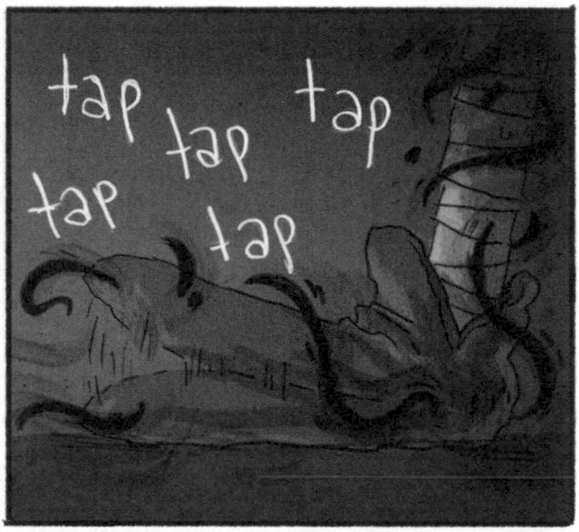
tap tap tap
tap tap

It's too **dangerous!**

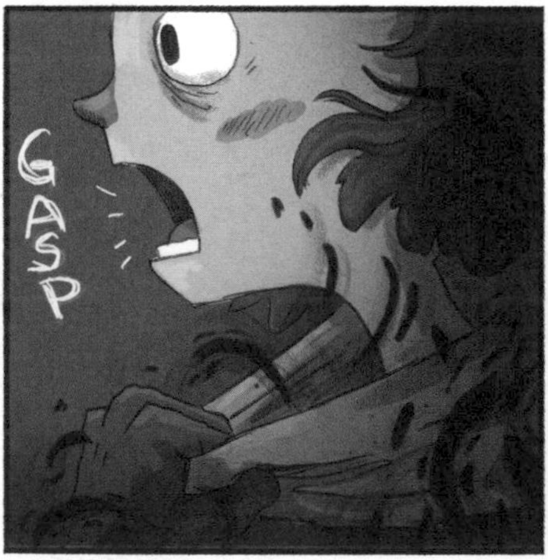
GASP

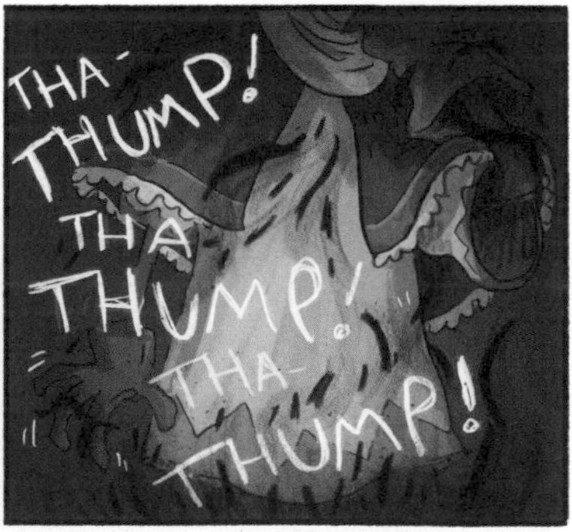
THA-THUMP!
THA-THUMP!
THA-THUMP!

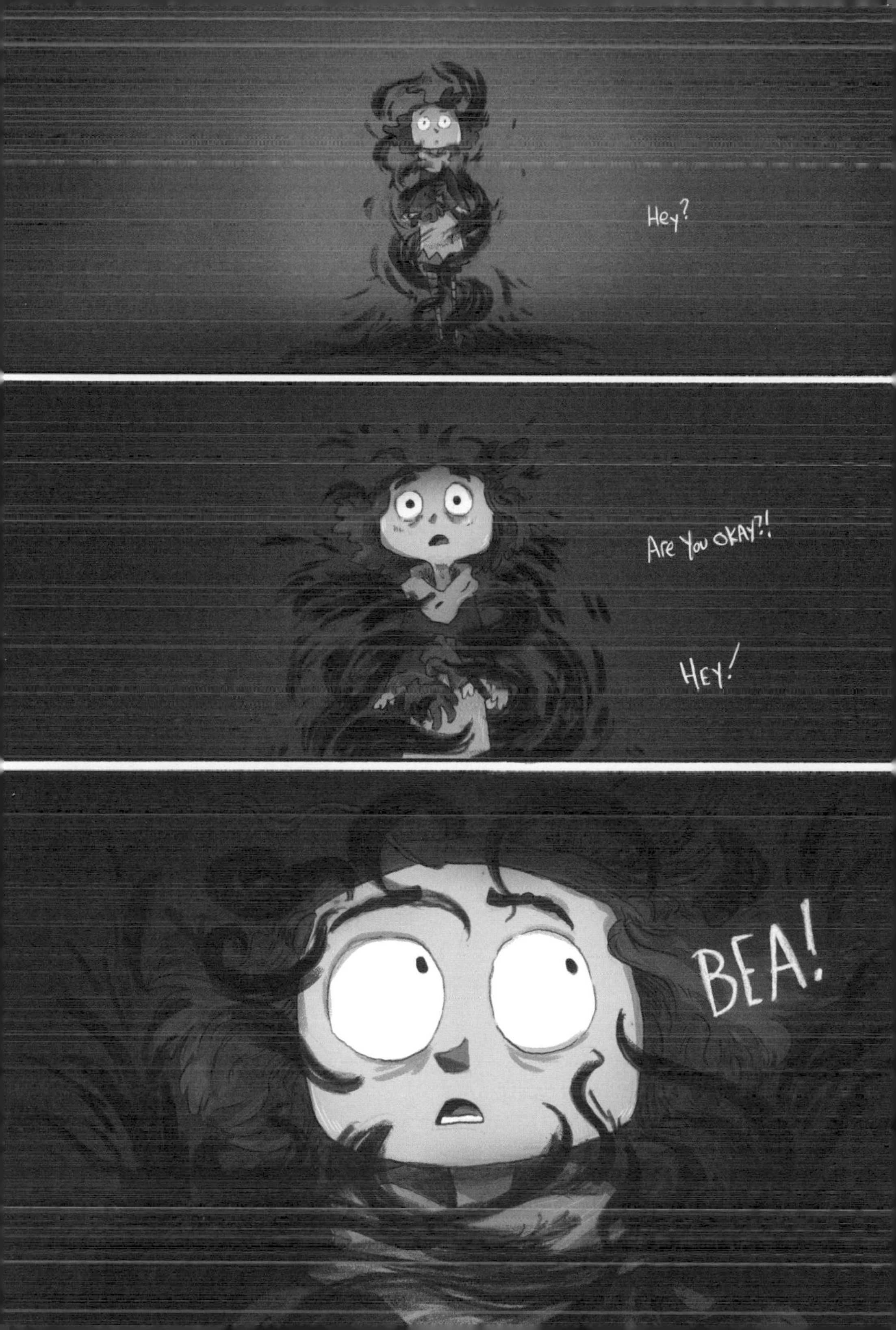
Hey?
Are You OKAY?!
HEY!
BEA!

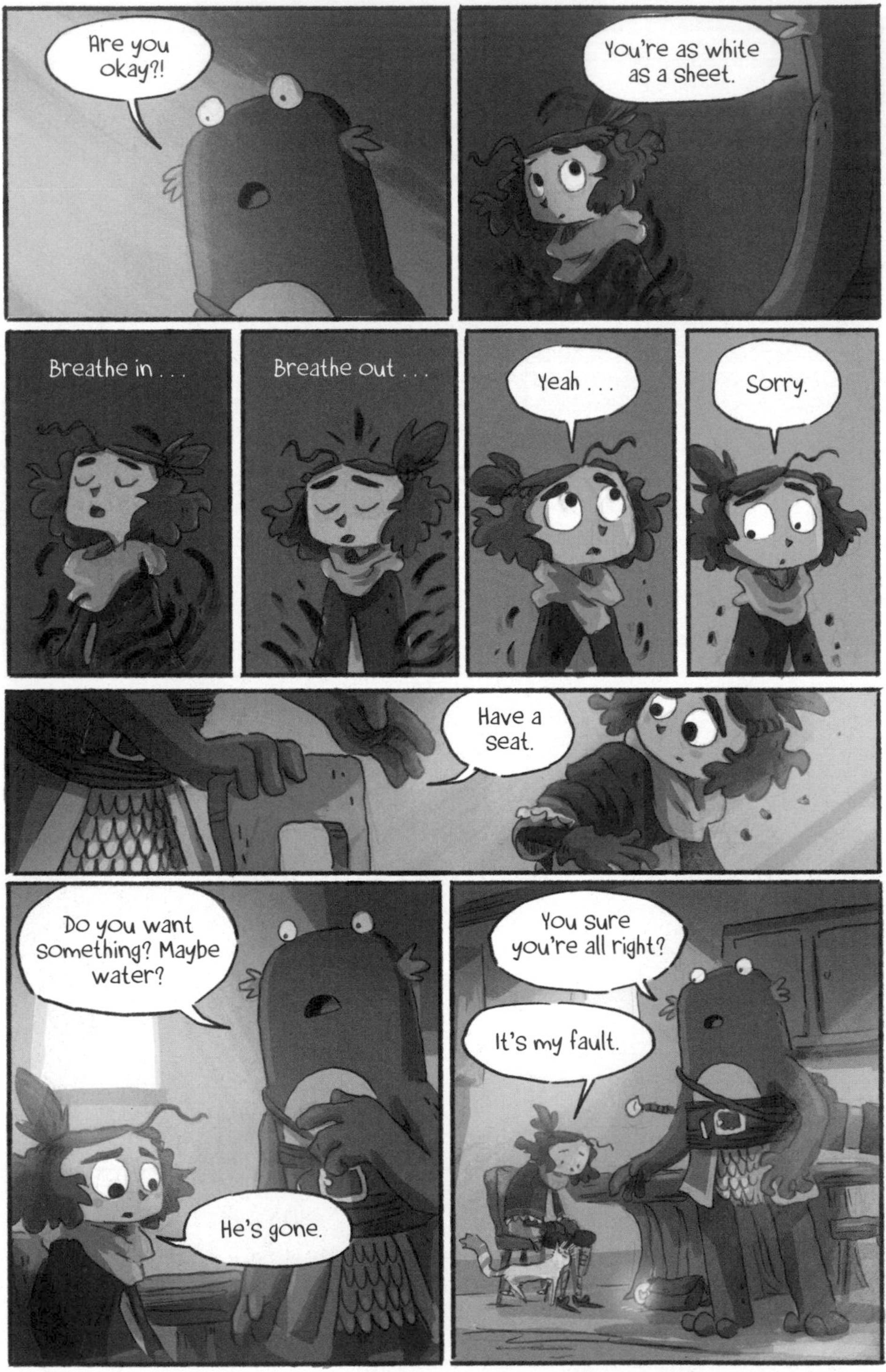
Are you okay?!
You're as white as a sheet.
Breathe in . . .
Breathe out . . .
Yeah . . .
Sorry.
Have a seat.
Do you want something? Maybe water?
He's gone.
You sure you're all right?
It's my fault.

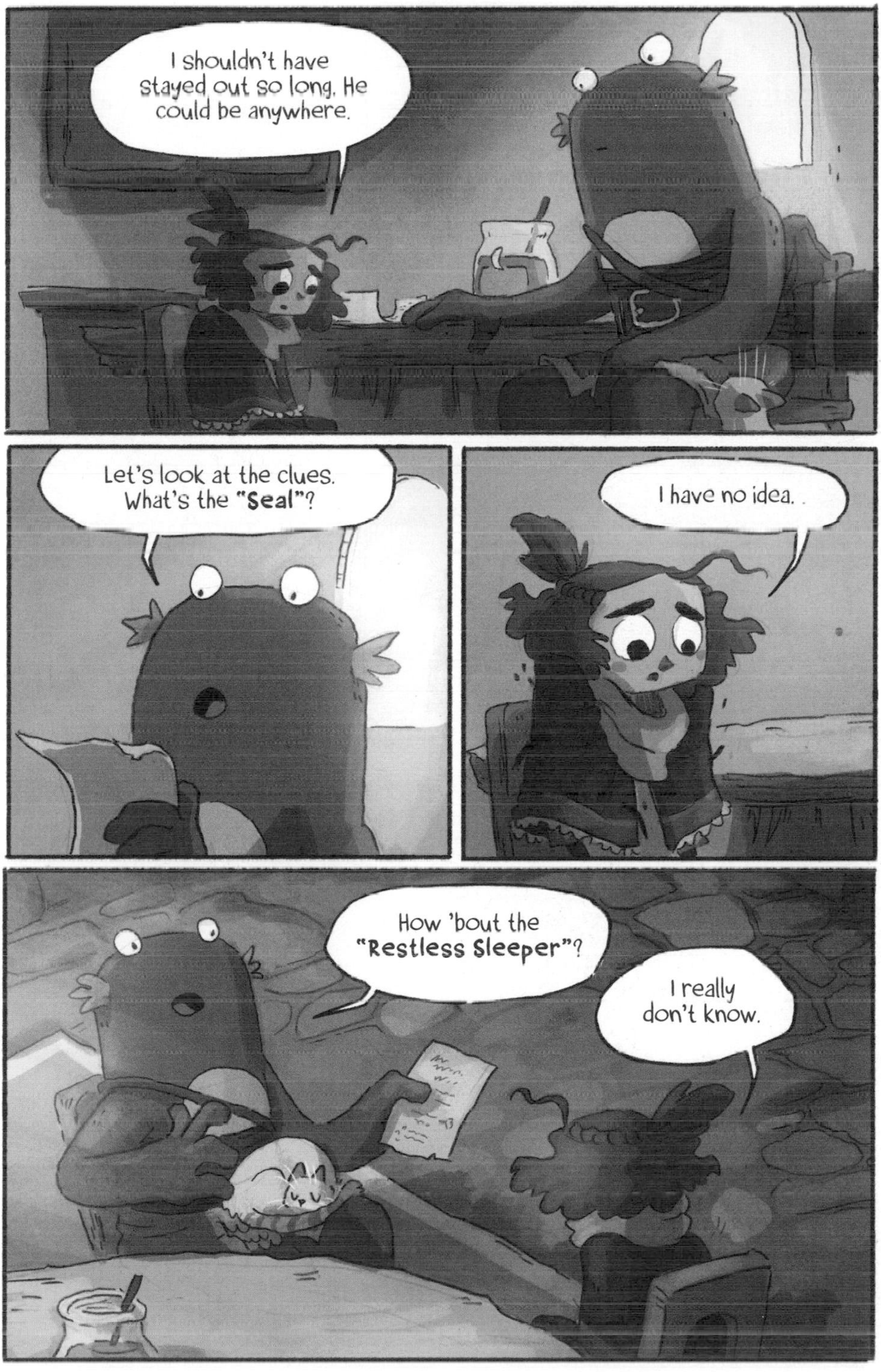
I shouldn't have stayed out so long. He could be anywhere.
Let's look at the clues. What's the **"Seal"**?
I have no idea. .
How 'bout the **"Restless Sleeper"**?
I really don't know.

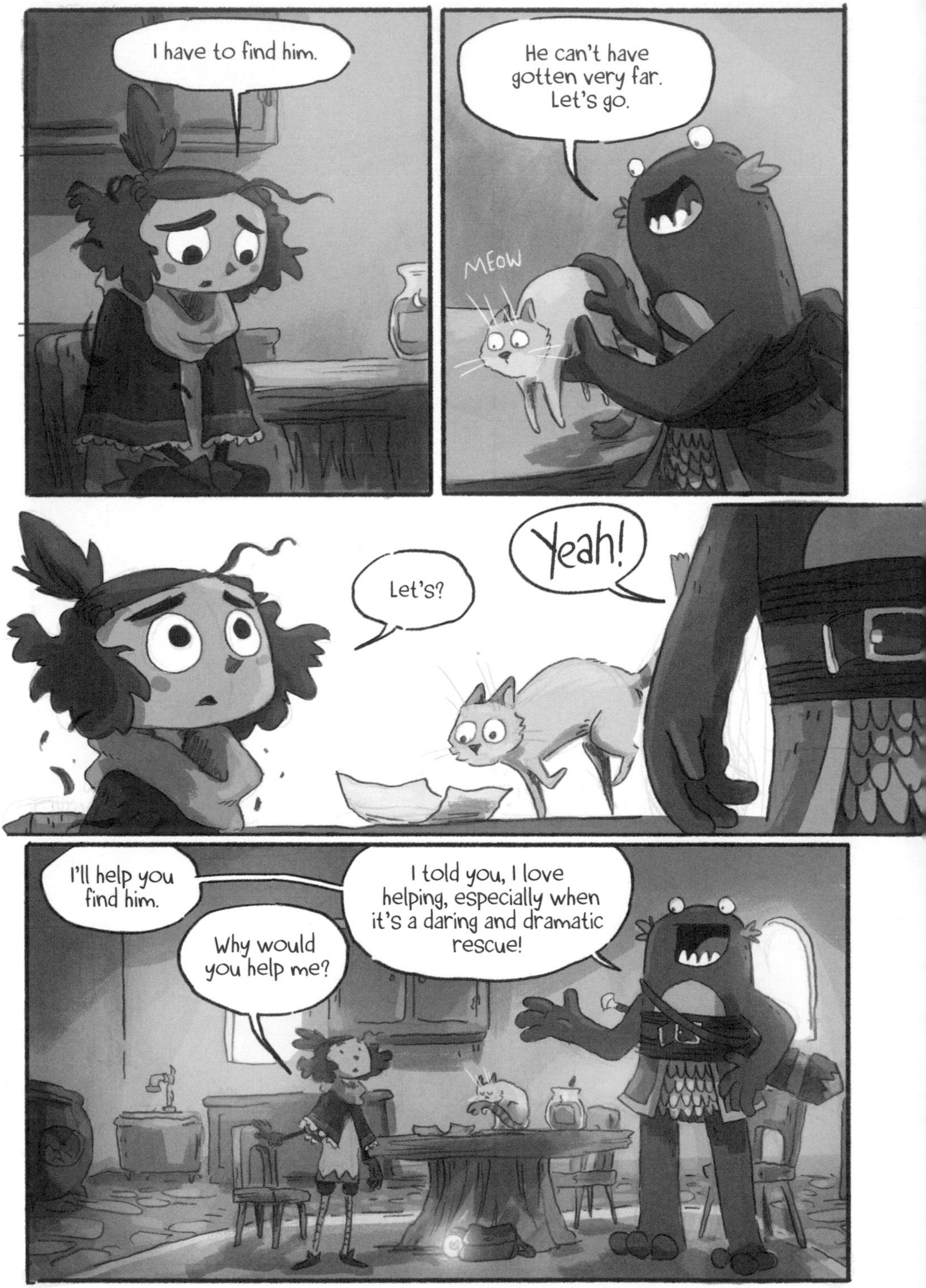
I have to find him.
He can't have gotten very far. Let's go.
MEOW
Let's?
Yeah!
I'll help you find him.
Why would you help me?
I told you, I love helping, especially when it's a daring and dramatic rescue!

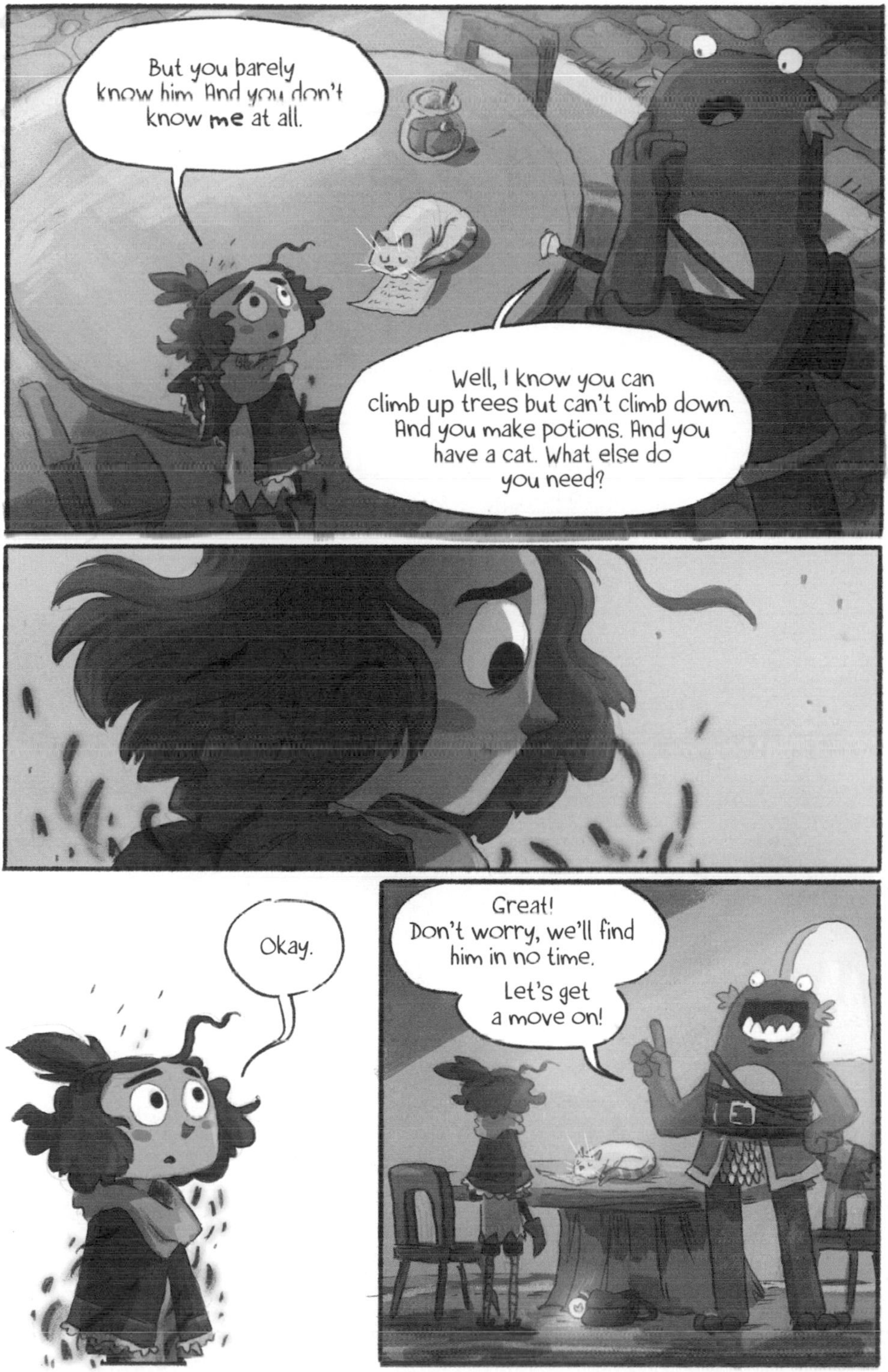
But you barely know him. And you don't know **me** at all.
Well, I know you can climb up trees but can't climb down. And you make potions. And you have a cat. What else do you need?
Okay.
Great! Don't worry, we'll find him in no time.
Let's get a move on!

BANG!
CLOSED
BE BACK
BANG!
CLICK!
FOR
MISS OBELTREE
CLOSED
BE BACK
SOON!

You got enough stuff?

Do you think I need more?!

Nope.
You look ready to take on the world.

You ready, Nimm?

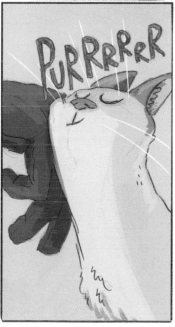

PuRRRRRR

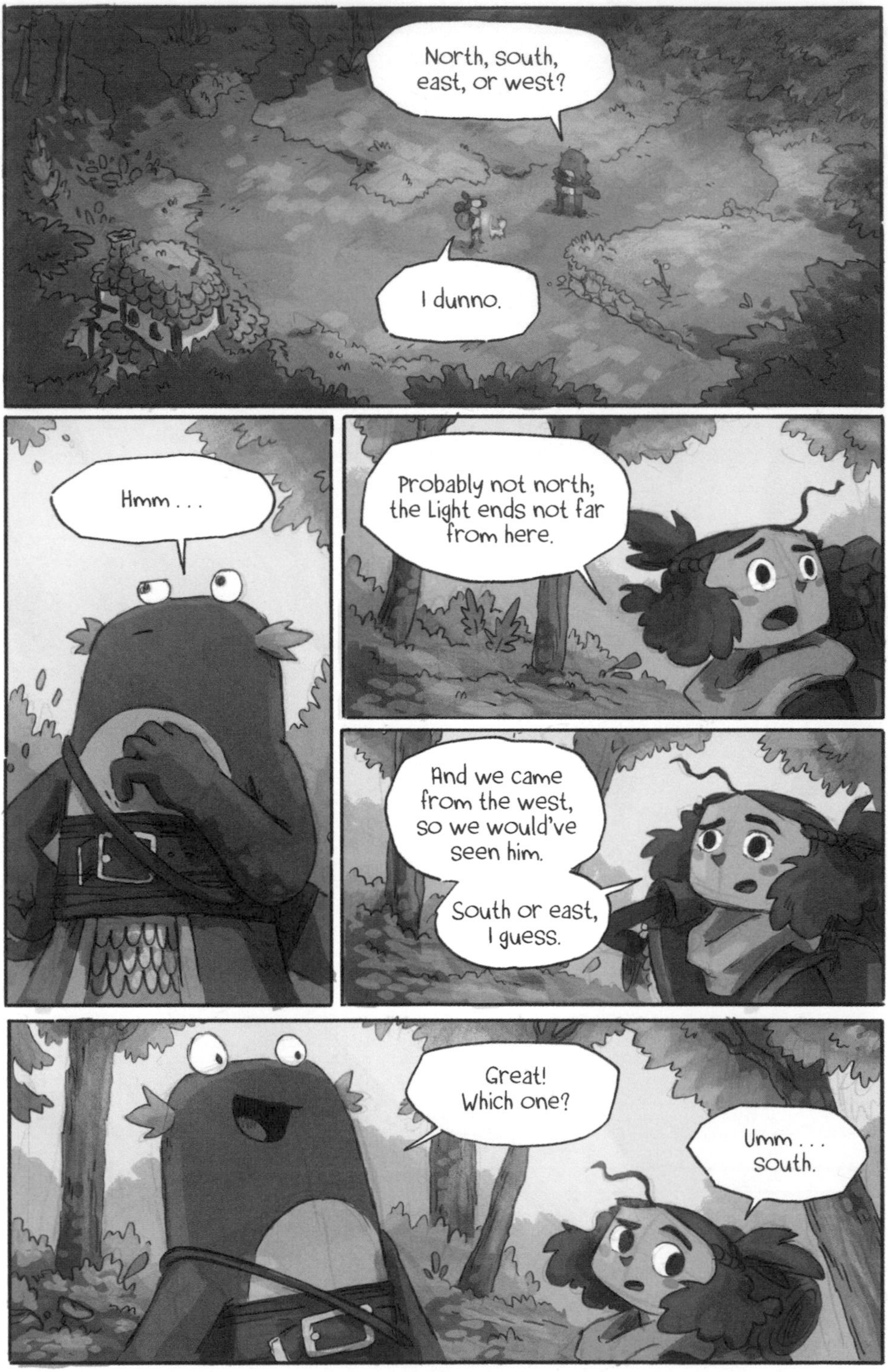
North, south, east, or west?
I dunno.
Hmm . . .
Probably not north; the Light ends not far from here.
And we came from the west, so we would've seen him.
South or east, I guess.
Great! Which one?
Umm . . . south.

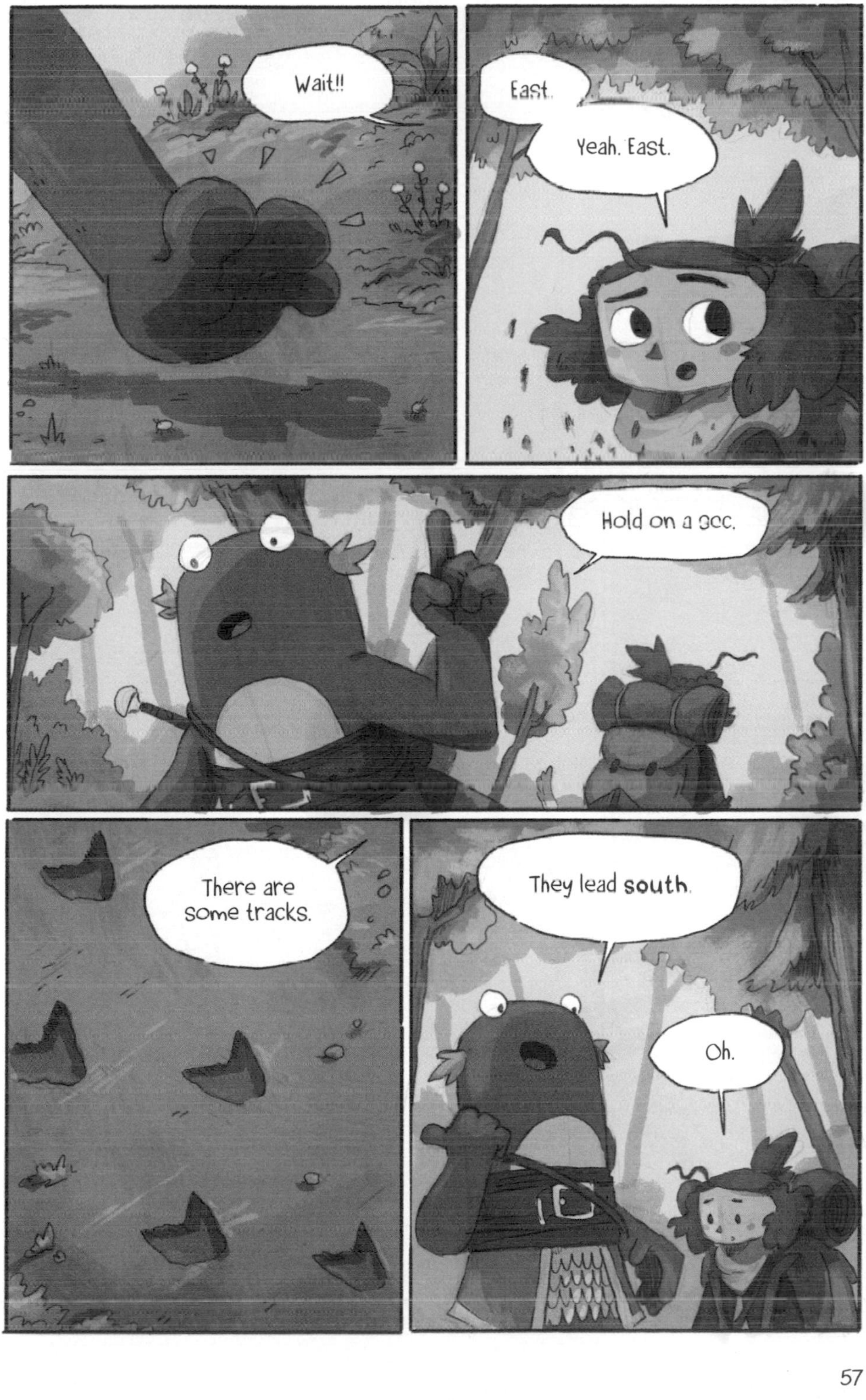
Wait!!
East.
Yeah. East.
Hold on a sec.
There are some tracks.
They lead **south**.
Oh.

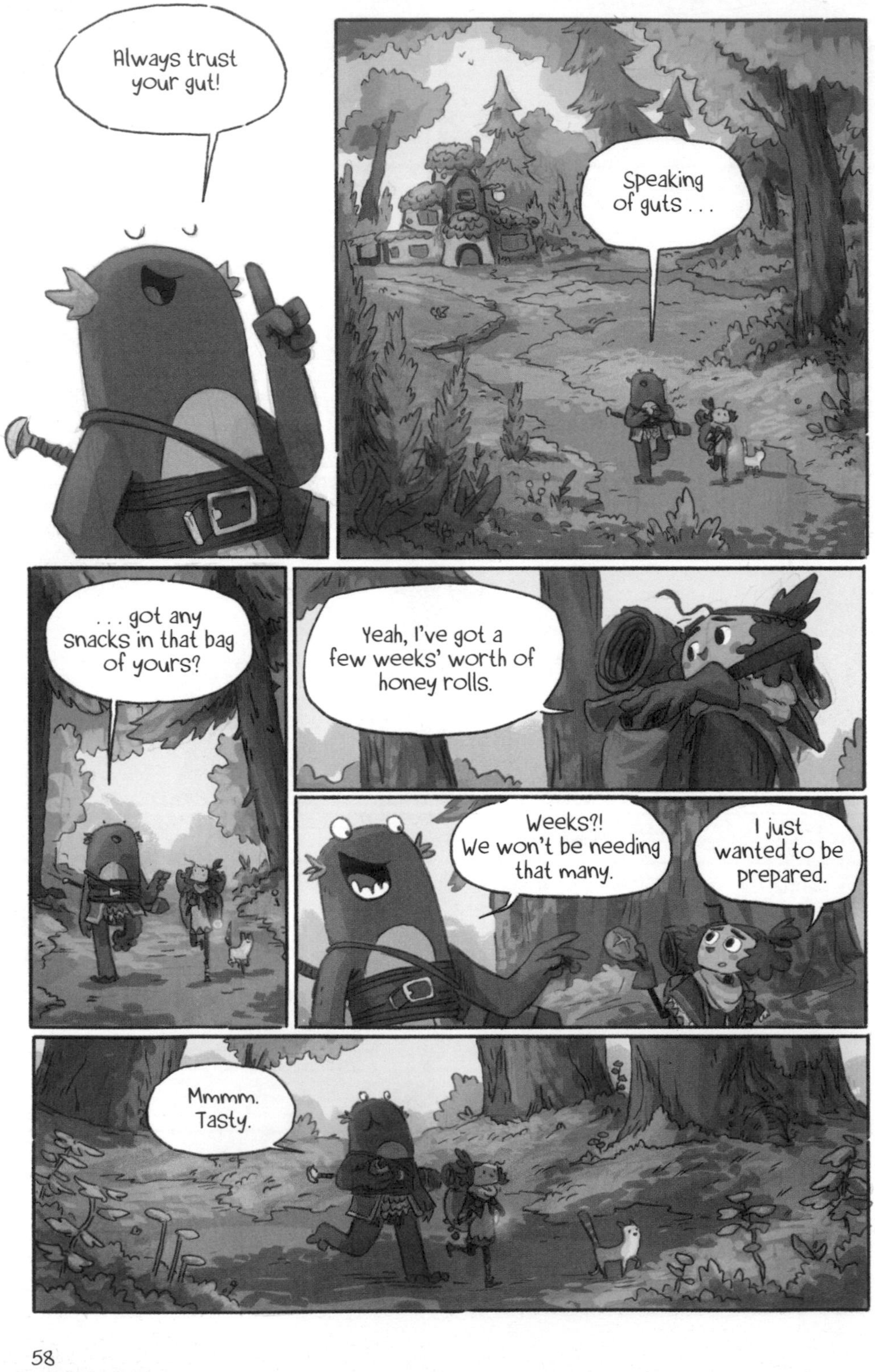

Always trust your gut!
Speaking of guts . . .
. . . got any snacks in that bag of yours?
Yeah, I've got a few weeks' worth of honey rolls.
Weeks?! We won't be needing that many.
I just wanted to be prepared.
Mmmm. Tasty.

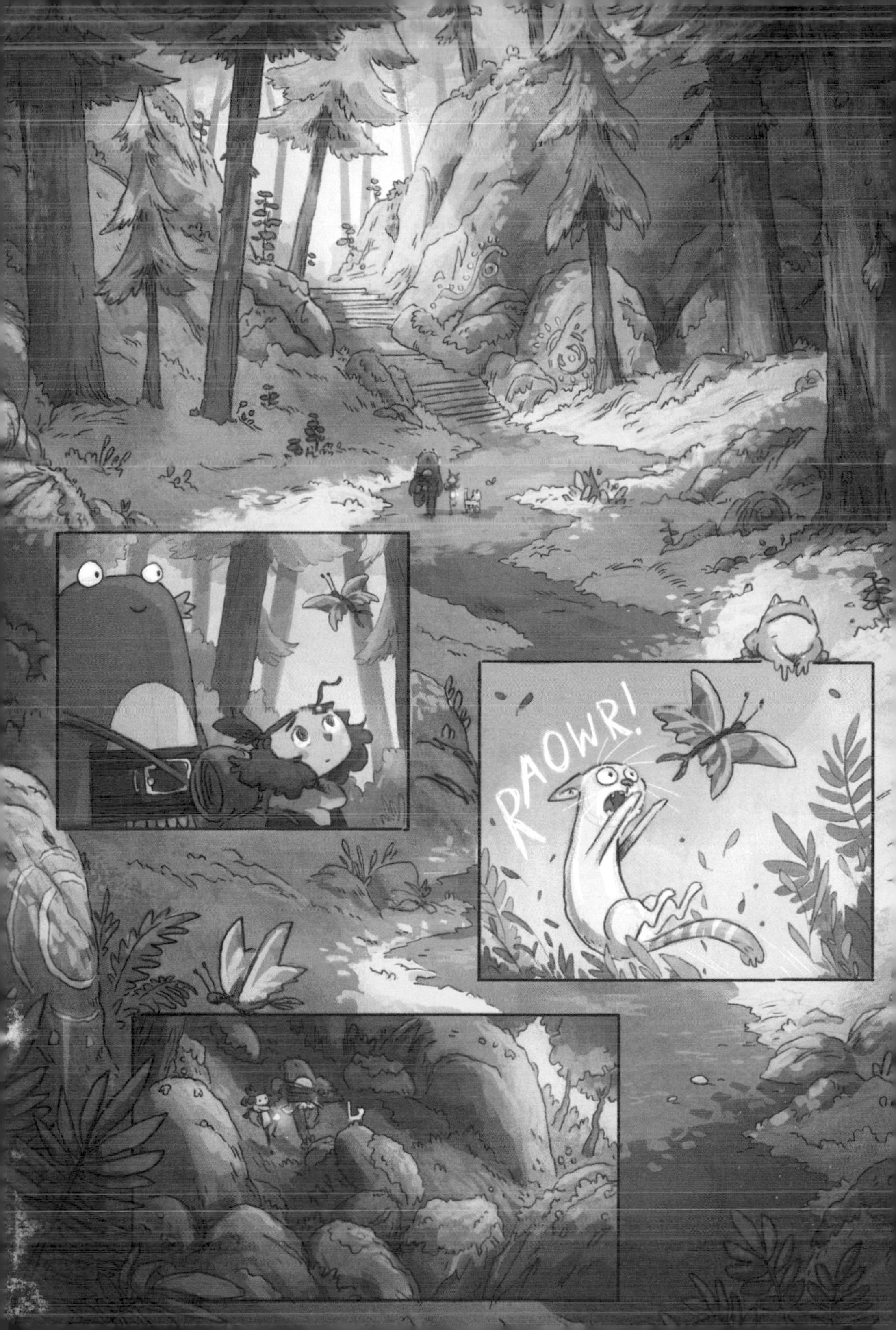
RAOWR!

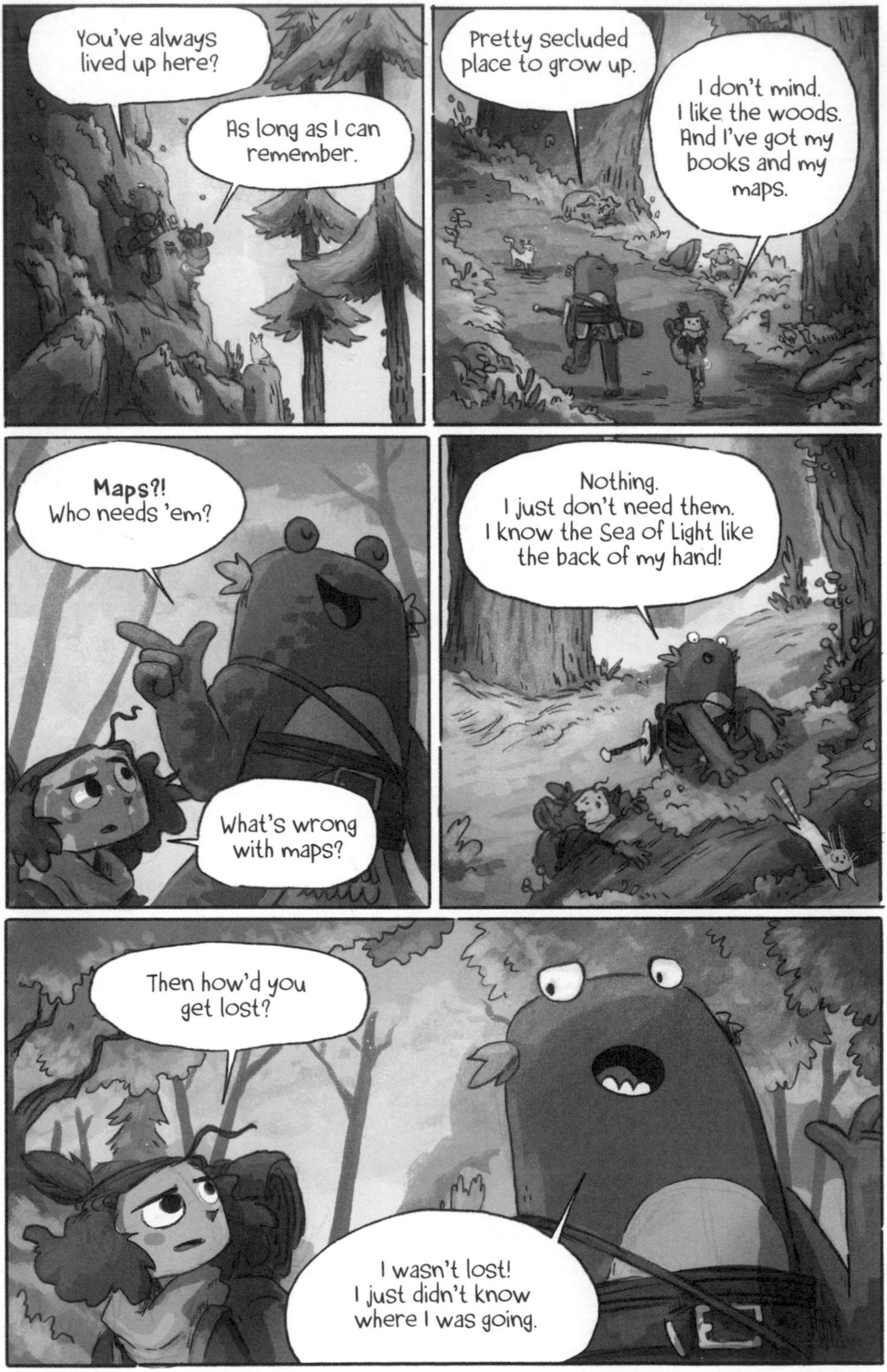
You've always lived up here?
As long as I can remember.
Pretty secluded place to grow up.
I don't mind. I like the woods. And I've got my books and my maps.
Maps?! Who needs 'em?
What's wrong with maps?
Nothing. I just don't need them. I know the Sea of Light like the back of my hand!
Then how'd you get lost?
I wasn't lost! I just didn't know where I was going.

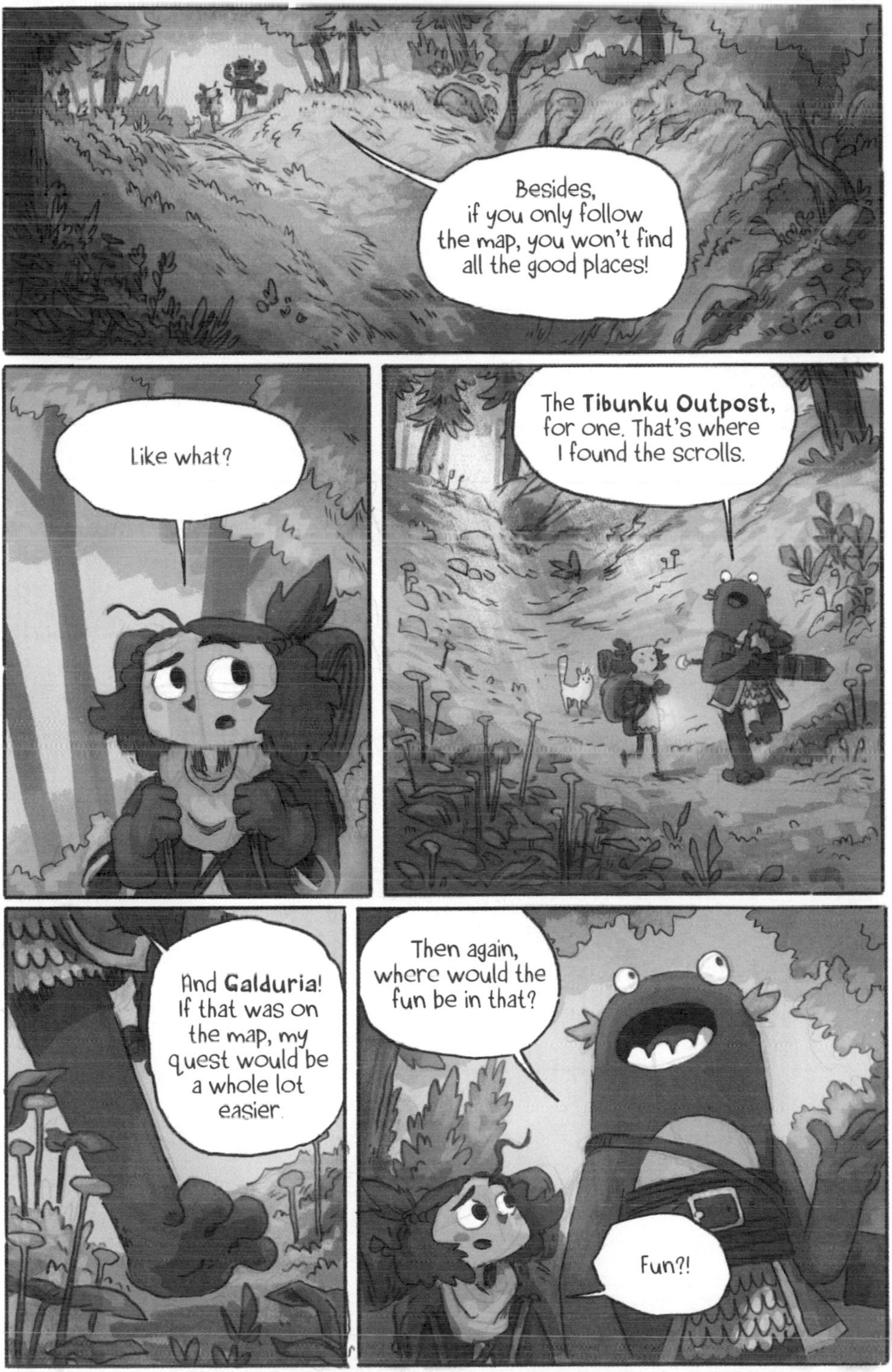
Besides, if you only follow the map, you won't find all the good places!
Like what?
The **Tibunku Outpost**, for one. That's where I found the scrolls.
And **Galduria**! If that was on the map, my quest would be a whole lot easier.
Then again, where would the fun be in that?
Fun?!

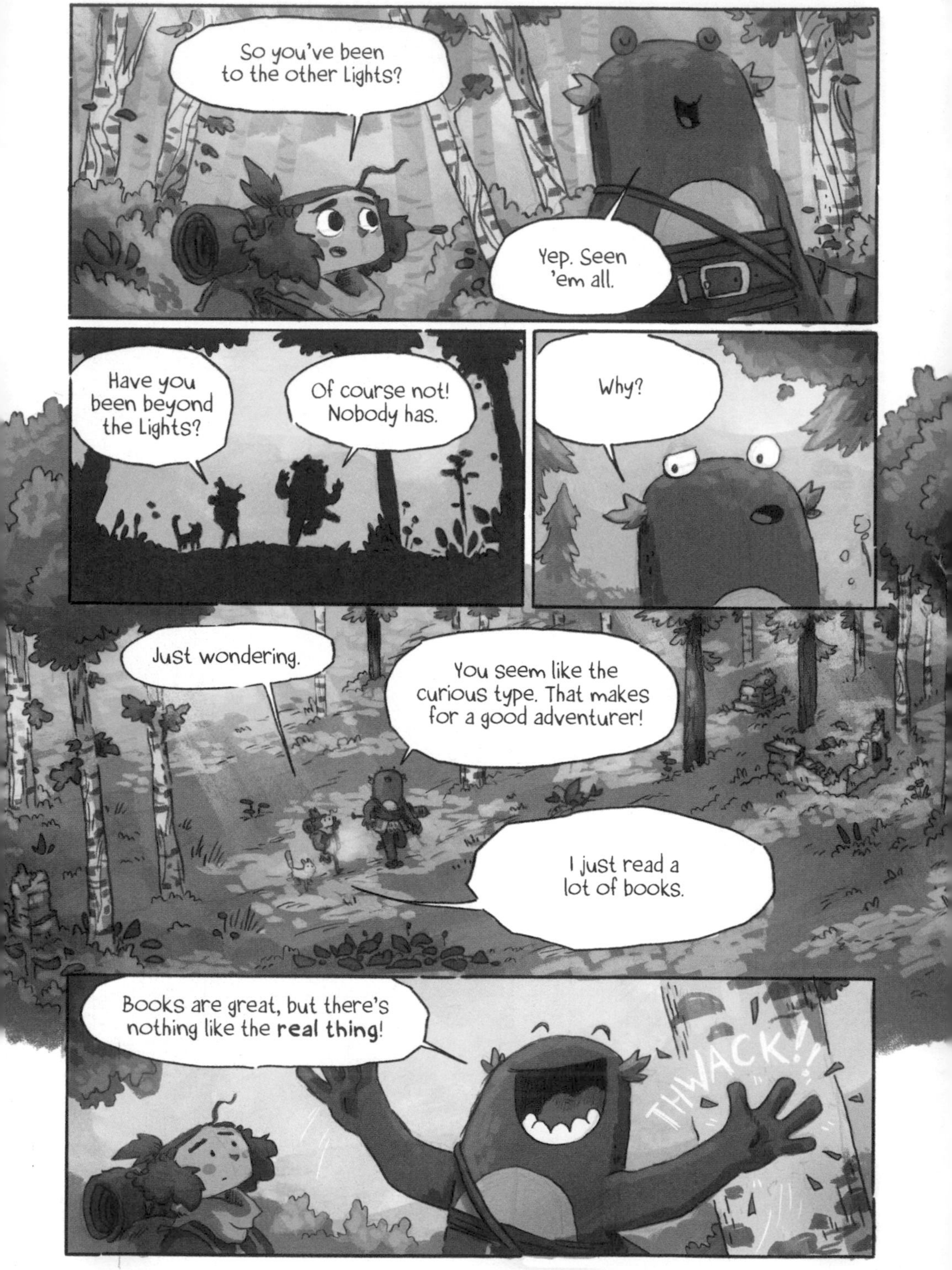
So you've been to the other Lights?
Yep. Seen 'em all.
Have you been beyond the Lights?
Of course not! Nobody has.
Why?
Just wondering.
You seem like the curious type. That makes for a good adventurer!
I just read a lot of books.
Books are great, but there's nothing like the **real thing**!
THWACK!!

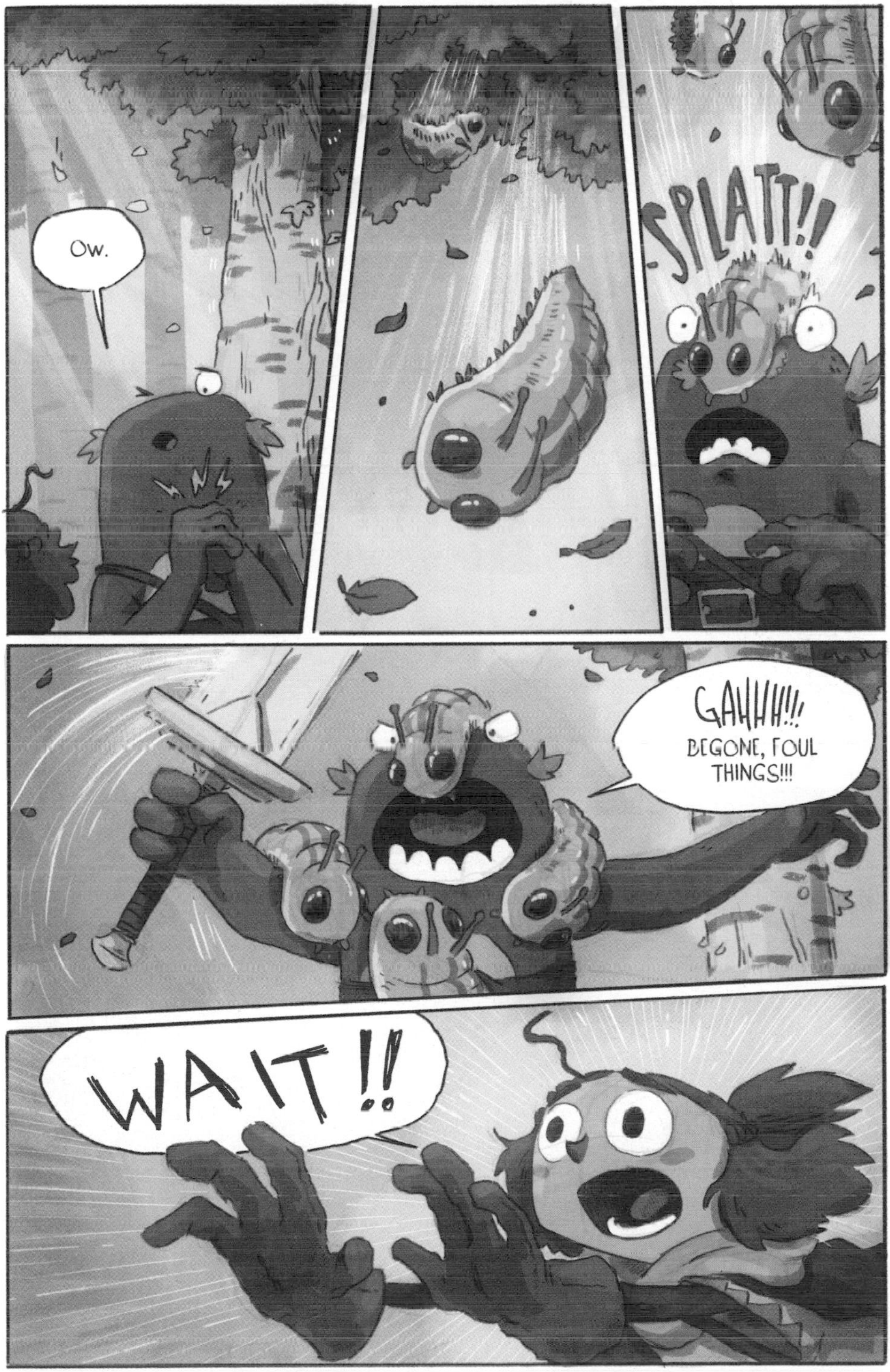
Ow.
SPLATT!!
GAHHH!!!
BEGONE, FOUL THINGS!!!
WAIT!!

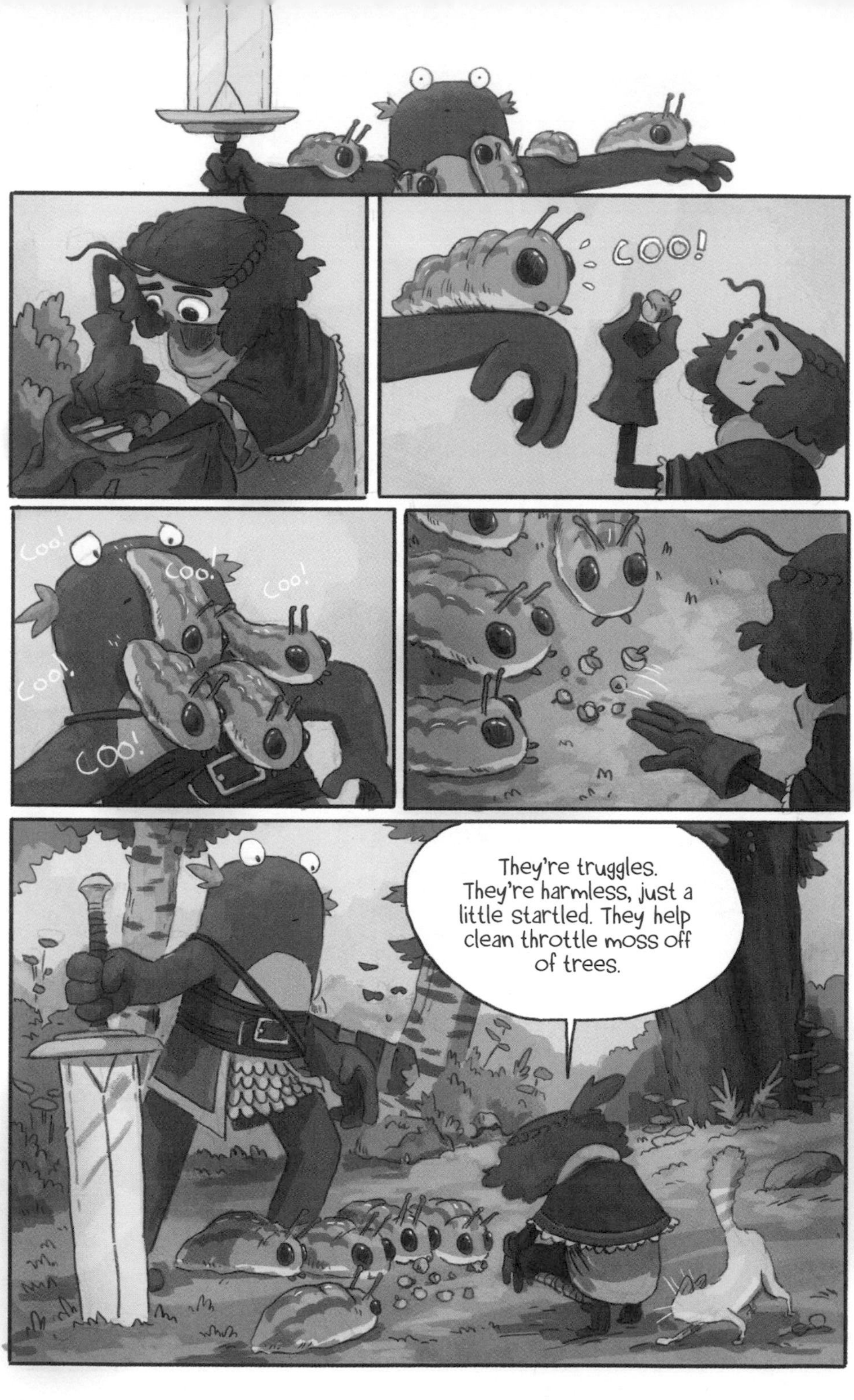
COO!
COO!
COO!
COO!
COO!
COO!
They're truggles. They're harmless, just a little startled. They help clean throttle moss off of trees.

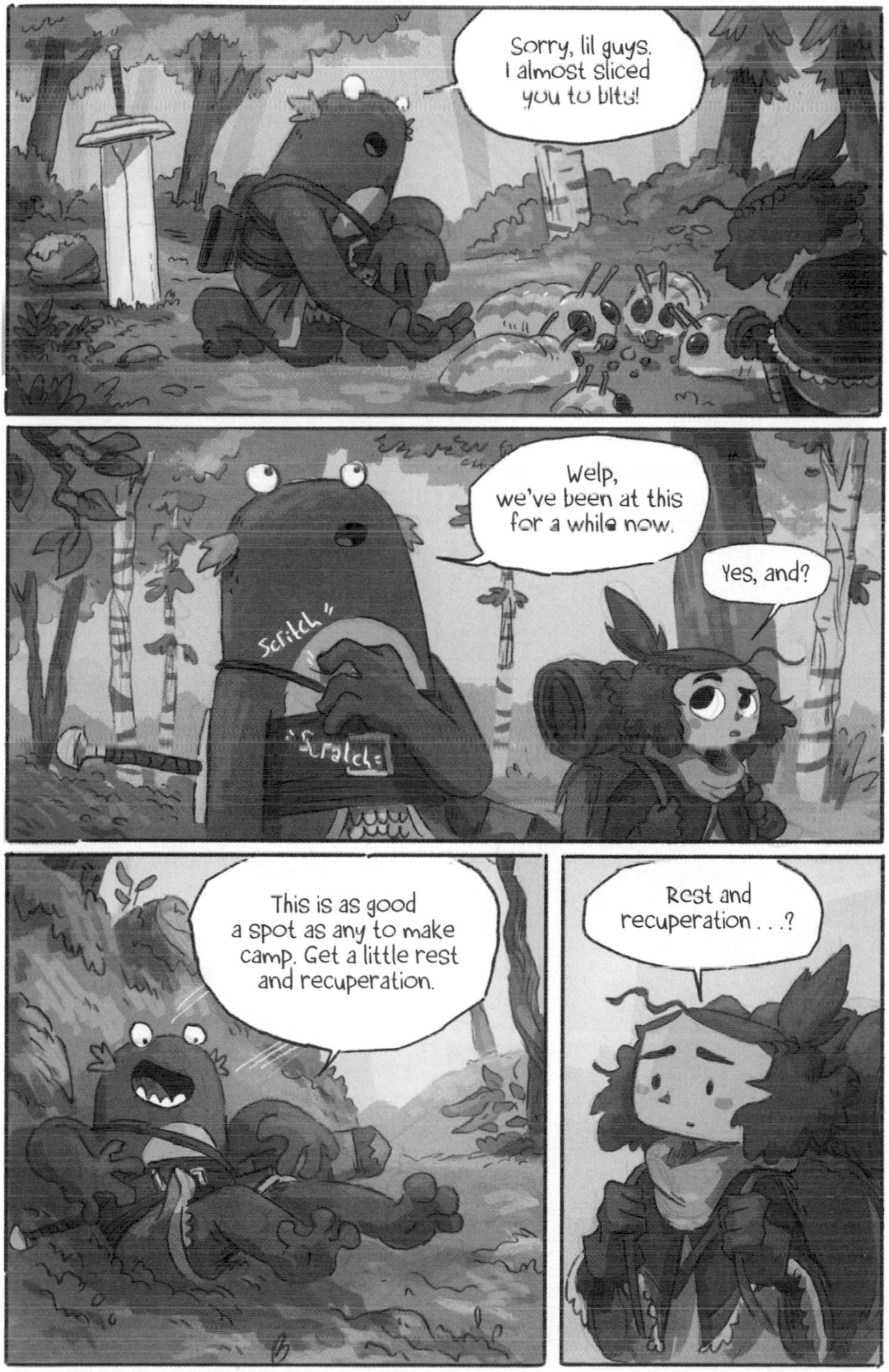
Sorry, lil guys. I almost sliced you to bits!
Welp, we've been at this for a while now.
Scritch
Scratch
Yes, and?
This is as good a spot as any to make camp. Get a little rest and recuperation.
Rest and recuperation . . .?

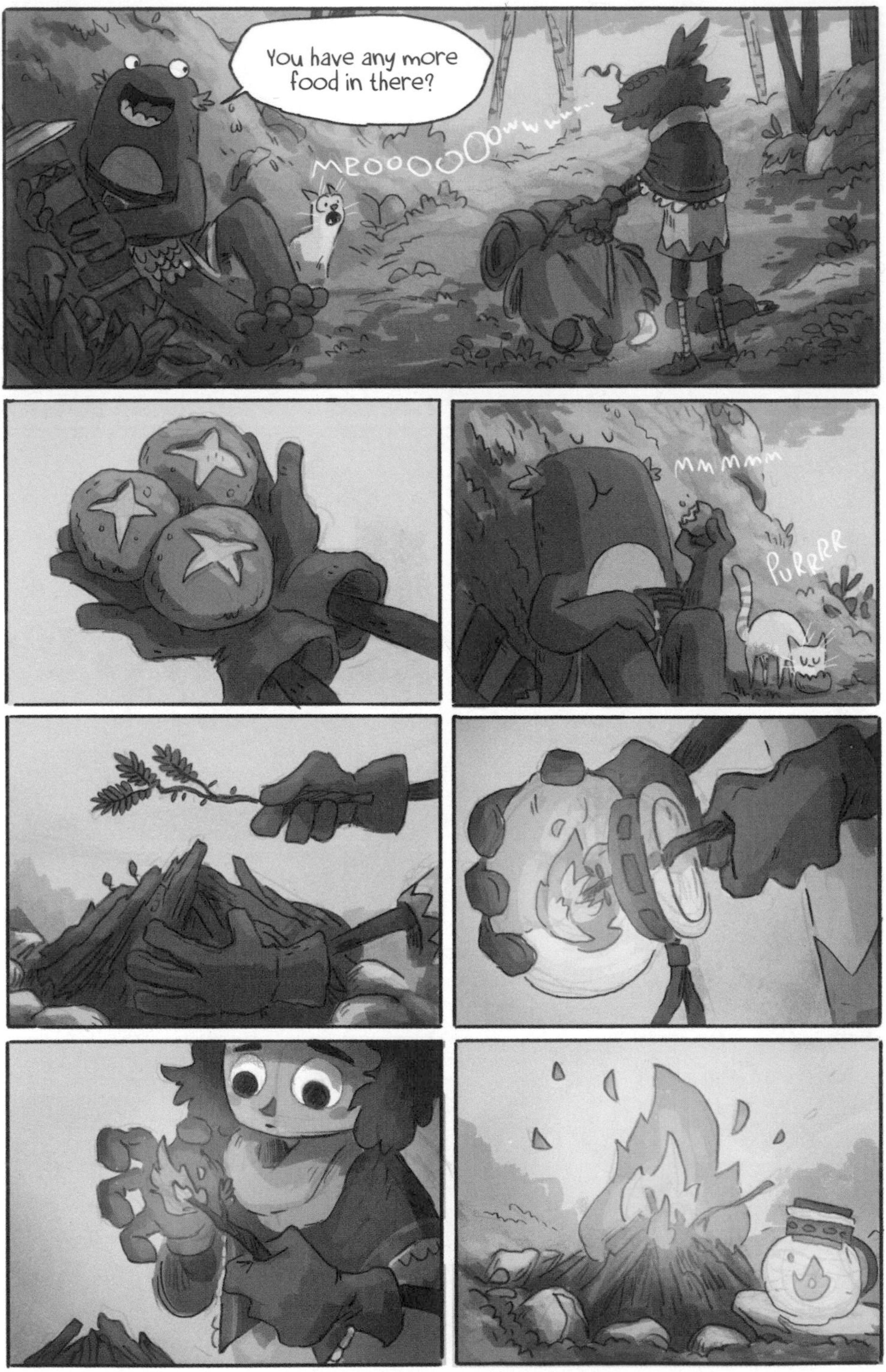
You have any more food in there?
MEOOOOOOwwww...
MMMMM
PURRRR

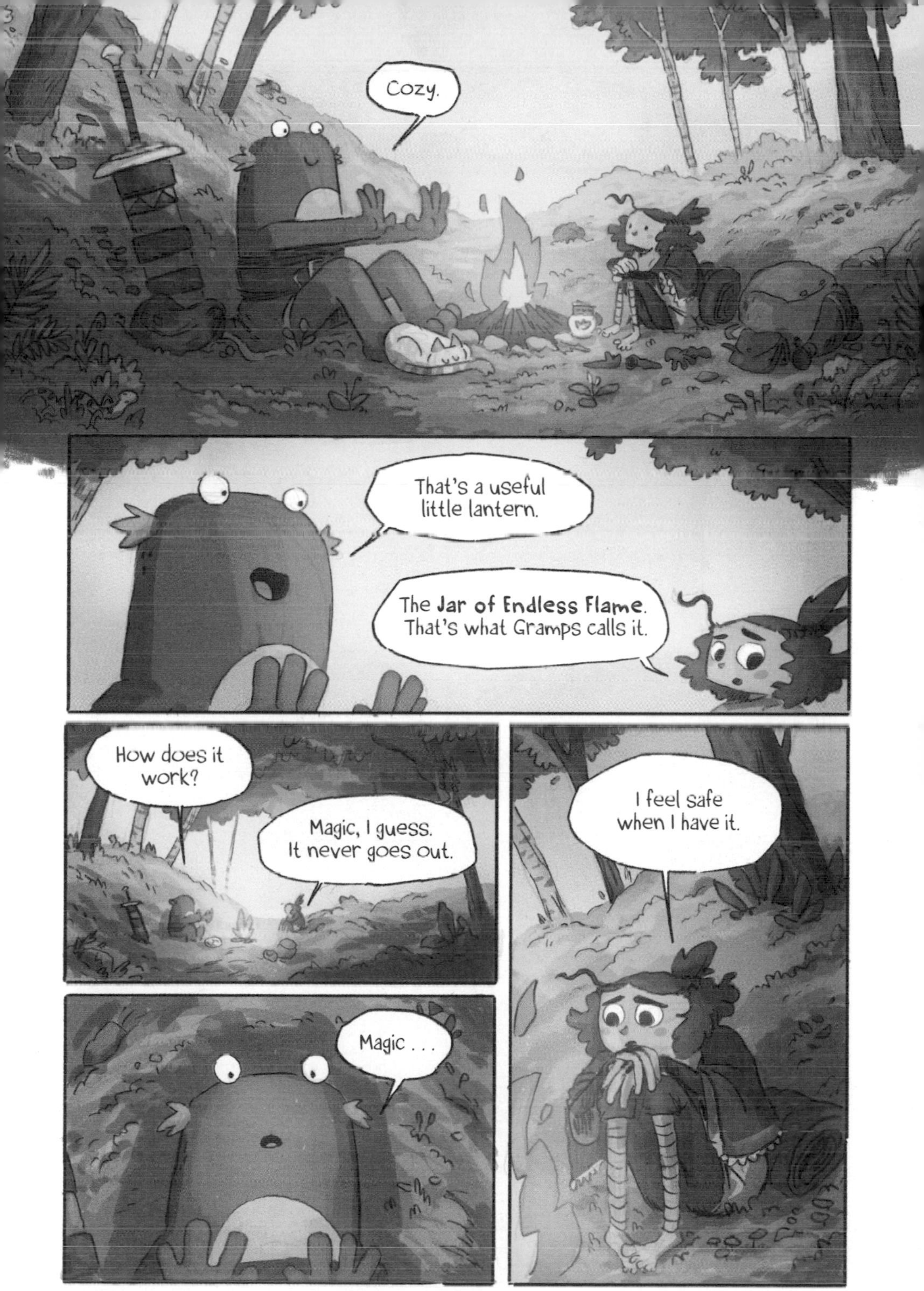
Cozy.
That's a useful little lantern.
The **Jar of Endless Flame**. That's what Gramps calls it.
How does it work?
Magic, I guess. It never goes out.
I feel safe when I have it.
Magic . . .

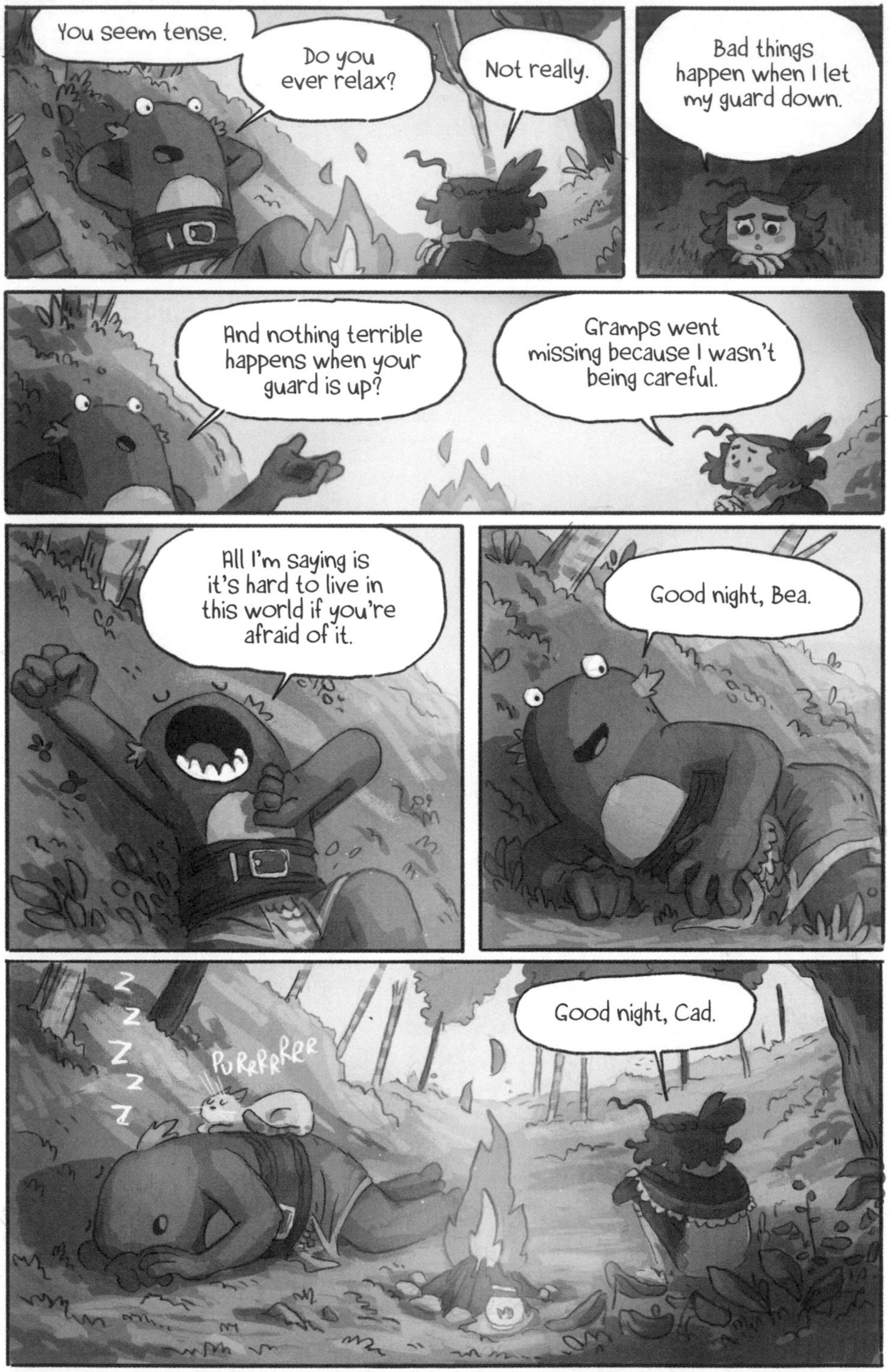
You seem tense.
Do you ever relax?
Not really.
Bad things happen when I let my guard down.
And nothing terrible happens when your guard is up?
Gramps went missing because I wasn't being careful.
All I'm saying is it's hard to live in this world if you're afraid of it.
Good night, Bea.
Z Z Z Z Z
PURRRRRRR
Good night, Cad.

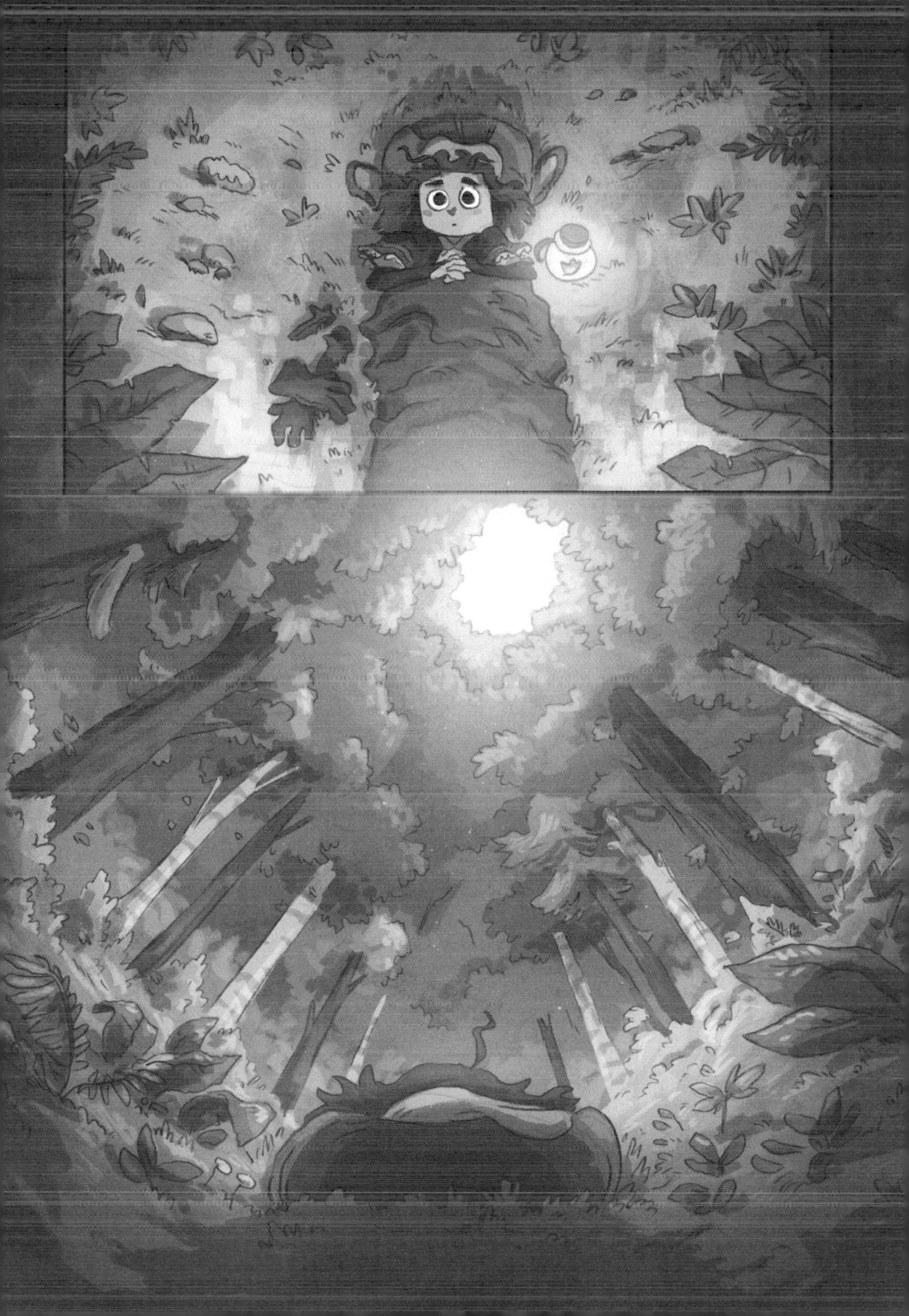

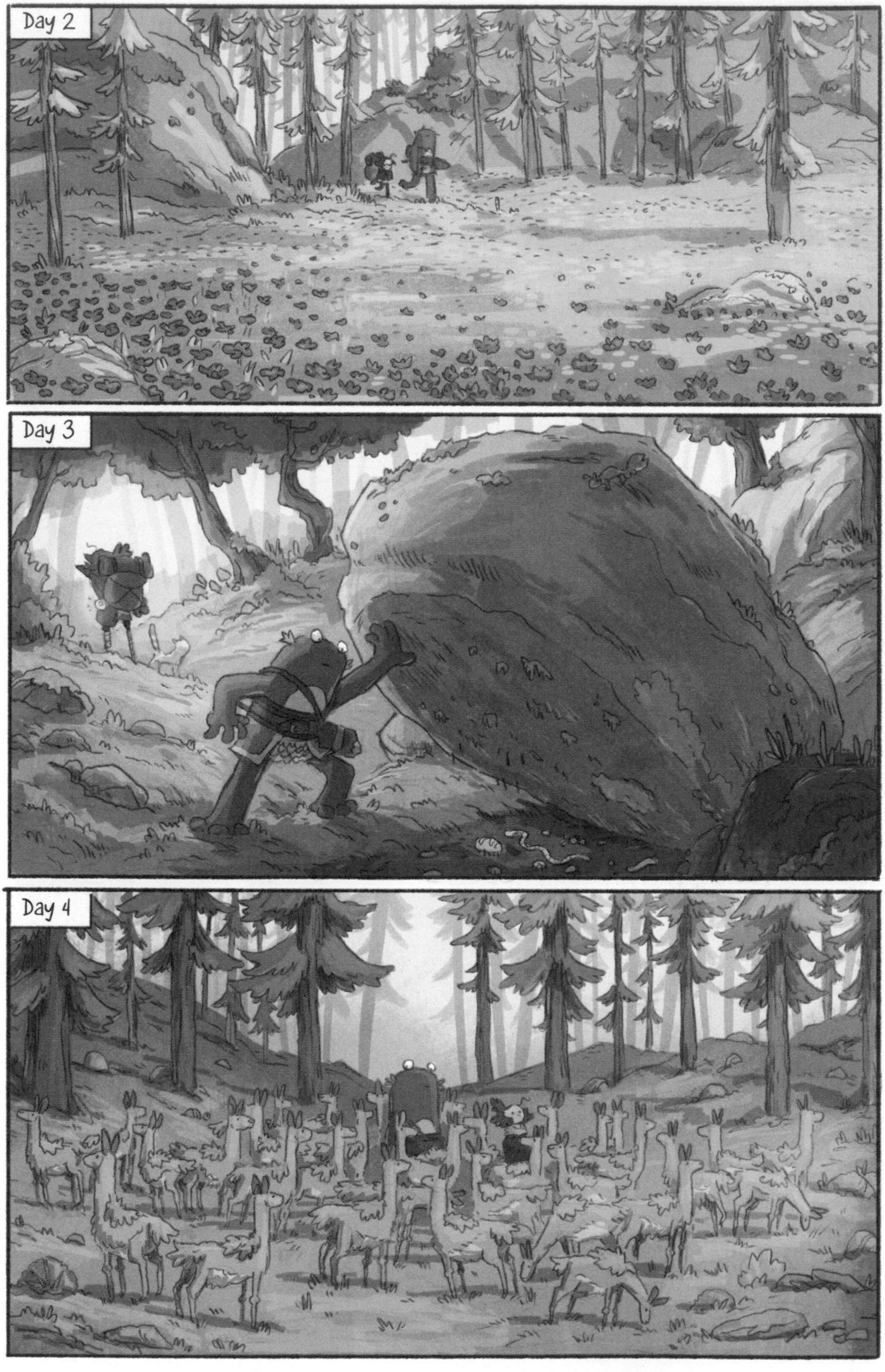
Day 2
Day 3
Day 4

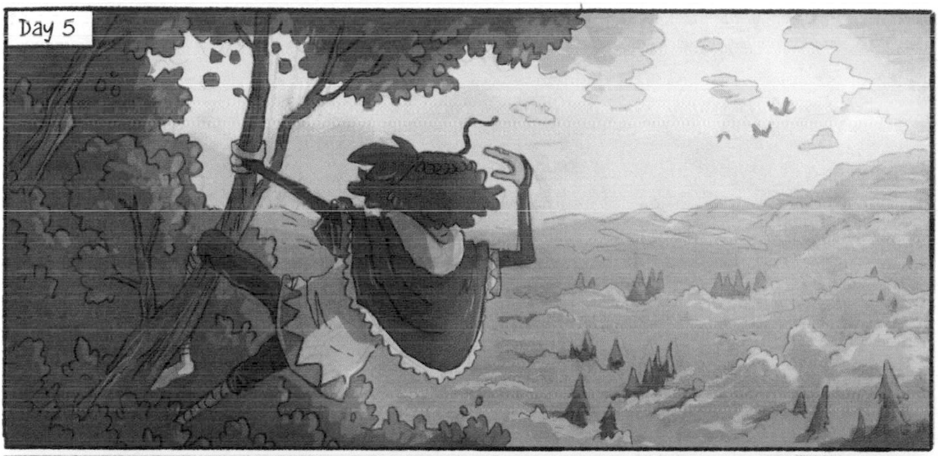
Day 5

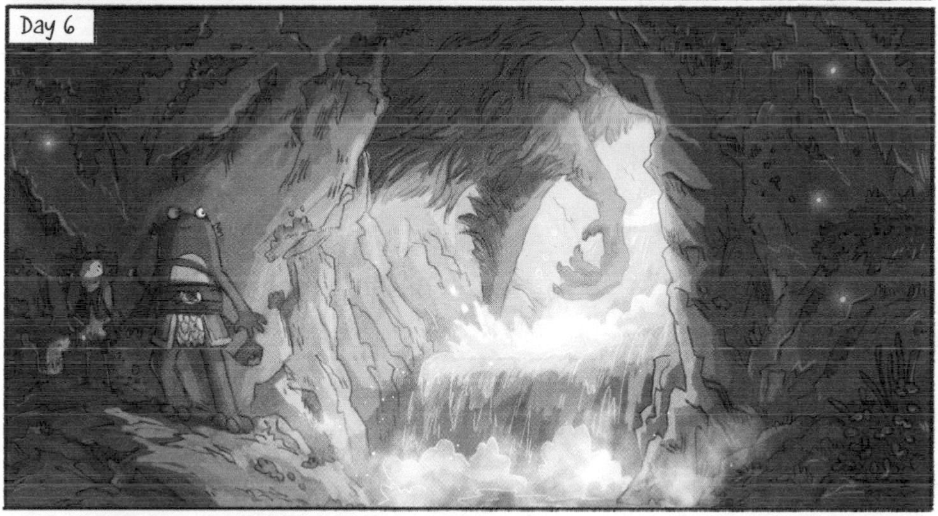
Day 6

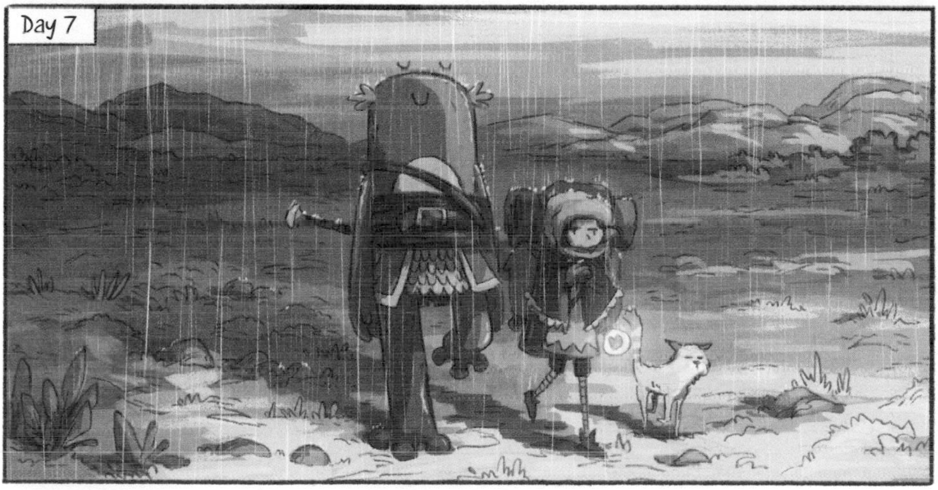
Day 7

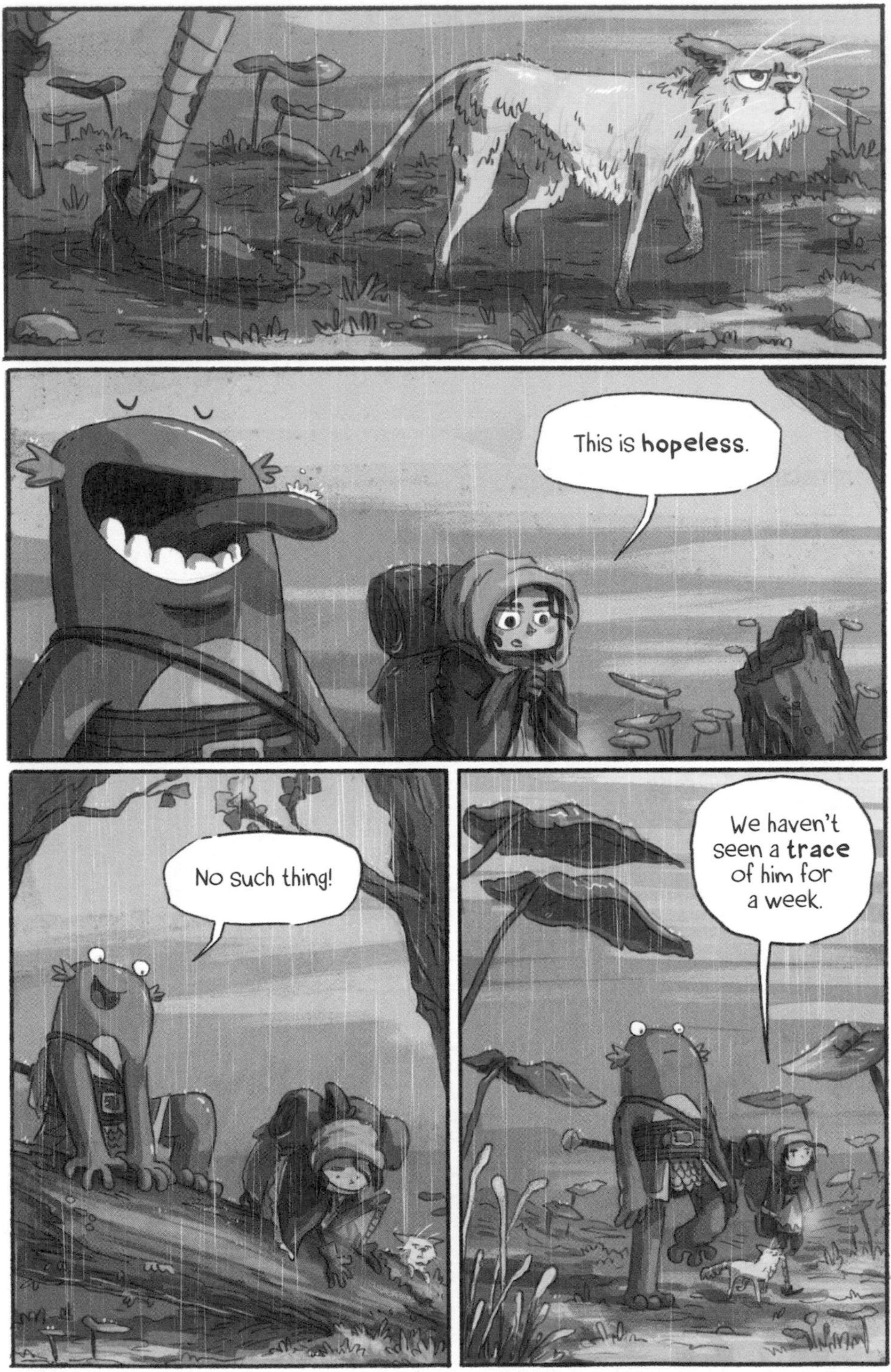
This is **hopeless**.
No such thing!
We haven't seen a **trace** of him for a week.

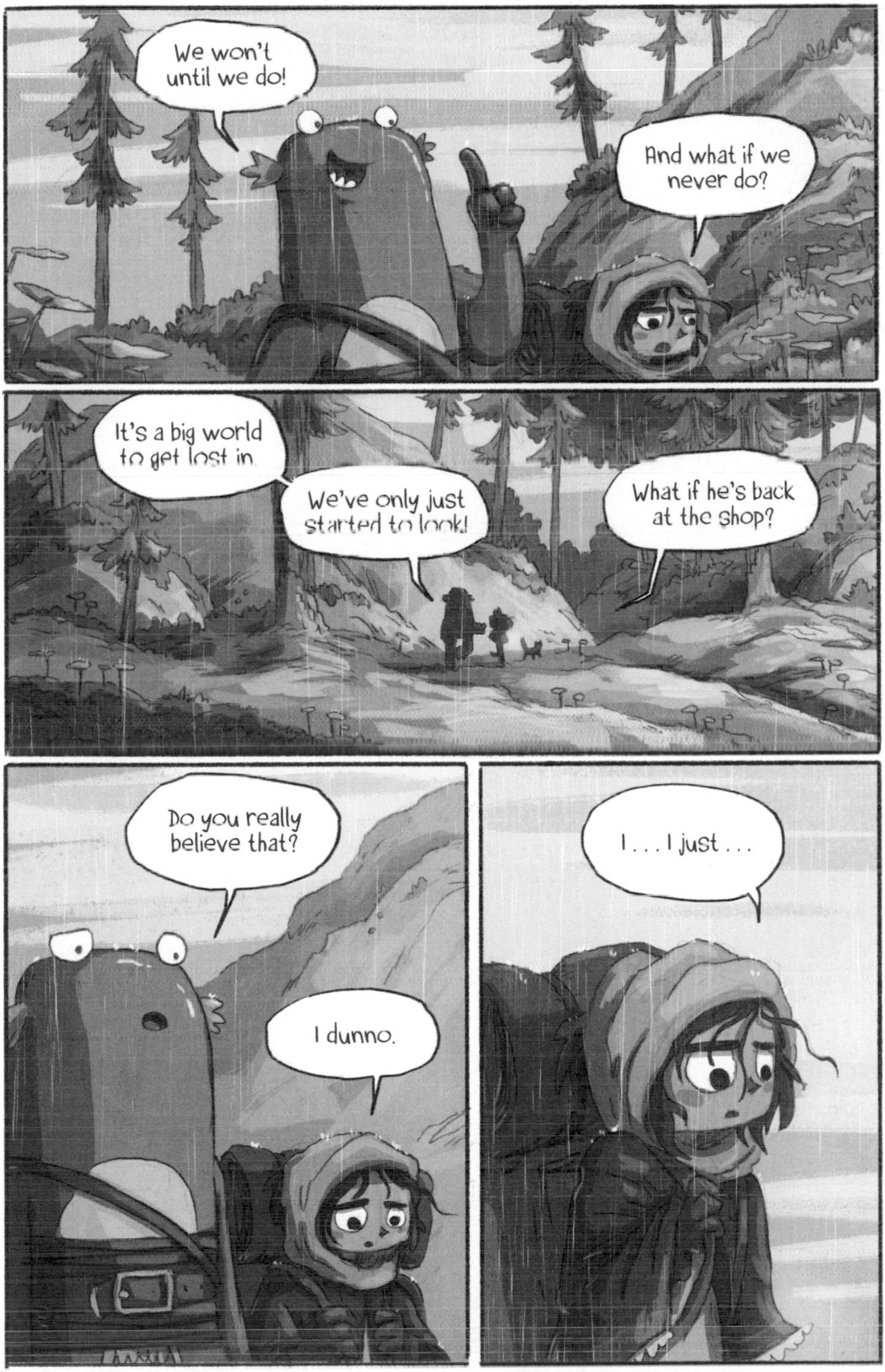
We won't until we do!
And what if we never do?
It's a big world to get lost in.
We've only just started to look!
What if he's back at the shop?
Do you really believe that?
I dunno.
I . . . I just . . .

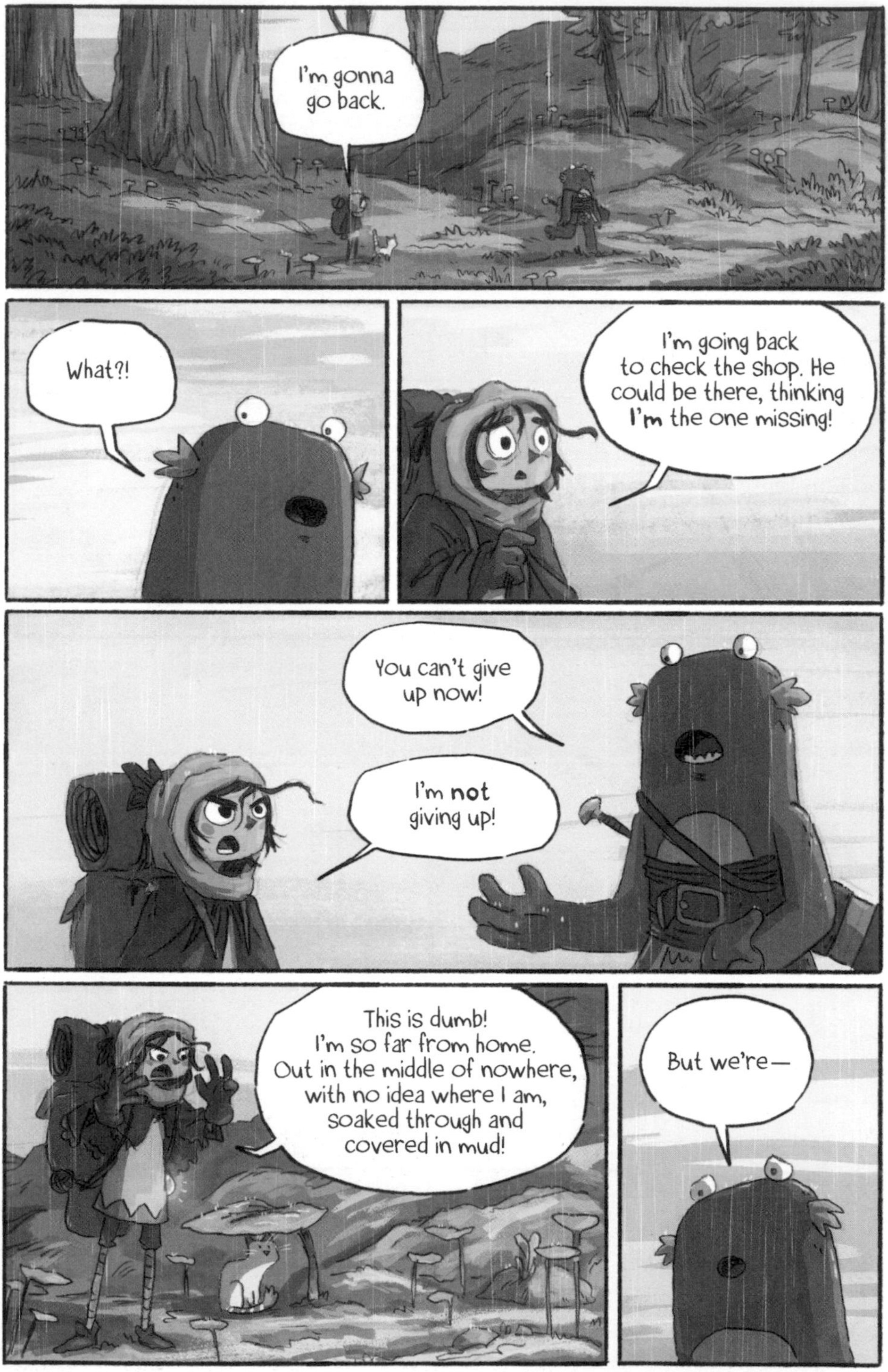
I'm gonna go back.
What?!
I'm going back to check the shop. He could be there, thinking **I'm** the one missing!
You can't give up now!
I'm **not** giving up!
This is dumb! I'm so far from home. Out in the middle of nowhere, with no idea where I am, soaked through and covered in mud!
But we're—

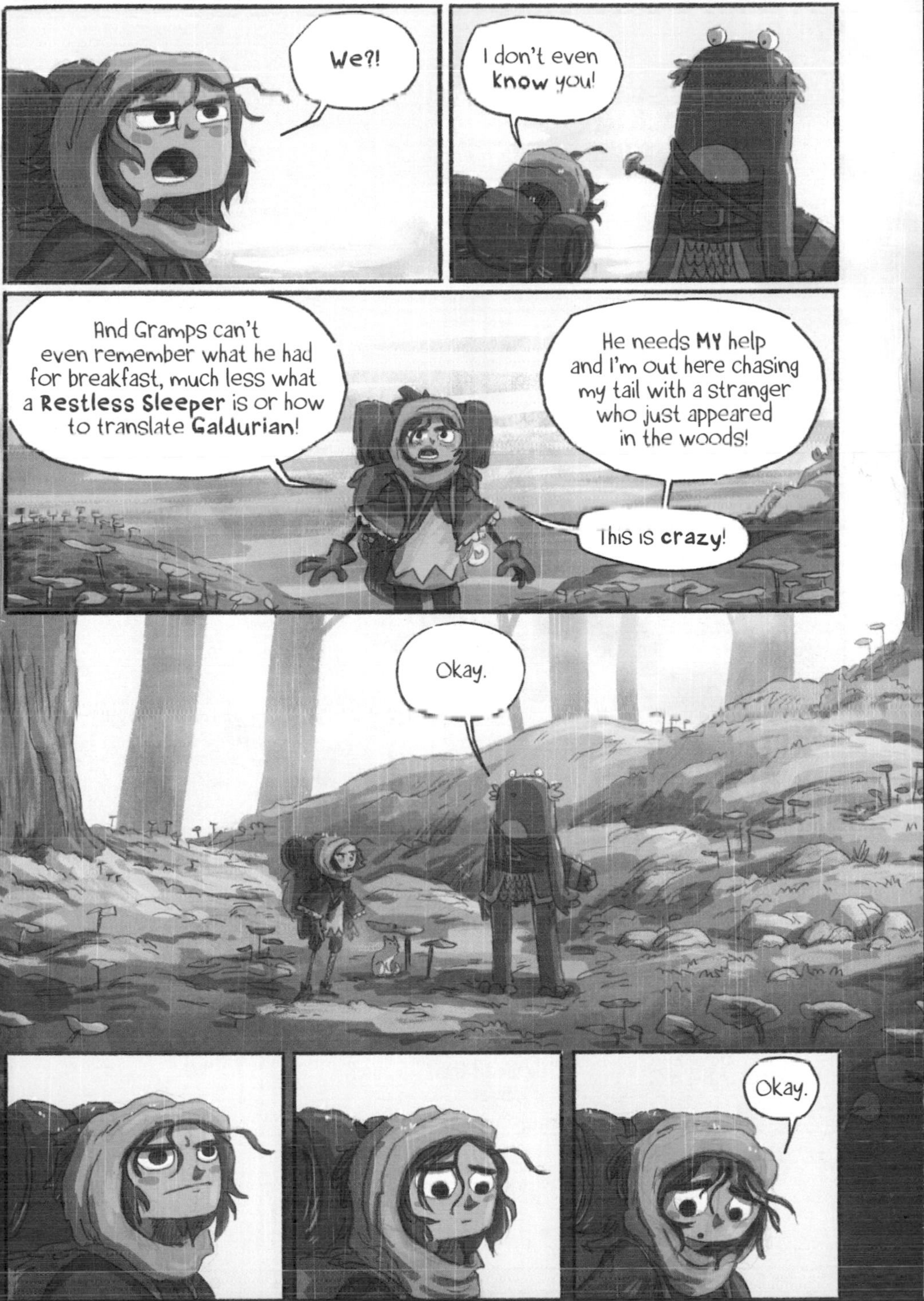
We?!
I don't even know you!
And Gramps can't even remember what he had for breakfast, much less what a Restless Sleeper is or how to translate Galdurian!
He needs MY help and I'm out here chasing my tail with a stranger who just appeared in the woods!
This is crazy!
Okay.
Okay.

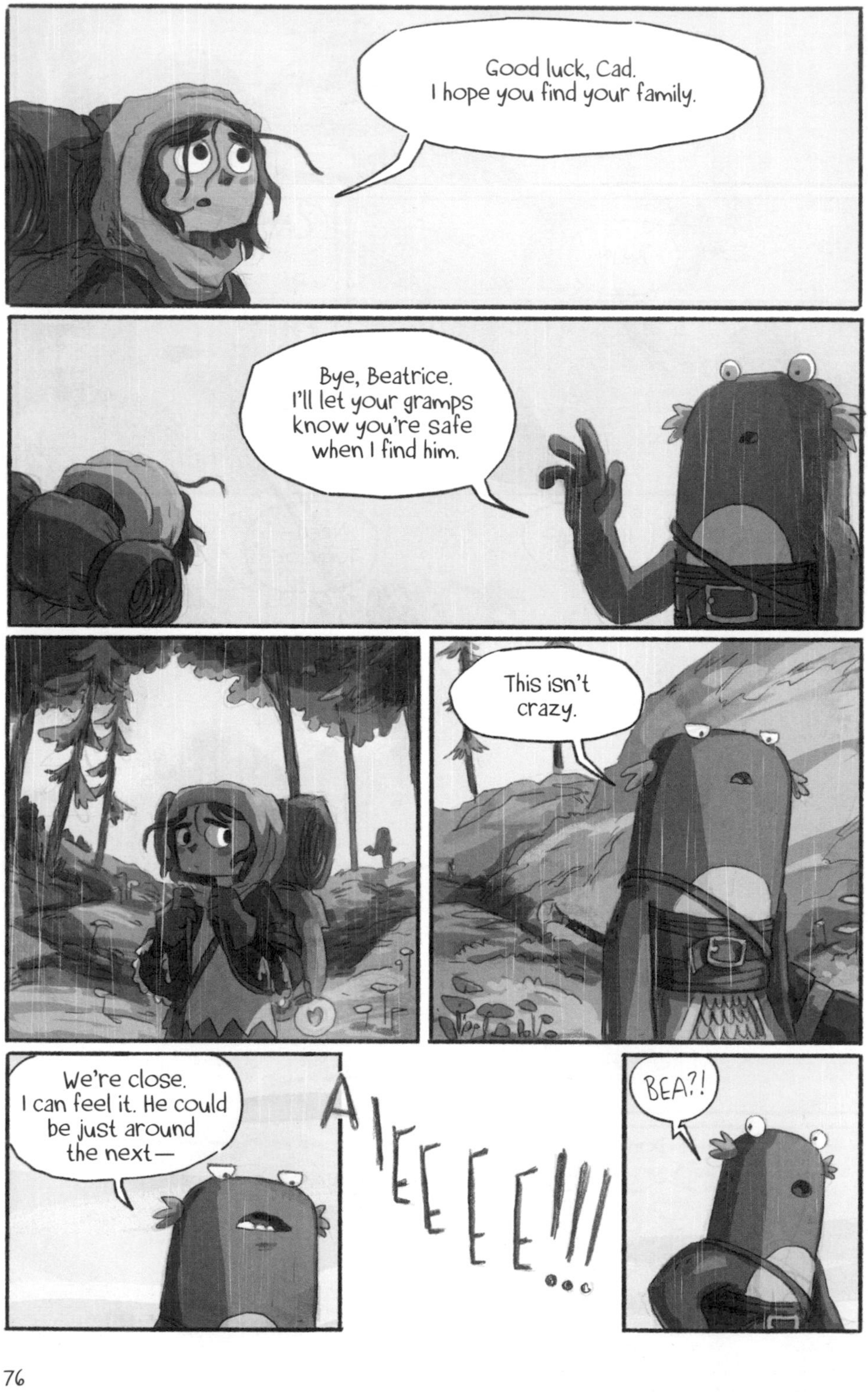
Good luck, Cad.
I hope you find your family.
Bye, Beatrice.
I'll let your gramps know you're safe when I find him.
This isn't crazy.
We're close. I can feel it. He could be just around the next—
AIEEEEE!!!...
BEA?!

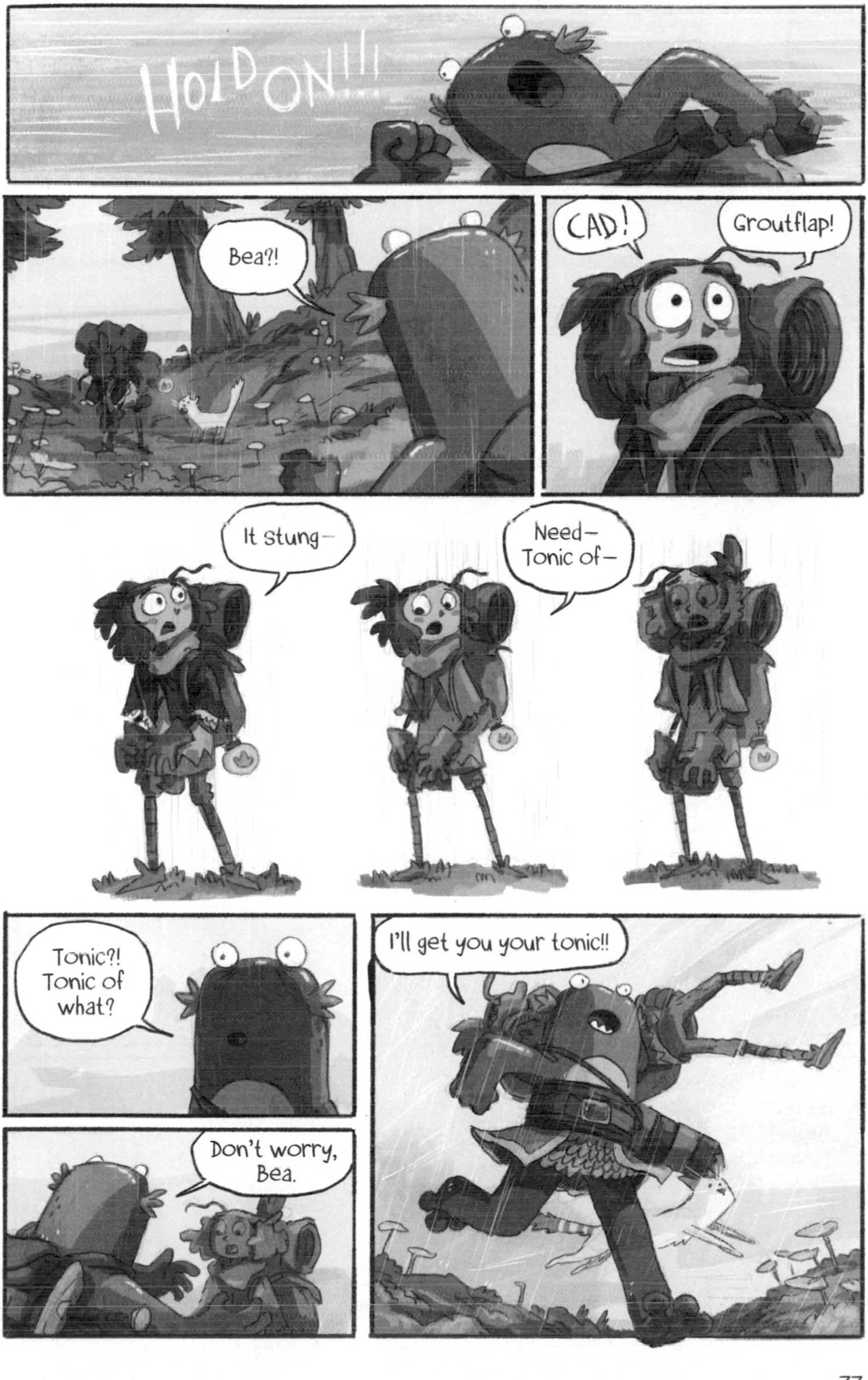
HOLD ON!!!
Bea?!
CAD!
Groutflap!
It stung—
Need—
Tonic of—
Tonic?! Tonic of what?
Don't worry, Bea.
I'll get you your tonic!!

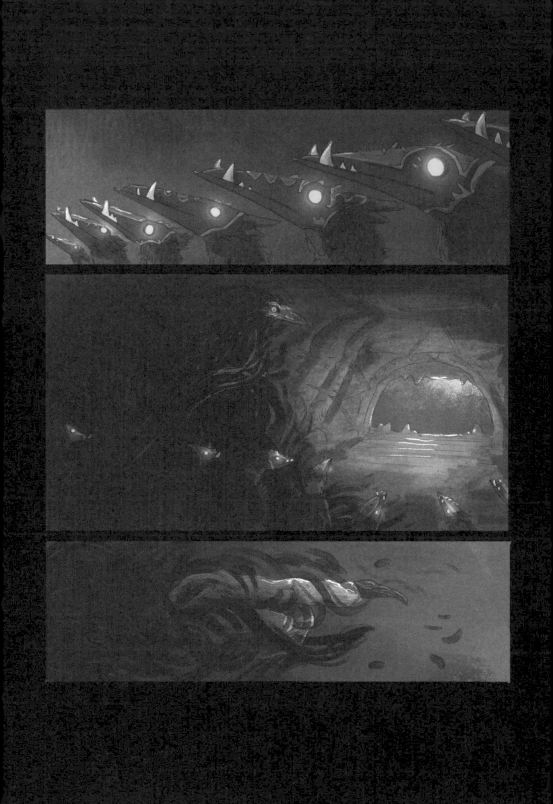

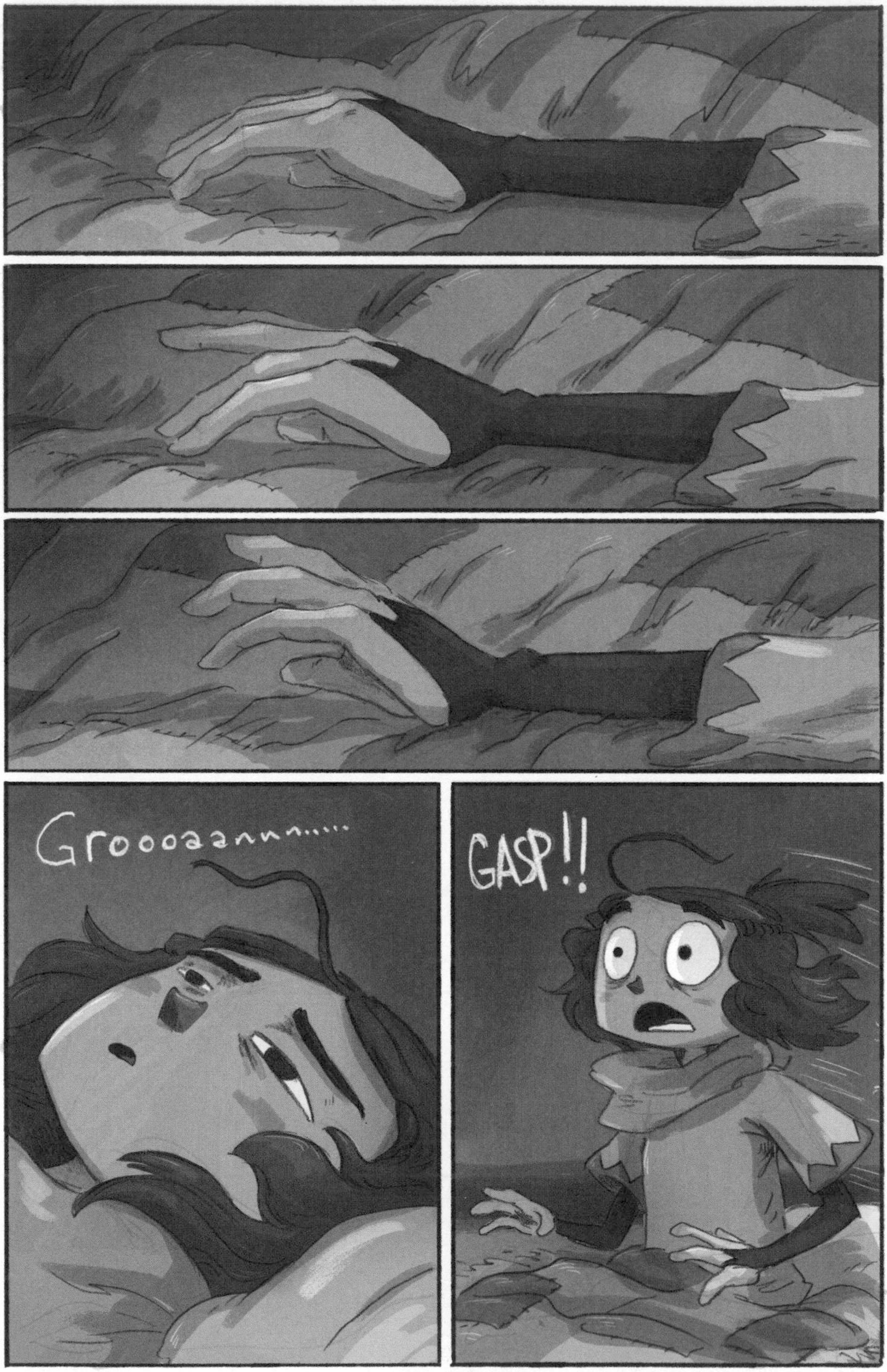
Grooaann.....
GASP!!

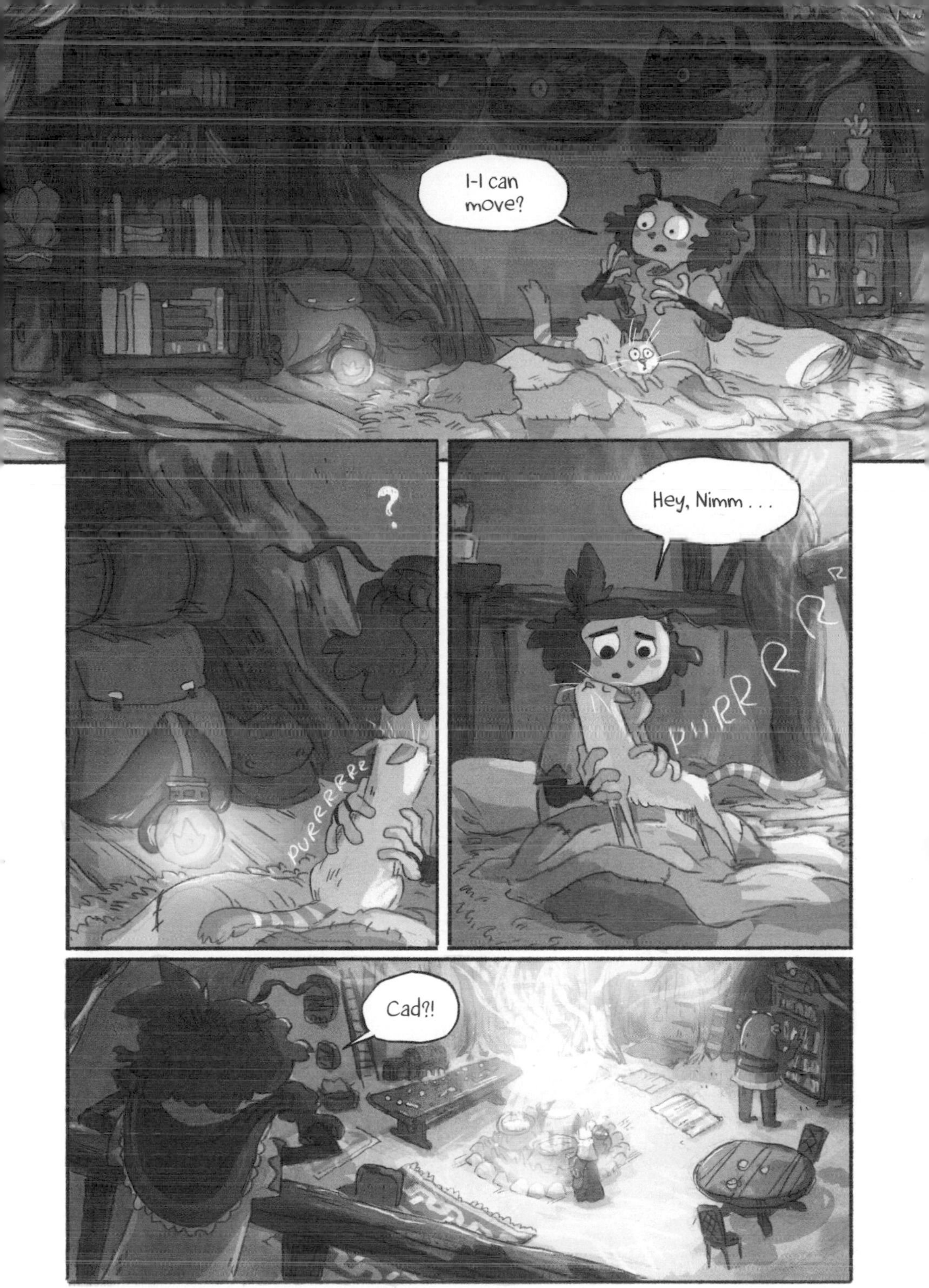
I-I can move?
?
PURRRRR
Hey, Nimm . . .
PURRRRR
Cad?!

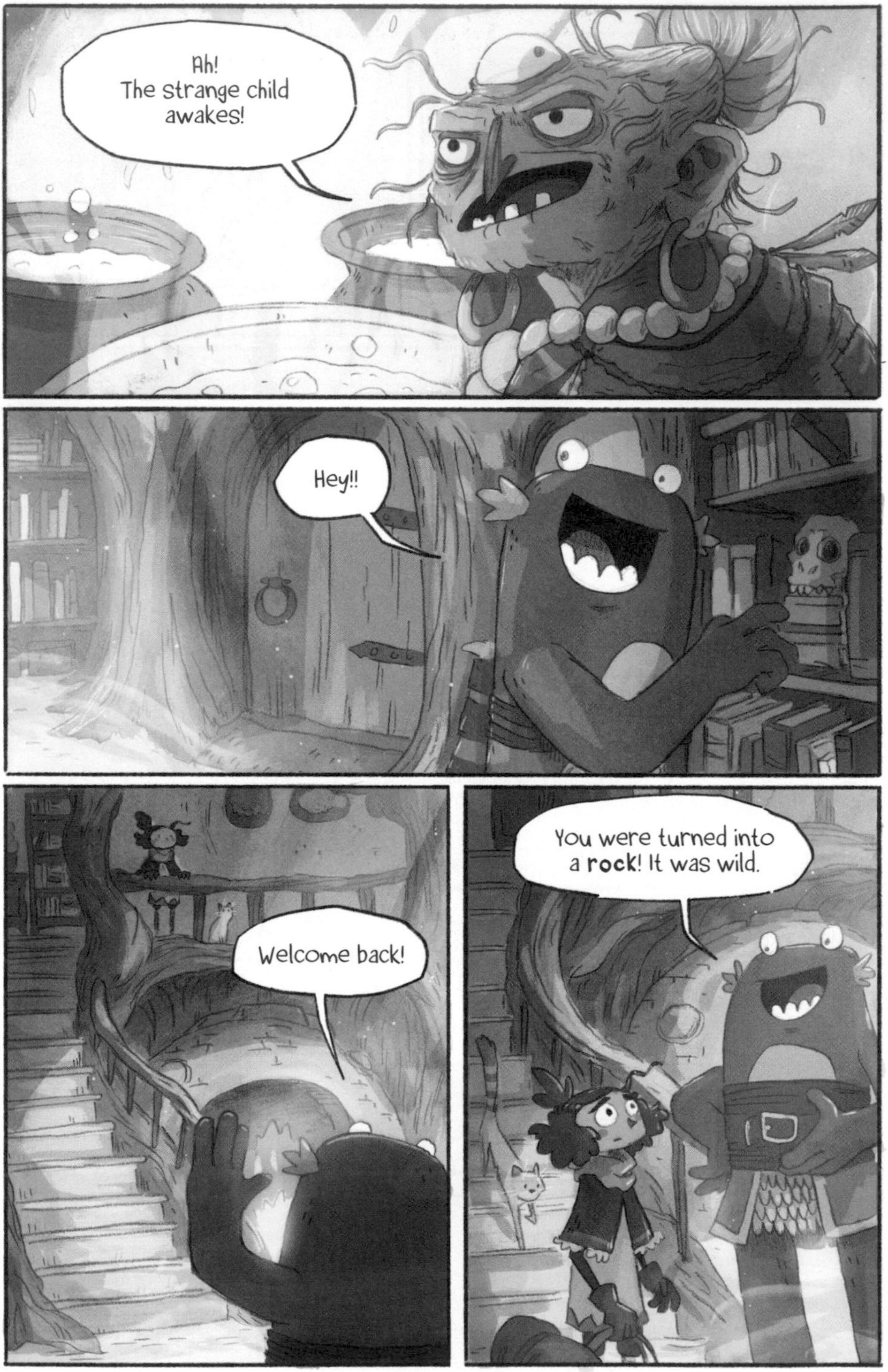
Ah!
The strange child
awakes!
Hey!!
Welcome back!
You were turned into
a **rock**! It was wild.

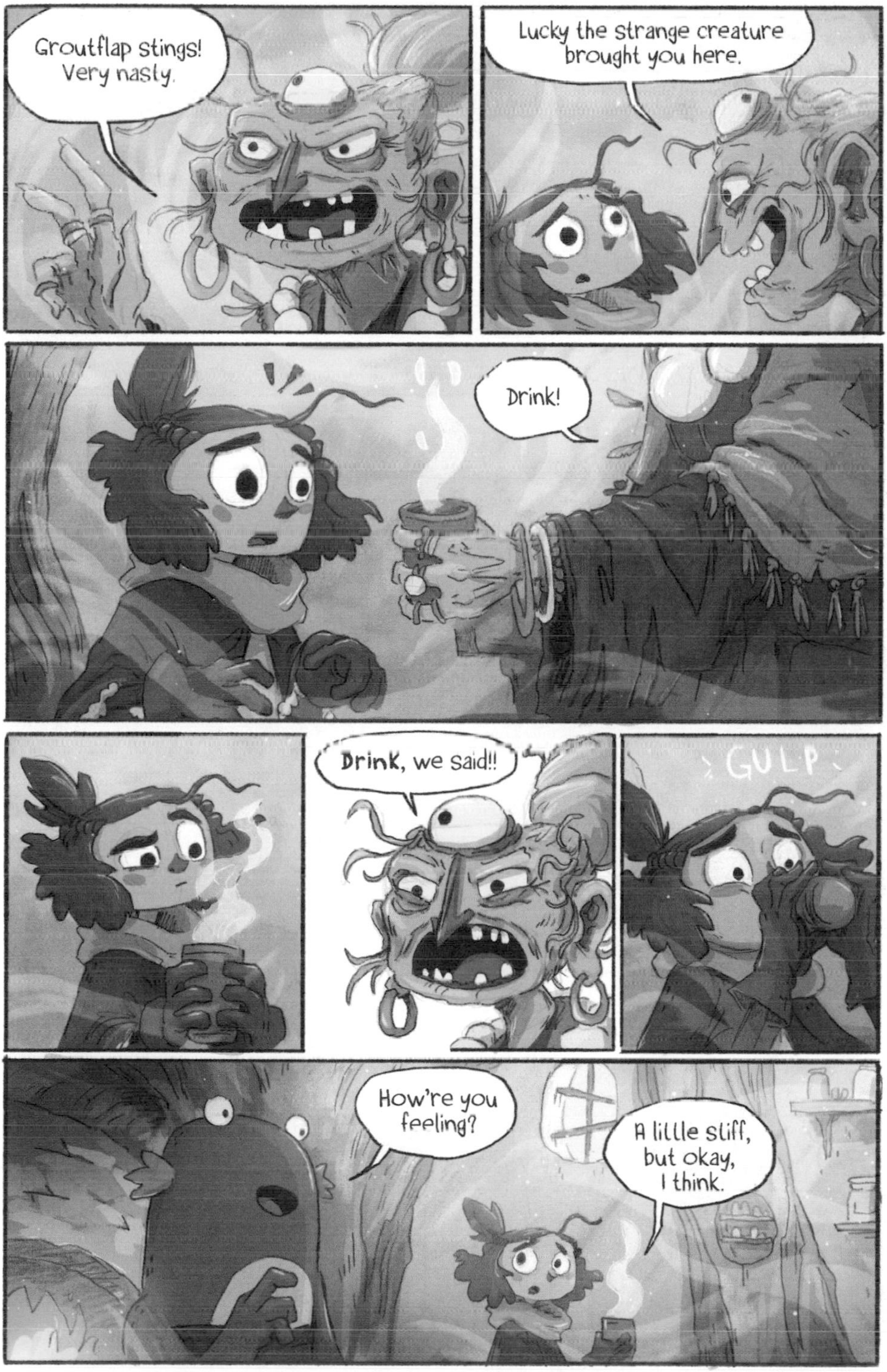
Groutflap stings! Very nasty.
Lucky the strange creature brought you here.
Drink!
Drink, we said!!
GULP
How're you feeling?
A little stiff, but okay, I think.

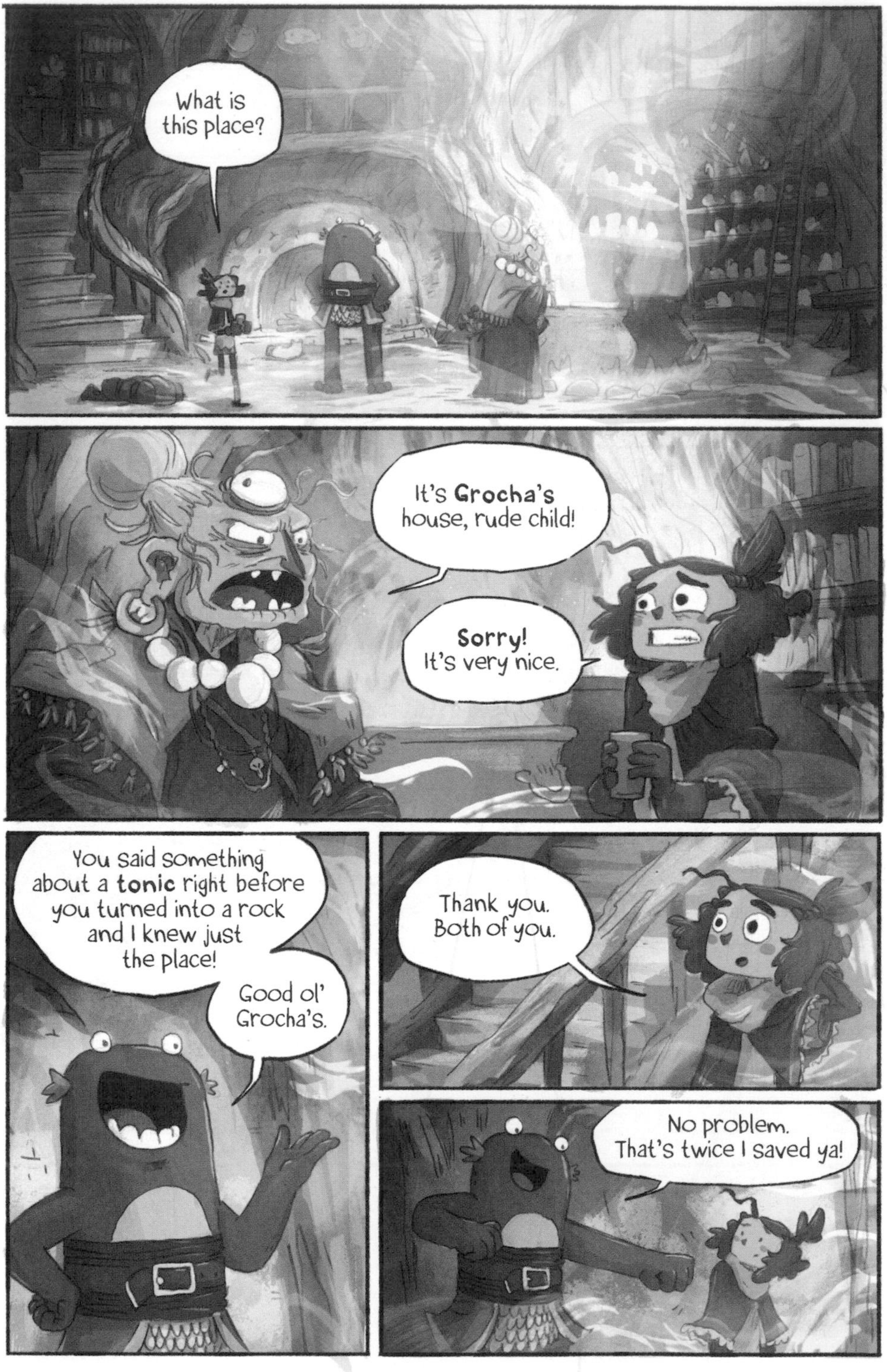
What is this place?
It's **Grocha's** house, rude child!
Sorry! It's very nice.
You said something about a **tonic** right before you turned into a rock and I knew just the place!
Good ol' Grocha's.
Thank you. Both of you.
No problem. That's twice I saved ya!

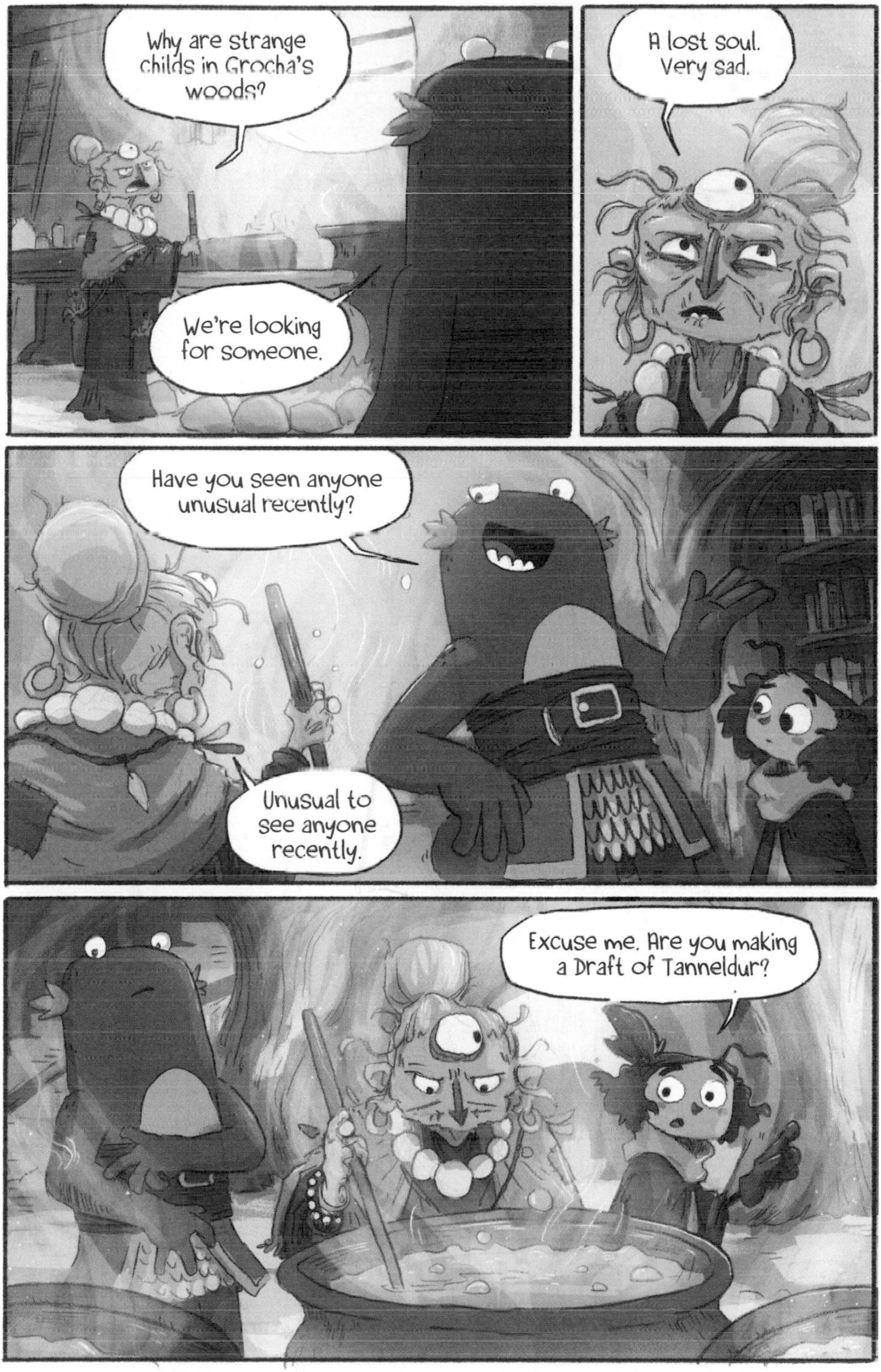
Why are strange childs in Grocha's woods?
We're looking for someone.
A lost soul. Very sad.
Have you seen anyone unusual recently?
Unusual to see anyone recently.
Excuse me. Are you making a Draft of Tanneldur?

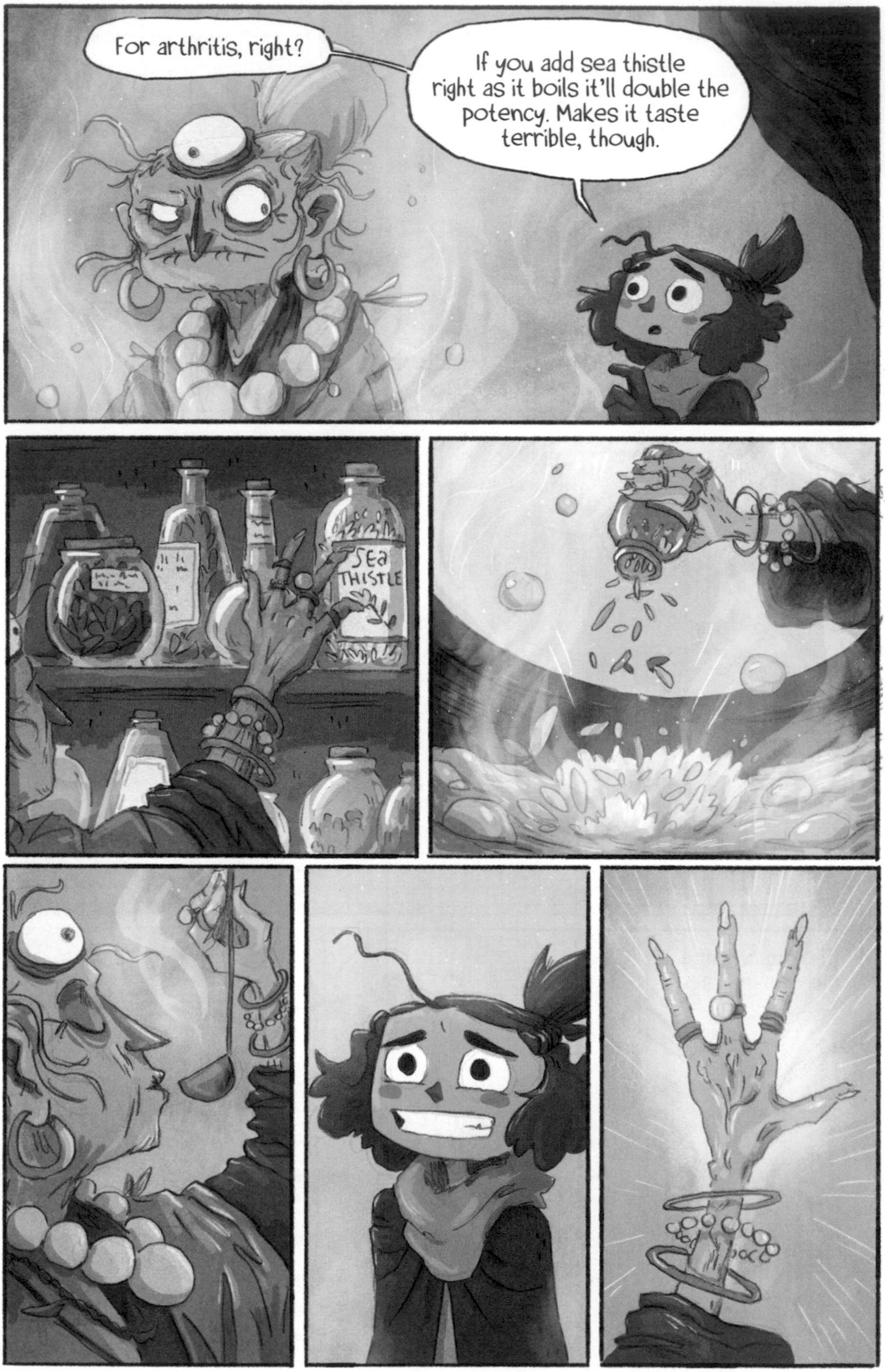
For arthritis, right?
If you add sea thistle right as it boils it'll double the potency. Makes it taste terrible, though.
SEA THISTLE

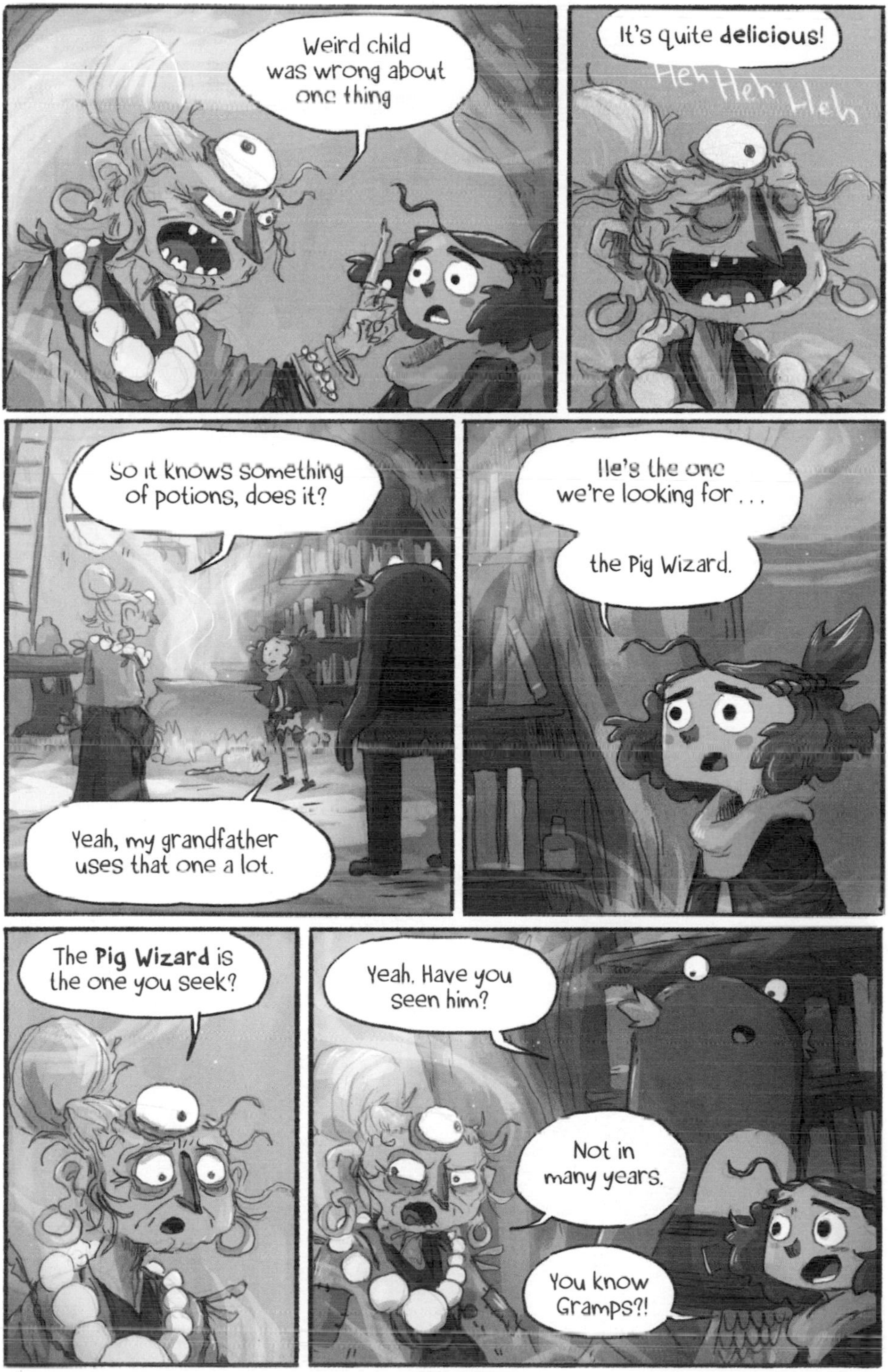
Weird child was wrong about one thing
It's quite **delicious**!
Heh Heh Heh
So it knows something of potions, does it?
Yeah, my grandfather uses that one a lot.
He's the one we're looking for . . .
the Pig Wizard.
The **Pig Wizard** is the one you seek?
Yeah. Have you seen him?
Not in many years.
You know Gramps?!

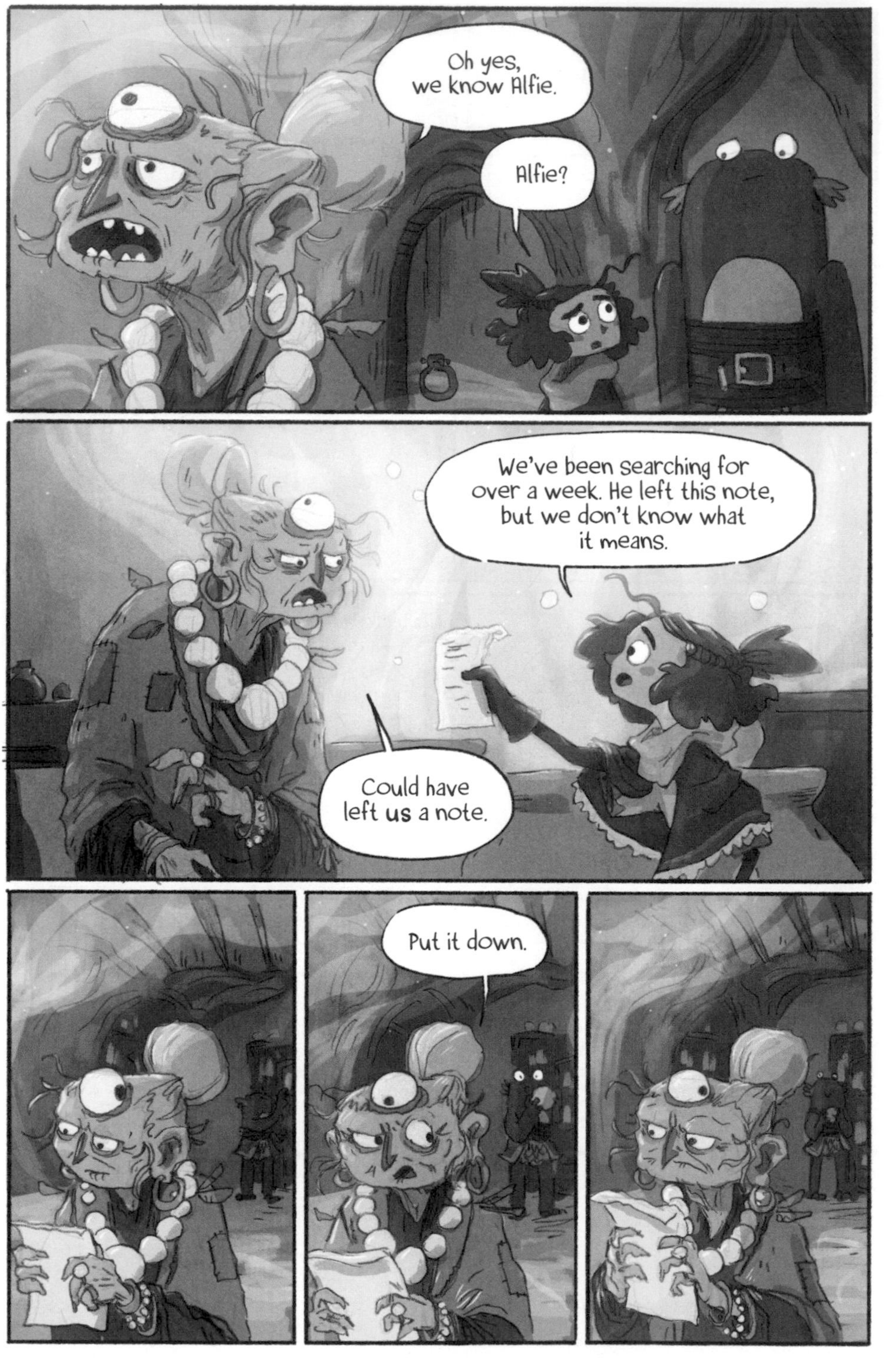
Oh yes,
we know Alfie.
Alfie?
We've been searching for
over a week. He left this note,
but we don't know what
it means.
Could have
left **us** a note.
Put it down.

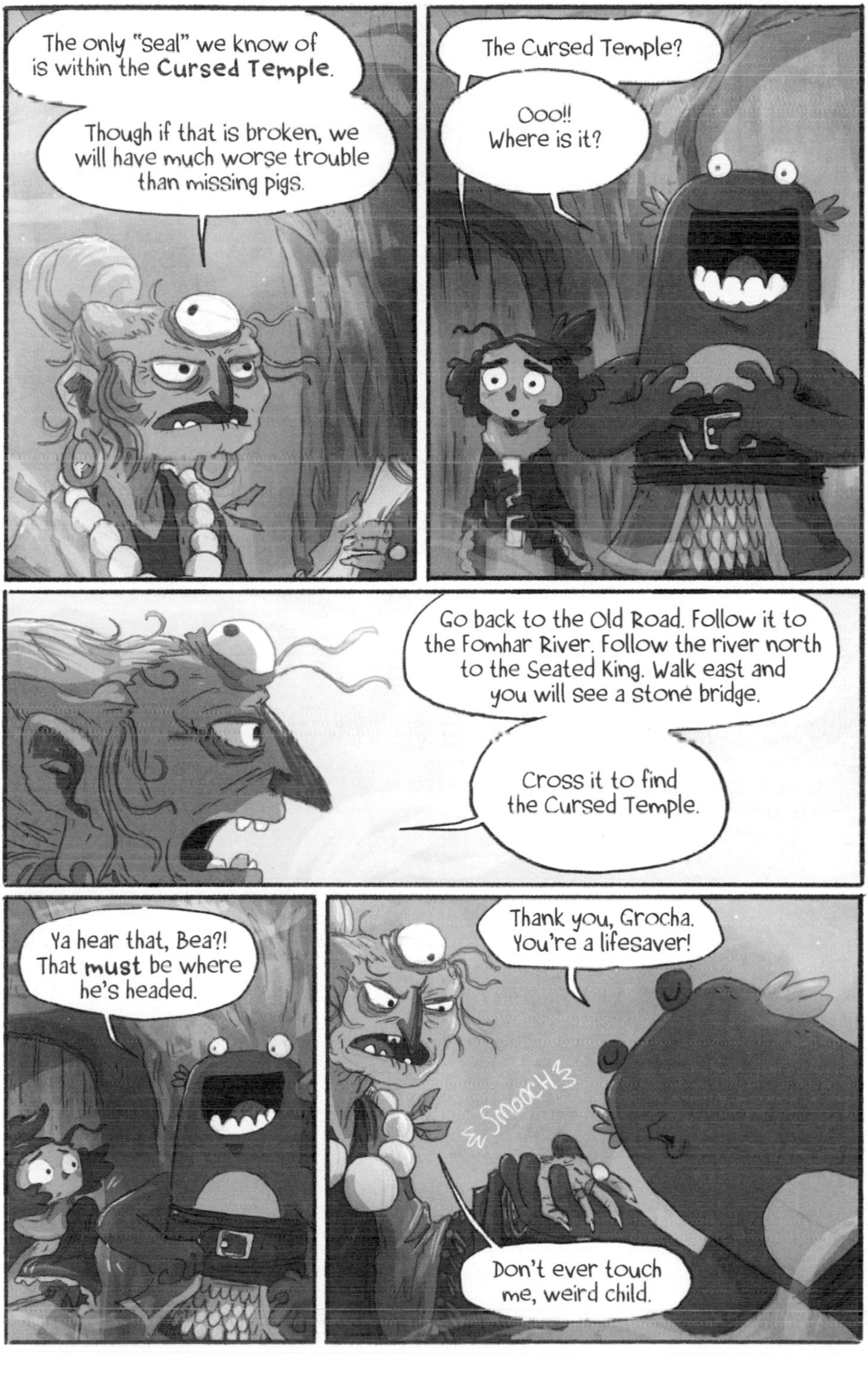

The only "seal" we know of is within the **Cursed Temple**.
Though if that is broken, we will have much worse trouble than missing pigs.
The Cursed Temple?
Ooo!! Where is it?
Go back to the Old Road. Follow it to the Fomhar River. Follow the river north to the Seated King. Walk east and you will see a stone bridge.
Cross it to find the Cursed Temple.
Ya hear that, Bea?! That **must** be where he's headed.
Thank you, Grocha. You're a lifesaver!
SMOOCH
Don't ever touch me, weird child.

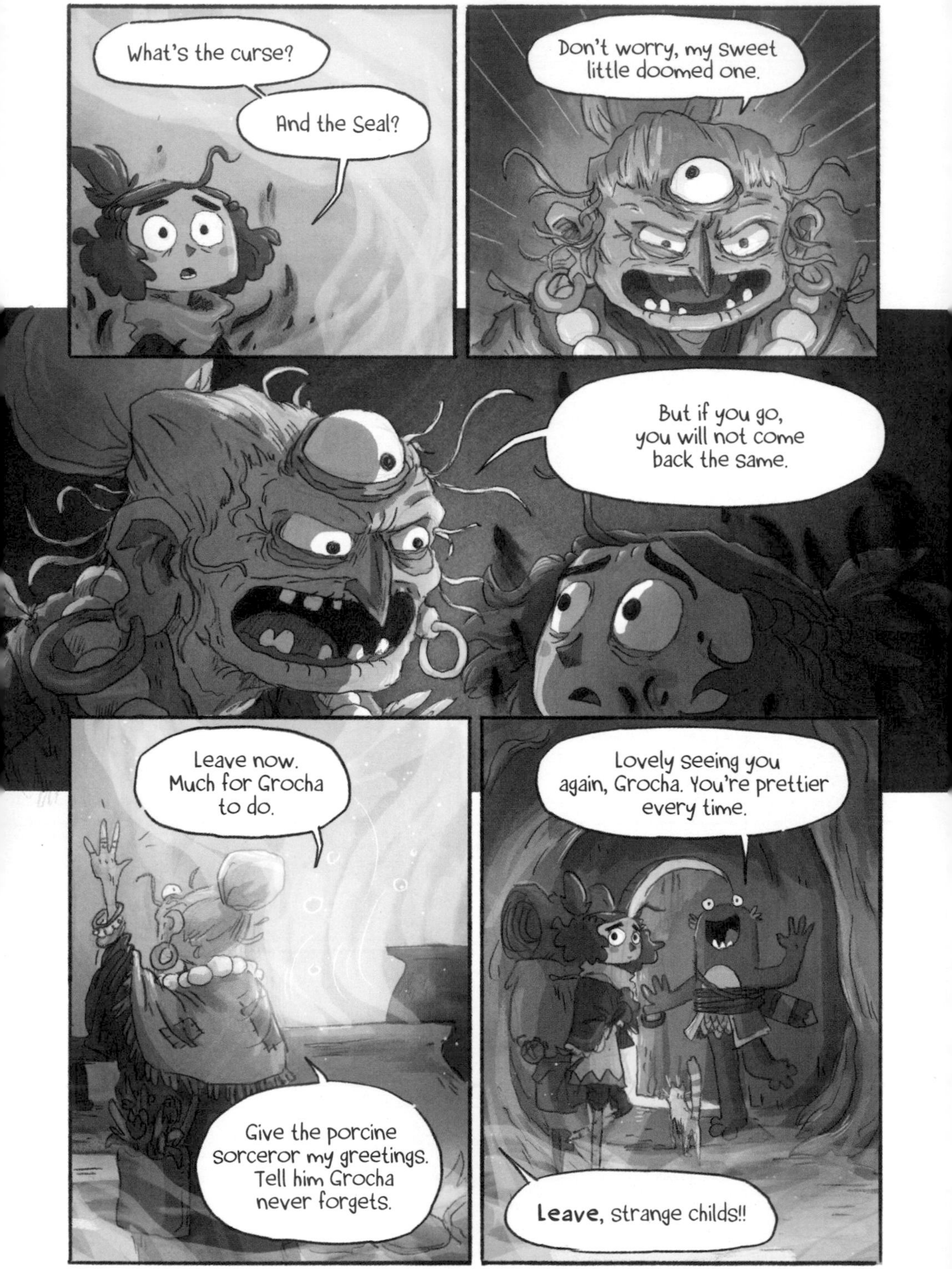
What's the curse?
And the Seal?
Don't worry, my sweet little doomed one.
But if you go, you will not come back the same.
Leave now. Much for Grocha to do.
Give the porcine sorceror my greetings. Tell him Grocha never forgets.
Lovely seeing you again, Grocha. You're prettier every time.
Leave, strange childs!!

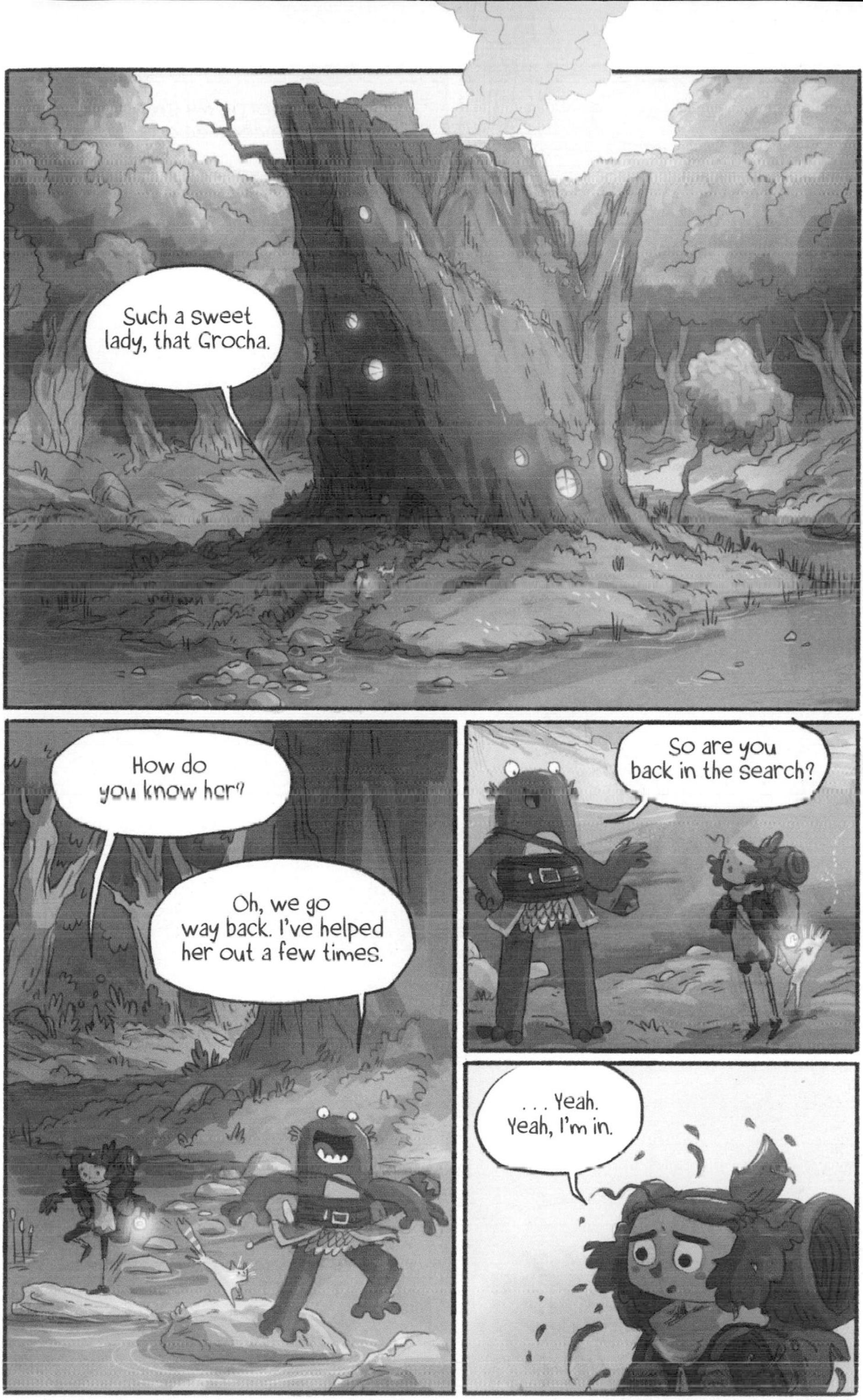
Such a sweet lady, that Grocha.
How do you know her?
Oh, we go way back. I've helped her out a few times.
So are you back in the search?
. . . Yeah. Yeah, I'm in.

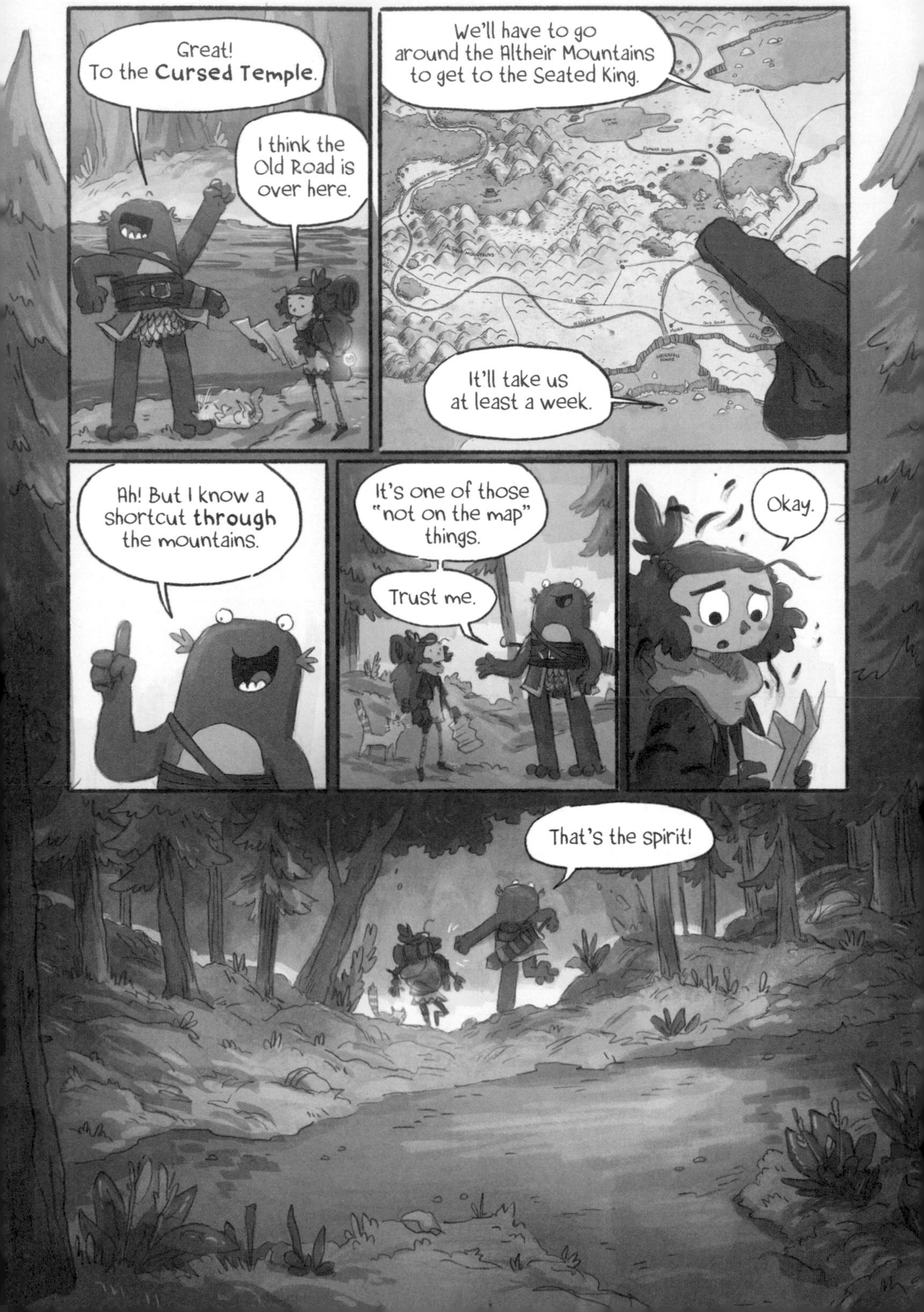

Great! To the **Cursed Temple**.
I think the Old Road is over here.
We'll have to go around the Altheir Mountains to get to the Seated King.
It'll take us at least a week.
Ah! But I know a shortcut **through** the mountains.
It's one of those "not on the map" things.
Trust me.
Okay.
That's the spirit!

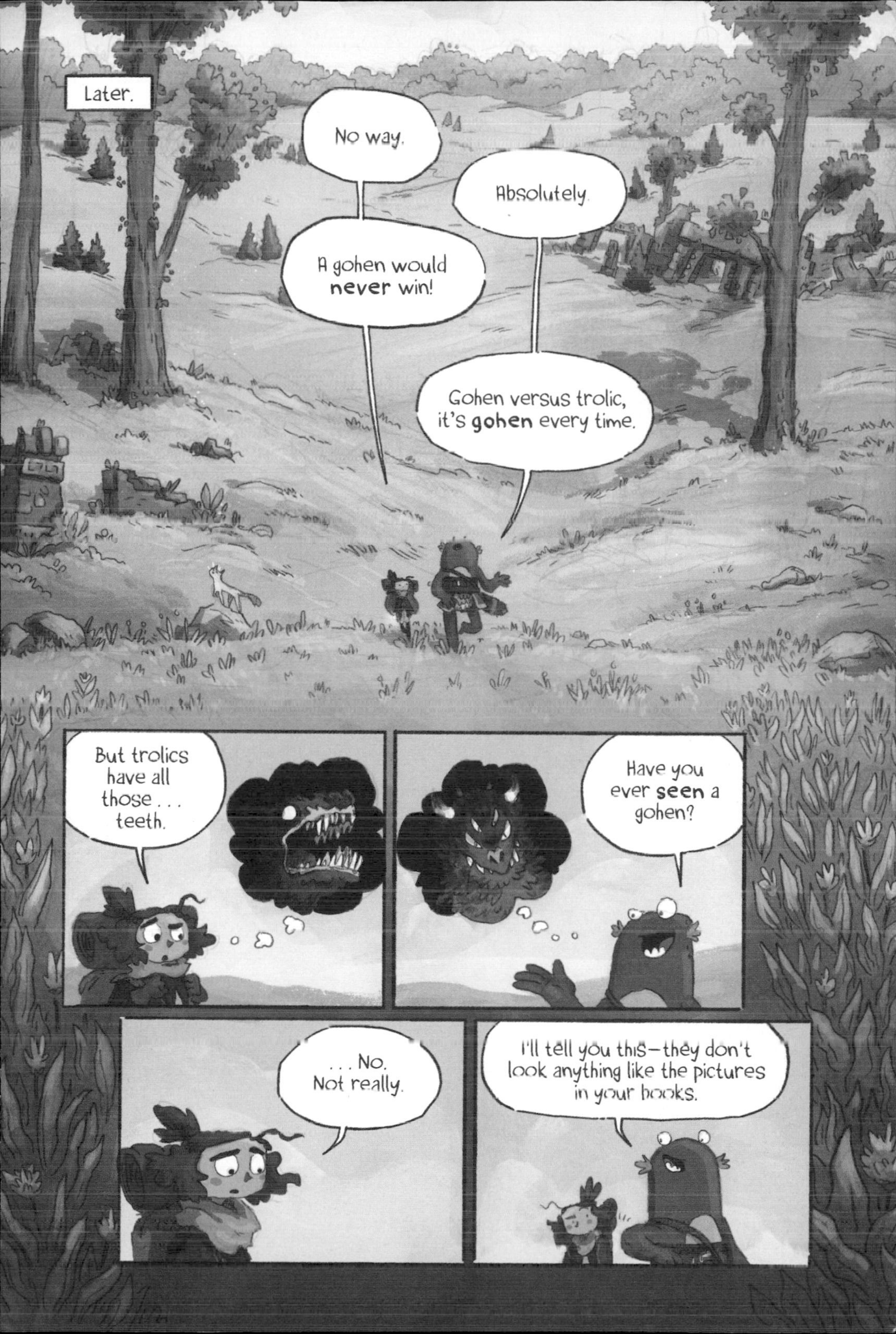
Later.
No way.
Absolutely.
A gohen would **never** win!
Gohen versus trolic, it's **gohen** every time.
But trolics have all those . . . teeth.
Have you ever **seen** a gohen?
. . . No. Not really.
I'll tell you this—they don't look anything like the pictures in your books.

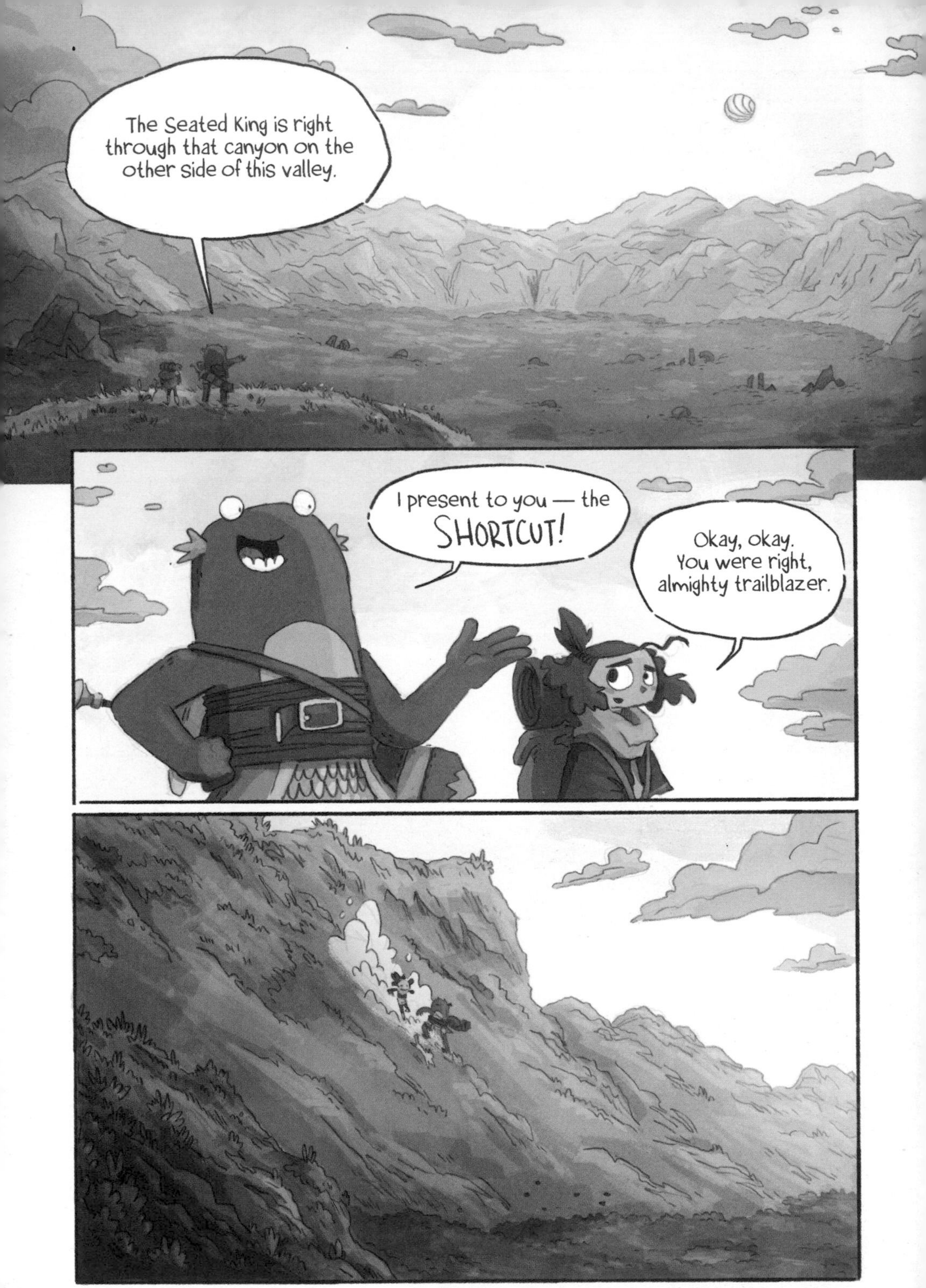
The Seated King is right through that canyon on the other side of this valley.
I present to you — the SHORTCUT!
Okay, okay. You were right, almighty trailblazer.

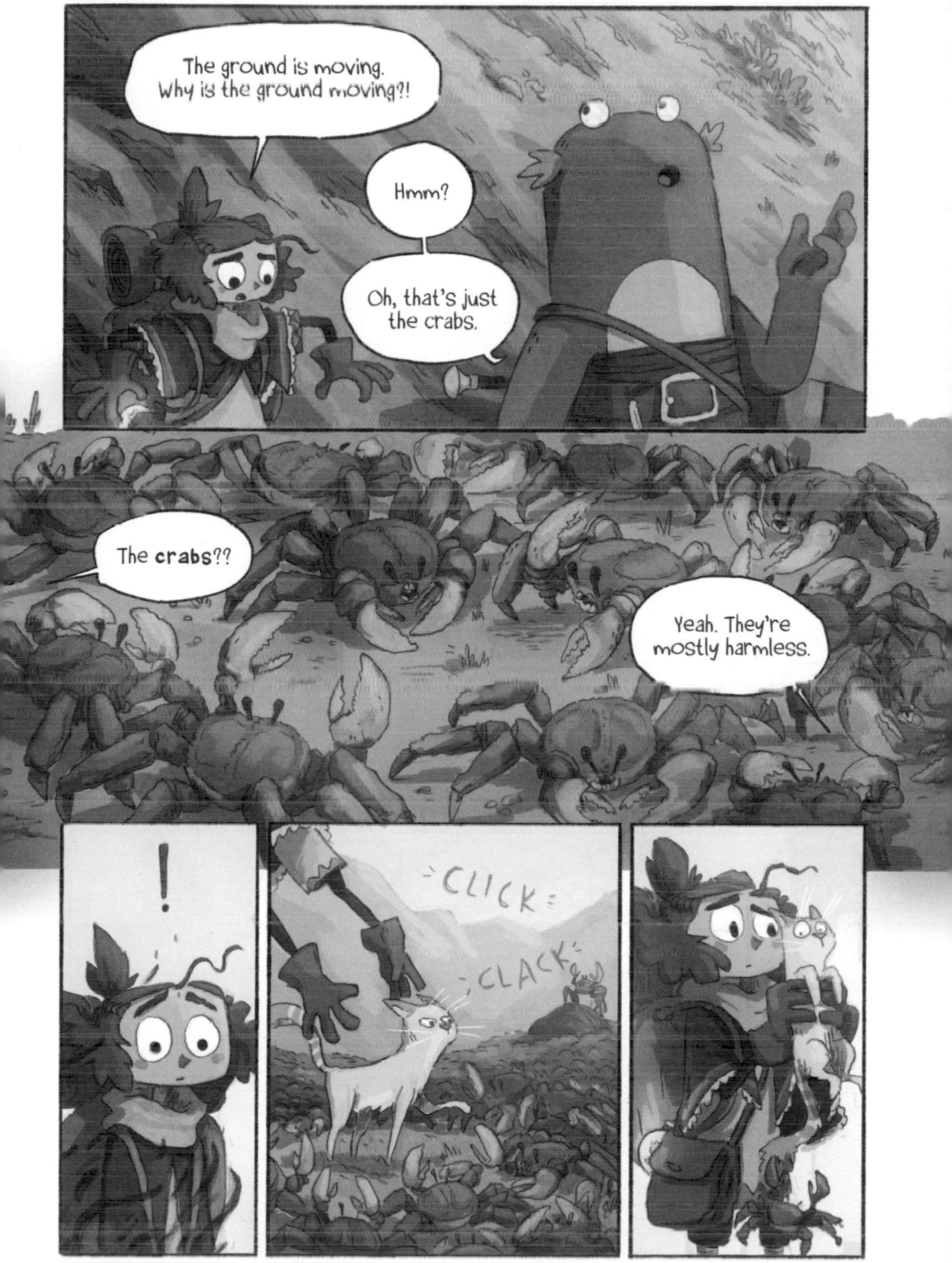
The ground is moving.
Why is the ground moving?!
Hmm?
Oh, that's just the crabs.
The **crabs**??
Yeah. They're mostly harmless.
!
CLICK
CLACK

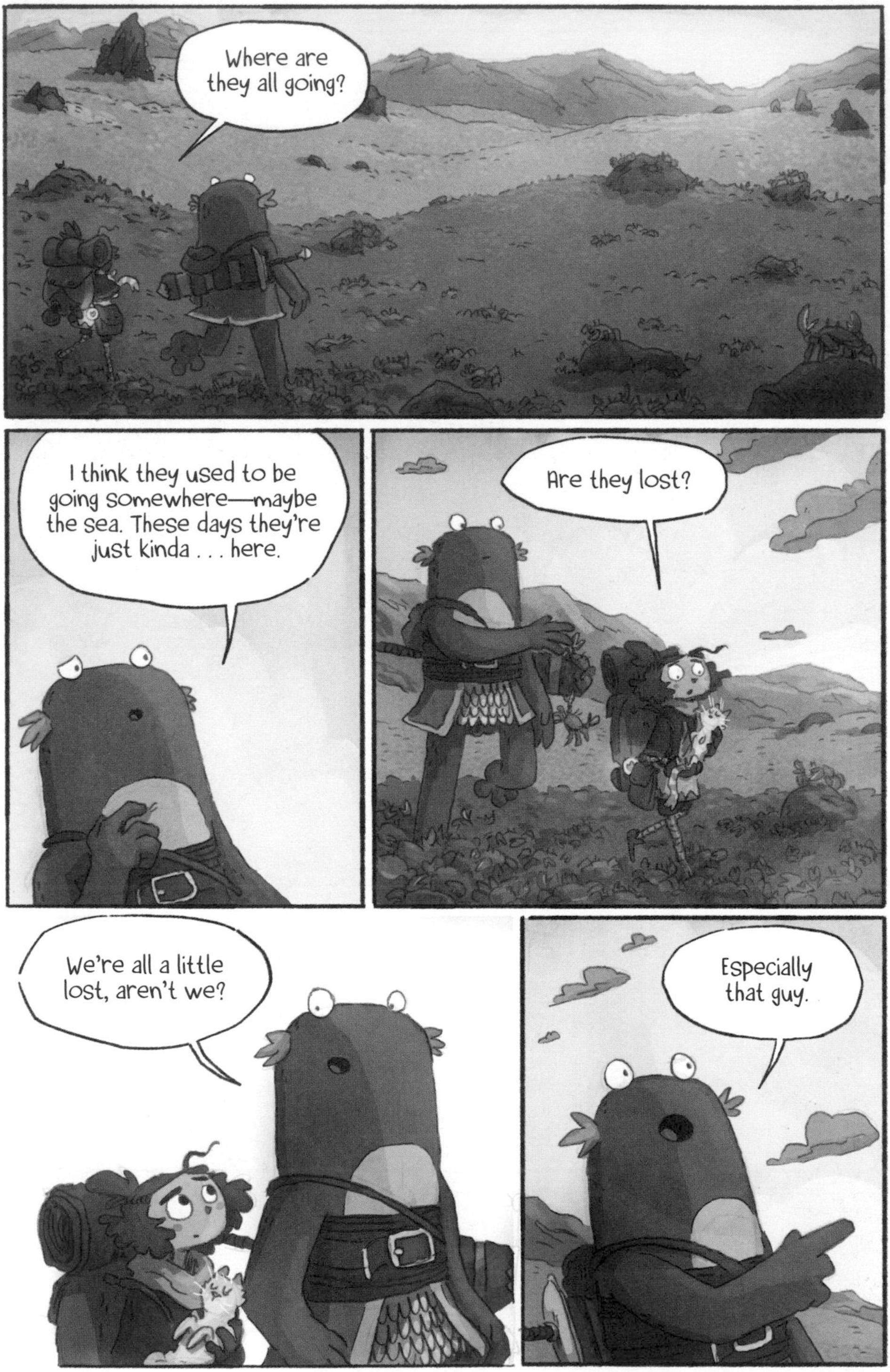
Where are they all going?
I think they used to be going somewhere—maybe the sea. These days they're just kinda . . . here.
Are they lost?
We're all a little lost, aren't we?
Especially that guy.

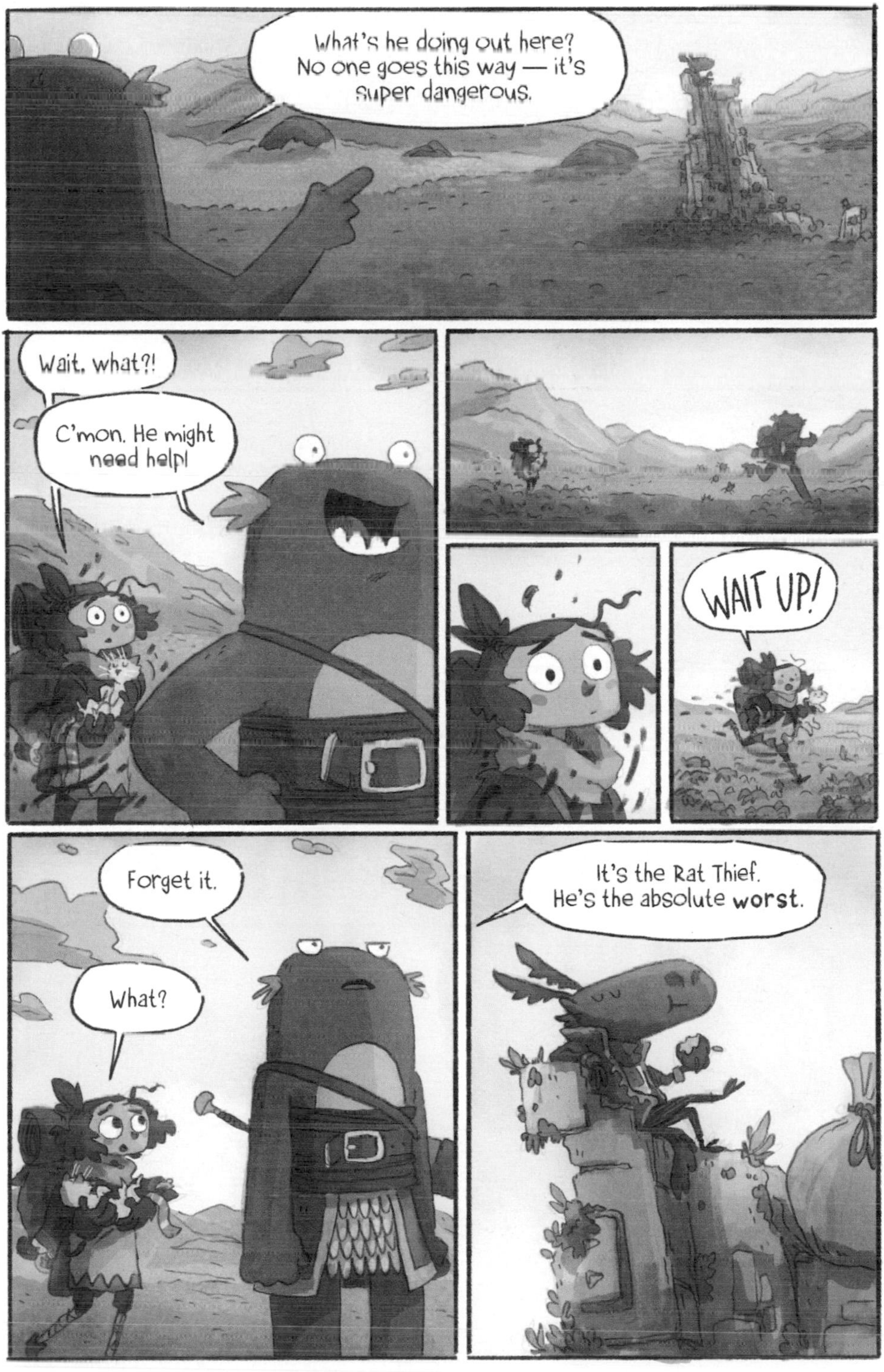
What's he doing out here? No one goes this way — it's super dangerous.
Wait, what?!
C'mon. He might need help!
WAIT UP!
Forget it.
What?
It's the Rat Thief. He's the absolute **worst**.

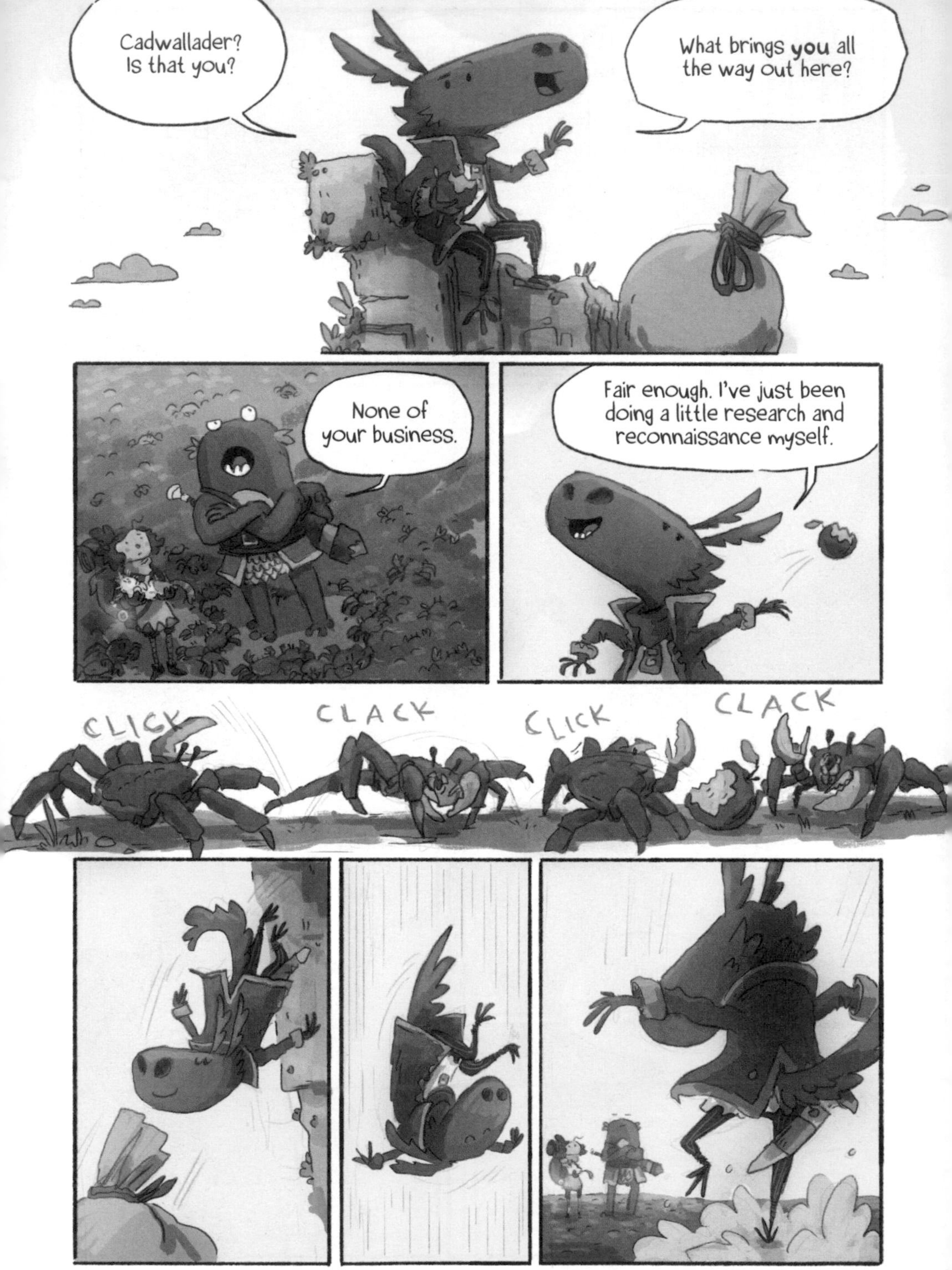
Cadwallader? Is that you?
What brings you all the way out here?
None of your business.
Fair enough. I've just been doing a little research and reconnaissance myself.
CLICK
CLACK
CLICK
CLACK

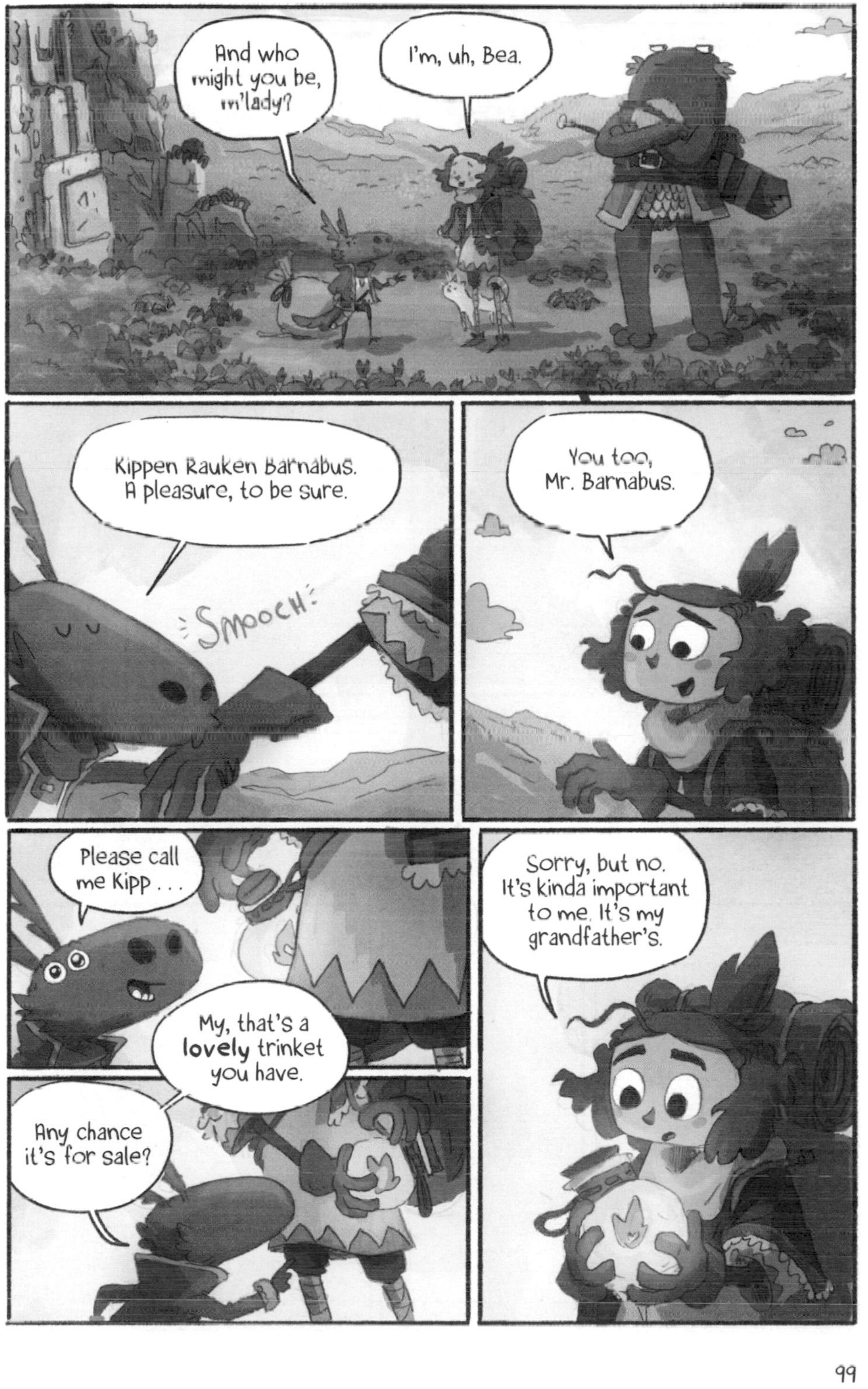
And who might you be, m'lady?
I'm, uh, Bea.
Kippen Rauken Barnabus. A pleasure, to be sure.
SMOOCH
You too, Mr. Barnabus.
Please call me Kipp . . .
My, that's a **lovely** trinket you have.
Any chance it's for sale?
Sorry, but no. It's kinda important to me. It's my grandfather's.

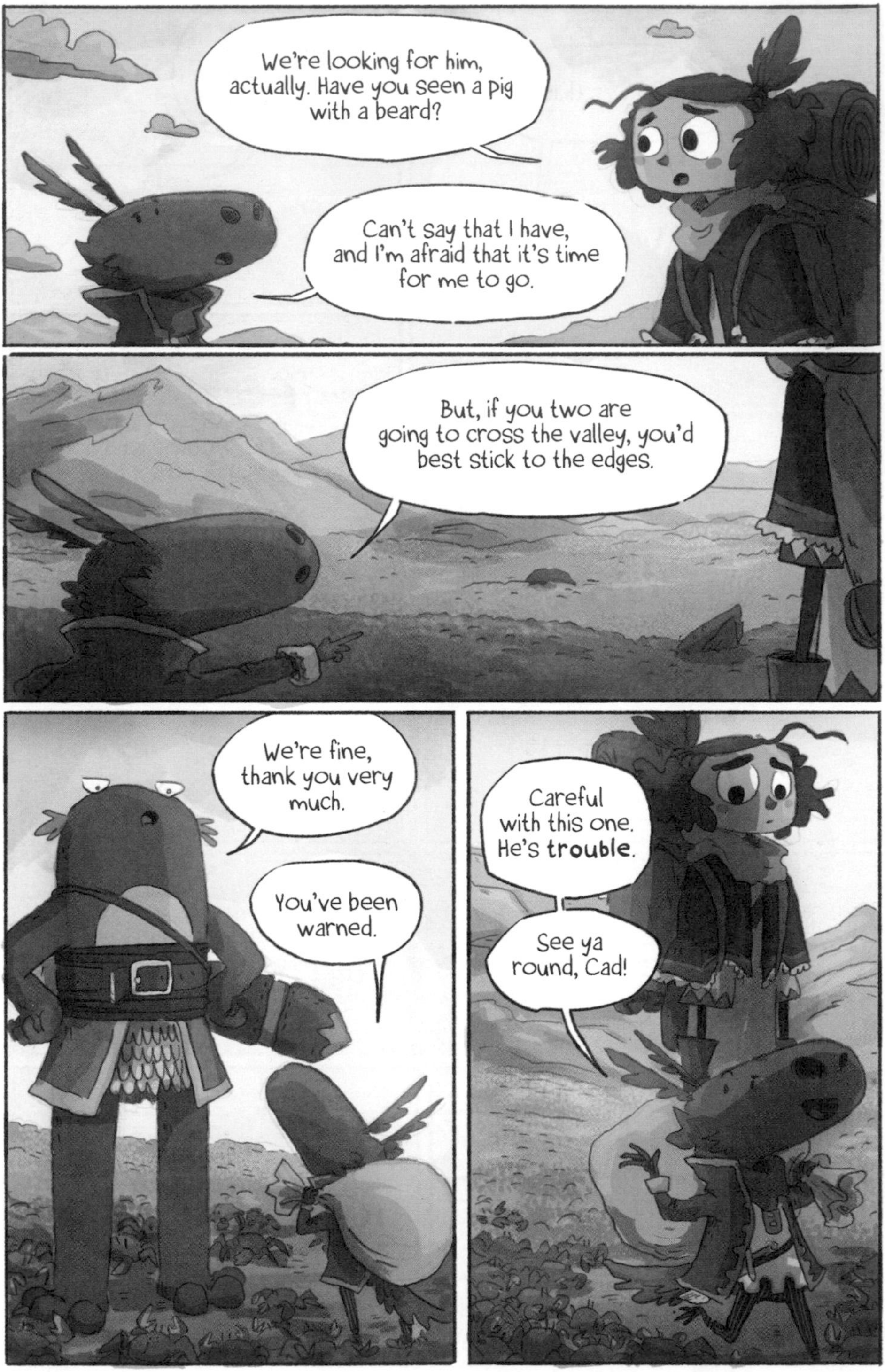

We're looking for him, actually. Have you seen a pig with a beard?
Can't say that I have, and I'm afraid that it's time for me to go.
But, if you two are going to cross the valley, you'd best stick to the edges.
We're fine, thank you very much.
You've been warned.
Careful with this one. He's **trouble**.
See ya round, Cad!

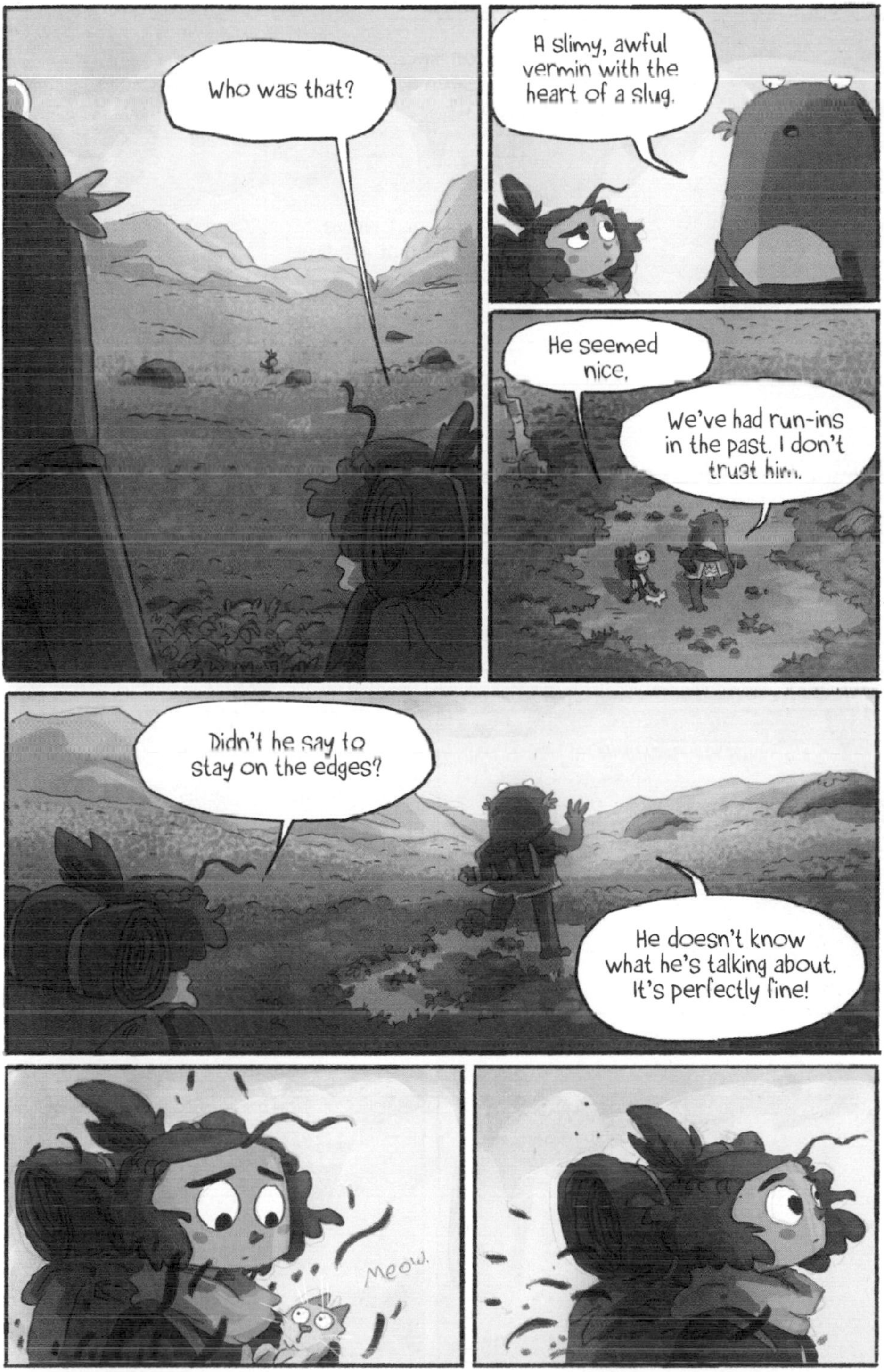
Who was that?
A slimy, awful vermin with the heart of a slug.
He seemed nice.
We've had run-ins in the past. I don't trust him.
Didn't he say to stay on the edges?
He doesn't know what he's talking about. It's perfectly fine!
Meow.

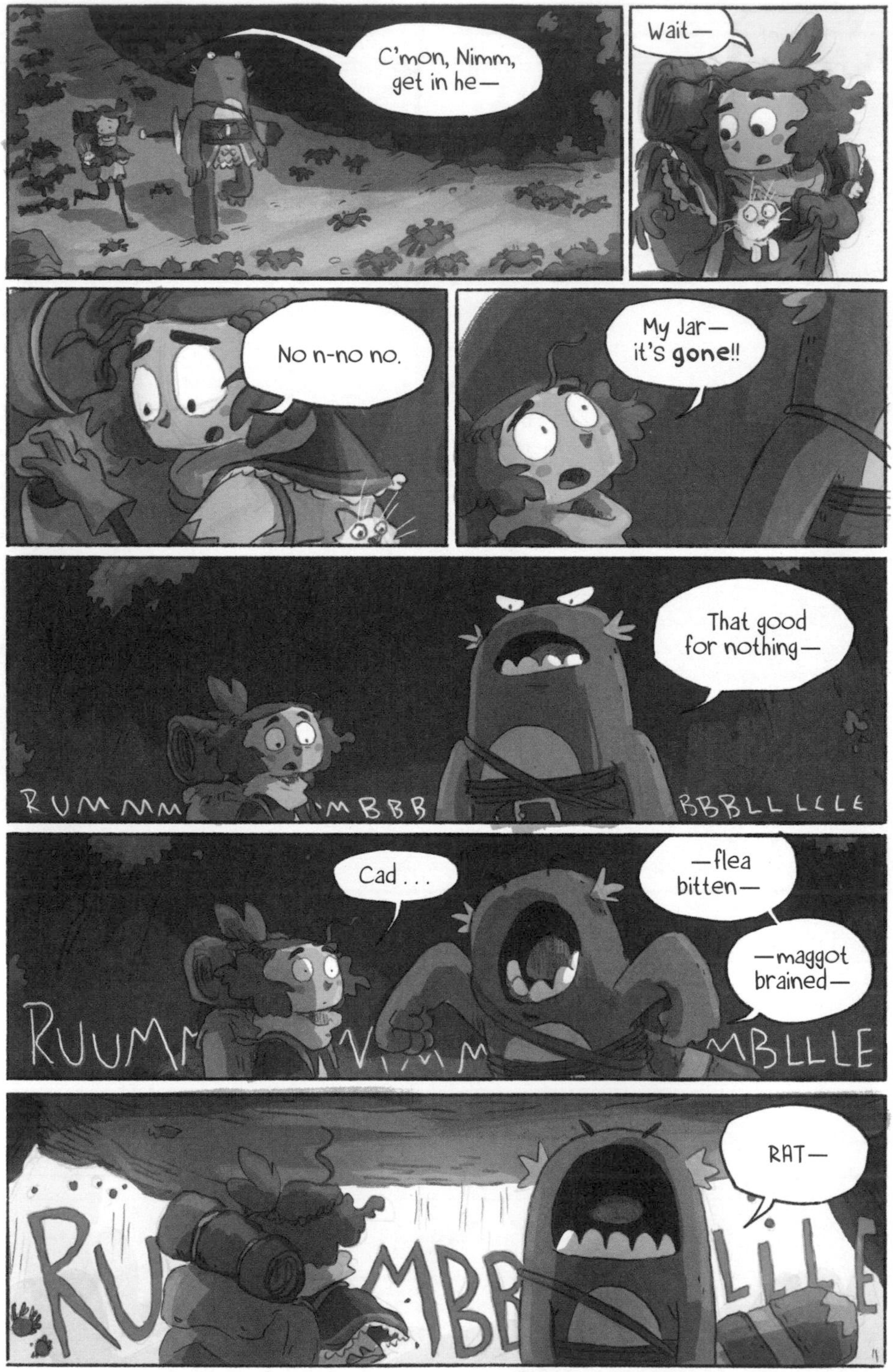
C'mon, Nimm, get in he—
Wait—
No n-no no.
My Jar— it's **gone**!!
That good for nothing—
RUMMMMBBBBBBLLLLLE
Cad . . .
—flea bitten—
—maggot brained—
RUUMMMMMBLLLE
RAT—
RUMBBLLLE

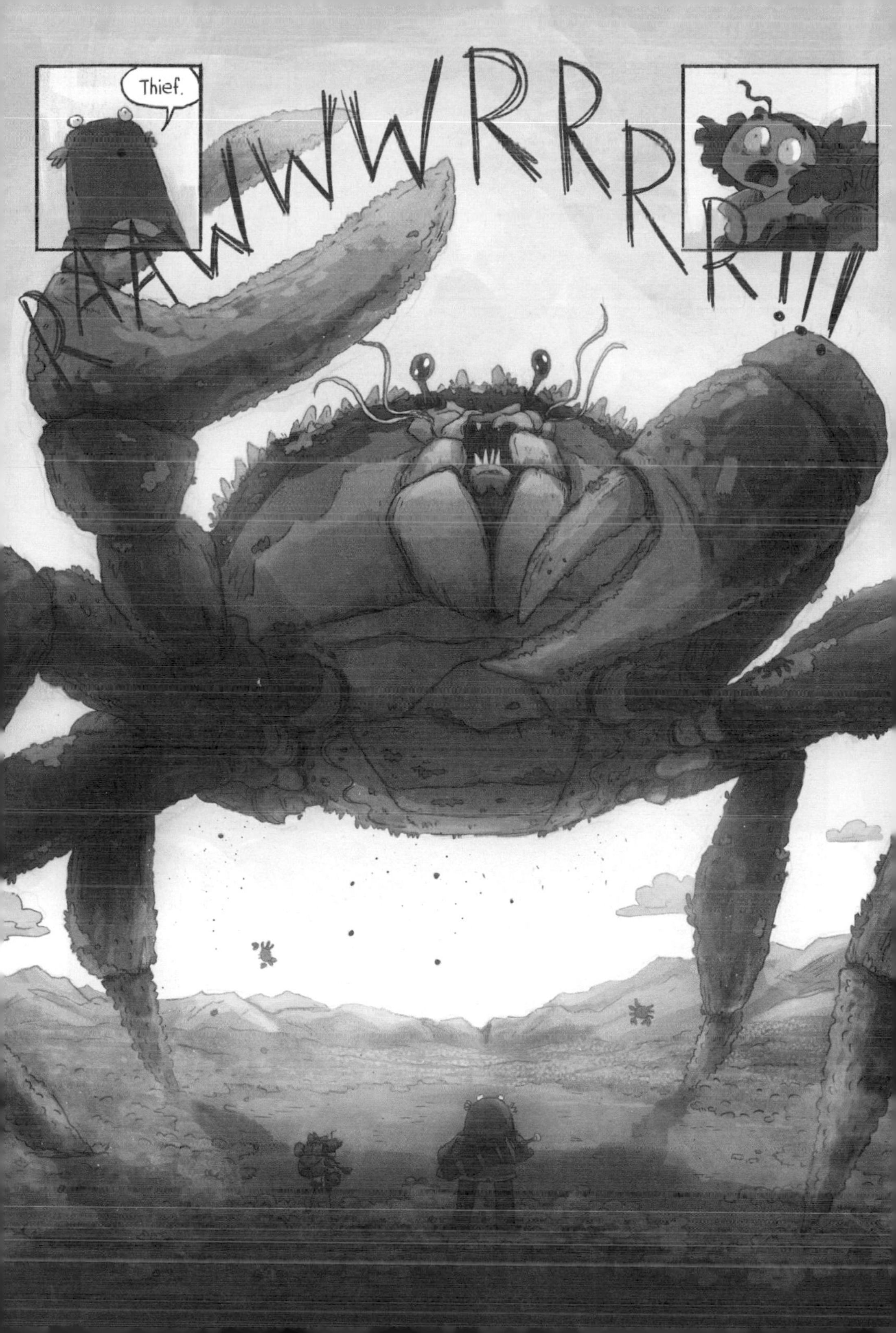

Thief.
RAAWWWRRRR!!!

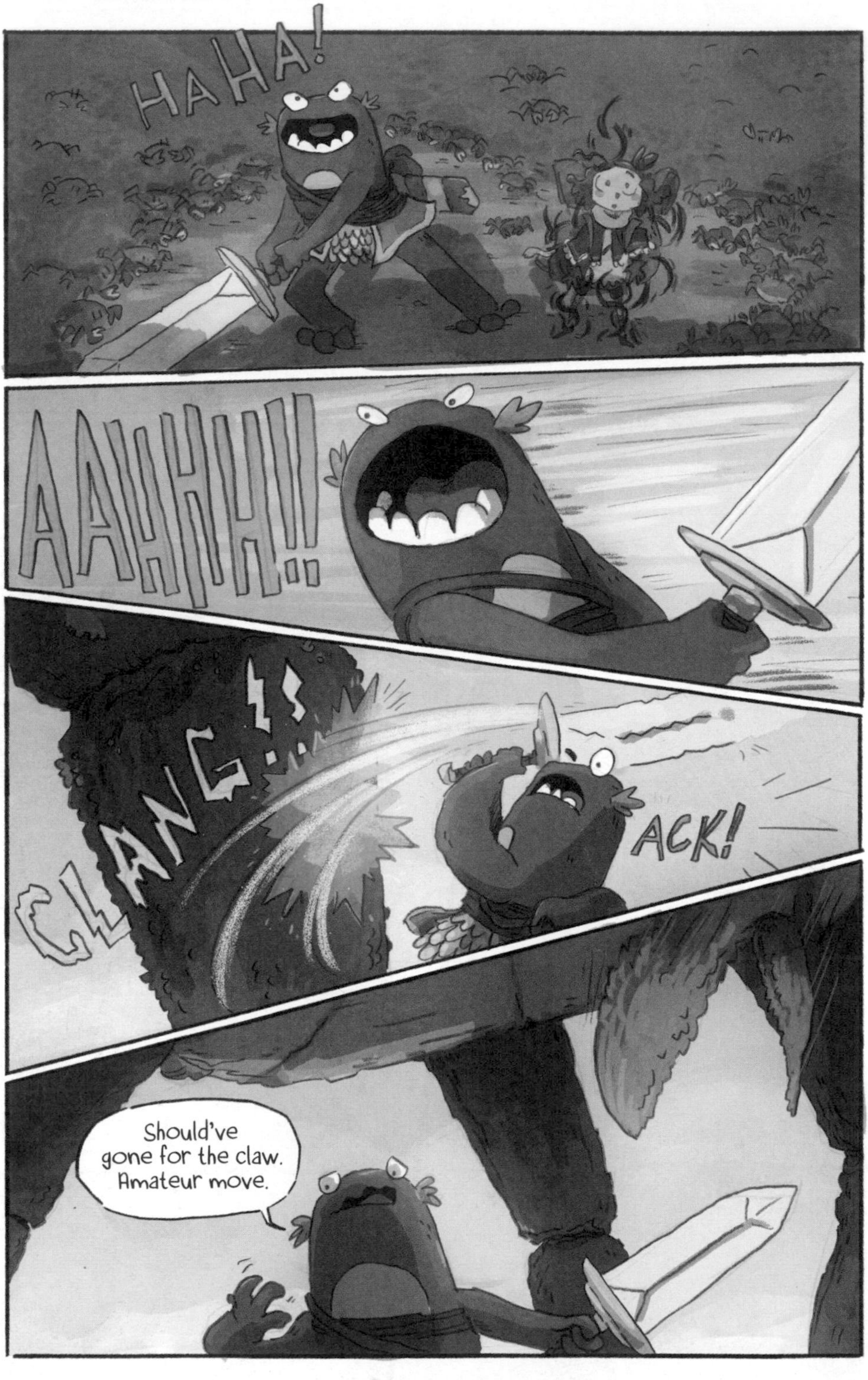
HAHA!
AAHHH!!
CLANG!!
ACK!
Should've gone for the claw. Amateur move.

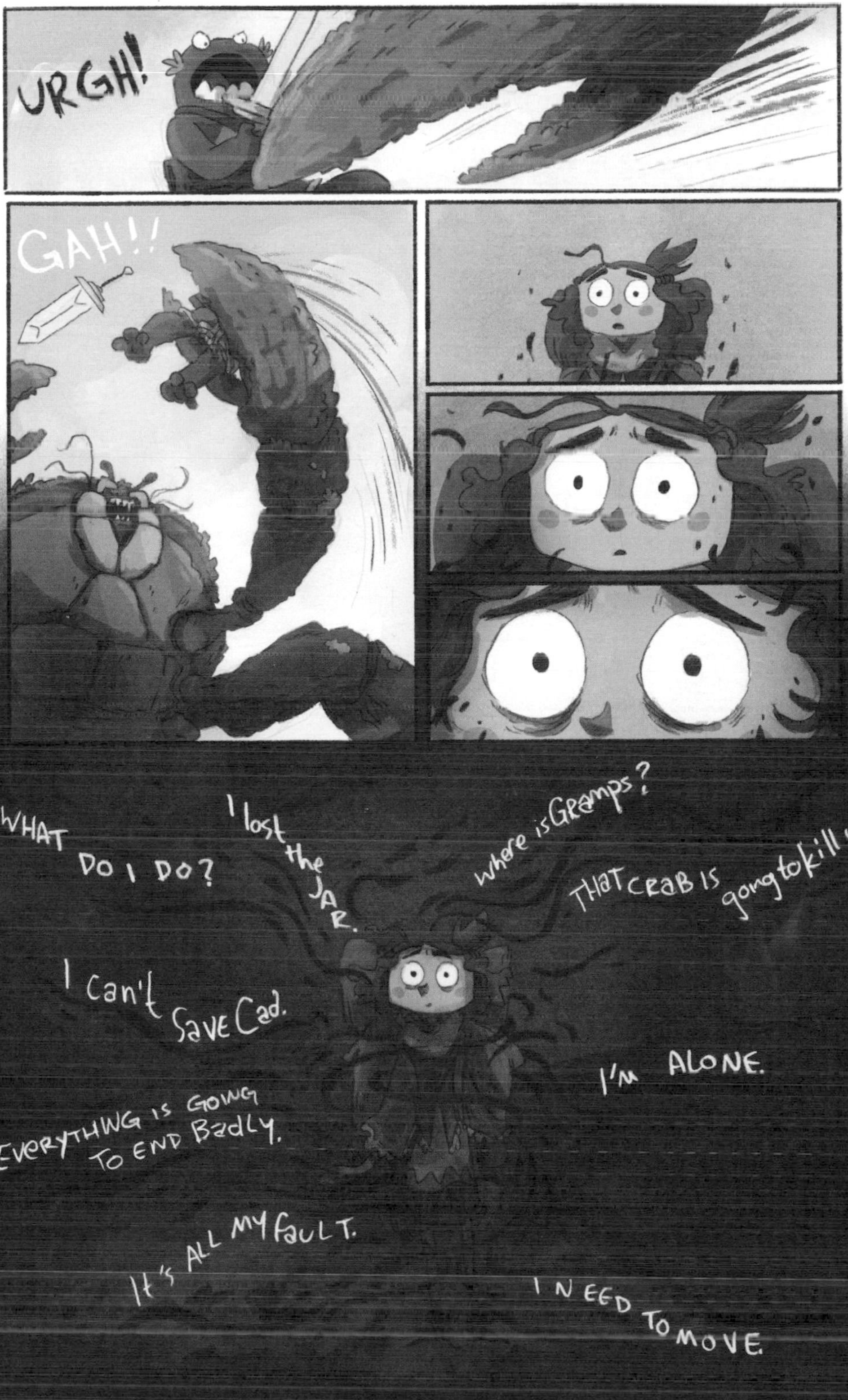
URGH!
GAH!!
WHAT DO I DO?
I lost the JAR.
where is Gramps?
THAT CRAB IS gong to kill us.
I can't save Cad.
I'M ALONE.
EVERYTHING IS GOING TO END BADLY.
It's ALL MY fault.
I NEED TO MOVE.

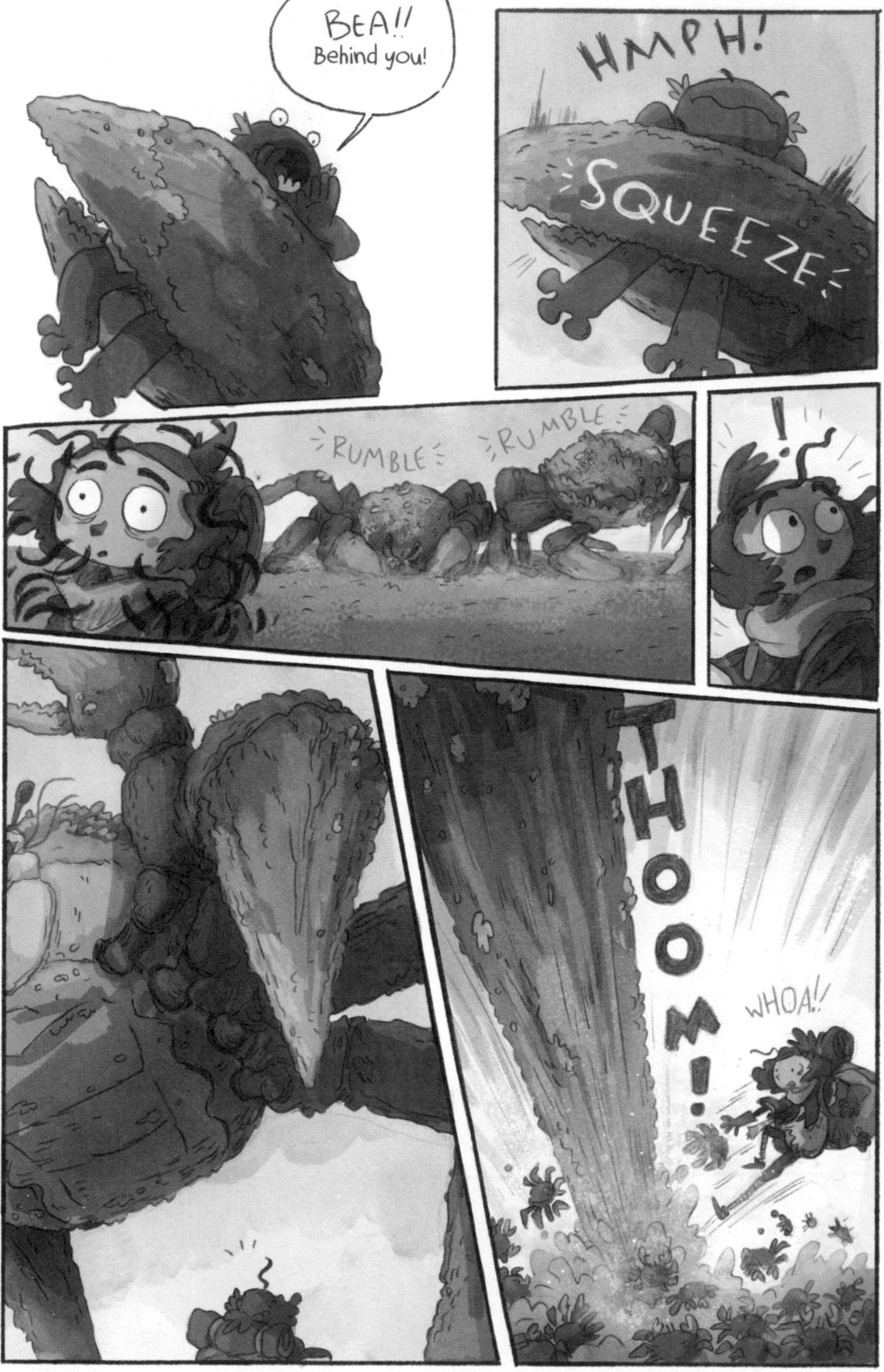
BEA!!
Behind you!
HMPH!
SQUEEZE
RUMBLE
RUMBLE
!
THOOM!
WHOA!!

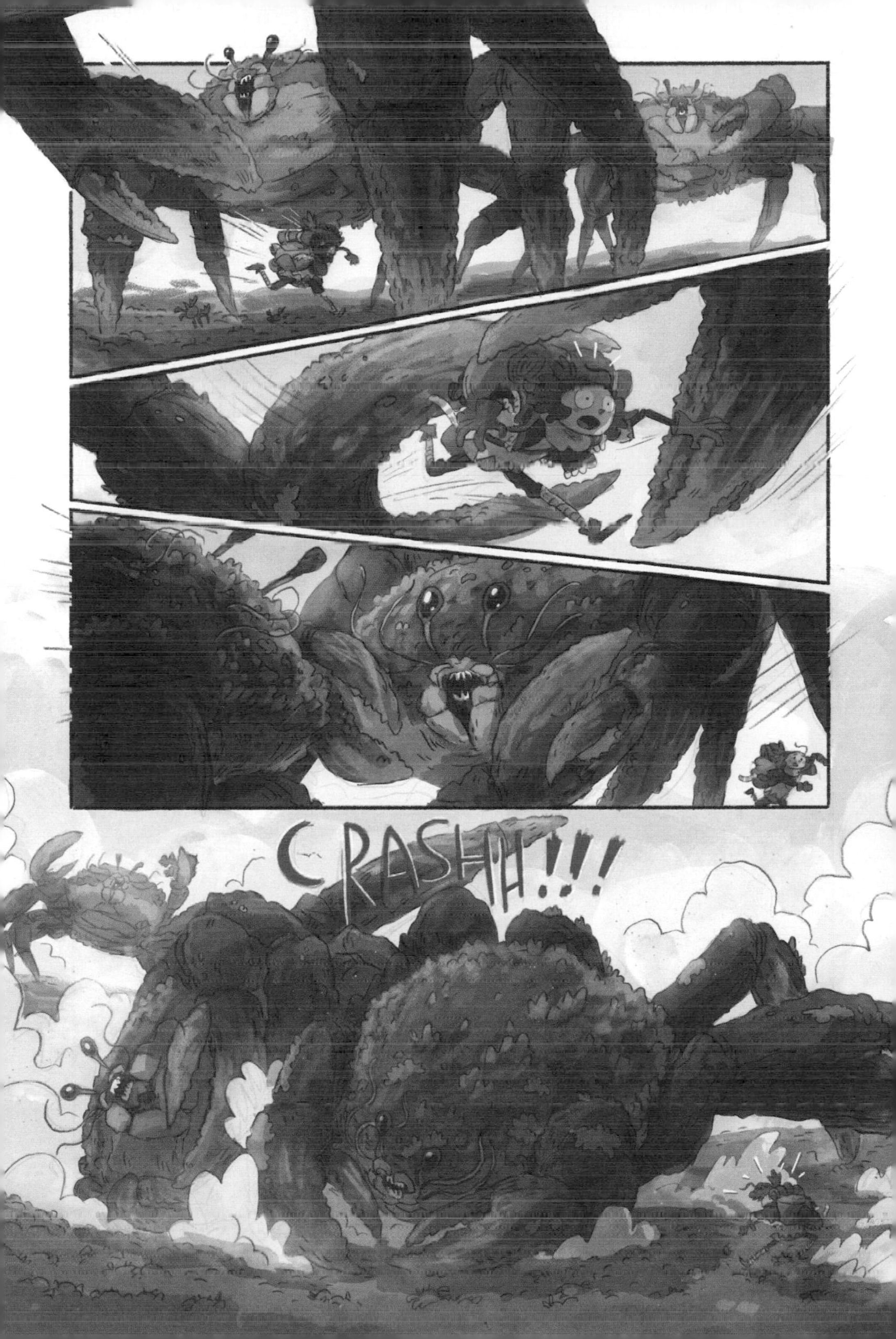
CRASHH!!!

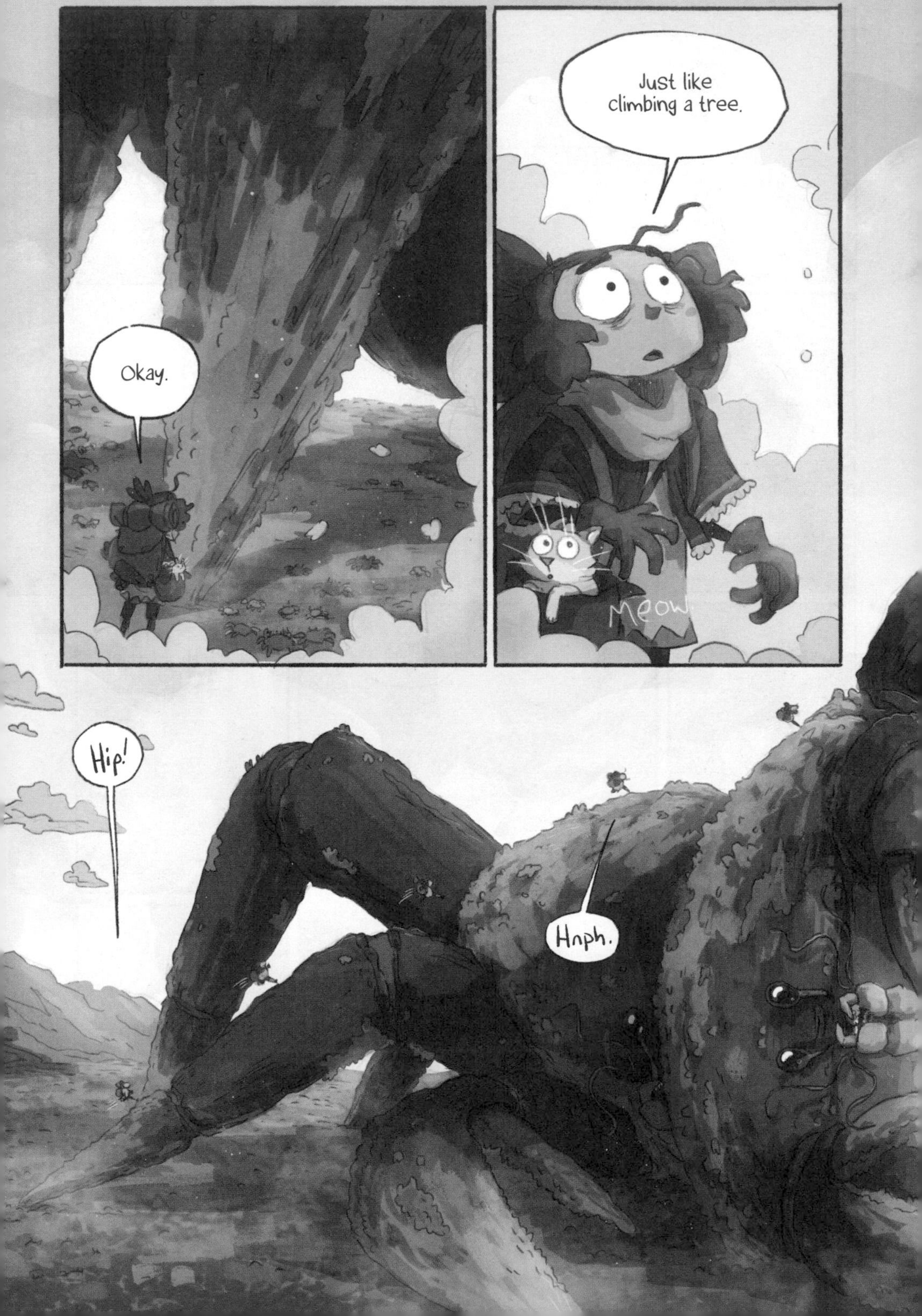
Okay.
Just like climbing a tree.
Meow.
Hip!
Hnph.

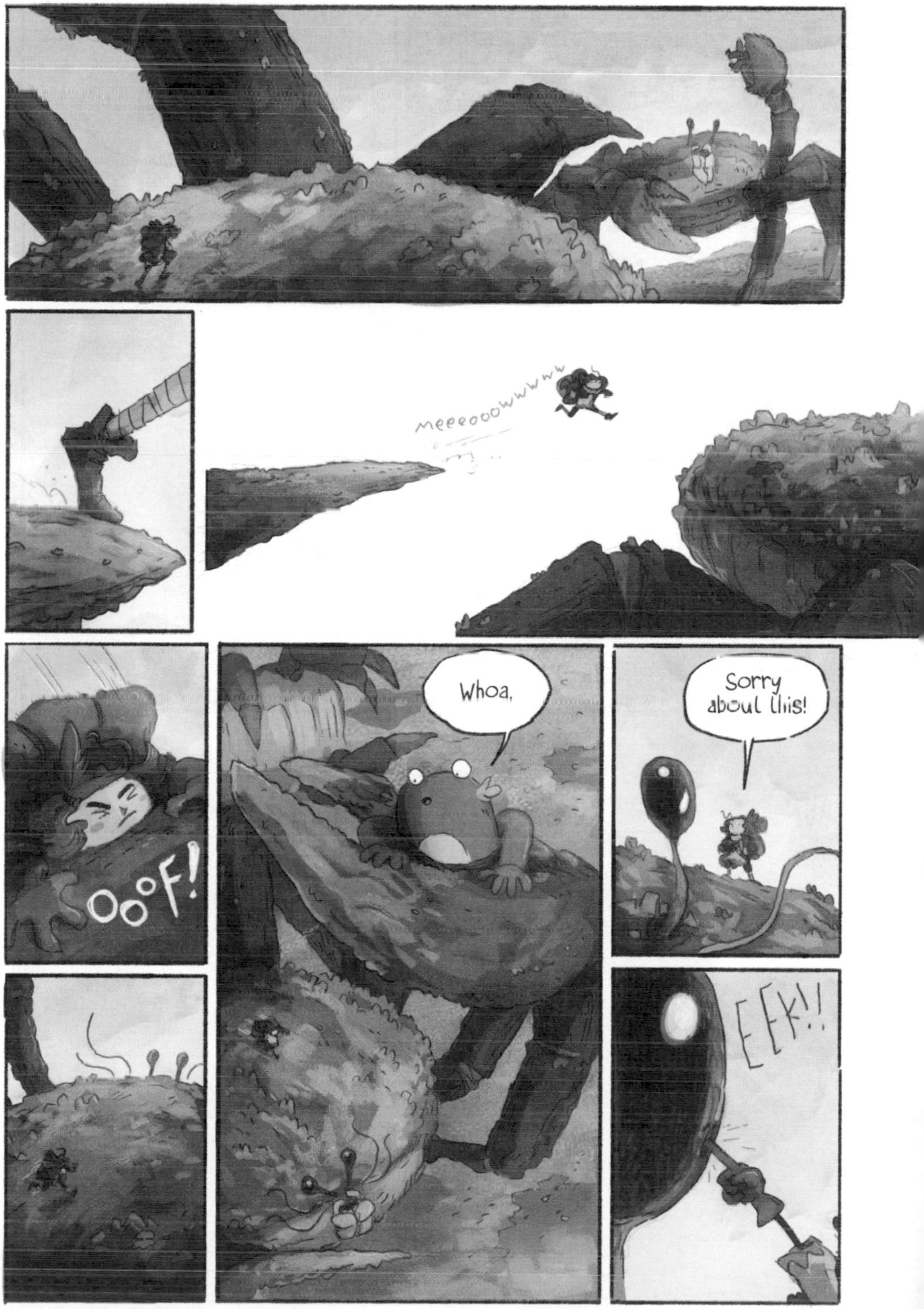
meeeooowwwww
OoOF!
Whoa,
Sorry about this!
EEK!!

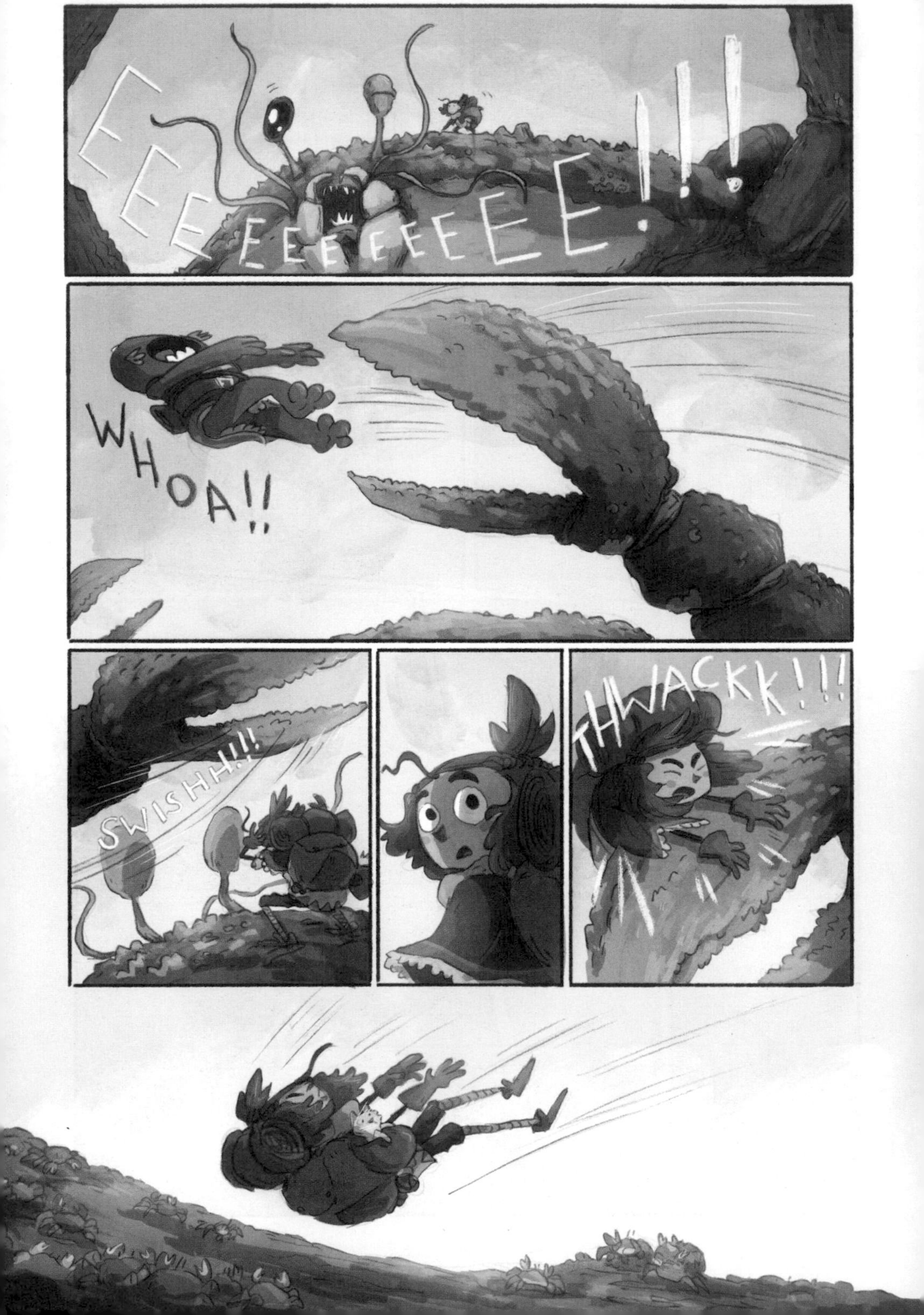
EEEEEEEEEE!!!
WHOA!!
SWISHH!!
THWACKK!!!

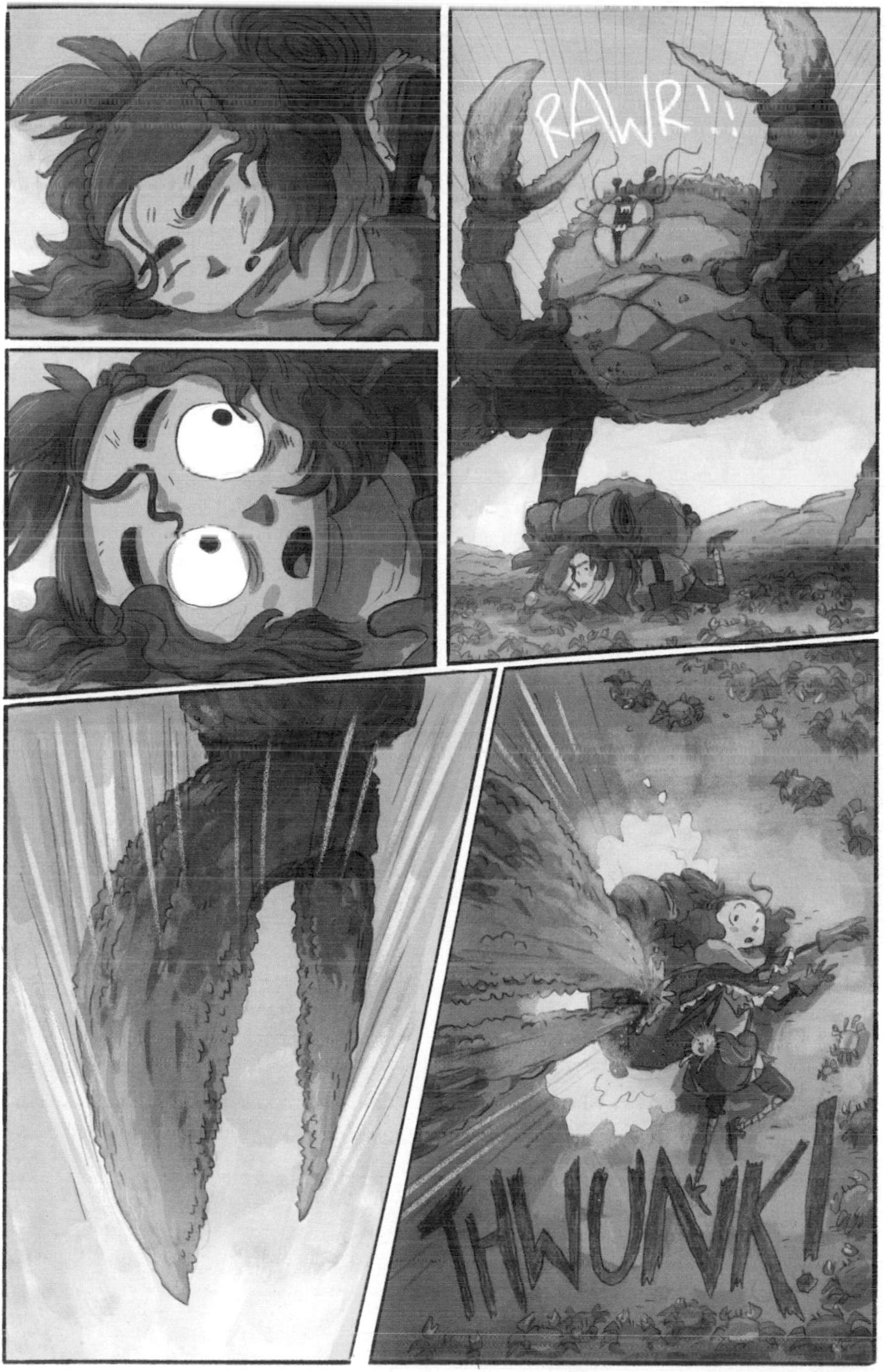
RAWR!!
THWUNK!

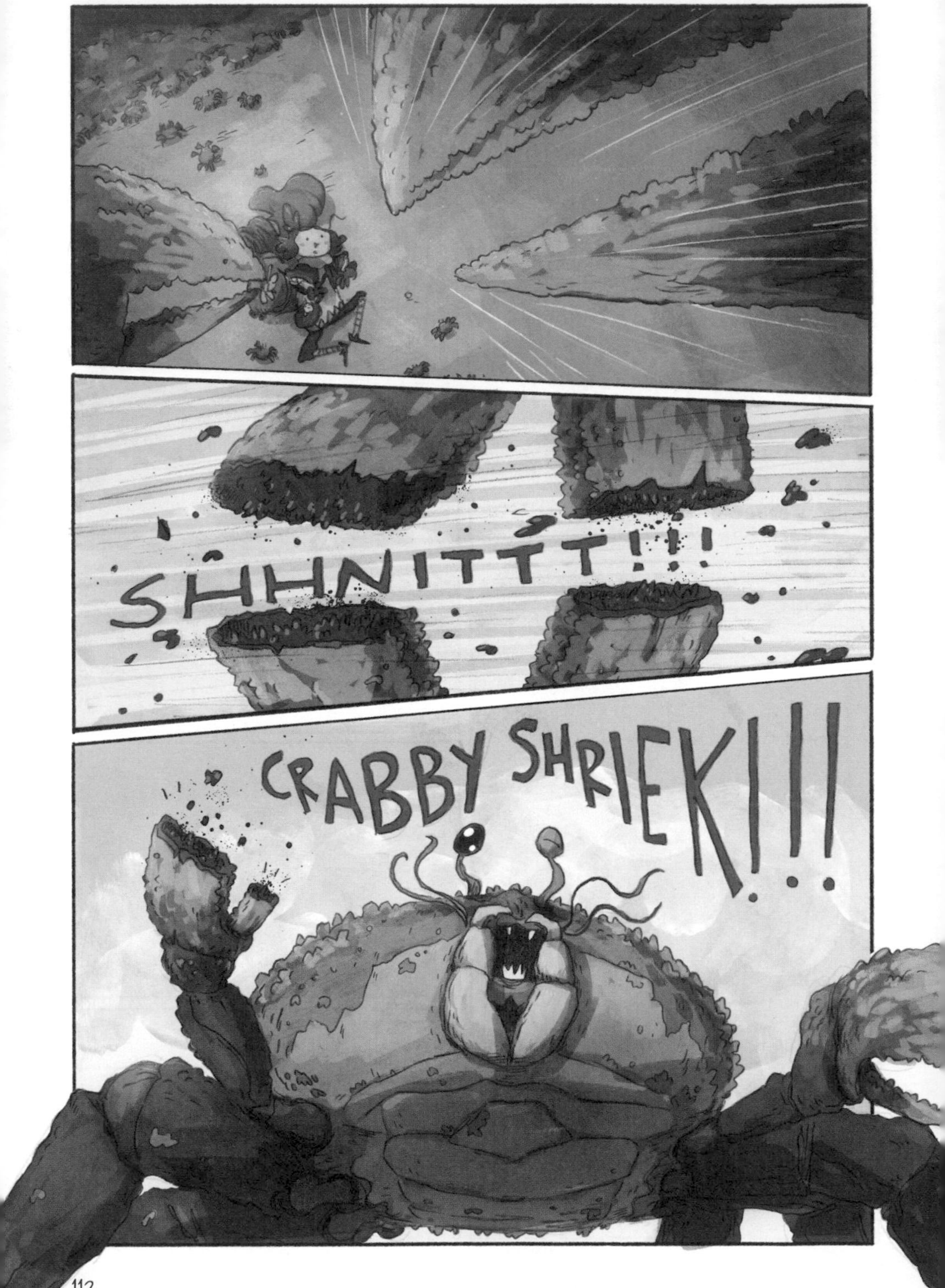
SHHNITTT!!!
CRABBY SHRIEK!!!

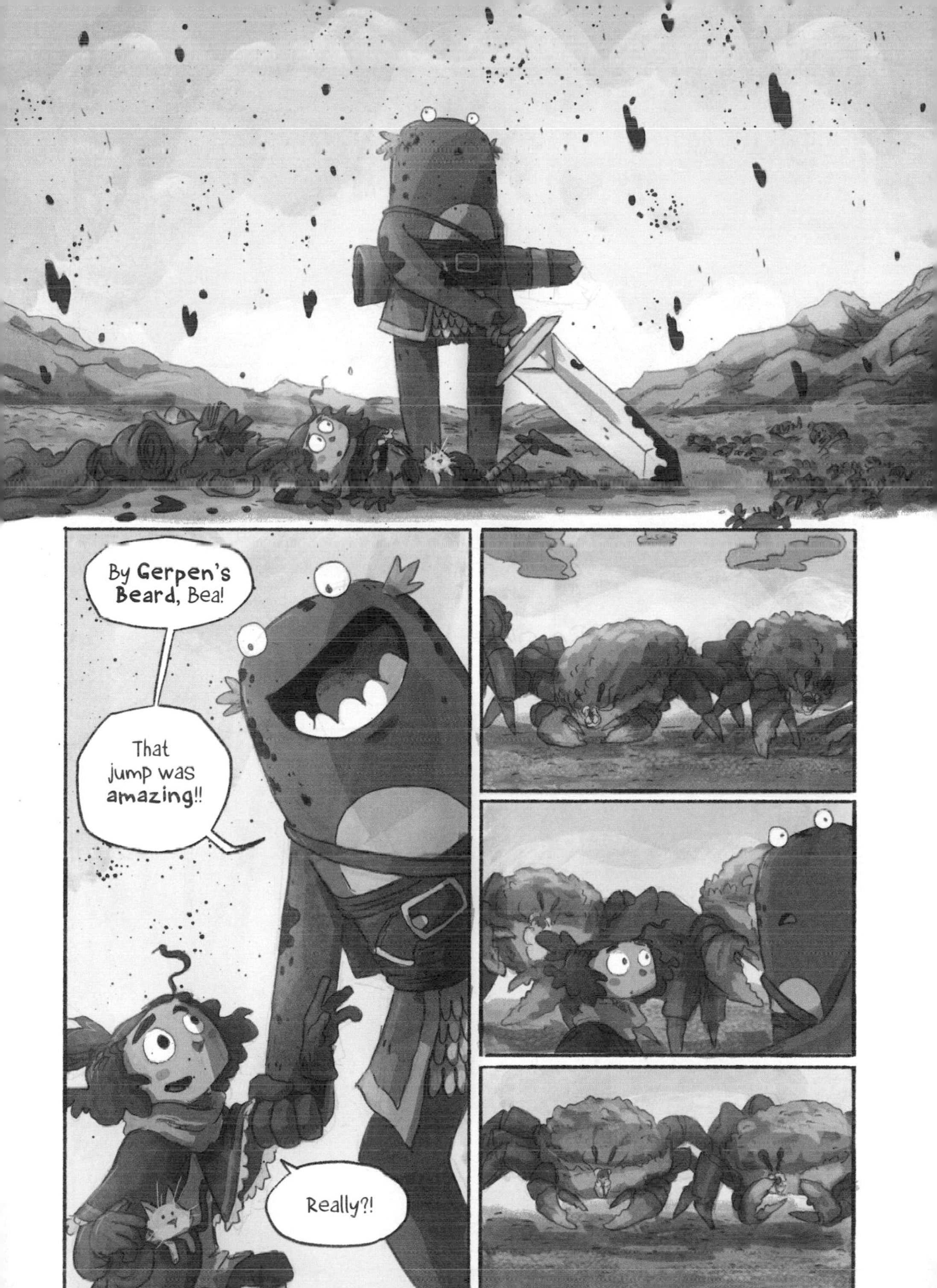
By Gerpen's Beard, Bea!
That jump was amazing!!
Really?!

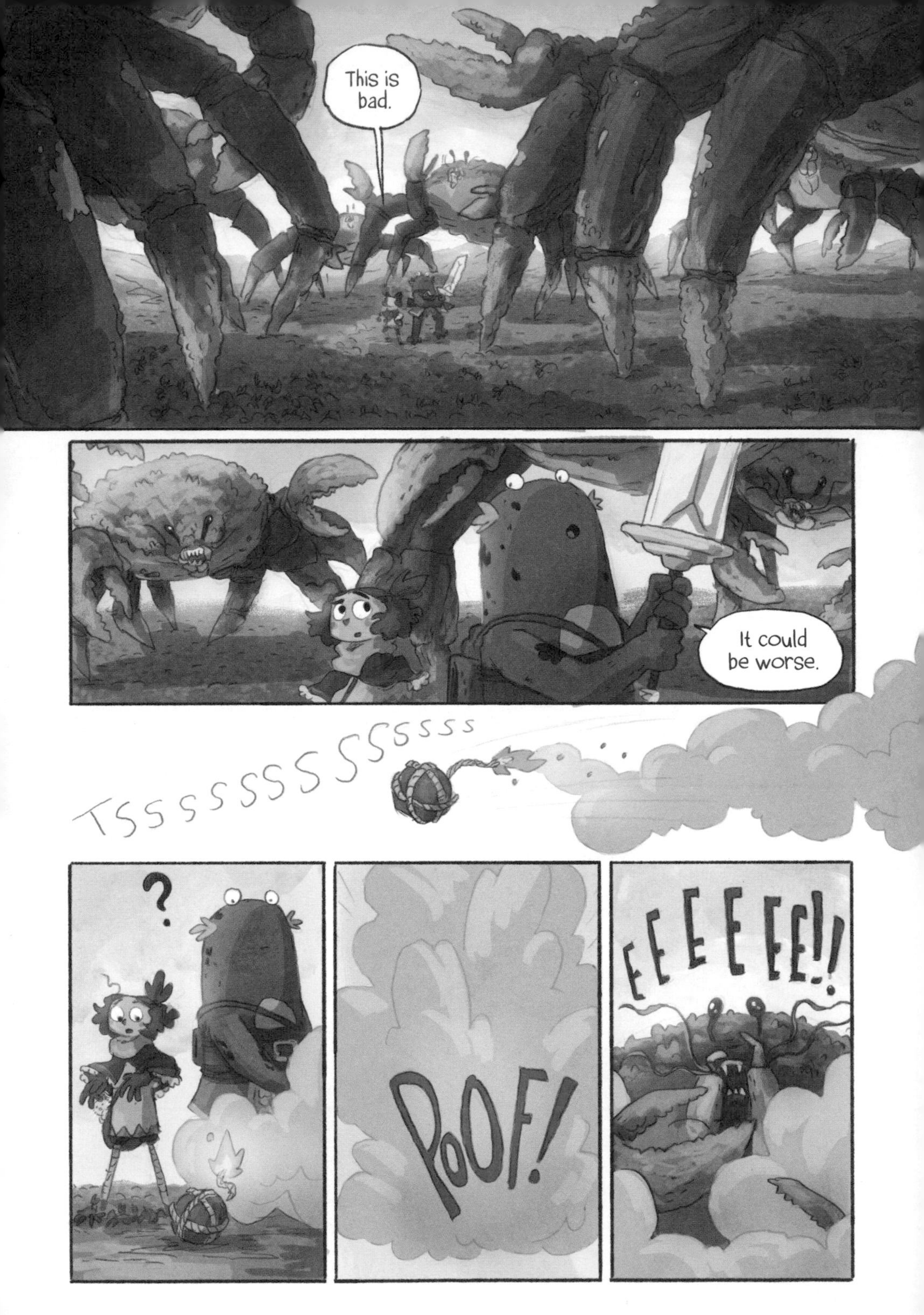
This is bad.
It could be worse.
TSSSSSSSSSSSSS
?
POOF!
EEEEEE!!

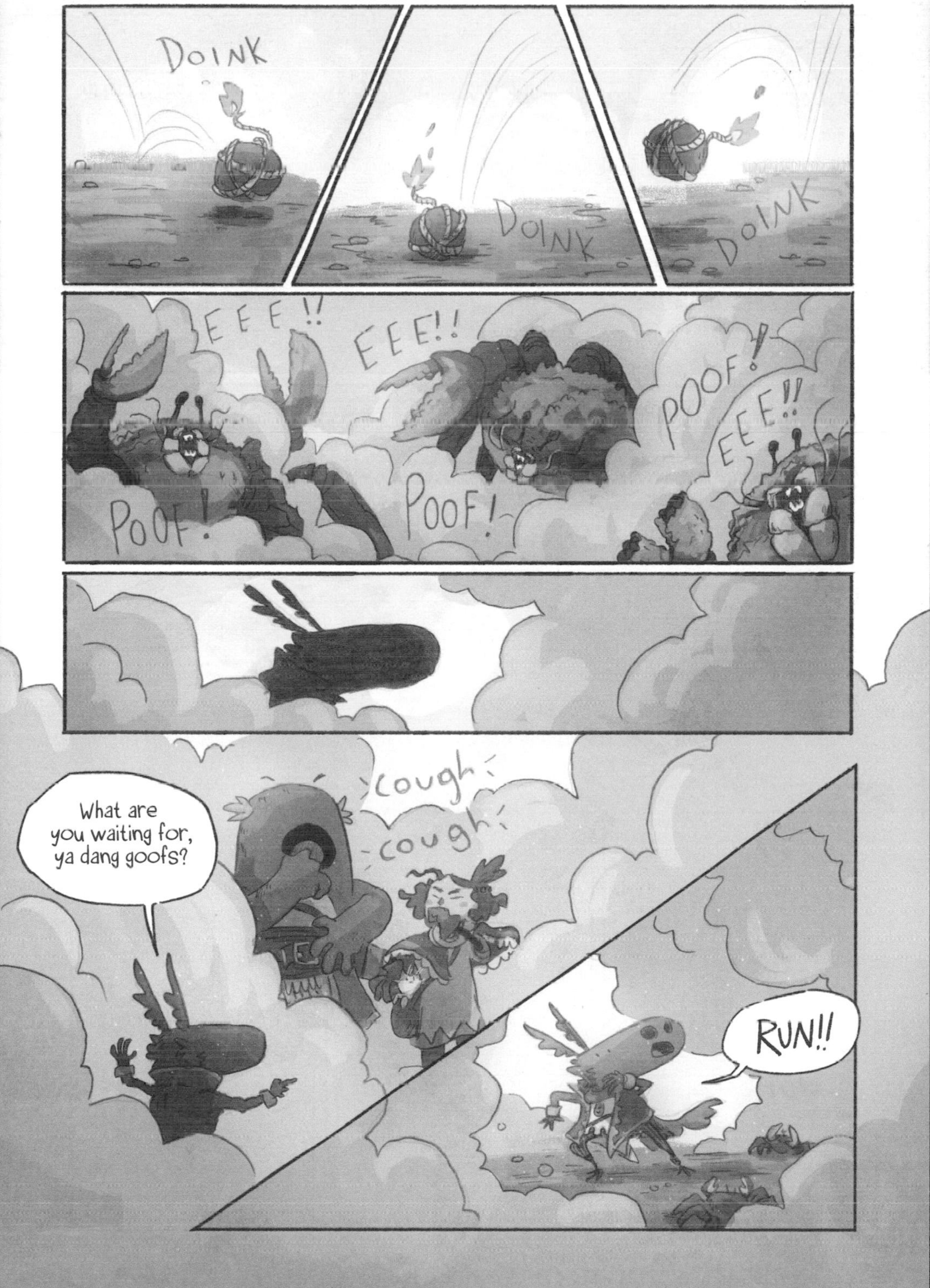
DOINK
DOINK
DOINK
EEE!!
EEE!!
POOF!
POOF!
POOF!
EEE!!
cough
cough
What are you waiting for, ya dang goofs?
RUN!!

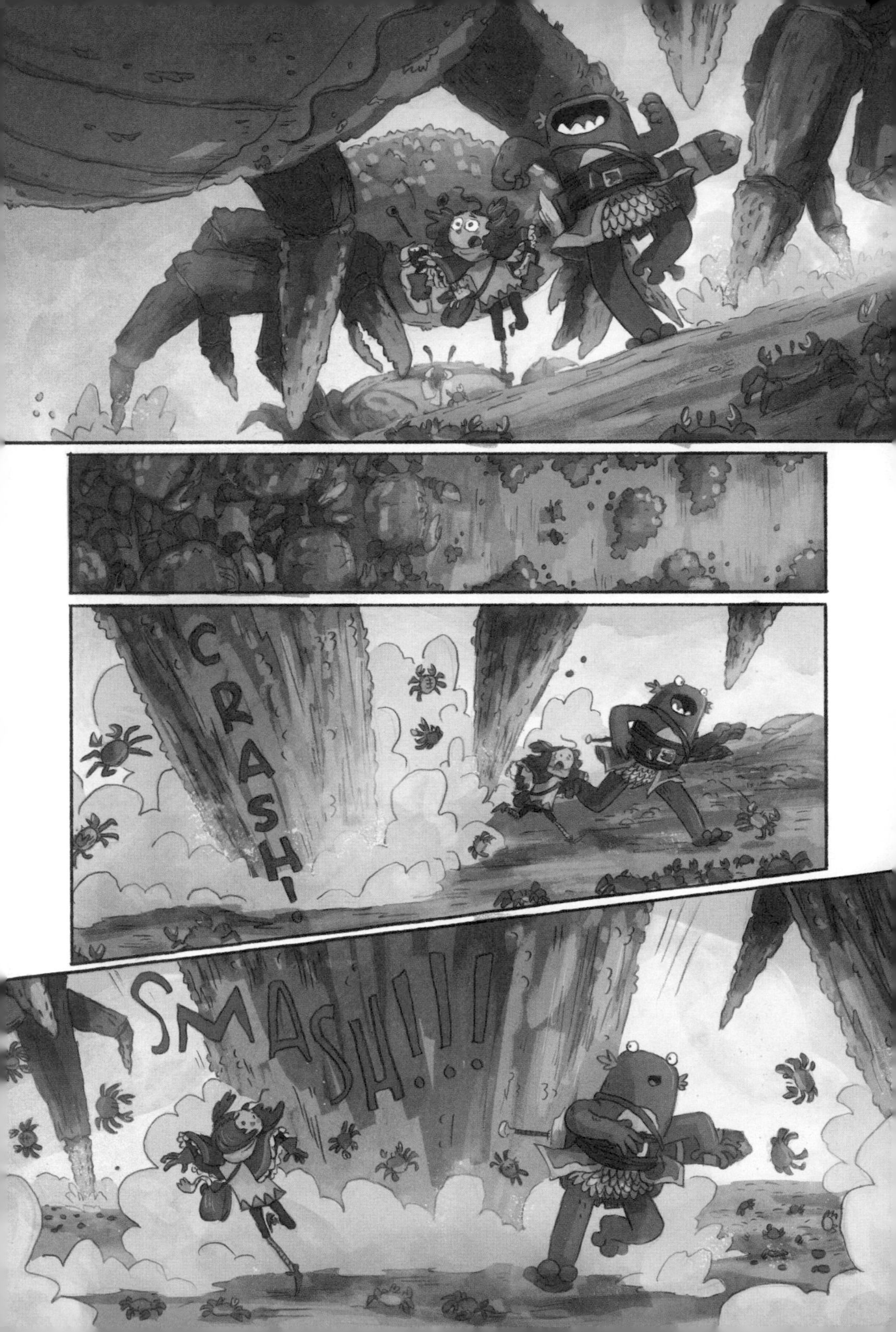
CRASH!
SMASH!!!!

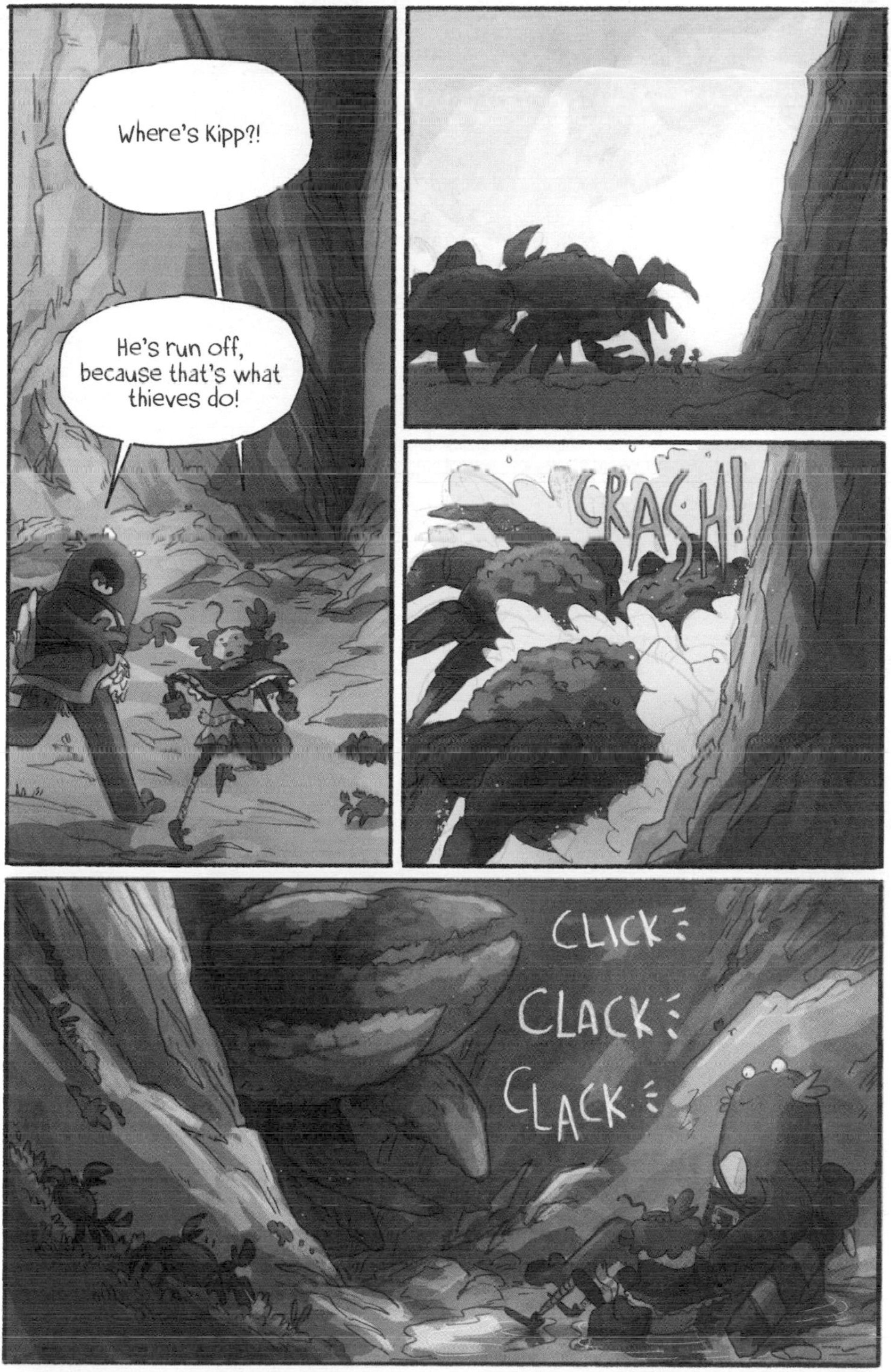
Where's Kipp?!
He's run off, because that's what thieves do!
CRASH!
CLICK
CLACK
CLACK

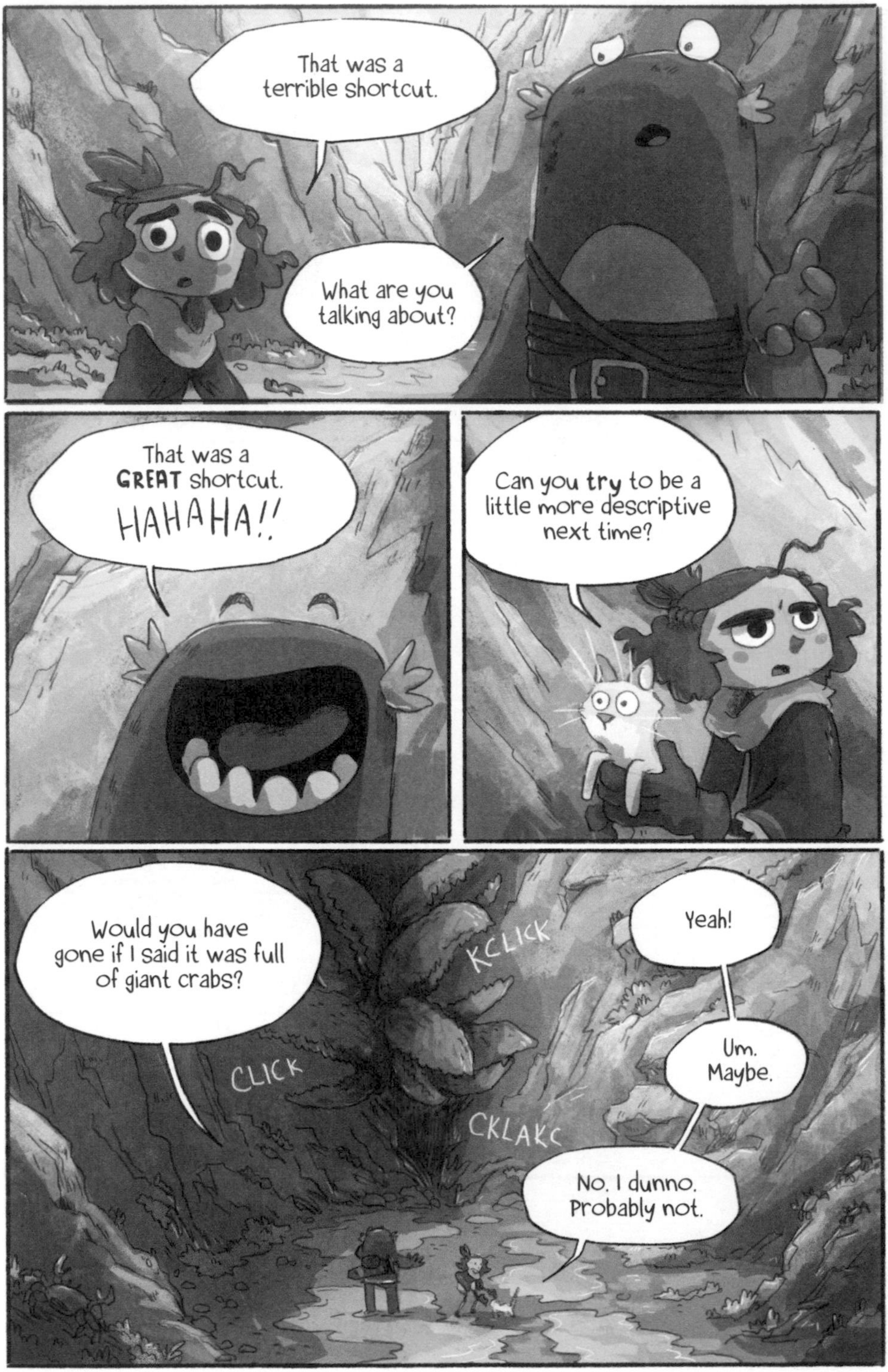
That was a terrible shortcut.
What are you talking about?
That was a **GREAT** shortcut.
HAHAHA!!
Can you **try** to be a little more descriptive next time?
Would you have gone if I said it was full of giant crabs?
KCLICK
CLICK
CKLAKC
Yeah!
Um. Maybe.
No. I dunno. Probably not.

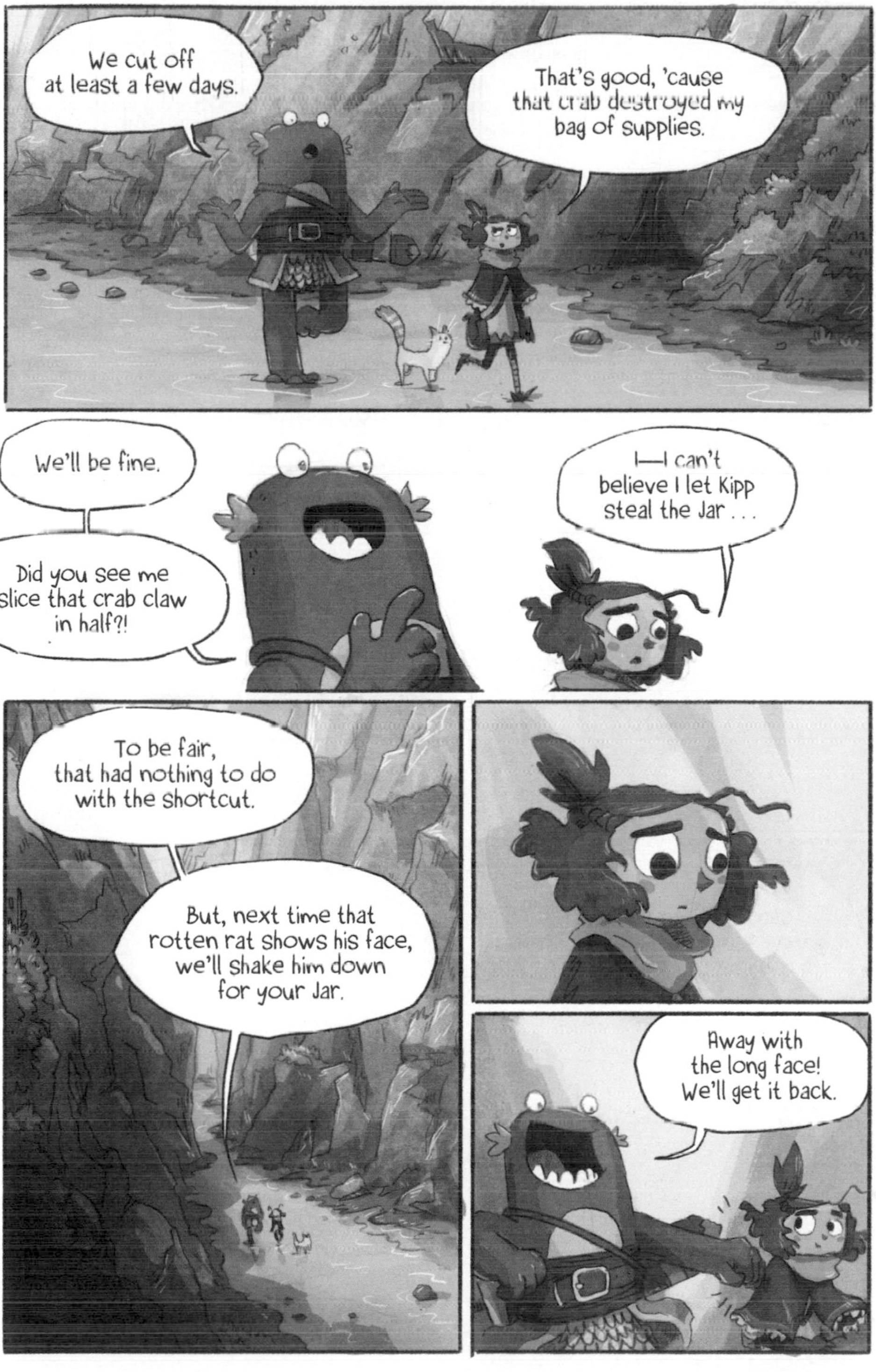
We cut off at least a few days.
That's good, 'cause that crab destroyed my bag of supplies.
We'll be fine.
Did you see me slice that crab claw in half?!
I—I can't believe I let Kipp steal the Jar . . .
To be fair, that had nothing to do with the shortcut.
But, next time that rotten rat shows his face, we'll shake him down for your Jar.
Away with the long face! We'll get it back.

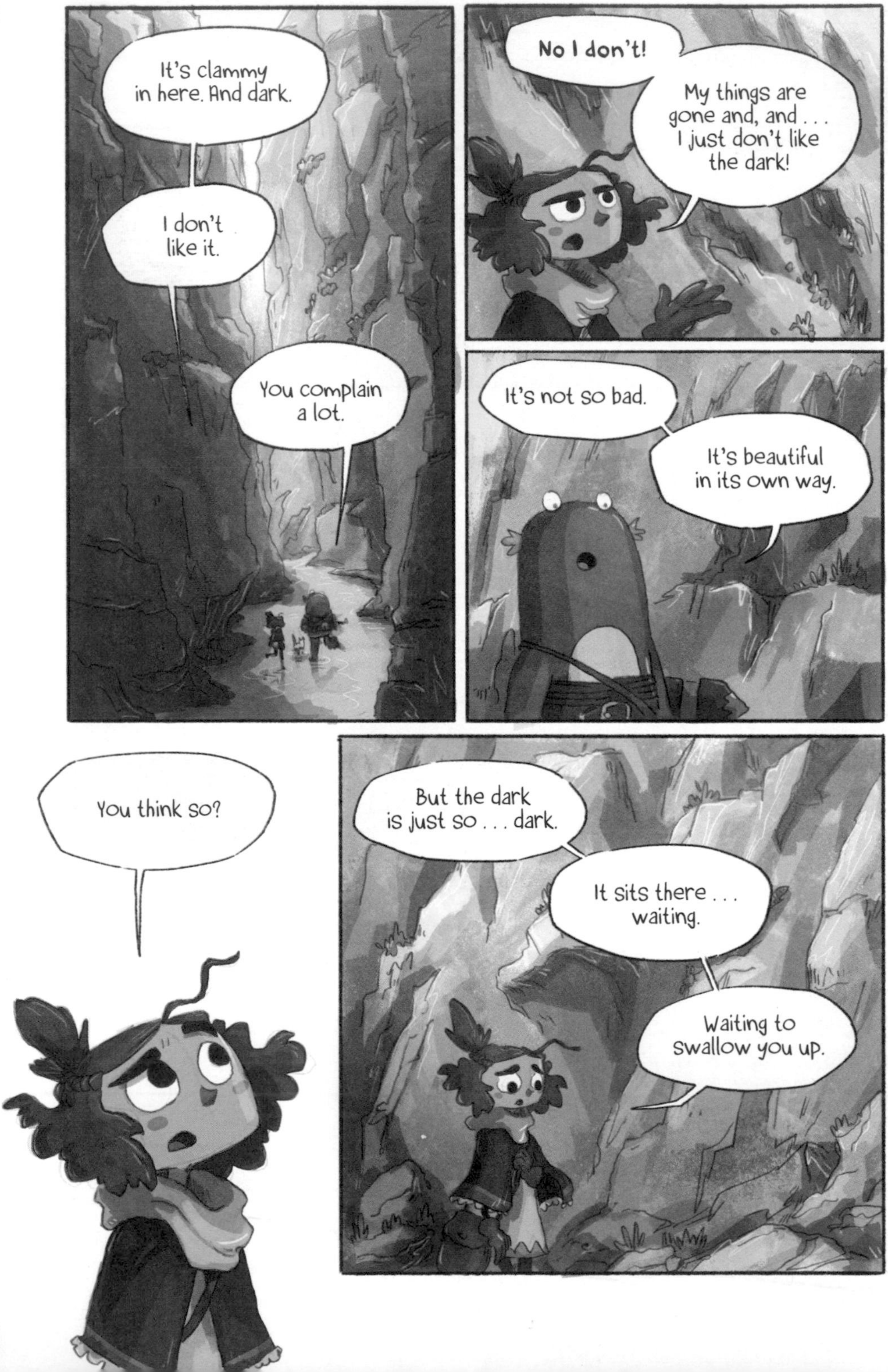
It's clammy in here. And dark.
I don't like it.
You complain a lot.
No I don't!
My things are gone and, and . . . I just don't like the dark!
It's not so bad.
It's beautiful in its own way.
You think so?
But the dark is just so . . . dark.
It sits there . . . waiting.
Waiting to swallow you up.

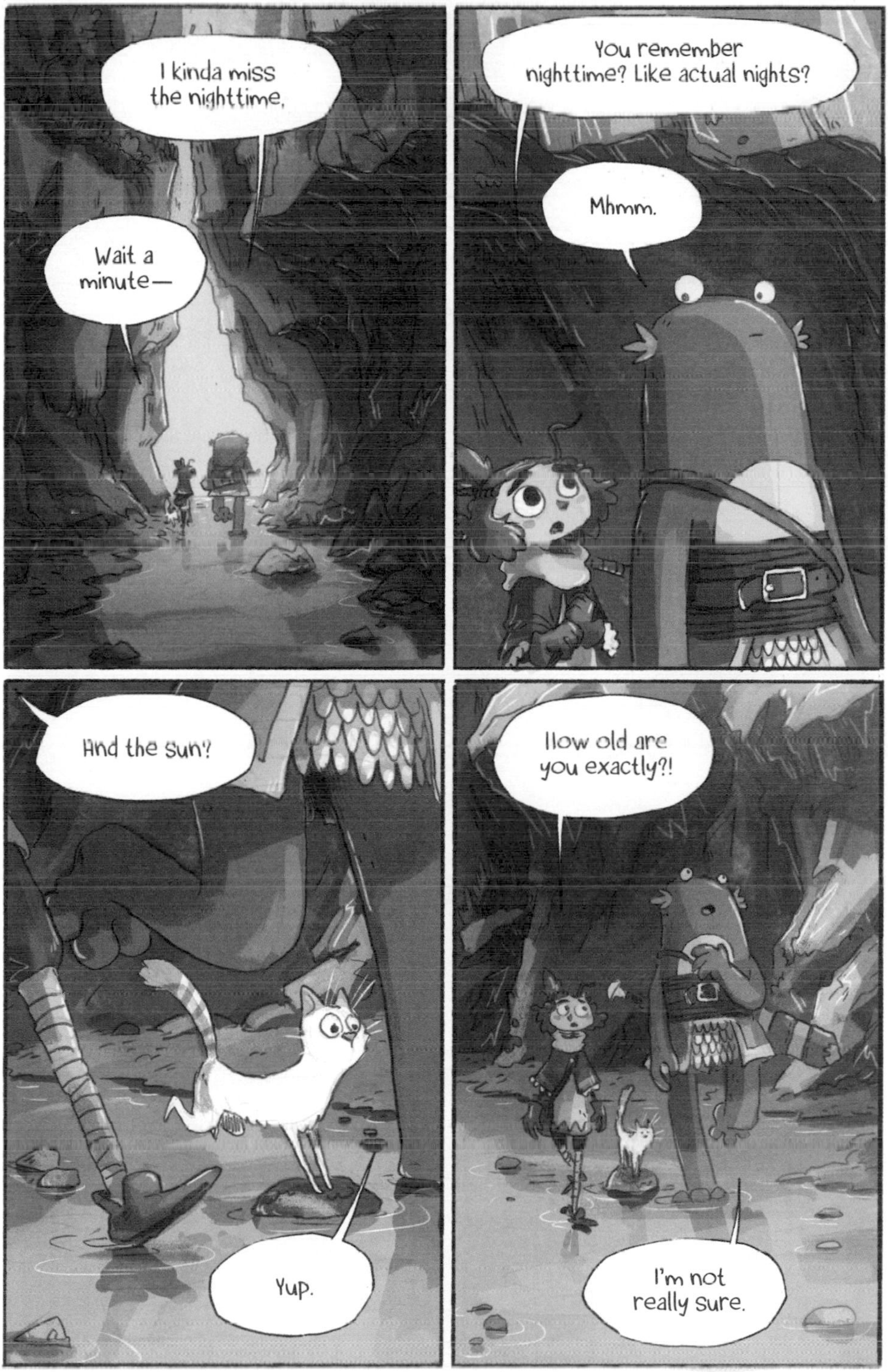
I kinda miss the nighttime.
Wait a minute—
You remember nighttime? Like actual nights?
Mhmm.
And the sun?
Yup.
How old are you exactly?!
I'm not really sure.

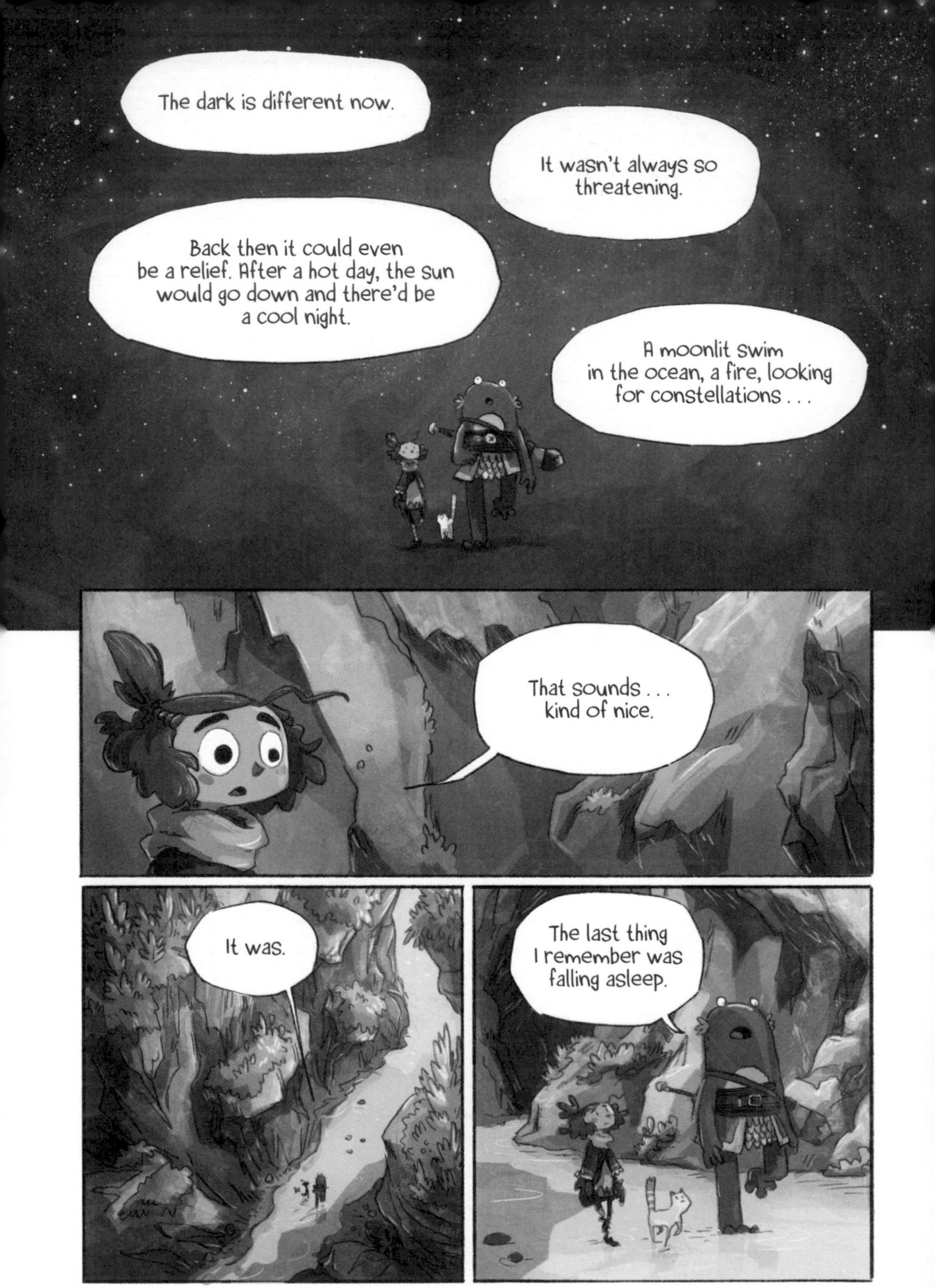
The dark is different now.
It wasn't always so threatening.
Back then it could even be a relief. After a hot day, the sun would go down and there'd be a cool night.
A moonlit swim in the ocean, a fire, looking for constellations . . .
That sounds . . . kind of nice.
It was.
The last thing I remember was falling asleep.

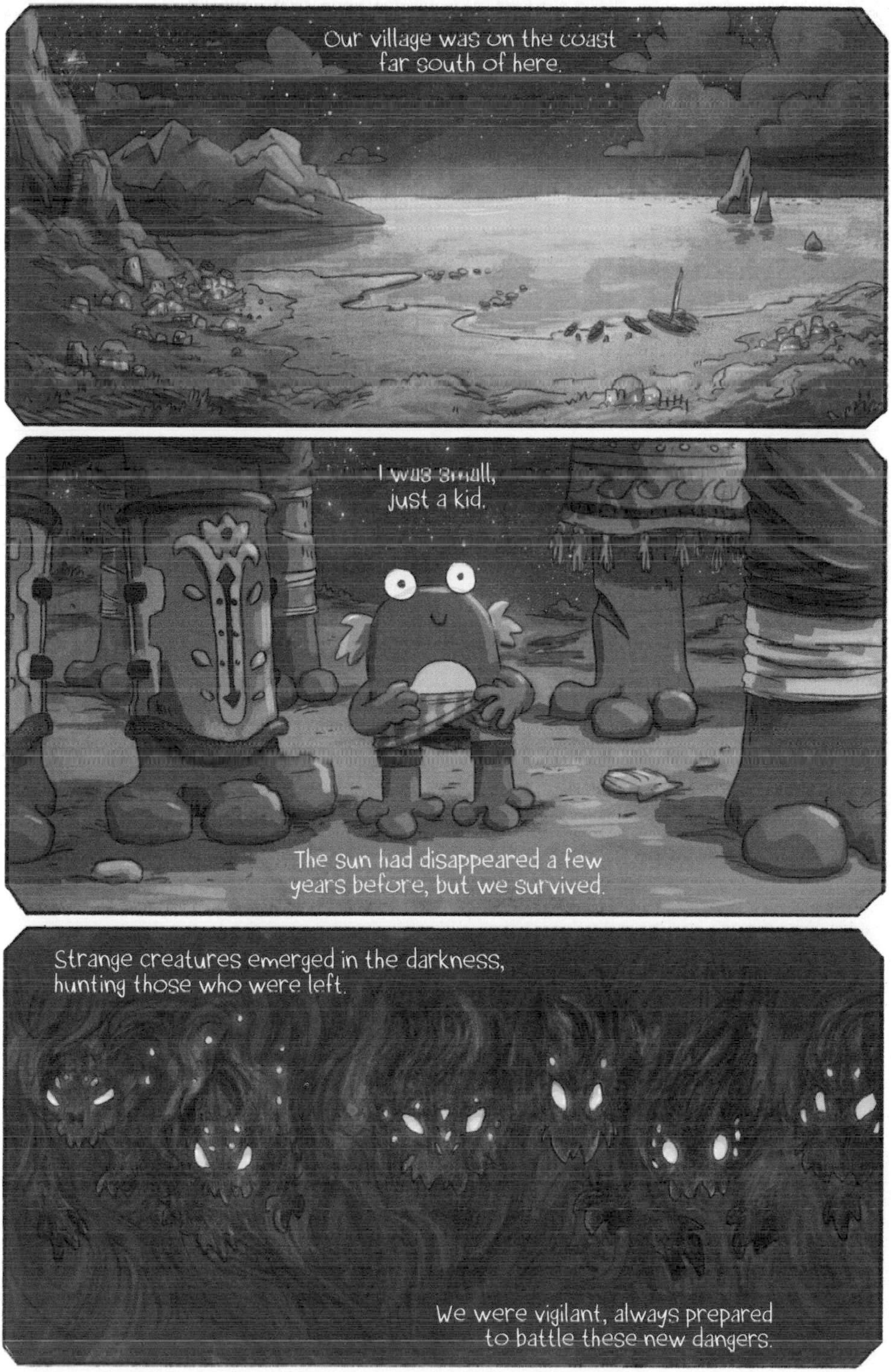
Our village was on the coast
far south of here.
I was small,
just a kid.
The sun had disappeared a few
years before, but we survived.
Strange creatures emerged in the darkness,
hunting those who were left.
We were vigilant, always prepared
to battle these new dangers.

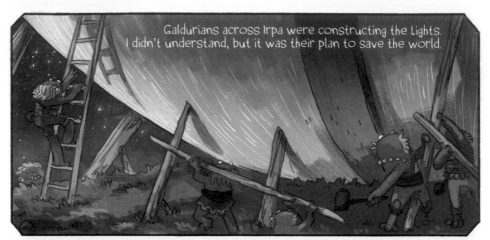
Galdurians across Irpa were constructing the Lights. I didn't understand, but it was their plan to save the world.

Our village's was to be the grandest of them all.

I liked to help, but mostly just watched. One day I fell asleep.

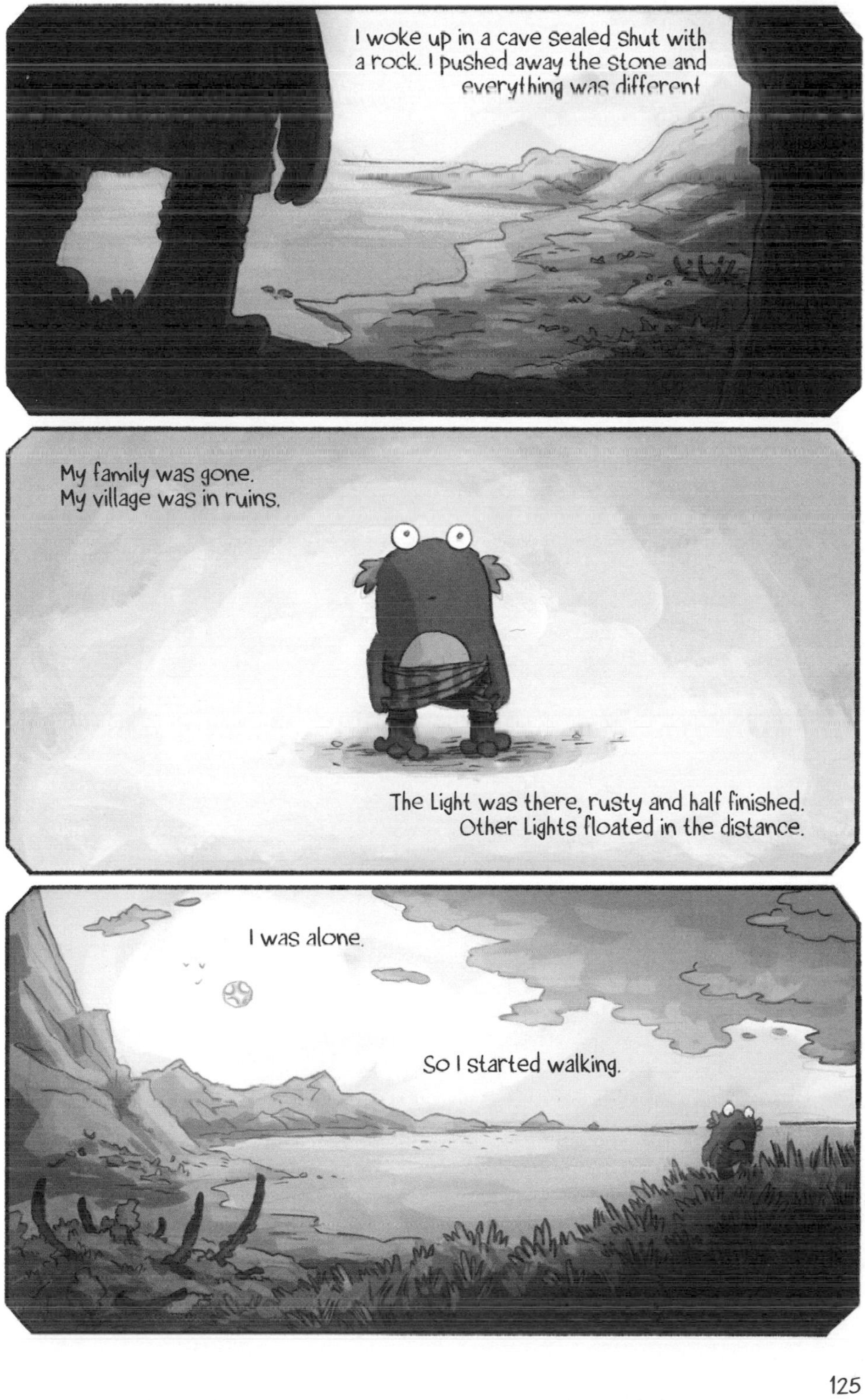
I woke up in a cave sealed shut with a rock. I pushed away the stone and everything was different
My family was gone. My village was in ruins.
The Light was there, rusty and half finished. Other Lights floated in the distance.
I was alone.
So I started walking.

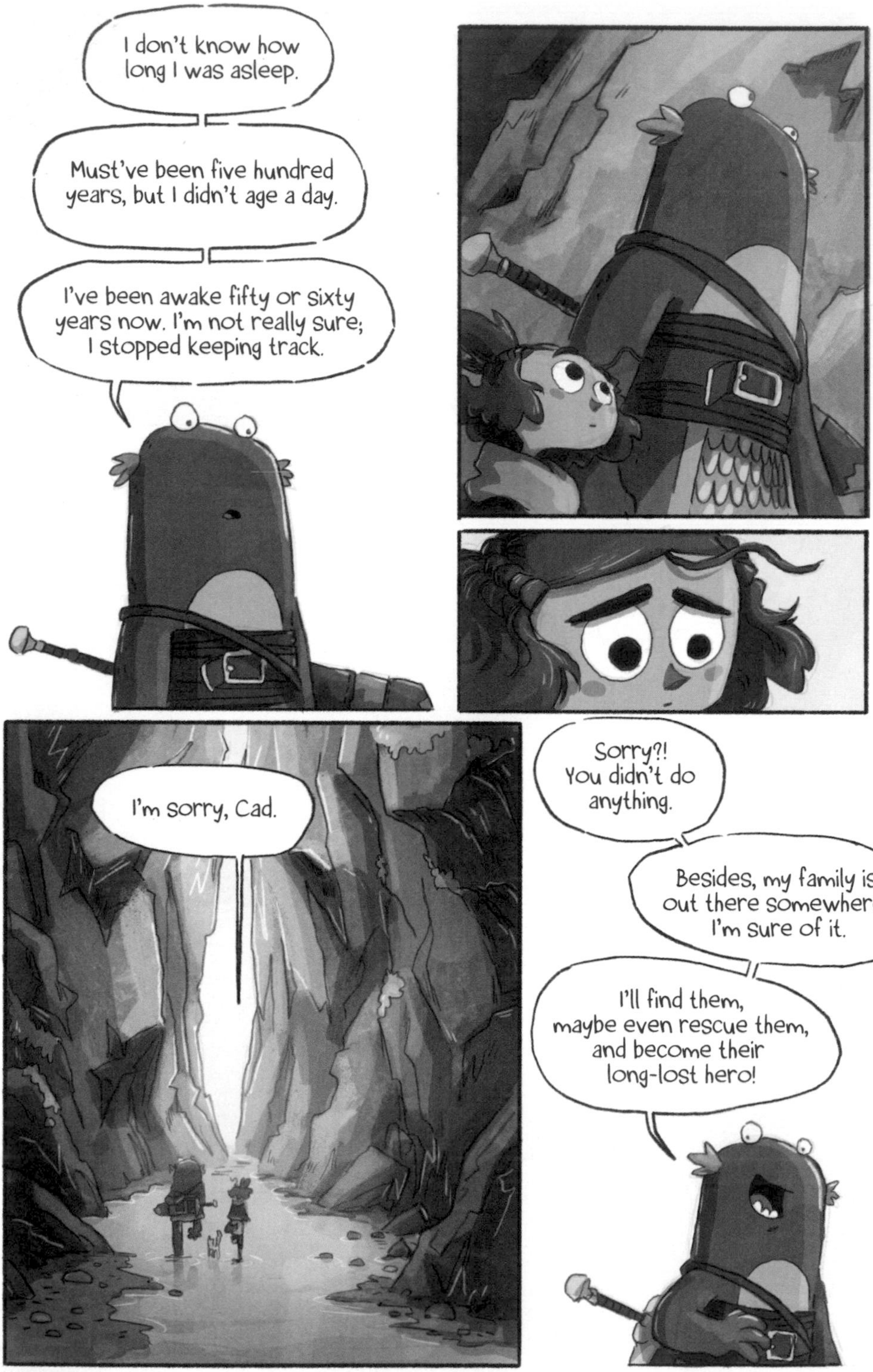
I don't know how long I was asleep.
Must've been five hundred years, but I didn't age a day.
I've been awake fifty or sixty years now. I'm not really sure; I stopped keeping track.
I'm sorry, Cad.
Sorry?! You didn't do anything.
Besides, my family is out there somewhere. I'm sure of it.
I'll find them, maybe even rescue them, and become their long-lost hero!

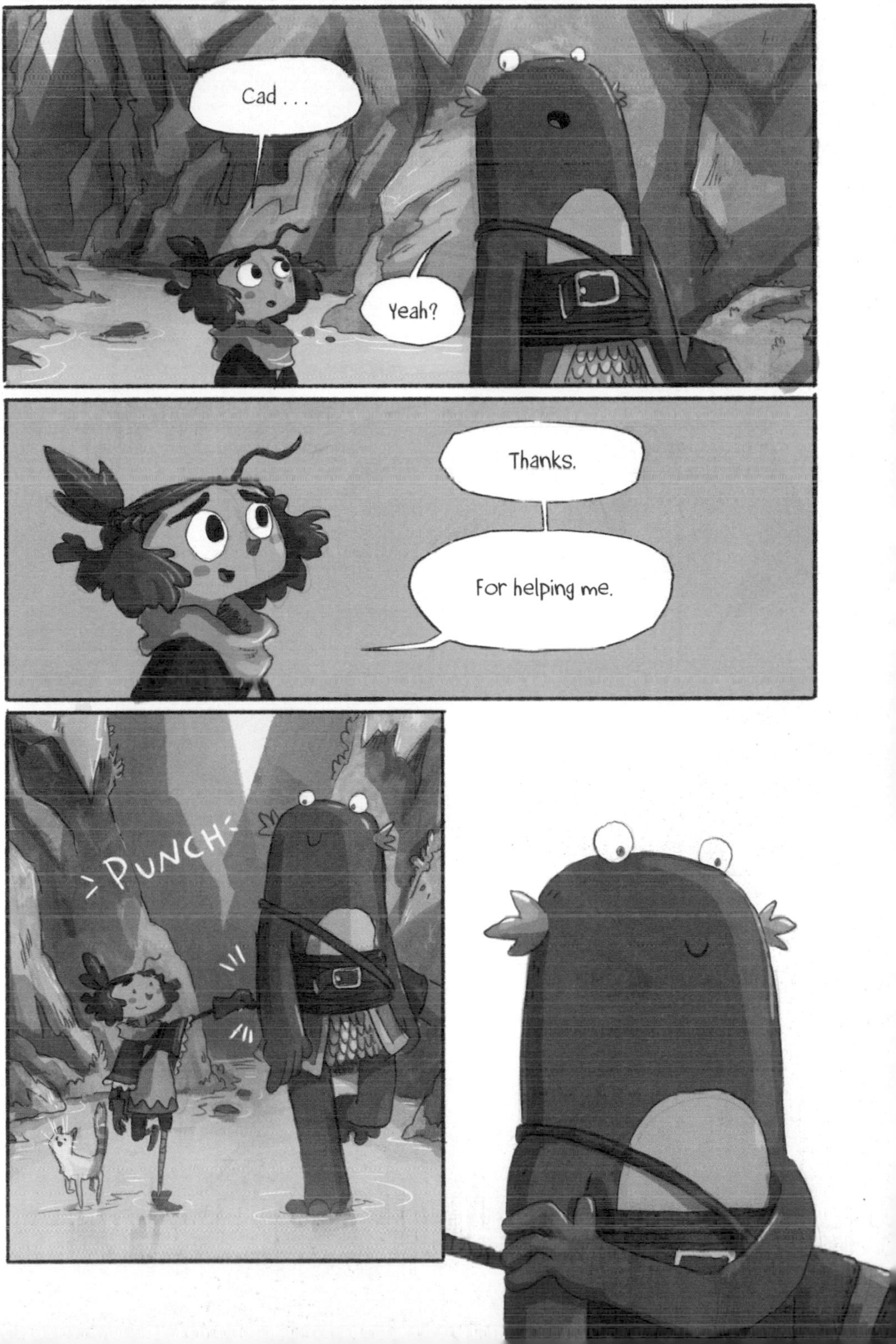
Cad . . .
Yeah?
Thanks.
For helping me.
PUNCH

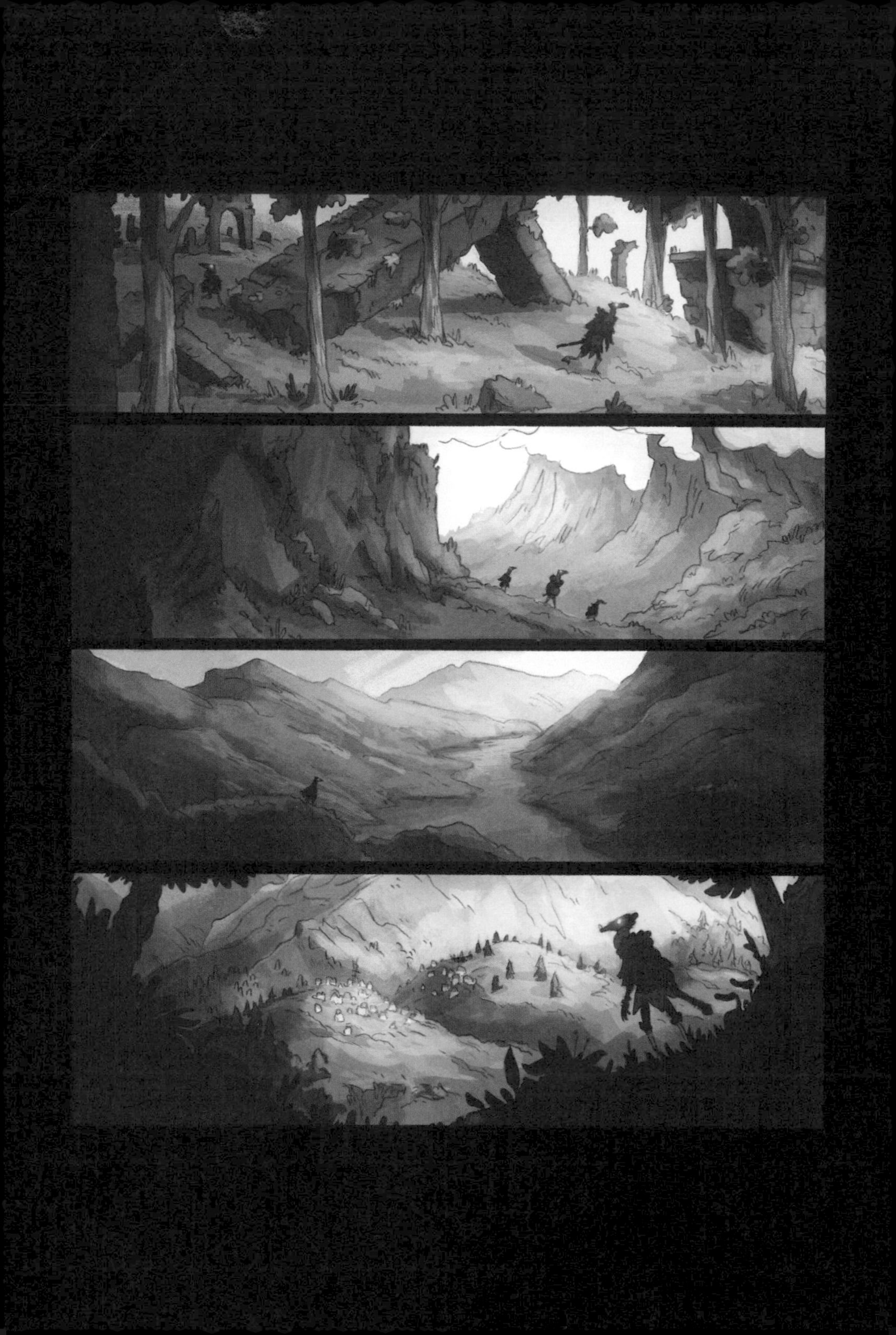

DING
DING
DING

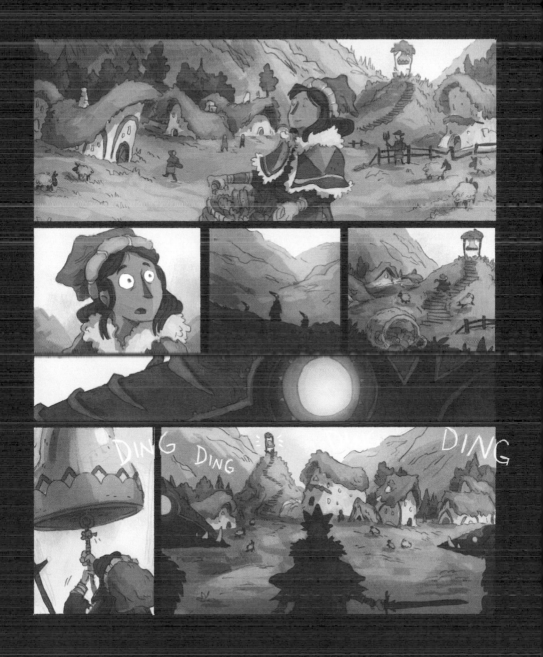

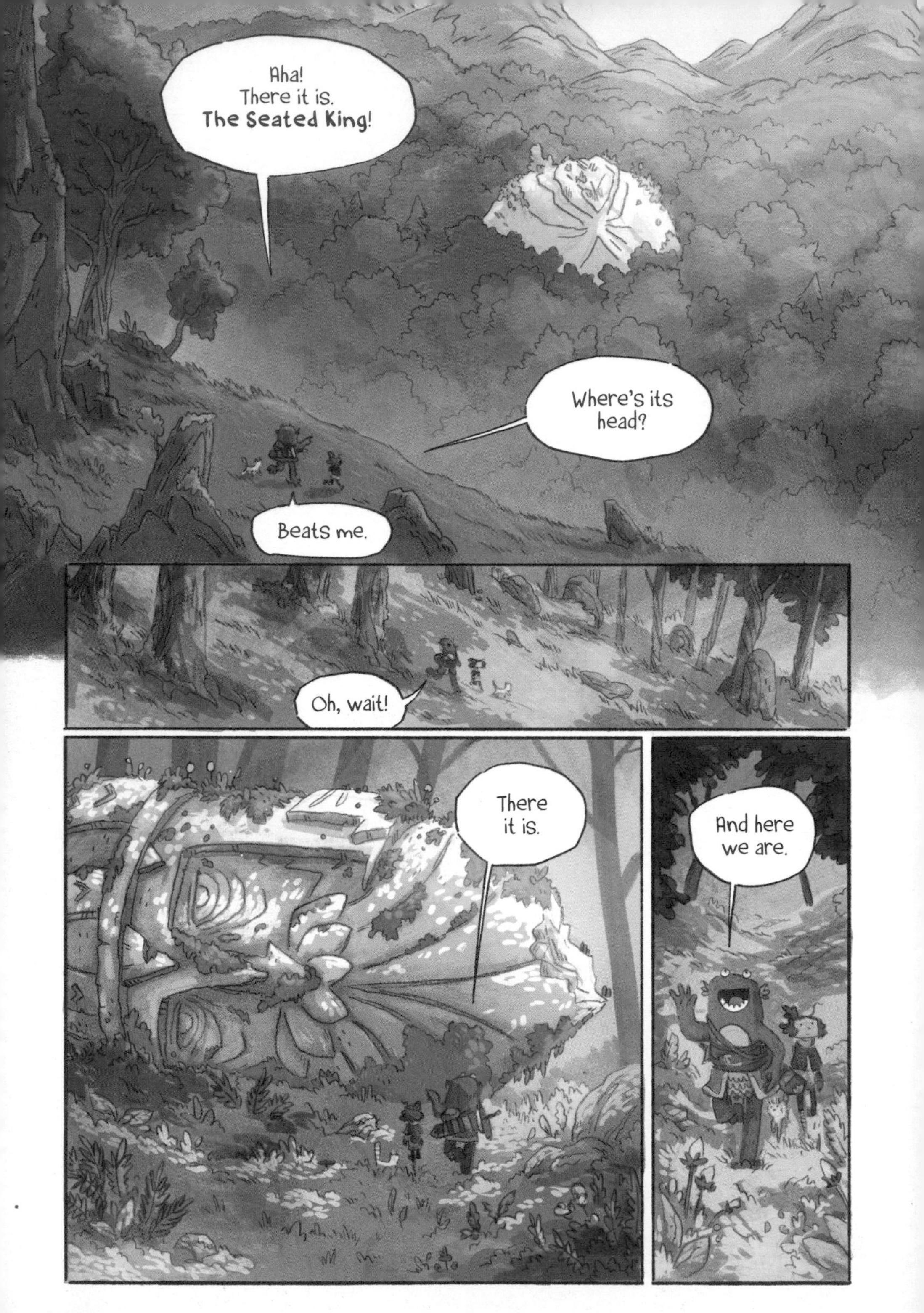
Aha!
There it is.
The Seated King!
Where's its head?
Beats me.
Oh, wait!
There it is.
And here we are.

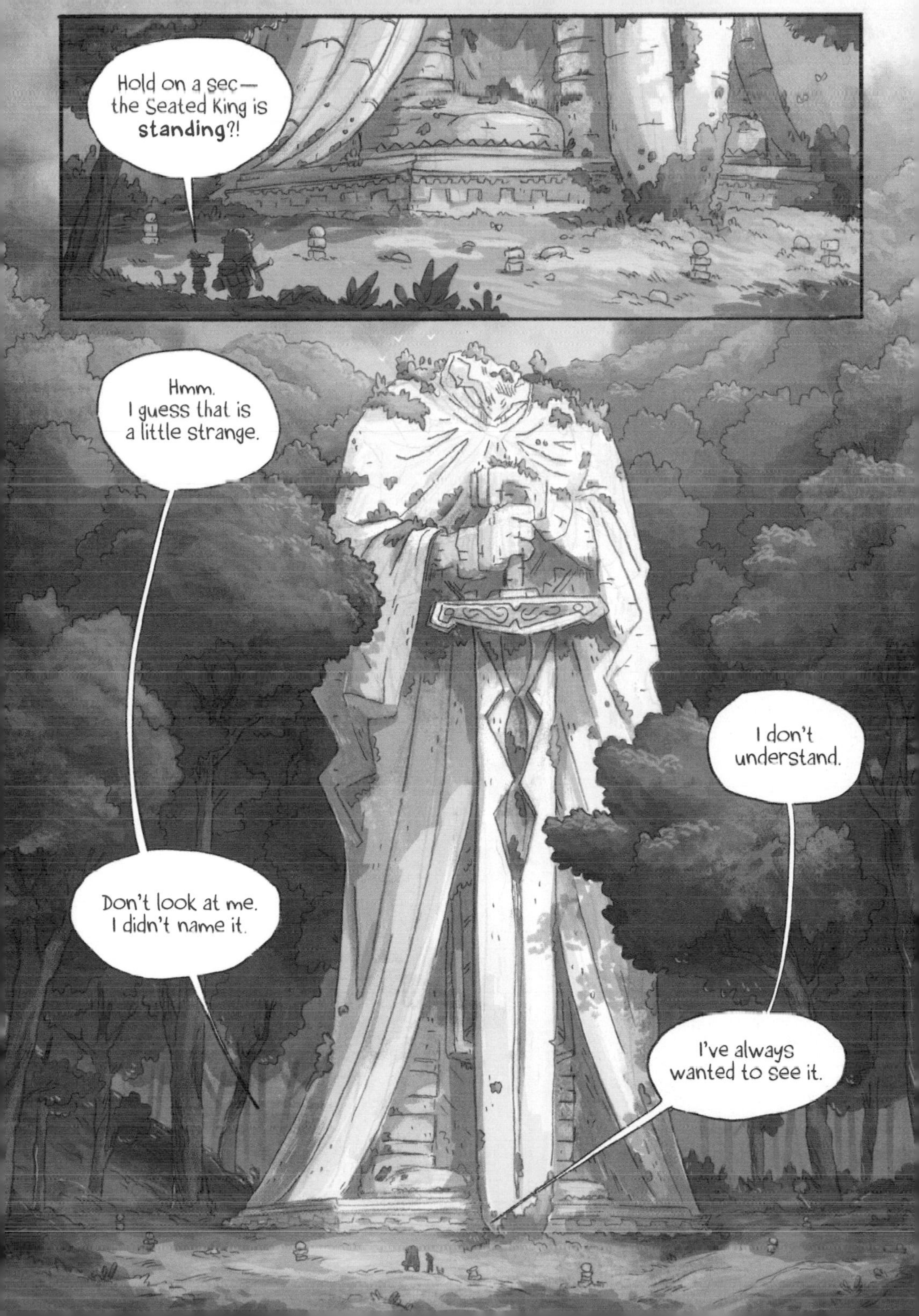
Hold on a sec—the Seated King is **standing**?!
Hmm. I guess that is a little strange.
Don't look at me. I didn't name it.
I don't understand.
I've always wanted to see it.

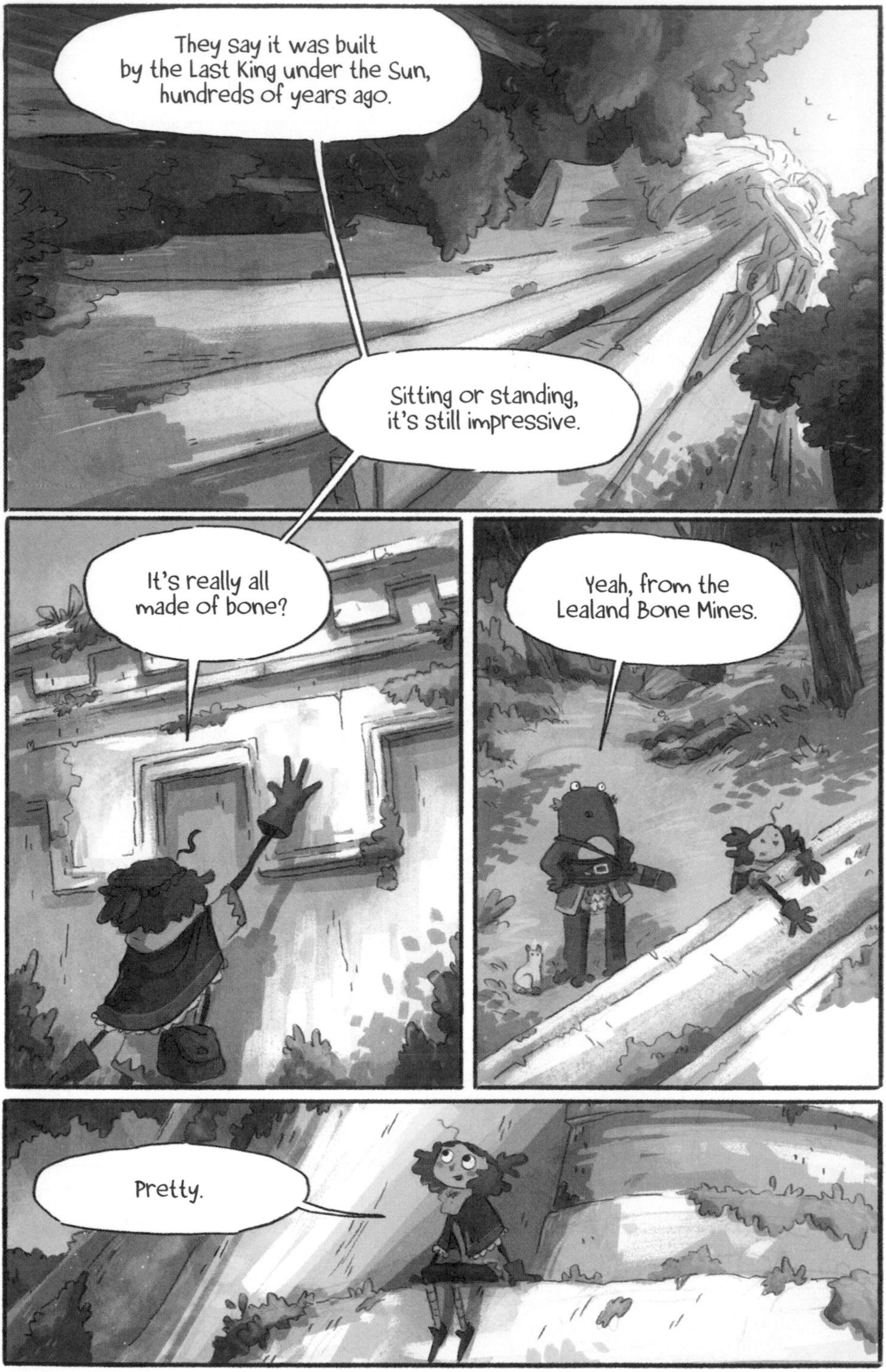
They say it was built by the Last King under the Sun, hundreds of years ago.
Sitting or standing, it's still impressive.
It's really all made of bone?
Yeah, from the Lealand Bone Mines.
Pretty.

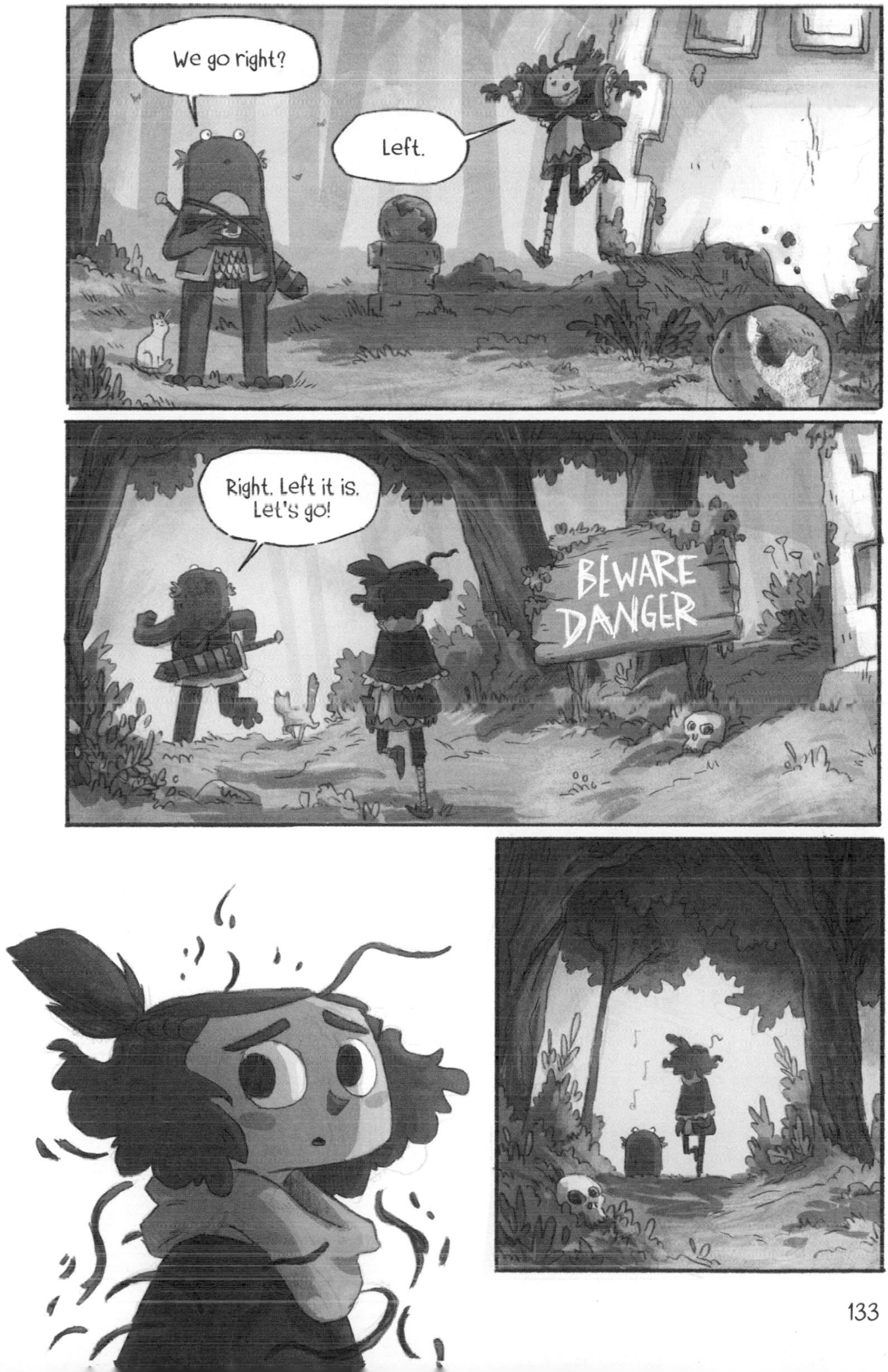
We go right?
Left.
Right. Left it is. Let's go!
BEWARE DANGER

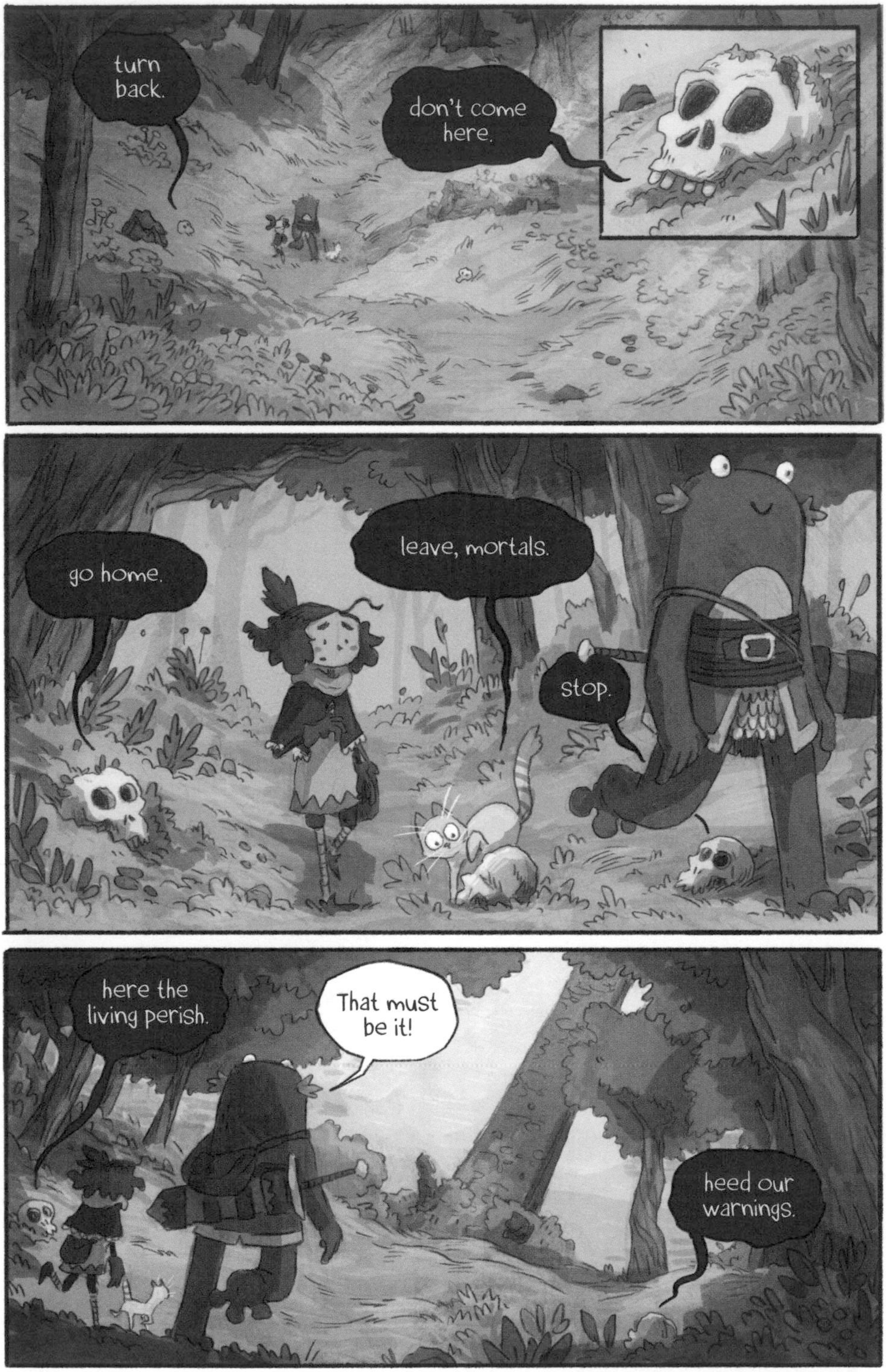
turn back.
don't come here.
go home.
leave, mortals.
stop.
here the living perish.
That must be it!
heed our warnings.

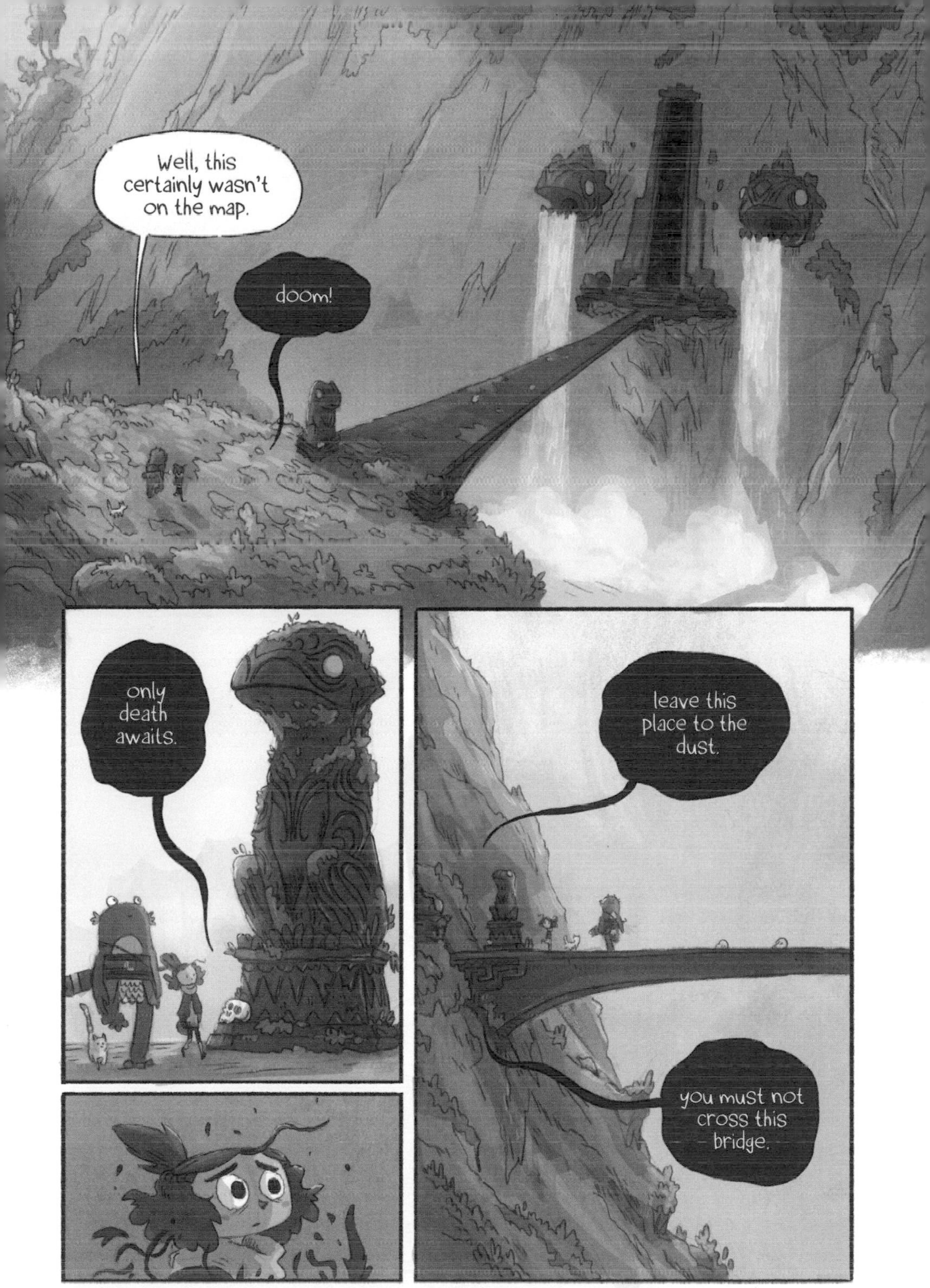

Well, this certainly wasn't on the map.
doom!
only death awaits.
leave this place to the dust.
you must not cross this bridge.

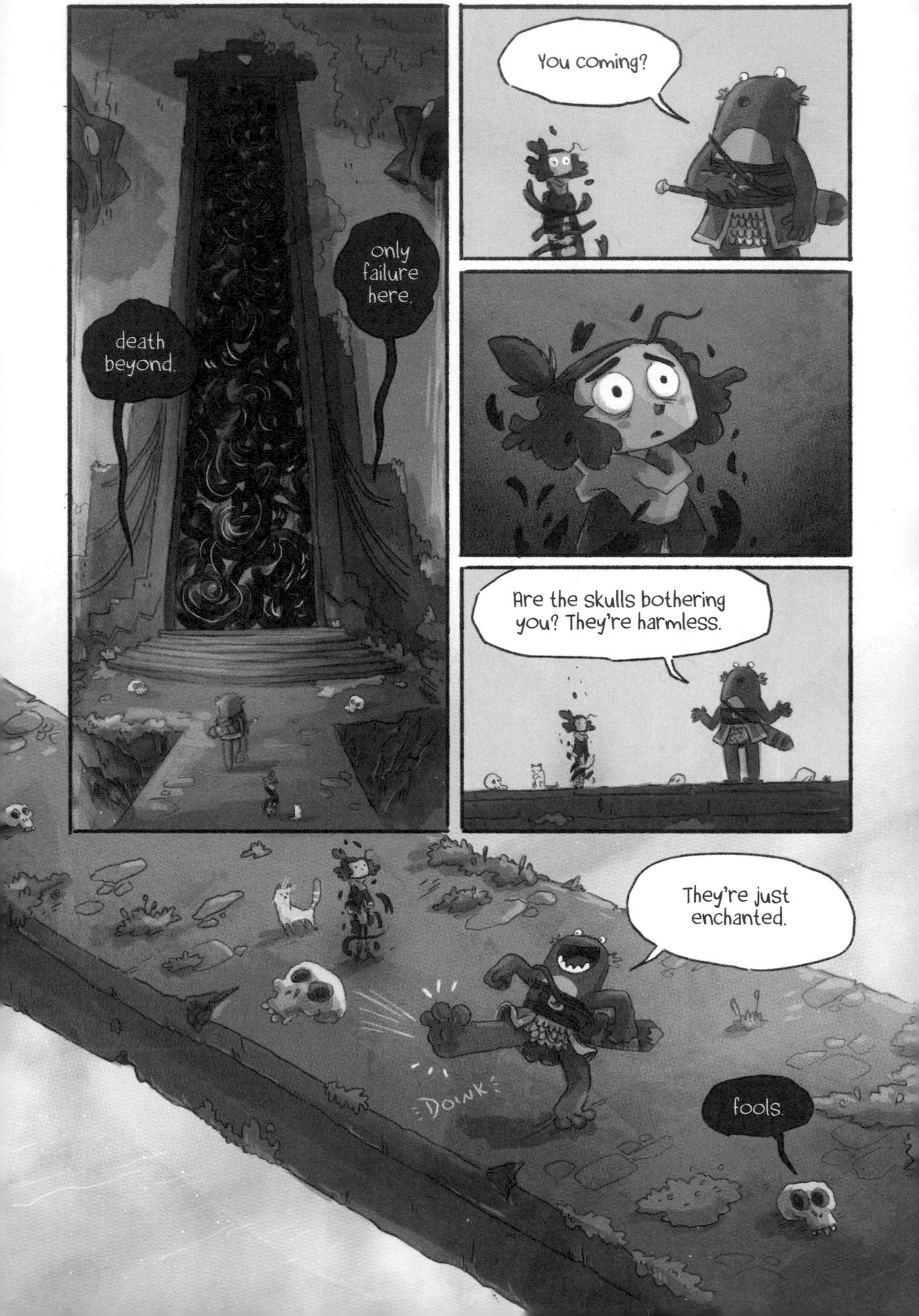
only failure here.
death beyond.
You coming?
Are the skulls bothering you? They're harmless.
They're just enchanted.
DOINK
fools.

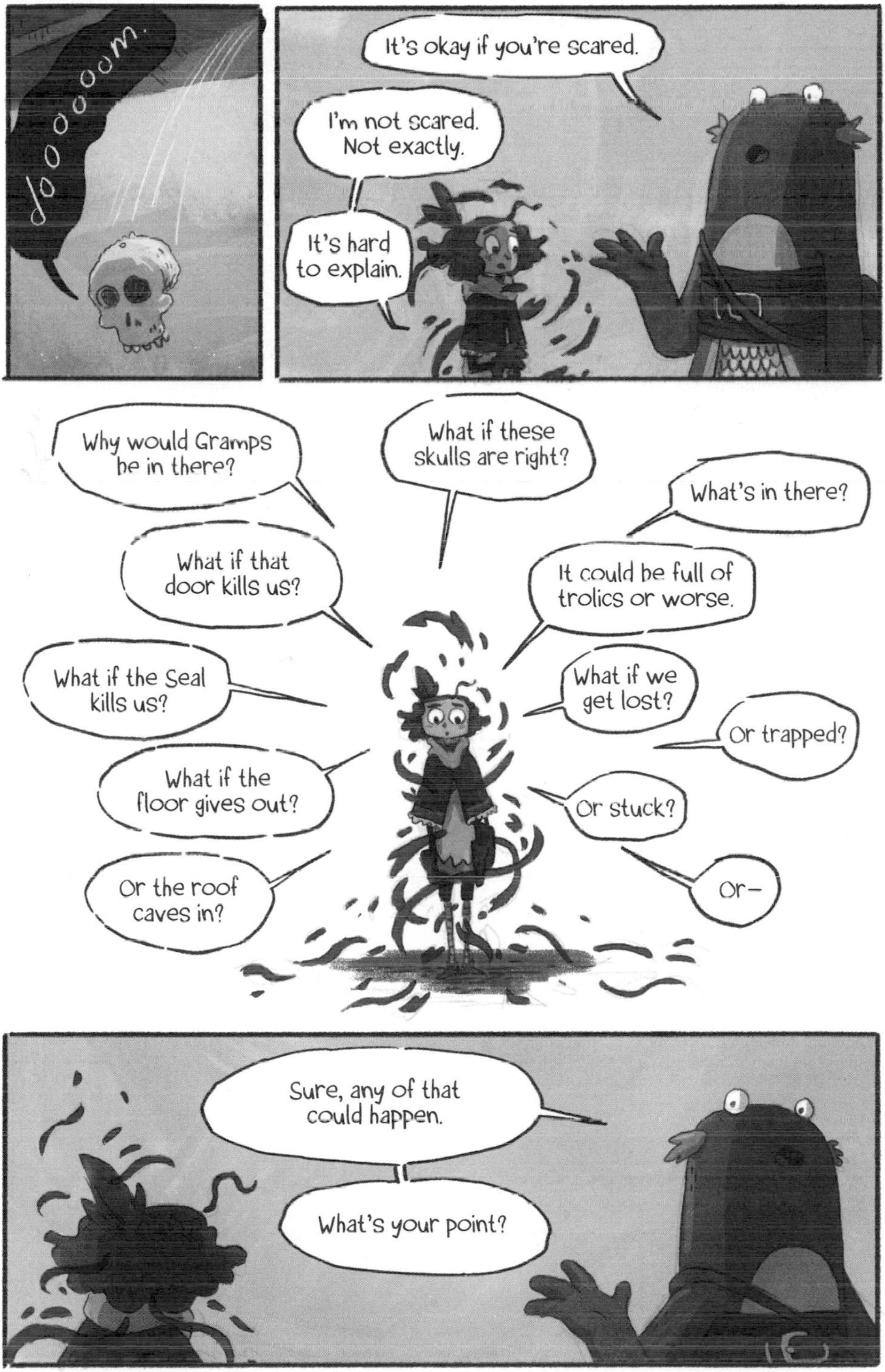
Doooom.
It's okay if you're scared.
I'm not scared. Not exactly.
It's hard to explain.
Why would Gramps be in there?
What if these skulls are right?
What's in there?
What if that door kills us?
It could be full of trolics or worse.
What if the Seal kills us?
What if we get lost?
Or trapped?
What if the floor gives out?
Or stuck?
Or the roof caves in?
Or–
Sure, any of that could happen.
What's your point?

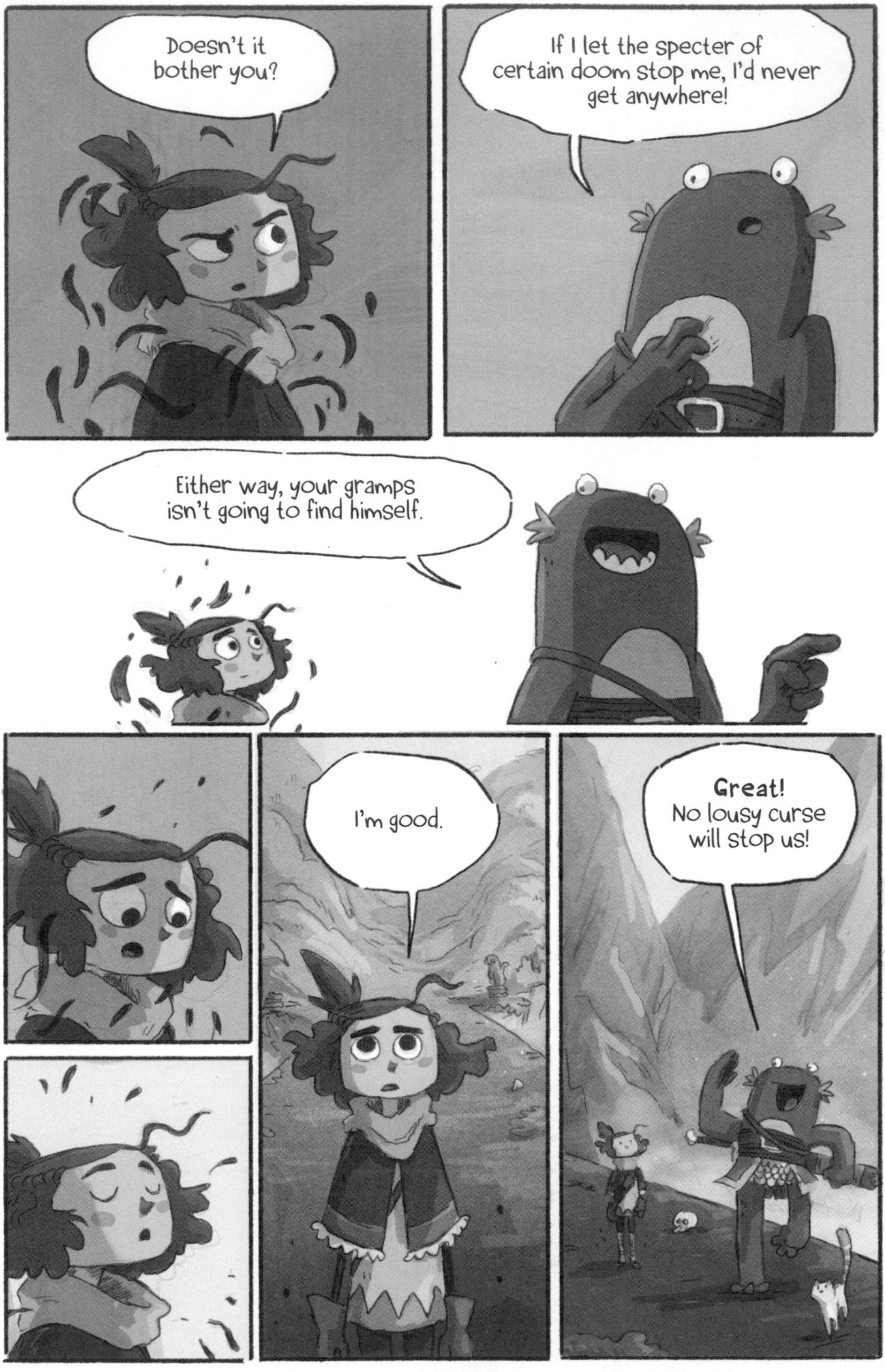

Doesn't it bother you?
If I let the specter of certain doom stop me, I'd never get anywhere!
Either way, your gramps isn't going to find himself.
I'm good.
Great! No lousy curse will stop us!

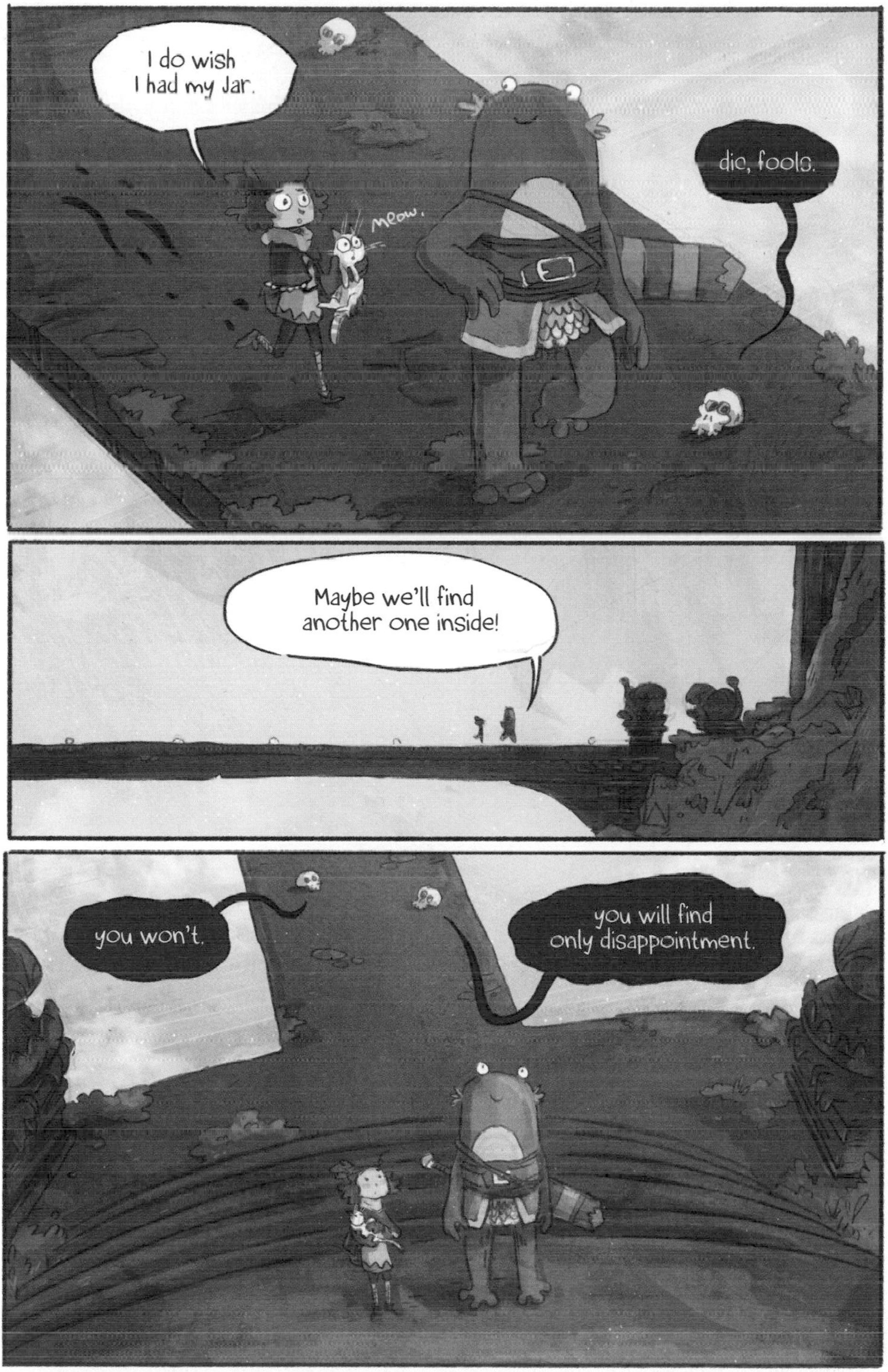
I do wish
I had my Jar.
meow.
die, fools.
Maybe we'll find
another one inside!
you won't.
you will find
only disappointment.

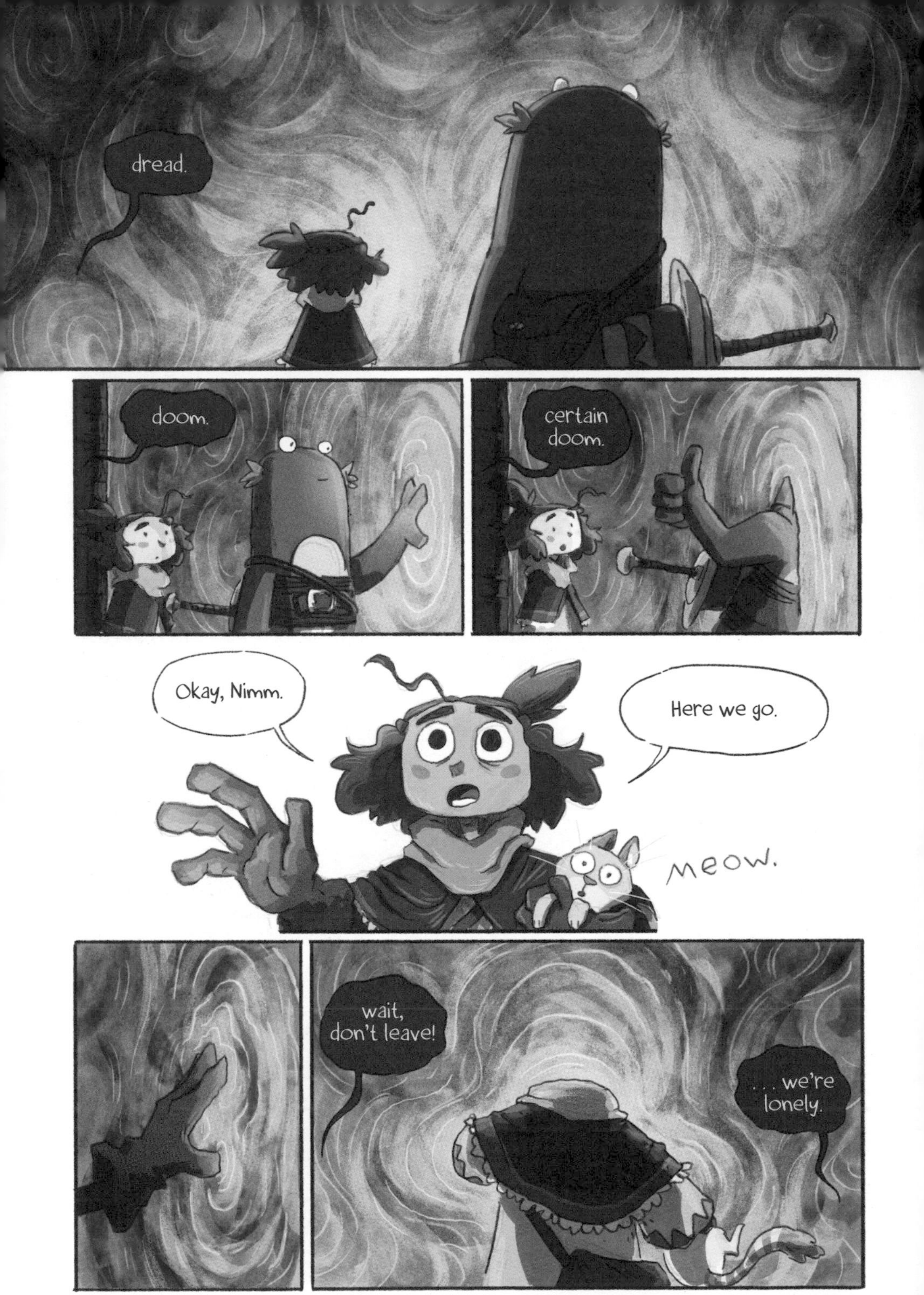
dread.
doom.
certain doom.
Okay, Nimm.
Here we go.
meow.
wait, don't leave!
. . . we're lonely.

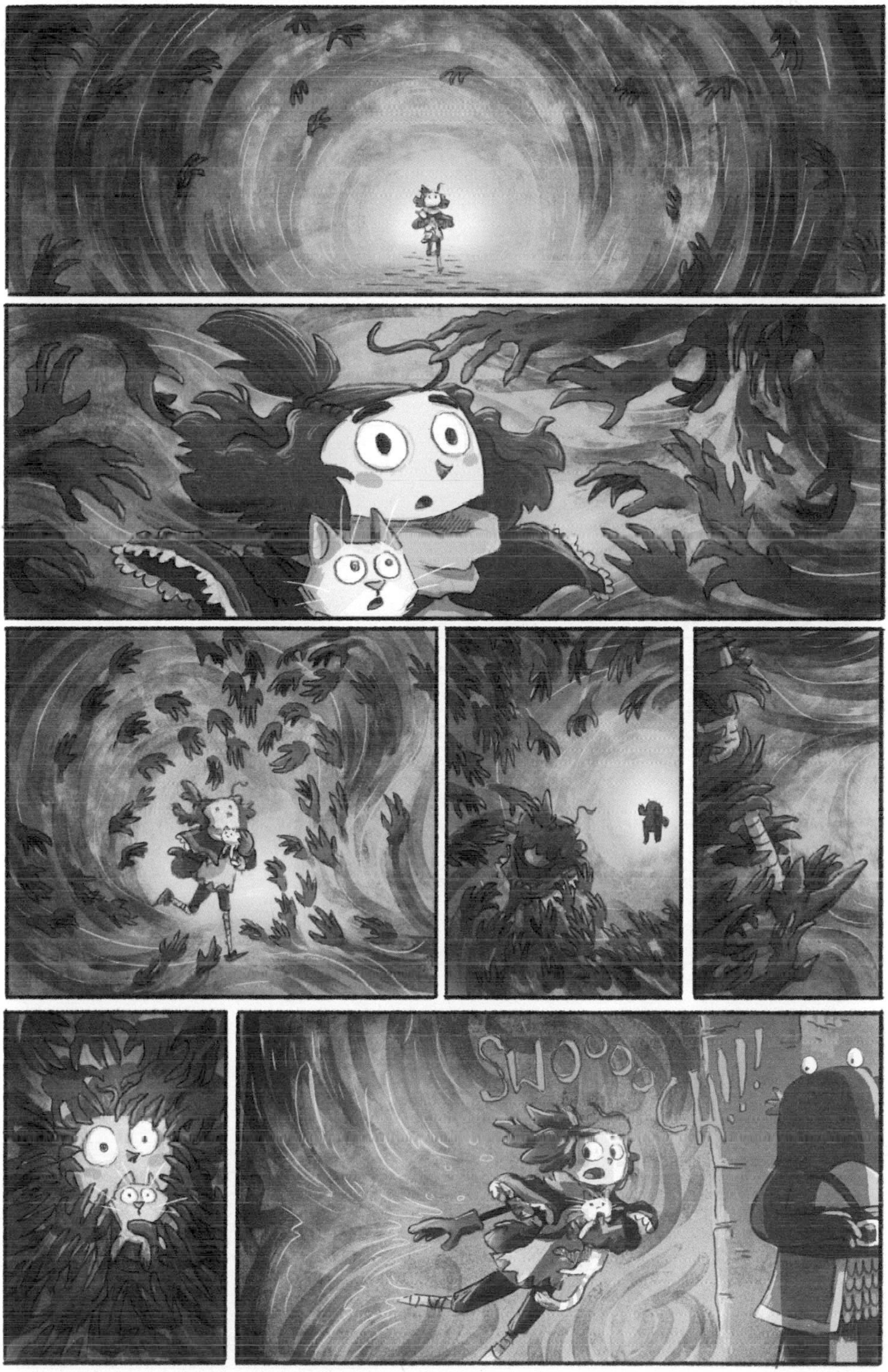
SWOOOOCH!!

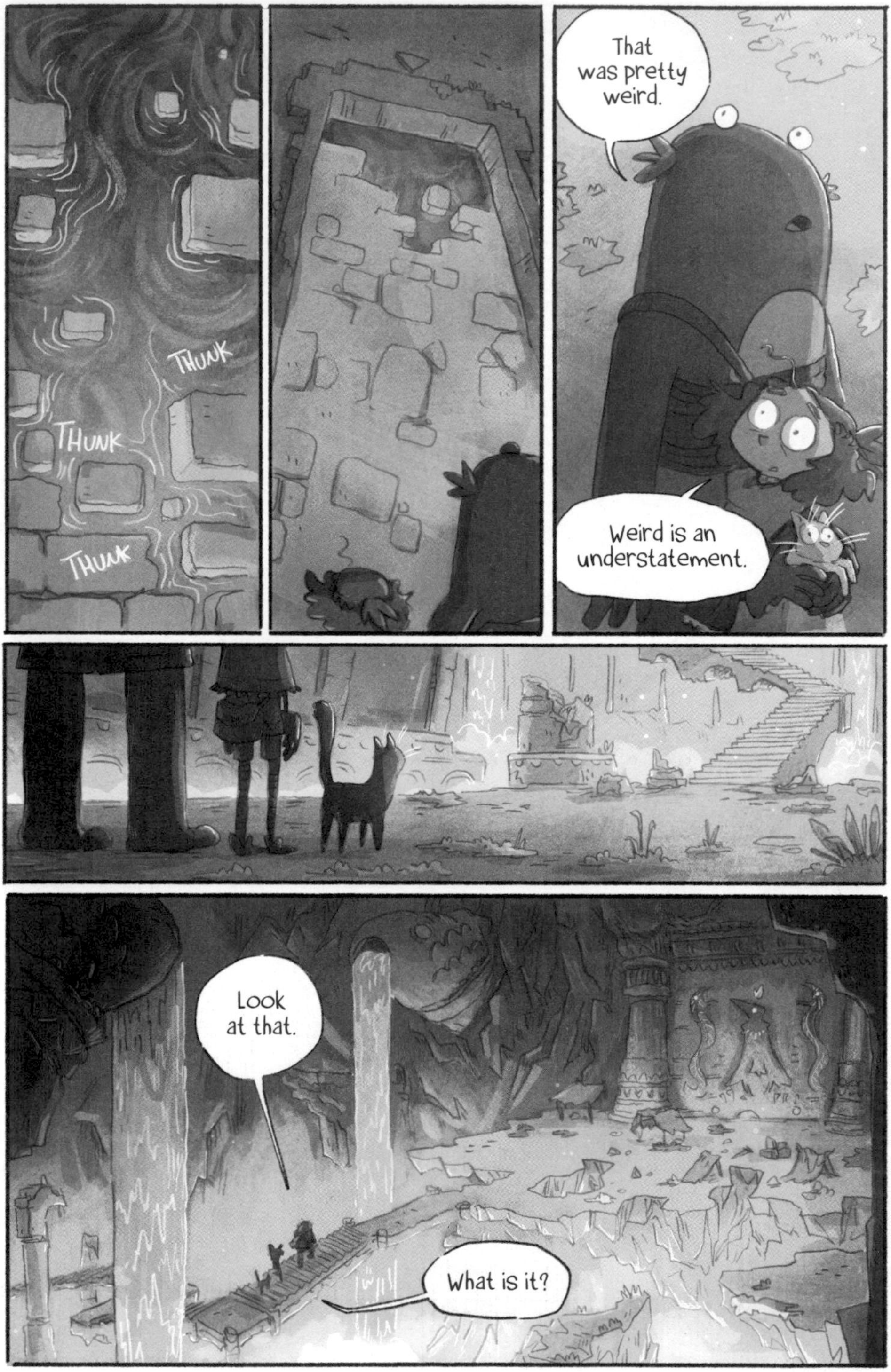
THUNK
THUNK
THUNK
That was pretty weird.
Weird is an understatement.
Look at that.
What is it?

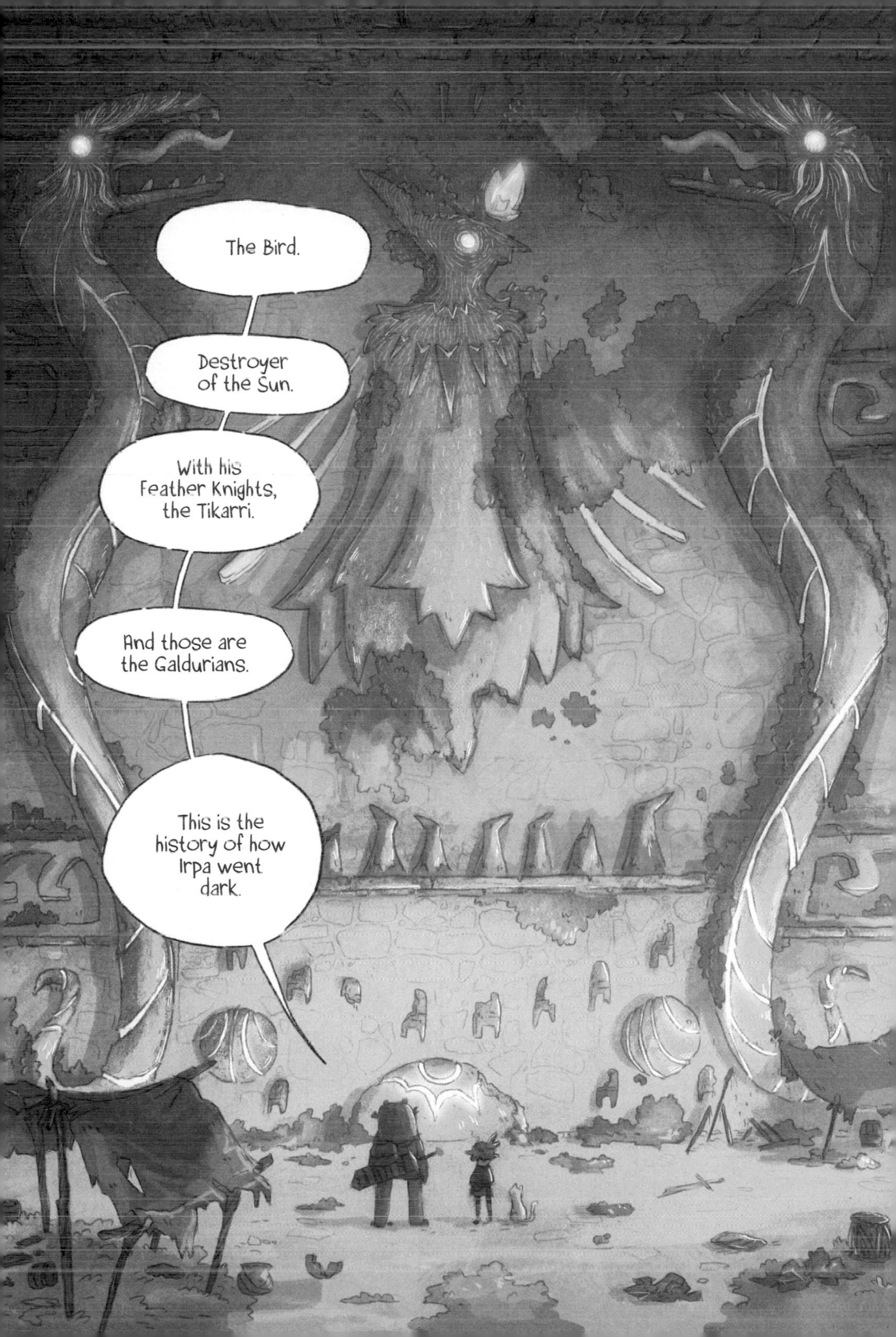
The Bird.
Destroyer of the Sun.
With his Feather Knights, the Tikarri.
And those are the Galdurians.
This is the history of how Irpa went dark.

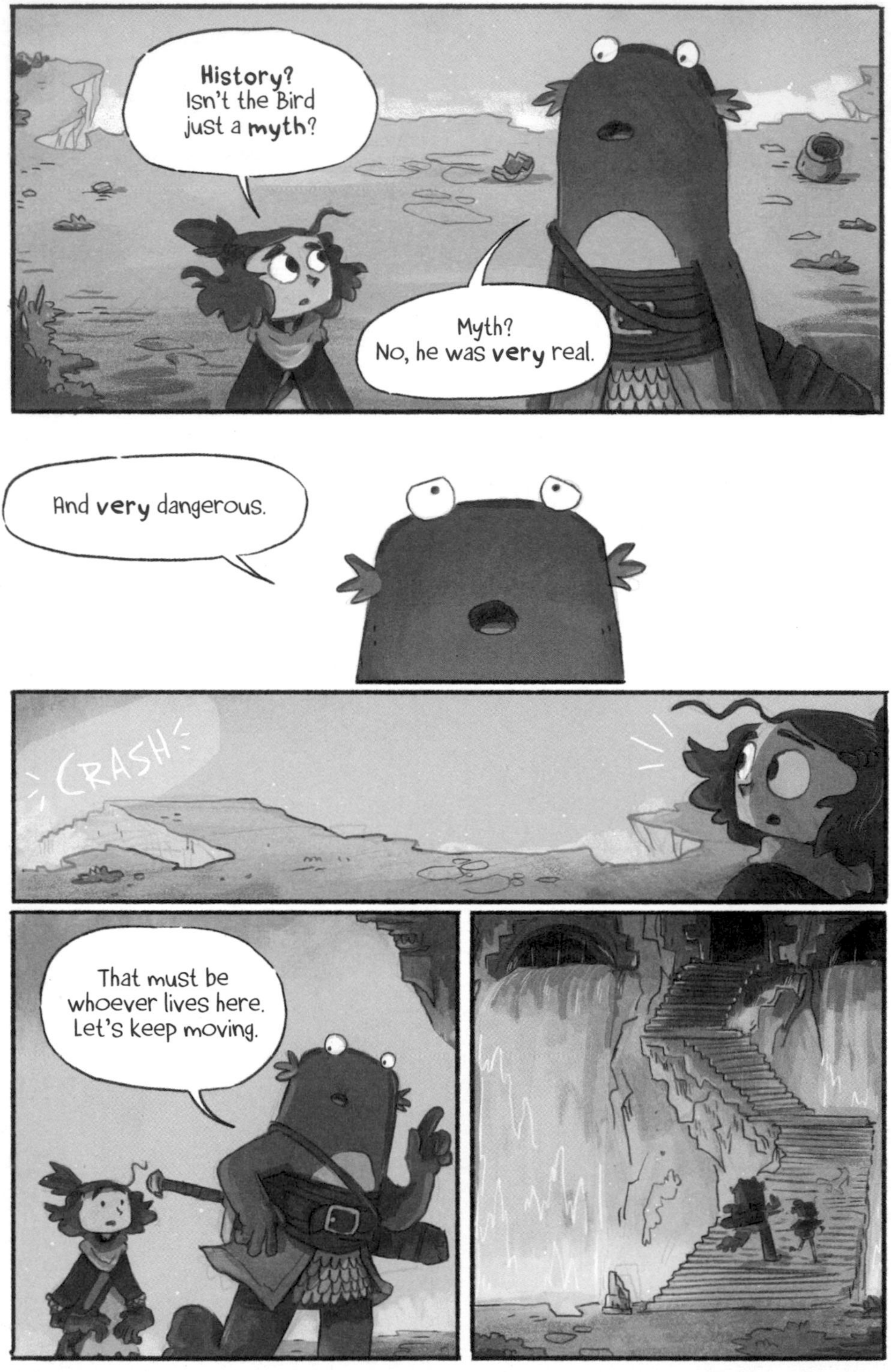
History? Isn't the Bird just a myth?
Myth? No, he was very real.
And very dangerous.
CRASH
That must be whoever lives here. Let's keep moving.

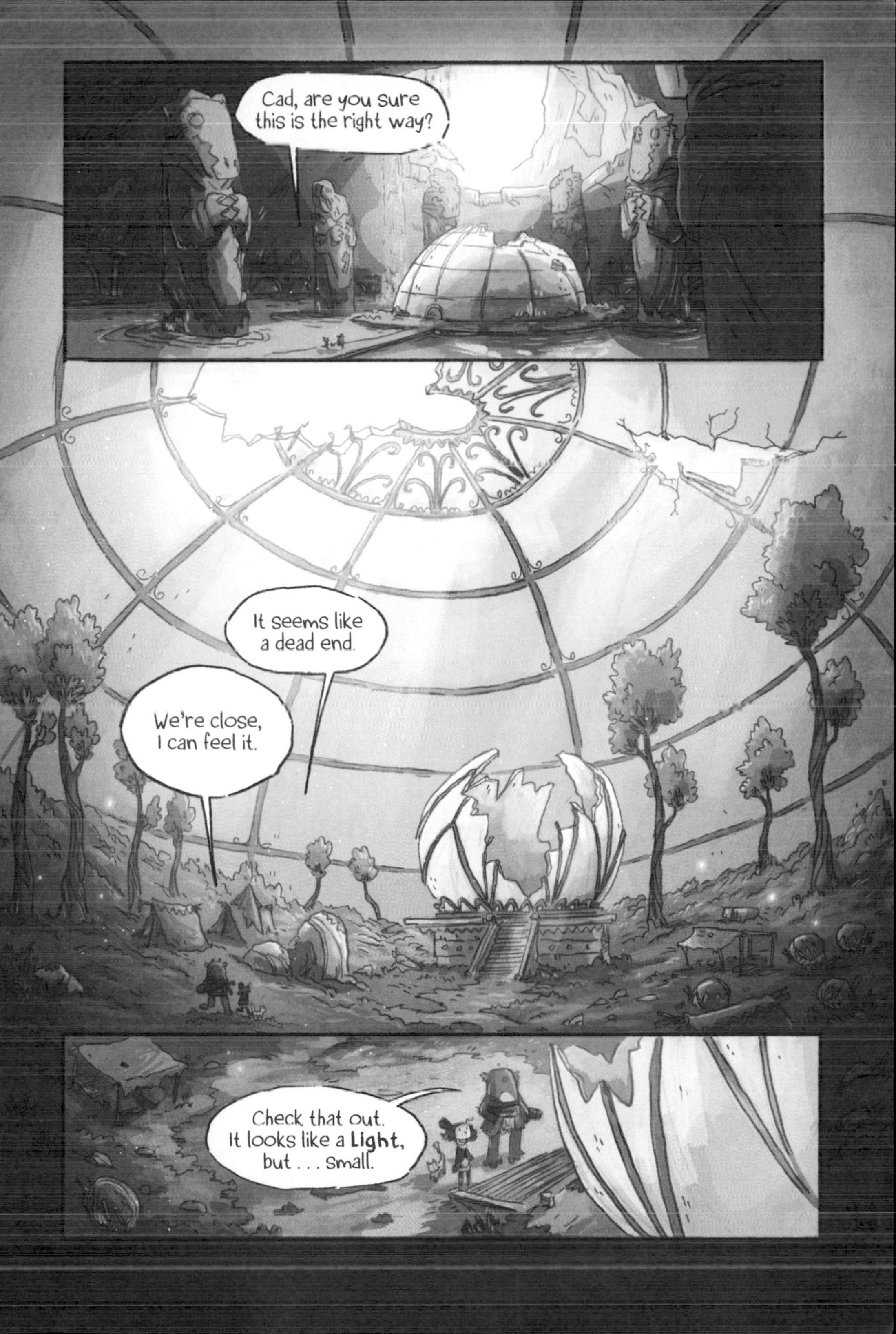
Cad, are you sure this is the right way?
It seems like a dead end.
We're close, I can feel it.
Check that out. It looks like a **Light**, but . . . small.

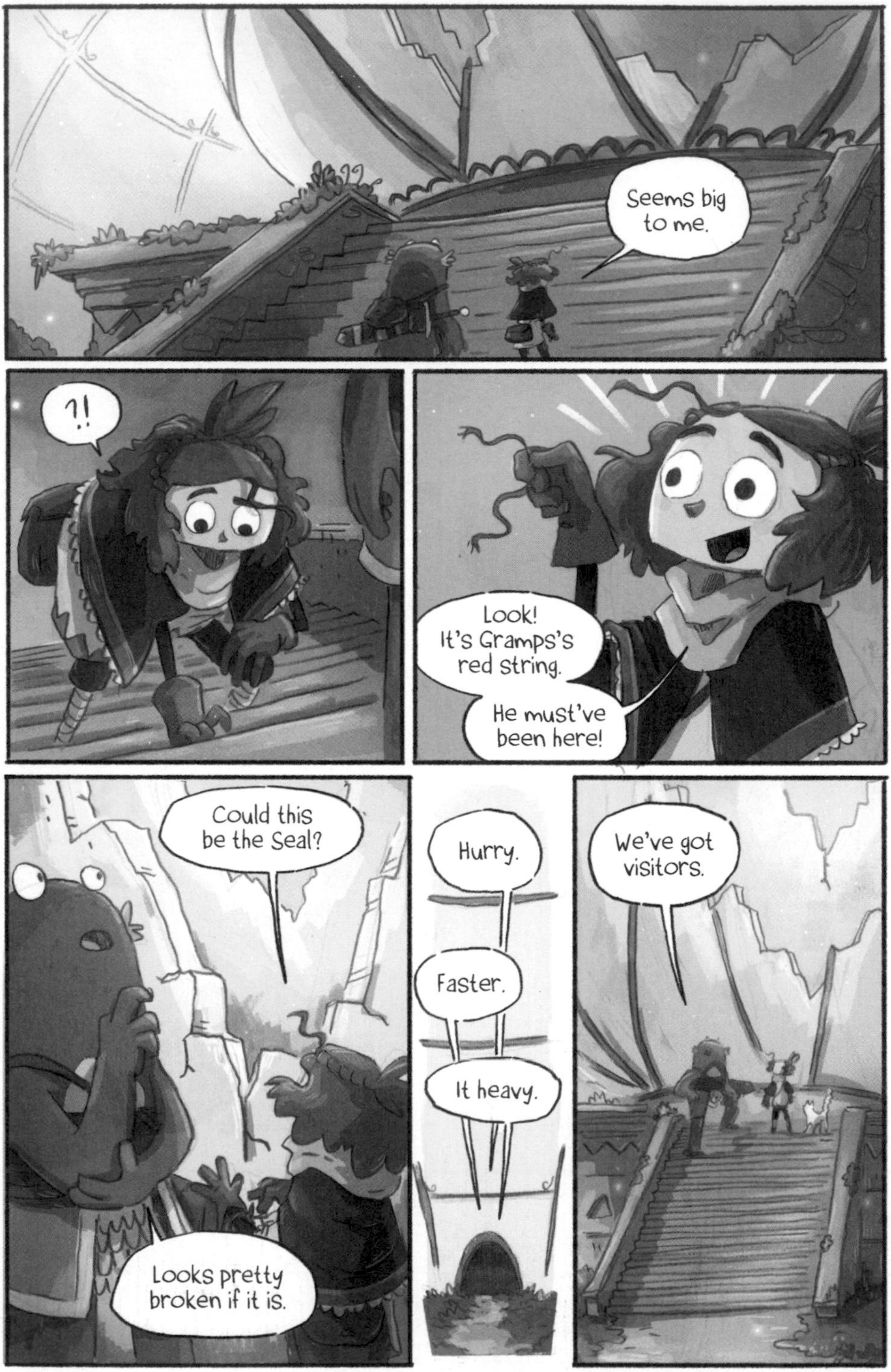
Seems big to me.
?!
Look! It's Gramps's red string.
He must've been here!
Could this be the Seal?
Looks pretty broken if it is.
Hurry.
Faster.
It heavy.
We've got visitors.

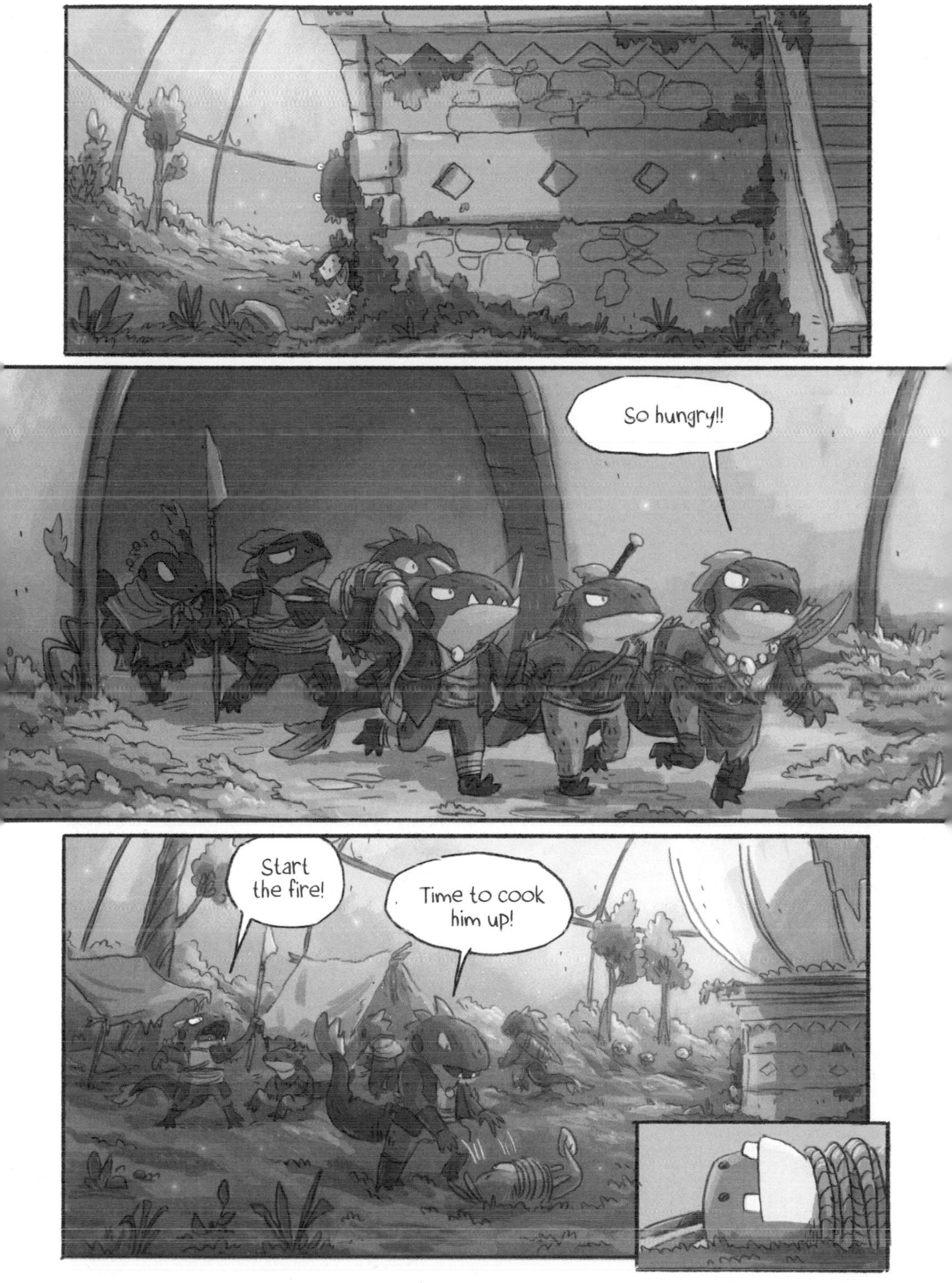
So hungry!!
Start the fire!
Time to cook him up!

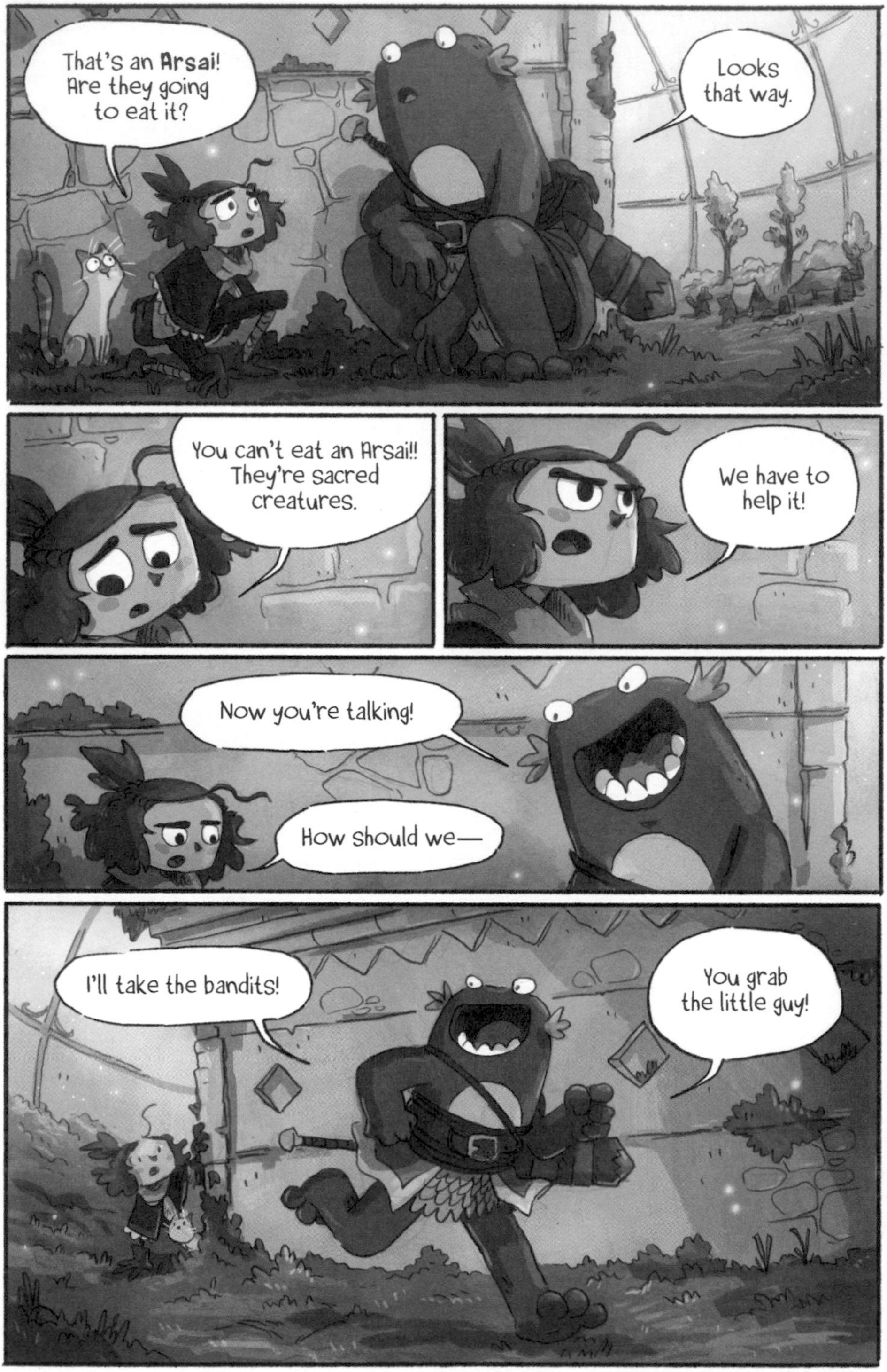
That's an **Arsai**! Are they going to eat it?
Looks that way.
You can't eat an Arsai!! They're sacred creatures.
We have to help it!
Now you're talking!
How should we—
I'll take the bandits!
You grab the little guy!

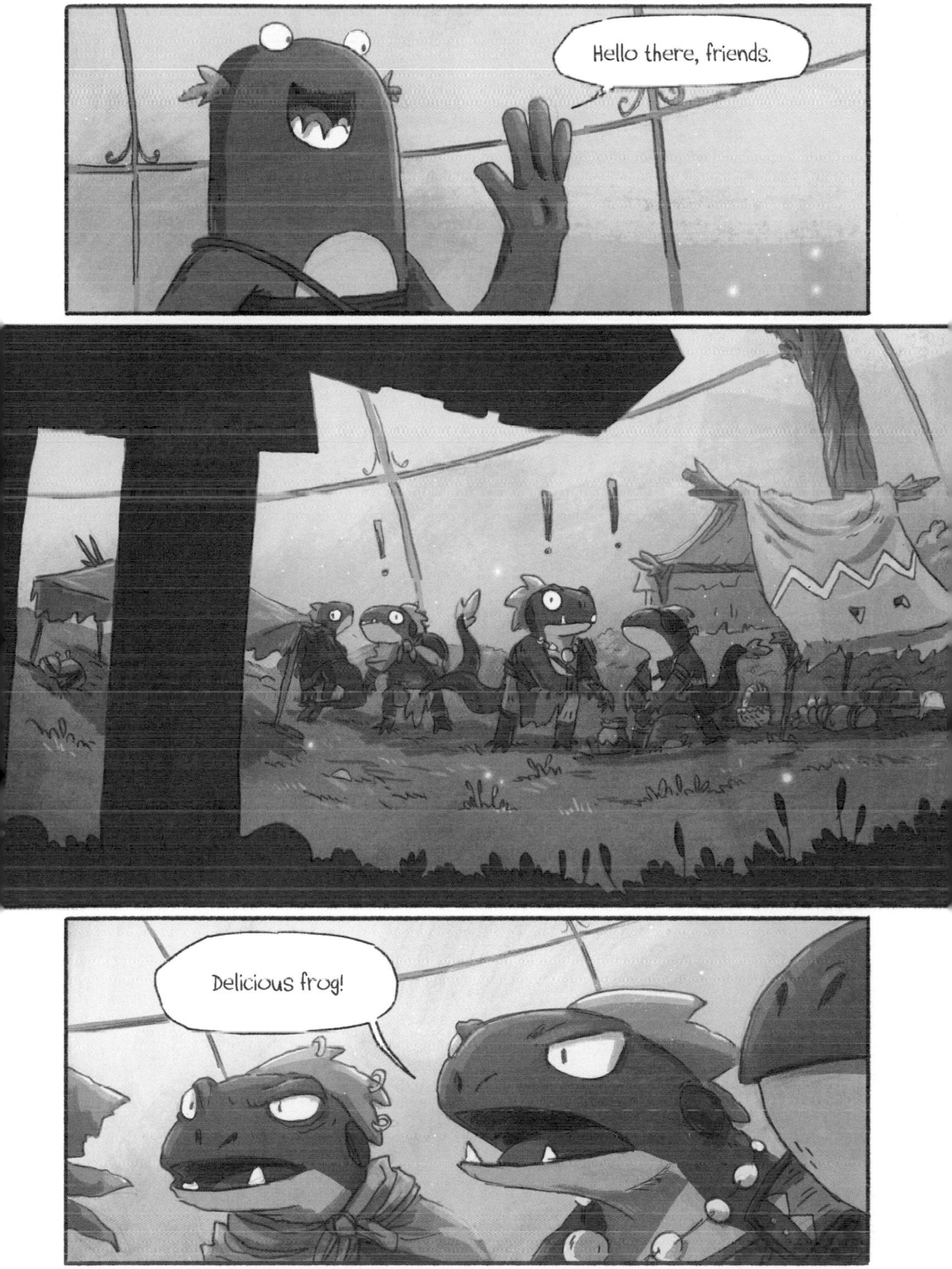
Hello there, friends.
!
!
!
Delicious frog!

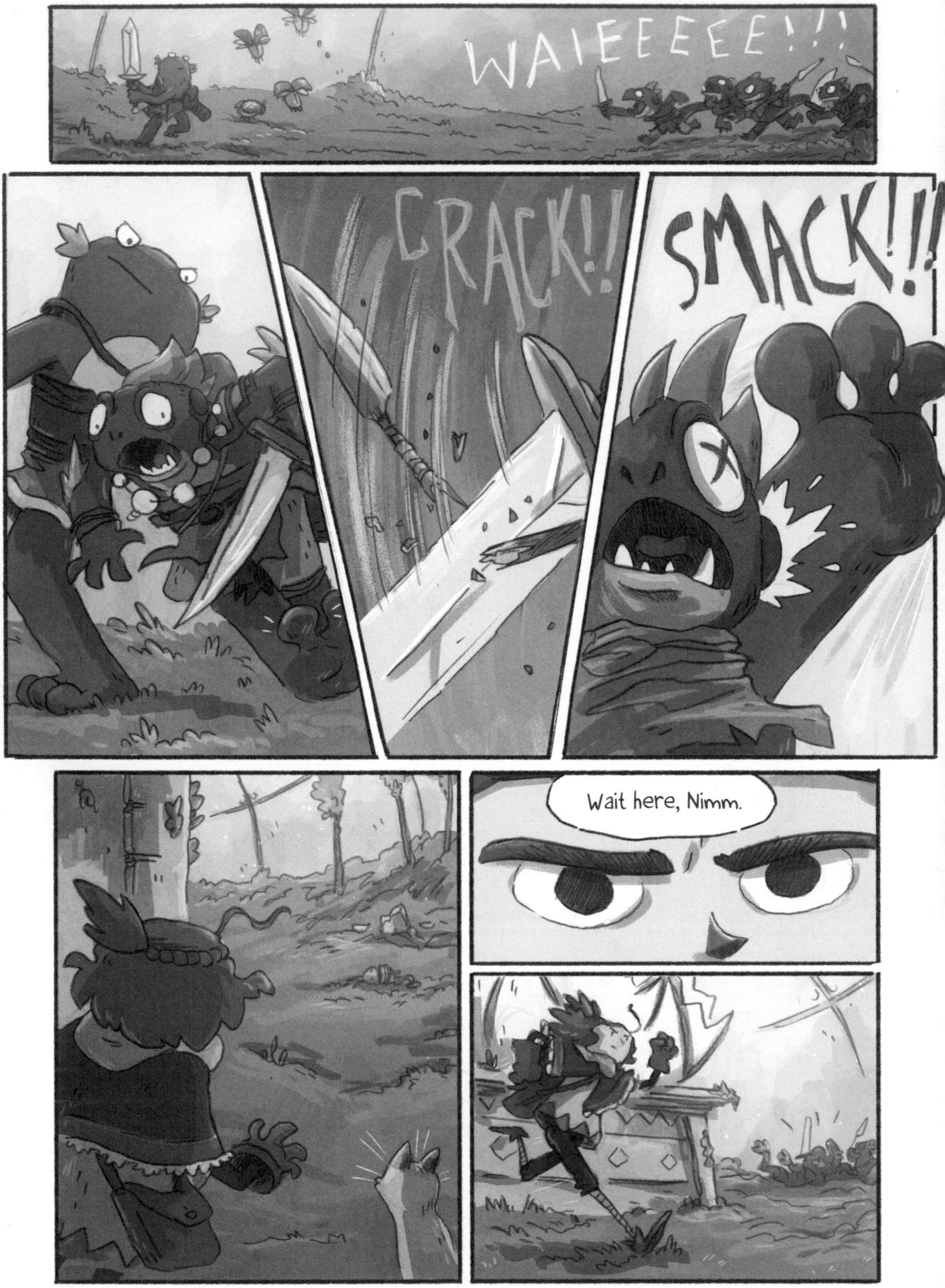
WAIEEEEE!!!
CRACK!!
SMACK!!!
Wait here, Nimm.

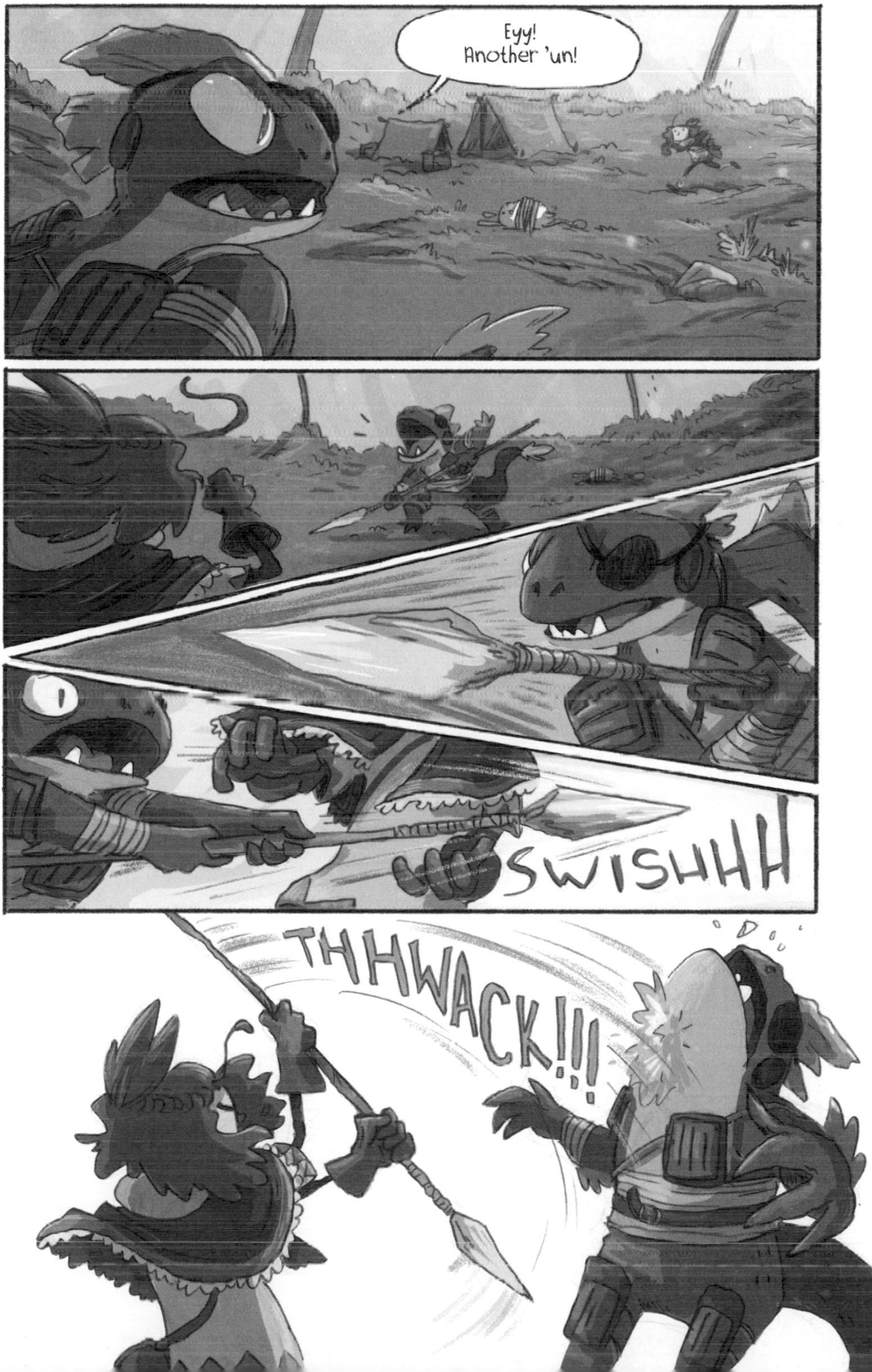
Eyy!
Another 'un!
SWISHHH
THHWACK!!!

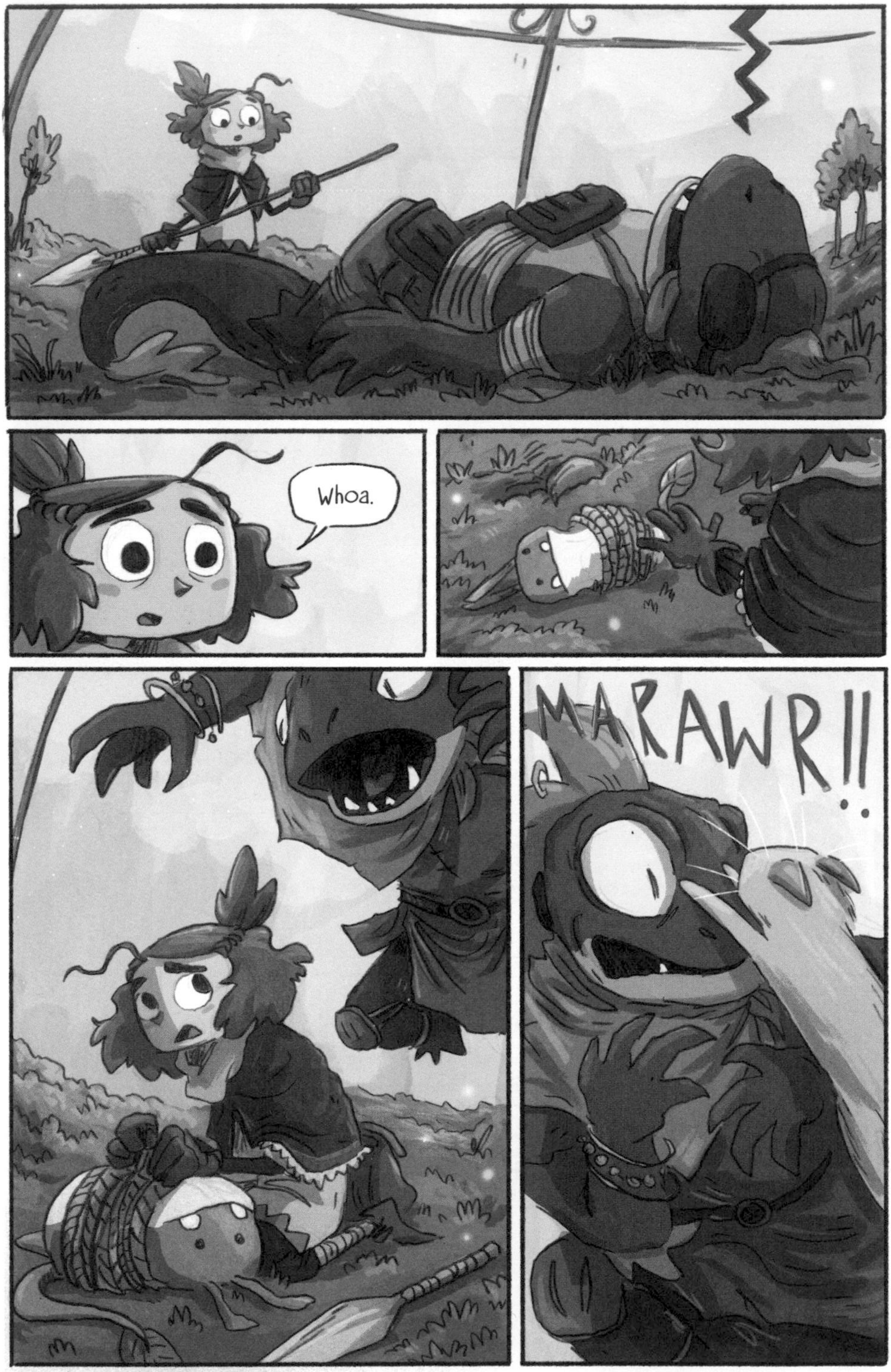
Whoa.
MARAWR!!

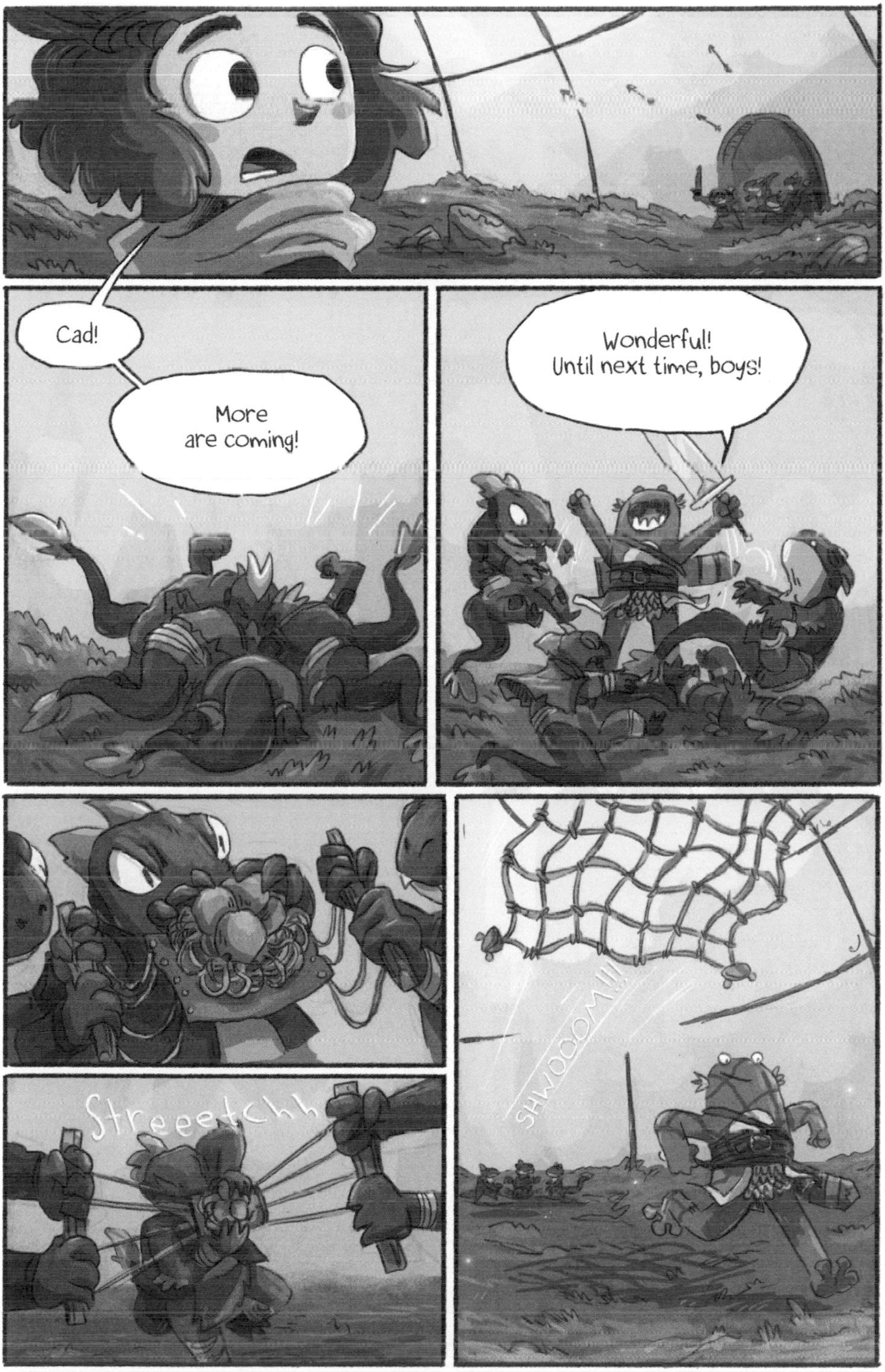
Cad!
More are coming!
Wonderful! Until next time, boys!
Streeetchh
SHWOOOM!!!

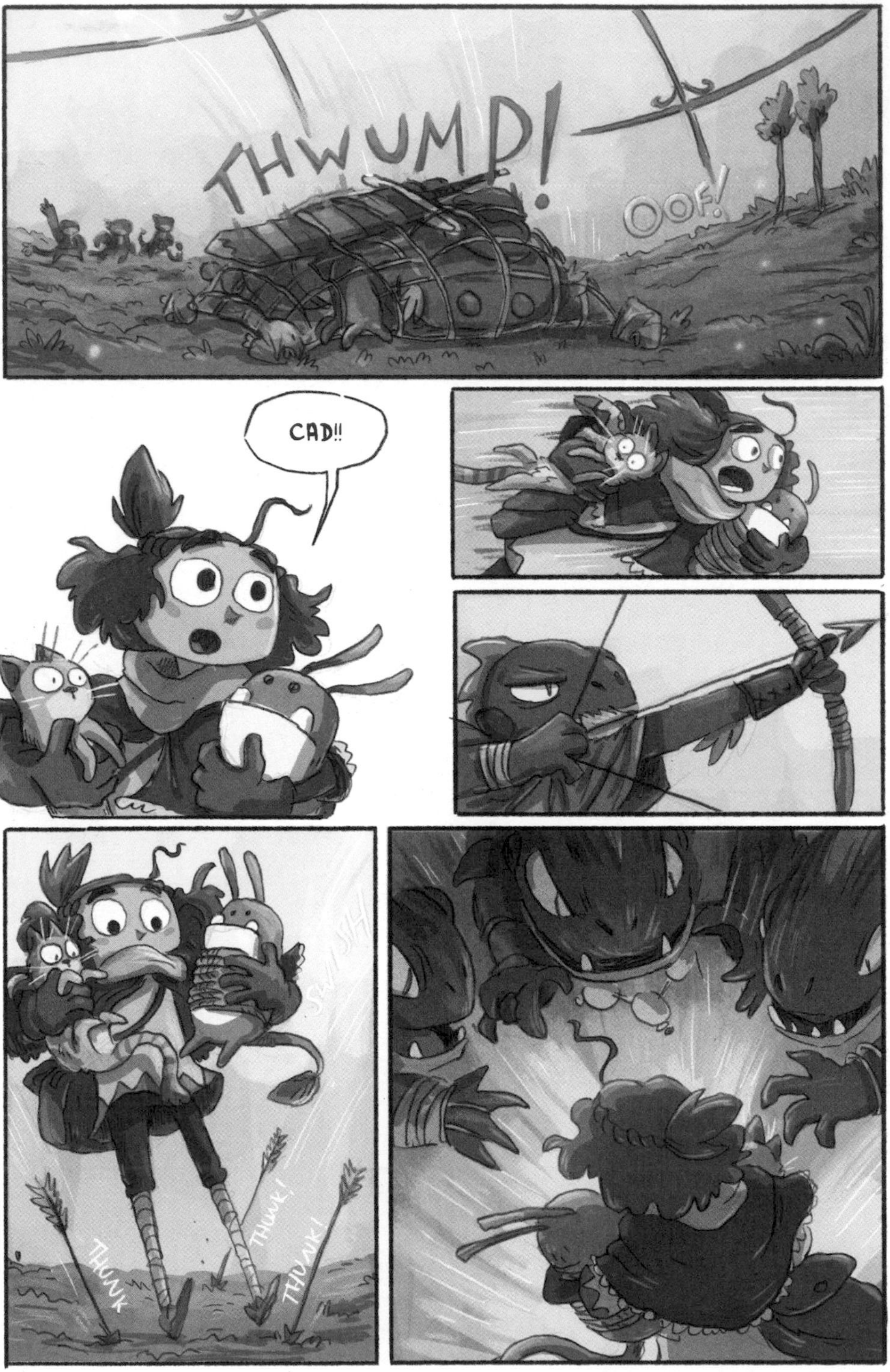
THWUMP!
OOF!
CAD!!
SWISH
THUNK
THUNK!
THUNK!

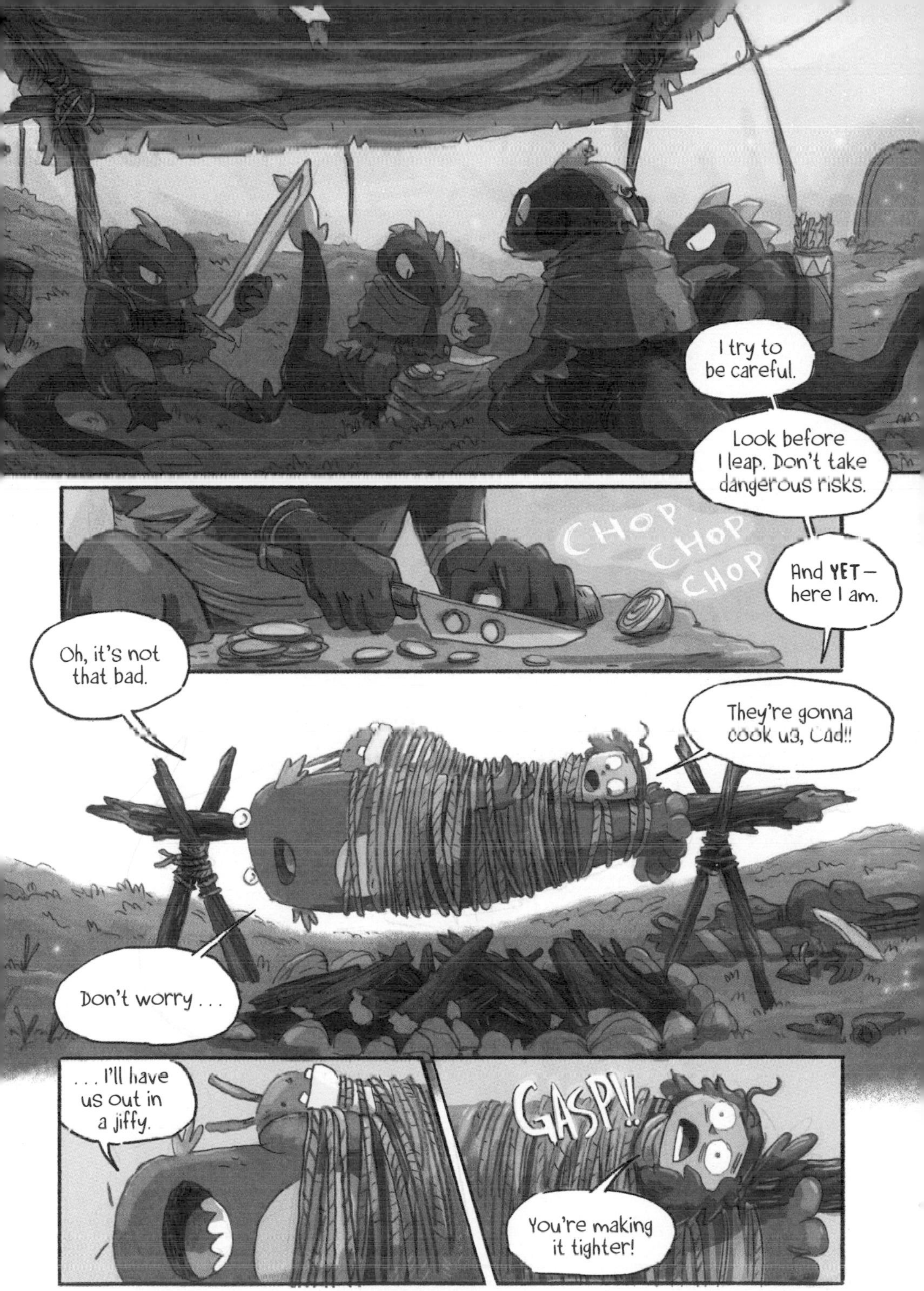
I try to be careful.
Look before I leap. Don't take dangerous risks.
CHOP CHOP CHOP
And YET— here I am.
Oh, it's not that bad.
They're gonna cook us, Cad!!
Don't worry . . .
. . . I'll have us out in a jiffy.
GASP!!
You're making it tighter!

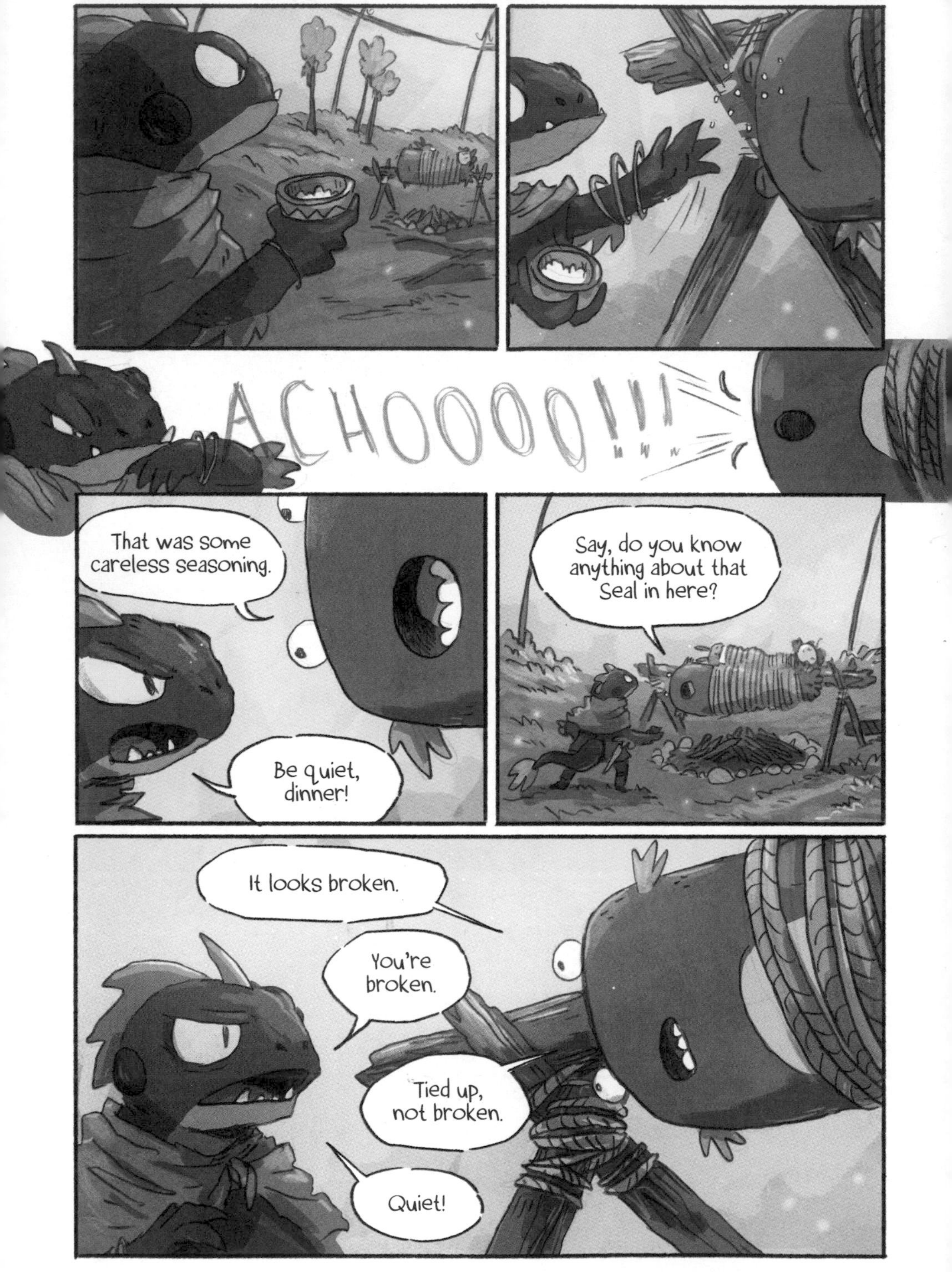
ACHOOOO!!!
That was some careless seasoning.
Be quiet, dinner!
Say, do you know anything about that Seal in here?
It looks broken.
You're broken.
Tied up, not broken.
Quiet!

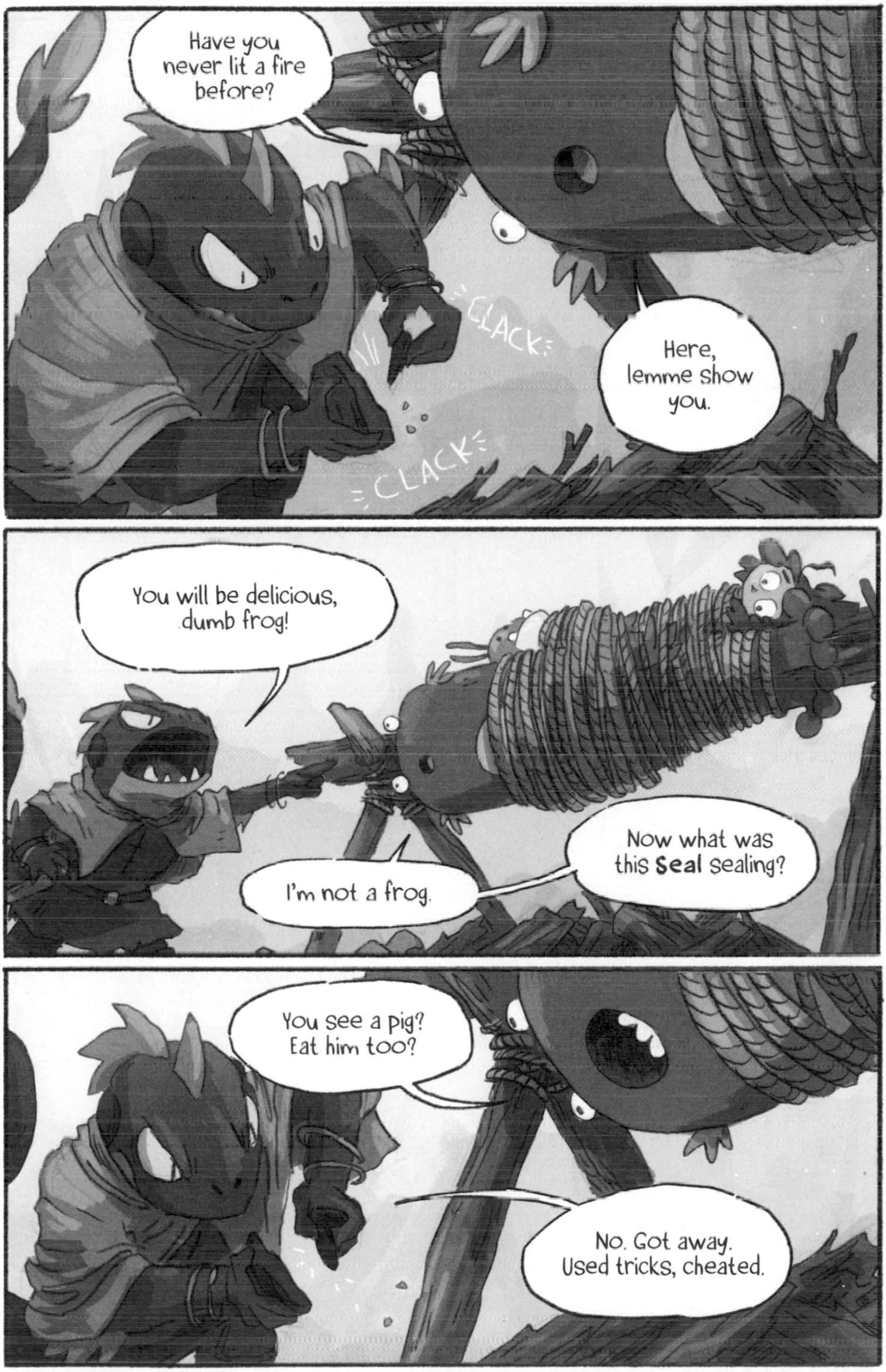

Have you never lit a fire before?
CLACK
CLACK
Here, lemme show you.
You will be delicious, dumb frog!
I'm not a frog.
Now what was this **seal** sealing?
You see a pig? Eat him too?
No. Got away. Used tricks, cheated.

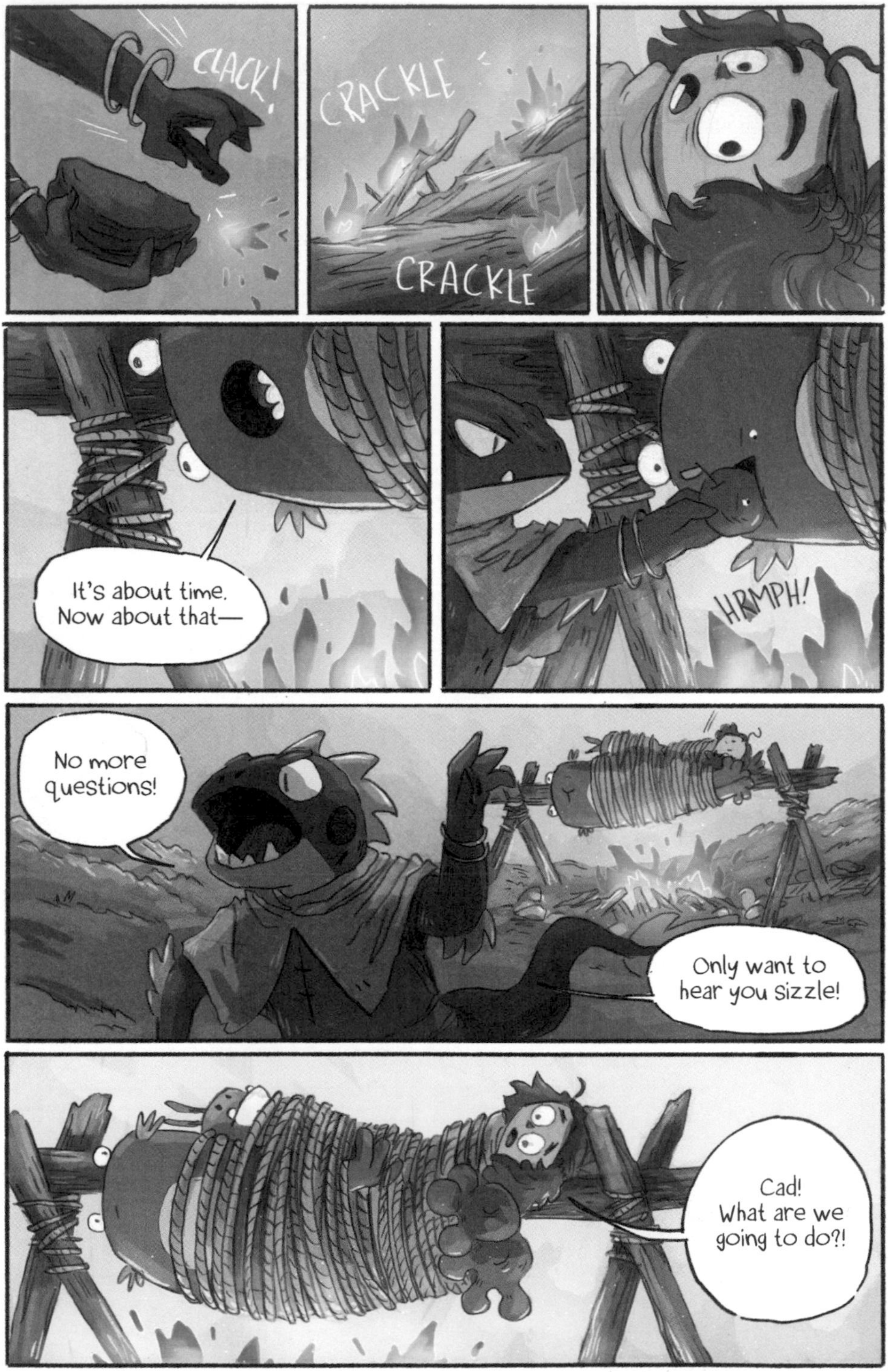
CLACK!
CRACKLE
CRACKLE
It's about time. Now about that—
HRMPH!
No more questions!
Only want to hear you sizzle!
Cad! What are we going to do?!

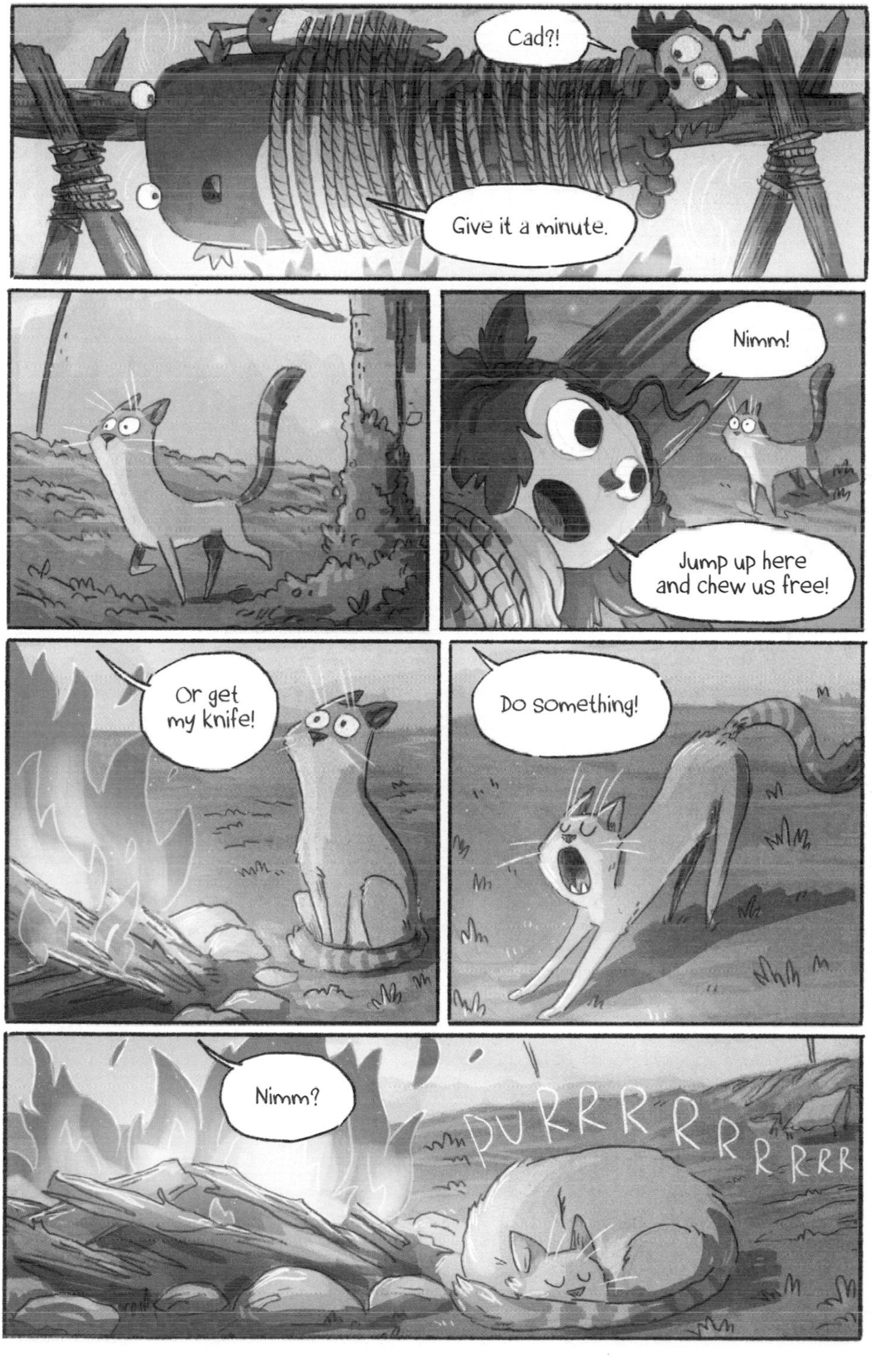
Cad?!
Give it a minute.
Nimm!
Jump up here and chew us free!
Or get my knife!
Do something!
Nimm?
PURRRRRRRRR

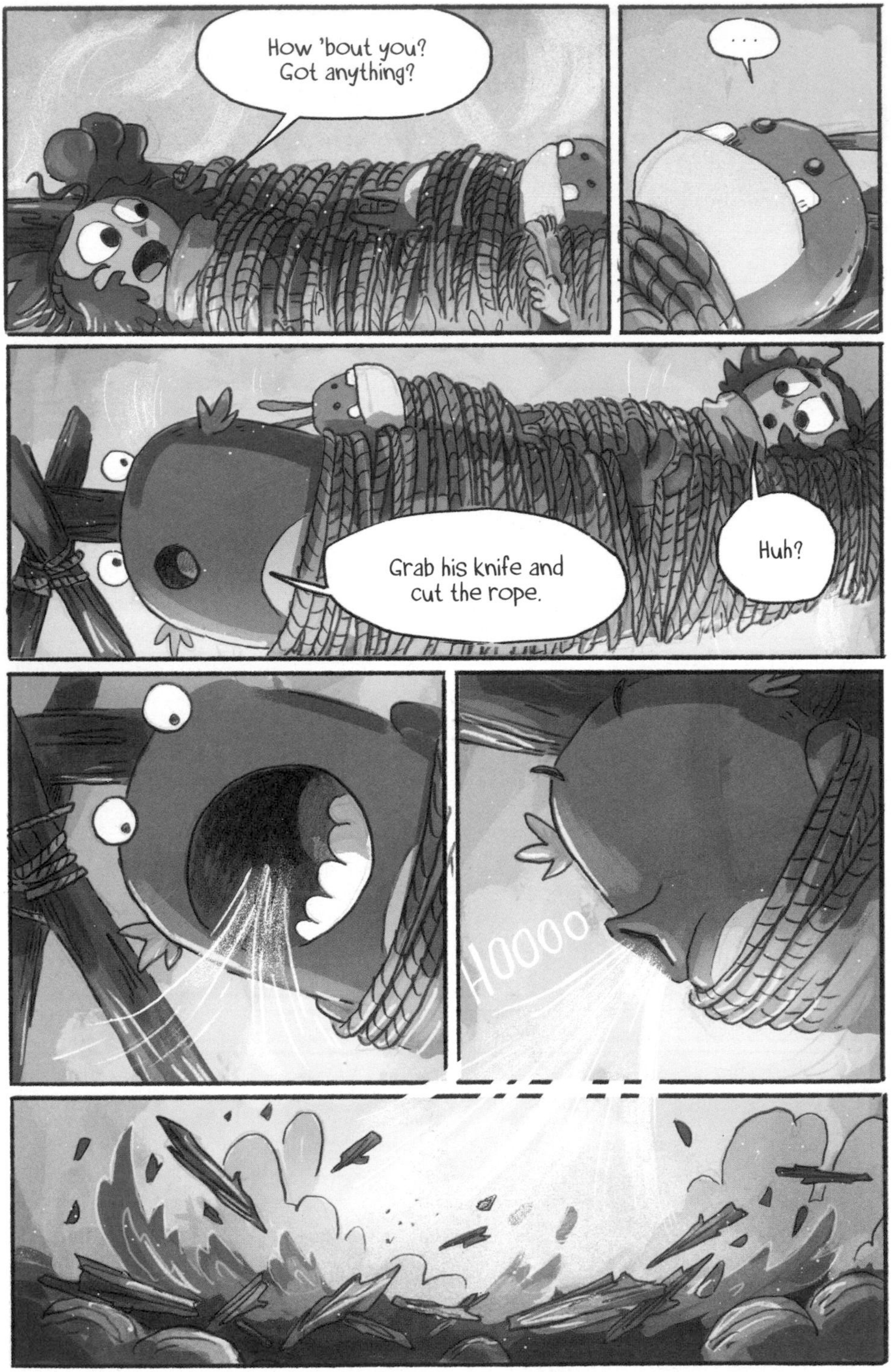
How 'bout you? Got anything?
...
Grab his knife and cut the rope.
Huh?
HOOOO

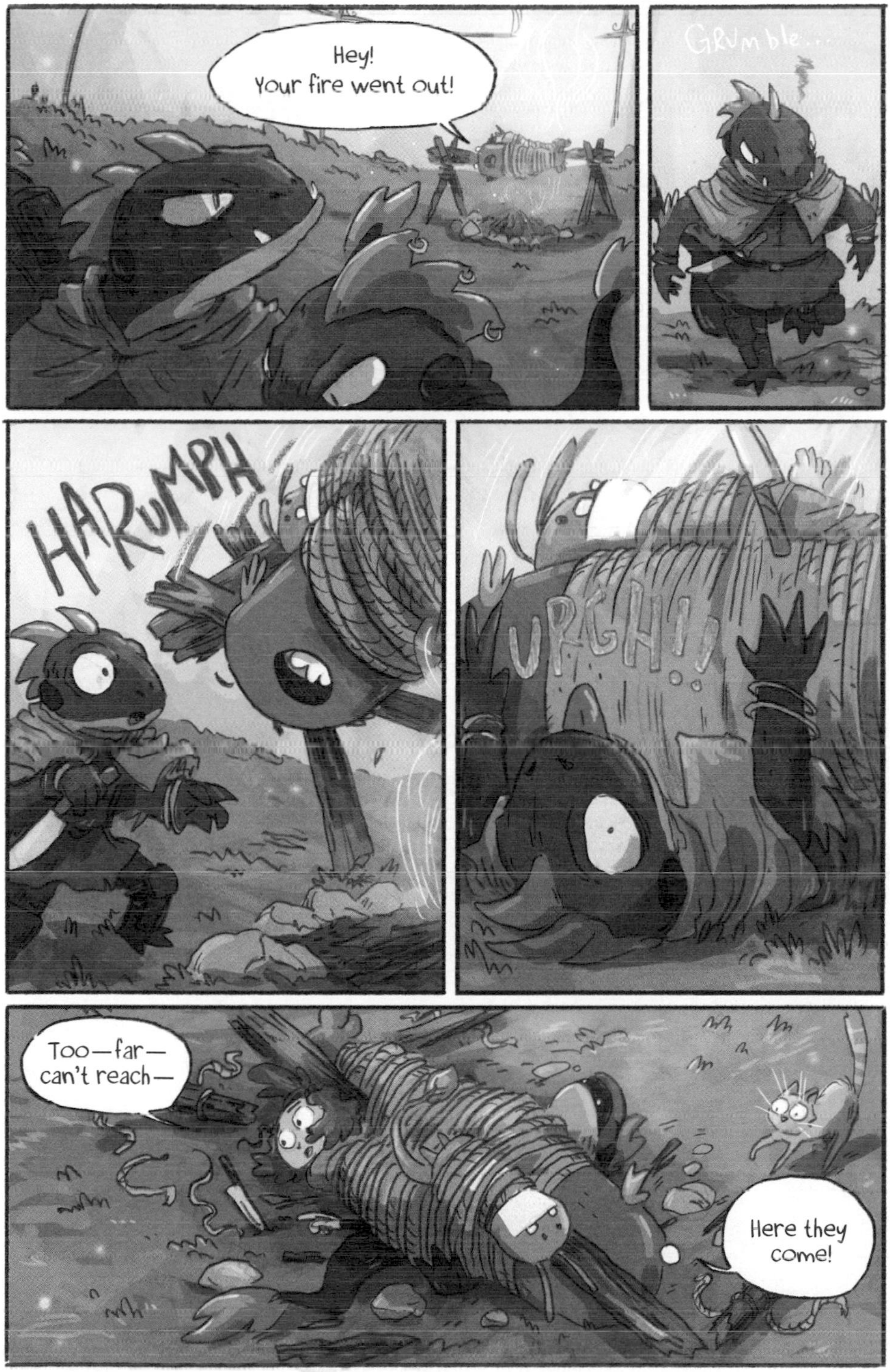
Hey!
Your fire went out!
GRUMble...
HARUMPH
URGH!!
Too—far—
can't reach—
Here they
come!

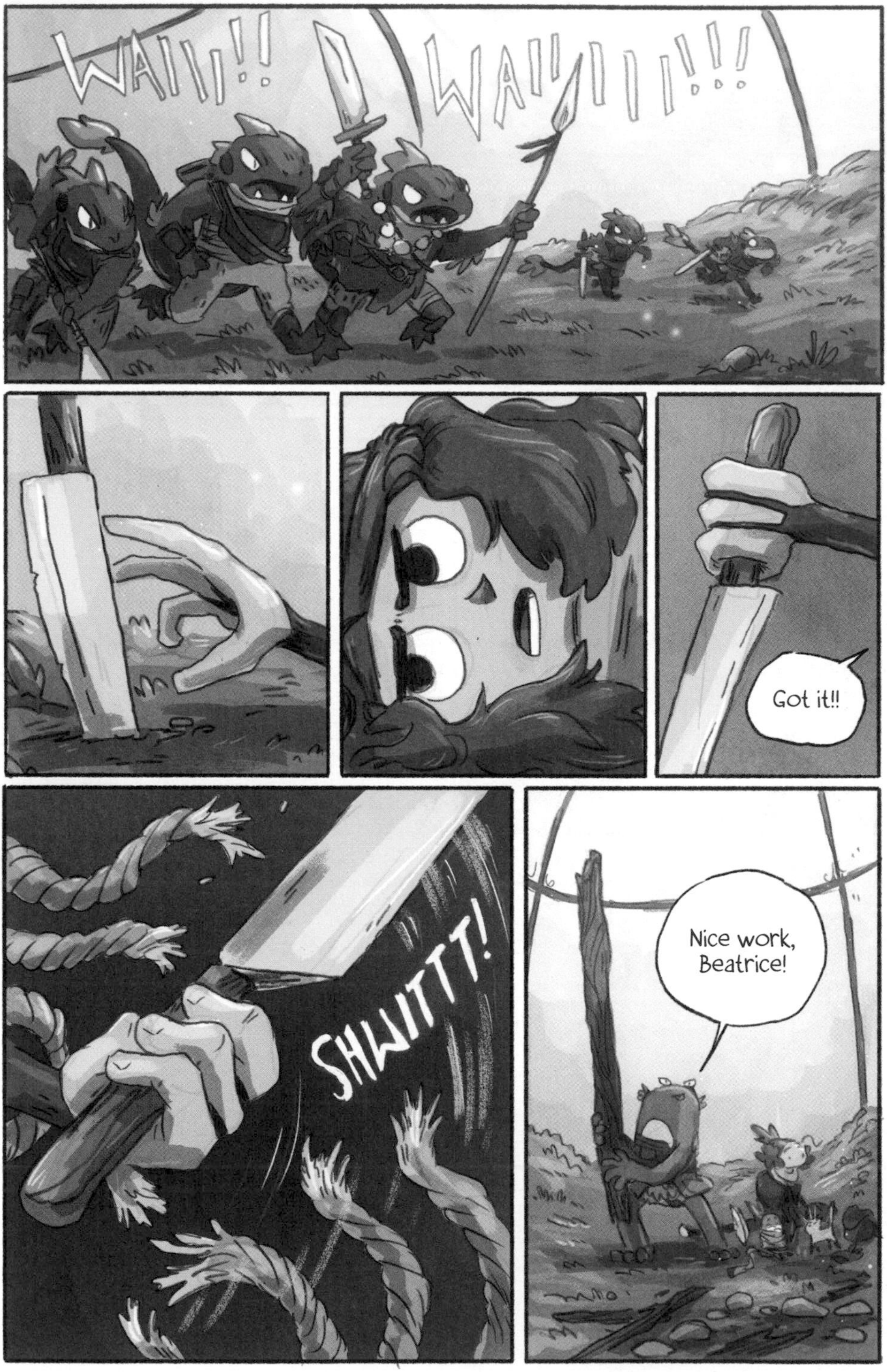
WAIII!! WAIIIIII!!!
Got it!!
SHWITTT!
Nice work, Beatrice!

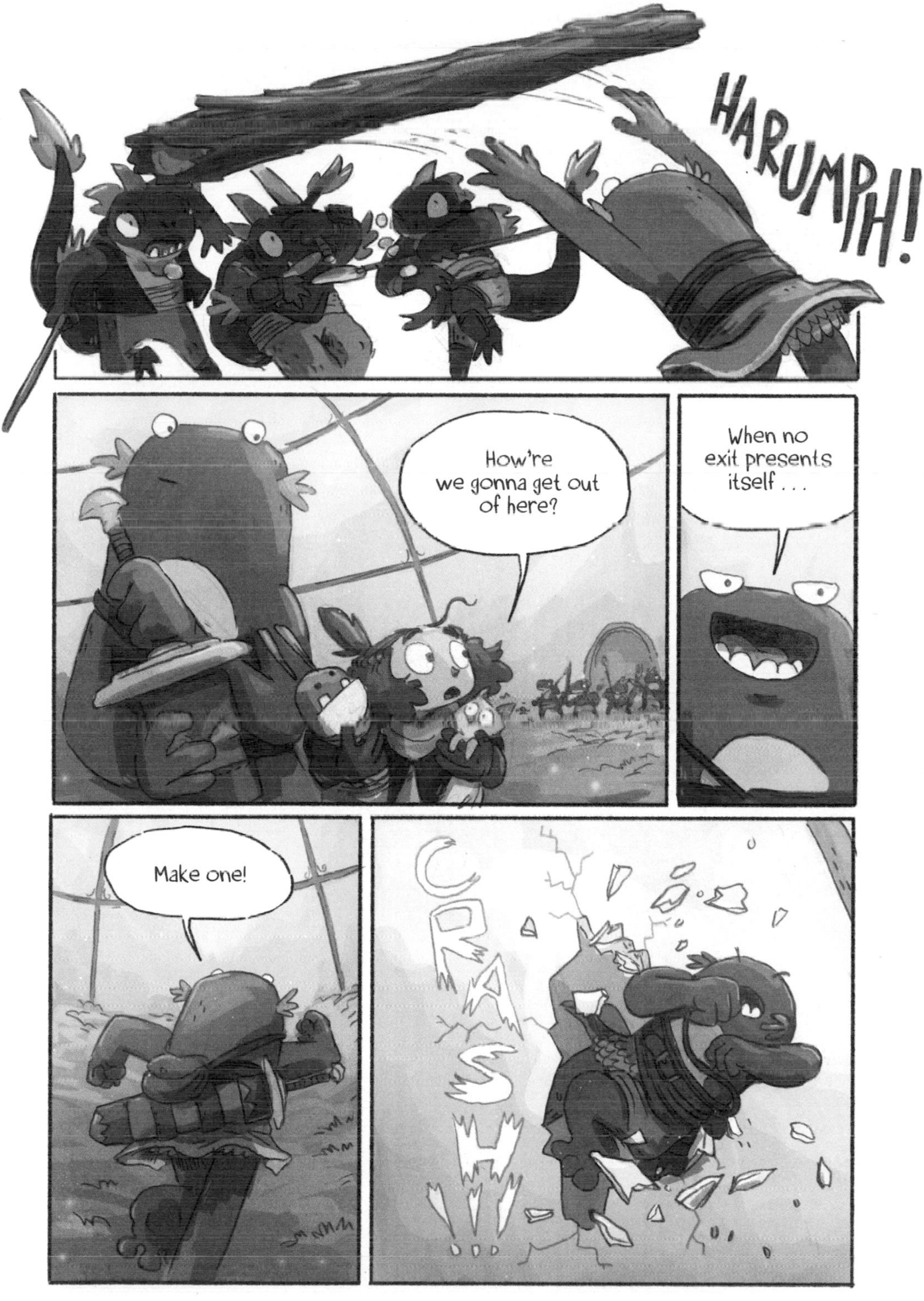
HARUMPH!
How're we gonna get out of here?
When no exit presents itself . . .
Make one!
CRASSH!!!

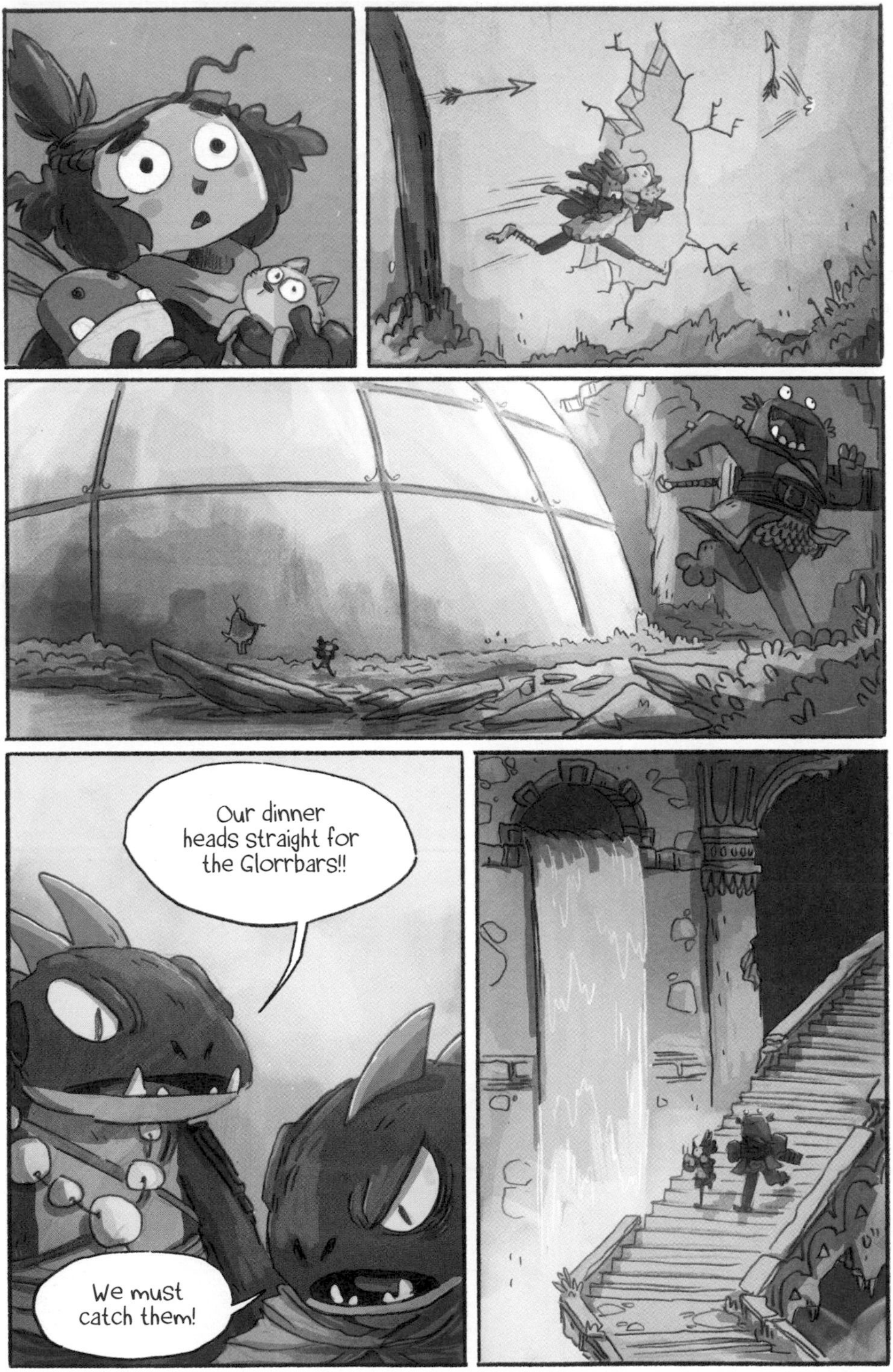
Our dinner heads straight for the Glorrbars!!
We must catch them!

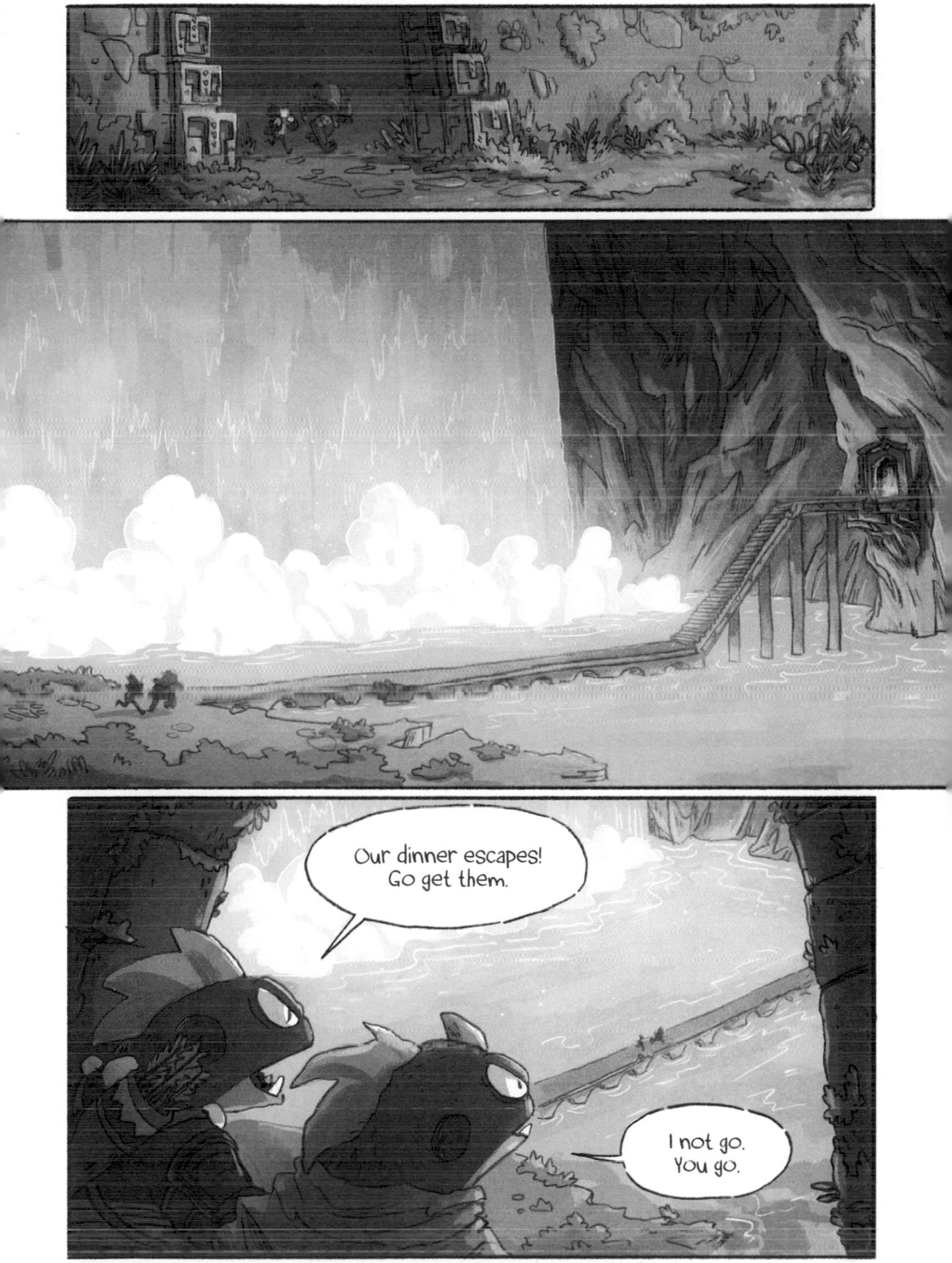
Our dinner escapes! Go get them.
I not go. You go.

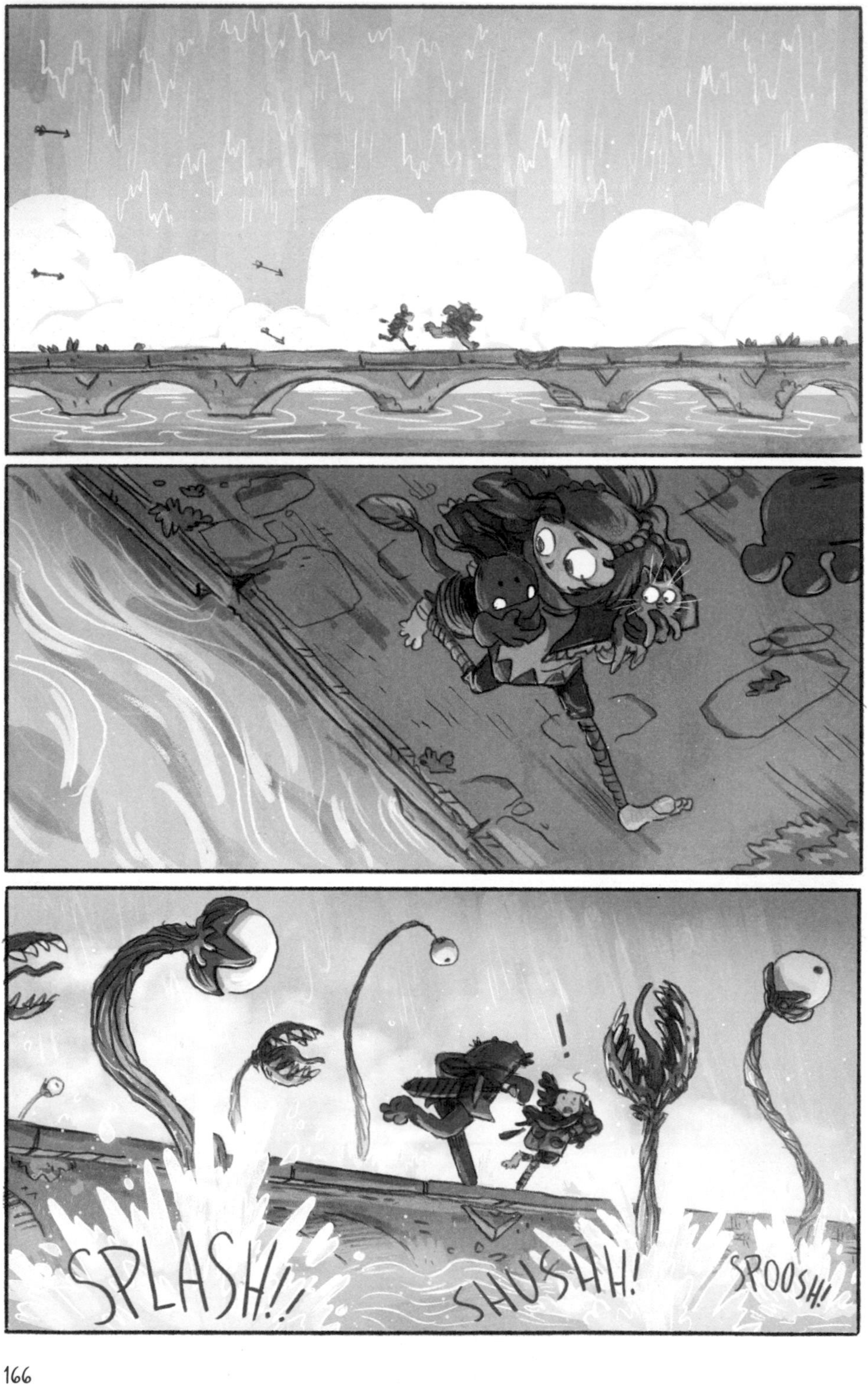
!
SPLASH!!
SHUSHH!
SPOOSH!

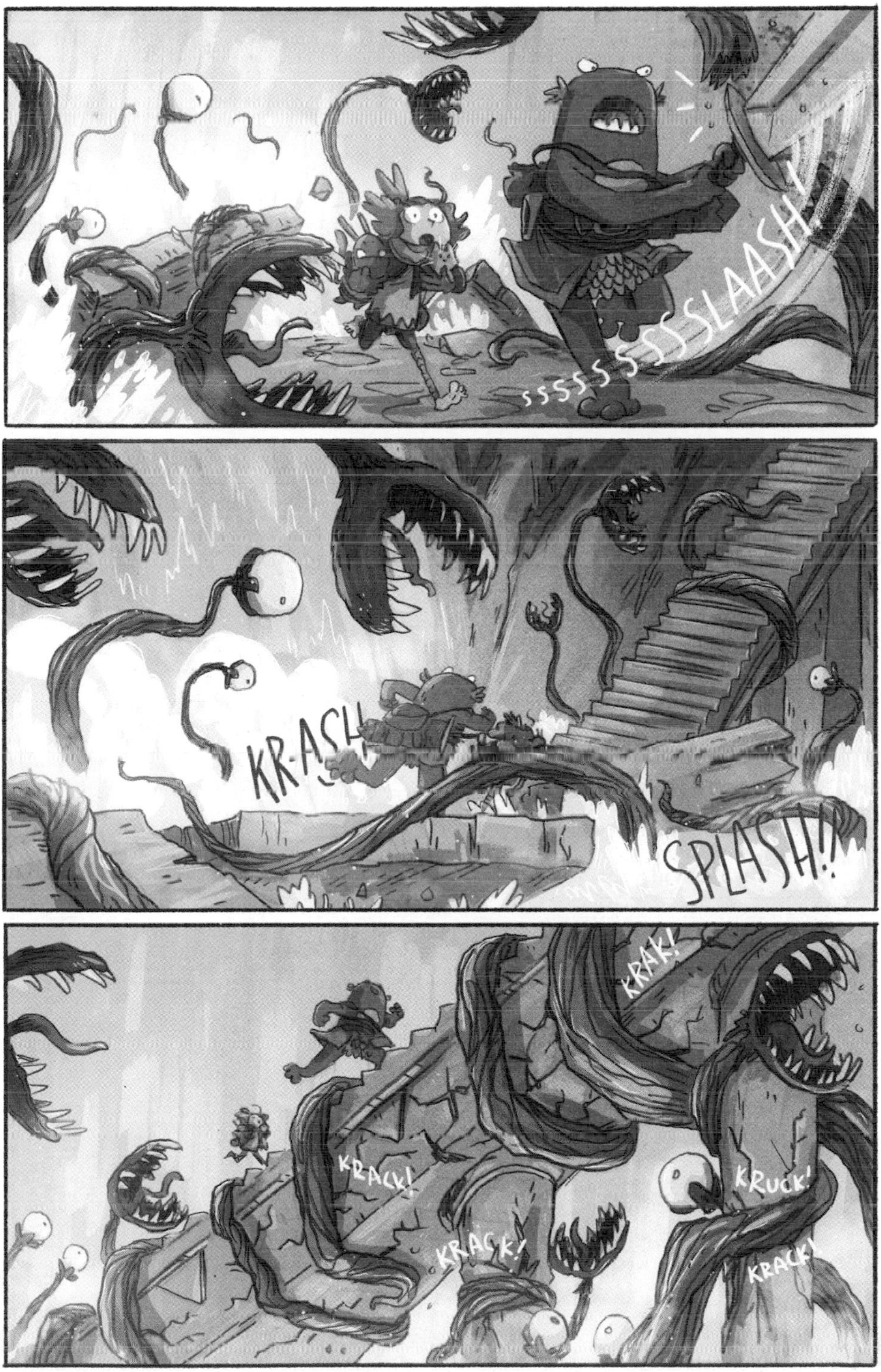
SSSSSSSSSLAASH!
KRASH
SPLASH!!
KRAK!
KRACK!
KRUCK!
KRACK!
KRACK!

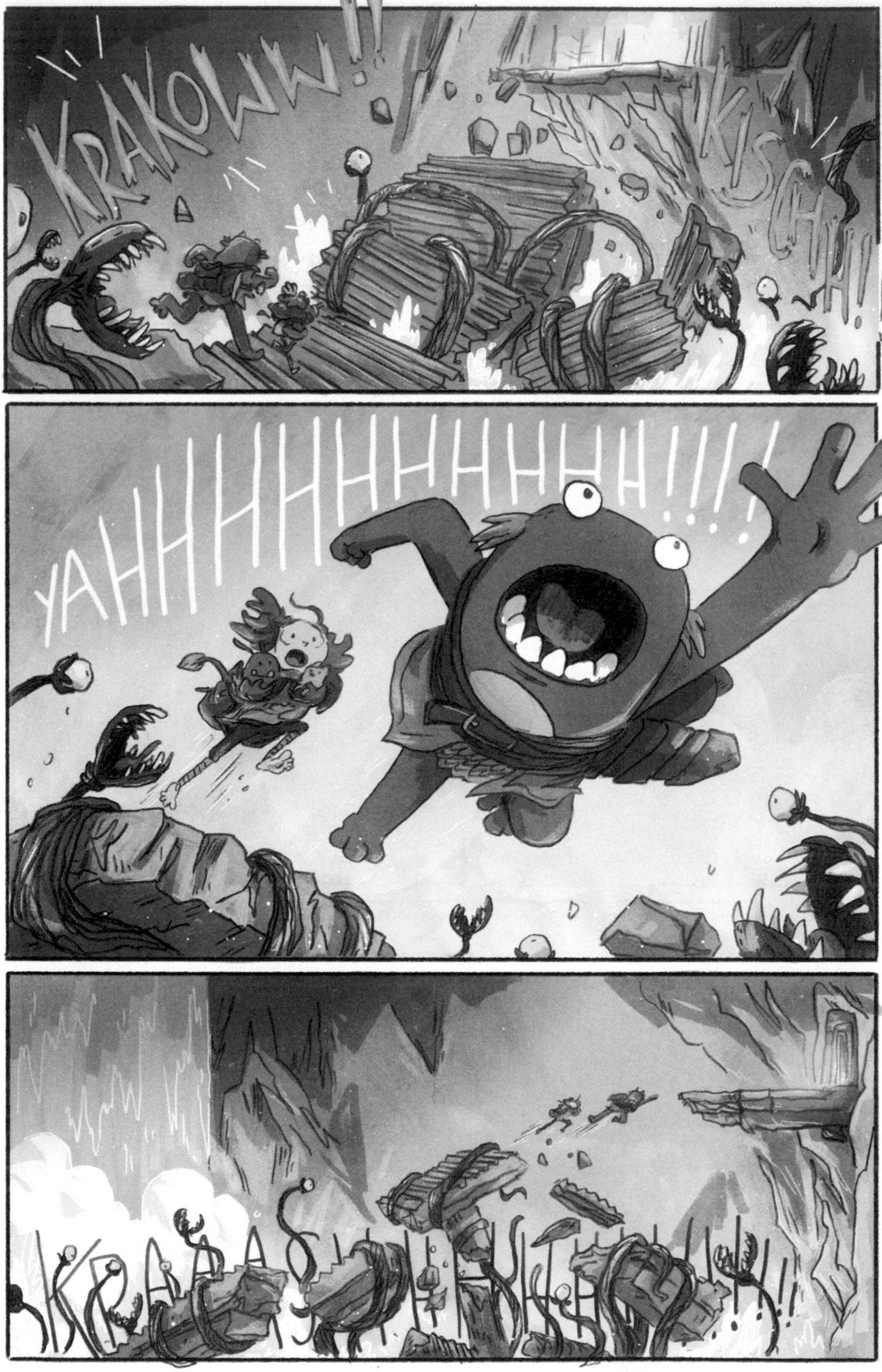
KRAKOWW!!
KISCH!!
YAHHHHHHHHHH!!!!
KRAAASHHHHHH!!

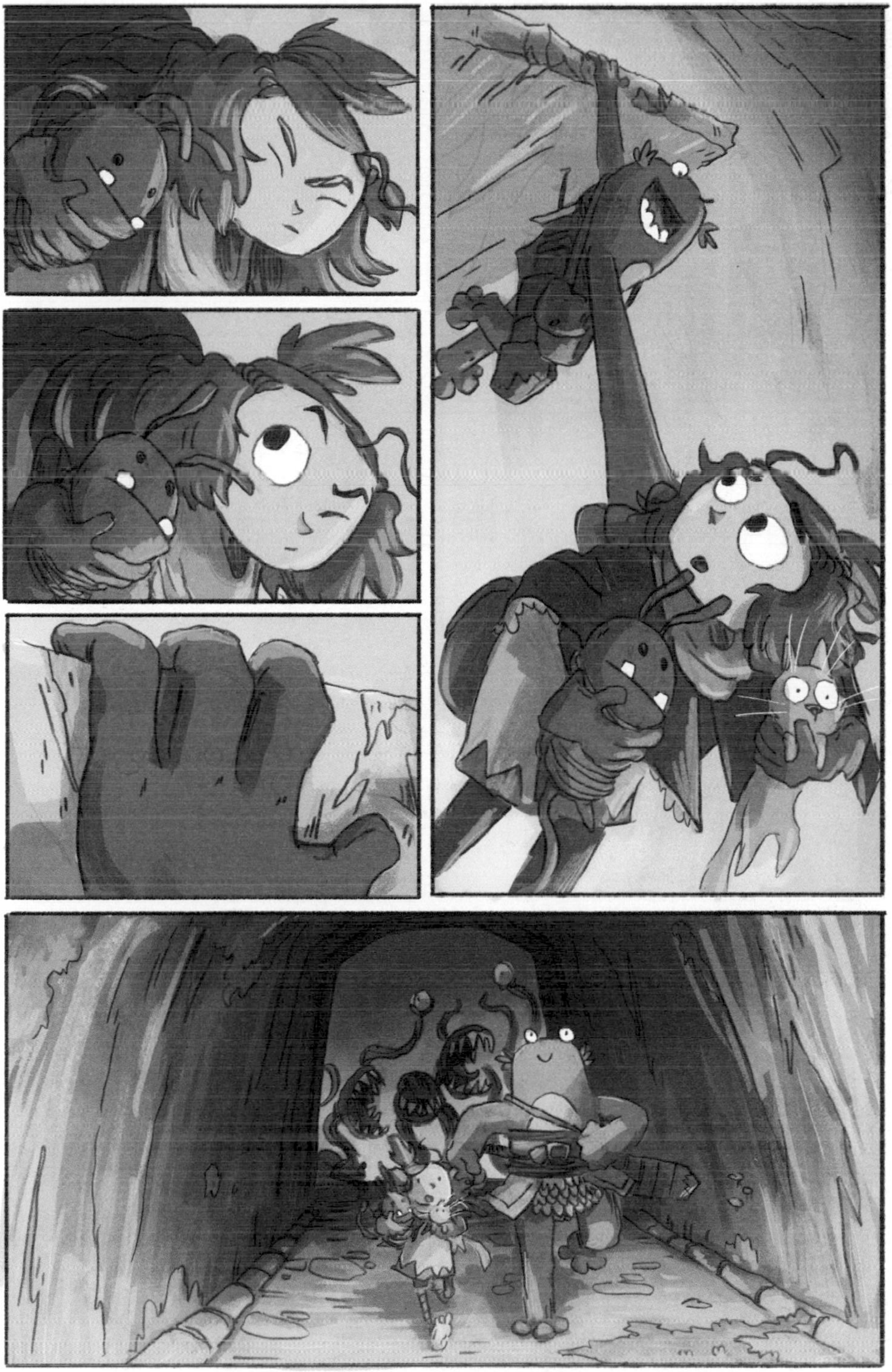

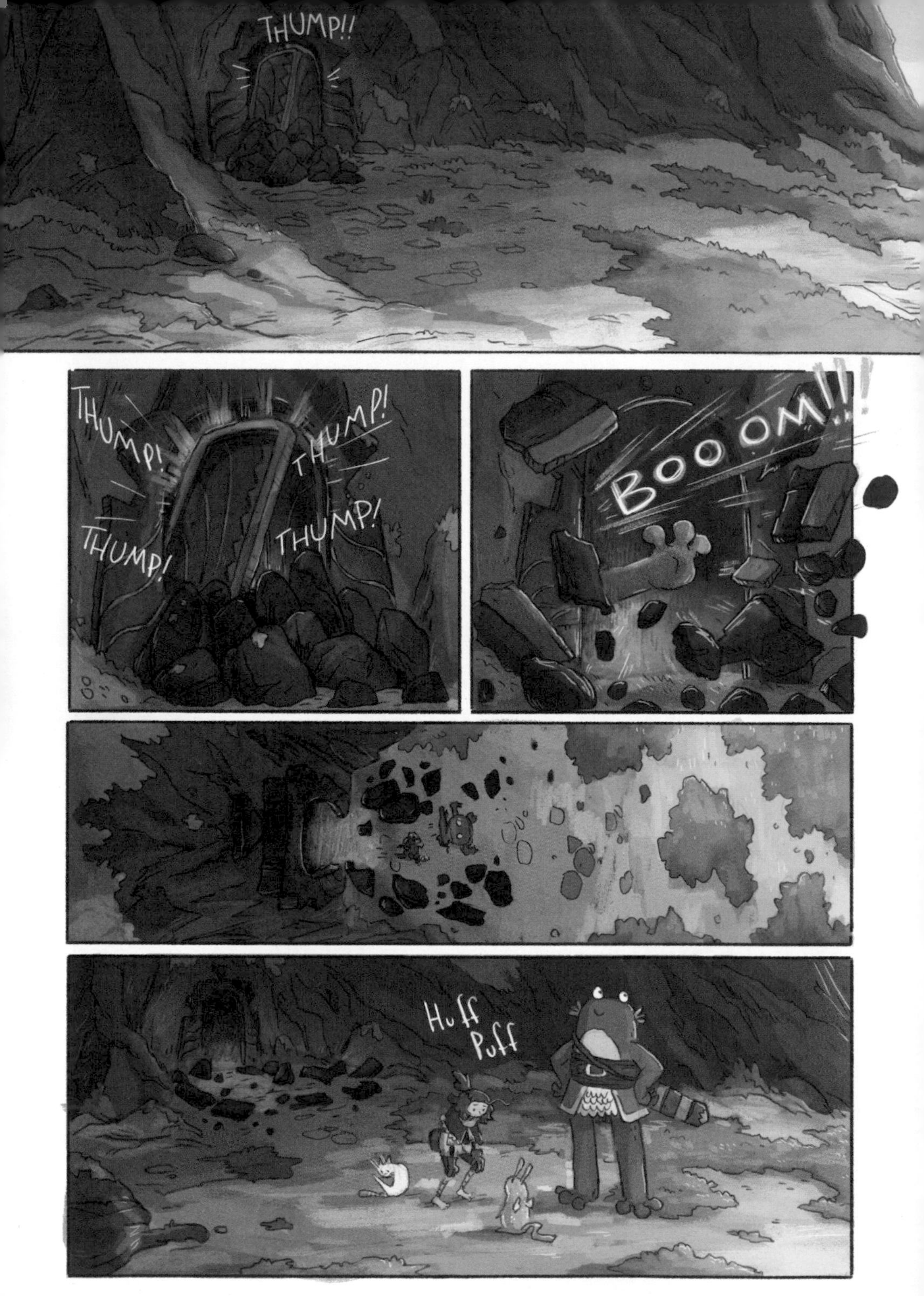
THUMP!!
THUMP!
THUMP!
THUMP!
THUMP!
BOOOOM!!
Huff
Puff

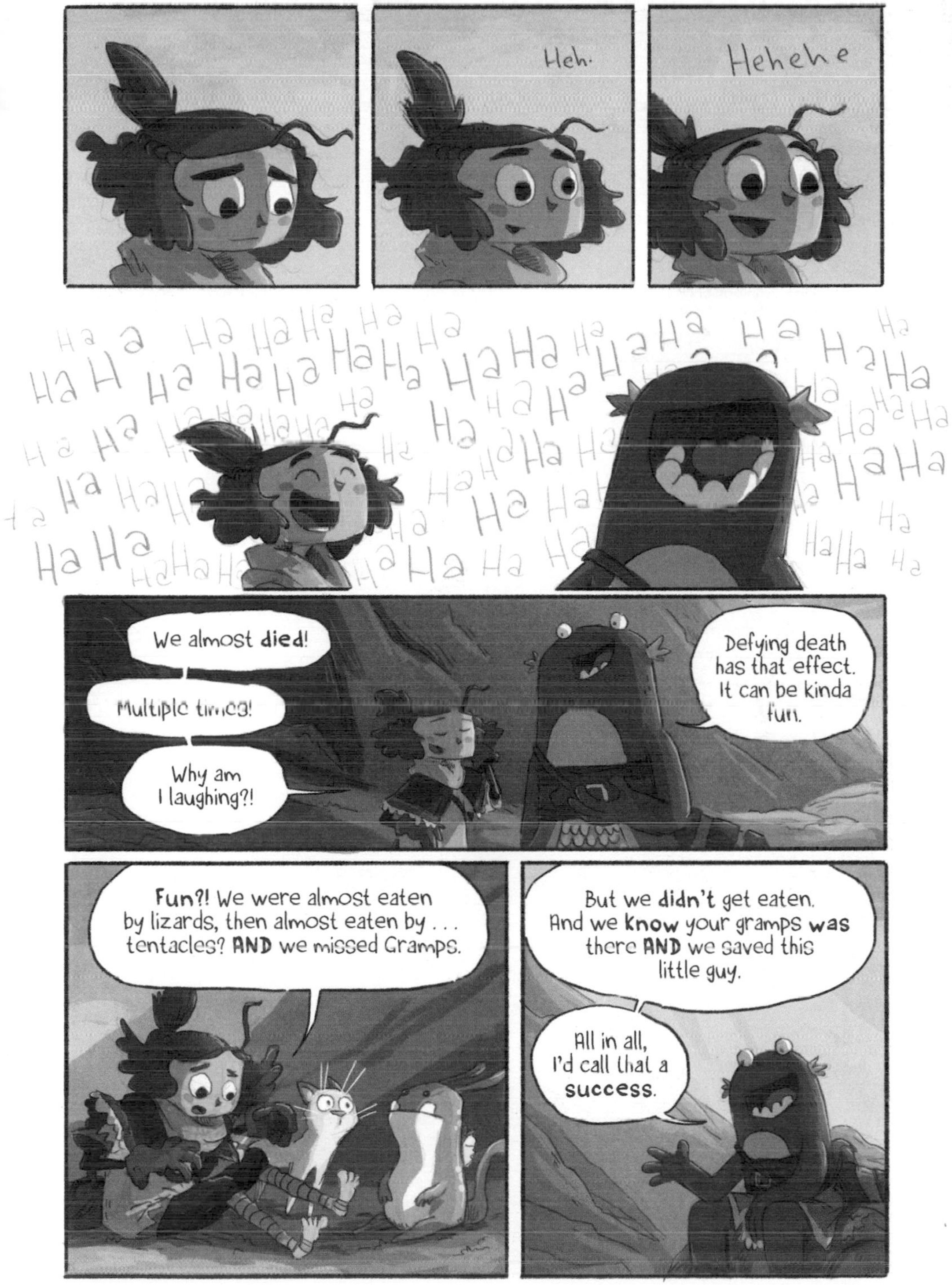
Heh.
Hehehe
Ha Ha Ha Ha Ha Ha
We almost **died**!
Multiple times!
Why am I laughing?!
Defying death has that effect. It can be kinda fun.
Fun?! We were almost eaten by lizards, then almost eaten by . . . tentacles? **AND** we missed Gramps.
But we **didn't** get eaten. And we **know** your gramps **was** there **AND** we saved this little guy.
All in all, I'd call that a **success**.

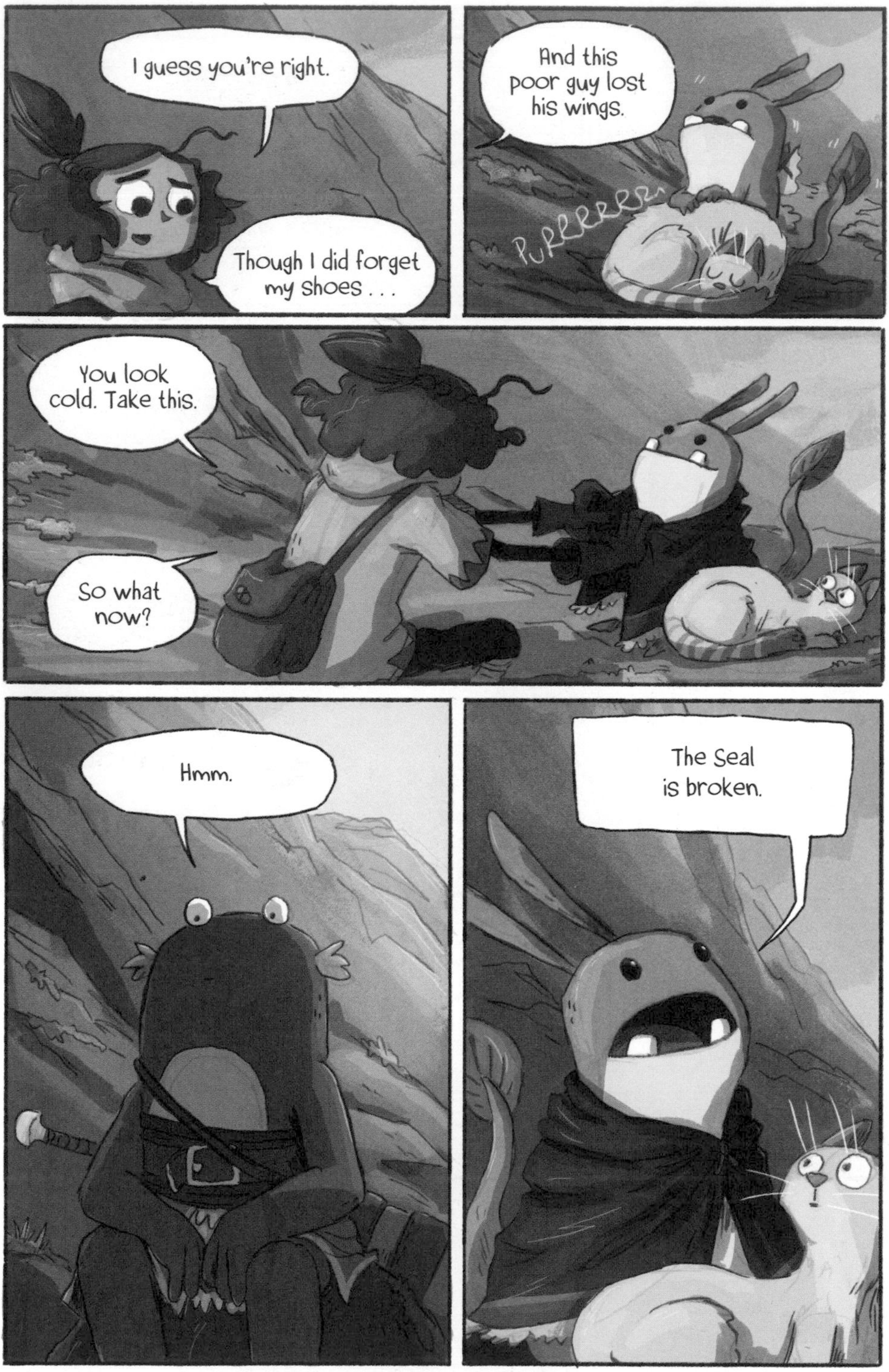

I guess you're right.
Though I did forget my shoes . . .
And this poor guy lost his wings.
PURRRRRR
You look cold. Take this.
So what now?
Hmm.
The Seal is broken.

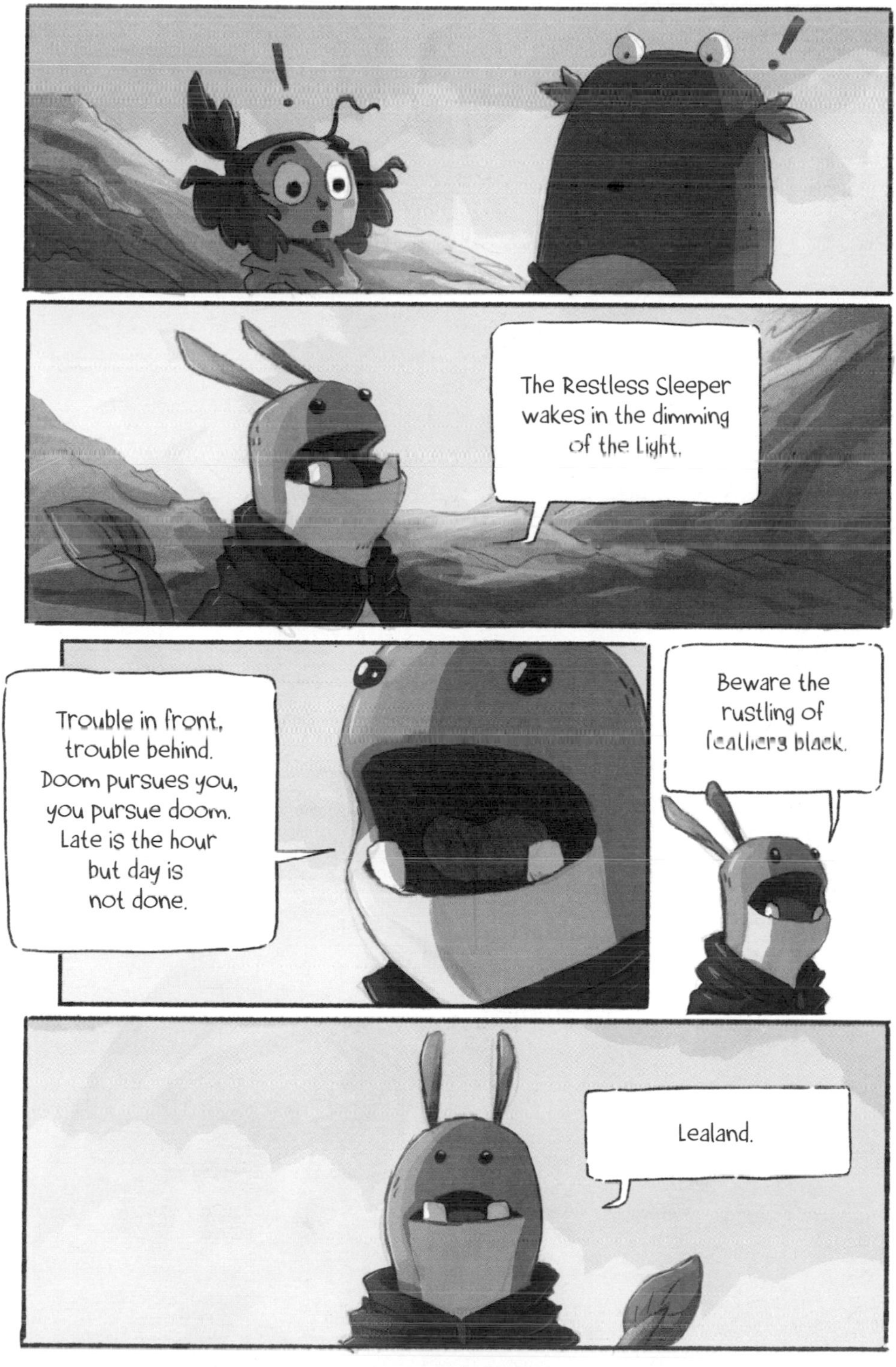
The Restless Sleeper wakes in the dimming of the Light.
Trouble in front, trouble behind. Doom pursues you, you pursue doom. Late is the hour but day is not done.
Beware the rustling of feathers black.
Lealand.

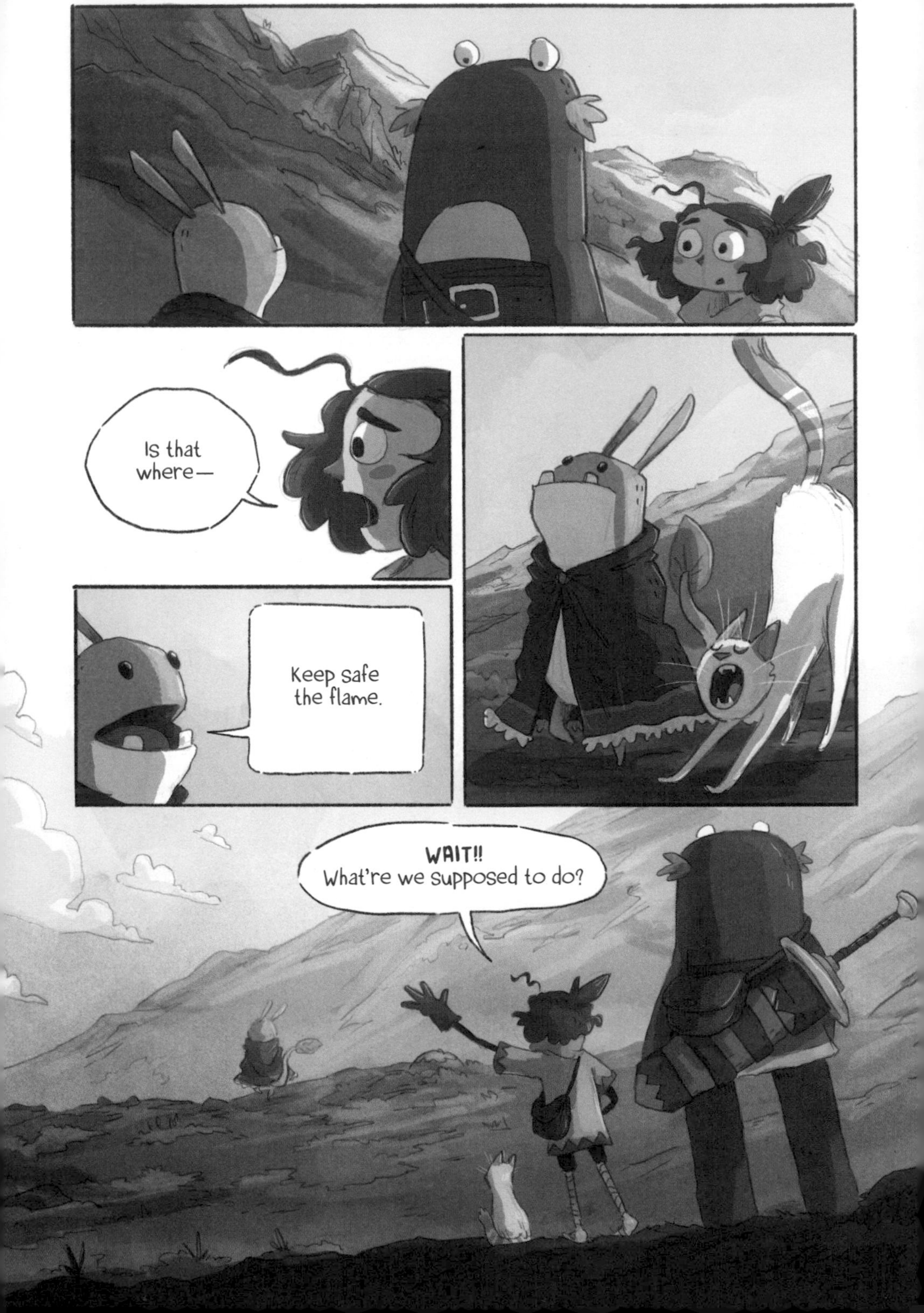
Is that where—
Keep safe the flame.
WAIT!!
What're we supposed to do?

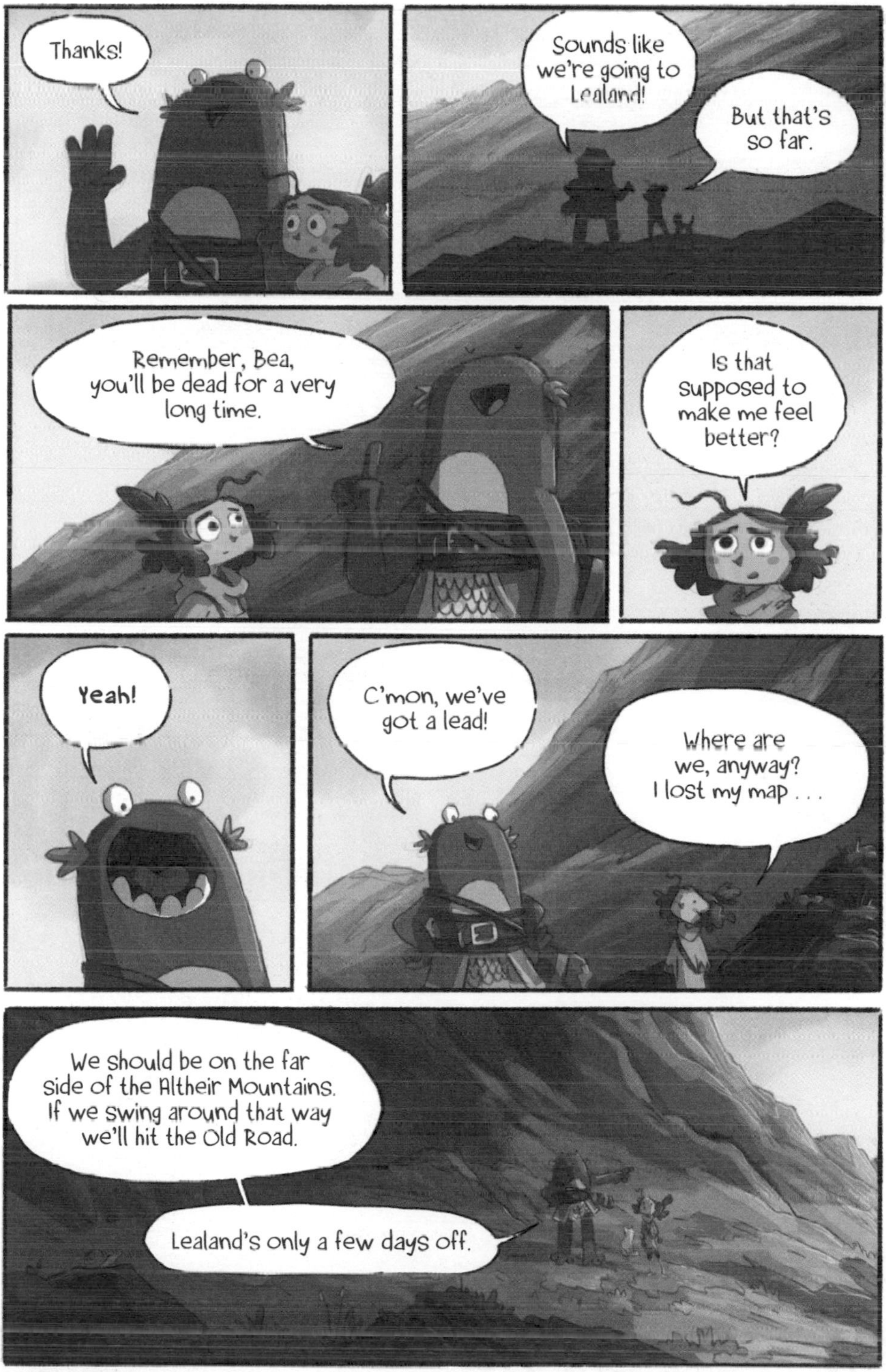
Thanks!
Sounds like we're going to Lealand!
But that's so far.
Remember, Bea, you'll be dead for a very long time.
Is that supposed to make me feel better?
Yeah!
C'mon, we've got a lead!
Where are we, anyway? I lost my map . . .
We should be on the far side of the Altheir Mountains. If we swing around that way we'll hit the Old Road.
Lealand's only a few days off.

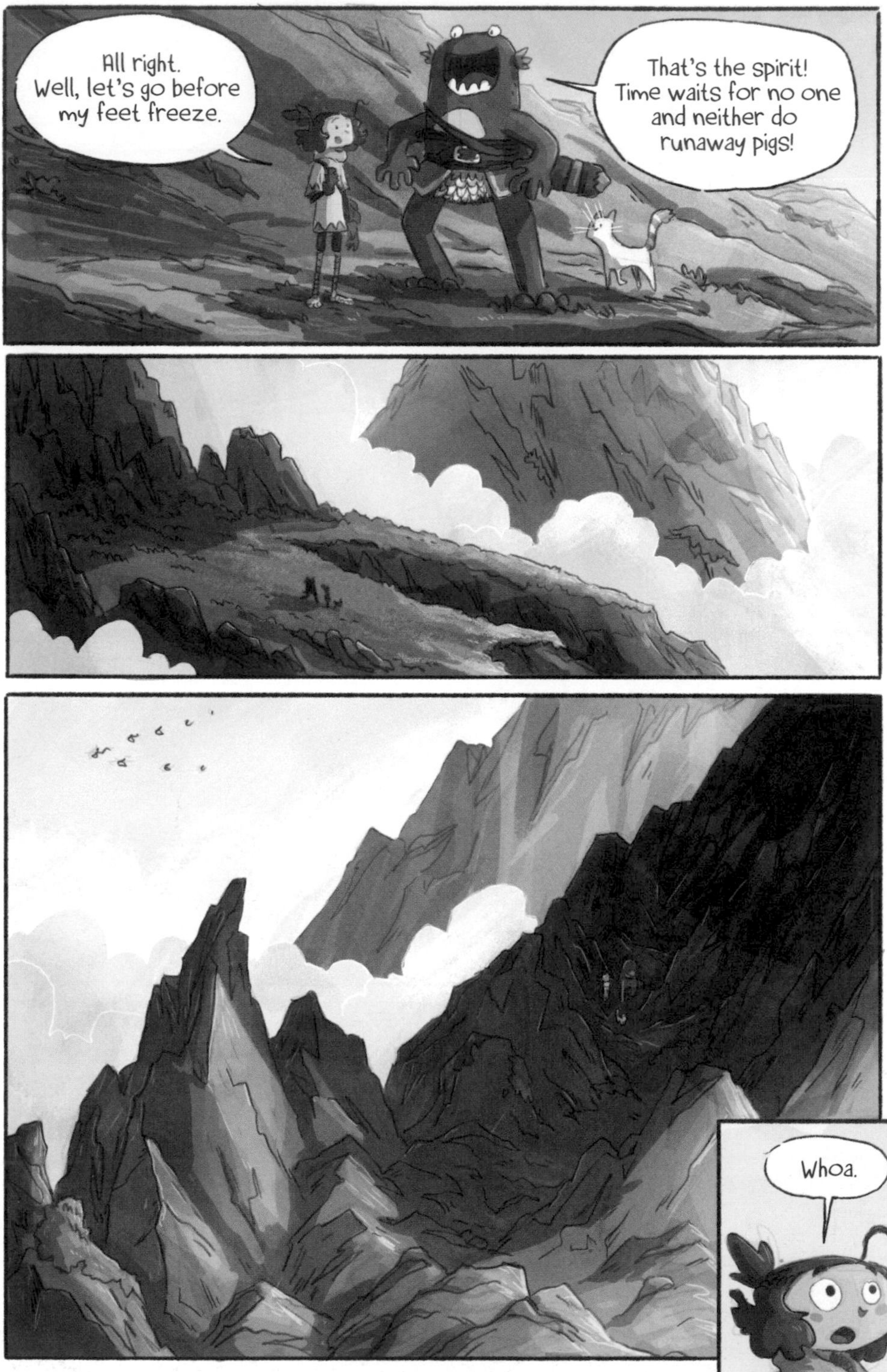
All right. Well, let's go before my feet freeze.
That's the spirit! Time waits for no one and neither do runaway pigs!
Whoa.

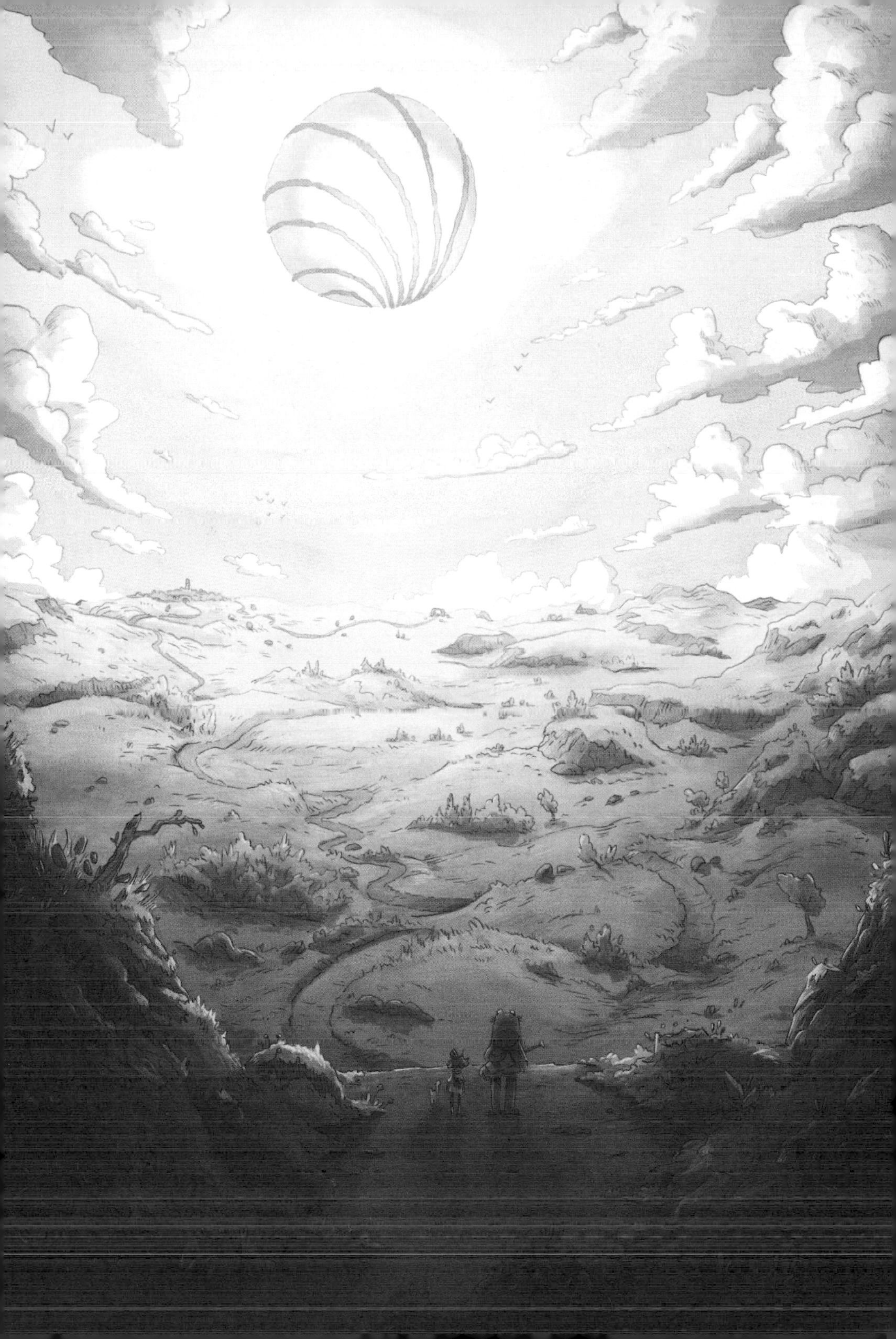

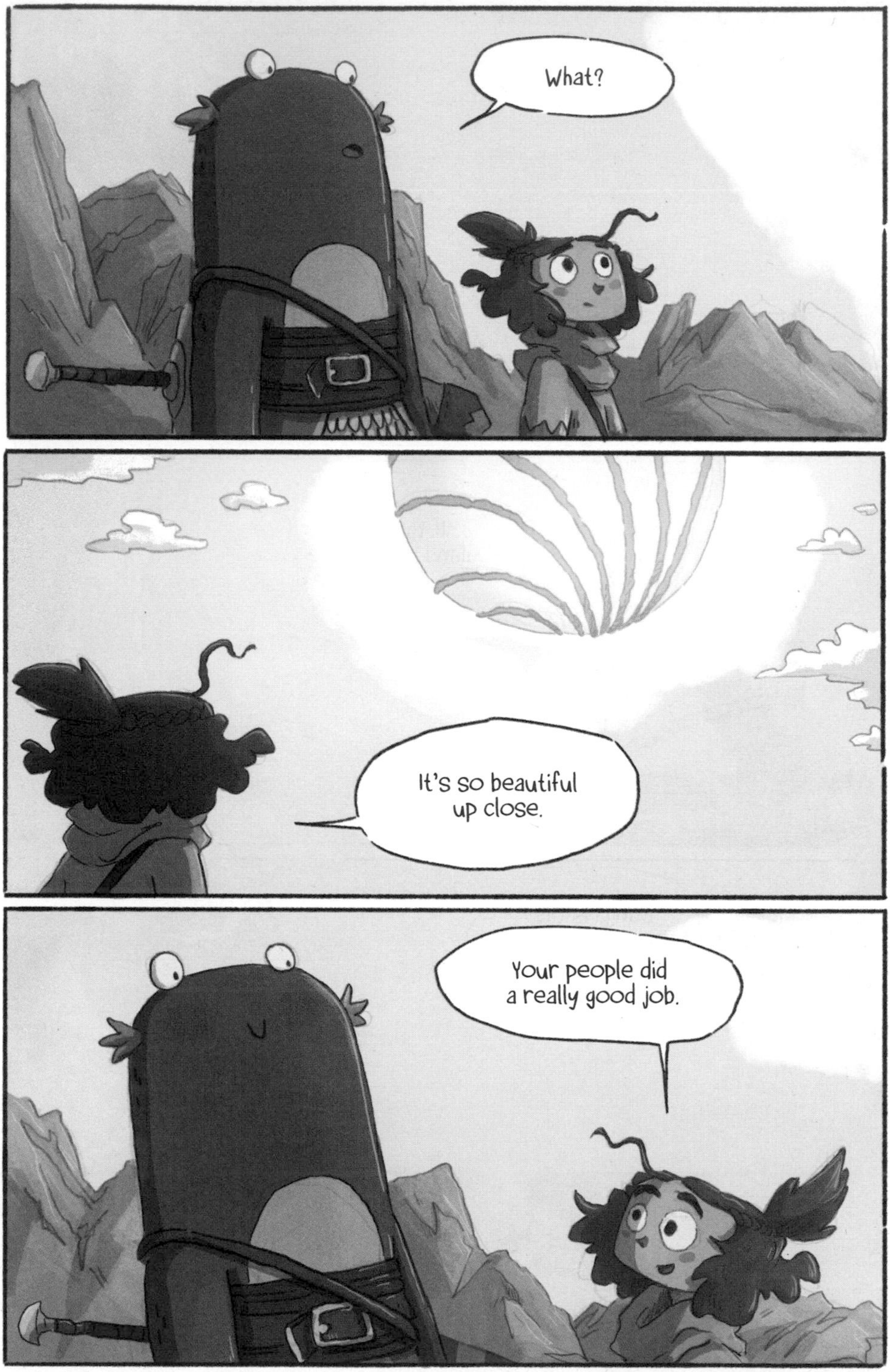
What?
It's so beautiful up close.
Your people did a really good job.

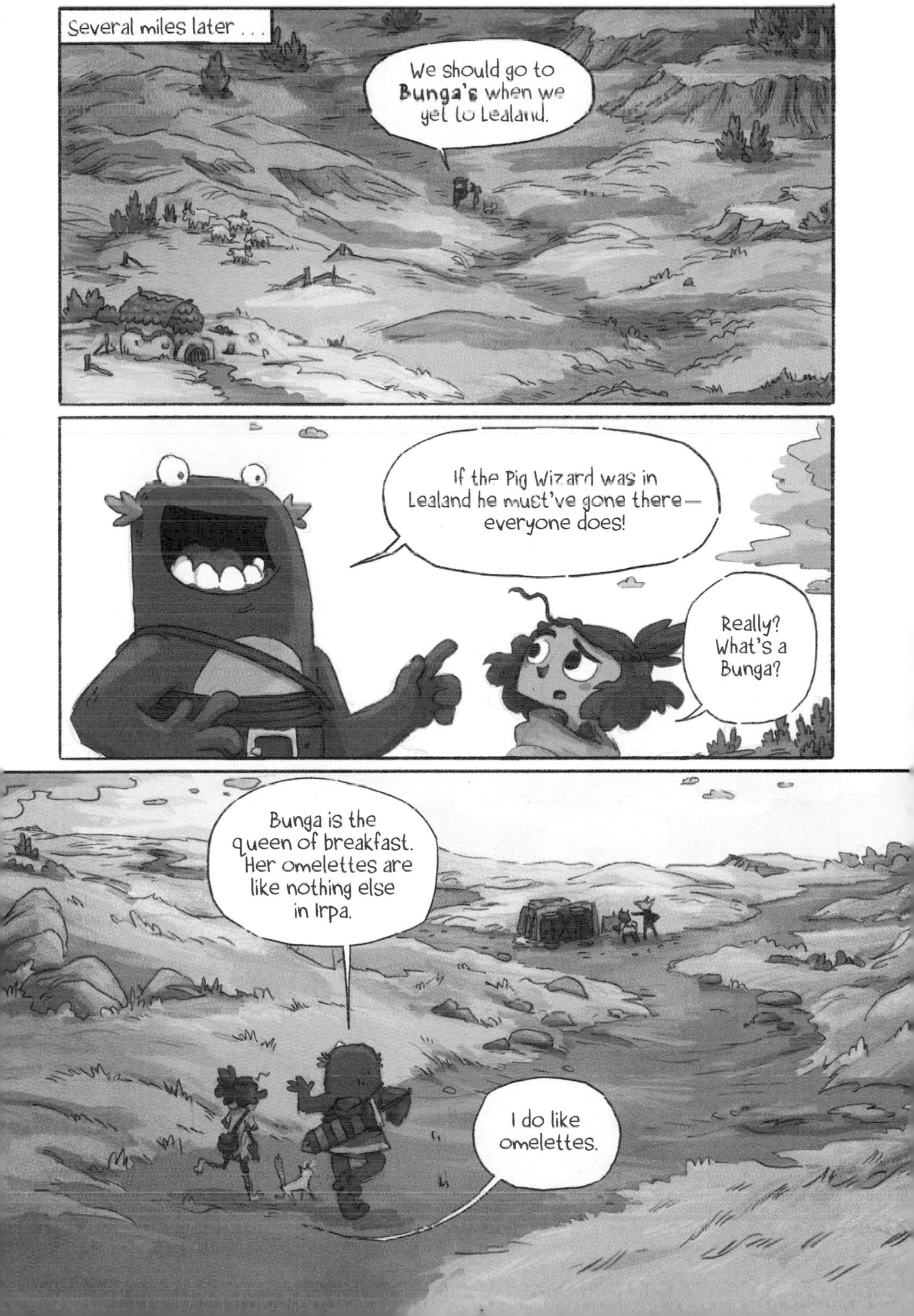
Several miles later . . .
We should go to Bunga's when we get to Lealand.
If the Pig Wizard was in Lealand he must've gone there— everyone does!
Really? What's a Bunga?
Bunga is the queen of breakfast. Her omelettes are like nothing else in Irpa.
I do like omelettes.

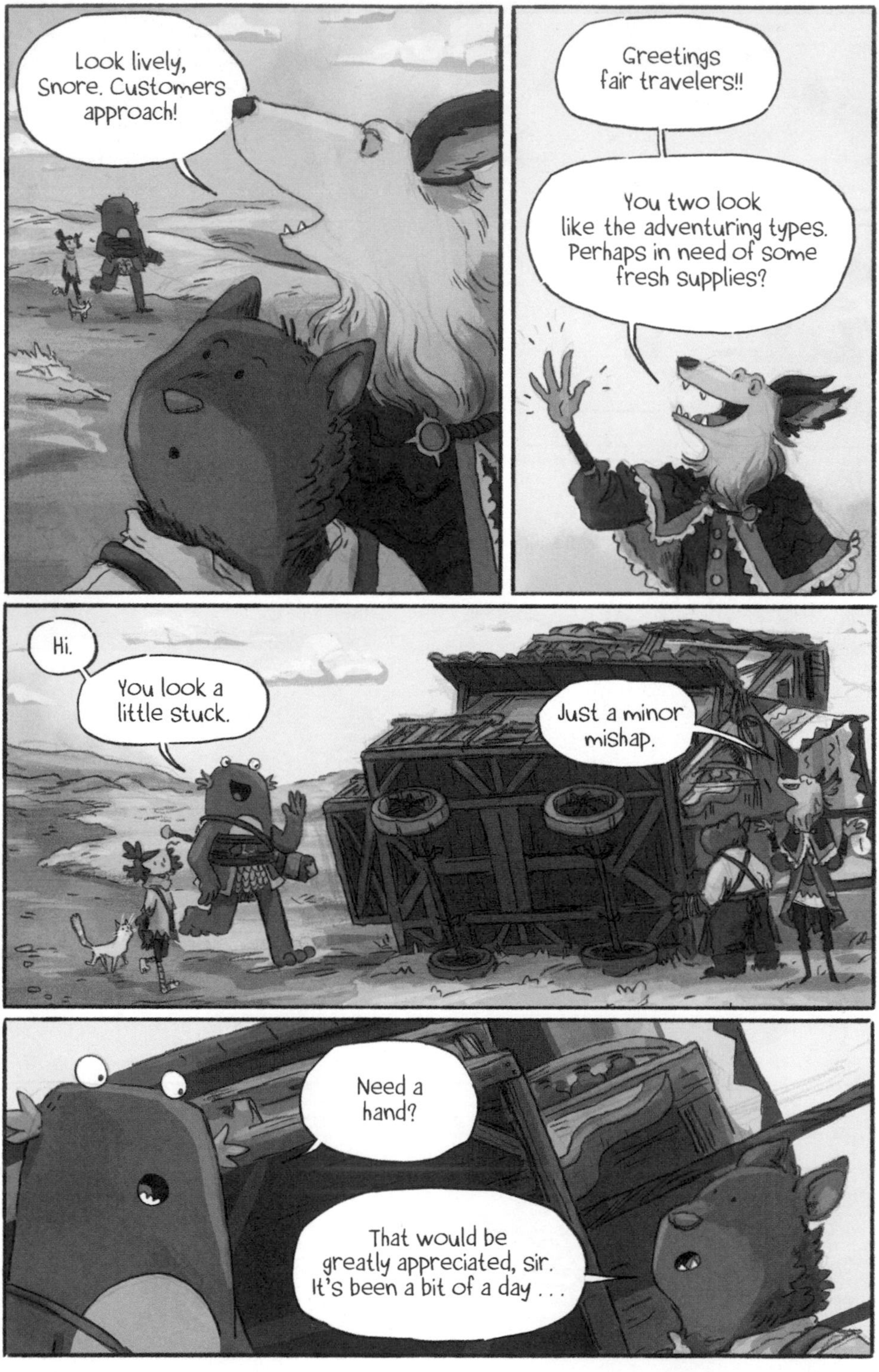
Look lively, Snore. Customers approach!
Greetings fair travelers!!
You two look like the adventuring types. Perhaps in need of some fresh supplies?
Hi.
You look a little stuck.
Just a minor mishap.
Need a hand?
That would be greatly appreciated, sir. It's been a bit of a day . . .

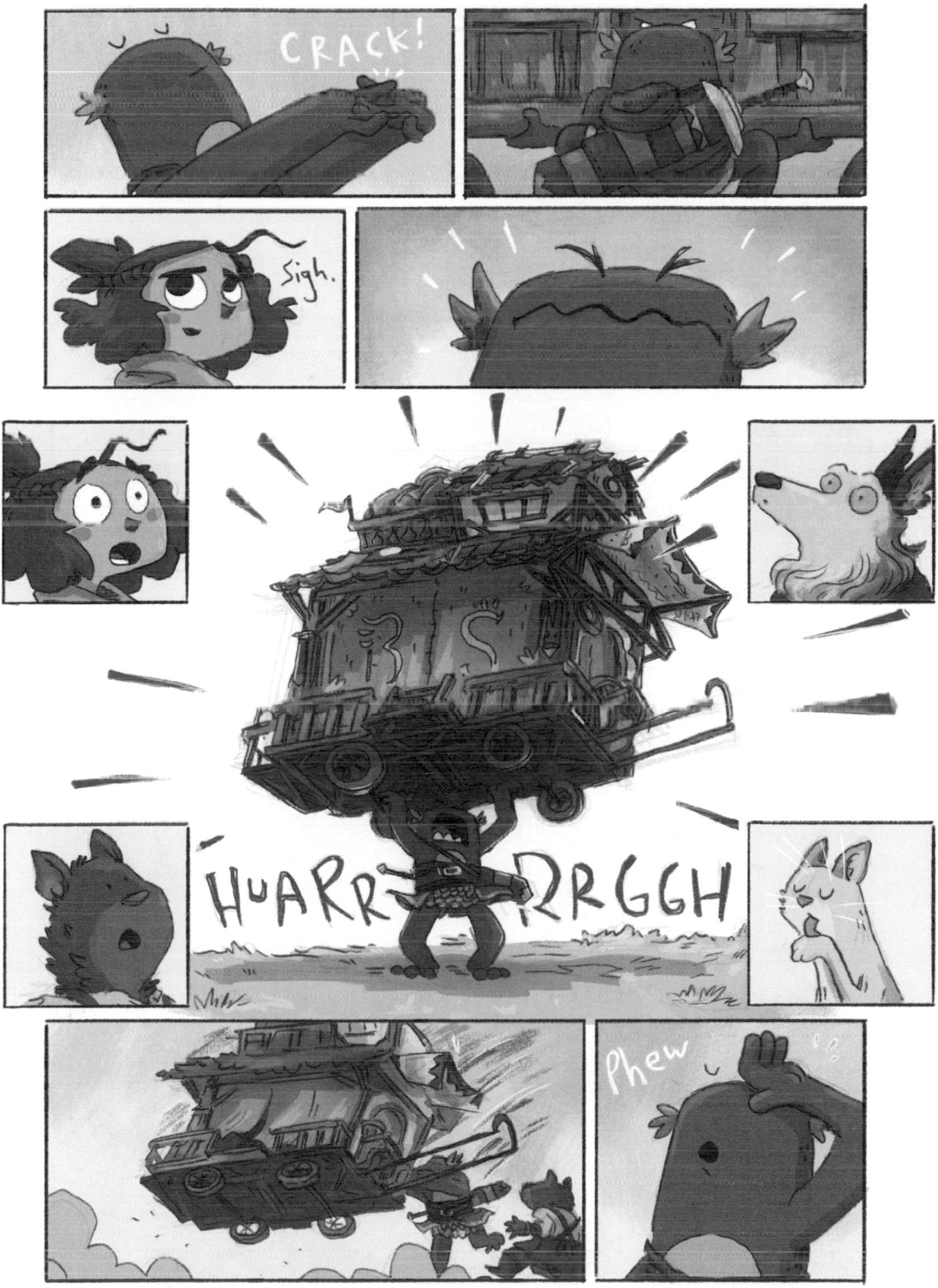
CRACK!
Sigh.
HUARR RRGGH
Phew

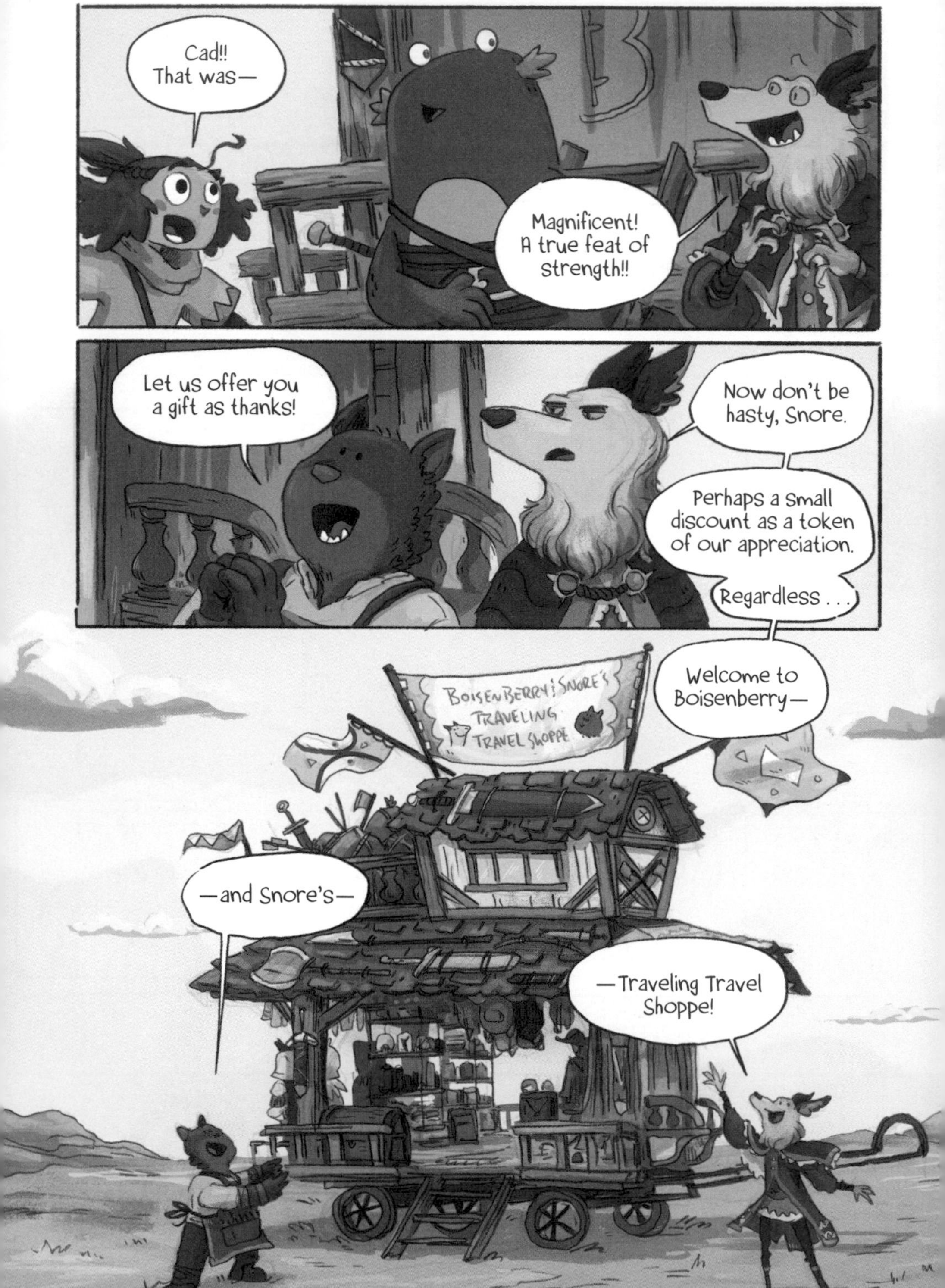
Cad!! That was—
Magnificent! A true feat of strength!!
Let us offer you a gift as thanks!
Now don't be hasty, Snore.
Perhaps a small discount as a token of our appreciation.
Regardless . . .
Welcome to Boisenberry—
BOISENBERRY & SNORE'S TRAVELING TRAVEL SHOPPE
—and Snore's—
—Traveling Travel Shoppe!

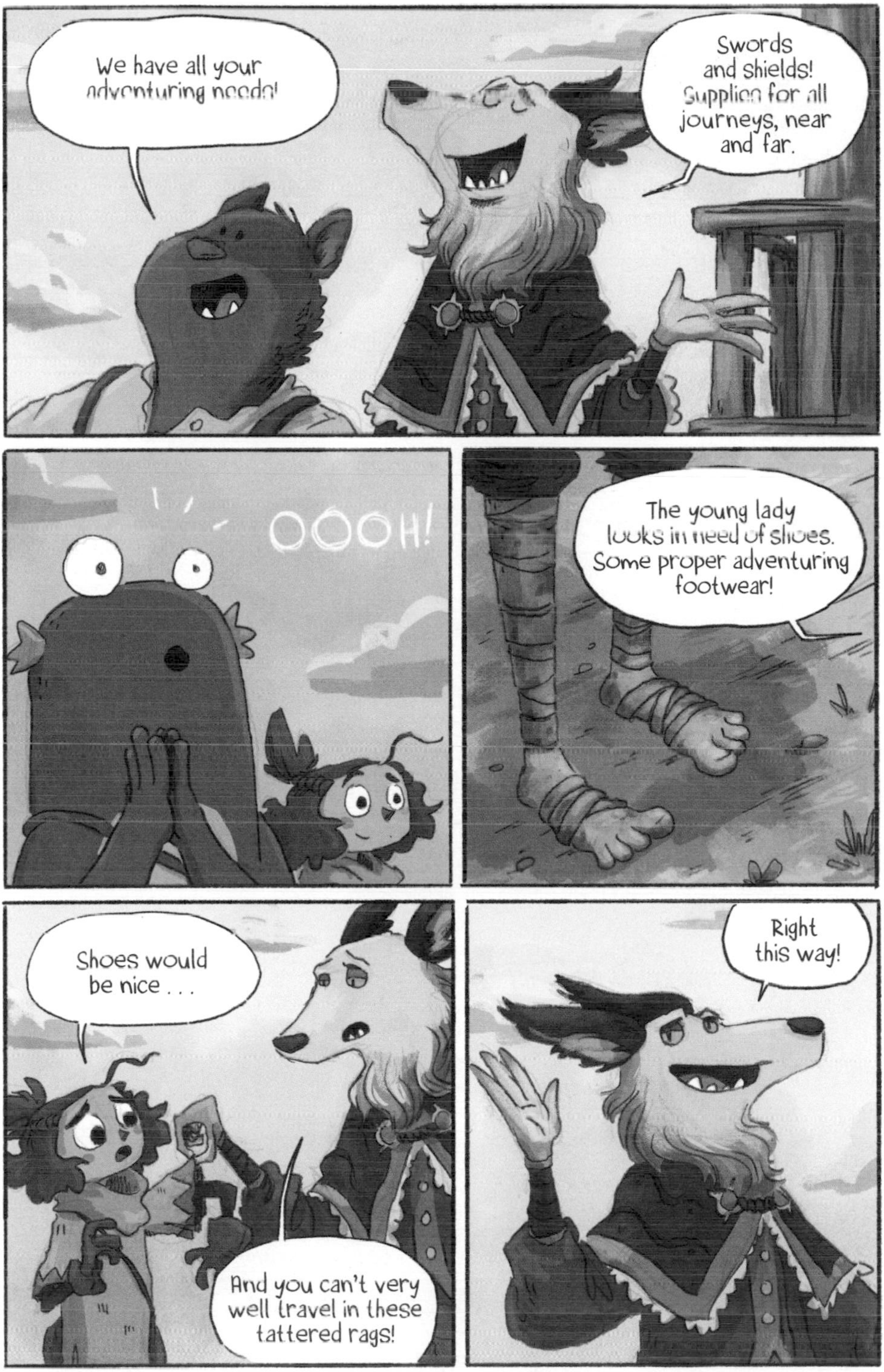
We have all your adventuring needs!
Swords and shields! Supplies for all journeys, near and far.
OOOH!
The young lady looks in need of shoes. Some proper adventuring footwear!
Shoes would be nice . . .
And you can't very well travel in these tattered rags!
Right this way!

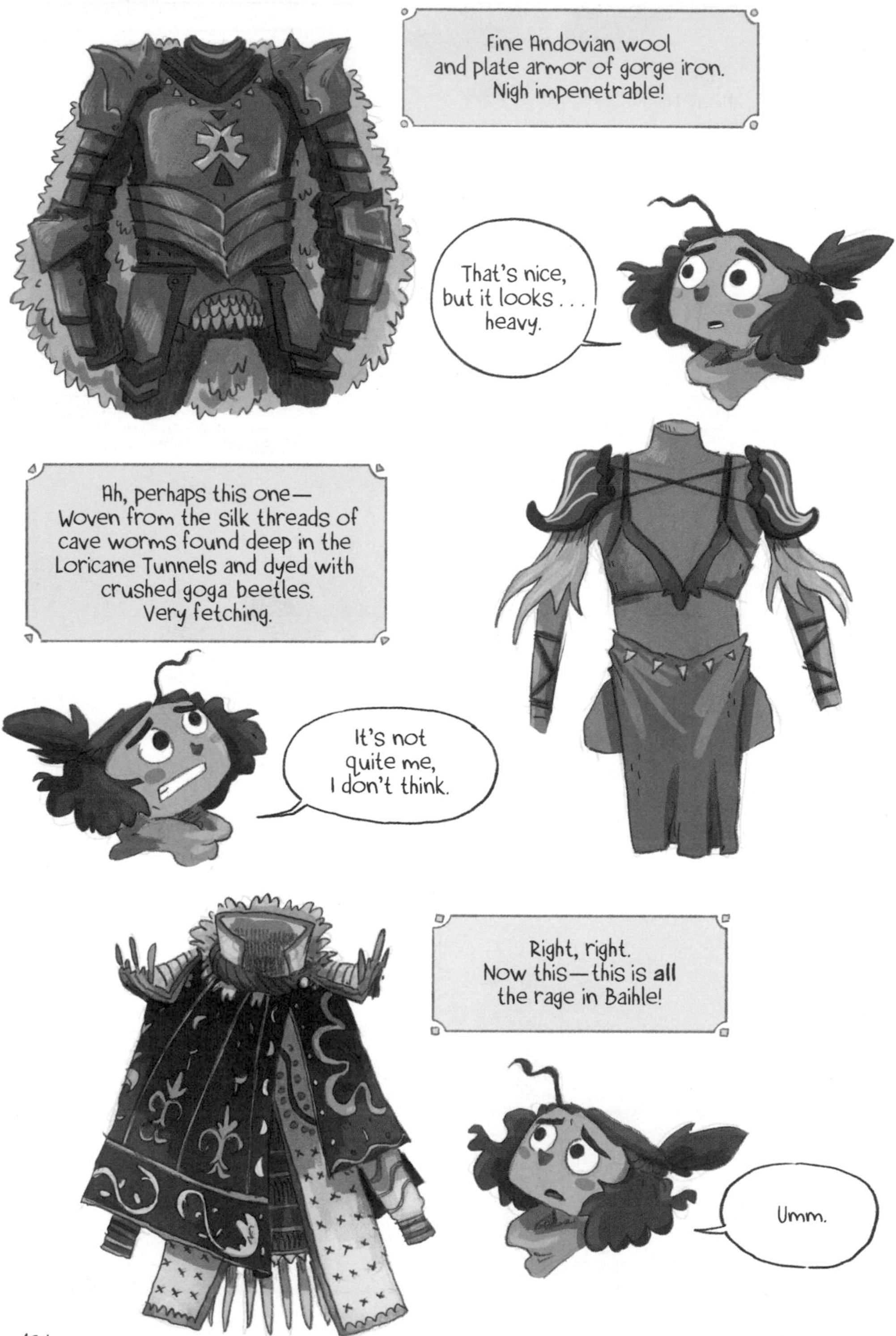
Fine Andovian wool and plate armor of gorge iron. Nigh impenetrable!
That's nice, but it looks . . . heavy.
Ah, perhaps this one— Woven from the silk threads of cave worms found deep in the Loricane Tunnels and dyed with crushed goga beetles. Very fetching.
It's not quite me, I don't think.
Right, right. Now this—this is **all** the rage in Baihle!
Umm.

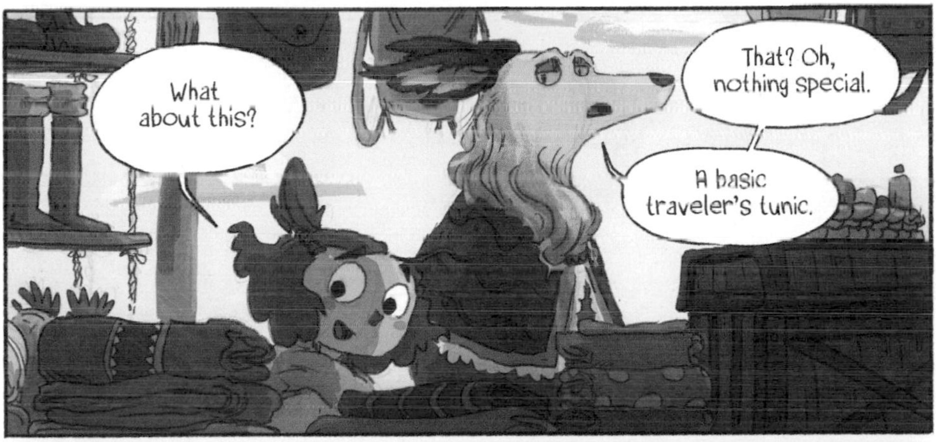
What about this?
That? Oh, nothing special.
A basic traveler's tunic.

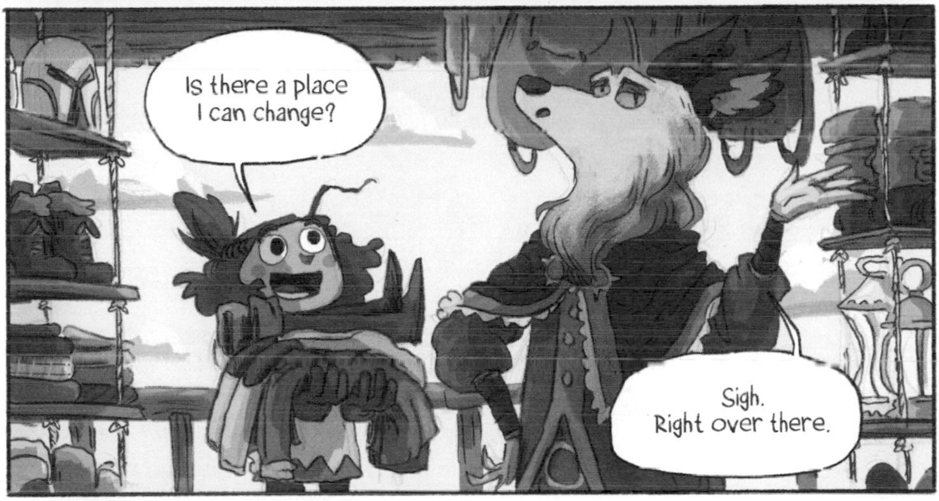
Is there a place I can change?
Sigh. Right over there.

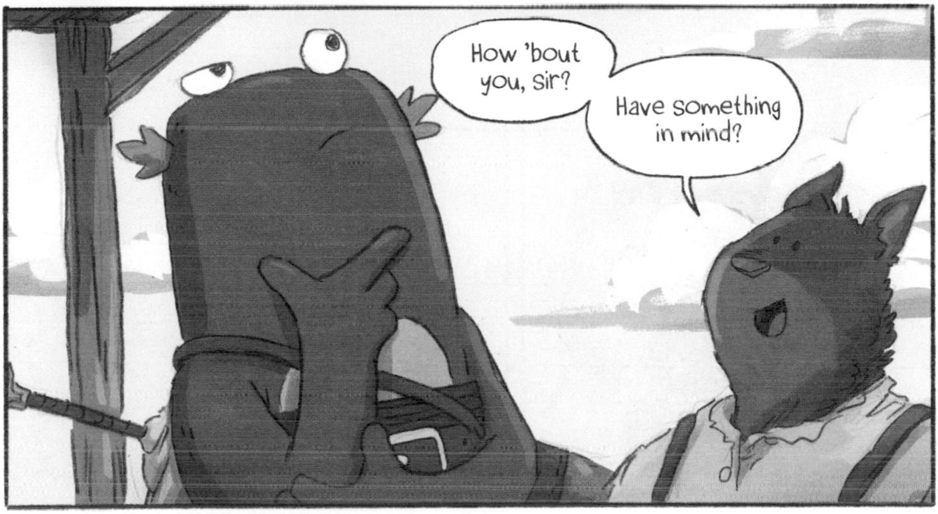
How 'bout you, sir?
Have something in mind?

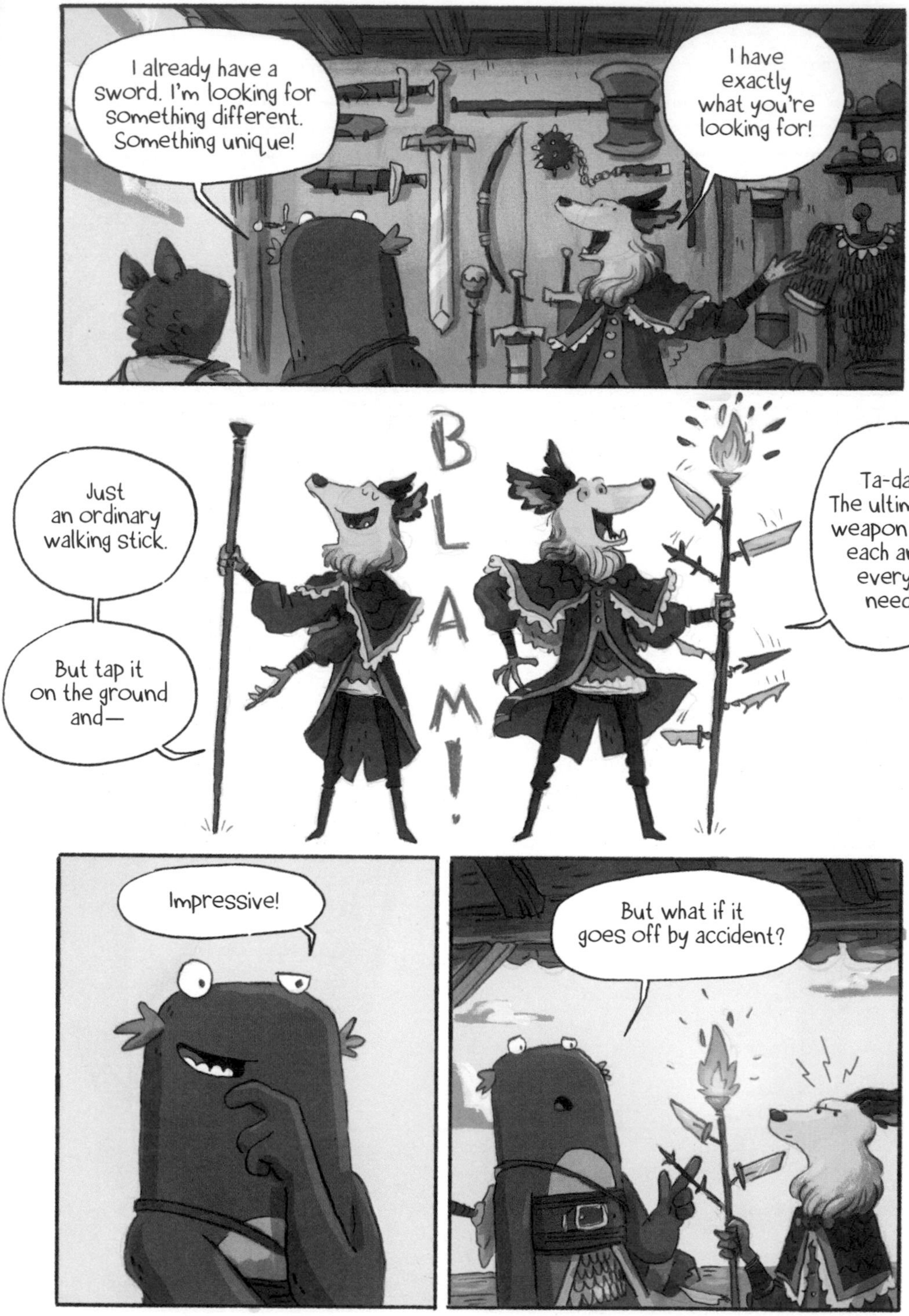
I already have a sword. I'm looking for something different. Something unique!
I have exactly what you're looking for!
Just an ordinary walking stick.
But tap it on the ground and—
BLAM!
Ta-da! The ultimate weapon for each and every need!
Impressive!
But what if it goes off by accident?

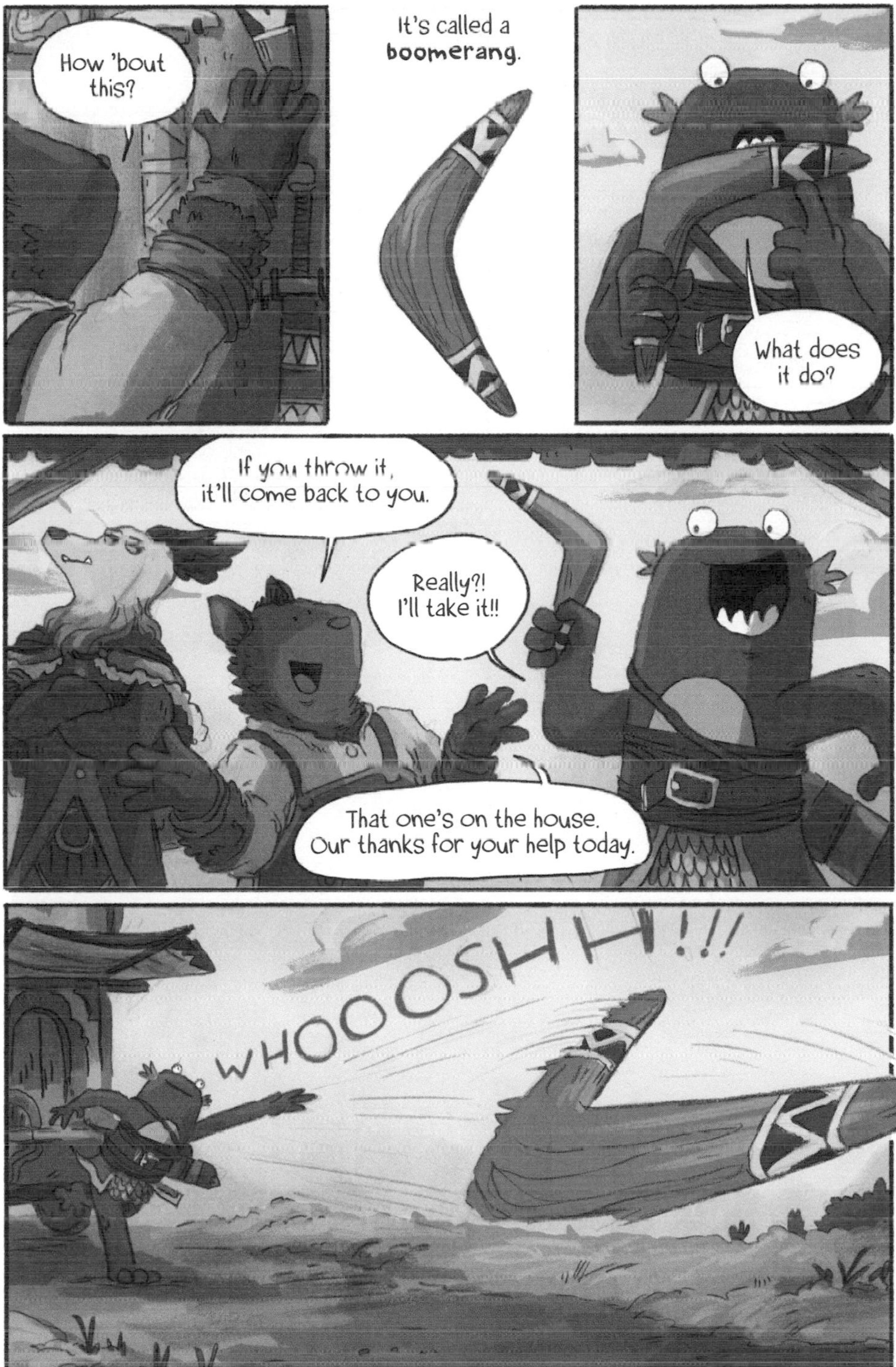
How 'bout this?
It's called a **boomerang**.
What does it do?
If you throw it, it'll come back to you.
Really?! I'll take it!!
That one's on the house. Our thanks for your help today.
WHOOOOSHH!!!

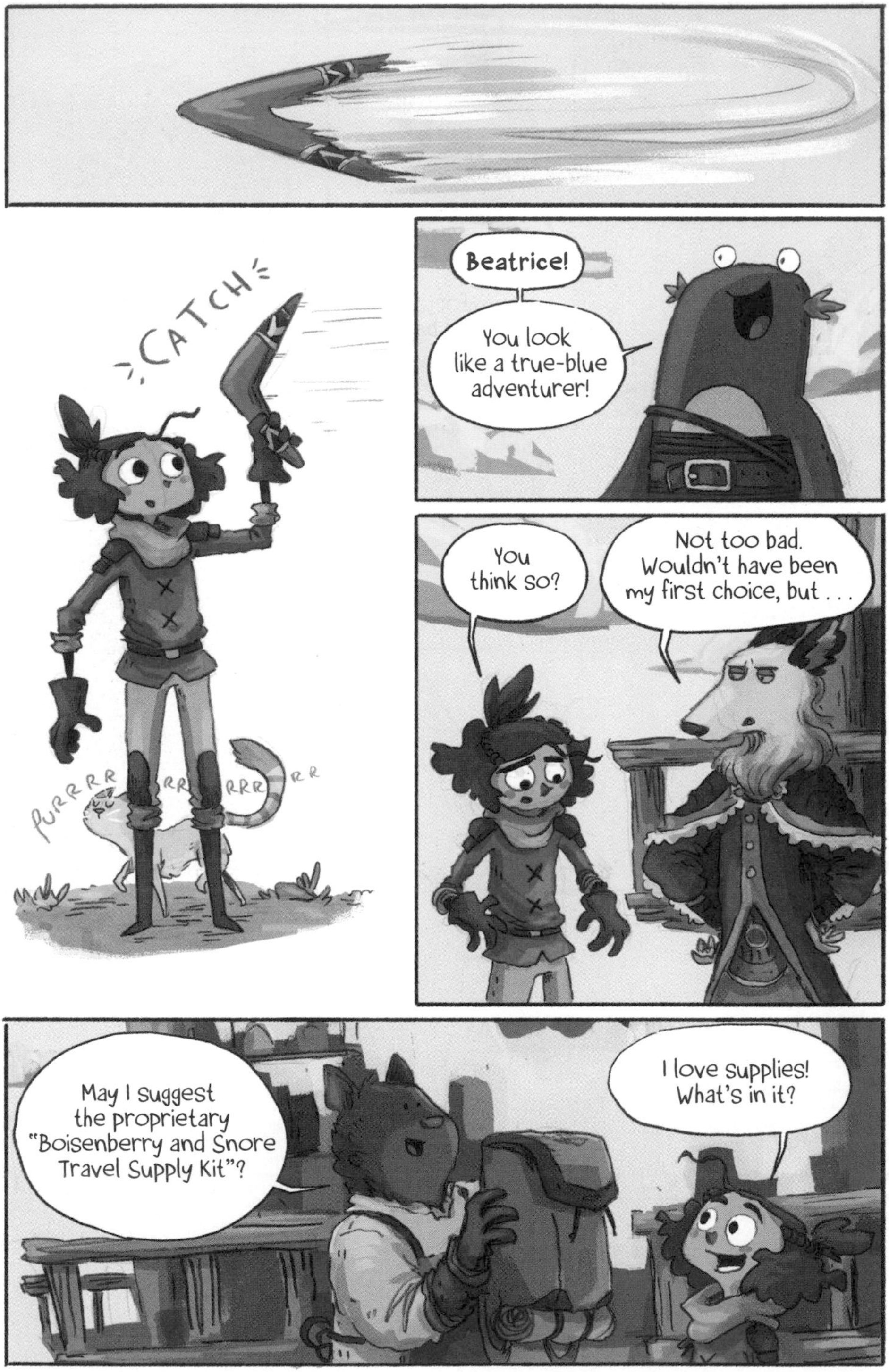
CATCH
PURRRRRRRRRRRRR
Beatrice!
You look like a true-blue adventurer!
You think so?
Not too bad. Wouldn't have been my first choice, but . . .
May I suggest the proprietary "Boisenberry and Snore Travel Supply Kit"?
I love supplies! What's in it?

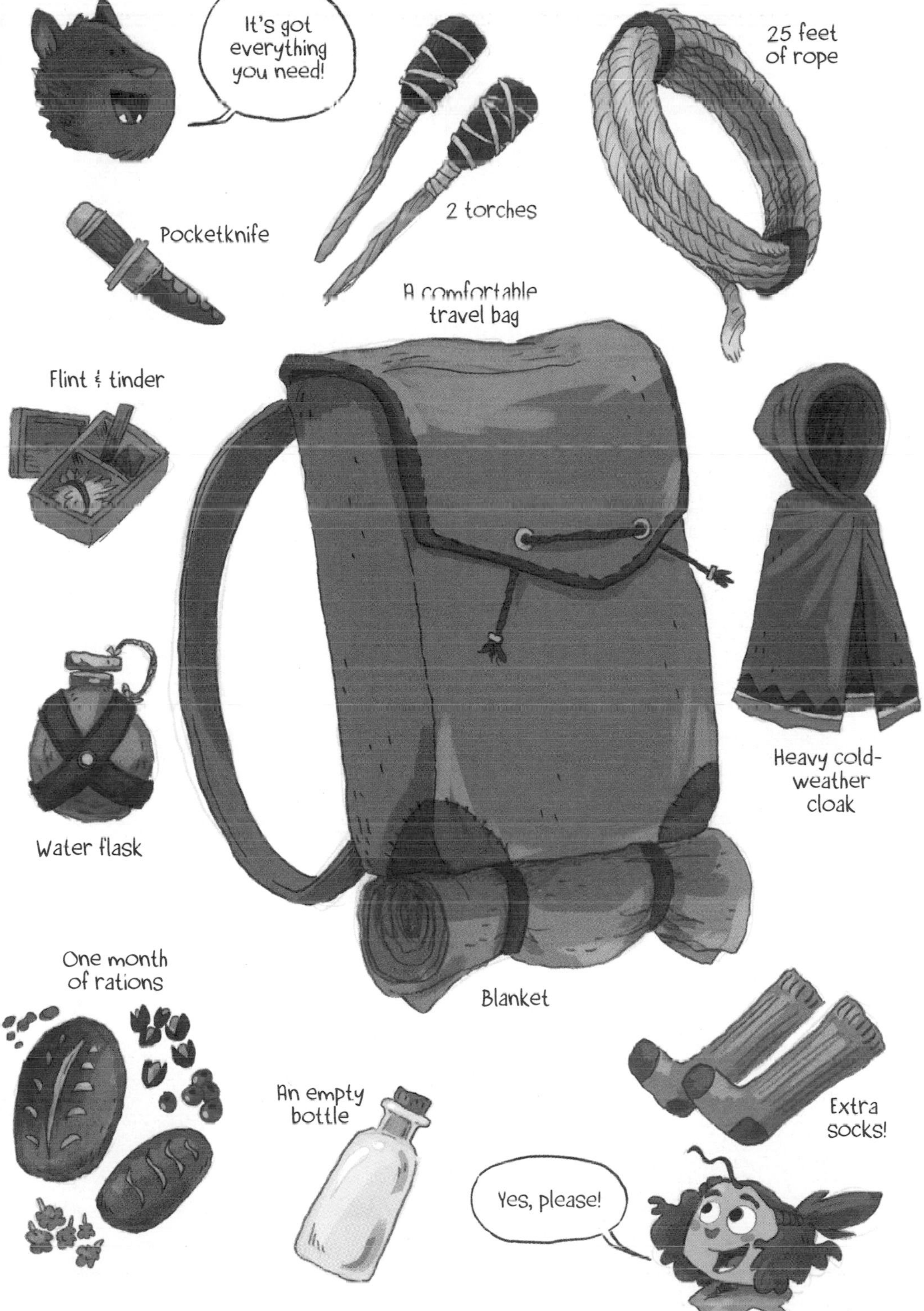
It's got everything you need!
Pocketknife
2 torches
25 feet of rope
A comfortable travel bag
Flint & tinder
Heavy cold-weather cloak
Water flask
Blanket
One month of rations
An empty bottle
Extra socks!
Yes, please!

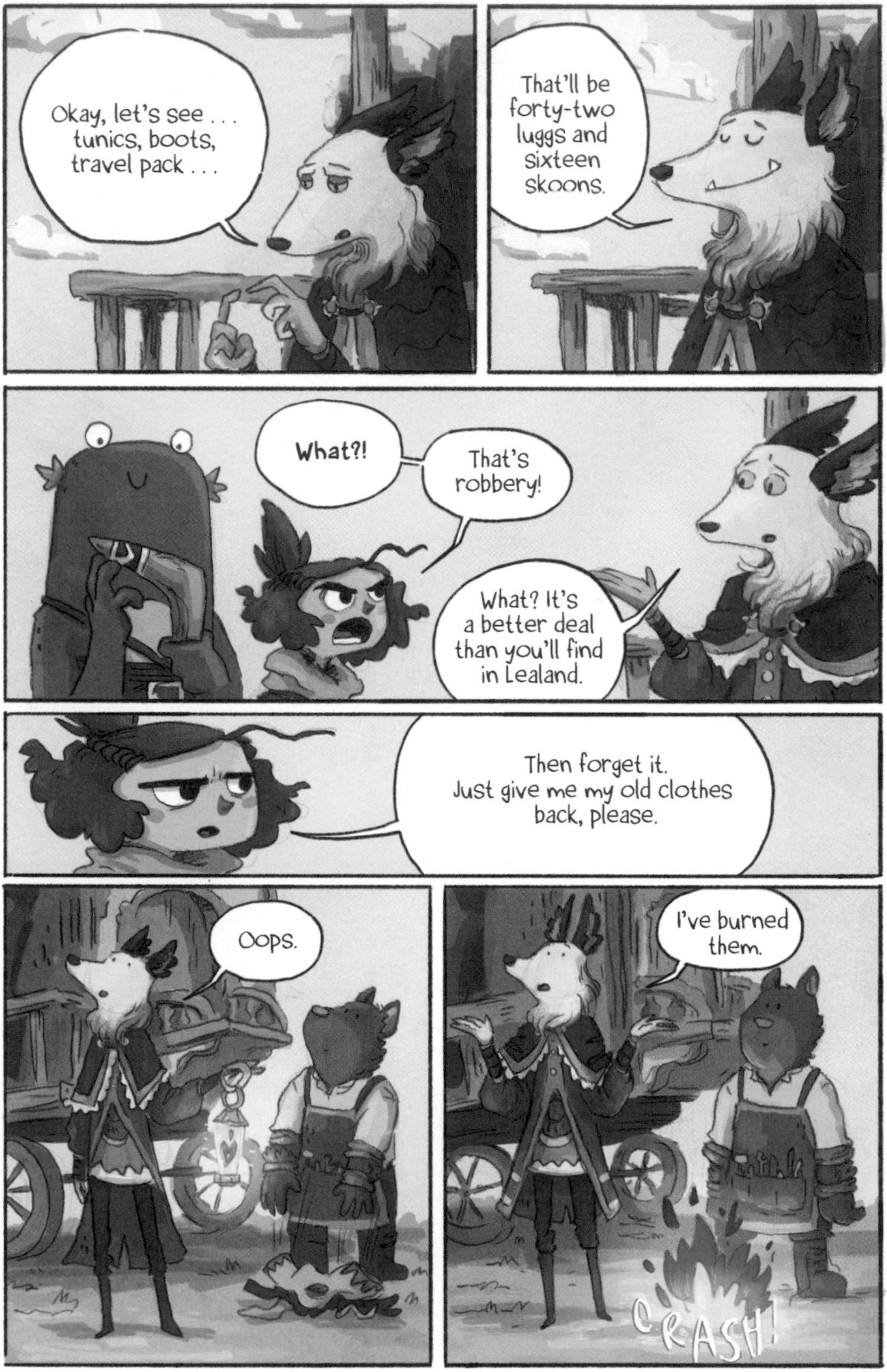
Okay, let's see . . . tunics, boots, travel pack . . .
That'll be forty-two luggs and sixteen skoons.
What?!
That's robbery!
What? It's a better deal than you'll find in Lealand.
Then forget it. Just give me my old clothes back, please.
Oops.
I've burned them.
CRASH!

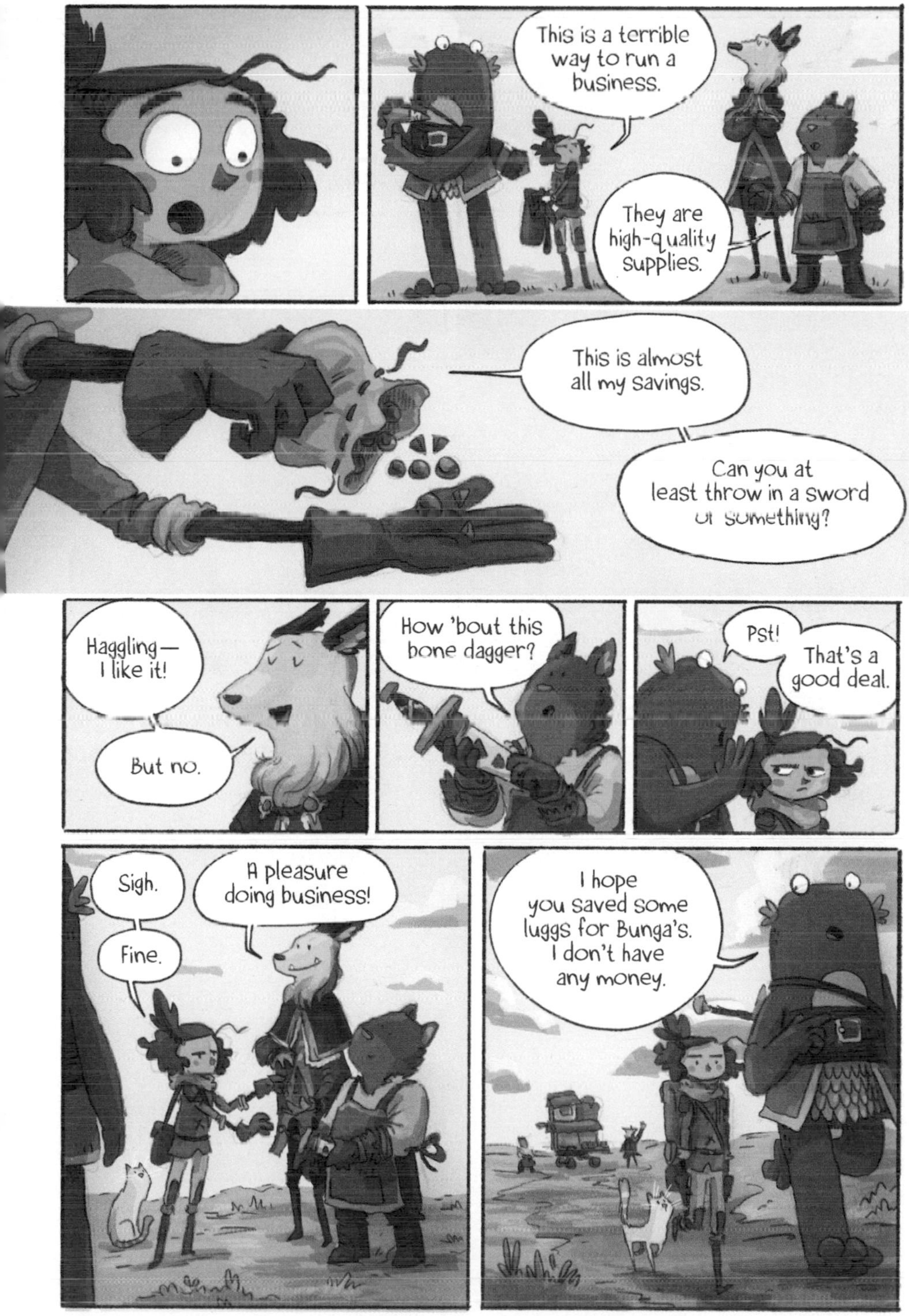
This is a terrible way to run a business.
They are high-quality supplies.
This is almost all my savings.
Can you at least throw in a sword or something?
Haggling— I like it!
But no.
How 'bout this bone dagger?
Pst!
That's a good deal.
Sigh.
Fine.
A pleasure doing business!
I hope you saved some luggs for Bunga's. I don't have any money.

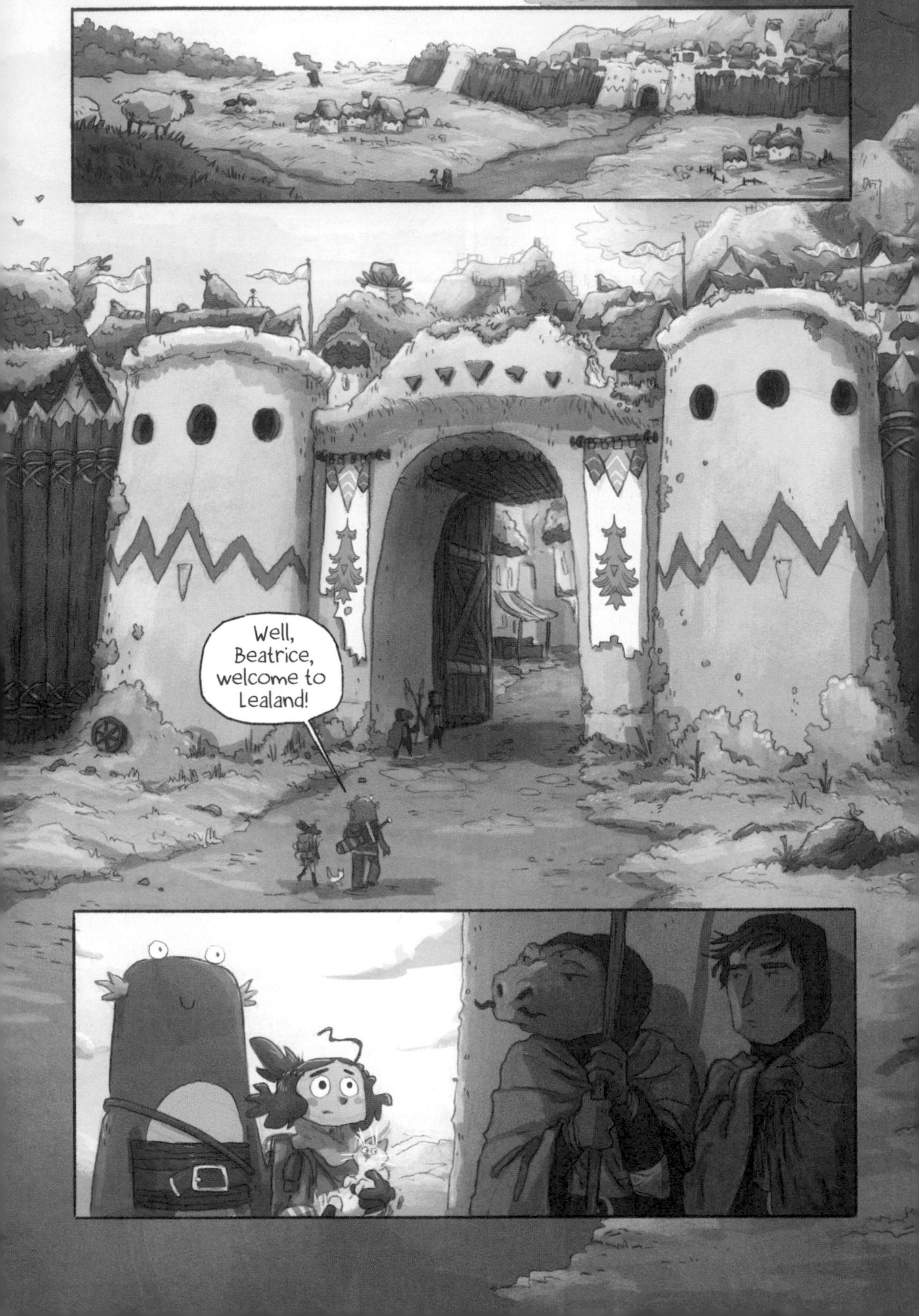
Well, Beatrice, welcome to Lealand!

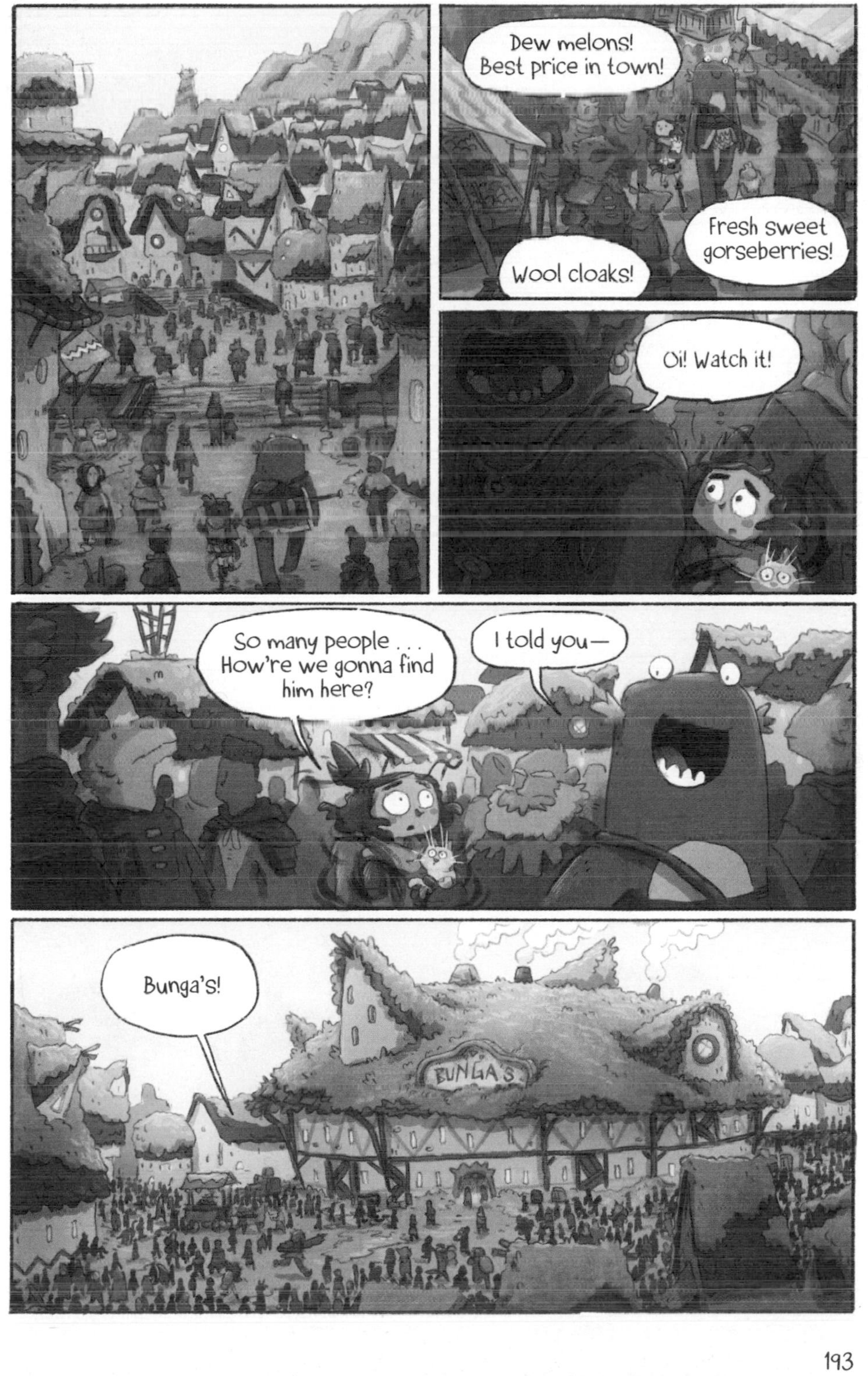
Dew melons!
Best price in town!
Wool cloaks!
Fresh sweet gorseberries!
Oi! Watch it!
So many people . . . How're we gonna find him here?
I told you—
BUNGA'S
Bunga's!

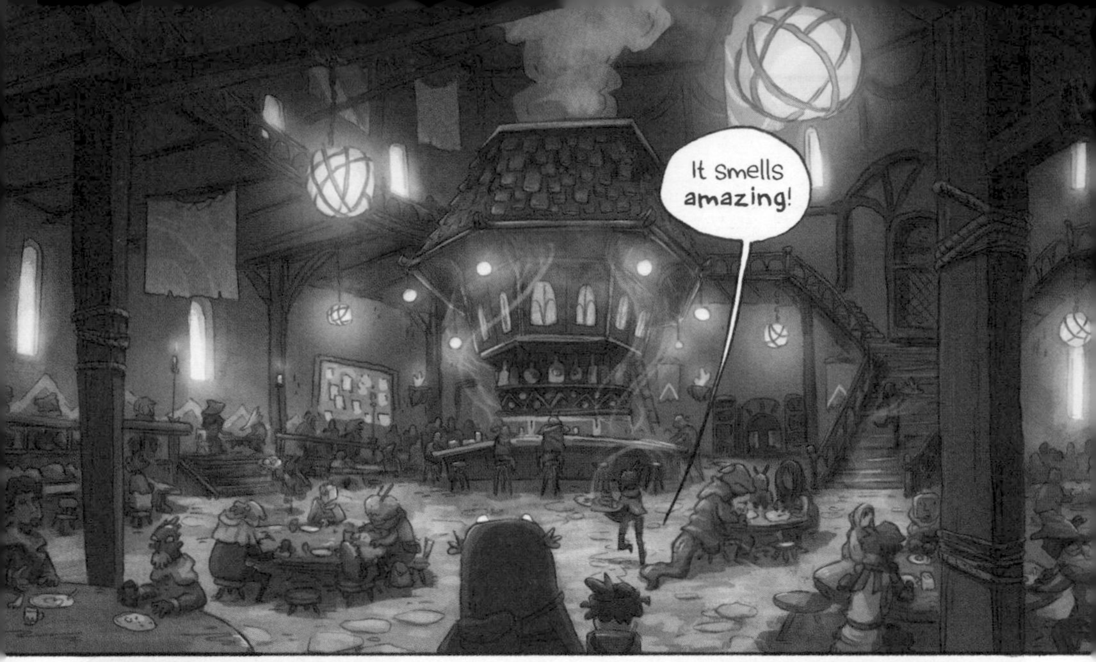
It smells amazing!

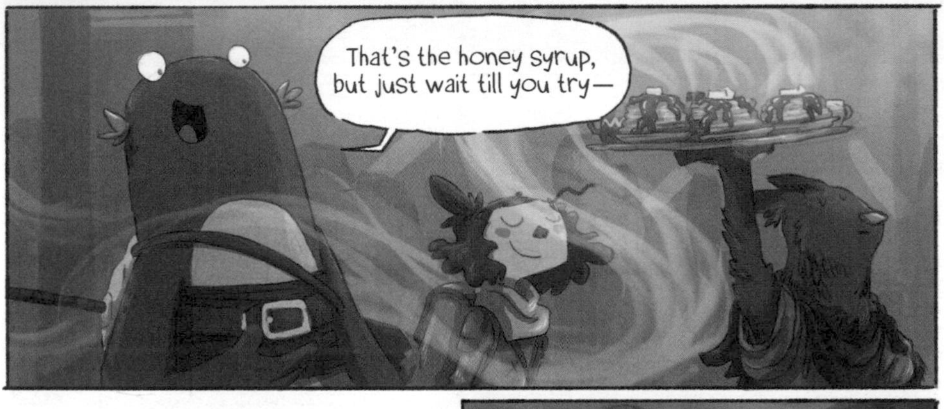
That's the honey syrup, but just wait till you try—

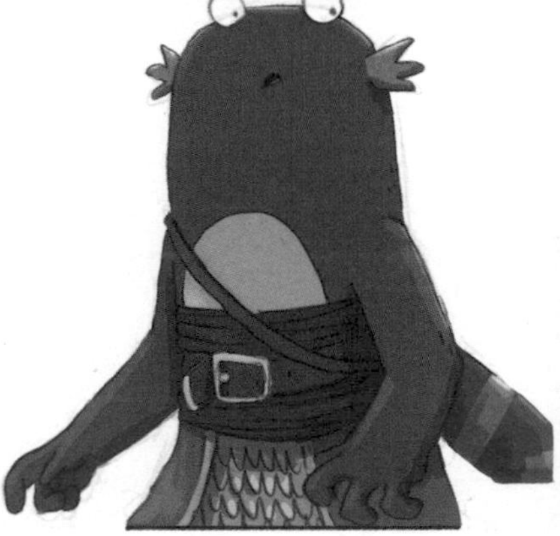

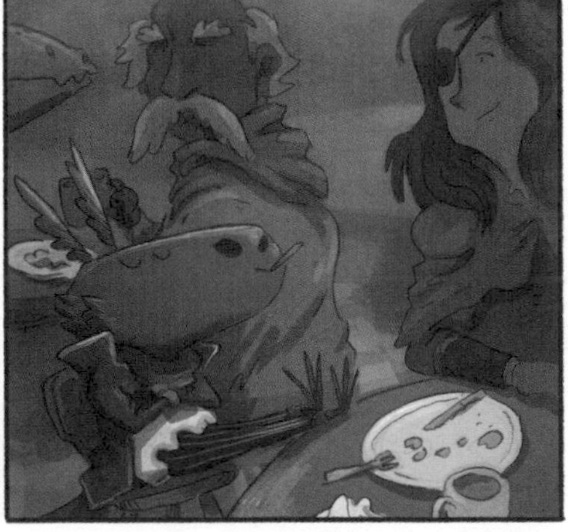

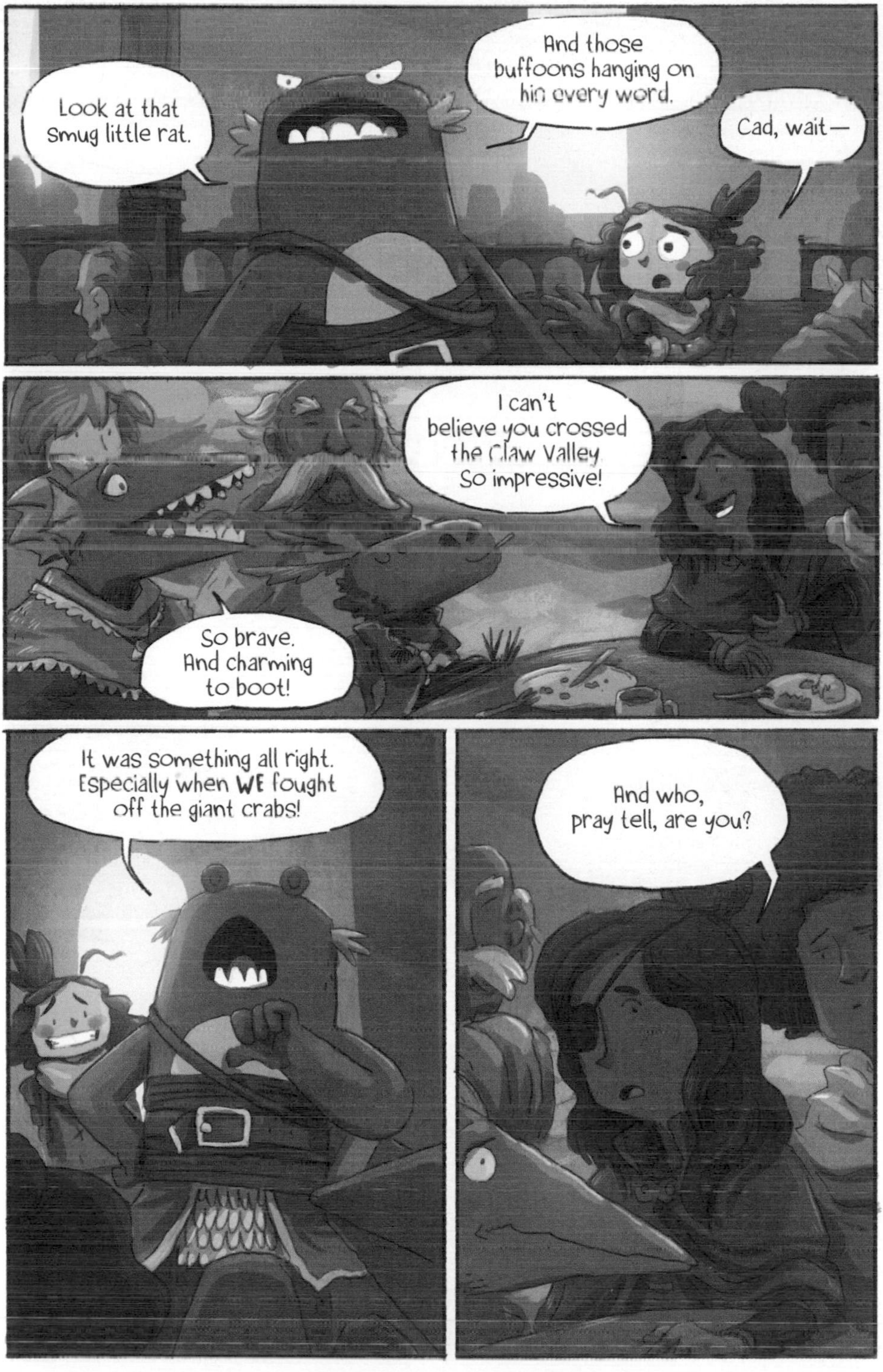
Look at that smug little rat.
And those buffoons hanging on his every word.
Cad, wait—
I can't believe you crossed the Claw Valley. So impressive!
So brave. And charming to boot!
It was something all right. Especially when **WE** fought off the giant crabs!
And who, pray tell, are you?

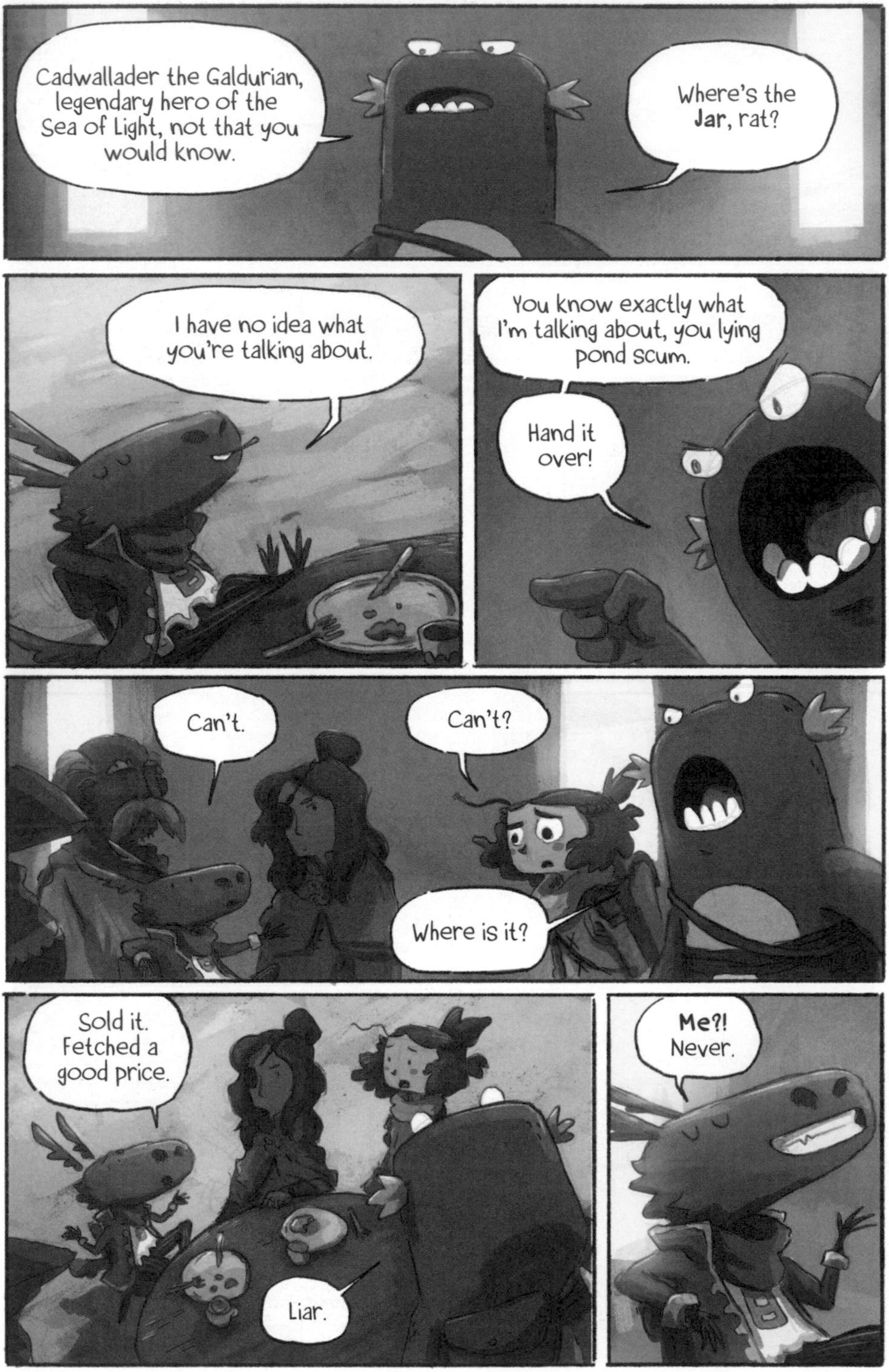
Cadwallader the Galdurian, legendary hero of the Sea of Light, not that you would know.
Where's the **Jar**, rat?
I have no idea what you're talking about.
You know exactly what I'm talking about, you lying pond scum.
Hand it over!
Can't.
Can't?
Where is it?
Sold it. Fetched a good price.
Liar.
Me?! Never.

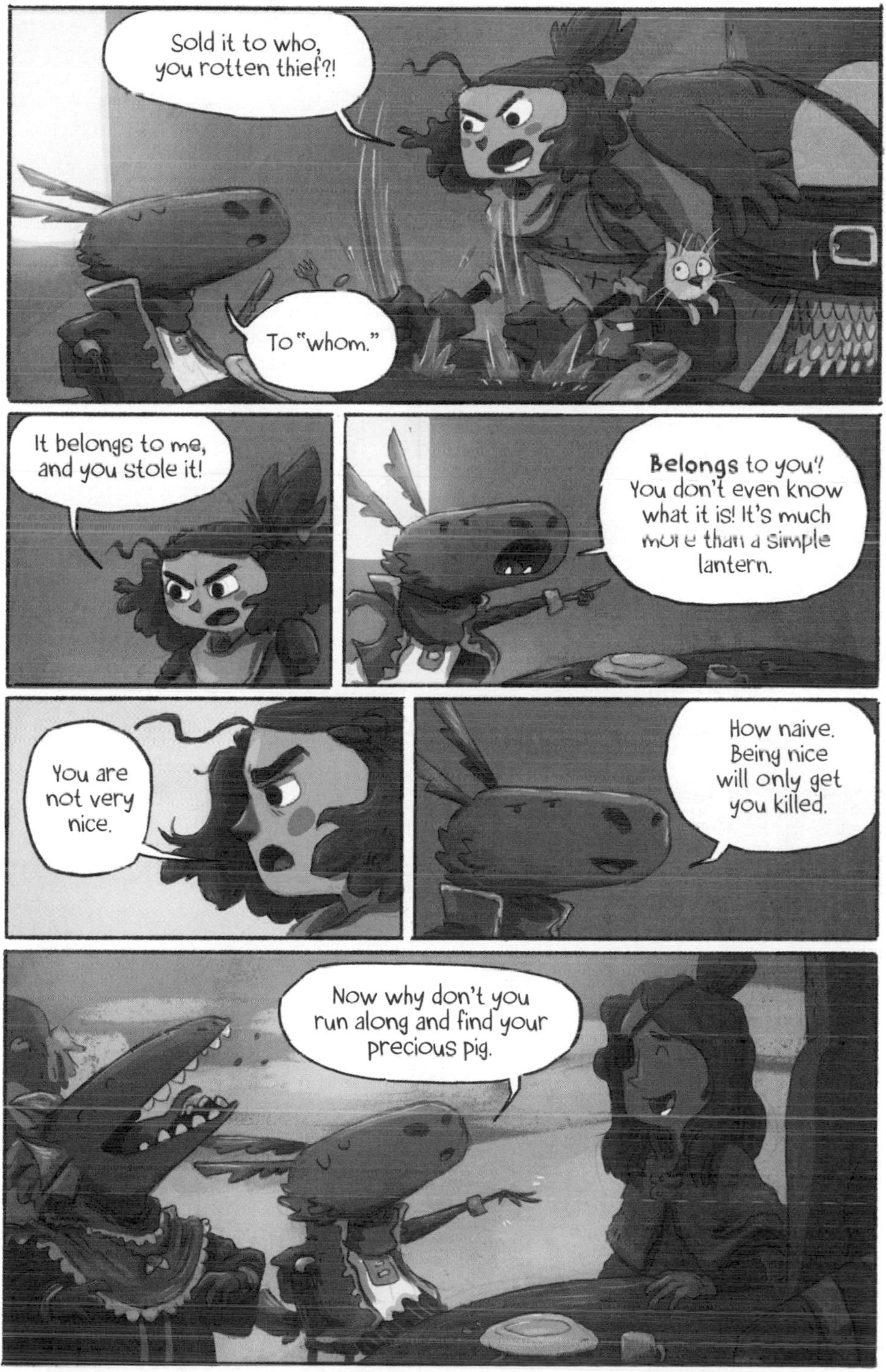

Sold it to who, you rotten thief?!
To "whom."
It belongs to me, and you stole it!
Belongs to you? You don't even know what it is! It's much more than a simple lantern.
You are not very nice.
How naive. Being nice will only get you killed.
Now why don't you run along and find your precious pig.

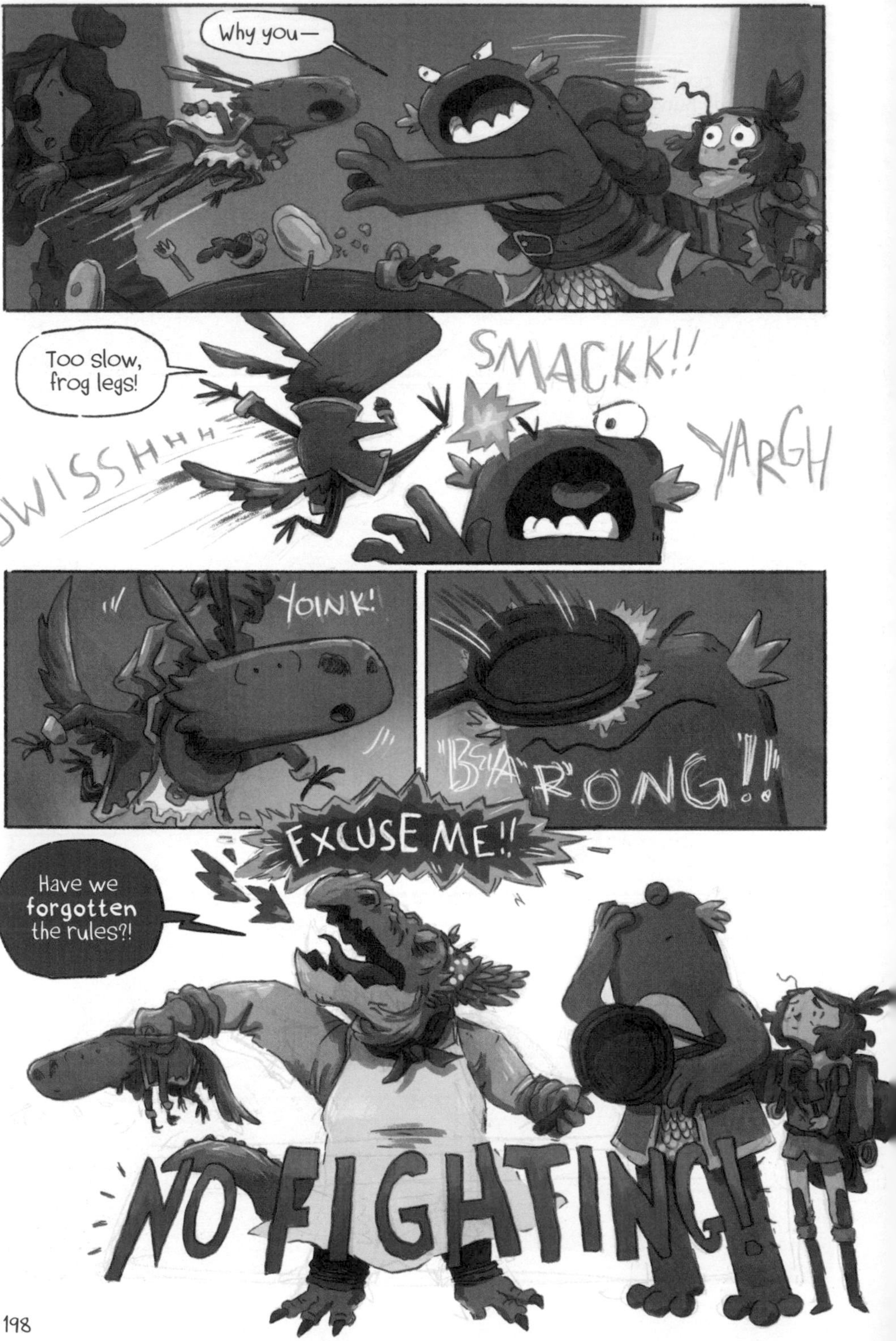

Why you—
Too slow, frog legs!
SMACKK!!
SWISSHHH
YARGH
YOINK!
BSA-RONG!!
EXCUSE ME!!
Have we **forgotten** the rules?!
NO FIGHTING!!

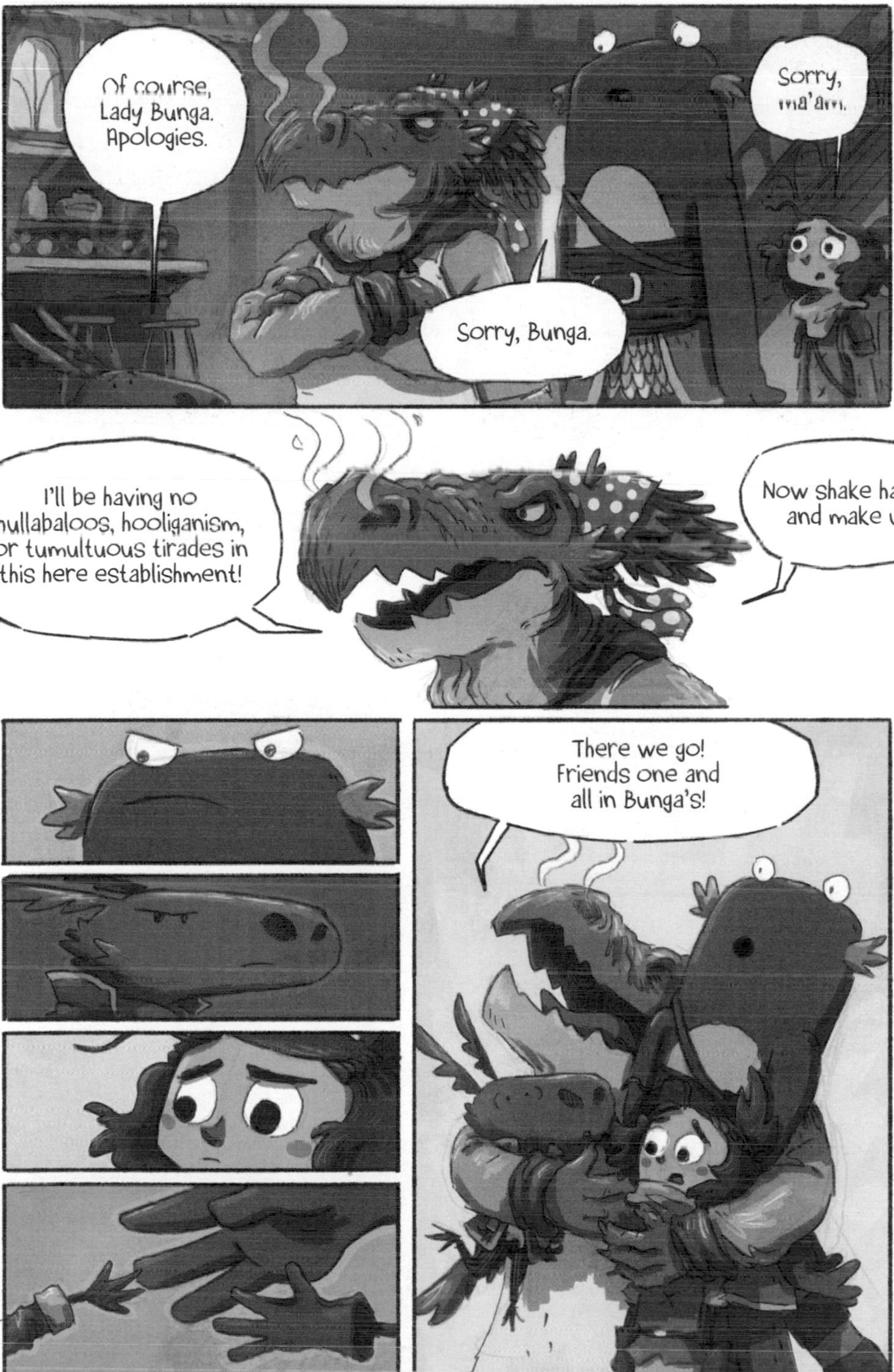

Of course, Lady Bunga. Apologies.
Sorry, Bunga.
Sorry, ma'am.
I'll be having no hullabaloos, hooliganism, or tumultuous tirades in this here establishment!
Now shake hands and make up.
There we go! Friends one and all in Bunga's!

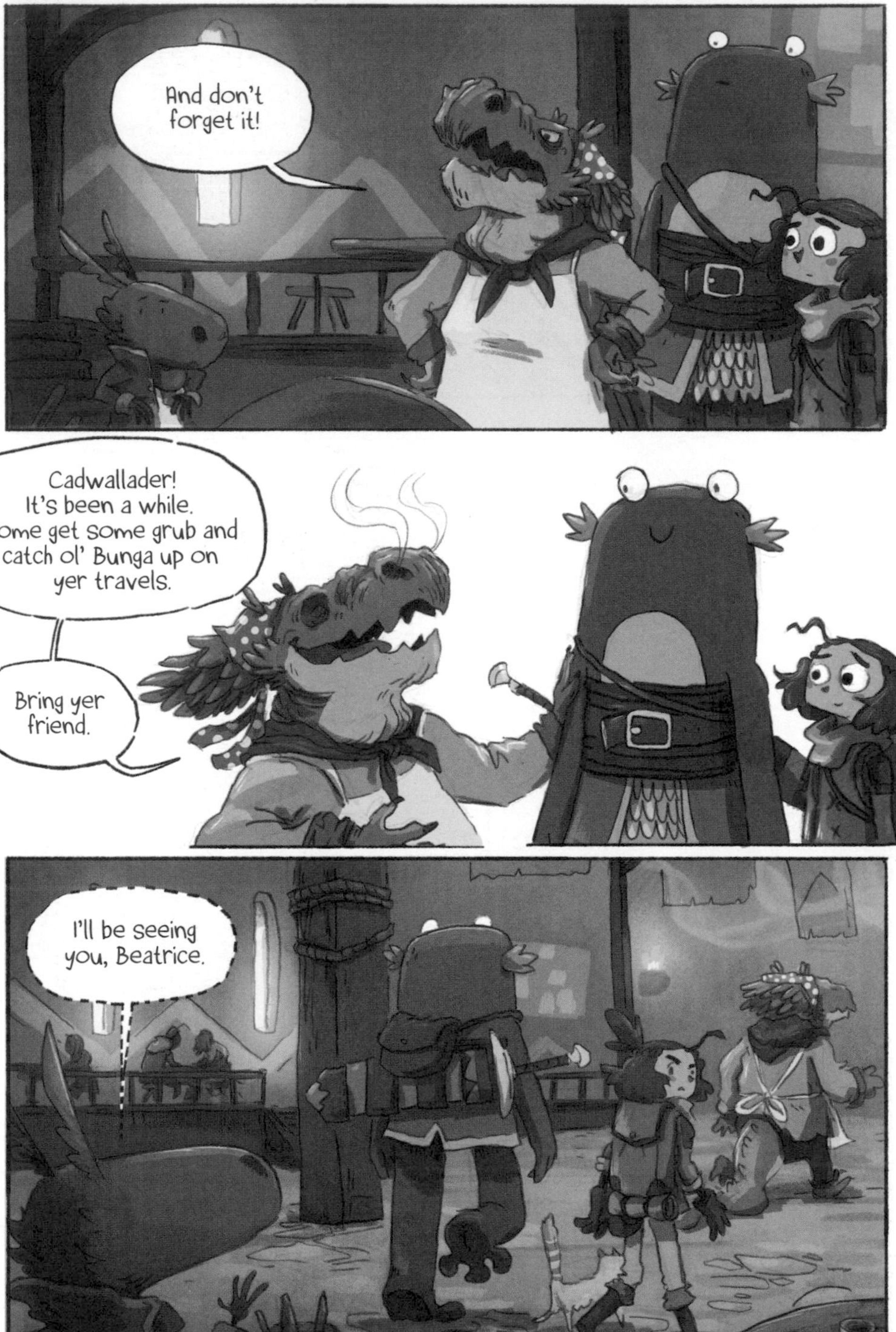
And don't forget it!
Cadwallader! It's been a while. Come get some grub and catch ol' Bunga up on yer travels.
Bring yer friend.
I'll be seeing you, Beatrice.

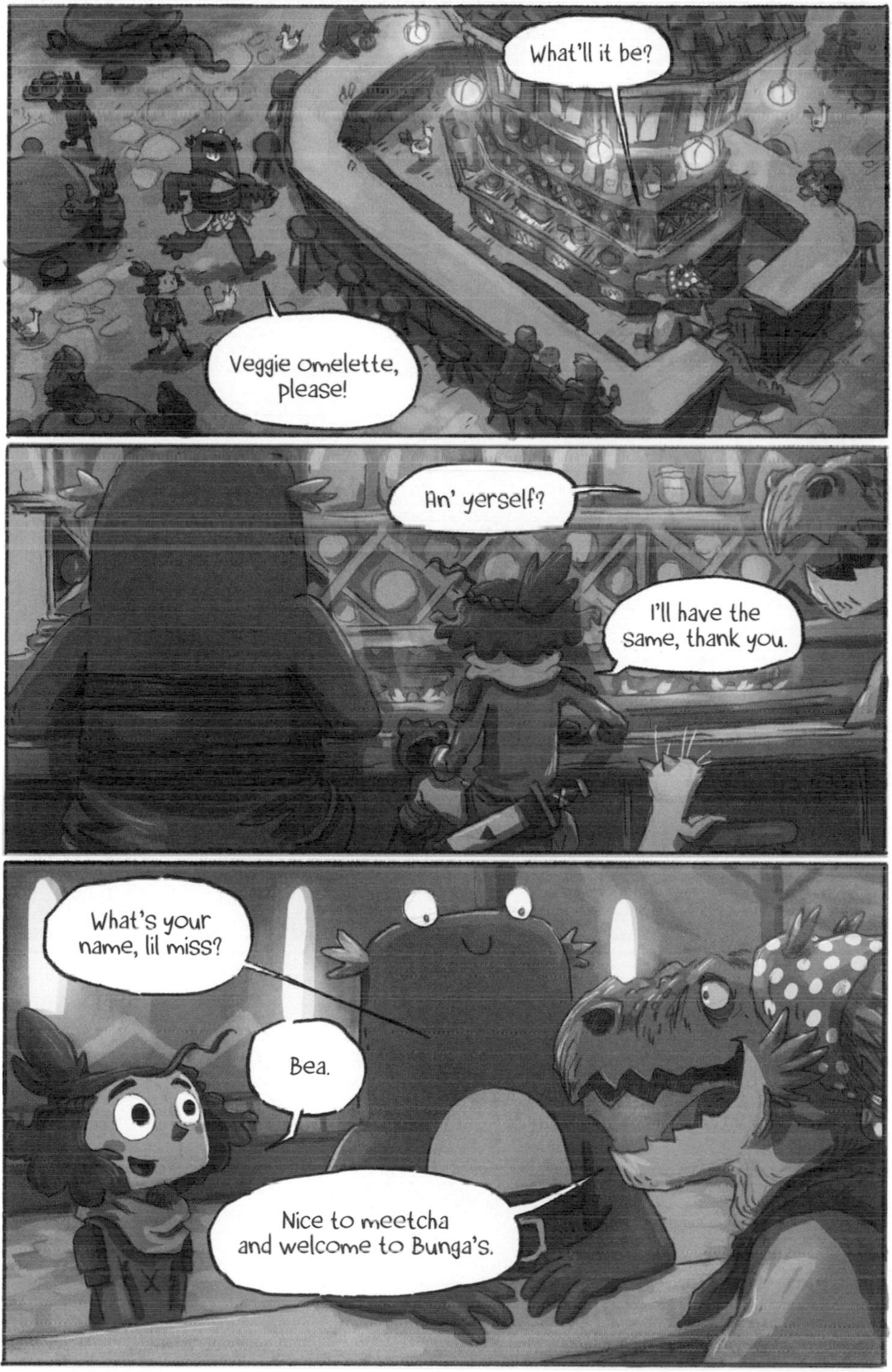
What'll it be?
Veggie omelette, please!
An' yerself?
I'll have the same, thank you.
What's your name, lil miss?
Bea.
Nice to meetcha and welcome to Bunga's.

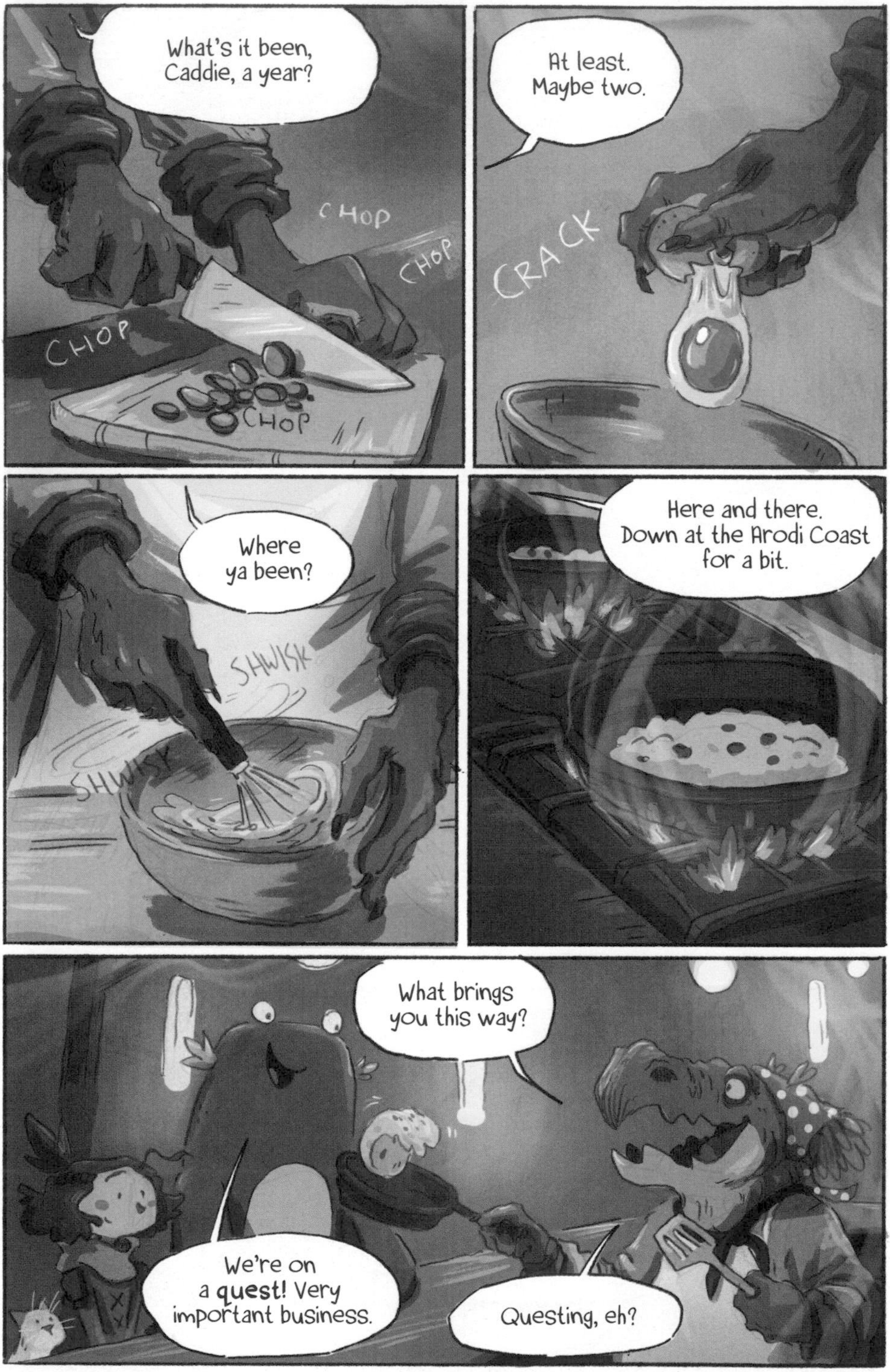
What's it been, Caddie, a year?
CHOP
CHOP
CHOP
CHOP
At least. Maybe two.
CRACK
Where ya been?
SHWISK
SHWISK
Here and there. Down at the Arodi Coast for a bit.
What brings you this way?
We're on a **quest!** Very important business.
Questing, eh?

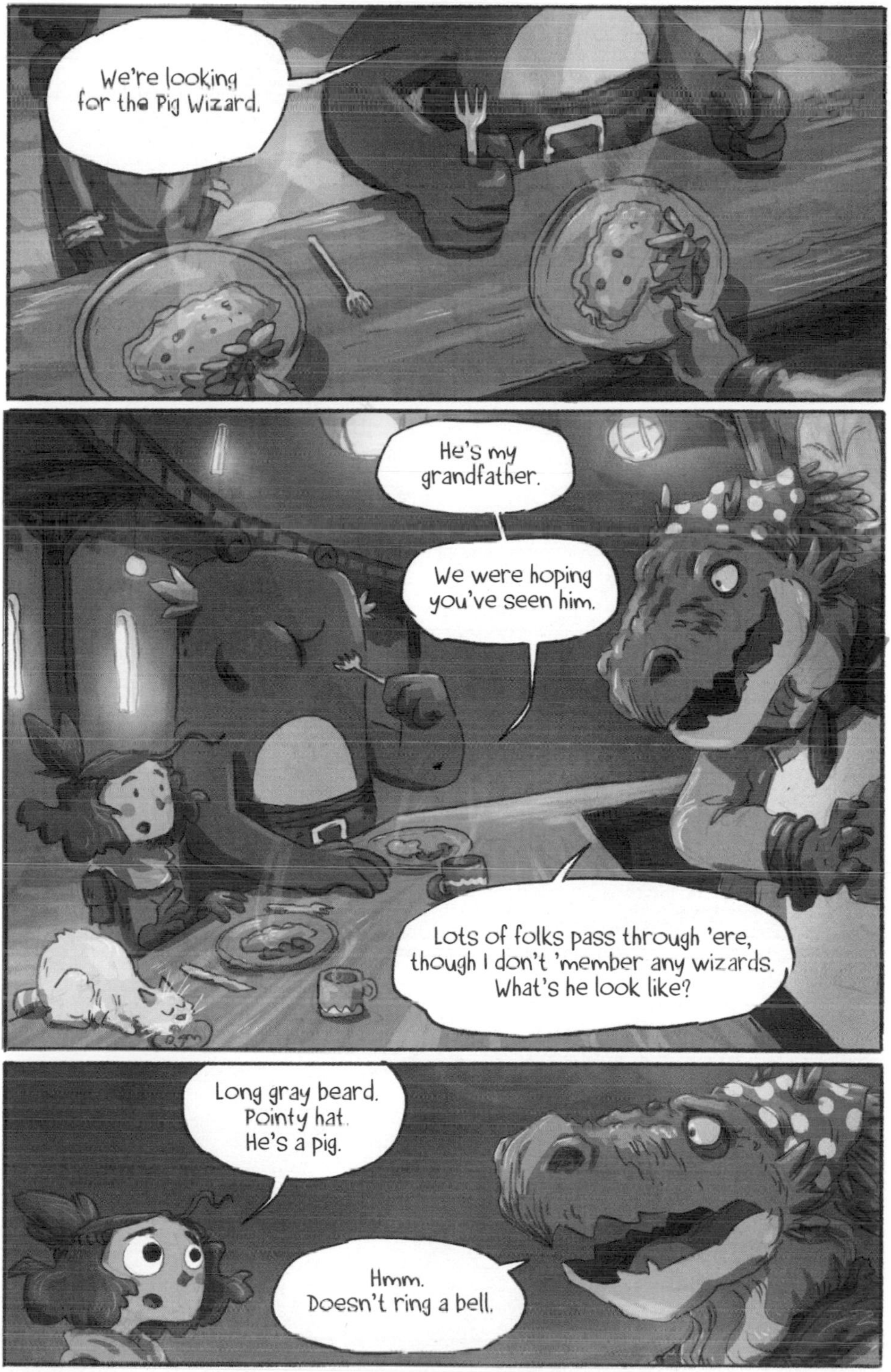
We're looking for the Pig Wizard.
He's my grandfather.
We were hoping you've seen him.
Lots of folks pass through 'ere, though I don't 'member any wizards. What's he look like?
Long gray beard. Pointy hat. He's a pig.
Hmm. Doesn't ring a bell.

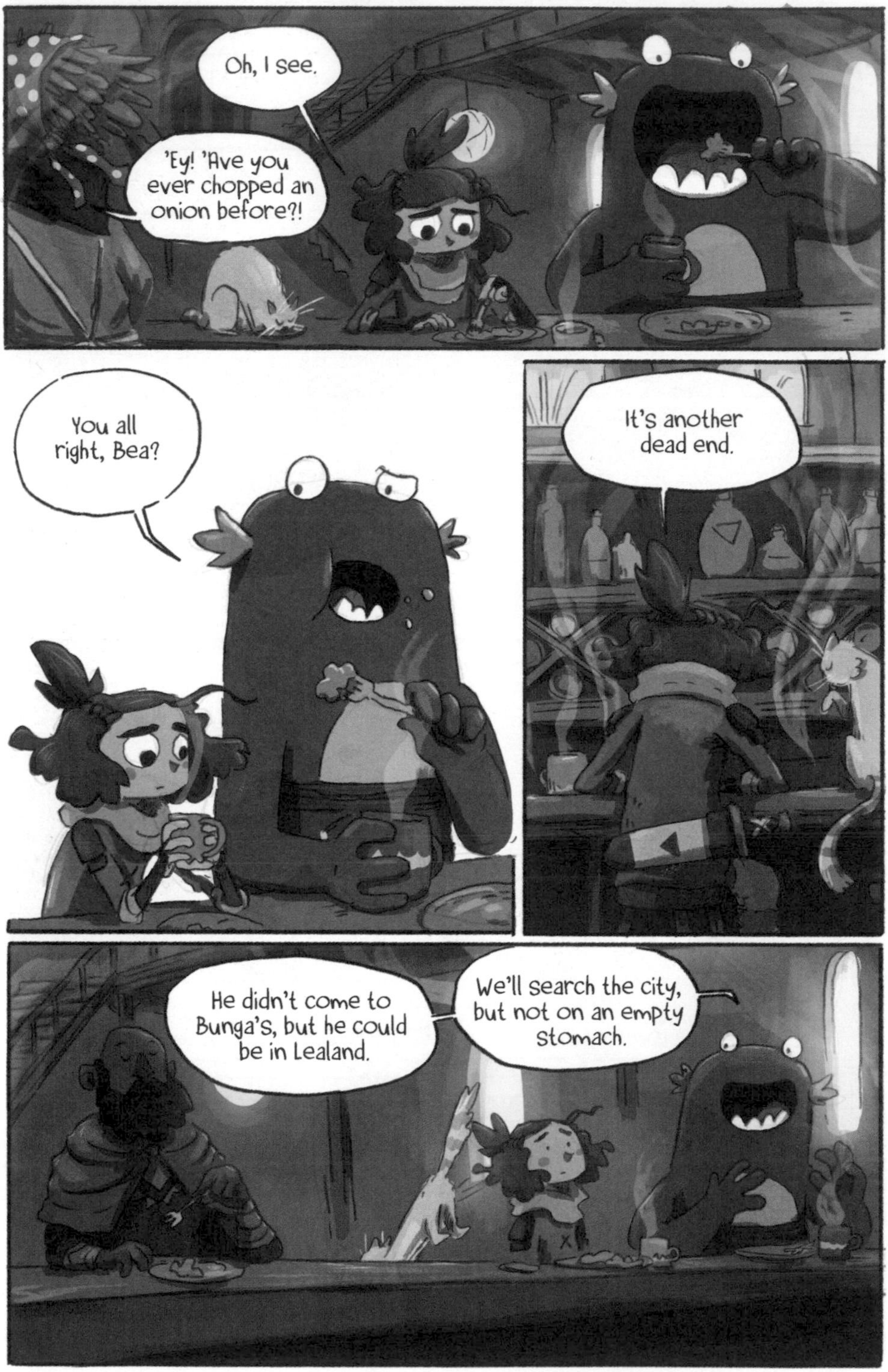
Oh, I see.
'Ey! 'Ave you ever chopped an onion before?!
You all right, Bea?
It's another dead end.
He didn't come to Bunga's, but he could be in Lealand.
We'll search the city, but not on an empty stomach.

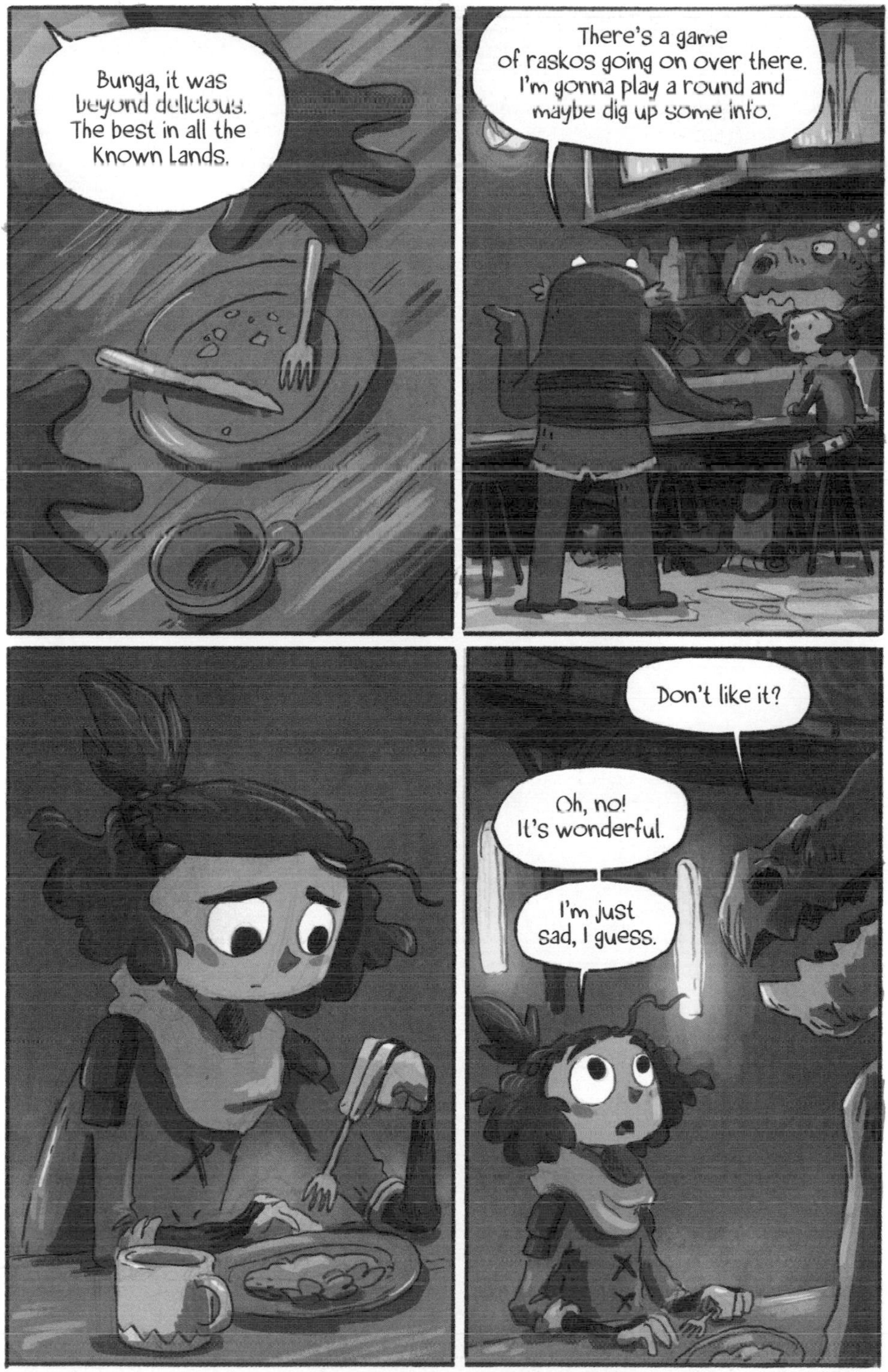
Bunga, it was beyond delicious. The best in all the Known Lands.
There's a game of raskos going on over there. I'm gonna play a round and maybe dig up some info.
Don't like it?
Oh, no! It's wonderful.
I'm just sad, I guess.

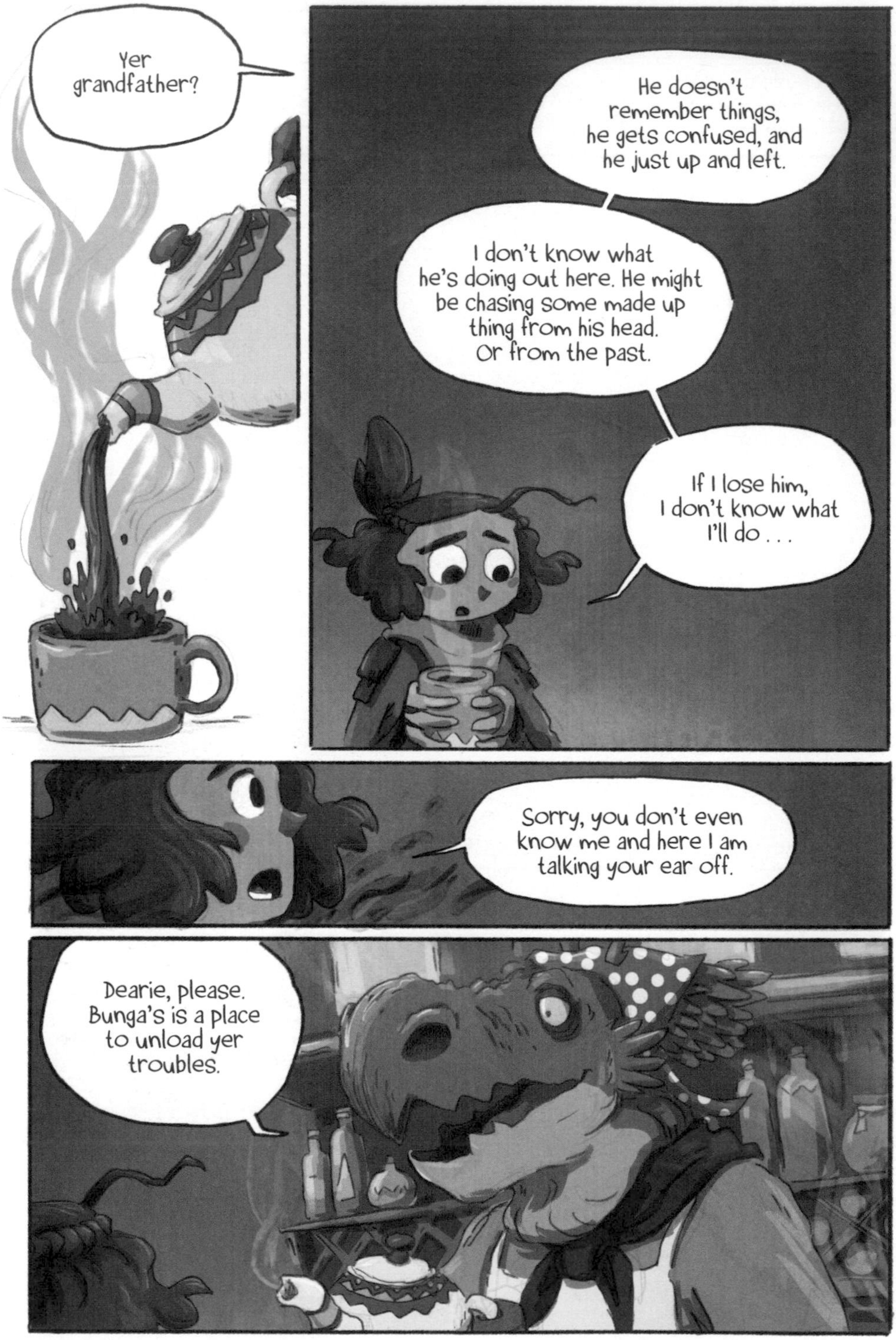
Yer grandfather?
He doesn't remember things, he gets confused, and he just up and left.
I don't know what he's doing out here. He might be chasing some made up thing from his head. Or from the past.
If I lose him, I don't know what I'll do . . .
Sorry, you don't even know me and here I am talking your ear off.
Dearie, please. Bunga's is a place to unload yer troubles.

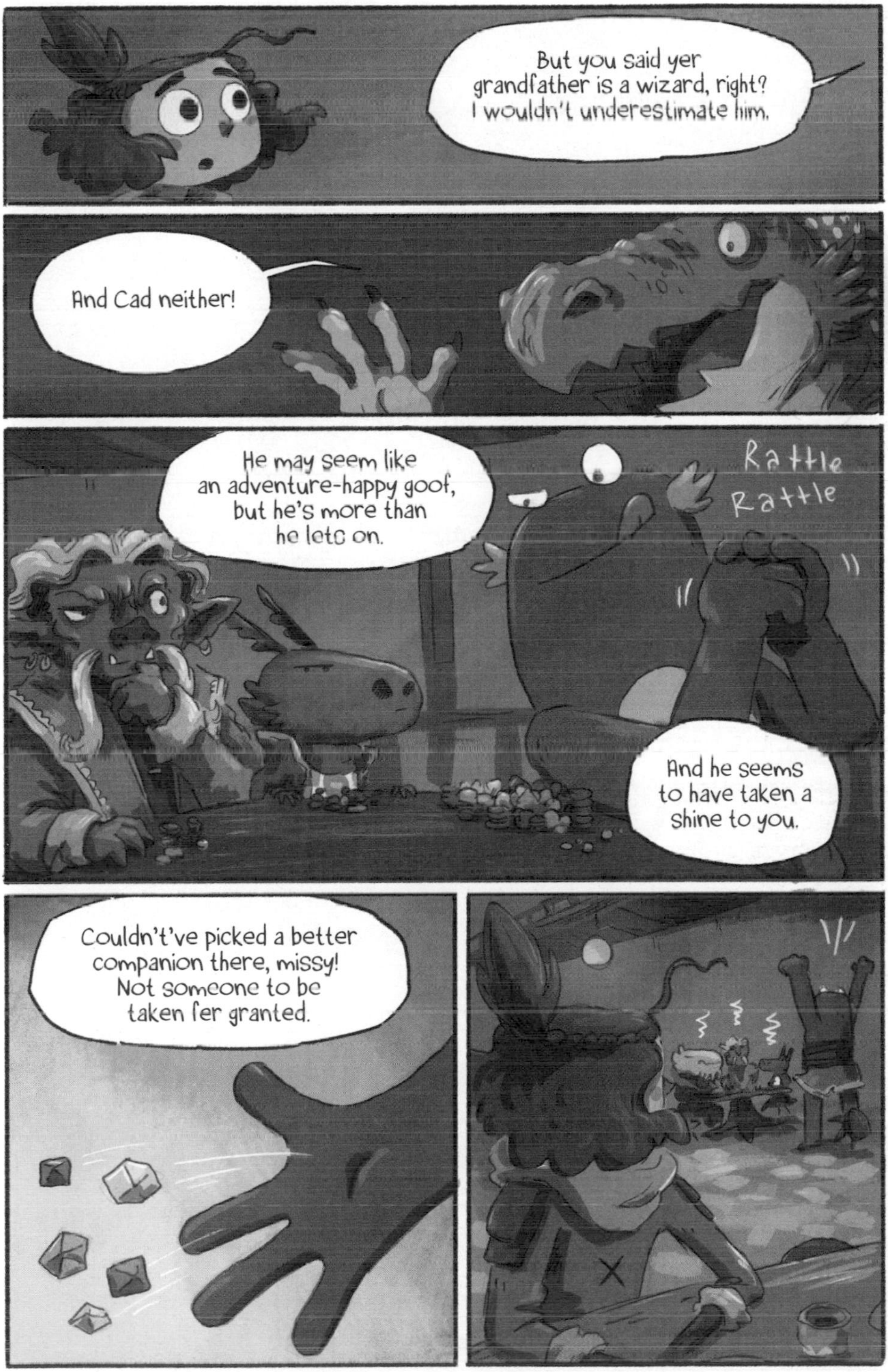

But you said yer grandfather is a wizard, right? I wouldn't underestimate him.
And Cad neither!
He may seem like an adventure-happy goof, but he's more than he lets on.
Rattle Rattle
And he seems to have taken a shine to you.
Couldn't've picked a better companion there, missy! Not someone to be taken fer granted.

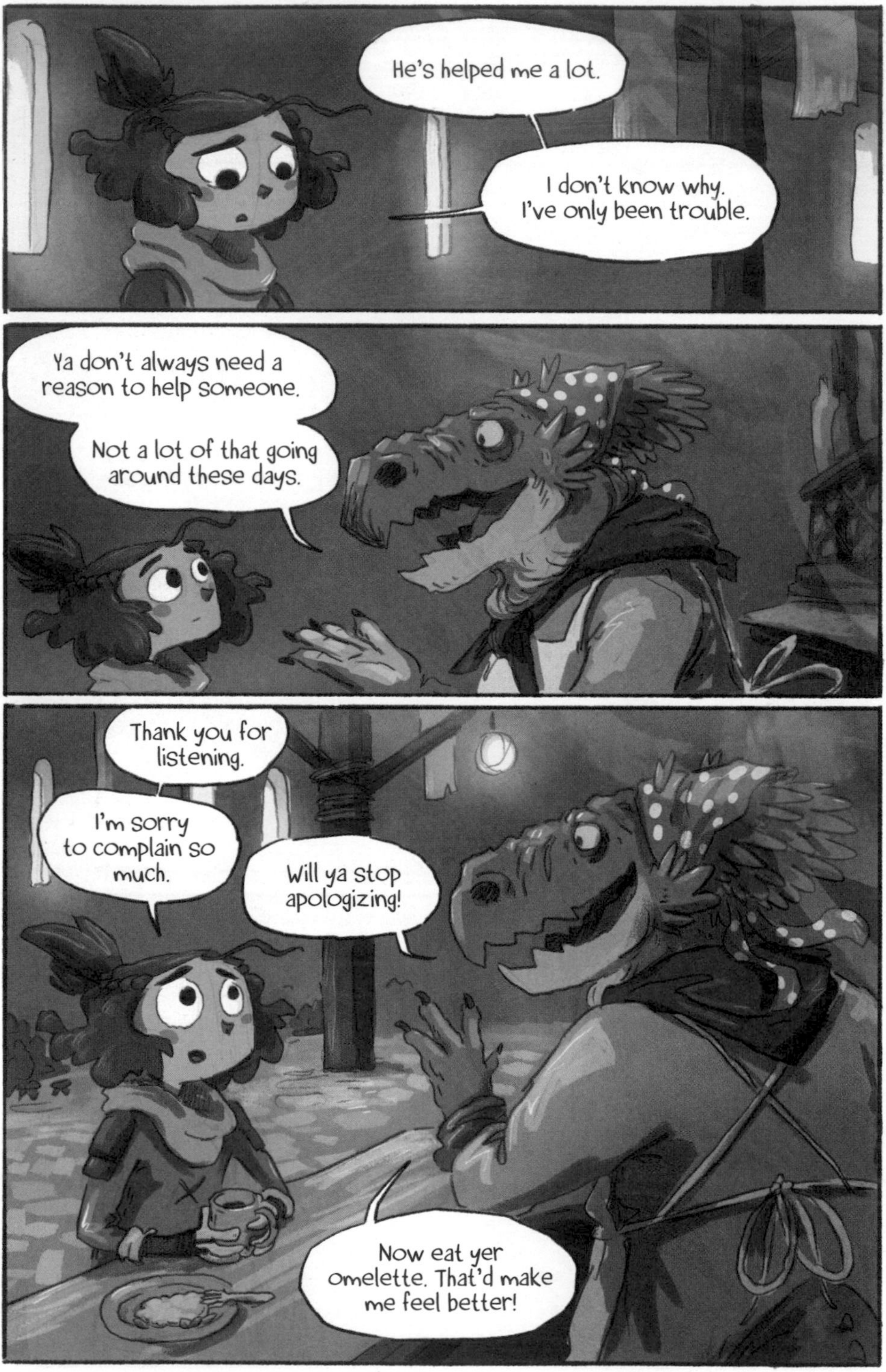
He's helped me a lot.
I don't know why. I've only been trouble.
Ya don't always need a reason to help someone.
Not a lot of that going around these days.
Thank you for listening.
I'm sorry to complain so much.
Will ya stop apologizing!
Now eat yer omelette. That'd make me feel better!

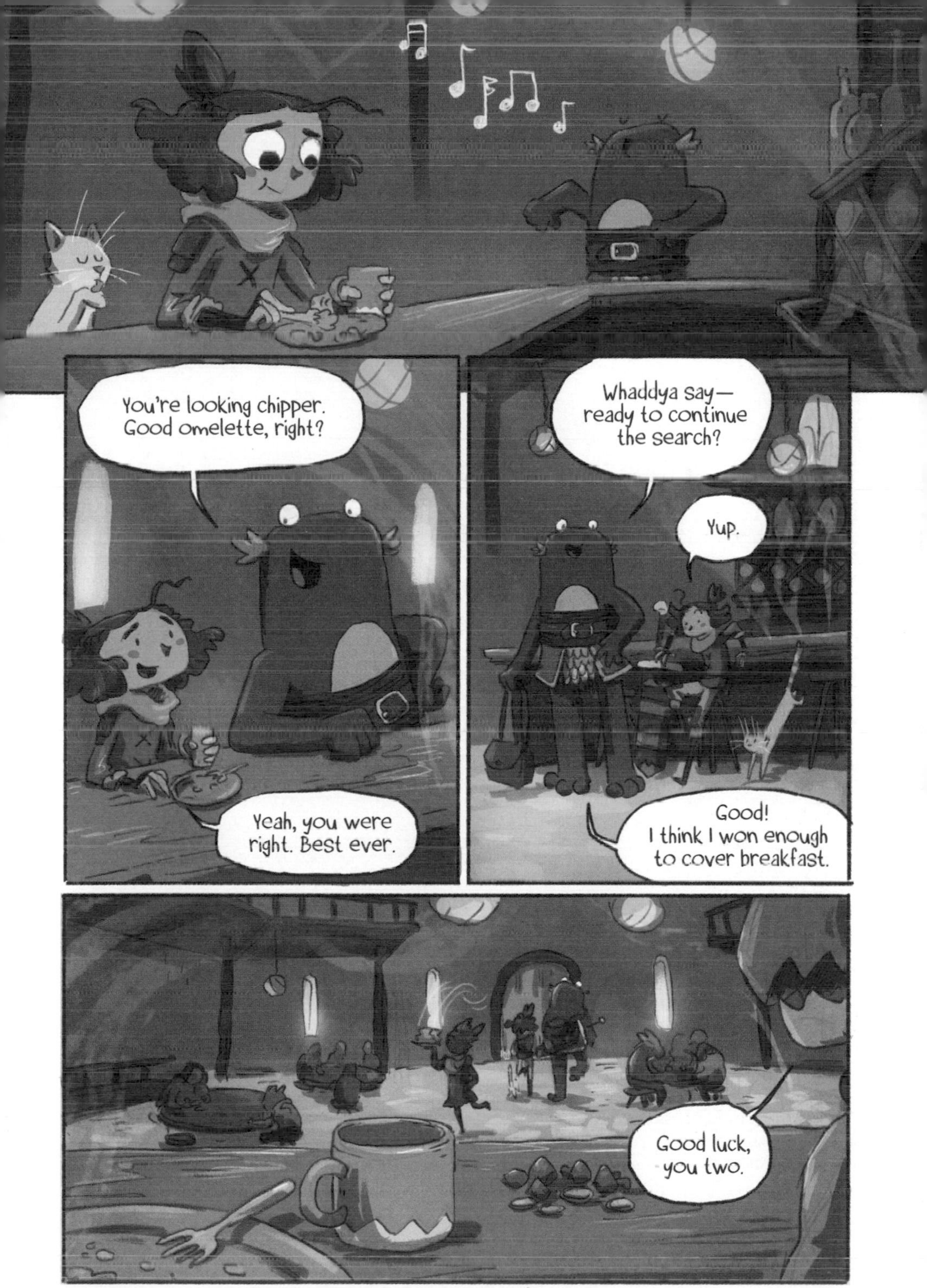
You're looking chipper. Good omelette, right?
Yeah, you were right. Best ever.
Whaddya say—ready to continue the search?
Yup.
Good! I think I won enough to cover breakfast.
Good luck, you two.

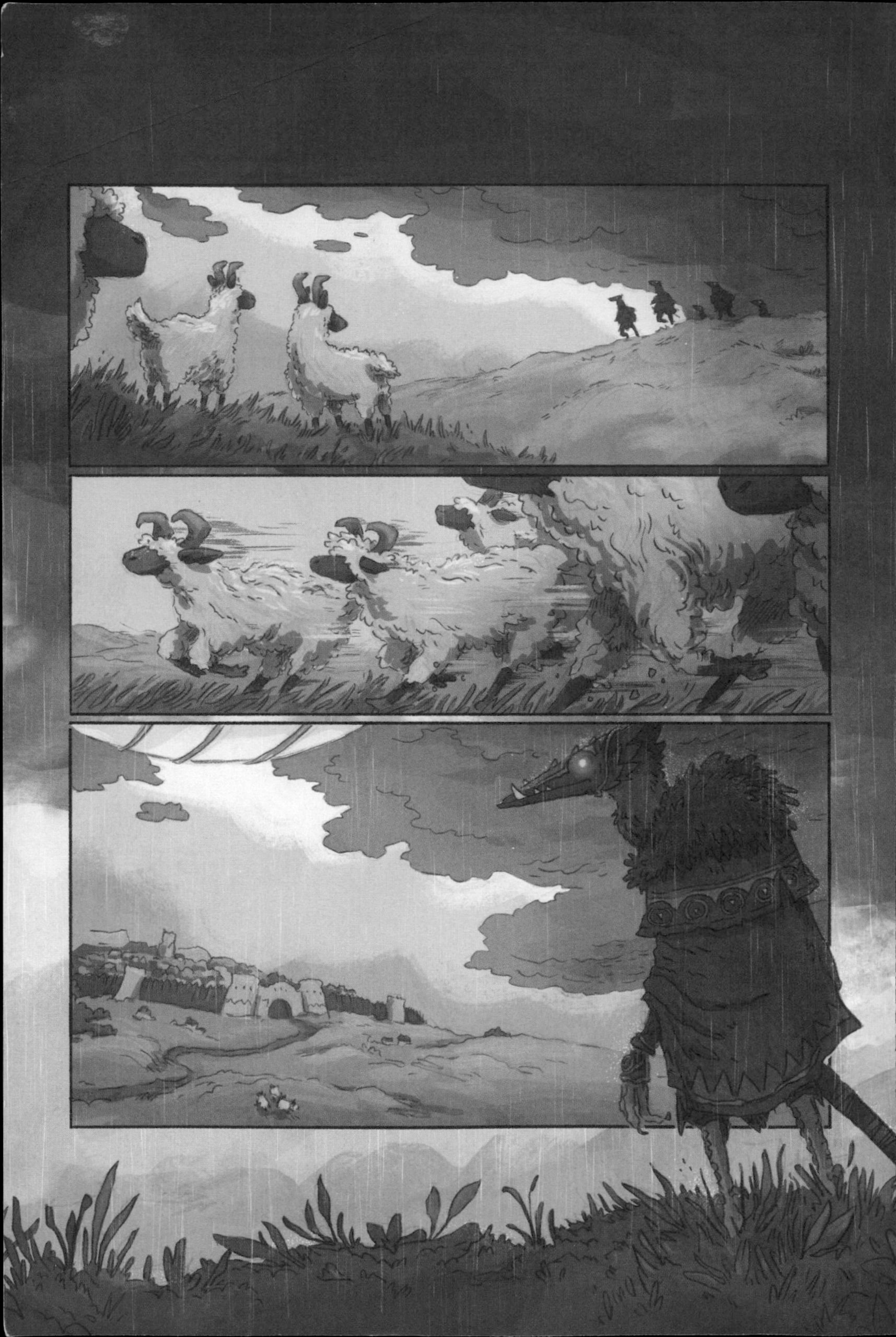

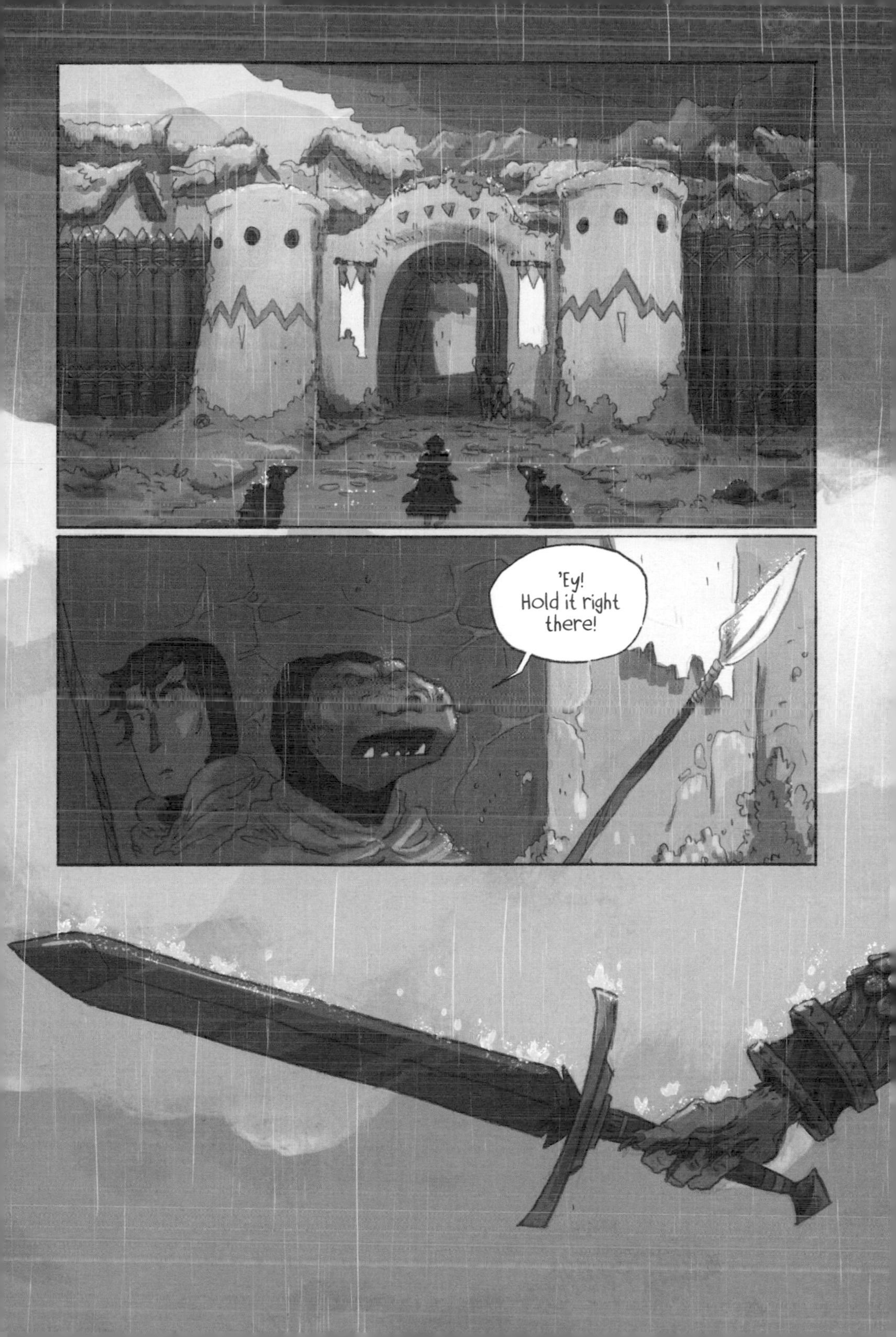
'Ey! Hold it right there!

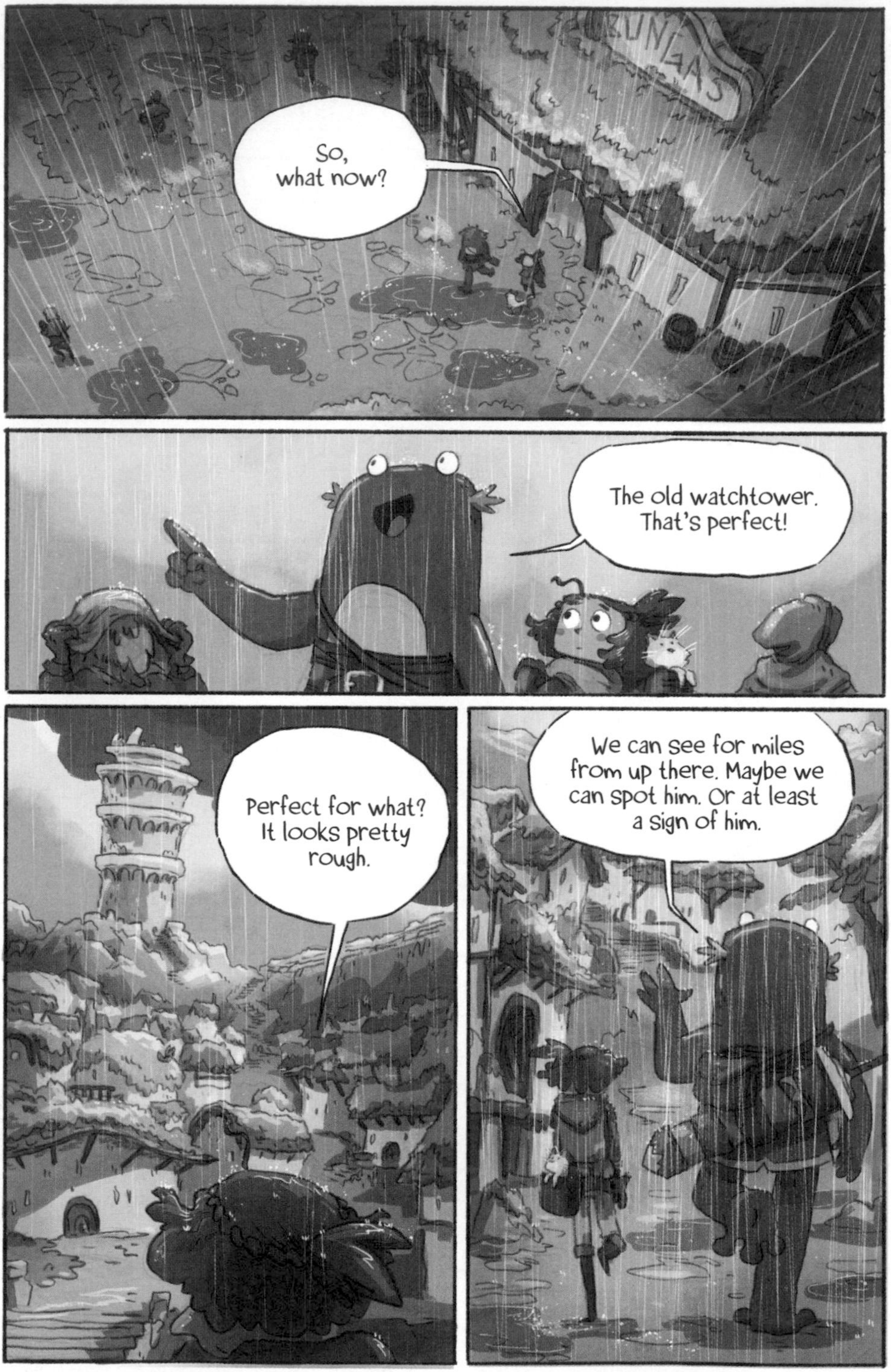

So, what now?
The old watchtower. That's perfect!
Perfect for what? It looks pretty rough.
We can see for miles from up there. Maybe we can spot him. Or at least a sign of him.

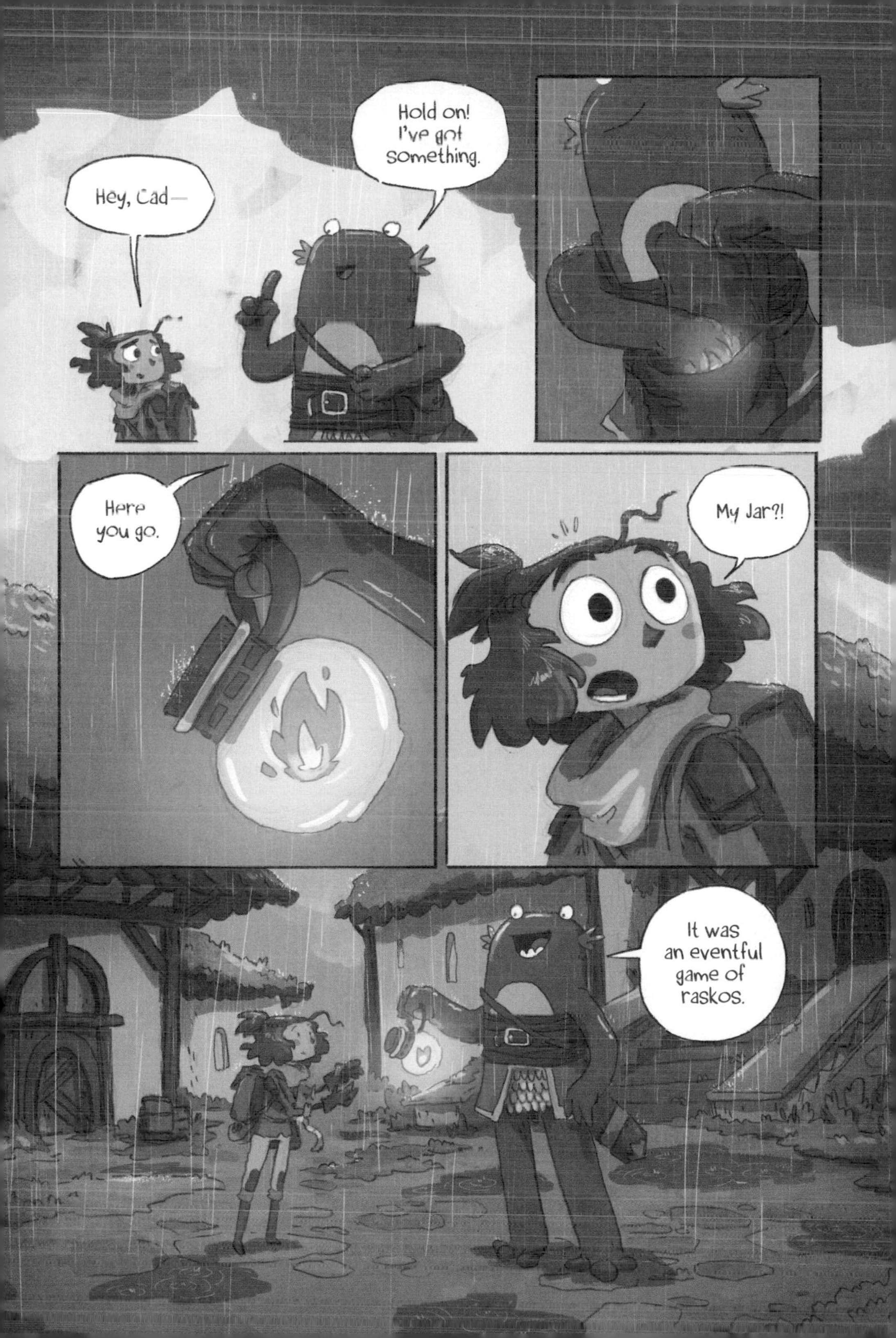
Hey, Cad—
Hold on! I've got something.
Here you go.
My Jar?!
It was an eventful game of raskos.

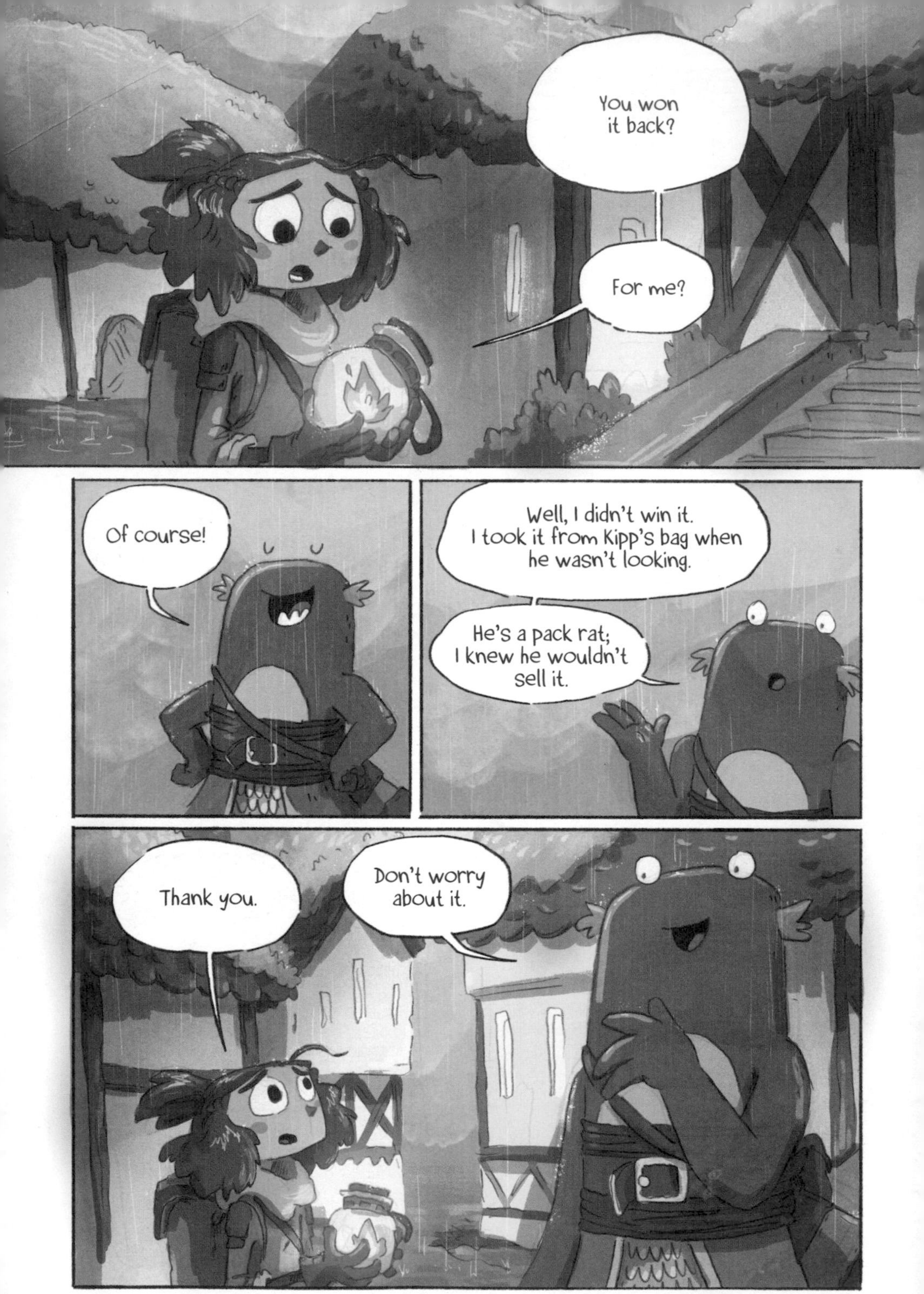
You won it back?
For me?
Of course!
Well, I didn't win it. I took it from Kipp's bag when he wasn't looking.
He's a pack rat; I knew he wouldn't sell it.
Thank you.
Don't worry about it.

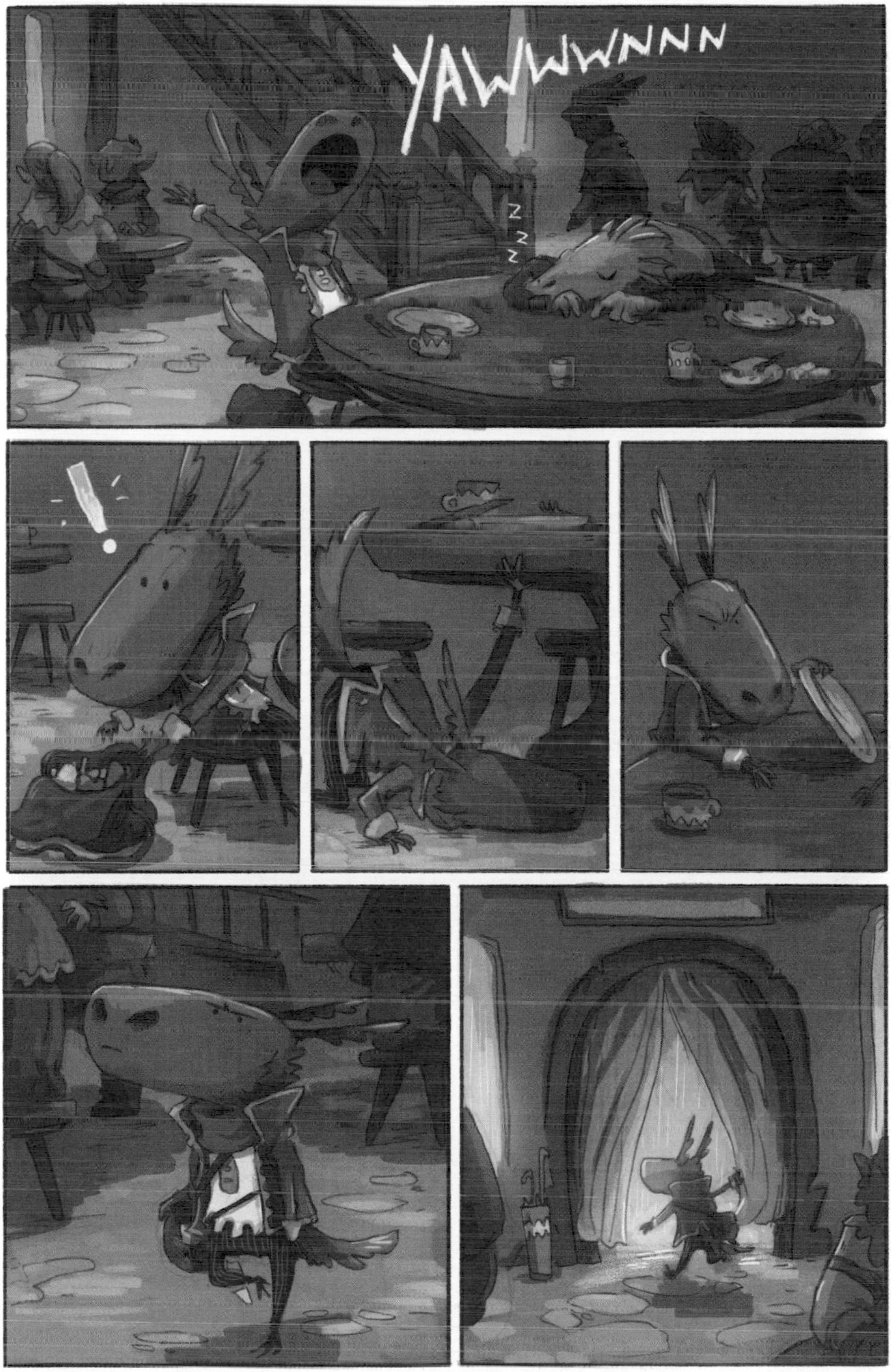
YAWWWNNN
Z
Z
Z
!

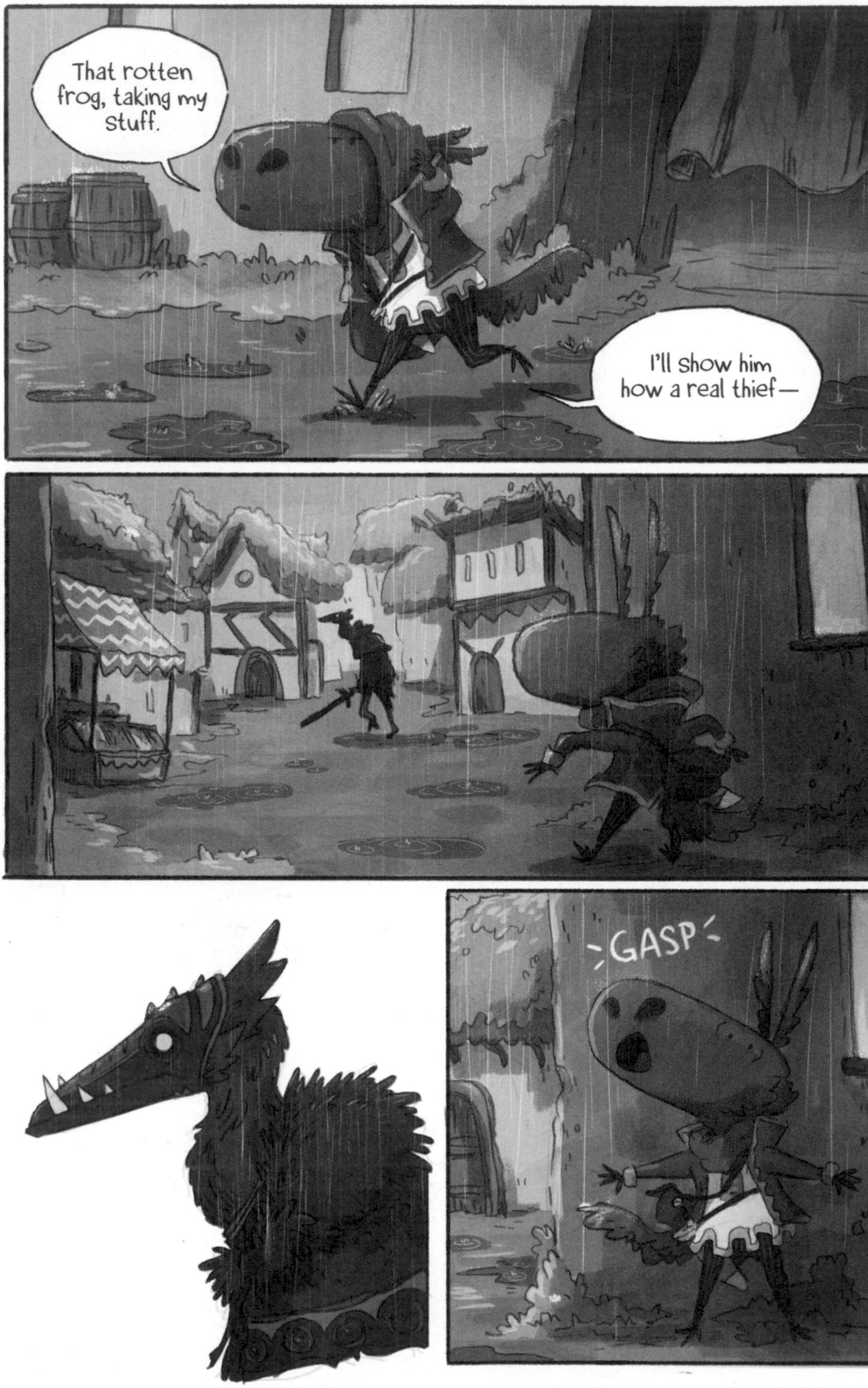
That rotten frog, taking my stuff.
I'll show him how a real thief—
GASP

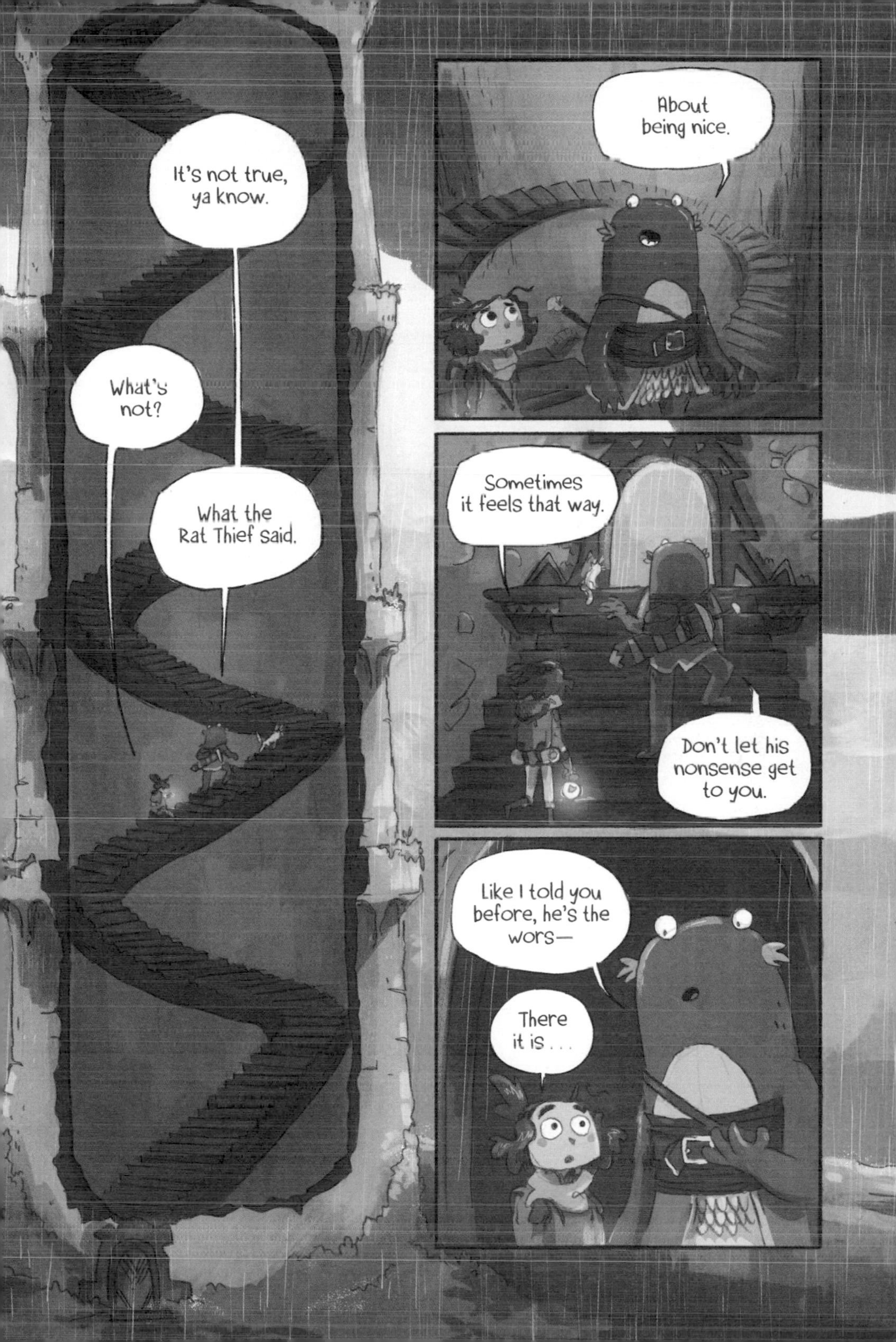
It's not true, ya know.
What's not?
What the Rat Thief said.
About being nice.
Sometimes it feels that way.
Don't let his nonsense get to you.
Like I told you before, he's the wors—
There it is . . .

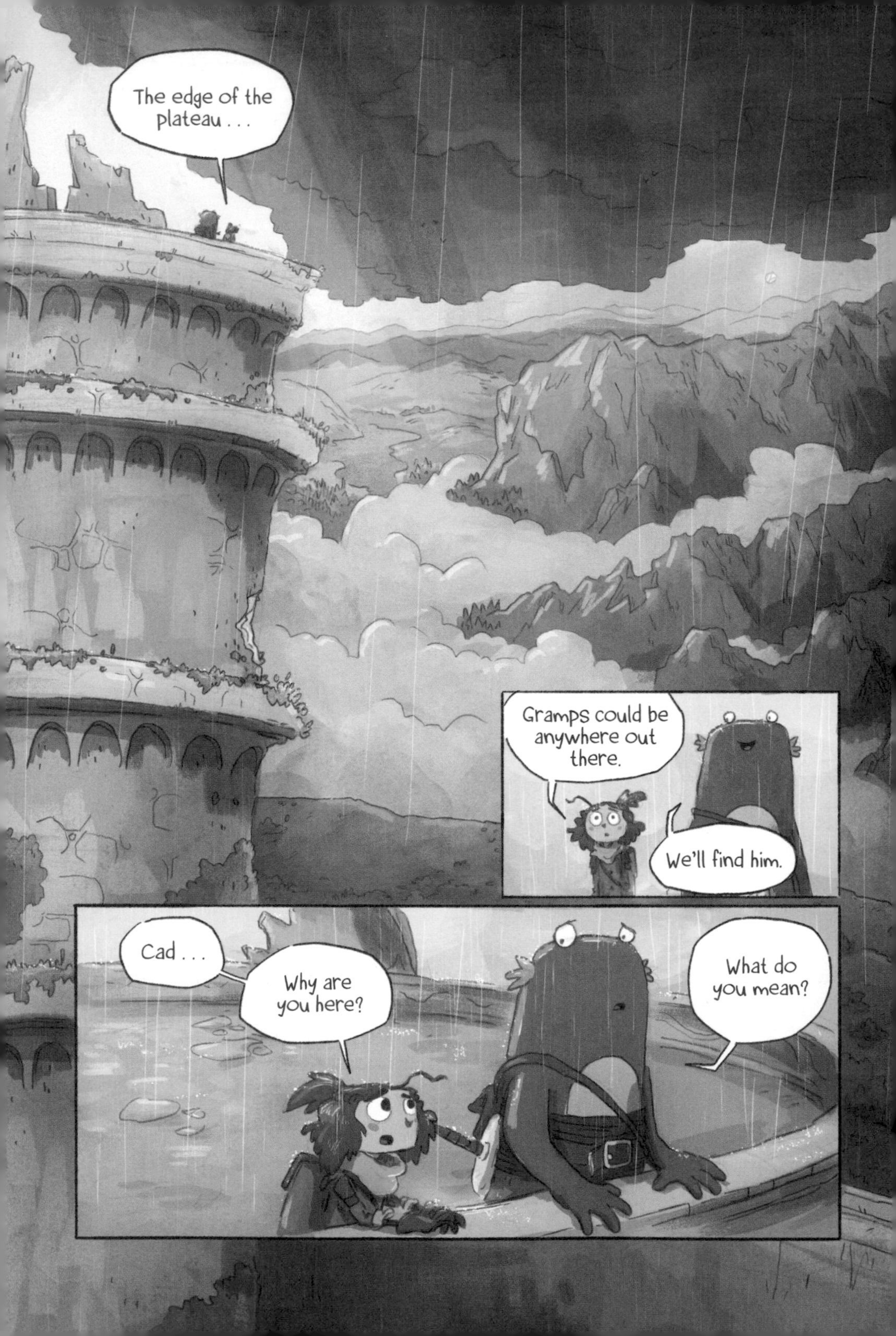

The edge of the plateau . . .
Gramps could be anywhere out there.
We'll find him.
Cad . . .
Why are you here?
What do you mean?

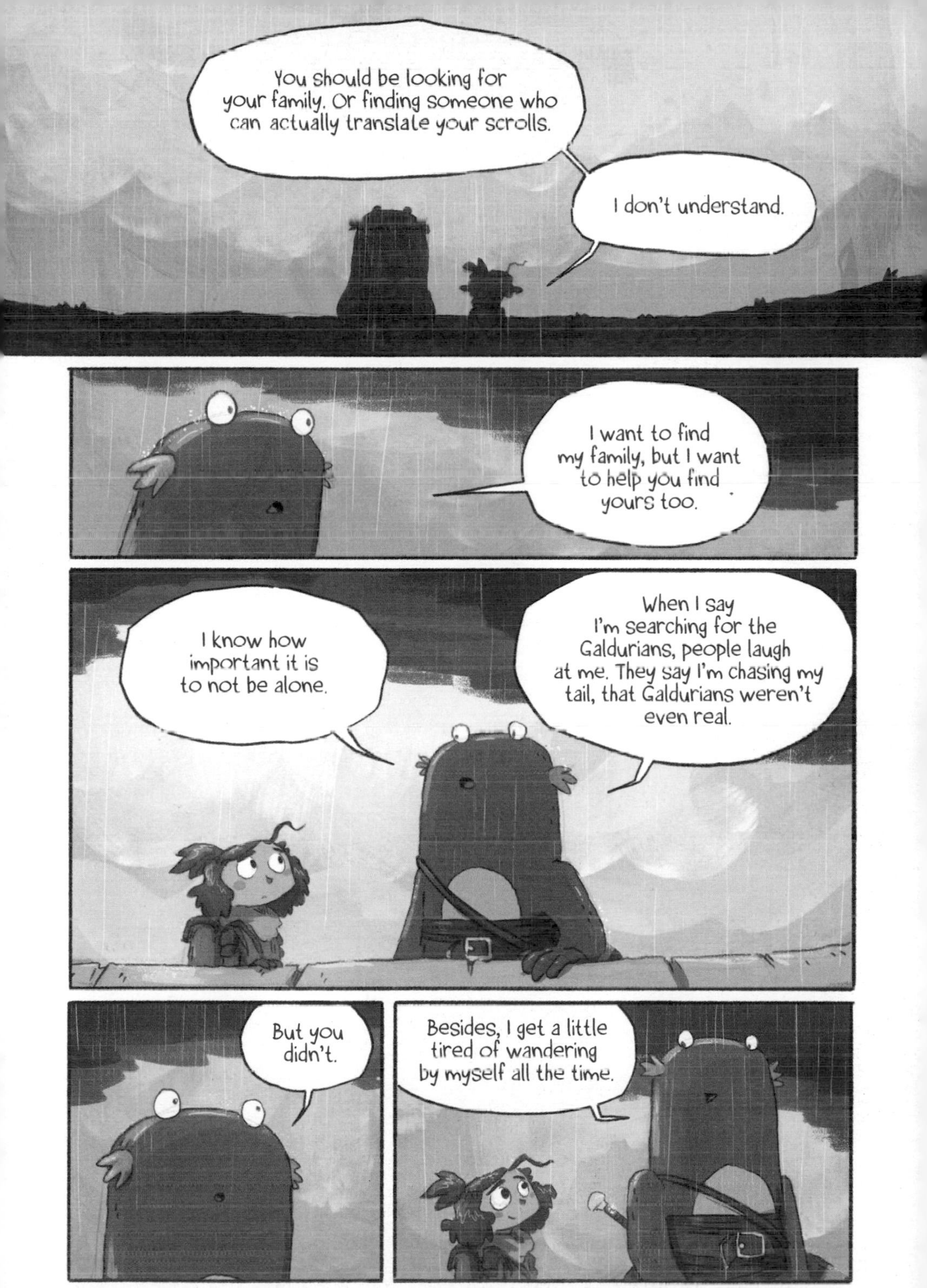
You should be looking for your family. Or finding someone who can actually translate your scrolls.
I don't understand.
I want to find my family, but I want to help you find yours too.
I know how important it is to not be alone.
When I say I'm searching for the Galdurians, people laugh at me. They say I'm chasing my tail, that Galdurians weren't even real.
But you didn't.
Besides, I get a little tired of wandering by myself all the time.

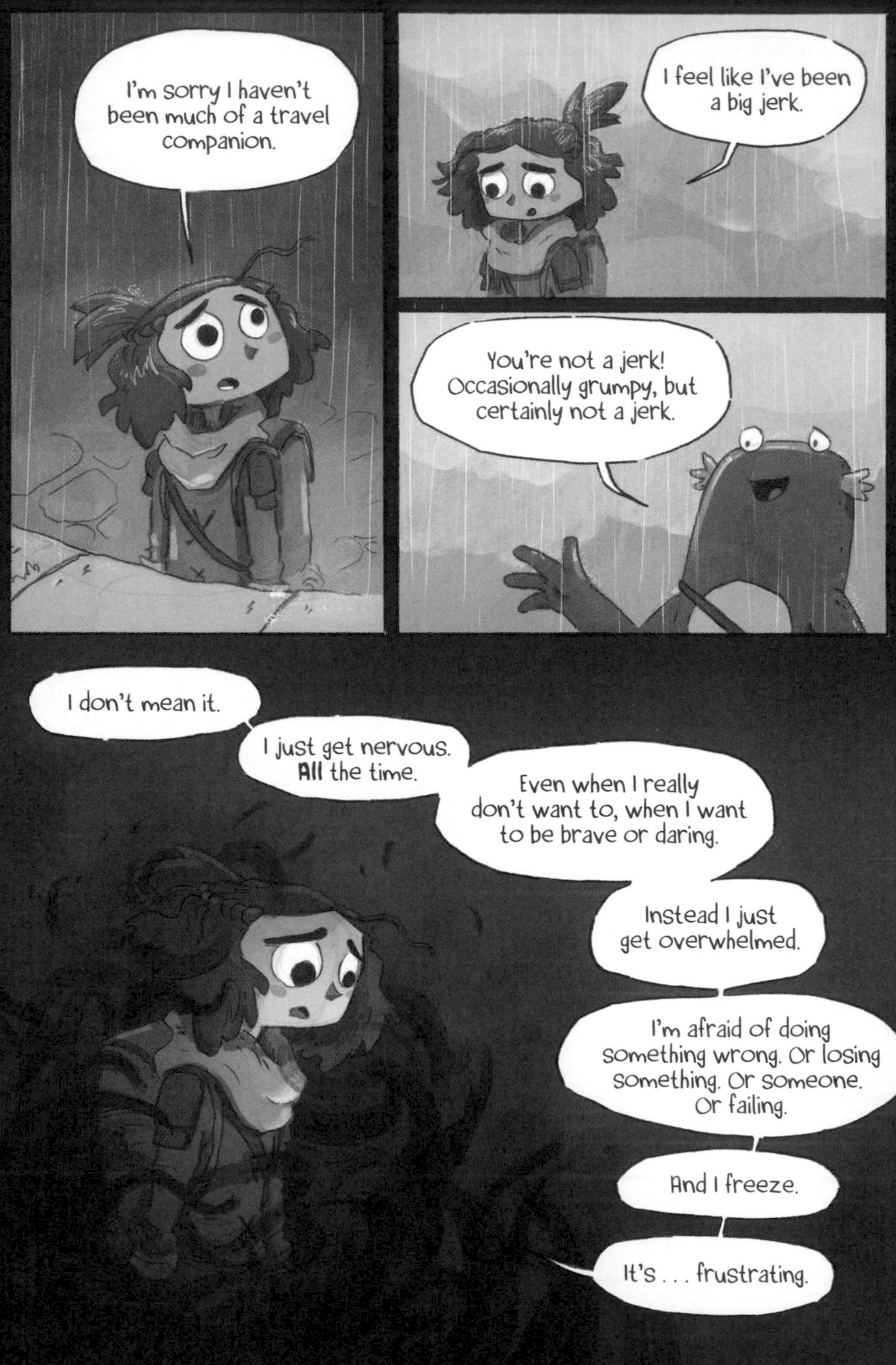
I'm sorry I haven't been much of a travel companion.
I feel like I've been a big jerk.
You're not a jerk! Occasionally grumpy, but certainly not a jerk.
I don't mean it.
I just get nervous. **All** the time.
Even when I really don't want to, when I want to be brave or daring.
Instead I just get overwhelmed.
I'm afraid of doing something wrong. Or losing something. Or someone. Or failing.
And I freeze.
It's . . . frustrating.

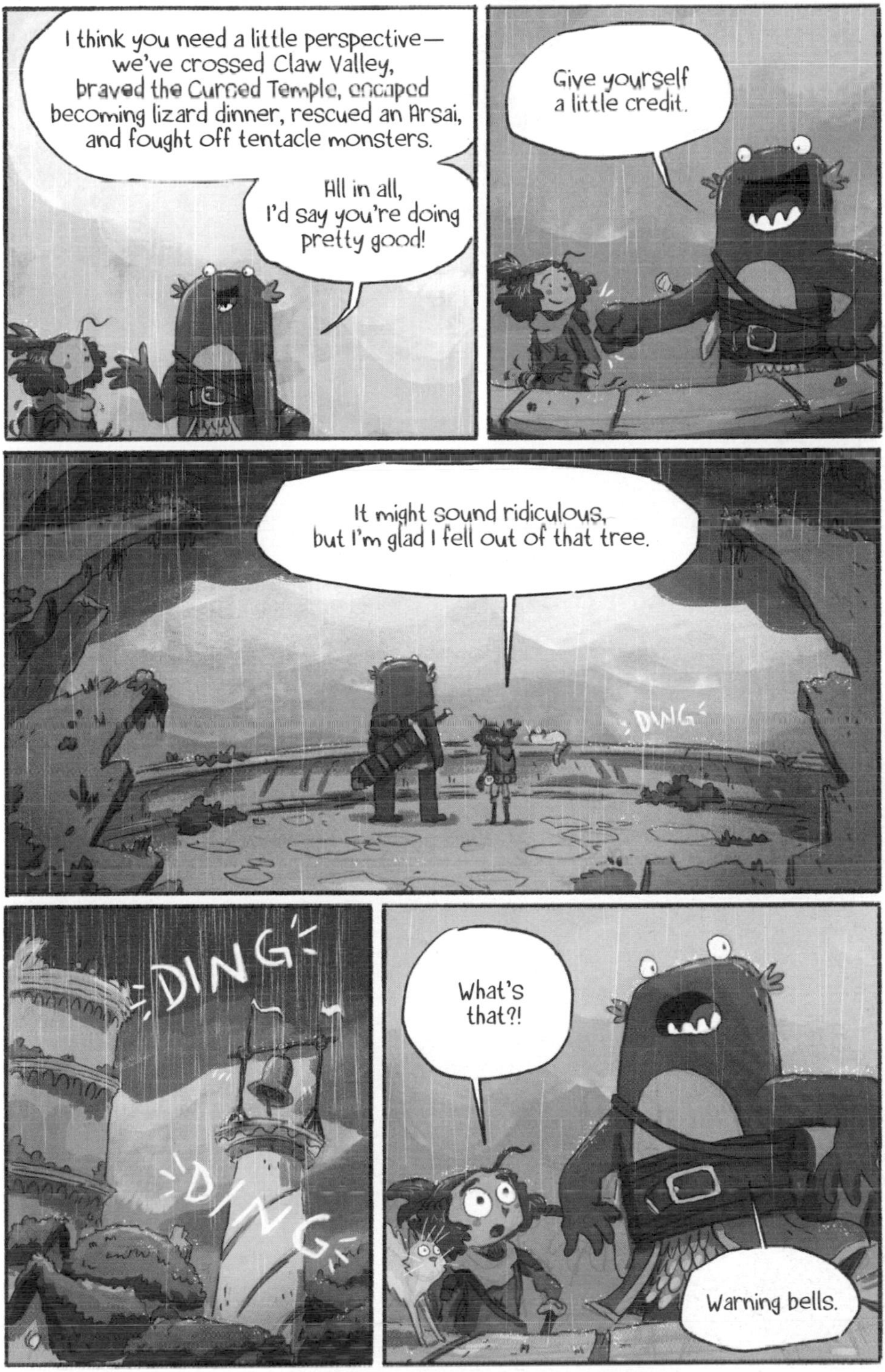

I think you need a little perspective—we've crossed Claw Valley, braved the Cursed Temple, escaped becoming lizard dinner, rescued an Arsai, and fought off tentacle monsters.
All in all, I'd say you're doing pretty good!
Give yourself a little credit.
It might sound ridiculous, but I'm glad I fell out of that tree.
DING
DING
DING
What's that?!
Warning bells.

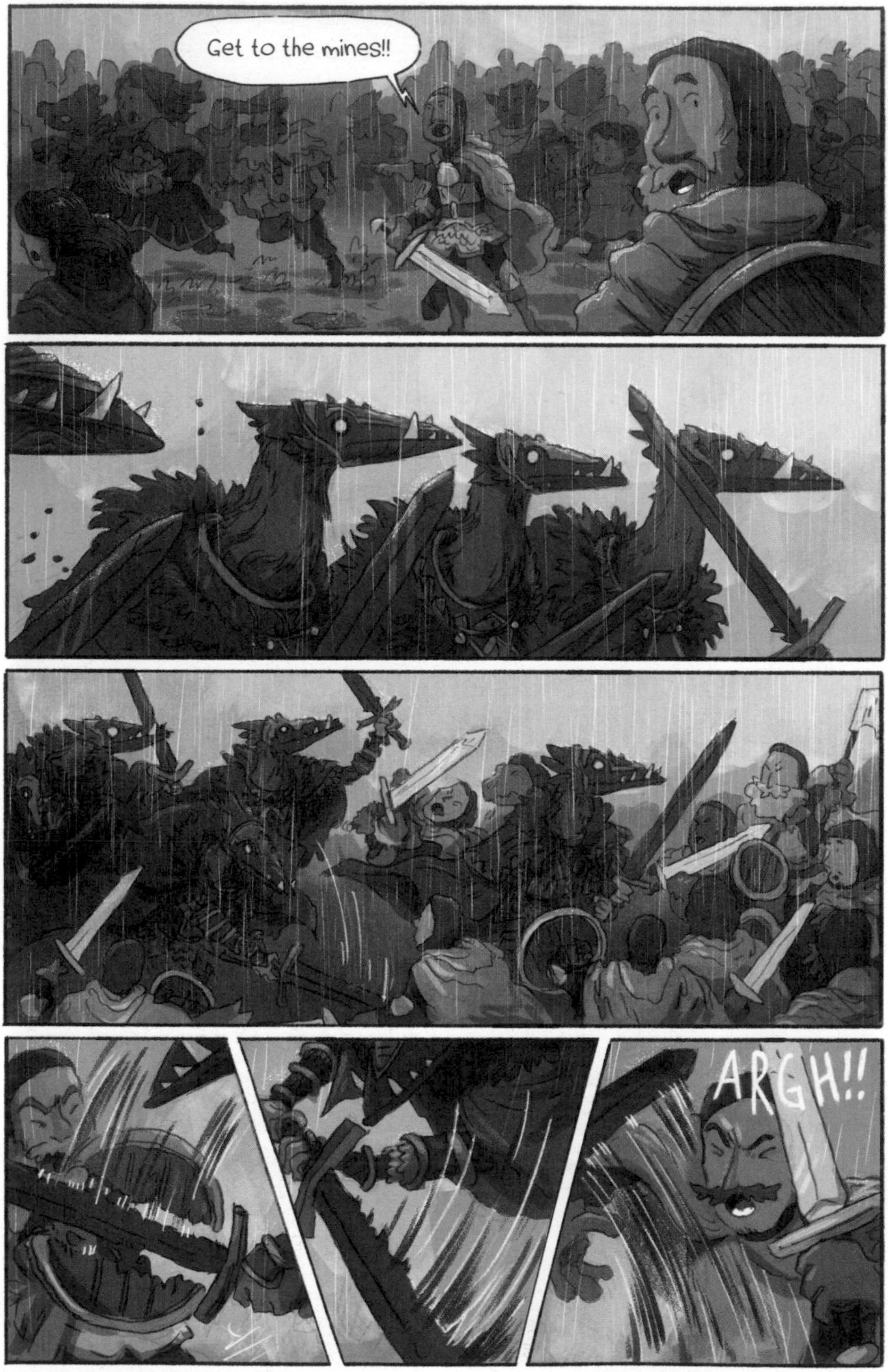
Get to the mines!!
ARGH!!

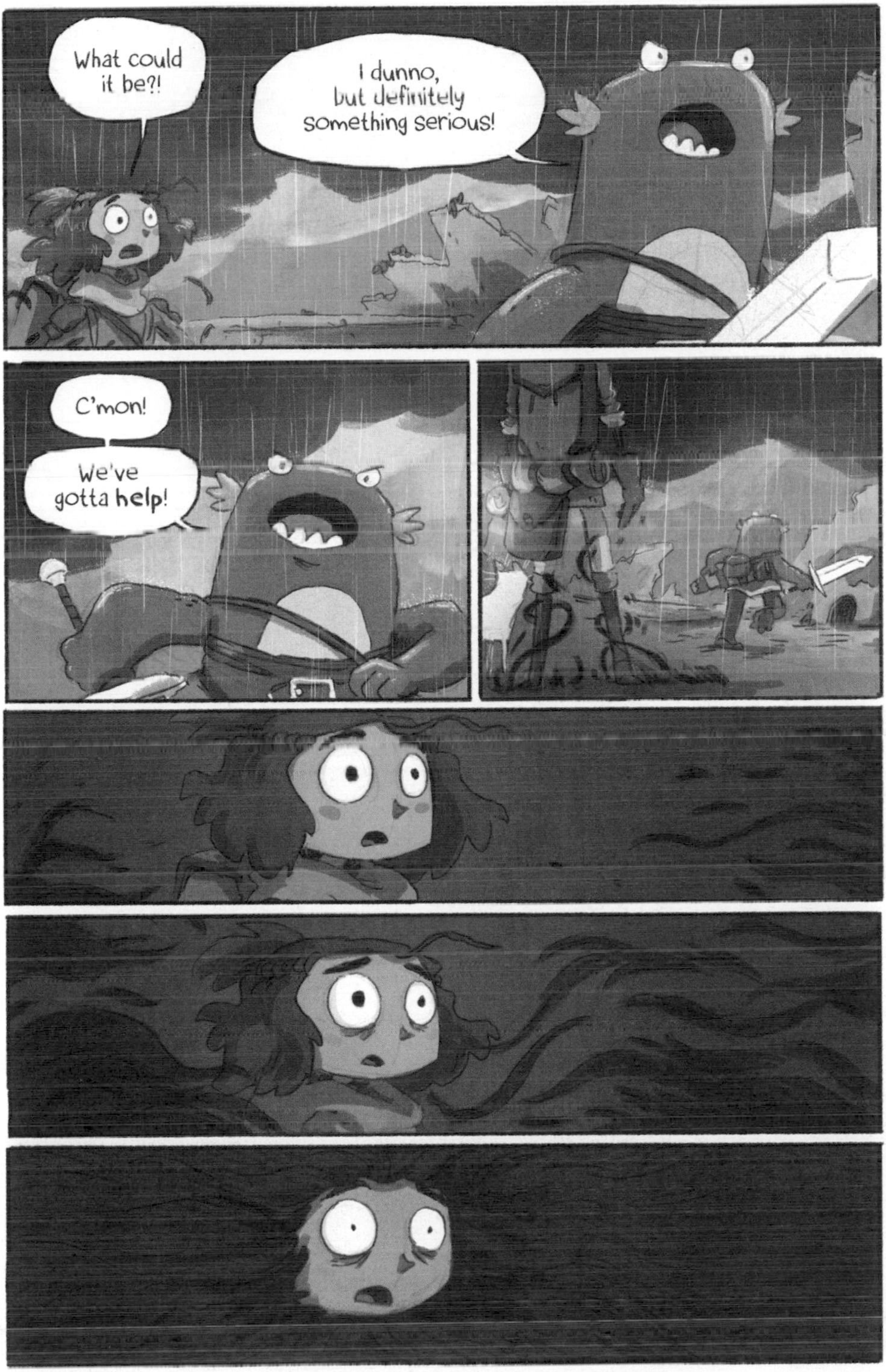
What could it be?!
I dunno, but definitely something serious!
C'mon!
We've gotta **help**!

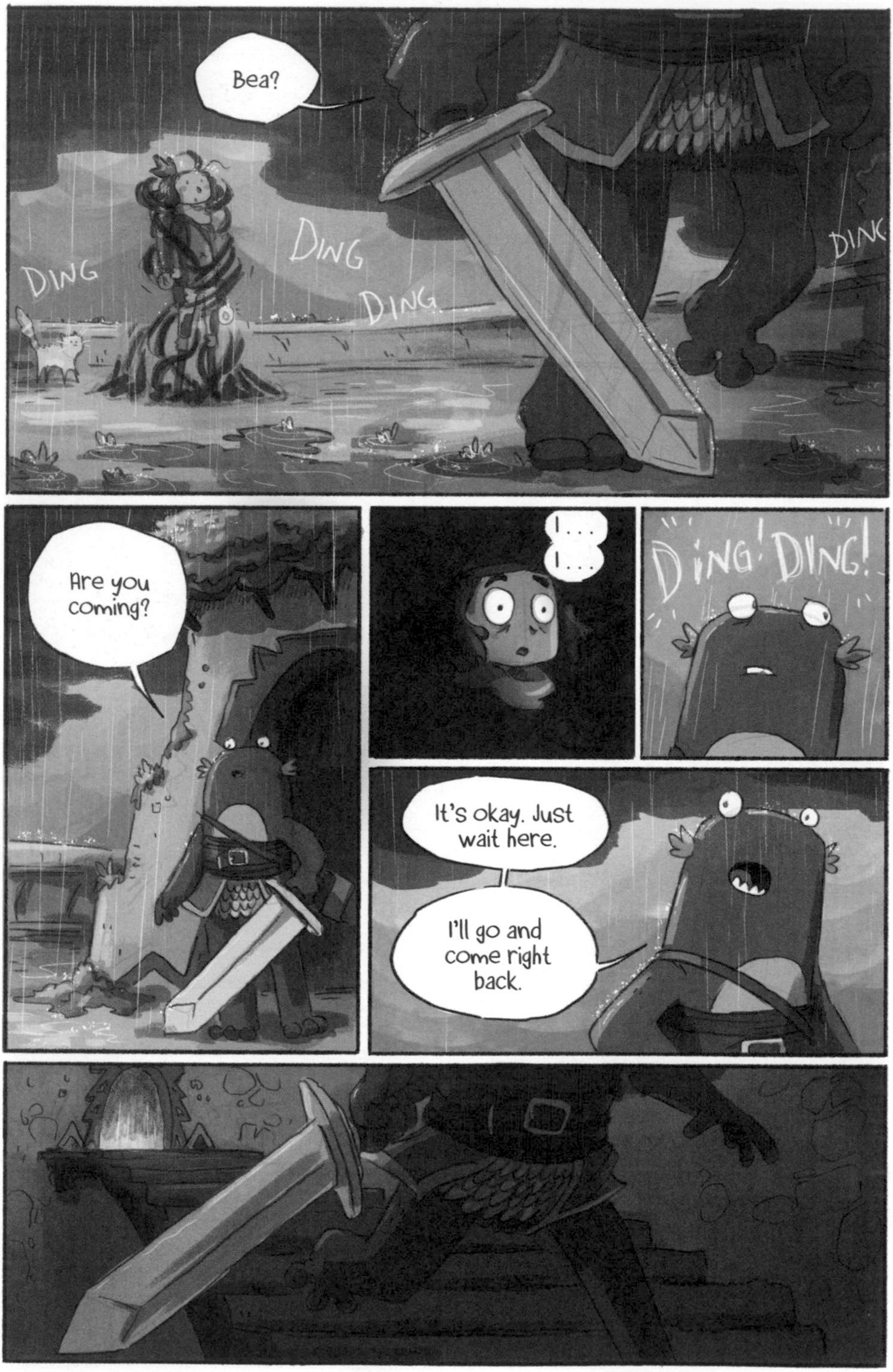
Bea?
DING
DING
DING
DING
Are you coming?
I...
I...
DING! DING!
It's okay. Just wait here.
I'll go and come right back.

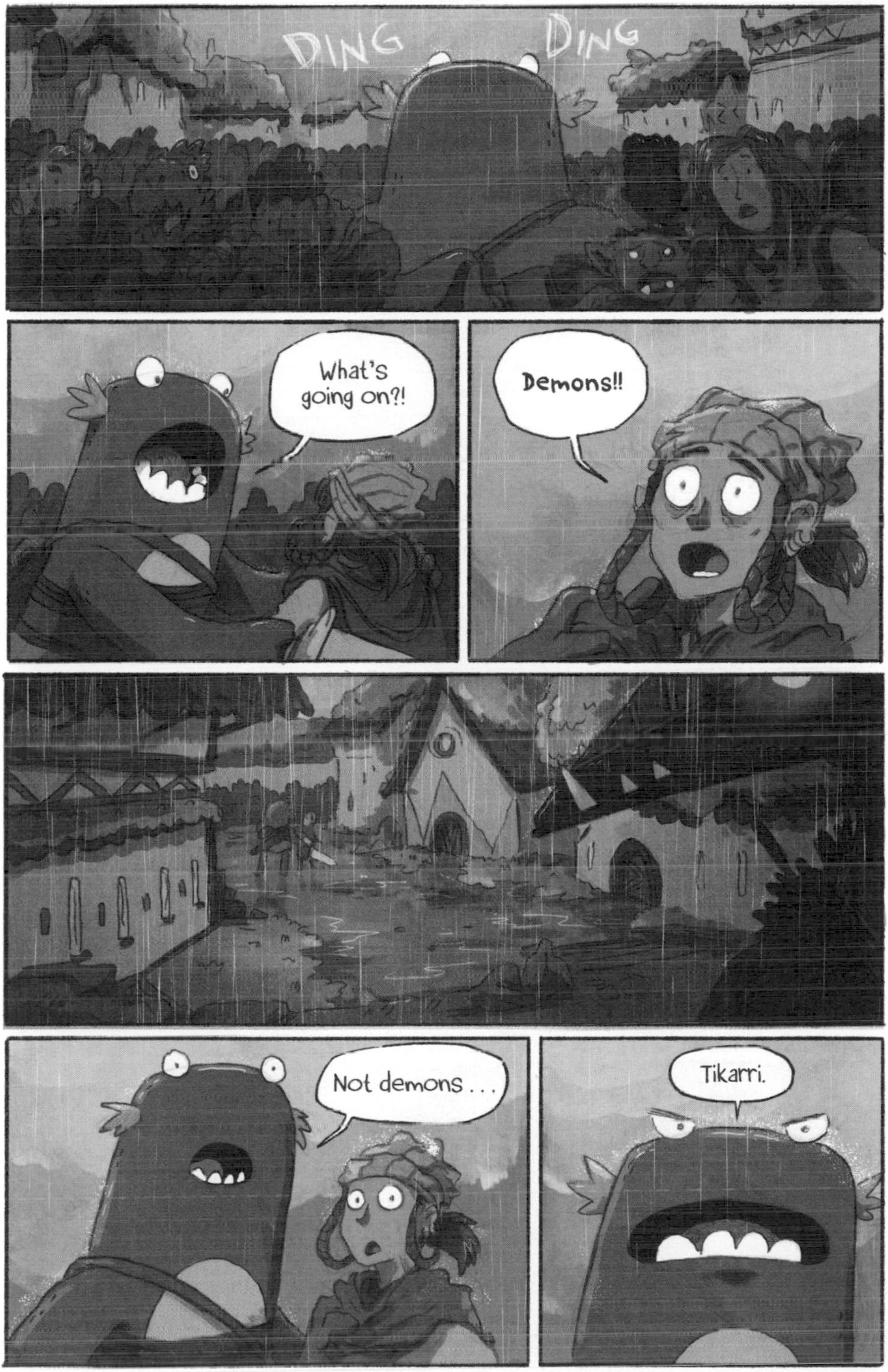
DING
DING
What's going on?!
Demons!!
Not demons . . .
Tikarri.

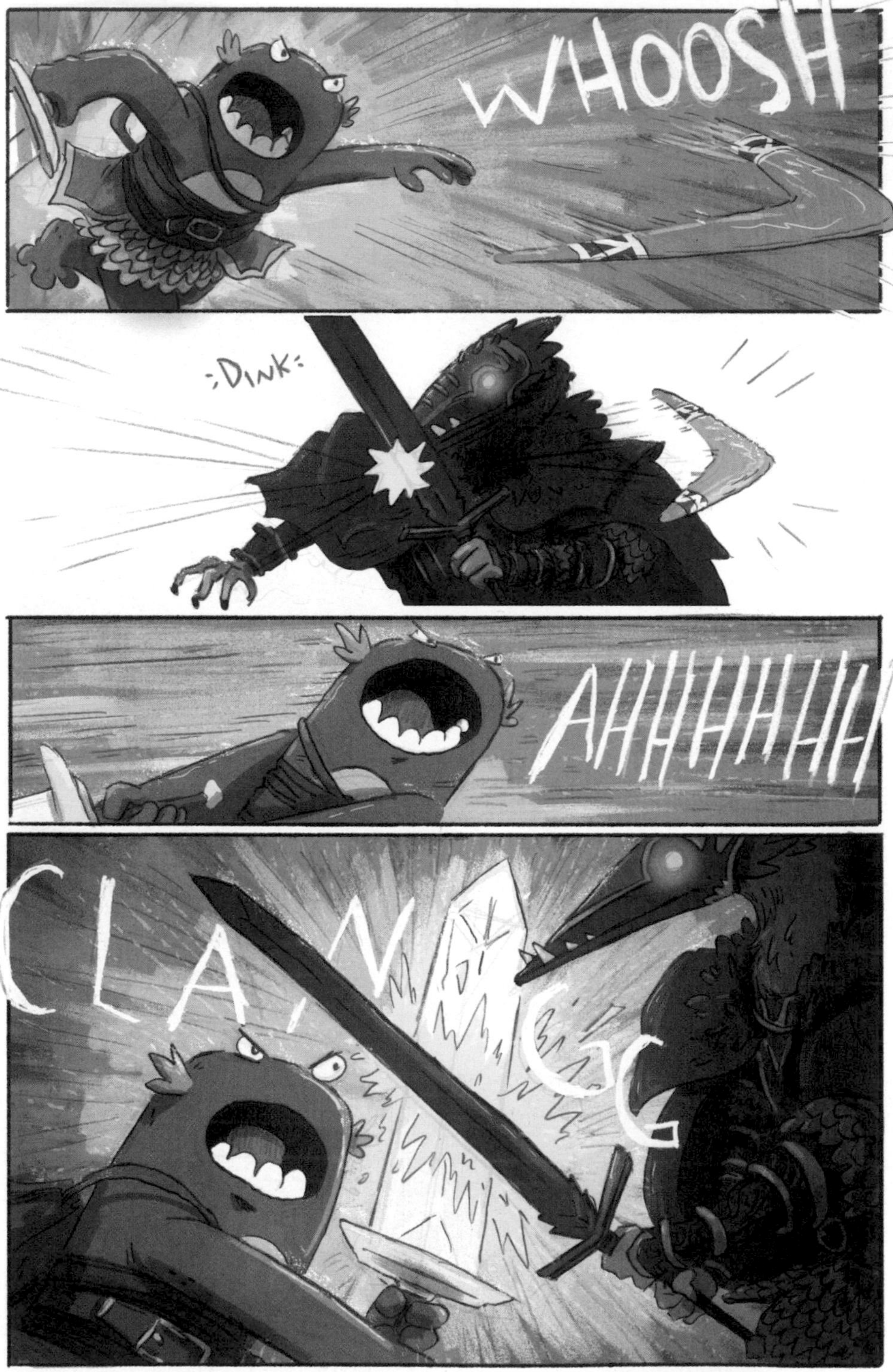
WHOOSH
DINK
AHHHHHHH
CLANGG

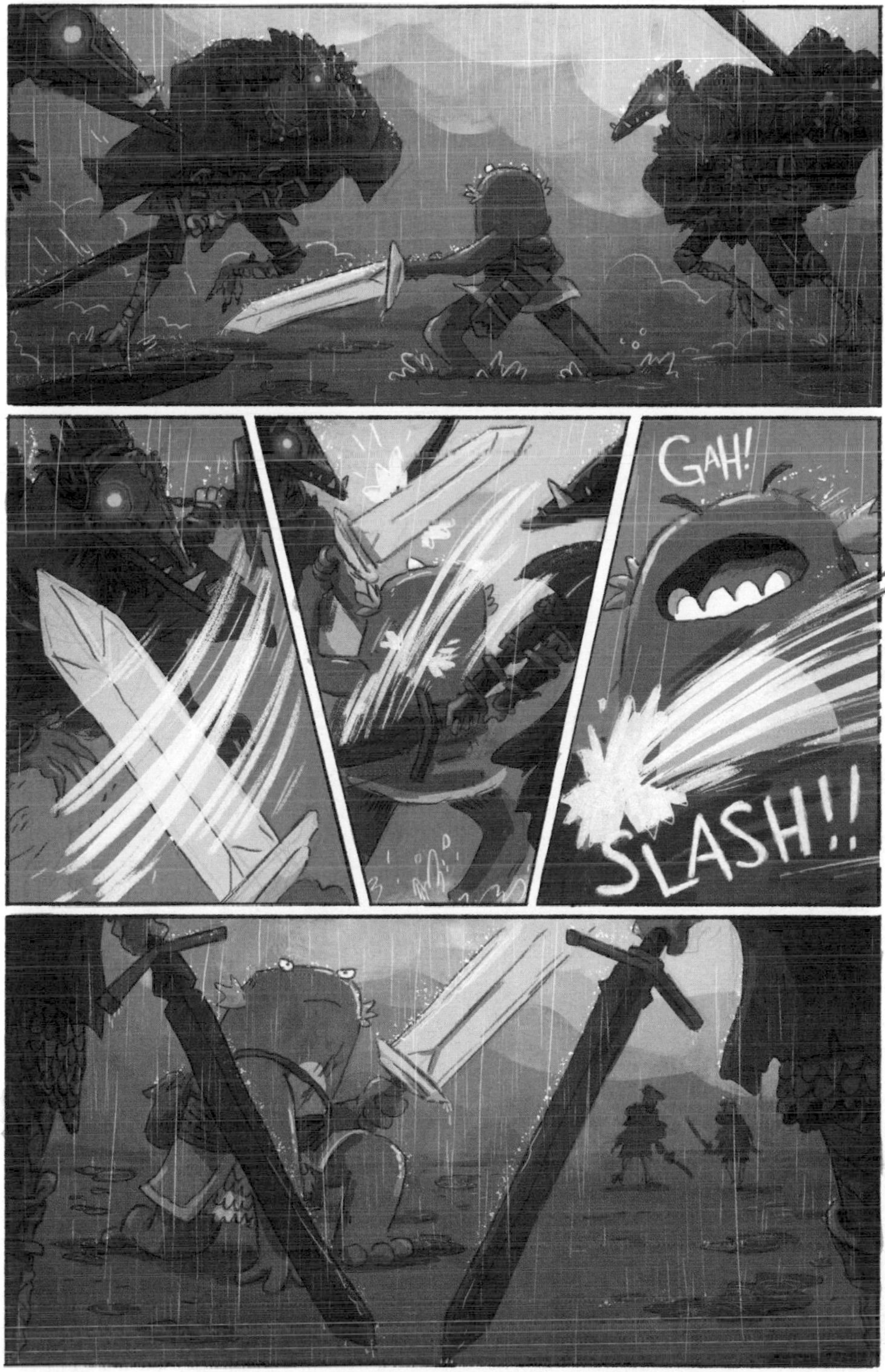
GAH!
SLASH!!

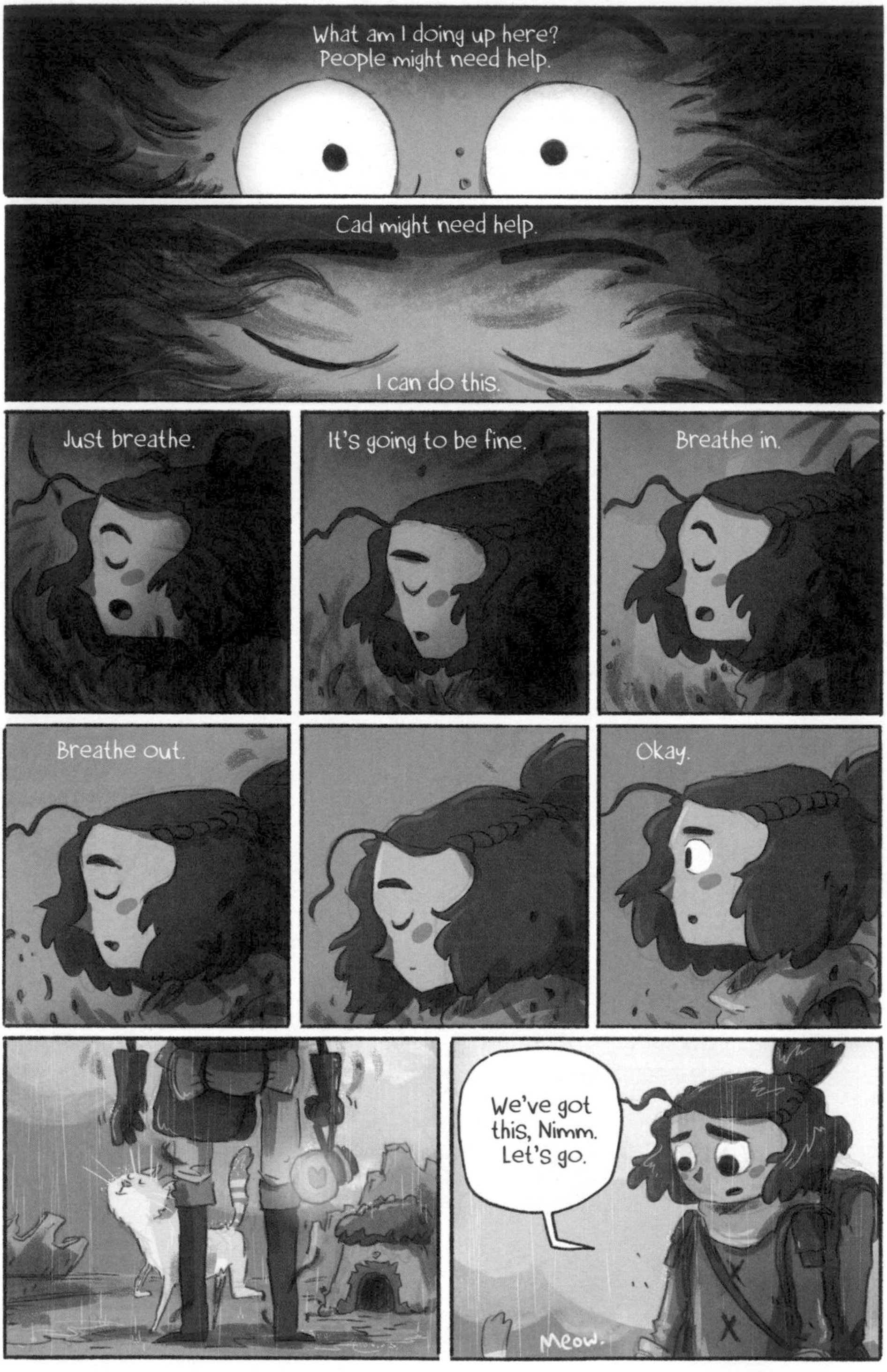
What am I doing up here?
People might need help.
Cad might need help.
I can do this.
Just breathe.
It's going to be fine.
Breathe in.
Breathe out.
Okay.
We've got this, Nimm. Let's go.
Meow.

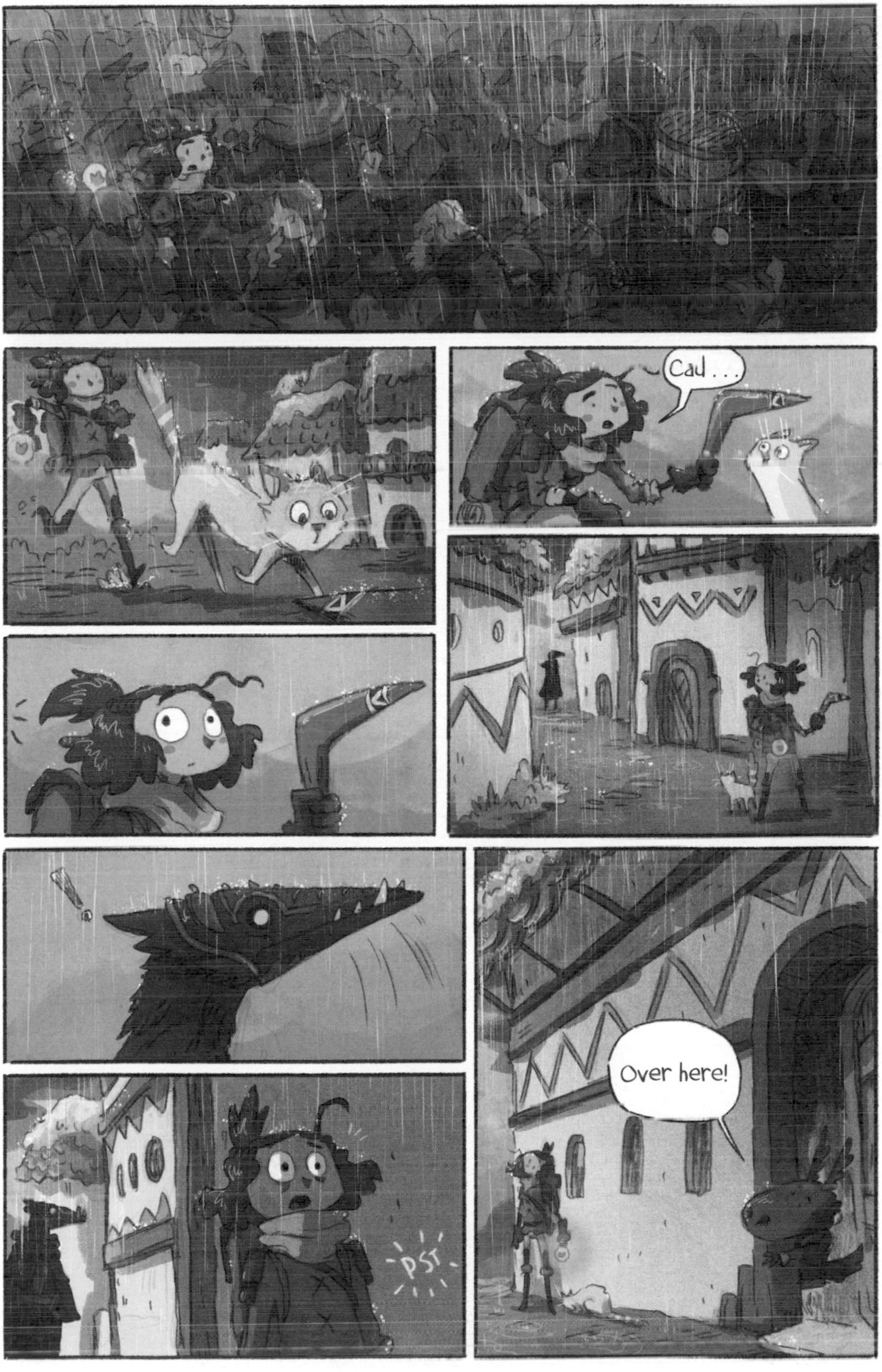
Cau . . .
PST
Over here!

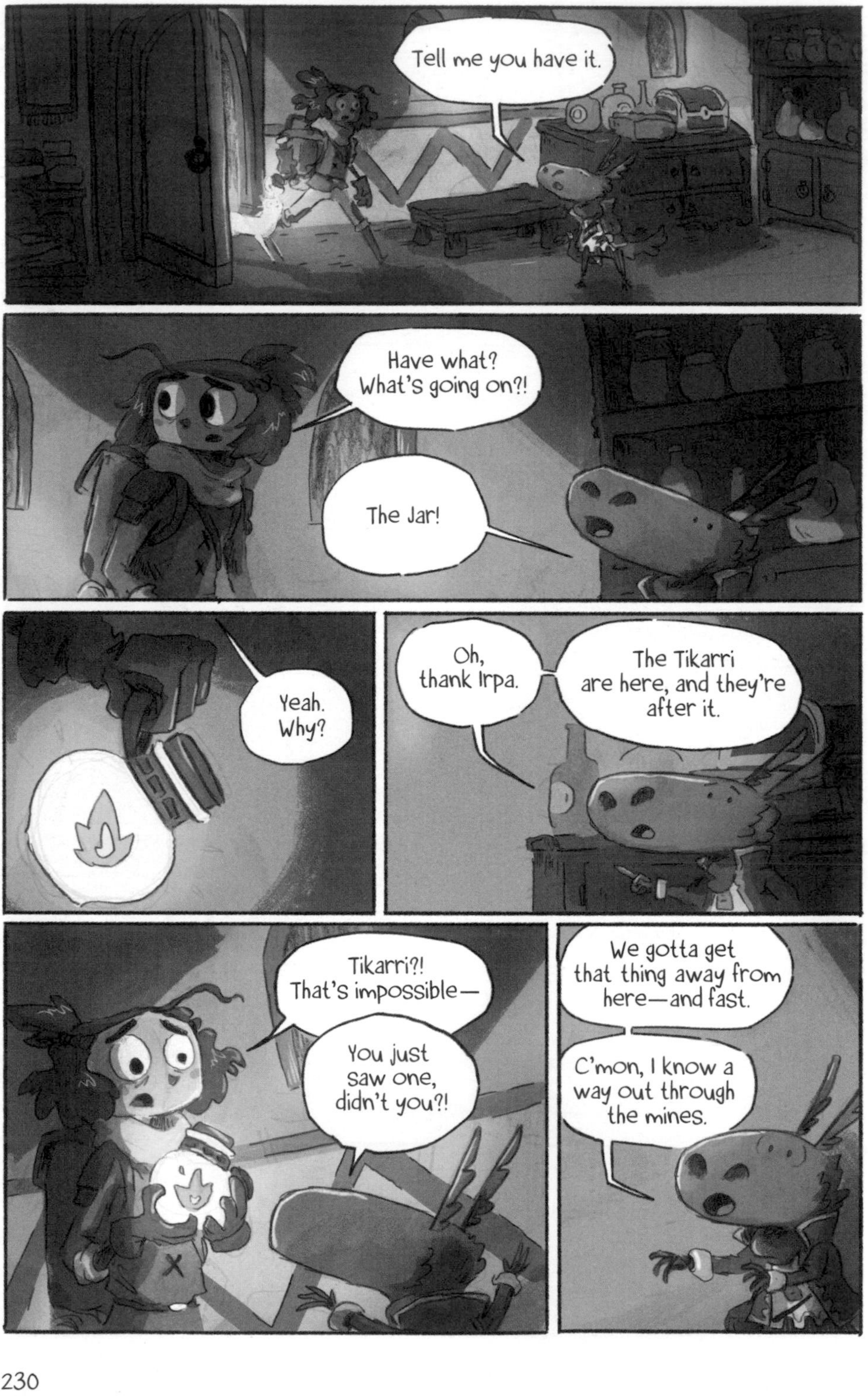
Tell me you have it.
Have what? What's going on?!
The Jar!
Yeah. Why?
Oh, thank Irpa.
The Tikarri are here, and they're after it.
Tikarri?! That's impossible—
You just saw one, didn't you?!
We gotta get that thing away from here—and fast.
C'mon, I know a way out through the mines.

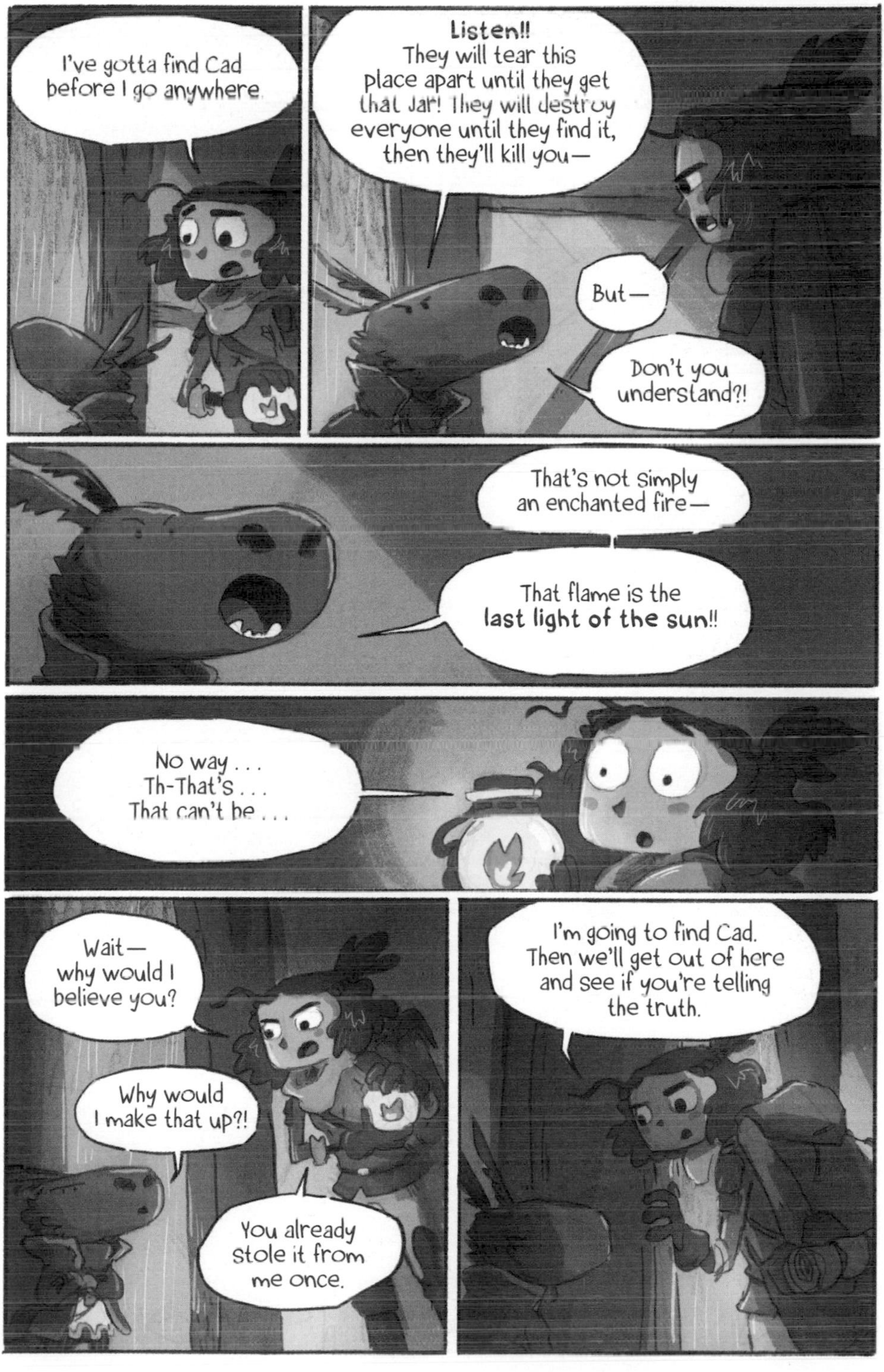
I've gotta find Cad before I go anywhere.
Listen!! They will tear this place apart until they get that Jar! They will destroy everyone until they find it, then they'll kill you—
But—
Don't you understand?!
That's not simply an enchanted fire—
That flame is the **last light of the sun**!!
No way . . . Th-That's . . . That can't be . . .
Wait— why would I believe you?
Why would I make that up?!
You already stole it from me once.
I'm going to find Cad. Then we'll get out of here and see if you're telling the truth.

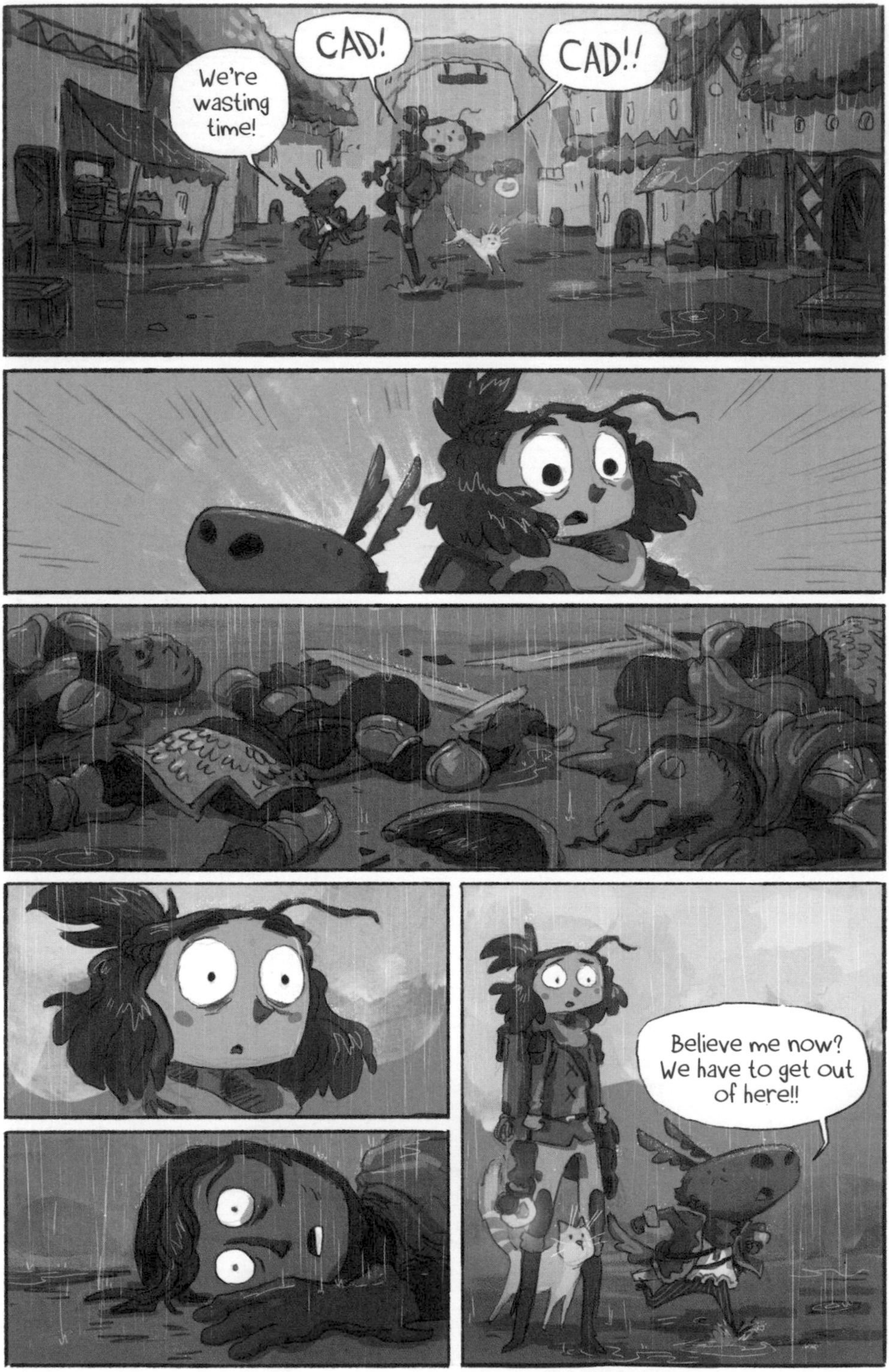
We're wasting time!
CAD!
CAD!!
Believe me now? We have to get out of here!!

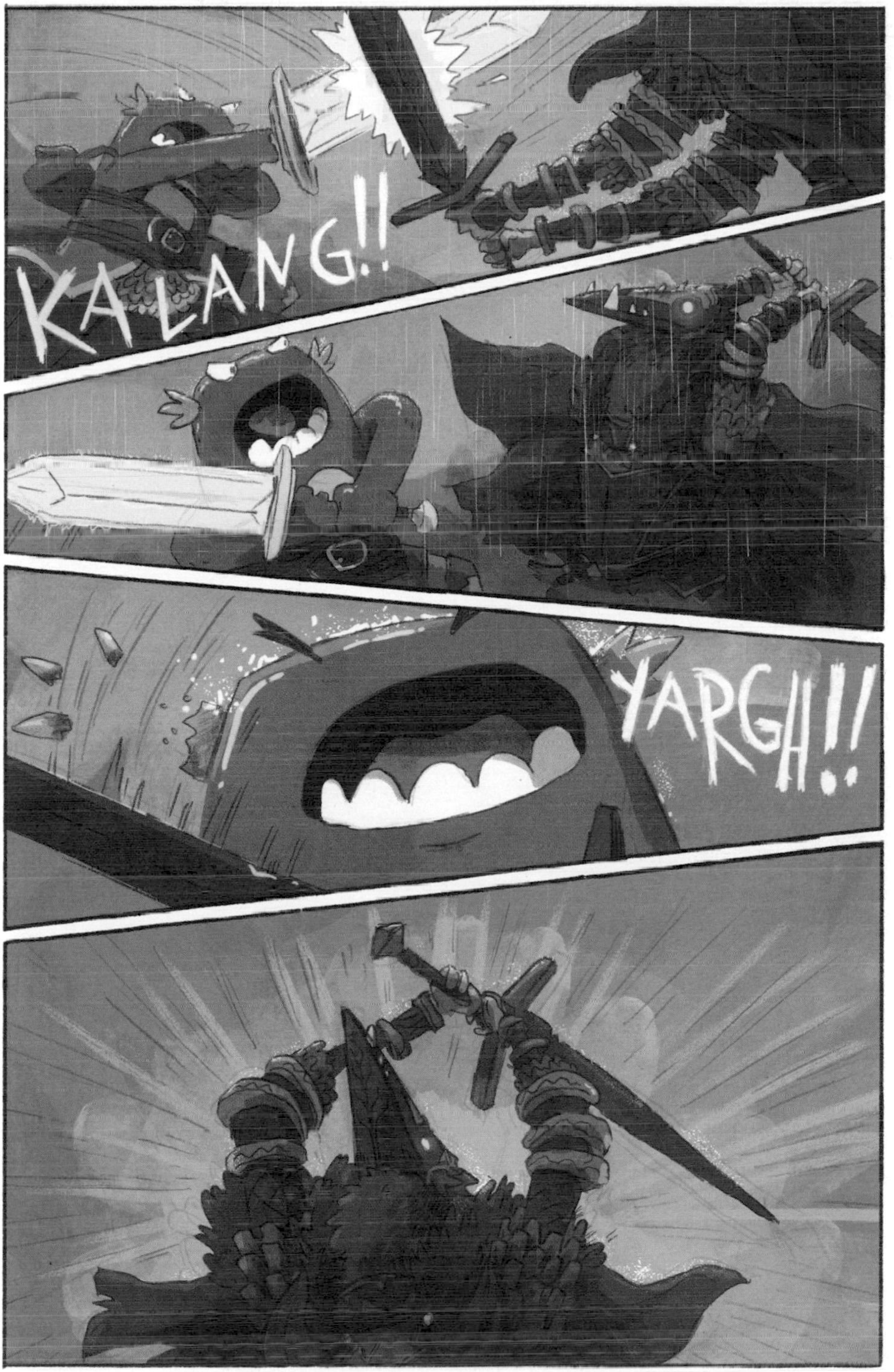
KALANG!!
YARGH!!

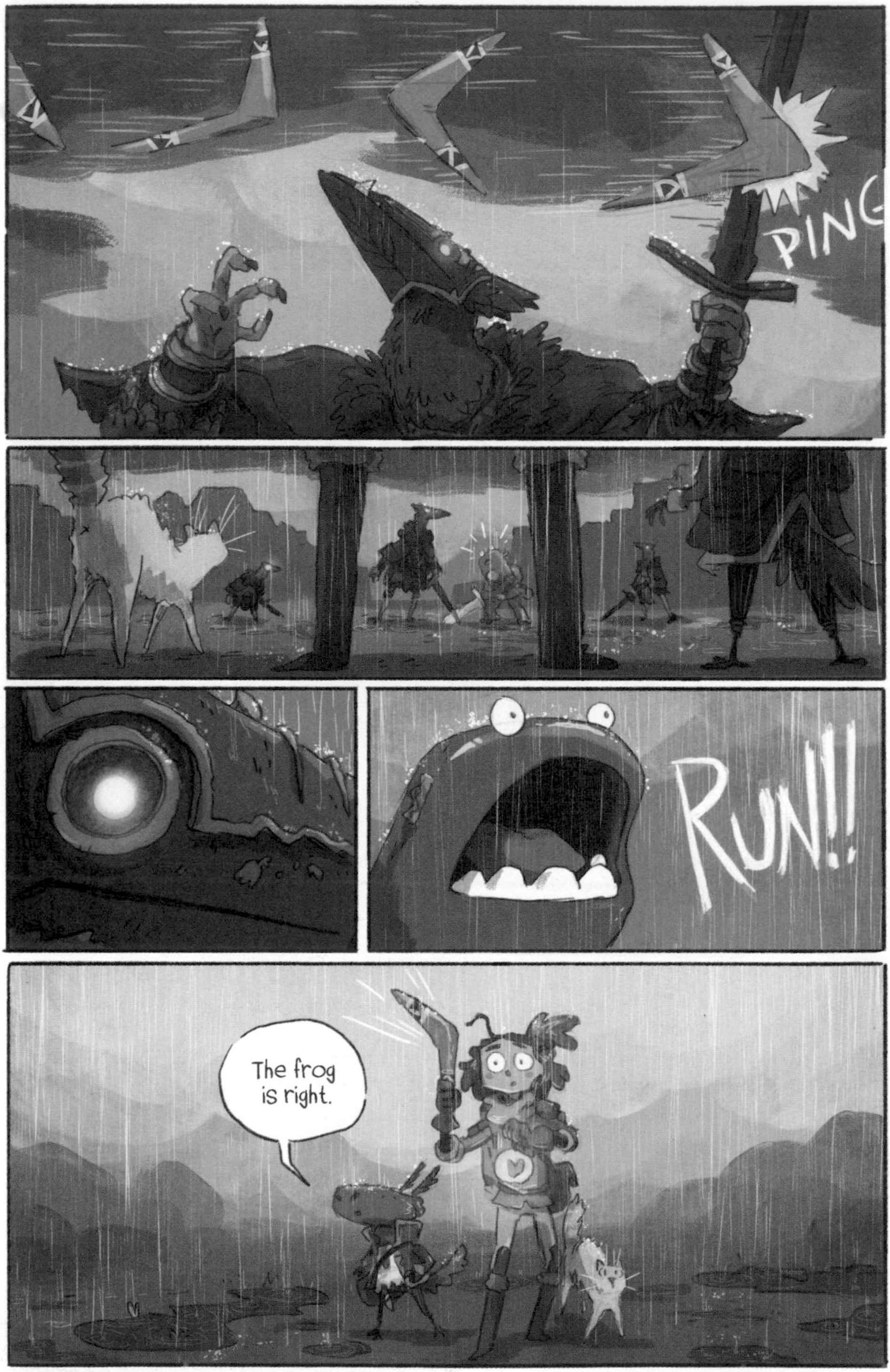
PING
RUN!!
The frog is right.

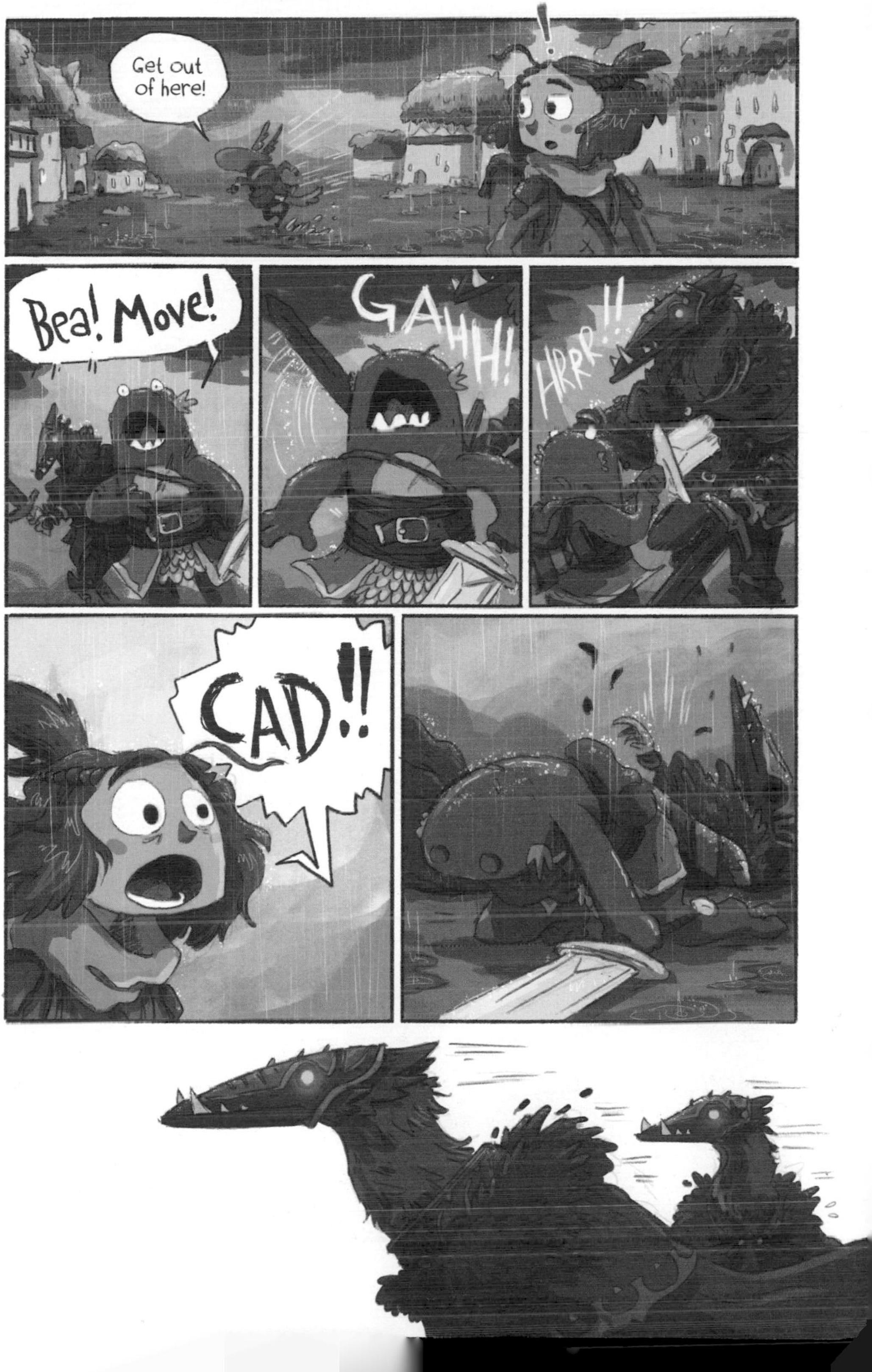

Get out of here!
!
Bea! Move!
GAHH!
HRRR!!
CAD!!

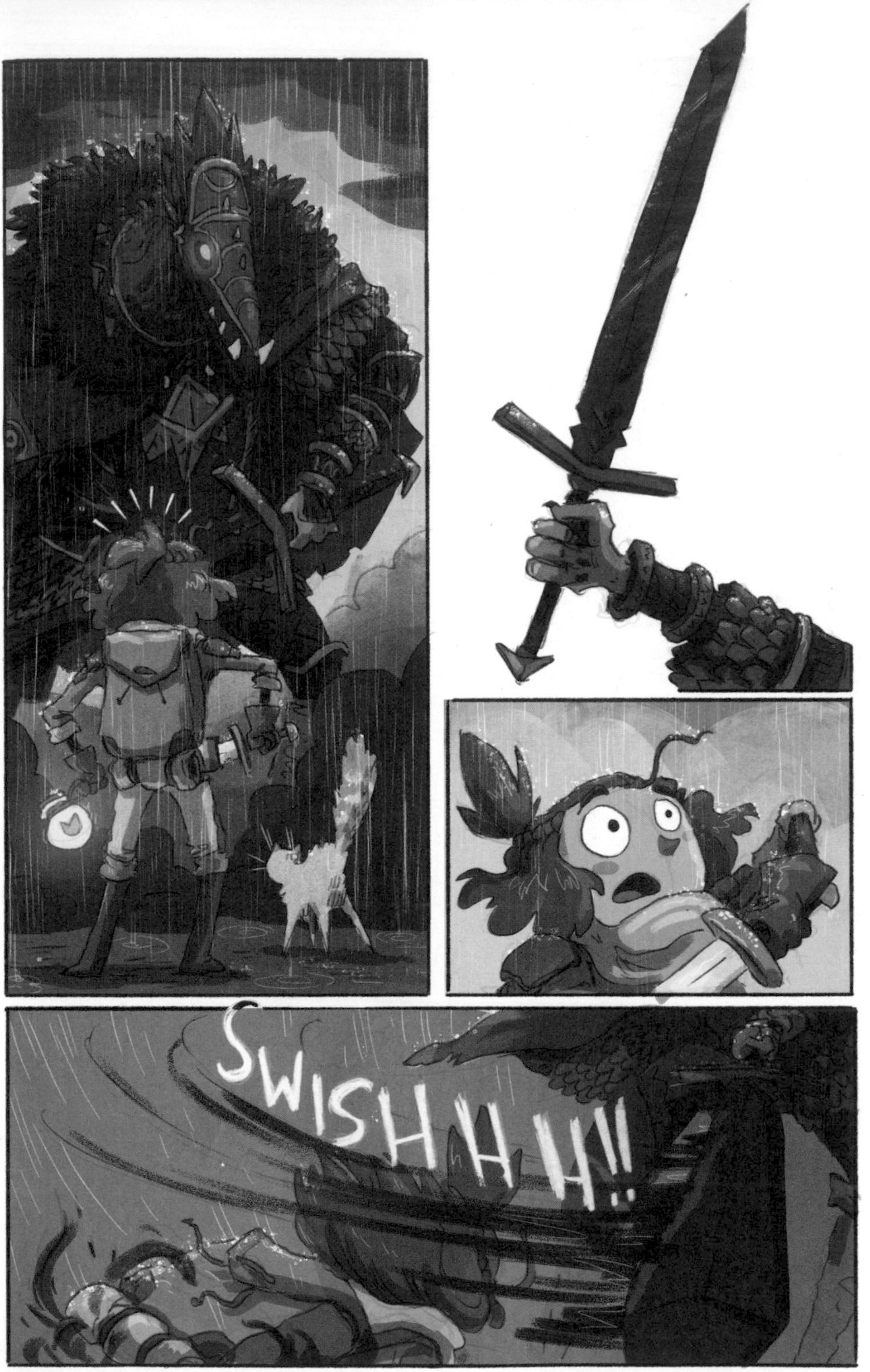
SWISHHH!!

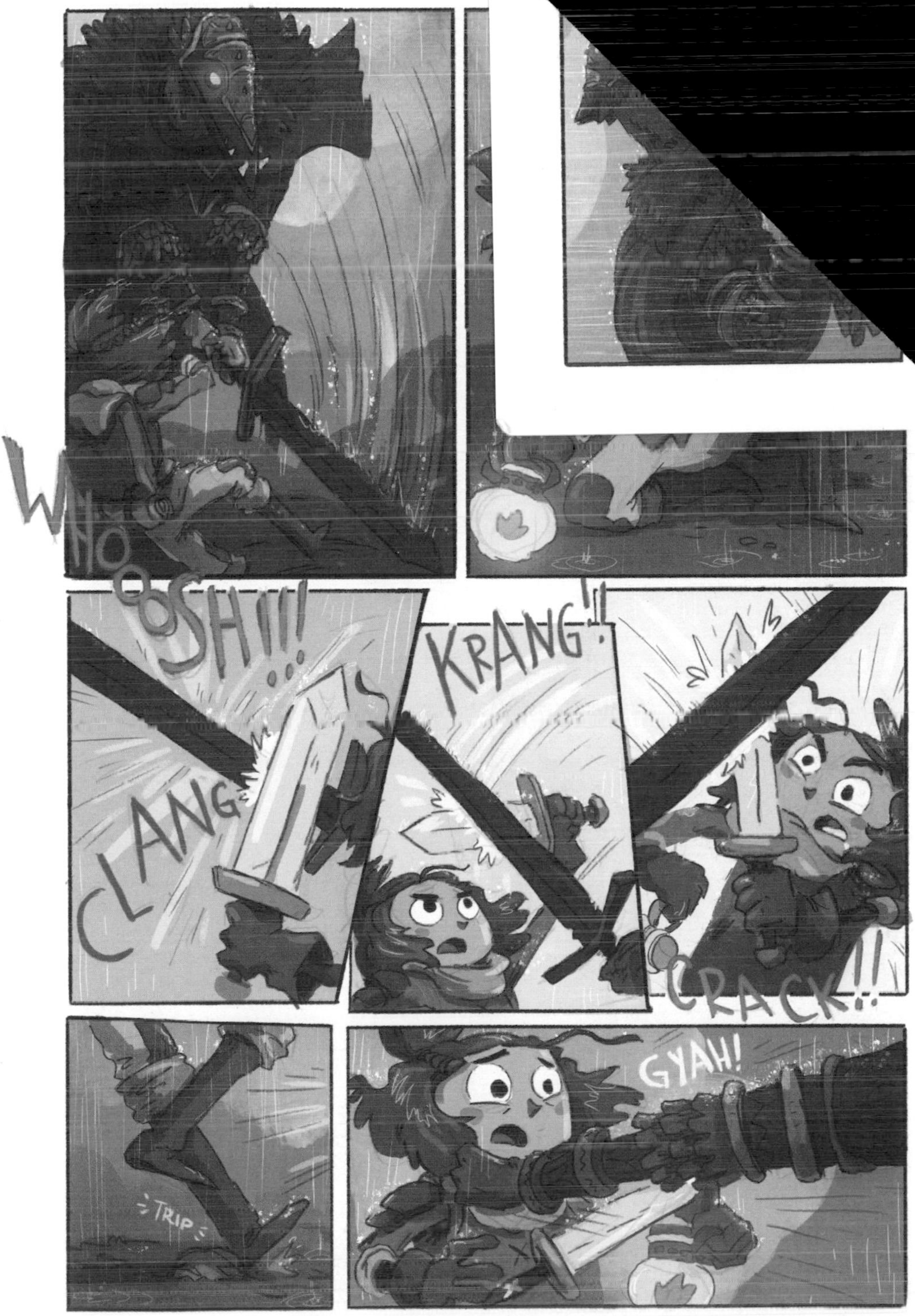
WHOOSH!!!
CLANG
KRANG!!
CRACK!!
TRIP
GYAH!

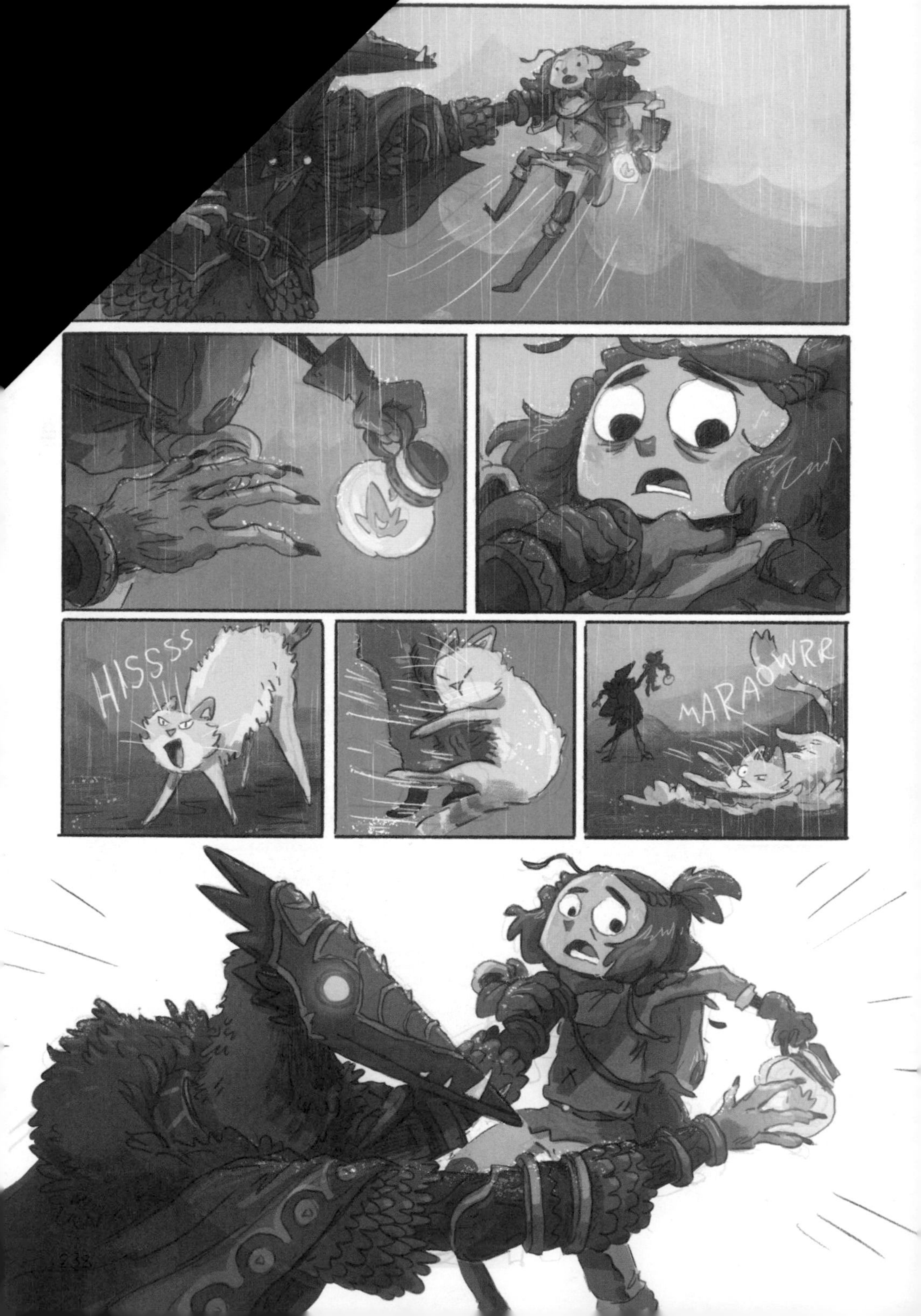
HISSSS
MARAOWRR

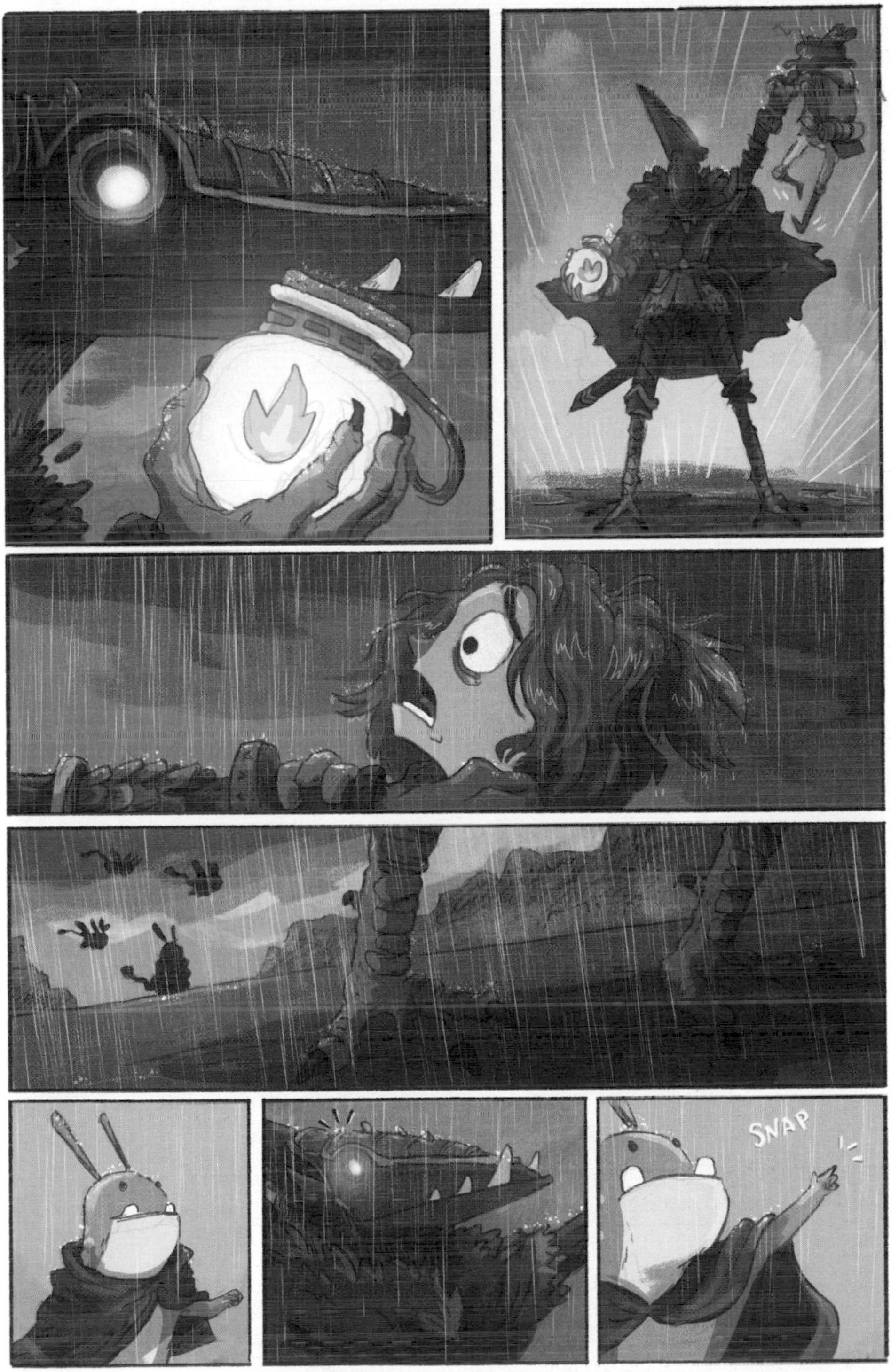
SNAP

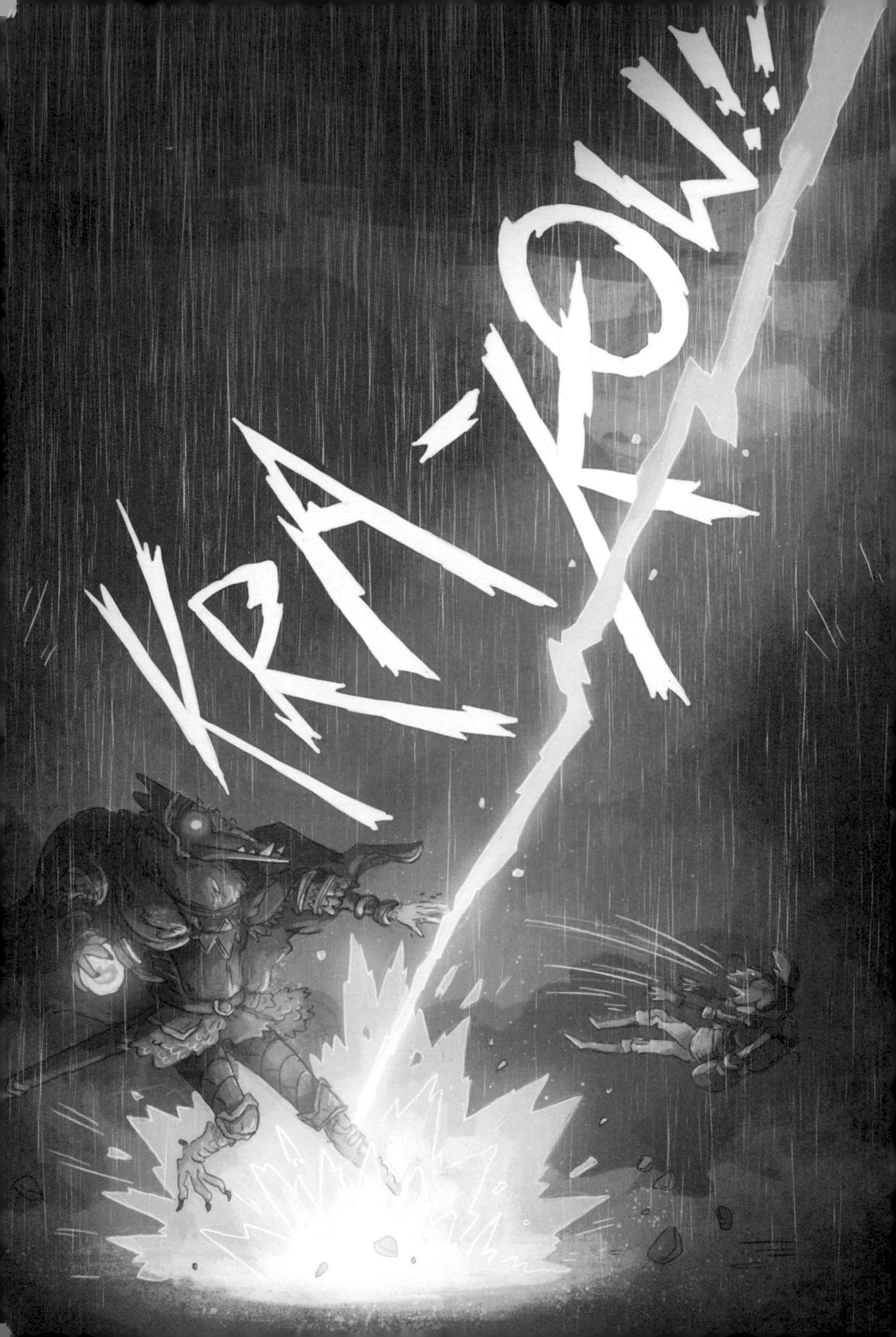
KRA-KOW!!

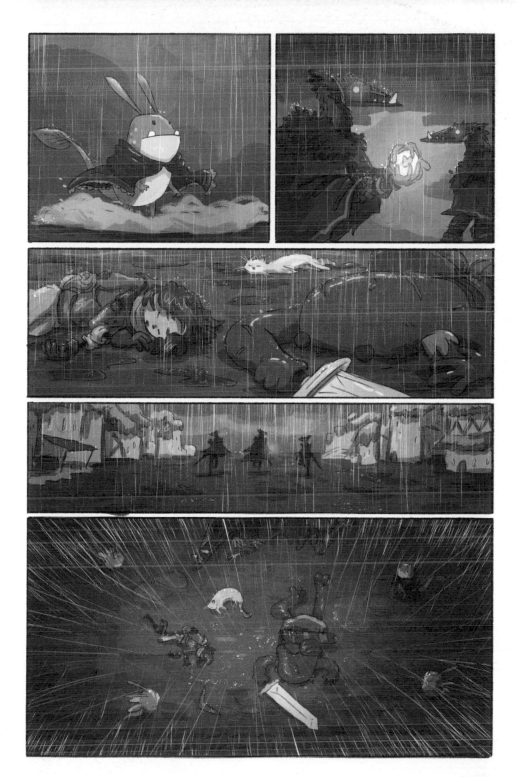

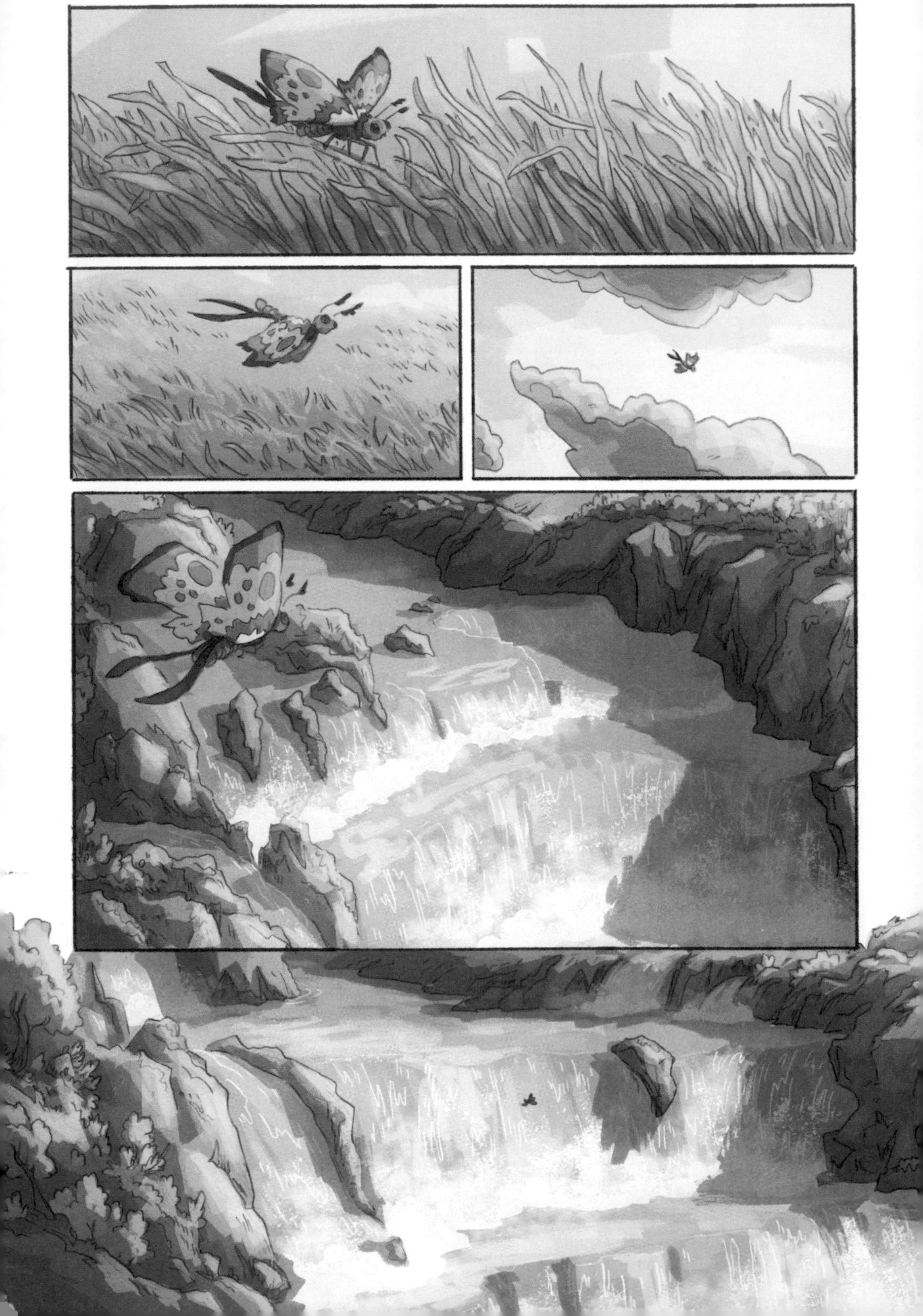

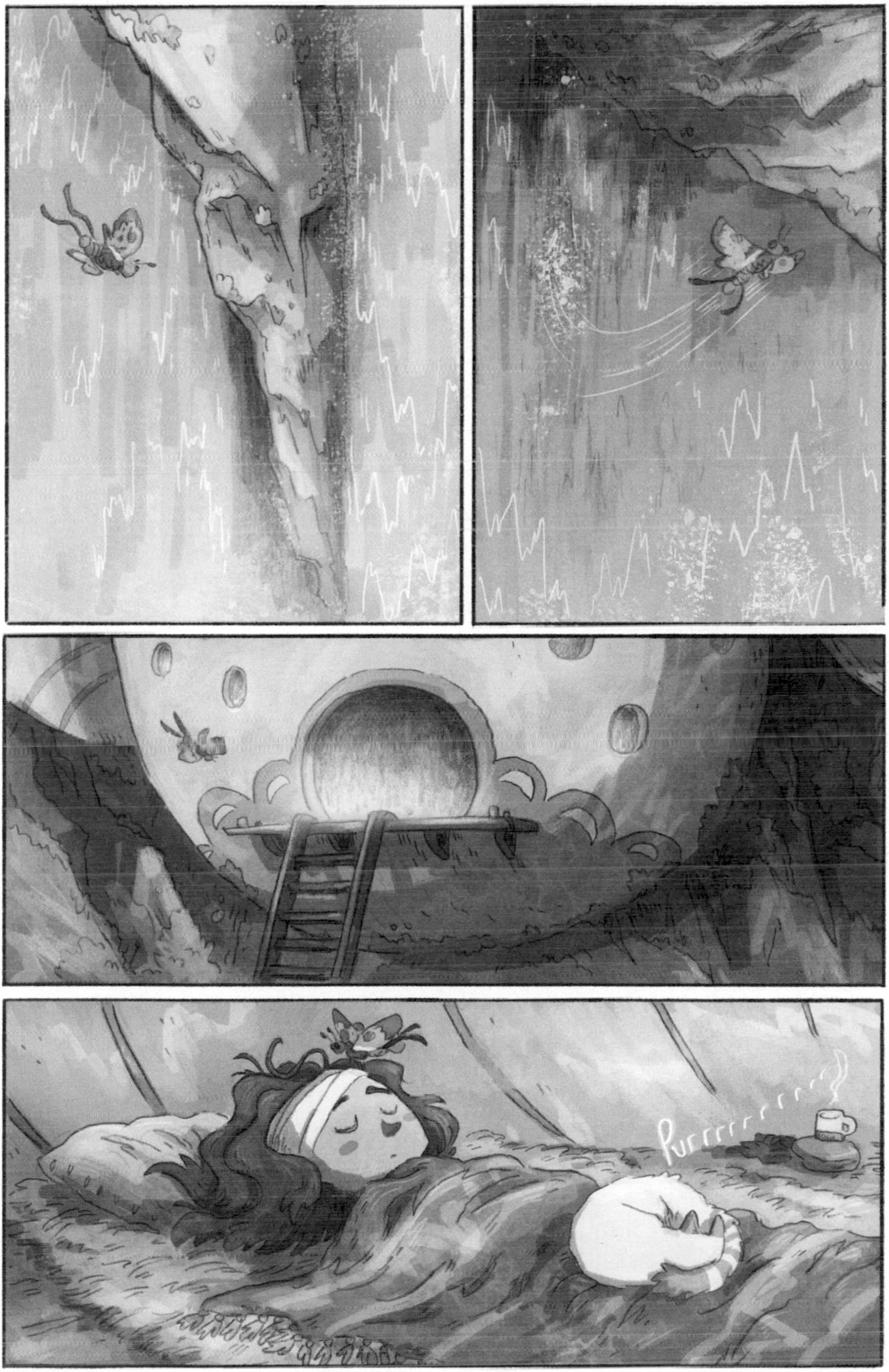
Purrrrrrrrrr

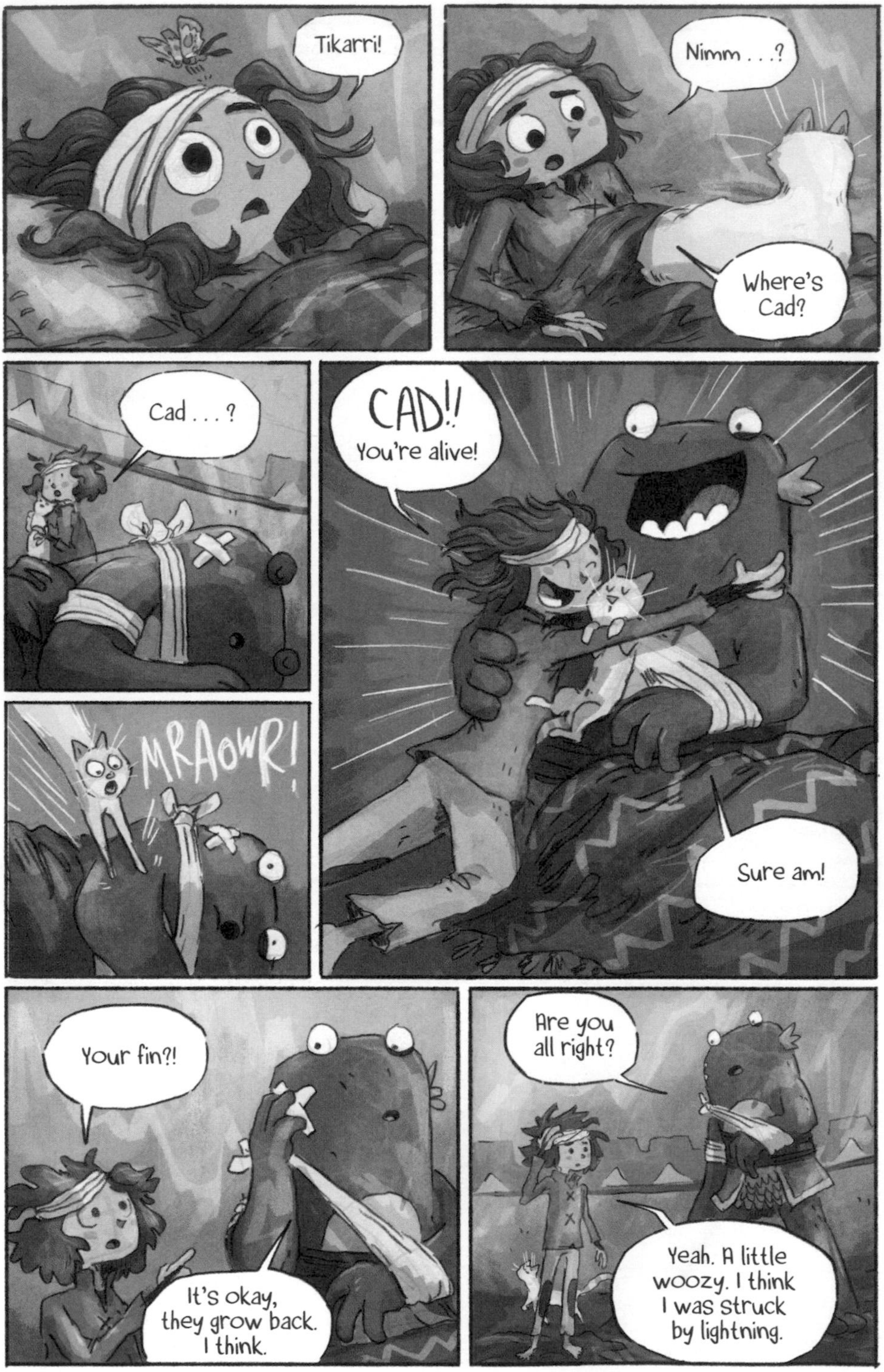
Tikarri!
Nimm . . .?
Where's Cad?
Cad . . . ?
MRAOWR!
CAD!! You're alive!
Sure am!
Your fin?!
It's okay, they grow back. I think.
Are you all right?
Yeah. A little woozy. I think I was struck by lightning.

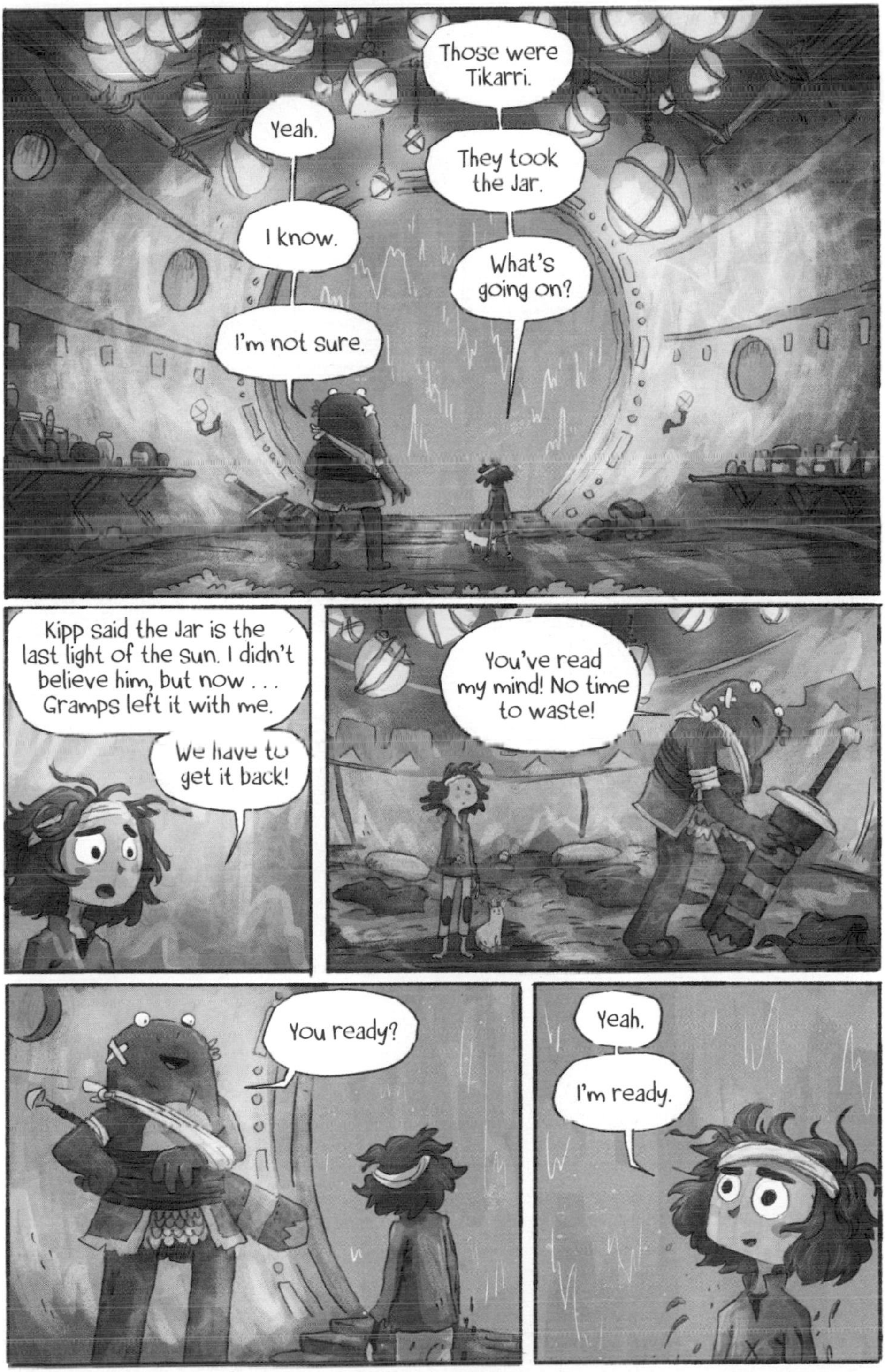
Those were Tikarri.
They took the Jar.
What's going on?
Yeah.
I know.
I'm not sure.
Kipp said the Jar is the last light of the sun. I didn't believe him, but now . . . Gramps left it with me.
We have to get it back!
You've read my mind! No time to waste!
You ready?
Yeah.
I'm ready.

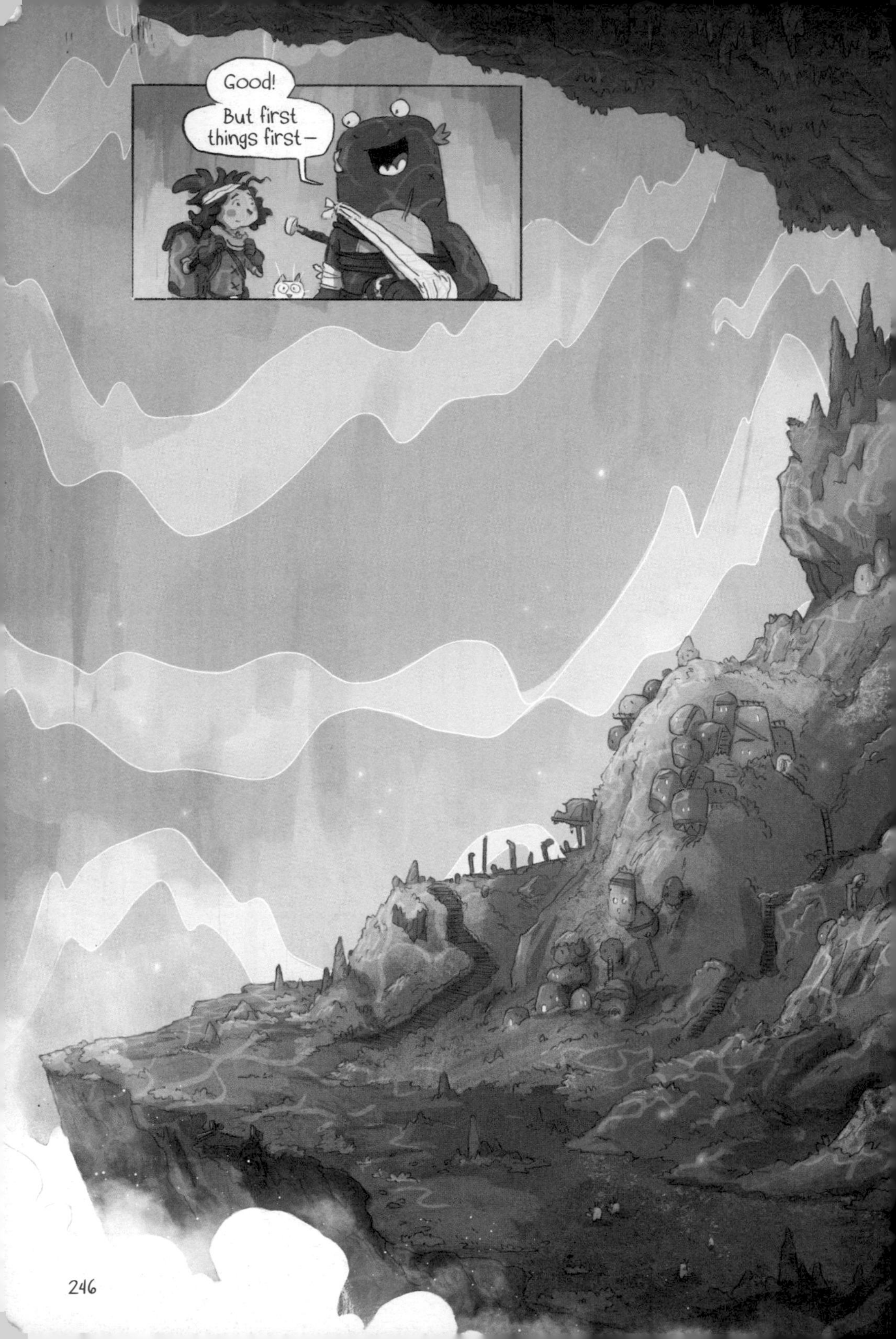
Good!
But first things first—

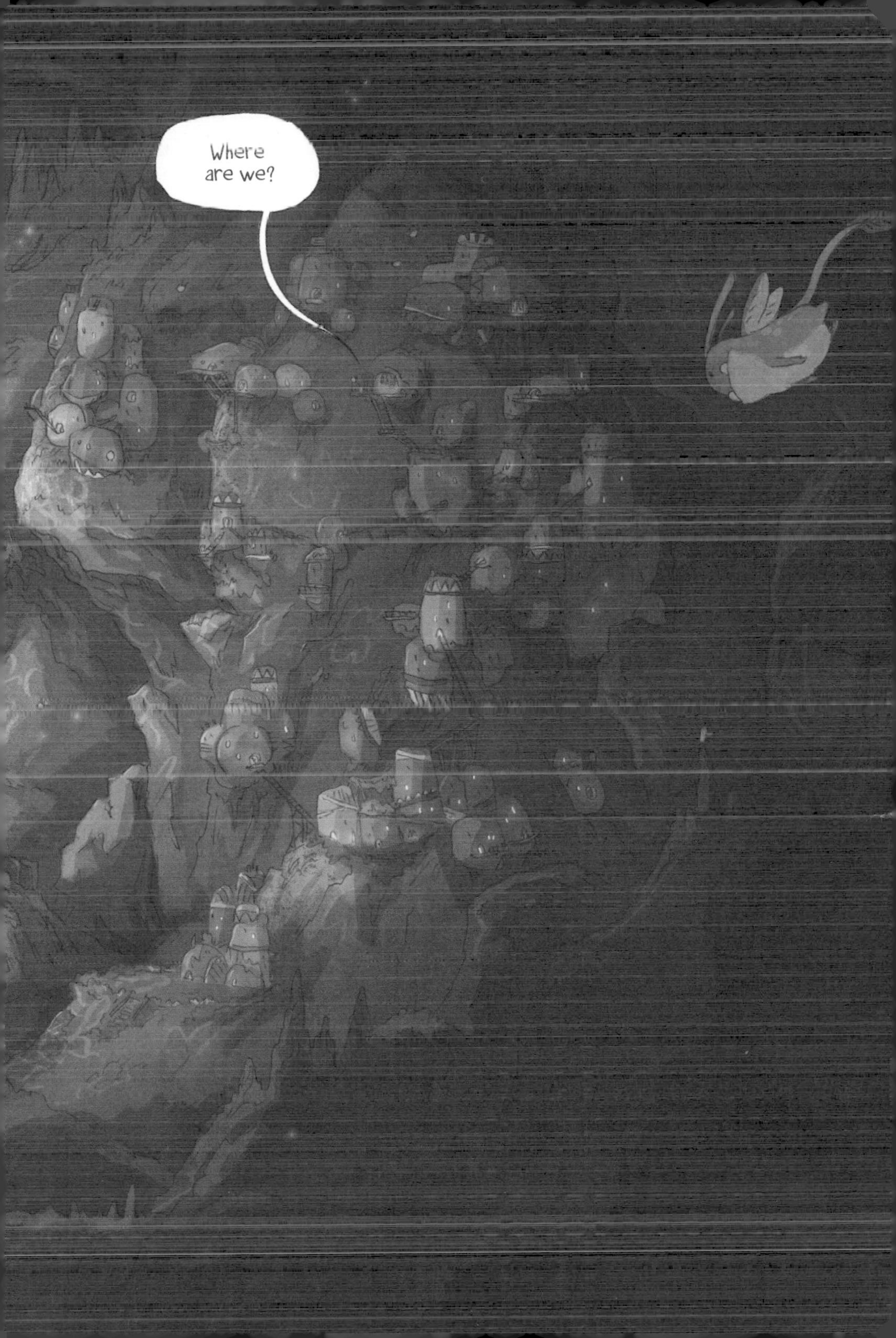
Where are we?

For Beau and Thor, loyal studio mates.

Thanks to
Mom and Dad, Sean, Tara, MK, Ted and Alice, Kate;
Grams and Bryan for helping flat; Joe Burrascano,
Heather Tilert; Andrew Arnold, Erica De Chavez,
Rose Pleuler, Caitlin Lonning, and the team at HarperAlley.
And Jodi.

HarperAlley is an imprint of HarperCollins Publishers.

Lightfall: The Girl & the Galdurian
Copyright © 2020 by Tim Probert
All rights reserved. Manufactured in Italy.
No part of this book may be used or reproduced in any manner
whatsoever without written permission except in the case of
brief quotations embodied in critical articles and reviews. For
information address HarperCollins Children's Books, a division
of HarperCollins Publishers, 195 Broadway, New York, NY 10007.
www.harperalley.com

Library of Congress Control Number: 2019957936
ISBN 978-0-06-299047-1 — ISBN 978-0-06-299046-4 (pbk.)

The artist used Prismacolor pencil, mechanical pencil, and
Photoshop to create the digital illustrations for this book.
Typography by Tim Probert and Erica De Chavez
20 21 22 23 24   RTLO   10 9 8 7 6 5 4 3 2 1
❖
First Edition

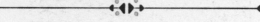